BURT BACHARACH
SONG BY SONG

The ultimate Burt Bacharach reference for fans, serious record collectors, and music critics.

by Serene Dominic

NEW YORK/LONDON/PARIS/SYDNEY/TOKYO/BERLIN/COPENHAGEN/MADRID

Cover photo: Lawrence K. Ho/Los Angeles Times/Retna USA, Ltd.

Schirmer Trade Books
A Division of Music Sales Corporation, New York

Exclusive Distributors:
Music Sales Corporation
257 Park Avenue South, New York, NY 10010 USA
Music Sales Limited
8/9 Frith Street, London W1D 3JB England
Music Sales Pty. Limited
120 Rothschild Street, Rosebery, Sydney, NSW 2018, Australia

Order No. SCH 10118
International Standard Book Number: 0.8256.7280.5

Printed in the United States of America
by Vicks Lithograph and Printing Corporation

CONTENTS

Make It Easy on Yourself: Collecting the Essential Bacharachiana 7

A Little Bacharach Background 11

A Little Hal David Background 12

Section One
MAGIC MOMENTS (1952–1959) 13

Section Two
ANY DAY NOW (1960–1962) 43

Section Three
MAKE IT EASY ON YOURSELF (1962–1963) 81

Section Four
WHAT THE WORLD NEEDS NOW (1964–1965) 119

Section Five
THE LOOK OF LOVE (1966–1967) 159

Section Six
PROMISES, PROMISES (1968–1970) 197

Section Seven
THE LOST HORIZON (1972–1979) 231

Section Eight
THAT'S WHAT FRIENDS ARE FOR (1980–1991) 255

Section Nine
PAINTED FROM MEMORY (1991–2001) 289

Section Ten
QUESTION ME AN ANSWER 321

Bacharach Backchat 322

Library of Congress List of Bacharach Songs 332

Bacharach Off the Record 339

New Jack Bacharach: Always Sampling There to Remind Me... 344

Bacharach Network TV Specials 347

Acknowledgments

It's impossible to collect Burt Bacharach music without making friends around the globe. For the better part of four years it's been a pleasure trading music and information with Stefan Wesley who has the most comprehensive Bacharach website The Hitmaker Archive (http://listen.to/burt), and the largest collection of Bacharach cover versions anywhere, Davide Bonori, Roberto Pinard, Mark Meister for his great A House Is Not a Homepage. Thanks for the personal insights of Shawn Phillips, Joanie Sommers, David Hennings, Tom Jones, Tony Bennett, Charlie Gracie, Mari Iijima, Johnny Rivers, Allison Ravenscroft at Linda Dozoretz and Associates, Chrissy Swearingen at Hal Leonard Corporation, Donna Fields, David Jenkins (www.harrywarren.org), Leonora Corate at Rhino Records, Rhonda Malmlund at Universal Music Special Markets, Betsy Brown at Warners Special Products, Wanda McSwain at Elektra Records, Beebe Born at Bourne Music, Peggy Flynn at Jim Beam Brands Public Relations Dept., Albin Ortega at Atlantic Records, Frank Lopez at EMI, Harry Young at RPM and Nick Vianizi at Global Communications, Canada.

All chart positions courtesy of *Billboard Publications, Inc.*

Thanks to Peter Gilstrap for picking me out of the crowd, Gil Garcia, Bob Mehr, Thomas Bond, Michelle Savoy, Jim Cherry, Sean Donovan, Jeremy Voas, Chris O'Connor, David Holthouse, Brian Smith and everyone who's kept my name in print the last ten years. And double thanks for Gil, Bob, and Jim for slogging through the rough drafts.

Personal thanks to Doreen and Joe for encouragement and letting me bring so much Bacharach into our home, Geri & John Sciortino and The Bronx Design Group, Fran & Enzo Zucchetto, Joseph and Grace Salerno ("cento di questi gioni"), Tres & Jen Ikner, Tom Travers, Michelle & Brett, Matt Strangwayes, Duke Dosik, Maria Jeanene Verso, Cristianajoy & Gardner Cole, Bill Barrett, Danny Pearl, Brigit Barton, Ms. B, Jim Speros, and the Torchbearers.

A big shout out to Tracks In Wax in Phoenix (http://members.cox.net/tracksinwax) for supplying many of the 45s and album jackets herein.

Also a big appreciative thanks Maryglenn McCombs at Omnibus, Larry Birnbaum, Dan, Alison, and everyone at Schrimer Trade Books.

And again to Burt for all the great music and not forgetting Hal, Mack, John, Paul, Peter, Norman, Sammy, Wilson, Sydney, Bob, Carole, Tonio, and Elvis for the words.

For Joseph Thaddeus Salerno, the coolest kid in the universe

Make It Easy on Yourself: Collecting the Essential Bacharachiana

At what point in time do you realize you're an adult? Is it the first time someone calls you "sir," and it's a cop ten years your junior? Is it when you mysteriously start wearing sweaters with elbow patches? When you find yourself offering homespun wisdom no one's asked you for? When Wilfred Brimley starts dropping by unannounced at your house to talk hot oatmeal? No, my friend, those are merely the first telltale signs of feeling old, which luckily can be avoided if you keep your heart open to anything and everything. Adulthood has a little something to do with putting aside selected childish things (no more mooning, f'rinstance); moreover, it's an acceptance that maybe some of the old ways were right. Your music collection will tell you when you've reached that considered age—when you find yourself trading in some CD on Matador that you supposedly liked but never actually played for a *Best of Peggy Lee* collection. Or when, like me, you find yourself gradually collecting Burt Bacharach.

Since the late Nineties, the words "resurgence" and "Burt Bacharach" have found their way into a lot of the same sentences. There's been an avalanche of press coverage on the composer, partly because of the stepped-up use of his Sixties-era classics in recent cinema blockbusters like *My Best Friend's Wedding, Forrest Gump, The First Wives Club* and the three *Austin Powers* movies, where the Maestro even made cameo appearances. But if lucrative copyrights and movie cameos alone were enough to spark this kind of belated appreciation, we'd be in the midst of a James "I Feel Good" Brown resurgence as well. While newly commissioned works for *Stuart Little* and *Isn't She Great?* and Bacharach's recent songwriting collaborations with Elvis Costello are partly responsible for renewed media interest, it's Burt's rich back catalog that continues to garner a groundswell of worship from a new generation of young fans. Some journalists have attributed this Gen-X interest in Burt to the already passé space-age-bachelor-pad music movement or offered up glib kids-dig-him-because-Oasis-does rationales. In doing so, they grossly underestimate how timeless his songs actually are.

On an almost daily basis, Bacharach and his incomparable lyricist, Hal David, sat in a windowless cubicle and saw the outside world in intricate time signatures, diminished chord sequences, soaring melodies and thought-provoking prose, creating songs that were anything but the hackwork most of their Brill Building brethren were churning out. Taken instrumentally, Bacharach's music screams with passion. From the mightiest orchestral swell to the quietest keyboard glissando, you are always made to feel as if you're either about to be loved or about to be left. Whether it's that first glance or the last door slam is of little consequence. You feel a part of something—something big.

As the perfect complement, Hal David brilliantly translated that big feeling into small words that carried a lot of weight. David was well into his forties by the time the Summer of Love rolled around, yet he said way more about love in a lyric like "Alfie" than those under 30 trying their damnedest to pass for "groovy." And because neither he nor his partner let fashion do the dictation, their words and music seem even more magical and otherworldly in the 21st century, where people beg off asking what the world needs now and tell you that the world just plain stinks. Maybe a Bacharach resurgence is the first tangible evidence that even the most hardened cynic needs music that betrays the existence somewhere of love sweet love, and that maybe a haunting melody is something to be savored, not just sampled in seven-second intervals.

There's something in Burt's revival for easily led easy-listening adults as well. For decades, adult music has meant divas who record only threadbare material designed not to upstage their roller-coaster voices, choosing showcases instead of songs. While radio, in its bland current state, doesn't have a format to accommodate the new songs Burt Bacharach and Elvis Costello recorded for their long-awaited collaboration *Painted from Memory,* winning the Grammy went some distance toward making good on Costello's claim to *Billboard* that "Burt and I are here to kick Celine Dion's ass."

Shipped to record emporiums at the same time as *Painted from Memory* was Rhino's *The Look of Love: The Burt Bacharach Collection*, the first comprehensive anthology of Bacharach hits as recorded by the artists (37 of them) who made them chart-worthy. Brilliantly compiled and annotated, this essential 3-CD set makes a compelling case for the unique team of Bacharach and David, who single-handedly manned the middle ground between Tin Pan Alley (Rodgers and Hammerstein, George and Ira Gershwin), the Brill Building (Leiber and Stoller, Goffin and King) and modern pop (Lennon and McCartney, Brian Wilson). No other songwriting team could create gritty R&B hits for Chuck Jackson, the Drifters and Etta James, fashion torchy ballads for Dionne Warwick and Dusty Springfield, and then turn around and write a Tony Award–winning musical and an Oscar-winning best song, all in the same decade. Their enterprise during the Sixties was positively breathtaking.

If *The Look of Love*'s roster of artists seems like a pop who's who, it pales beside the complete list of almost 1,000 recording artists who have recorded Bacharach songs. Nat King Cole, Patti Page, Margaret Whiting, Mel Tormé, Doris Day, Jerry Lewis (?), Keely Smith, Johnny Mathis, Andy Williams, Joe Williams, Stan Getz, Del Shannon, Petula Clark, the Beatles, Herman's Hermits, Love, Smokey Robinson and the Miracles, Gladys Knight and the Pips, Bobby Darin, the Supremes, Peter Sellers and the Hollies (together at last!), the Searchers, the Walker Brothers, Peter and Gordon, Chrissie Hynde, Carly Simon, Barbra Streisand, Isaac Hayes, Dick Van Dyke (??), Frank Sinatra, Elvis Presley—all household names to be sure. Then there are those forgotten names—June Valli, Gals & Pals, Mary Mayo, Brian Foley, Babs Tino, Anita Harris, Rosemary June—artists whom Bacharach thought enough of to give the first shot at first-rate compositions. Certainly songs like "Close to You" and "Alfie" were mandatory selections for every adult-contemporary singer in the rock era, and many of the pop and R&B groups of the Sixties and Seventies took at least one stroll through the house of Bacharach. He's virtually inescapable. If you were to play the infamous Kevin Bacon game with Burt Bacharach, six degrees of separation would be at least three too many.

Perhaps the most fun you'll have searching for unheard-of tracks is finding the unmistakable Bacharach quality of "What the World Need Now Is Love" or "Any Day Now" in cuts like Johnny Mathis' "Warm and Tender," Joe Williams' "That Kind of Woman," Etta James' "Waiting for Charlie to Come Home" or Dionne Warwick obscurities like "The Wine Is Young" and "I Smiled Yesterday" that no one else saw the wisdom of covering. This laborious search for little-known Bacharach compositions will force you to investigate singers you probably never heard of (Jane Morgan, Babs Tino), great artists you know very little about (Chuck Jackson, Patti Page, Timi Yuro), non-rock rock-era artists you thought you never liked but will come away with a grudging respect for (Bobby Vinton, Perry Como) and artists you will never like despite their having recorded a Bacharach song. You'll have to read this tome to find my personal pariahs.

Until now, there have been no books detailing Bacharach's amazing body of work. While you can probably find dozens of Beatles discographies in print offering intense critical analyses of every B-side, every cover version and every outtake, there has been no reference book dedicated to Bacharach and David or to Bacharch alone, outside of a few incomplete songbooks. While Bacharach gets a mention in the hundreds of biographies of celebrities he time-traveled with through the Fifties and Sixties (Neil Simon, Marlene Dietrich, et al.), rarely do these books contain musical trivia beyond Burt's being married to Angie Dickinson when he wrote many of his hits. Any musical information, studio dates, places and musicians seemed exclusively the stuff of CD reissue liner notes and scattered interviews.

Even with the slew of Bacharach CD collections following in *The Look of Love*'s wake (many with the same dozen songs), there is no record company in the galaxy with enough patience or licensing prowess to collect all these recorded works in one exhaustive fell swoop, as the Bear Family label of Germany did for the complete works of Rosemary Clooney. If you want to hear this stuff for yourself (and want to you should), you'll have to do all the digging, trading and home taping. But that's what *Burt Bacharach: Song by Song* is for. This handy reference book will lead you through a 50-year tour of popular music's peaks and valleys, as well as Bacharach's triumphs and troughs. If you are to become a serious Bacharachaholic, you will find yourself collecting scores of records, many times buying whole CDs for just for one hard-to-find song. Hunting down these rare pop gems is half the fun, and the listening is more than adequate payback. For myself, this proved a personally rewarding and invigorating pastime and taught me a lot about music, love and love of music.

Burt Bacharach: Song by Song will provide you with new insight into this composer's incredible half-century career. While it might not change your life entirely, if it prevents even one of you out there from ever listening to Celine Dion records again, it will have been worth it.

Serene Dominic, 2003

A Little

Bacharach

Background...

When asked by radio reporter Fred Robbins where his son Burt—or "Happy," as he was nicknamed in his younger years—got his musical talent, Bert Bacharach gave full credit to his wife. "I've never been musical," he readily admitted. "I can whistle a little. I can hum a song in the shower. But Irma was very gifted and could have had a career in show business if she hadn't married me and wasted the whole thing."

Burt Freeman Bacharach was born on May 12, 1929, in Kansas City, the son of Bert Bacharach—syndicated columnist and author of the household hints book *How to Do Everything*—and his wife, Irma Freeman Bacharach. Besides singing, Irma could play piano by ear, but she gave up any professional ambitions after "Hap" was born and the family moved to Forest Hills, New York. Her gift for music would now be matched by her ability to tirelessly badger her son to practice the cello, the drums and, finally, the piano. "Those two were fighting constantly. Irma wanted him to practice and Burt wanted to play football," recalled his father. "But he really got the bug when [his] little five-man unit played a Saturday dance at a Catholic church in Forest Hills. There were 20 pretty young girls hanging around the piano. They weren't at the drums or the saxophone. So I think that influenced him into becoming a musician."

Several other influences were at work. Hearing Ravel's *Daphnis et Chloé* suite eliminated his dislike for classical music, and patronizing Manhattan jazz clubs (with the help of a fake ID) fostered his love for bebop. While his level of music appreciation soared, his grades took a nosedive. After graduating from Forest Hills High School, he continued his music studies at McGill University in Montreal. During that time he wrote his first song, "The Night Plane to Heaven," which was published but never recorded. Later he would study under French classical composer Darius Milhaud at the Mannes School of Music in New York. According to his mother, "Burt wanted to do serious music; he wanted to be a serious composer. But I'll bet he's glad he got off that track."

Milhaud may have expedited that process by pointing out Bacharach's gift for melodic phrases and encouraging him to "never be afraid to write music that people can whistle." But writing popular songs would have to wait a few years, as Bacharach was drafted into the army in 1950. Whatever action the young pianist might have seen during the Korean conflict was confined to the inside of an officer's club on Governor's Island in New York Harbor. His unique tour of duty included donning a tuxedo and tickling the ivories. Often he'd stretch out his "Bach to Bacharach" program with pseudo-classical noodling he tried to palm off as an unpublished work by Debussy.

Upon his discharge from the army, he began playing piano bars around New York, like Nino's Continental on 53rd Street and the Bayview on Fire Island. Then he got a prestigious gig conducting for singer Vic Damone. "Vic taught me where the loot and the real scenes were in the music business," Burt told *Billboard* magazine in a 1964 interview. "I got into arranging and conducting for Vic, and through him I got the same kind of gigs with the Ames Brothers, Polly Bergen, Imogene Coca, Georgia Gibbs and Tony Bennett." Damone was also the first person to fire Bacharach from a job, a crushing disappointment that drove the young musician to achieve a level of professionalism he'd soon demand from the musicians in his orchestra pit. During this time he would also play piano accompaniment at auditions for actress Paula Stewart, who'd become the first Mrs. Burt Bacharach.

Somewhere in this flurry of activity, an instrumental the young composer had written found its way onto a 10-inch LP by Nat "King" Cole.

The Ames Team. Found on the back cover of the *Ed Ames Sings the Songs of Bacharach and David* album is this photo from Burt's conducting days with the Ames Brothers. Later, Bacharach would serve as conductor for the Harlem Globetrotters, which begs the question "How many different ways can you arrange 'Sweet Georgia Brown'?"

"Searching Wind" b/w "Roseanne." Little is known about this 45 in which Burt Bacharach makes like Roger Williams under the orchestration of Marion Evans. "Rosanne," composed by Dick Manning with Glen and Edna Osser, was also recorded by Vic Damon in 1952. "Searching Wind" was a Famous Music composition from 1946, written by Edward Heyman and Victor Young.

Hal David Songbook. The non-Bacharach selections contained in this 1990 collection include "Broken Hearted Melody," "American Beauty Rose," "Sea of Heartbreak," "To All the Girls I've Loved Before," "It Was Almost Like a Song" and "99 Miles From L.A." WHAT—no "Johnny Get Angry"?

A Little

Hal David

Background...

Once Burt F. Bacharach was officially under contract as a songwriter for Paramount's Famous Music publishing company, it was Eddie Wolpin who paired him up with Hal David and other songwriters, including Hal's older brother Mack. According to every popular retelling of the historic Burt and Hal teaming, Bacharach had already written some songs with Mack, whose credits included "Cherry Pink and Apple Blossom White" (a No. 1 hit in 1955 for Pérez Prado), "I Don't Care If the Sun Don't Shine," (a No. 1 hit for Patti Page in 1950), "A Dream Is a Wish Your Heart Makes" (from the 1948 Disney animation feature *Cinderella*) and the English translation lyrics for "La Vie En Rose." The earliest recorded evidence of Burt and Mack's collaborations doesn't show up until spring 1958 and the theme from *Hot Spell.* However, several songs by Burt Bacharach and Hal David appear as early as 1956.

Hal David was born May 25, 1921, in New York City, where his first writing job was for the school newspaper at Thomas Jefferson High School. In his senior year he became editor and went on to study journalism at New York University, eventually landing a copyediting job at the *New York Post*. Having studied the violin at an early age, Hal was adept enough to play in various borscht belt bands on weekends.

Like Bacharach, Hal David served the armed forces in an entertainment capacity; upon his return to civilian life, he gave professional songwriting a try at the encouragement of his brother Mack. For a while Hal toiled away writing lyrics in his Lyndhurst, New Jersey, apartment, while his schoolteacher wife, Eunice, supported them. He didn't have to wait too long to sell his first song, a ditty called "Isn't This Better Than Walking in the Rain," to bandleader Sammy Kaye, who also recorded Hal's next song, "The Four Winds and the Seven Seas," a huge hit in 1949. David wrote that song with Guy Lombardo's vocalist Don Rodney, who showed it to his boss. The song elicited five competing Top 20 versions, with Lombardo, Vic Damone, Herb Jeffries and Mel Tormé all in the running, but it was Sammy Kaye who would best the competition, going all the way up to No. 3.

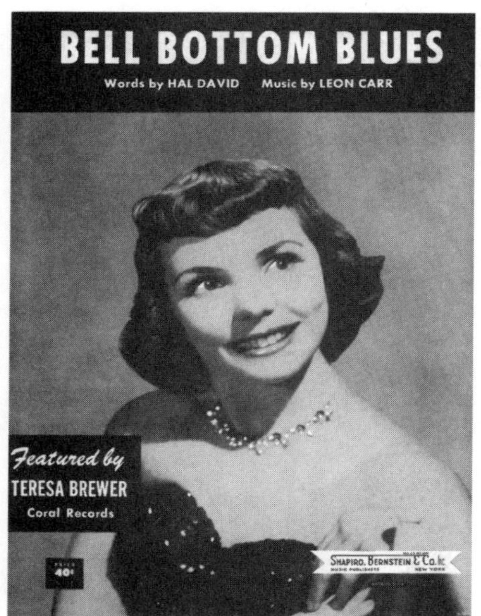

Bell Bottom Blues. Not to be confused with the Derek & the Dominoes hit in 1970. C'mon, do you really wanna see Teresa Brewer crawl across the floor and beg you please to stay?

The following year, Frank Sinatra had a Top 30 hit with Hal's "American Beauty Rose," and "Bell Bottom Blues" would be a Top 20 hit for Teresa Brewer in 1954. "Bell Bottom Blues" would also be a Top 5 UK hit for Alma Cogan. David had enough clout to be writing on a song-by-song basis for several different publishers as well as having his pick of collaborators. Hal continued to collaborate with Lee Pockriss, Sherman Edwards and a host of others. Even after Bacharach and David scored back-to-back hits with Perry Como's "Magic Moments" and "Marty Robbins' "The Story of My Life" in early 1958, no one was referring to them as a team until 1963.

In 1959, David and Edwards gave Sarah Vaughan the biggest hit of her career, the million-seller "Broken-Hearted Melody," which Vaughan chose to record but then shelved for a year. It was issued on the B-side of "Misty," but popular taste flipped the record over, and "Broken-Hearted Melody" rose to No. 7. While David would continue to have hits with other partners besides Bacharach, after 1963 there would be no looking back.

Among Hal David's awards are an Oscar for "Raindrops Keep Falling on My Head," a Grammy for *Promises, Promises,* the NARM Presidential Award and inductions into the Songwriters Hall of Fame and the Nashville Songwriters Hall of Fame International. David and Bacharach received the Founders Award from ASCAP, where Hal served as president from 1980 to 1986.

SECTION ONE

MAGIC MOMENTS (1952-1959)

...or when Burt met Hal

Don't panic if you don't see Dionne Warwick's name in this section—it's a roundup of all known Fifties Bacharach recordings, from "Keep Me in Mind" to "Faithfully," many of which never escaped the time period they were written and recorded for. Since Bacharach didn't do any arranging or producing on these sides, almost none contain the trademark sounds he would later be known for. Nonetheless, they provide a fascinating journey through all the steps leading up to those later triumphs, including his first collaboration with Hal David and sporadic pairings with other Tin Pan Alley lyricists. You'll find trivia on at least a dozen white-bread male and female vocalists who would not see a hit past the Kennedy administration and discover Burt's earliest forays into film themes and the rock 'n' roll idiom.

Section One: Magic Moments (1952–1959)

1. *"Once in a Blue Moon"* . . . . *Nat "King" Cole*
2. *"Keep Me in Mind"* . . . . *Patti Page*
3. *"The Desperate Hours* . . . . *Mel Tormé*
4. *"Tell the Truth and Shame the Devil"* . . . . *Harry Carter Singers*
5. *"Peggy's in the Pantry"* . . . . *Sherry Parsons*
6. *"The Morning Mail"* . . . . *The Gallahads*
7. *"I Cry More* . . . . *Alan Dale*
8. *"Beauty Isn't Everything"* . . . . *June Valli*
9. *"How About"* . . . . *Della Reese*
10. *"Warm and Tender"* . . . . *Johnny Mathis*
11. *"Underneath the Overpass* . . . . *Jo Stafford*
12. *"Wild Honey"* . . . . *Cathy Carr*
13. *"Presents from the Past"* . . . . *Cathy Carr*
14. *"The Story of My Life"* . . . . *Marty Robbins*
15. *"Sad Sack"* . . . . *Jerry Lewis*
16. *"Winter Warm"* . . . . *Gale Storm*
17. *"Uninvited Dream"* . . . . *Peggy Lee*
18. *"Magic Moments"* . . . . *Perry Como*
19. *"Humble Pie"* . . . . *Four Preps*
20. *"Country Music Holiday"* . . . . *Bernie Nee*
21. *"Hot Spell"* . . . . *Margaret Whiting*
22. *"It Seemed So Right Last Night"* . . . . *Mary Mayo*
23. *"Sitting in a Tree House"* . . . . *Marty Robbins*
24. *"The Night That Heaven Fell"* . . . . *Tony Bennett*
25. *"Oooh My Love"* . . . . *Vic Damone*
26. *"The Blob"* . . . . *The Five Blobs*
27. *"Saturday Night in Tia Juana"* . . . . *The Five Blobs*
28. *"Wendy Wendy"* . . . . *The Four Coins*
29. *"The Last Time I Saw My Heart"* . . . . *Marty Robbins*
30. *"Dream Big"* . . . . *Sonny James*
31. *"Loving Is a Way of Giving"* . . . . *Steve Lawrence*
32. *"Make Room for the Joy"* . . . . *Jack Jones*
33. *"Paradise Island"* . . . . *The Four Aces*
34. *"Moon Man"* . . . . *Gloria Lambert*
35. *"The Hangman"* . . . . *John Ashley*
36. *"The Net"* . . . . *John Ashley*
37. *"Don't Unless You Love Me"* . . . . *Paul Hampton*
38. *"Write Me (Lonely Girl)"* . . . . *Paul Hampton*
39. *"Young and Wild"* . . . . *The Five Blobs*
40. *"With Open Arms"* . . . . *Jane Morgan*
41. *"Heavenly"* . . . . *Johnny Mathis*
42. *"That Kind of Woman"* . . . . *Joe Williams*
43. *"Faker Faker"* . . . . *The Eligibles*
44. *"In Times Like These"* . . . . *Gene McDaniels*
45. *"Faithfully"* . . . . *Johnny Mathis*

"Once in a Blue Moon" (Burt F. Bacharach)
Recorded by Nat "King" Cole
Capitol H-332 10-inch album *Penthouse Serenade*
Released 1952

Hot on the heels of his signature hit, "Unforgettable," came Nat "King" Cole's first instrumental excursion without the King Cole Trio, released in part to silence the jazz critics who bemoaned his recent commercial strategy of "more singing, less playing." Even today, few fans realize that Cole's distinctive swing piano playing heavily influenced Oscar Peterson, Art Tatum and Ray Charles, no slouches at the piano bench themselves. But by the time Cole's popular television show was first aired in 1956, it's doubtful the viewing audience knew he could do considerably more with a piano than just lean against it.

***Penthouse Serenade,* 10-inch LP (1952).** Question: If this was an eight-song album in its 10-inch configuration, and four songs were added to the 12-inch version in 1954, how many songs would total on the five-inch compact disc?

It's not surprising then that the sprightly "Once in a Blue Moon" should remain one of Burt Bacharach's most obscure compositions, its lack of recognition compounded by the fact that he is rarely given the proper label credit for it. Since the melody is an adaptation, perhaps credit is a moot point. When the tune was originally issued on the *Penthouse Serenade* 10-inch LP, the label stated that it was "based on Rubenstein's Melody in F" and arranged by Cole. The expanded 12-inch version issued two years later was Cole's first ever full-length album release, and pressings alternated between crediting "Burt F. Bacharach" and "The Maestro." Now, in its compact disc incarnation, it's mistakenly attributed to "Jerome Kern /Anne Caldwell," who wrote an altogether different "Once in a Blue Moon" for the 1923 musical *Stepping Stones*.

Despite his father's protest of no musical talent, Burt recalls this title instantly as having the senior Bacharach's participation: "That was a song I wrote with my dad when I was in college. And Nat 'King' Cole recorded it. Actually, it's Rubenstein's Melody in F, so it was a real cop or a hat's off. Or maybe it was public domain. I can't even say. Jerome Kern also had a song with that title, but you can't copyright titles," he adds. "If you look it up, you'll see there are 15 songs with the title 'I Love You Baby.'"

True! Witness how many lackluster songs have "The Look of Love" for a title.

***Penthouse Serenade* (1998).** Answer: An additional seven bonus cuts bolster the CD edition to a total of 19 tracks, including alternate vocal versions of "Unforgettable" and "Too Young." Cole would release two more instrumental long players, *Piano Stylings* (1954) and *The Piano Style of Nat King Cole* (1956).

"Keep Me in Mind" (Jack Wolf - Burt F. Bacharach)
Recorded by Patti Page
Mercury 70579-X45, released March 1955

As mentioned earlier, Bacharach's first job out of the army was playing piano and conducting for Vic Damone. "When I got fired, which I did, I went to work for the Ames Brothers," Bacharach recounts in the book *Off the Record: An Oral History of Popular Music*. "The songs that used to come in for them were so deceptively simple—songs like 'You You You' [the group's 1953 hit, which spent eight weeks at No. 1]—that I thought, Jeez, I ought to be able to write four or five of these a day. Well, I went a year without getting anything published. What I learned, of course, was that it's the hardest thing in the world to write a simple melody that's fresh and doesn't sound stolen."

1955

The Voices of Patti Page. This LP sported three carbon-copied Pages, the most ever allowed on any Patti Page cover. "Keep Me in Mind" first appeared here with the correct "Bacharach-Wolf" writers' credit, which Mercury managed to botch on the 45. (See below).

Bacharach's persistence eventually paid off. A tune he'd written with lyricist Jack Wolf (who co-wrote "I'm a Fool to Want You" with Frank Sinatra) was recorded by Patti Page, the woman overzealous press agents dubbed "the Singing Rage" because of her gimmick of double-tracked vocals. She called attention to her multitracking ways by appearing in double image on album covers; as if that wasn't enough, one of her earliest sound-on-sound experiments, "With My Eyes Wide Open I'm Dreaming," carried this unwieldy label credit: "Vocals by Patti Page, Patti Page, Patti Page and Patti Page." Maybe she was hoping the same shoddy bookkeeping that credited "Keep Me in Mind" to "Zing/Wexler" on the label of the 45 would also result in her getting paid four times by ASCAP.

In hindsight, Bacharach would've probably preferred that the credit for his all-important first work remain with Zing and Wexler. In interviews, he doesn't ever refer to this tune by name: "It was awful" is generally his first and last word on the matter. While far from groundbreaking material, "Keep Me in Mind" is hardly the musical hemorrhage its composer maintains it is. That is, unless you have a low tolerance for dated lyrics that depict women as willing standbys, ready to interpret any bang on a ceiling or yell down the hall as an invitation to romance and willing to forgive any indiscretion while under the hypnotic power of a wedding ring.

Perhaps what irritates the finicky arranger now is the jumping jive arrangement typical of most up-tempo pre-rock songs of the day. Bacharach also regrets how often he capitulated to the demands of record companies, record producers and even artists at this early juncture. "I ran into things with A&R men when they'd say 'Well, I'll give you the record of that song, but first you've got to change this from a three-bar phrase to a four-bar phrase. Then it makes sense.' And I would ruin the song, y'know?"

"Keep Me in Mind." The record plays Bacharach and Wolf's "Keep Me in Mind" but the label reads otherwise. Zing-Wexler did indeed write a song entitled "Keep Me in Mind," which Peggy Lee and Mitch Miller recorded. The B-side of Bacharach's first pop single, prophetically enough, was a song called "Little Crazy Quilt," written by Leon Carr and Hal David.

Whatever fiddling was done to "Keep Me in Mind" didn't guarantee Bacharach's song placement in the Top 100, despite being issued between two sizable Top 20 Page hits, "Let Me Go Lover" and "Croce Di Oro." Its failure hardly registered a blip in the singer's ongoing career. During the Fifties, Page hosted television shows on all three networks, and her string of Top 40 hits for Mercury Records that began in the late Forties showed no signs of abating. Bacharach has admitted in numerous interviews that the hardships he incurred trying to break into the world of popular songwriting meant time away from home that cost him his marriage to his first wife, Paula Stewart—another possible reason this innocuous song left such a bad taste in his mouth.

Next in line to cover "Keep Me in Mind" was British chanteuse Alma Cogan. Coincidentally enough, her first hit was a novelty tune co-written by Hal David called "Bell Bottom Blues" which reached No. 5 on the British charts in 1954. Cogan's saucy material earned her the nickname of "the girl with the laugh in her voice." In fact, Cogan's voice had a frequent squeak to it that some listeners might liken more to a fingernail against a chalkboard than a laughing kewpie doll.

Other Versions: *Alma Cogan • Buddy Greco (1965)*

"The Desperate Hours" (Wilson Stone - Burt Bacharach)
Recorded by Mel Tormé
From a promotion for the Paramount movie *The Desperate Hours,* October 1955

In the Fifties, using music as a movie-marketing tool was a limited option. Only musicals merited full-blown soundtracks, and the suspense thriller *The Desperate Hours,* a torrid tale of three convicts holding a suburban family hostage, was hardly fodder for a catchy commercial tune. Instead, Paramount Pictures assigned two of its Famous Music writers to whip up what was called an "exploitation song," meant to promote the movie's title on radios and jukeboxes but not figure on a single frame of celluloid.

With nothing but a title to go on, the temporary songwriting team of Wilson Stone and Burt F. Bacharach set to work on "The Desperate Hours," a slow, swanky torch song—replete with vibraphone and horns—that would've made a great theme for a Mickey Spillane flick. Two minutes and 12 seconds of warbling time doesn't leave much room for Mel Tormé to trip out the customary shoo-bee-dweedle-dops, so instead the Velvet Fog delivers the bad news to himself with unadorned resignation, only daring once to stretch out the word "desperate" to seven syllables.

Mel Tormé at the Movies. "The Desperate Hours" is titled "These Desperate Hours" for some reason on this 1999 Rhino compilation. This odd stereo version confines Tormé's vocals to the left speaker and the instrumental track on the right. Karaoke singers who enjoy playing with the balance on their receivers should "shoo-bee-doo-bee-dwadda" along at their own peril.

With lines like "the girl is missing and mister, that's doom," the song nearly lapses into lounge-lizard camp but is rescued mainly through the cool baritone's expert delivery of lyricist Stone's series of downtrodden film-noir images: *"The blues are draggin' me back to my room / And I climb every stair with a heart that's as bare as a tomb / Desperate hours..."*

Catchy, yes. But exploitative? Nah. "The Desperate Hours" turned up on neither single nor album anytime soon. Since some recollections in Tormé's 1988 autobiography, *It Wasn't All Velvet,* are jumbled (he recalls being in the offices of Atlantic Records in 1963 and seeing a Led Zeppelin poster), one can't expect him to recall a song that doesn't even appear in his book's comprehensive discography.

As for Bacharach's first film assignment, consider it a very early dry run for the *Casino Royale* and *After the Fox* scores, where his jazzier excursions would meet with far greater acclaim. Bacharach would pen several songs with Stone that went unrecorded, including "I Need You, " "Go 'Way, Mister Moon," "The Woman Who Wasn't Mine," "Send Me Letters Filled with Kisses" and one that works in Bacharach's boyhood nickname, "Happy and His One-Man Band"

"The Desperate Hours." Bacharach's first "exploitation" song, and its headache-inducing sheet music cover. This artwork is better suited to the music that was actually played under the film's VistaVision opening credits. That theme kicked off with machine guns providing percussion!

"Tell the Truth and Shame the Devil" (Margery S. Wolpin/Martita - Hal David - Burt Bacharach)
Recorded by the Harry Carter Singers
Hudson 223 F T8461, released March 1956

1956

Sherry Parsons. Looks can be deceiving. This enchantress actually has an urgent hair-pulling, eye-gouging engagement in the pantry. Run, Peggy, run!

Extremely little is known about this odd chorale recording, which originated during Bacharach's earliest days at Famous Music. Hardly a gospel song, it sounds more like the byproduct of some long-forgotten Paramount Picture, thanks to its Salvation Army–band marching beat. It's hard to imagine much demand for a standalone song where flat-voiced glee club singers and one particularly hilarious soprano advocate not taking the road that leads to "the devil's hideaway" and urge listeners to "make the angels proud of you."

While the record is inexorably stupid, it's entwined with a tragedy befitting a song with a Shakespearean title. While interviewing Bacharach for this book, a casual mention that the ASCAP files carry a writing credit for Eddie Wolpin's late wife Margery, then still Margery Cummings, momentarily stuns him. "Margery Wolpin's credited as a writer? That doesn't make any sense at all. [long pause] I don't know what kind of marriage they had. I just know that when Eddie was walking home from the Brill Building whatever day she jumped out the window, it was just about the time he'd be coming home. At the Gotham Hotel, I think it was. She was a bright woman. Just pretty crazy."

Margery Wolpin is credited with having written music to three Mack David lyrics. "My Jealous Eyes (That Turned from Blue to Green)," from January 1953, and "Spring Never Came Around This Year," from July 1954, were written when she was still Margery Cummings. Only "Una Momento," from December 1956, was written while she was Margery Wolpin (and published under the pseudonym Martita). Her name appears first on all three copyrights, so it's possible Burt was brought in to help flesh the song out after some work had been already done with Hal. Whatever the circumstances concerning her involvement, this song was the catalyst that brought Bacharach and David together.

"Peggy's in the Pantry" (Burt Bacharach - Hal David)
First recorded by Sherry Parsons
RKO Unique 361, flip side of "I'm Sorry for Someone"
Released June 1956

Who was the first artist to have the honor of recording a Burt Bacharach and Hal David tune? All signs point to Sherry Parsons, the singer of "Peggy's in the Pantry," frequently cited by the composer in interviews these days as one of his earliest abominations.

Compared to other woman-done-wrong songs of the day, "Peggy's in the Pantry" is an anarchic chick's call to arms. In this forerunner of Little Eva's "Keep Your Hands Off My Baby" and Leslie Gore's "Judy's Turn to Cry" (not to mention Blondie's "Rip Her to Shreds"), Parsons plays the jilted girl at the party who suspects that promiscuous Peggy in the strapless gown is picking on something in the pantry—and it isn't a chicken bone! Against a swinging hepcat beat, Parsons manages to sound sweet while threatening that tramp Peggy with irreparable bodily harm: *"Gonna tear her hair out, gonna scratch her eyes out / Peggy, Peggy, Peggy leave my guy alone!"* Guess the world wasn't ready for this sort of forthright woman-to-woman chat in 1957.

Ridiculously likeable, "Peggy's in the Pantry" is more a jump tune than a bona fide rocker. While Bacharach's aversion to simplistic early rock 'n' roll kept him from totally committing to the savage within, Hal David had no qualms about penning the occasional Neanderthal violence-is-love anthem. Witness Joanie Sommers' 1962 smash "Johnny Get Angry," written one of with David's other partners, Sherman Edwards.

Not the Gallahads—the Gallahads! Whoever they were, they were the first white vocal group to record a Bacharach-David tune. Or "David-Bacharach" tune, as the pecking order continued to read until the mid-Seventies.

"The Morning Mail" (Burt Bacharach - Hal David)
Recorded by the Gallahads
Jubilee 5252, flip side of "The Fool"
Released August 1956

This set of Gallahads recorded for Capitol, Jubilee and Vik Records in the Fifties and should not be confused with the popular East L.A. Chicano doo-wop group of the same name, fronted by Jimmy Pipkin, which recorded for Del-Phi, Donna, Beechwood and Starla in the early Sixties. By then the used name hardly mattered, since the first set of Gallahads failed to rack up any substantial hits anyway.

More's the pity, since "The Morning Mail" could've established the Gallahads as a white vocal group à la the Four Freshman but with a firm rockabilly beat behind them. Certainly the tune is bouncy enough. From its delightfully goofy opening (the bass vocalist announcing, *"Oh, the morn-ing may-uuuullll!"* like a train conductor) to its carefree whistling call-and-responses, it's the sort of jollity a postman might pull off on his appointed rounds if no ravenous canines were around. Of note is the persistently cheerful whistling that would later be the hallmark of the first two Bacharach-David hits, "The Story of My Life" by Marty Robbins and "Magic Moments" by Perry Como.

Hal David's lyrics outline all sorts of communiqués that arrived via the postal service in the days when not every household had a telephone to reach out and touch someone: *"Aunt Josie sent a jar of honey, Cousin Jimmy wants some money."* But it's the absence of the singer's true honey which has him complaining *"I've got not one word from you-hoo,"* while the bass vocalist rubs it in behind him: *"No! No! Not one word!"*

And yet this charming Bacharach-David morsel was relegated to the flip side of a boring, repetitive cover of "The Fool" that completely ignored the Gallahads' harmonies so evident on "The Morning Mail." It was common practice in those days for recording artists and record labels to release competing versions of a surefire hit. If the caddish Gallahads meant to beat Phoenix singer Sanford Clark out of what would become his signature song, they failed. His "Fool" made it all the way to No. 7 while the Gallahads continued to toil in relative anonymity—except perhaps when they played for relatives like Aunt Josie and Cousin Jimmy.

"I Cry More" (Burt Bacharach - Hal David)
Recorded by Alan Dale
From the Columbia Pictures production *Don't Knock the Rock*
Coral 61699, released September 1956

1956

Promo still for *Don't Knock the Rock.* Once these gals realize that Alan Dale isn't really a rock star, they'll run screaming for the nearest Trenier!

Ever since Irving Berlin asked "How Deep Is the Ocean?" pop songwriters have been using nature as the Great Quantifier—gauging how much one can be expected to love and how much one can expect to cry by examining the boundless expanses of nature. Leave it to Hal David to break the infinitesimal down into concrete terms: *"There are 91,000 raindrops in a shower," "23,000 drops in every ripple,"* but only *"4,200 dewdrops on a flower."* Naturally they all pale in comparison to the number of teardrops falling from Alan Dale's eyes, making even the "96 Tears" cried by Question Mark seem like a drop in the bucket.

B-movie producer Sam Katzman followed up his previous year's riot-inciting *Rock Around the Clock* with a second rock exploitation film, *Don't Knock the Rock*, although we use the term "rock exploitation" loosely. In a film that has genuine rock luminaries like Little Richard, Bill Haley and the Comets, the Treniers and Alan Freed, Katzman decides that the real rock story begging to be told is the rise to fame of...*Arnie Haynes?!!* The fictional icon is portrayed by Coral recording artist Alan Dale, a guy who couldn't rock if you stood him on the San Andreas Fault and sawed off the heel of his left shoe. Not even performing the first Bacharach-David motion picture song could prevent Dale from getting his passport to obscurity furiously stamped.

This recording marks the first appearance of an early Bacharach trademark, vocalists aping the percussive sound of a musical instrument. In this case the "choo-ch-ch-choo" sound simulates not a train but the opening and closing of a hi-hat cymbal, clearly illustrated in close-ups during its performance in the opening of *Don't Knock the Rock*. Probably a feature of the original voice and piano demo, it became the final recording's most distinctive hook. Unfortunately, the rest of the arrangement sounds less like rock and more like the champagne music of Dale's label mate at Coral, Lawrence Welk.

"I Cry More" surely deserved better than Dale, who steps all over David's breezy lyrics with his Broadway belting and incessant mugging. Thirty-nine seconds into his performance, Dale's voice clutches up on what sounds like a flat note. The song is dispensed with in the first scene of the film, with girls screaming as unconvincingly as if they were being poked with a stick. During Dale's twitching gyrations, there's a reaction shot of Alan Freed looking at his watch. That says it all.

Strangely enough, Bacharach and David do not get a screen credit. Considering their well-documented disdain for three-chord wonders like Bill Haley, maybe that's a fortunate thing.

June Valli. This Valli girl's peak, chart performance wise, was a number 4 for "Crying In the Chapel" that must've left Sonny Till and the Orioles hissing in the pews.

"Beauty Isn't Everything" (Burt F. Bacharach - Edward Heyman)
Recorded by June Valli
RCA 6662, released fall 1956

It takes a pretty lass to keep a song like "Beauty Isn't Everything" from becoming a comedy number, and luckily June Valli was no Medusa. Having gotten her start by winning on the *Arthur Godfrey's Talent Scouts* program, this Bronx singer soon secured an RCA Victor contract and began racking up hits like "Strange Sensation," "I Understand" and her cover version of Sonny Till and the Orioles' "Crying in the Chapel," which bested the original on the pop charts in 1954, going all the way up to No. 4. After the hits stopped coming, Valli would demonstrate a different commercial appeal as the voice of Miss Chiquita Banana.

Luck might've helped where beauty failed to carry the day, since "Beauty Isn't Everything," a warm but fairly innocuous slow shuffle, didn't crack the Top 100. Sounding very much like a fairy godmother giving a pep talk to an ugly duckling Cinderella, Valli advises, *"It isn't what your face has got, it's what you've got inside.* This is Bacharach's only known collaboration with Edward Heyman, the man who wrote the timeless lyrics to such Victor Green ballads as "When I Fall in Love" and "Love Letters," as well as co-writing the lyrics of the jazz standard "Body and Soul" with Robert Sour and Frank Eyton to music by Johnny Green.

Bacharach's first recording under his own name, on the little known Cabot label, was a cover of Heyman and Victor Young's beautiful "Searching Wind."

Warm and Tender. This Bacharach-David song was featured in the Eleanor Parker film called Lizzie, the story of a girl who had considerably less fun with her triple personalities than a Patti Page album cover might've.

"How About" (Jack Wolf - Burt F. Bacharach)
Recorded by Della Reese
Jubilee 5278, released early 1957

Decades before her role as divine intervener on the popular CBS drama series *Touched by an Angel*, Della Reese was quite an accomplished belter of gospel, blues and torch songs. Like many black vocalists of the day vying for a white pop audience, Reese had a penchant for enunciating every syllable, a trait that lyricists loved but R&B listeners might find unnerving. Reese's trio of Top 40 chart hits in the Fifties were all dramatically articulated ballads, heavy on the bombast. "How About" is the complete antithesis of what she'd soon be known for. It's a jazzy pop tune not dissimilar to the Crew Cuts' "Sh-Boom." Over a low-down striptease beat, Della positively growls these Jack Wolf lyrics, which demand to know her lover's intentions for their future. It's a perfect showcase for Reese's jazzy, trumpet-emulating vocalization.

One other Wolf-Bacharach collaboration was copyrighted in 1955, a song called "The Secret of Staying Young," while another, aptly tagged "Forgotten Music," wasn't officially registered until 1964. Two other Wolf-Bacharach titles are known to exist in the ASCAP files—"My Heart Will Still Be Yours" and "It's Great to Be Young." As for Jack Wolf, he would go on to write such hits as "Paper Roses" for Anita Bryant and such obscurities as "I'll Never Learn to Cha Cha" and "We Want a Rock and Roll President" for someone less fortunate.

"Warm and Tender" (Burt Bacharach - Hal David)
Recorded by Johnny Mathis
From the Paramount motion picture *Lizzie*
Columbia 40851, flip side of "It's Not for Me to Say"
Released March 1957

1957

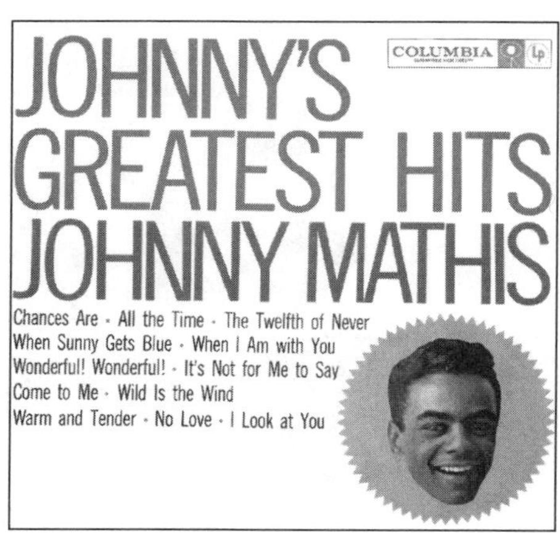

Heeeere's Johnny! Re-released in the Eighties on with a modern-day sleeve photo of Johnny, here's the original cover for Johnny's Greatest Hits, with its widely imitated disembodied head plopping through a sunburst design. You couldn't keep singers' heads on their bodies for years after that!

Chances are you already own this obscure but positively enthralling Bacharach-David collaboration. It first appeared as the B-side of Johnny Mathis' first Top 5 hit, "It's Not for Me to Say." Mathis could be seen crooning both sides of that single in a little-remembered film called *Lizzie*. The final resting place for "Warm and Tender" was a fortuitous one—*Johnny's Greatest Hits.* This phenomenally successful 1958 compilation logged a staggering 490 weeks in the Top 100 album charts, a Guinness World Record that would stand until Pink Floyd's *Dark Side of the Moon* eclipsed Johnny's chart performance with an unbelievable 730-week stay.

Since the Columbia recording studio on Manhattan's West 30th Street was a converted temple, many of the label's records from this golden period have more than their share of natural reverb. Sometimes it sounds as if a canyon of echo was compounded on top of that. Certainly the dark, heavy tom-toms that open "Warm and Tender" couldn't have been murkier if they'd been pounded from the bottom of a well. But hey, it works. Pushing the haunt count ever upward is an eerie soprano vocal (a carryover from Johnny's first hit, "Wonderful, Wonderful") and a heavenly harp plucking away.

One has to be impressed by Mathis' dexterity as he maneuvers his vibrato from hushed trepidation to wonderment. Then to the surprise of everybody but his opera coach, Mathis belts out the closing tag line like something out of *Porgy and Bess. "Wontcha make me yours! Make me yours! Make me yours!"* he implores, now taking his vocal direction straight from Hal David's lyric. Once "Misty" becomes his signature tune, this demanding blast of baritone will become a most rare commodity on a Johnny Mathis record.

In early 1957, arranger and pianist Peter Matz double-booked himself with Noel Coward and Marlene Dietrich. Matz recommended that his friend Bacharach take his place for the Dietrich engagement. It was in the first week of their association that Bacharach played "Warm and Tender" for Dietrich, and she felt compelled to forward the song to pal Frank Sinatra and tell him he ought to record it. Well, nobody chides the Chairman, not even a pushy German broad. Old Blue Eyes would not record a Bacharach tune until the 1964 Reprise album *It Might As Well Be Swing*, where he conspired with Count Basie and arranger Quincy Jones to pummel "Wives and Lovers" out of waltz time.

Other Versions: *Leroy Holmes & His Orchestra & Chorus (1957)*

Jo Stafford. Jo and her beau make love in the shadows underneath the overpass, where no passing commuters can spoil the mood by yelling "Hey! Get a room!"

"Underneath the Overpass" (Burt Bacharach - Hal David)
Recorded by Jo Stafford
Columbia 40926, flip side of "I'll Be There (When We Get Lonely)
Released May 1957

Speaking of savages, Jo Stafford and her nightly smooching companion require little in the way of romantic accouterments, just "a little bench, a patch of grass" and, oh yes, a busy overpass where all who traverse are oblivious to the carnal clickety-clack beneath the railroad tracks.

"While others go to lover's lane, we go where we hear a train a-chuggin' while we're huggin," she coos in double-tracked voice, with Hal David's rhythmic rhymes suggesting the shuffling arrangement.

Stafford, a onetime vocalist for Tommy Dorsey's vocal group the Pied Pipers, had enjoyed a staggering 78 Top 40 hits as a solo artist between 1944 and 1956, plus ten more chart entries singing duets with Gordon MacCrae. Sadly for this talented vocalist, that lengthy streak would end at the start of 1957. Stafford, in a rare 1999 interview for the Internet magazine *Songbirds*, faulted Mitch Miller for giving longtime Columbia artists "inappropriate" songs to sing. "A lot of the material he gave me to record—it was not my cup of tea. I couldn't do it justice. One was called 'Chow, Willy.' And then there was one called 'Underneath the Overpass.' If you can believe it."

The late Fifties would find the charts dominated by male singers, with only a one female soloist (Debbie Reynolds singing "Tammy") nabbing a No. 1 hit for the remainder of the decade. In the next five years, 16 different female vocalists would record Bacharach tunes, and only one would get within spitting distance of the Top 40 (Jane Morgan, with a meek No. 39 showing for "With Open Arms"). It would take the girl-group power of the Shirelles to break the Top 30 Bacharach blockade in 1961 with "Baby It's You," but not until the arrival of Dionne Warwick would luck be a lady for Burt.

Cathy Carr. Bacharach and David's first weepie, and first waltz. Coupled with an equally dejected A-side, this little 45 must've provided the soundtrack to many a teenage girl's mope-a-thon.

"Wild Honey" (Burt Bacharach - Hal David)
Recorded by Cathy Carr
Fraternity 765, released May 1957

The previous spring, Cathy Carr had climbed to No. 2 with the ballad "Ivory Tower." From that lofty perch there would be nowhere for this Bronx singer to go but down—and dirty. The song is structured like a stuttering I-IV-V blues, with the first and second lines repeating. Carr aggressively purrs *"w-i-i-i-i-i-l-l-l-l-d honnn-nnney"* at the top of each verse but winds down by verse's end, sounding more conquered than conquering. Clearly her stinger of a beau has the upper hand in this relationship, *"flitting and flirtin' all over this town,"* leaving her to wonder, *"How can I claim / A love I cannot tame / Even though we have kissed you insist you are free."* Ultimately, it's one of those you're-a-creep-but-how-can-I-help-but-love-you songs that's not meant to be taken seriously, especially since the wronged lass seems more than willing to put up with her man's insensitivity as long as it's bookended with kisses.

The circular, scale-climbing guitar line in "Wild Honey" recalls the circular, scale-climbing line of "Flight of the Bumblebee," albeit at a considerably slower speed. Just imagine a little drone that's either been drugged or hit with a newspaper. A minor charmer.

Cathy Carr. In a chart catfight over "Ivory Tower" with *My Little Margie* star Gale Storm, Carr would win by a whisker.

"Presents from the Past" (Burt Bacharach - Hal David)
Recorded by Cathy Carr
Fraternity 782, flip side of "House of Heartache"
Released September 1957

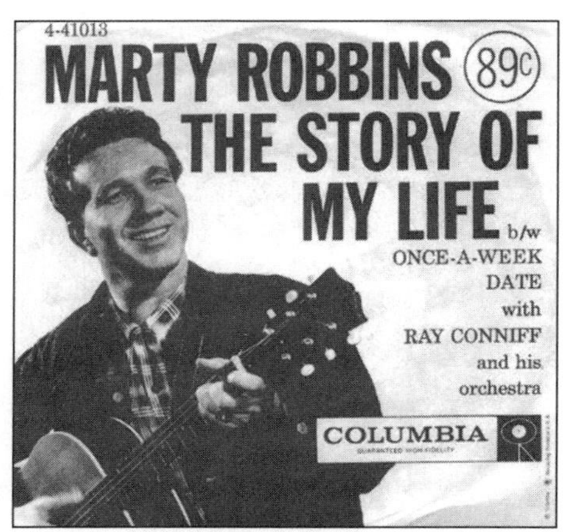

Marty Robbins. Because Columbia wanted to market Robbins as a country artist, Mitch Miller encouraged his latest pop discovery Guy Mitchell to cover Robbins' hits "Singing the Blues" and "Knee Deep in the Blues" for the pop market. Robbins was furious when Mitchell's version of the former sat at No. 1 for nine weeks while he had to settle for No. 17. That's when he decided to come to New York and record with the Ray Conniff Singers to secure some pop hits of his own.

Here's another early B-side, this one notable only for being the first truly unhappy Bacharach and David composition to be etched in wax. Like a despondent cousin to the soon-to-be hit "Magic Moments," this song finds Cathy Carr ruminating over a locket, a pressed rose and a high school sweater, all mementos that no longer hold any more magic for her. The arrangement is even less magical, fashioned by some staff producer to sound exactly like "Tennessee Waltz," with the half-step key change coming in right when you expect it to. Bacharach would find greater success when he returned to the waltz idiom for the jazzy "Wives and Lovers," the snazzy "What's New Pussycat?" and the classy "What the World Need Now Is Love".

"The Story of My Life" (Burt F. Bacharach - Hal David)
First recorded by Marty Robbins
Columbia 40864 (*Billboard* pop #15, country #1)
Released November 1957

Bacharach and David's first Top 40 entry yielded their first No. 1 hit—on the country charts! It was Robbins' sixth country chart-topper and his third appearance in the pop Top 20. Remembered chiefly as a country music artist, this versatile native of Glendale, Arizona, managed to record gospel, rockabilly, calypso, Hawaiian music and string-laden ballads—all within the first half decade of his recording career.

While a small-scale guitar that sounds like a ukulele and the Ray Conniff Singers' cheerful whistling most readily characterizes "The Story of My Life," it's the clever lyrical outline that best recommends it. Here Robbins' romantic yet selective memory recounts the only significant events of his life, beginning and ending with his true love and omitting all that messy birth, school, work and death stuff in between. The only hint of turmoil occurs in the bridge, when the happy couple actually break up, only to make up in the next line so that they can marry and this likeable galoot's story can indeed end happily ever after. Three years later Bacharach and David would be fashioning mostly tortured life stories where the Book of Love/Life is irrevocably shut tight whenever a lover leaves. "Without your love, I would die" is a popular sentiment found in many Hal David lyrics ("The Last One to Be Loved," "This Guy's in Love With You," "Take a Broken Heart," "Another Night," "A Lifetime of Loneliness," etc.). But for now the girl returns, the whistlers reign supreme, the fluff gets up your nose.

Michael Holliday. British audiences apparently wanted to hear "The Story of My Life" told with a local accent. Unfortunately the story ended rather grimly for the once-popular British singer, who committed suicide in November 1963 rather than witness the tide of British groups push him any further into chart obsolescence.

Meanwhile back in the UK, the record-buying public continued its peculiar practice of bypassing the original American version whenever confronted with inferior British sound-alike covers. Liverpudlian Michael Holliday reached No. 1 with his retelling of "The Story of My Life," while shaky-voiced Gary Miller also made the Top 20 with a slightly more eccentric production featuring background vocals emulating castanets.

No copycat claims can be made about the odd version Herman's Hermits offered on its 1966 *Best of Herman's Hermits, Volume 2* collection. In an attempt to make the song sound more western, the Hermits' version begins with an Indian tom-tom and a slide guitar track that Jimmy

Page probably doesn't remember ever cutting, just before it shifts into chunky Merseybeat sounds for the bridge.

Other Versions: *Bruce Adams (1958) • Paul Anka (1966) • Apollo 100 (1973) • Don Cherry (1966) • Gerry & the Pacemakers (1983) • Herman's Hermits (1966) • Michael Holliday (1958) • Cacka Israelsson – "Boken Om Mitt Liv" (1958) • Dave King (1958) • Frankie Laine (1967) • Jenny Luna (1958) • Siw Malmkvist - "Boken Om Mitt Liv" • Werner Overheidt – "Die Story von Uns Zwei'n" (1958) • Rod McKuen (1976) • Gary Miller (1957) • Bobby Vee (1965)*

Jerry Lewis. Folks always pledge big for the annual Muscular Dystrophy Association Telethon whenever the host sings himself to tears with "You'll Never Walk Alone." But imagine how much more financial support Lewis could extort from viewers by threatening to sing "Sad Sack" over and over unless the tote board numbers improved.

"Sad Sack" (Burt F. Bacharach - Hal David)
Recorded by Jerry Lewis
From the Paramount movie *Sad Sack*
Decca 30503, released November 1957

Before Capitol signed Dean Martin to a record deal in 1948, the laid-back crooner from Steubenville had released several titles on tiny record labels like Diamond, Apollo and Embassy. One incentive for Capitol to ink a deal with the commercially unproven Dean in the first place was that it gave them an option to also release comedy records by Martin and Lewis, the world's most successful comedy duo at that time. Capitol's enthusiasm waned when the pair's first release, "That Certain Party," only racked up laughable sales figures. Thereafter, the Hollywood-based label banished Lewis' hyperactive participation to the occasional movie soundtrack EP.

After the acrimonious Martin and Lewis split in 1956, Jerry wasted no time in trouncing Dean's post-breakup chart performances by scoring a Top 10 hit with "Rock-A-Bye Your Baby with a Dixie Melody." Jerry even managed to score a Top 3 album for Decca with *Jerry Lewis Just Sings.* Top 3!! Dean wouldn't even have a Top *40* album until *Everybody Loves Somebody* in 1964. Imagine if he'd issued an album called *Dean Martin Just Mugs.*

Despite this early solo success, the novelty of hearing Jerry Lewis warble on a piece of plastic had worn off completely by the time the stooge's second solo flick, *Sad Sack,* hit theaters the following fall. Here's the first of many instances where Hal David shows his knack for encapsulating two hours of film stock in two minutes of song, in this case by letting Lewis sing about what a lovable schlub he is: *"I take her dancing and step on her shoes / I fix her toaster and I blow a fuse / Then I get seasick when we take a cruise / I'm the genuine original, first edition copy of Sad Sack."*

Once again the Bacharach trait of having background vocalists ape a musical instrument is repeated. In the days before he cut fully produced demos, he would vocally suggest instrumentation that would eventually become a hook in the song. This time, male singers mimic the track's baritone sax behind Jerry's singing. You couldn't call Jerry's droll singing melodic—on the turnarounds, he moans *"How can I make her love me"* as if he is being shaken awake after swallowing too many sleeping pills. With the minimal number of notes to work with, Bacharach fashions a bluesy I-IV-V progression that lopes along to that laid-back beat kids

Perry Como. The RIAA introduced gold-record awards in 1958, the year RCA issued this Como compilation. Only one seven-inch included here was awarded a gold record—"Catch a Falling Star," which had the added incentive of "Magic Moments" on the flip side.

were doing "The Stroll" to at that time. There's even a hint of rock guitar on the break, but not even nearsighted teens who thought they were purchasing a Jerry Lee Lewis record could send this lovable stinker into the Top 40.

"Winter Warm" (Burt Bacharach - Hal David)
Recorded by Gale Storm
Dot 15666, flip side of "Go Away from My Window"
Released November 1957

Hollywood leading lady Gale Storm transferred her silver-screen stardom of the Forties to the small screen in the Fifties with television shows like "My Little Margie" and "The Gale Storm Show," remaining on the air until 1962. Around the time "Margie" was ending its run in 1955, Gale made a beeline for the pop charts. Taking her cure from the first successful TV-star-turned-recording-artist, Ricky Nelson, Storm also covered an R&B hit the first time out. It was Smiley Lewis' "I Hear You Knocking" that kicked off Storm's streak of six consecutive Top 20 hits. Producer Randy Wood set the commercial strategy of having Storm alternate between trying to woo the adults who appreciated a good Doris Day tune and suckering in the kids whose radios didn't make scheduled stops at black stations. Neither strategy was working for her by mid-summer 1957, giving this soothing lullaby B-side minimum exposure.

"Winter Warm," with its spare glockenspiel-and-harp arrangement, is also noteworthy for being one of the first Bacharach songs to sport an unexpected and deliberately shortened measure. After two lines Storm has already reached the tag line (*"in your arms, I'm winter warm"*). In this extremely streamlined structure, David's economical lyrics still manage to convey an idyllic *"snowy, glowy kind of day,"* those moments when love feels like a comfy sweater with a steamy cup of cocoa waiting nearby.

Other Versions: *Betty Bryant Trio (2002) • Trudi Mann (2000)*

Gale Storm. As a public service for people who don't need a beat, My Little Margie also rerecorded Frankie Lymon and the Teenagers' "Goody Goody" and "Why Do Fools Fall in Love." Goody indeed!

"Uninvited Dream" (Burt Bacharach - Sammy Gallop)
Recorded by Peggy Lee
Capitol 3811, flip side of "Listen to the Rockin' Bird"
Released late 1957

At this point in Peggy Lee's illustrious career, she'd returned to Capitol after a successful spell at Decca. Despite attempts like "Listen to the Rockin' Bird," Lee would not connect with the newly identified rock 'n' roll market until her 1958 cover of Little Willie John's "Fever." This seductive B-side deftly demonstrates the appeal of Lee's barely-above-a-whisper delivery, which would give rise to her biggest rock-era hit.

"Uninvited Dream" sounds like the drowsy last-call number that dance bands strike while the final few chairs are being stacked up on tables. In it, Lee portrays a woman whose nocturnal visitor delights her in dreams but breaks her heart the rest of the time. Sammy Gallop, whose lyrical credits include "Maybe You'll Be There," "Somewhere Along the

Way," "Autumn Serenade" and "Wake the Town and Tell the People," as well as the infrequently heard words to "Holiday for Strings," perfectly captures the painful bliss of a woman under an uncontrollable spell: *"I see him smiling in an uninvited dream / why does he find me, why does he remind me that I can't be free / Break the chains that bind me to a memory."*

Perry Como. Unlike other contemptuous adult contemporaries, Como gave his paternal nod to rock 'n' roll by giving early TV exposure to Fats Domino, the Everly Brothers, the Teddy Bears and Conway Twitty.

While "Uninvited Dream" proved a one-off Gallop collaboration, Bacharach would furnish Lee with another exclusive song in 1971, the instantly forgettable "My Rock and Foundation."

"Magic Moments" (Burt Bacharach - Hal David)
First recorded by Perry Como
RCA 7128, flip side of "Catch a Falling Star" (*Billboard* pop #4)
Released January 1958

Hot on the heels of the successful "Story of My Life" came another whistling anthem, with Perry Como the resident pucker-up-and-blower. A direct descendant of the Bing Crosby school of croon, Como managed to maintain his high standing on the pop charts during the early onslaught of Presley mania. Unlike other adult singers who'd try to remain afloat by bastardizing R&B hits, Como rang up sales with the youngsters by aligning old-school pop to the kind of nonsensical lyrics that were all the rage in doo-wop. Among Como's hits were such novelty numbers as "Hot Diggity (Dog Ziggity Boom)," "Jukebox Baby," "Ko-Ko-Mo (I Love You So)" and "Chee Chee-Oo Chee (Sang the Little Bird)."

However, on Bacharach and David's "Magic Moments," the heir o'parent is unmistakable. Recalling the Four Lads' 1955 nostalgic checklist on "Moments to Remember," Como rattles off happy Norman Rockwell scenarios, from the floor of his car falling through to hugging his honey on the sleigh ride to keep warm. Combined with the quizzical bassoon, the whistling and the ghastly white shadings of the Ray Charles Singers, these distant recollections must seem like occurrences on another planet to later generations. Those who wish to keep believing that *"time can't erase the memories of these magic moments"* are advised to stay away from Erasure's ironic cover of the song. Sadly, it's hard to imagine music this trouble-free being written by anyone ever again.

***Connie Francis Sings Bacharach and David* (1968).** The back cover contains a signed note from the songwriters she once snubbed: "Dear Connie, We are pleased and proud that you recorded an album of our songs. You have always been one of our favorites. Many thanks, Burt Bacharach, Hal David." But don't believe everything you read: although the cover lists "Wishin' and Hopin'," the record doesn't include it.

The B-side to Como's No. 1 hit "Catch a Falling Star," "Magic Moments" managed to climb all the way to No. 4 on its own merits. In Britain, the song did even better, shooting past the A-side all the way to No. 1, bumping Michael Holliday's "Story of My Life" down to second place. This gave Bacharach and David the top two positions on the UK pop charts for most of March 1958 as well as the honor of two consecutive No. 1's, a feat they would never duplicate at home.

Despite the success of "Magic Moments," Bacharach and David would not return to the American Top 5 as a team until "The Man Who Shot Liberty Valance" in 1962. Needing a hit during that dry spell, they turned to the girl *Billboard* called "Pop music's No. 1 female vocalist from the late Fifties to the mid-Sixties." Bacharach delights in telling concert audiences the story of a snotty young vocalist who ripped the needle off one of their demos after letting it play for a few seconds, then blurted, "What else have you got?" The composer diplomatically omits the identity of the singer, but she was one "Who's Sorry Now" lady who atoned after her hits dried up in 1968 by recording an album called *Connie Francis Sings Bacharach and David.* It contained the team's newest hit "Promises, Promises," as well as its oldest golden oldie, "Magic Moments."

Other Versions: *Jula De Palma • Sandy Duncan - TV special (1972) • Erasure (1995) • Film Score Orchestra • Connie Francis (1968) • Gerry & the Pacemakers (1983) • Ronnie Hilton (1958) • Shauna Hicks - part of "A Bacharach Love Story Medley" (1998) • Nelson Riddle (1962) • Royal Marines (1974) • Snuff (1997) • Starlight Orchestra (aka Starshine Orchestra) (1995) • Billy Vaughn*

The Four Preps. Among this clean-cut group's members was Ed Cobb, the writing and producing brains behind the Standells' "Dirty Water," "Why Pick on Me," "Have You Ever Spent the Night in Jail" and "Sometimes the Good Guys Don't Wear White." Or letterman sweaters!

"Humble Pie" (Burt Bacharach - Hal David)
Recorded by the Four Preps
From the album *The Four Preps,* Capitol T994
Released winter 1958

The Four Aces, the Four Lads, the Four Naturals, the Four Coachmen, the Four Voices, the Four Esquires, the Four Coins, the Four Freshmen, and the Four Preps—you need four eyes and four years of college just to tell 'em apart. Here's all you need to know of a Bacharachian nature: only three of these gangs of four had material written specifically for them by Bacharach and David—two Pennsylvanian foursomes, the Four Aces and the Four Coins, and a quartet of seniors from Hollywood High called the Four Preps.

Because of their youth, the Four Preps had more of a natural inclination to rock and swing like the Spaniels or the Diamonds than the other arcane barbershop quartets mentioned above. To prove it, there's a Sambo bass voice and a snazzy semi-hollow-bodied guitar solo on "Humble Pie," a scholarly meditation on eating crow and an exercise in baby-I'm-sorry-I'm-such-a-fool couple counseling. This could be filed away in the forget-me vault if it weren't for one great Hal David line that almost sounds like Elvis Costello: *"I found my tongue and lost my head."*

"Country Music Holiday" (Burt Bacharach - Hal David)
Recorded by Bernie Nee
From the film *Country Music Holiday*
Columbia 41132, flip side of "State of Happiness"
Released March 1958

A low-budget country-western musical aimed at cashing in on Elvis Presley's recent celluloid success, *Country Music Holiday* neither kick-started a country music boom in the pop world nor catapulted singer Ferlin Husky into the throne as teenyboppers' new hillbilly king. This rarely seen musical remains a curio largely because of its oddball cast. It co-starred Zsa Zsa Gabor as the Hungarian she-devil who owns 50 percent of the young singer's contract, Jesse White (the original Maytag repairman) as Ferlin's Colonel Tom of a manager, Patty Duke as his little sister, former heavyweight champ Rocky Graziano as a record company executive named Rocky who used to box, June Carter not-yet-Cash as the love interest, Faron Young as country music rival Clyde Woods and the Jordanaires as, well, guys who look and sing exactly like the Jordanaires.

It's inconceivable that Bacharach and David's infectious theme was not sung by this movie's star, especially when judged against the slim offerings on Husky's own *Country Music Holiday* EP. Imagine having one of the extras in an Elvis movie singing "Loving You" instead of the King. Co-star Bernie Nee does the honors, bringing bounce to David's lyrics about an ideal guilt-free holiday, one where school lets out at 1 P.M., there's *"a girl beneath the kissing tree,"* there's never any mention of relatives and everyone's playing guitars except Mr. Miller, whose promise of free ice cream sodas for even one day would surely spell financial ruin in the real world. Ironic that the only time David ever used the words *"we're gonna rock"* in a B&D song, it was in celebration of country music. And the rockin' was taking place around a fire pump!

By November, the song washed up on the British Isles and was promptly recorded by English pop singer Adam Faith (HMV POP 557). Not even coupling it with another American movie theme, "High School Confidential," could insure a placing in Britain's Top 100. And yet it remains another fine example of Bacharach-David bringing country music to the mother country.

Bernie Nee. The voice of the Five Blobs could also be found billed below Al Fisher and Lou Marks, the Jordanaires, Lonzo and Oscar, Drifting Johnny Miller and the LaDell Sisters in *Country Music Holiday.*

Other Versions: *Adam Faith (1958)*

"Hot Spell" (Burt Bacharach - Mack David)
First recorded by Margaret Whiting
Dot 45 15742, released May 1958

"Waitin' like a fool in vain, in vain, waitin' for the cool, cool rain"

Your waiter for this quasi-calypso rocker is Margaret Whiting, who is teamed with Jordanaires-like background vocalists echoing her every "waiting" with five or six of their own. Whiting's own hot spell, popularity-wise, spanned the years 1946 to 1954, before rock showed its infant face.

Meant to promote the Anthony Quinn film of the same name, Mack David's prose steered clear of *Hot Spell*'s steamy story of a married man threatening to run off with a 20-year-old bachelorette. Instead it focused on Whiting as an abandoned woman running hot while her love life remained decidedly cold. With a spirited Milton Rogers arrangement not unlike that of Buddy Holly's "Maybe Baby," this Paramount exploitation song would be as close to the rock idiom as a Bacharach tune would veer until he and Mack David paired up again to compose "The Blob" later the same year.

Ernie Felice and his quintet recorded a strange but far more interesting competing version, where discordant horns and strings drone in every time the title is sung to simulate the dizzying effect of sweltering heat. The idea of introducing such an unpleasant noise for even a second during a song was unheard of in those days, for fear it would turn listeners

1958

Marty Robbins. Contrary to claims made by head Kink Ray Davies on brother Dave's behalf, guitar fuzz as we know it was prominently first showcased on Robbins' hit "Don't Worry," which appeared four years before "You Really Got Me." Sorry, Ray.

off. One imagines this to be one of those risky Bacharach arrangement ideas that most producers of the time felt compelled to disregard vigilantly.

Other Versions: *Ernie Felice Quintet (1958) • The Plaids - part of a "Bacharach at the Movies" medley (1998)*

"It Seemed So Right Last Night" (Burt Bacharach - Hal David)
Recorded by Mary Mayo
Columbia 41190, flip side of "Memory Book"
Released July 1958

Not until Bacharach and David throw themselves full-bore into love-gone-irreversibly-wrong songs do they find their unique voice. By the same token, until the pair assumes the arranging duties full-time, their work bears more of the imprint of its producers than its authors. Unlike "Presents from the Past," whose bland, throwaway arrangement rightfully kept Cathy Carr's womanly woe buried on a B-side, this sobering number about the morning after got a sympathetic treatment certainly worthy of an A-side.

Things are kept to a stark minimum, the coloring little more than reverb-enhanced Spanish guitars, which give the track an exotic Mediterranean lilt. Another internal rhyming sequence, in which the second and third lines correspond, spares David from having to keep coming up with more rhymes with the word "night." For her part, Mayo gives an effective if sometimes over-dramatic low-register performance of the kind Dionne Warwick would later render with great frequency.

"Sitting in a Tree House" (Burt Bacharach - Hal David)
Recorded by Marty Robbins
Columbia 41208, flip side of "She Was Only Seventeen"
Released July 1958

As the follow-up to the successful "Story of My Life," Bacharach and David offered Marty Robbins the singalong-friendly "Sitting in a Tree House," which, like its predecessor, featured whistling after the first two lines of every verse. While Robbins turns in a characteristically solid vocal performance, the big problem here is casting. It's one thing for a 32-year-old man to sing lovingly about a girl who's only 17, as he does on the A-side. It's quite another to have the same grown man rushing out after supper to go kiss her in a tree house—it makes him seem like either a pervert or, worse, a cheap date. This couldn't have gone unnoticed by the honchos at Columbia, who would grudgingly encourage Robbins' subsequent move to gunslinger ballads and trail songs once the teen hits stopped coming. Six months after "Sittin' in a Tree House," Robbins would be noticeably more comfortable dangling from "The Hanging Tree."

Although Bacharach later employed children singing on "Saturday Sunshine" and on the *Lost Horizon* soundtrack, one wonders how violently he must've reacted upon first hearing the chipmunk background vocals grafted onto this song—with that cavernous Columbia echo, yet! Clearly an attempt by Columbia's powerful A&R man Mitch Miller to cash in on Ross "David Seville" Bagdasarian's recent No. 1 hit, "Witch Doctor," the resulting arrangement (easily Ray Conniff's most gimmicky to that date) sounds boldly infantile.

Tony Bennett. Like Bacharach, Bennett would find there was still a youth market out for there for "good songs" in the Nineties. Both men also enjoyed a healthy camaraderie with one of modern rock's best practitioners of "good songs," Elvis Costello. A hint to Sony/Legacy—this flip side is one of many that have yet to appear on CD.

"The Night That Heaven Fell" (Burt Bacharach - Hal David)
Recorded by Tony Bennett
Columbia 41237, flip side of "Firefly"
Released August 1958

When the Beatles needed to fill the 24 empty bars of "A Day in the Life," they arrived upon something that halfway resembled the opening and closing of "The Night That Heaven Fell," recorded by one of Bacharach's old conducting clients.

While cellos zoom from the lowest note upward, a team of violins saw away in unison from the highest note to the lowest, until both arrive at an amicable F major. On top of that, eerie sopranos do their ghostly best to impersonate a theremin, while a thoroughly awed Tony Bennett muses on how love has magically turned his whole world upside down and, even more amazing, that no one's gotten hurt.

No wonder Frank Sinatra named Bennett his favorite singer. When a song demands an audible smile, he radiates warmth that's genuine, even on songs where the spell of love is broken. Like "Warm and Tender" before it, "The Night That Heaven Fell" transcends its schlock horror movie production through a masterly vocal performance and otherworldly lyrics.

The only Bacharach exploitation song ever written for a film with English subtitles, *The Night Heaven Fell* is the name of a titillating French film released that year that starred a young Brigitte Bardot as a convent girl vacationing with relatives in Spain. When Tony Bennett sang about how *"paradise had just come down to earth to celebrate the birth of love,"* he couldn't have been thinking of our little Lolita, who ran off with the thug who murdered her uncle and seduced her aunt.

Blob, Italian Style! It creeps, it leaps, it rapes and pillages! Like most Italians, that "fluido mortale," better known as the Blob, has no trouble expressing itself. "The Blob" would become the second Bacharach movie theme in a year to be sung by Bernie Nee, which still didn't help the session singer's name recognition.

"Oooh My Love" (Burt Bacharach - Hal David)
Recorded by Vic Damone
Columbia 41245, flip side of "Forever New"
Released August 1958

Bacharach was too busy touring with Marlene Dietrich to notice that back home his old nemesis Vic Damone, the guy who had him fired from that all-important first gig, recorded one of his compositions on a B-side. It was the largely forgettable "Ooh My Love," a western ballad with heavily plonking electric bass and jingling tambourine that would constitute the standard "spaghetti western" sound in the late Sixties. It sounds as if Vic is about to face off against his darling in the middle of a dusty, deserted street, but he's no match for her warm, sweet lips and her tender touch.

Surrender seems imminent, almost immediate, but Damone's deep operatic baritone sounds ludicrous singing lines like "how I quiver" and "can't you feel me shake and shiver" without a Little Richard yelp or a Buddy Holly hiccup.

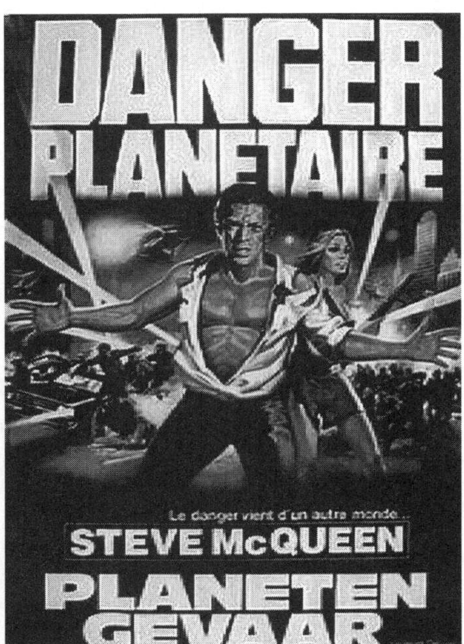

If it's Belgium, this must be *Planeten Gevaar*! Belgian poster for *The Blob*.

"The Blob" (Burt Bacharach - Mack David)
First recorded by the Five Blobs
From the Paramount movie The Blob
Columbia 41250 (Billboard pop #33)
Released September 1958

Could you be scared to death by a slimy parasitic space invader that "creeps and leaps and glides and slides" but looks like a tipped over vat of raspberry preserves? Someone at Paramount apparently hoped so and tapped Bacharach and Mack David to come up with a non-threatening theme that would prevent the faint of heart from going into nostril-flaring terror during the opening credits. Together the two men concocted "The Blob," a goofy musical creature that was one part "Temptation" to two parts "Tequila." Session singer Bernie Nee does the champagne-cork-popping honors by pulling his finger out of his cheeks seven times. Oddly enough, those opening credits omit any mention of Bacharach and David or the tune. Only Ralph Carmichael's score received a screen check, giving credence to the notion that the song was a last-minute addition.

Given its horror movie origins, it's no surprise that the Five Blobs turned out to be a phantom group that only pumped blood within the confines of a recording studio. In this case, the mystery band consisted of Bacharach, a bunch of musicians for hire and Nee, who tracked his voice five times to achieve that Karloff-esque quality.

The Blob. Mack David had some highly impressive writing credits even before "The Blob." Among them are "Cherry Pink and Apple Blossom White" (a No. 1 hit for Pérez Prado in 1955), "I Don't Care If the Sun Don't Shine," (a No. 1 hit for Patti Page in 1950), "A Dream Is a Wish Your Heart Makes" (from the 1950 Disney animated feature *Cinderella*) and the English translation of Edith Piaf's lyrics for "La Vie En Rose."

For those wishing to hear "The Blob" with female voices, the Zannies provide some quivering estrogen, Dracula impersonators and ghoulish "blob" sound effects that more closely resemble suppressed farts.

Extreme trivia note: Prior to "The Blob," Bernie Nee recorded several singles for Columbia (including "Feeling Foolish in Brazil," "Sleepy Sunday" and "Hey Liley Lelay Lo"), then continued to go undetected on Kapp Records for several more sides.

Other Versions: *Aqualads (2000) • Blob & the Blobettes • Casino Royale (1999) • Wolfman Jack • Guy Klucevsek (2000) • Little Stevie & The McQueen • The Plaids - part of a "Bacharach at the Movies" medley (1998) • Pumpkin Uglies (1996) • Tropicalisimo Apache • The Zannies (1971)*

"Saturday Night in Tia Juana" (Burt Bacharach - Hal David)
First recorded by the Five Blobs
Columbia 41250, flip side of "The Blob"
Released September 1958

In keeping with the "Tequila" feel of the A-side, the Five Blobs decide to finish out the recording date south of the border. A squeaky sax does most of the work along with some handclapping and Ray Conniff–style singers doing their horny best to emulate Tijuana brass. Although the song was originally credited solely to Bacharach, Hal David jotted down some lyrics for "Saturday Night in Tia Juana" before the year was up. The following year, the obscure duo of Cindy Lord and Lindy Doherty gave Hal David's travel tips a try. *"Tijuana teens in jeans are making eyes at the teenage queens,"* they charge to a cha-cha beat, repeating *"Tia Tia Tia Tia T'juana"* like stuttering mariachi brass.

Other Versions: *Cindy & Lindy (1959)*

Cindy and Lindy. Here's some info for all those budding Cindy and Lindy archivists out there. The duo recorded two singles on Pilgrim and another pair on ABC Paramount before landing on Coral. The second of their four singles for Coral was "Saturday Night in Tia Juana" (note the Fifties spelling of Tijuana). Its flip was the scholarly "You Can't Mail an Elephant."

"Wendy Wendy" (Burt Bacharach - Hal David)
Recorded by the Four Coins
Epic 9286 (*Billboard* pop #72)
Released September 1958

"Wendy Wendy" was the first of three Bacharach-David tunes written for the Four Coins. This rolling country-western ballad about a jealous fool begging Miss Wendy for forgiveness is typical of something Frankie Laine might've hollered at the time. Hal David provides some crazy frontier vernacular, like "just a-longin' for to hold you near," that almost convinces you that these young men of Greek descent are ranch hands on the Ponderosa—until they blow their cover by pronouncing "jealous" like Parthenon dwellers. But there's little time to notice, since you've got an insistent electric guitar twanging back every line with a counter-melody riff. Not a big money winner, but a strapping also-ran.

"The Last Time I Saw My Heart" (Burt Bacharach - Hal David)
Recorded by Marty Robbins
Columbia 41282, flip side of "Ain't I the Lucky One"
Released November 1958

Bacharach and David's last contribution to the Marty Robbins catalog was this pretty yet forlorn tango with clacking castanets, a harbinger of the Mexican flavor shortly to follow on Robbins releases like "El Paso" and "Devil Woman." Closer examination of David's lyrics might lead one to conclude that they were originally scribed for a woman to warble, what with Robbins forever swooning in his lover's arms and always having to climb his way up to her lips. No, this enchantress doesn't buy her clothes at the Big & Tall Gals section of the department store—she's in paradise, where she always has the home advantage over hapless Marty. When our boy comes down to earth again, his heart has been removed with a pick-pocket's precision. *"I can't believe you'd deceive someone who needs you so," he* weeps, never expecting such shabby treatment from a paradisiacal girl. Welcome to Loveland, Marty.

Although this Ray Conniff arrangement isn't totally immune to the usual Columbia tricks, at least it isn't as conspicuously gimmicky as the previous "Sittin' in a Tree House." To musically simulate Robbins' frequent flyer miles between paradise and earth, one busy keyboardist's hand trills up the ivories from low notes to high while the other cascades back down. This is the sort of contrivance that those dueling concert pianists Ferrante and Teicher would build an entire career around.

Marty Robbins. Mitch Miller created the "greatest hits" album concept during his tenure at Columbia. *Marty's Greatest Hits* was an obvious attempt to re-create the phenomenal success of *Johnny's Greatest Hits*. While Robbins' collection would not enjoy the chart longevity of the earlier Mathis set, at least he resisted the urge to push his disembodied head through that gold sunburst on the bottom right.

"Dream Big" (Burt Bacharach - Paul Hampton)
Recorded by Sonny James
Capitol F412, flip side of "Yo Yo"
Released January 1959

Like Marty Robbins, country star Sonny James found himself with a pop crossover hit in 1957, only to watch some Yankee beat him to No. 1 with a competing pop version of that same song. It was Tab Hunter's nearly identical cover of "Young Love" that robbed the Southern Gentleman of what should've been his rightful chart topper (James' version was stuck at No. 2). He would never get another chance: the follow-up "First Date, First Kiss, First Love" became his last pop hit, peaking at No. 25.

When further salvos lobbed at the teen market met with negligible results, James permanently funneled his attention toward the country charts, where his records still made the Top 10. This flip side caught him at the end of his rock 'n' roll tether. "Dream Big" was a fairly amiable Ricky Nelson sound-alike, complete with knockoff James Burton guitar licks booting it along. If the melody sounds suspiciously like Nelson's "Be Bop Baby," there's a truncated Bo Diddley beat in the intro being played furiously on the piano to throw people off the scent. This was Bacharach's first collaboration with Paul Hampton, a Canadian singer/composer who on occasion wrote both words and music.

Almost without exception, Bacharach and Hampton's collaboration was unremarkable. The sum of two musicians working together may have caused each to compromise more than usual or withhold more adventurous musical ideas in order to arrive at a finished product. On the sheet music for several Hampton-Bacharach compositions, both are credited with words and music. Judging by the evidence here, lyrics were neither man's strong suit. What kind of advice is "dream big" to give people who aren't happy or sad *and* to people whose wishes never come true?

"Loving Is a Way of Giving" (Burt Bacharach - Hal David)
Recorded by Steve Lawrence
ABC Paramount 10005, flip side of "Only Love Me"
Released March 1959

From his earliest recordings on labels like King and Coral, Steve Lawrence maintained a conscious duality never before necessary in popular music. On the one hand, vying for the rock-hating, easy-listening adults, he filled his albums with nightclub standards. For the teen market, he reserved the greasy kid stuff like "Party Doll," "Speedo," "Blah Blah Blah" and "Uh-Huh, Oh Yeah."

By 1959 the former Sidney Leibowitz was a steady regular on the Steve Allen–hosted "Tonight Show," where he'd already paired off with Eydie Gormé. While the middle of the road seemed like a foregone conclusion, the underside of his first recorded product for ABC Paramount demonstrated that he was still willing to bop for the younger set. Lawrence's one-time musical director fashioned for his old friend this melodic mid-tempo rocker, yet another in Bacharach and David's seemingly endless chain of little-known B-sides. Unusually for pop records of the day, stand-up bass is ditched in favor of electric bass and the two notes of the song's main riff are picked authoritatively with a plectrum, while Steve demonstrates he can "yeah, yeah, yeah" with credible chutzpah.

Sonny James. Although largely remembered as a one-hit wonder on the pop charts, James (pictured here on an early EP) had a streak of 16 consecutive No. 1 country hits, which was broken after he recorded Bacharach and David's "Only Love Can Break a Heart."

"Make Room for the Joy" (Burt Bacharach - Hal David)
Recorded by Jack Jones
From the film *Juke Box Rhythm*
Capitol F4161, released March 1959

Before there was a Charles Manson or a Marilyn Manson, there was Riff Manson. Producer Sam Katzman again repeated his objectionable *Don't Knock the Rock* movie formula: in a film with the Earl Grant Trio, the Treniers, the Nitwits and even Johnny Otis on hand to sing "Willie and the Hand Jive," who does Katzman pick to portray an aspiring rock star? Jack Jones!!!—the same guy who'd eventually warble "The Love Boat Theme," which rocked only slightly harder than the title theme to this extravaganza. Capitol wisely passed on releasing "Juke Box Rhythm" in any form, as well as on Jack's Paleozoic attempt at vogueing—a little-known dance craze called "The Freeze." Strike a pose, poseur!

Capitol did, however, sanction this single, essentially a mellower retread of "Magic Moments," if such an incredible feat can be believed. Its failure concluded Jones' hitless tenure at the label. But the crooner would do a lot better at Kapp Records, with further involvement from Bacharach and David.

"Paradise Island" (Burt Bacharach - Hal David - Paul Hampton)
First recorded by the Four Aces
Decca 30874, flip side of "Ciao Ciao Bambino"
Released April 1959

Steve Lawrence. Once a cool-rockin' daddy, always a cool-rockin' daddy. The evidence can be found on this Taragon reissue of his ABC greatest-hits album. Then, of course, there's always Steve and Eydie's lounge-meets-grunge (lunge?) cover version of Soundgarden's "Black Hole Sun." You can find that kitschy Lawrence on the 1997 collection *Lounge-a-Palooza.*

It's not certain whether Hal David was an eleventh hour addition to this Bacharach-Hampton effort, but it's his participation that prevented "Paradise Island" from becoming another throwaway. The three-way composition proved good enough to give to the Four Aces, who charted 29 Top 40 hits between 1951 and 1956. Everything about it—from the silly location (*"It's somewhere east of Steal-a-Kiss Ocean / Where the Bay of Devotion meets Ecstasy Lagoon"*) to the surreal imagery (*"a million moonlit palms seem to be waving their arms"*) to the imaginative rhyming of "desires" with "papayas"—smacks of David's clever ease.

Freed up from having to write lyrics, Bacharach and Hampton cook up an easygoing melody and a traditional sleepy Hawaiian steel guitar and ukulele arrangement. Of course, it wouldn't be a Fifties recording without some ghostly females wailing in the background and four guys whistling like they're standing on the corner watching all the girls go by (Oops! Sorry. That's the Four Lads!)

1959

The Four Aces. About to split up before being given "Love Is a Many Splendored Thing" in 1955, the Aces hung in there for an extra seven years. They've reunited countless times since then, though never as closely joined at the head as in this photo.

By now the proliferation of Four Aces imitators seemed to have lessened the public's appetite for hearing the four voices that were the source of all the mimicry. With lead singer Al Alberts' departure in 1957, the Aces' days were indeed numbered. As for "Paradise Island," not even its stowaway status on the "Ciao Ciao Bambino" single and the accompanying *Beyond the Blue Horizon* album could guarantee it much of an audience.

Other Versions: *Maki Kaaihiu & His Orchestra*

"Moon Man" (Burt Bacharach - Hal David)
Recorded by Gloria Lambert
Columbia 41402, flip side of "Anyone Would Love You"
Released May 1959

That so many Bacharach-David songs were languishing on B-sides can be viewed as a badge of honor when they are compared to the drivel they usually wound up supporting. The team took some lyrical chances with "Moon Man," serving up an unconventional song idea (earth woman seduces space invader) for the slow dancing set. Musically no more adventurous than your average slow and dreamy Fifties ballad, "Moon Man" was still demoted to the reverse side in favor of a conservative love song that left no lasting impression. With so many sci-fi enthusiasts proliferating in the late Fifties, "Moon Man" would've seemingly been a surefire bet had it been given the push.

Little is known about singer Gloria Lambert, except that she makes an engaging argument that Earth girls are indeed easy. Our alien is barely out of his flying saucer and she's already loosening the buttons of his space suit and promising to take him to her leader tomorrow, but only after she's given him the kind of kissing-in-gravity demonstration Captain Kirk would've insisted on anyway. Her hospitality includes letting an extraterrestrial place an astronomically expensive phone-home call and extending the use of her brush and comb set. Obviously the thought that it could be a mind-sucking android with reptilian features under a handsome "Moon Man" facade never crosses her mind—or that he's probably married to some moon maiden. Ya gotta love the Fifties!

The movie star...and the rest! Portuguese souvenir book for *The Hangman.* Couch potatoes will recognize sexy castaway Tina Louise as she's gingerly being manhandled by Robert Taylor. *The Hangman* also starred TV's Davy Crockett (Fess Parker) and Steve McGarrett (Jack Lord).

"The Hangman" b/w "The Net" (theme song) (Burt Bacharach - Hal David)
Recorded by John Ashley
Dot 15775, A-side "inspired by the film *The Hangman*"
Released June 1959

How many other pop songs of the Fifties had a guy carried away with this concern: *"If I find my man, I'll lose my love"*? Or a stirring chorus like *"a hangman wants to be loved like any other man"*?

The first-ever pairing of Bacharach-David tunes on a 45 promises momentous things and happily delivers to those who ferret this single out. Keeping in the Wild West feel of "Ooh My Love," Bacharach and David penned a pair of western themes sung by teen-magazine heartthrob John

Ashley. *The Hangman* was a none too highly regarded flick whose hackneyed plot entailed a U.S. Marshal (Robert Taylor) fixing to bring wanted man Johnny Bishop (Jack Lord) to a stringy end. The trouble is, Johnny's a reformed no-goodnick whom the whole community—even the sheriff (Fess Parker)—doesn't want to see dangling from the gallows. Tina Louise provides the necessary third side to the lovers' triangle that Hal David exploits in his "inspired by" lyrics for "The Hangman." Singing from the viewpoint of the stoic marshal, John Ashley is determined to get his man but knows it will cost him the woman who loves them both.

"The Net" may be an exploitation theme for the 1959 film *Man in the Net,* starring Alan Ladd and Carolyn Jones, about a man accused of murdering his vanished wife. Whatever the original impetus, it remains one of the most eccentric and fun of Bacharach's early compositions, mostly because it's arranged and conducted by Bacharach for a change, as was the A-side. The musically sparse chorus features only Ashley, some backup singers snapping their fingers and singing "doo doo doo doo doo doo doo" and a gnarly, reverb-laden guitar that sounds like it's being picked with a baseball card. The galloping verses tell the tale of a failed jewel thief in Yuma who is driven to these desperate measures by a femme fatale whose affections can't be sated by affections alone. Even Ashley's cracking voice in the low register adds to the fun, as does the corny key change.

Ashley would star in his share of drive-in second features in the ensuing decades, from *Hot Rod Gang* to *How to Make a Monster, Frankenstein's Daughter, High School Caesar, Revenge of Doctor X, Brides of Blood, Dragstrip Girl* and *Women Hunt,* before turning his attention to producing films. He suffered a fatal heart attack in 1997 while working on the production of *Scarred City.*

Paul Hampton. The young singer-songwriter made his film debut in the 1958 musical *Senior Prom,* which also starred Louis Prima & Keely Smith, Sam Butera & the Witnesses, Ed Sullivan and Mitch Miller. And its associate producer was everyone's favorite headbanger Stooge—Moe Howard!

"Don't Unless You Love Me" b/w "Write Me (Lonely Girl)" (Paul Hampton - Burt Bacharach)
Recorded by Paul Hampton
Columbia 41396, released June 1959

"I remember Paul Hampton," laughs Bacharach about his sometime writing partner between 1958 and 1960. "Oh yeah, shit. It was hard writing with him. He wasn't the easiest guy to work with. The method was the same as when I wrote with Elvis [Costello]. We both had different keyboards in the same room."

As mentioned earlier, Bacharach's collaborations with Paul Hampton constitute the most forgettable endeavors of his early period. Prior to this release, Columbia issued two Hampton singles, "Rockin' Doll" and "Play It Cool," that pegged him as a rockabilly cat. This release finds him morphing into a mild balladeer. Since Hampton isn't much of a singer, these back-to-back collaborations are of purely historical interest.

Without Hal David to interject interesting patter as he did on "Paradise Island," neither number ever rises above the mundane. Take the A-side, where Hampton pleads with a girl not to intrigue him or say she

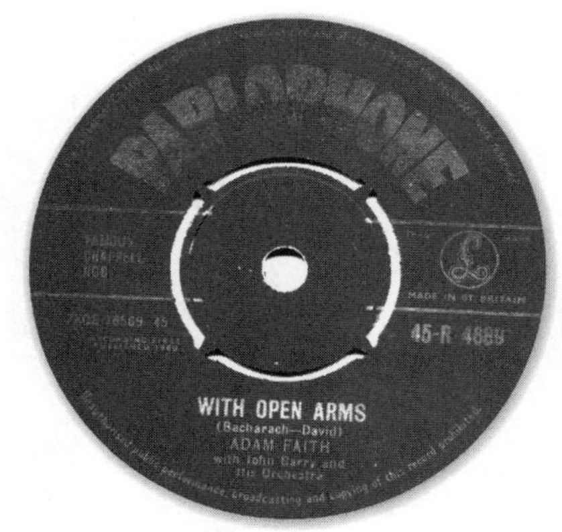

"With Open Arms." Britpop idol Adam Faith rerecorded this song for the British market, recasting himself as the uncaring sailor who loves catching fish more than kissing desperate women. Hey, England can't survive on chicks and chips alone.

adores him unless she loves him. If the listener's attention is to get any stimulation at all, it's invariably drawn to the backing track's yakety sax and to a detuned electric guitar whose bottom strings buzz against the fretboard.

Although ASCAP lists Bacharach as the co-writer of "Write Me," he isn't actually credited on the single or the sheet music. When you hear it you'll understand why. This mercifully brief throwaway resembles the kind of maudlin weepie that variety-show hosts used to haul out at the end of a telecast to keep those cards and letters coming. Singing to that very special "lonely girl" out there who pledges to adore *and* love Hampton, the singer gives explicit spoken instructions on how to write him: *"My name is Paul Hampton, 1619 Broadway, New York."* Sheet music collectors will recognize this as the address of the infamous Brill Building, where thousands of songs far superior to "Write Me" were being written.

"Young and Wild" (Burt Bacharach - Hal David)
Recorded by the Five Blobs
Joy 230, flip side of "Juliet"
Released June 1959

Evidently, someone in power thought the Five Blobs had a viable future beyond a one-shot hit single like "The Blob" and reassembled the faceless Bacharach-led studio aggregation once more to presumably cash in. Not until two singles on the Joy label ("Rockin' Pow Wow" and "Juliet") were allowed to crash and burn without a movie tie-in was this flimsy idea summarily dismissed. Still, for a 1959 record about teens who want to break free of their parental shackles, it's better than most:

"Why do they call me young and wild / When will they learn I'm not a child / I'm old enough to have the car to go out with / To just knock about with / They say I'm too young and wild"

Too bad the credible juvenile delinquent angle established in the early verses is blown rather disappointingly in the last minute of the song, when our young hood complains *"they never let me choose the clothes I desire."* Surely James Dean's mom never picked out his clothes!

"Young and Wild" follows the musical formula established by "The Blob"—a rockin' sax, Bernie Nee tracked five times in a hushed low register, handclaps and key changes but, alas, no finger popped through the cheek. Interestingly, the conductor for this Bacharach-David song is David's other frequent collaborator, Sherman Edwards.

"With Open Arms" (Burt Bacharach - Hal David)
First recorded by Jane Morgan
Kapp 284, released June 1959

"I pray all through the day that he'll return and make my life begin/ and when his boat comes in / I run to him with open arms"

It's hard to imagine a woman singing a song like "With Open Arms" today without having to work in a self-aware commentary about her low self-esteem just to keep credibility. Barring take-charge Gloria Lambert's close encounter, these were the dreams of the everyday housewife circa 1959. Jane Morgan breathes considerable oxygen into this lifeless shell of a woman, who only brightens when her fisherman returns from the salty sea and briefly pays attention to her. Even if you don't quite fathom her yearning, Bacharach's soaring melody and Morgan's passionate delivery make for a vividly cinematic song. Especially evocative are the strings, which sneak in after the second bridge like morning sun seeping through drawn blinds. Once again the Bacharach trait of having the background vocals imitate an instrument is present in the persistent "a-plicka-cha!" Whether it's supposed to be a simulated guitar strum or some percussive scraper is open to interpretation.

Jane Morgan. The first time Bacharach and David ever hit on a woman—on the charts, that is—was this release, which peaked at No. 39 on *Billboard*'s Top 40.

"With Open Arms" temporarily restored Bacharach and David to the Top 40 for just one week in early September 1959. It would be Morgan's last appearance in the upper chart regions, but she would record two more Bacharach tunes in the coming years while sustaining her initial success through TV, theater and nightclub appearances.

"With Open Arms" received a second chance across the sea, with Adam Faith playing the part of the sailor. Here the song takes on an appreciably less desperate tone, rather like an Old Spice commercial. For one thing, there's a whimsical tuba and some whistling—nothing to suggest the seaman has any reciprocal dependency to the needy girl with open arms waiting onshore. The plucky pizzicato strings and sweeping swells in the bridge come courtesy of John Barry, future musical director for another kiss-and-run-away male, James Bond.

Other Versions: *Adam Faith (1960)*

"Heavenly" (Burt Bacharach - Sydney Shaw)
Recorded by Johnny Mathis
From the album *Heavenly,* Columbia 8152
Released August 1959

Johnny Mathis. Johnny ranks just behind Sinatra and Elvis as the male singer with the most Top 10 and Top 40 albums in the rock era.

You might wonder why mint copies of early Johnny Mathis albums are so hard to find and why the ones that do turn up in thrift shops are so thoroughly scratched, soiled and pawed over. Back in the day, Mathis LPs were the prime soundtrack for necking sessions and other forms of, er…umph, long playing. Mathis' angelic voice was asexual enough not threaten male or female enjoyment of one another, and unlike earlier albums, *Heavenly* contained no head-scratching novelty productions like "Warm and Tender" to distract passionate young fornicators from the job at hand. *Heavenly* proved the most popular of Mathis' 60-some career albums, with song after lushly orchestrated song carrying the day and little left to chance.

Similarly, no risks are taken in the lyrical department. Sydney Shaw, who previously co-wrote the opening cut on Johnny's *Wonderful, Wonderful* album, "Will I Find My Love Today," would compose four songs with Bacharach. There's nothing particularly clever about Shaw's wordplay here: he manages to half rhyme "heavenly" with "breathlessly,"

1959

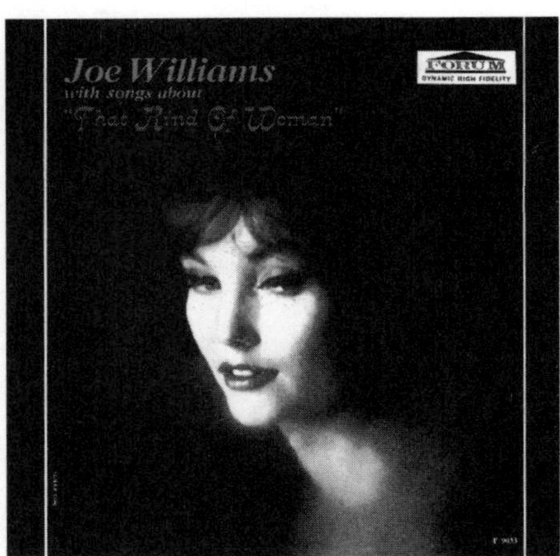

Joe Williams. Perhaps the Academy should've created a special "exploitation songs" category, given the high caliber of inspired-by-the-film songs Bacharach and David fashioned throughout their career ("Hot Spell," "The Man Who Shot Liberty Valance," "Wives and Lovers" and especially "That Kind of Woman").

"meant to be," "forever free," "happy as we" and "our hearts agree." Bacharach's melodic capabilities insure this innocuous old-school wordplay a safe and comfortable ride, with the piano and strings answering back the same three notes Mathis uses to sing each "heavenly."

Oddly enough for such a popular album cut, no one saw the logic in trying to capitalize on "Heavenly" as a single. The absence of cover versions demonstrated either that no one else felt Mathis' rendition could be bettered or that its charms seemed threadbare in less capable hands.

"That Kind of Woman" (Burt F. Bacharach - Hal David)
Recorded by Joe Williams and the Count Basie Orchestra
From the album *That Kind of Woman,* Roulette 4185
Released September 1959

That Kind of Woman was the second movie Carlo Ponti produced for his soon-to-be wife Sophia Loren—and the bombshell's second Carlo Ponti–produced bomb! Reportedly the most expensive film ($2.5 million) to be shot entirely in New York up to that time, it played three weeks to mostly empty theaters. Having an A-1 exploitation song like "That Kind of Woman," sung by the great Joe Williams, didn't put asses in theater seats, either.

It's just as well that a smoldering torch song like this wasn't used in the film. It would've been better suited to a movie like Alfred Hitchcock's *Vertigo*, where a man is tortured beyond relief by a woman who always keeps him at a distance. It hardly seems appropriate for a light comedy that struggles for 90 minutes to create chemistry between Loren and Tab Hunter.

Count Basie meanders around on the bottom piano keys, somberly underlining the vocals, while Williams negotiates Bacharach's tricky melody, scatting the lyrics as if they were a trumpet solo. Try singing (or breathing) along with Williams during the low-register passages and his leaps to the top of his range seconds later and you'll come away awed by his facility in negotiating this bumpy terrain.

Among the obscure Bacharach-David recordings, "That Kind of Woman" easily stands alongside their better-known works. It's also a recording that Burt Bacharach can't stand listening to, and his annoyance at how it was handled is still evident 42 years later. Of the songs that "got away," this was one where he insists the integrity of his original arrangement was sabotaged. To the unsuspecting ear it sounds beautiful, but he groans, "It would've been better if they'd just left it alone." Not even a second stab with the Jimmy Jones Orchestra did much to change the result.

Anyone holding out any hope of hearing the song Bacharach's way will probably turn three shades of blue waiting. "We did a demo version a long time ago, but all you've got now is 'That Kind of Woman' in its current version. Nobody else ever covered it. And nobody ever will!" he chuckles.

"Faker Faker" (Burt Bacharach - Hal David)
Recorded by the Eligibles
Capitol 4265, released September 1959

Earlier in 1959, the Eligibles had pushed a song called "Car Trouble" up to No. 107 on the charts. "Faker Faker" was its similarly underwhelming follow-up, a patty-cake rhythmic trifle about catching one's honey kissing someone else at the movies. Rather than sounding genuinely upset—like the Shirelles when they cry "cheat cheat" on "Baby It's You"—the Eligibles seem positively gleeful, their admonishments of *"faker faker"* and *"promise breaker"* carrying no weight unless you believe the heavily echoed handclaps that accompany them are some sort of violent retribution against a lying mate.

The lack of inspiration in this hopscotch singsong arrangement allows the Eligibles to spread their vocal "doo doo" over two whole instrumental verses, doing everything that the sax was managing quite well on its own, thank you. As with many Bacharach compositions of this period, one imagines that somewhere beneath all the fluoride smiles and whiter-than-white harmonies is a tortured R&B song struggling to get out.

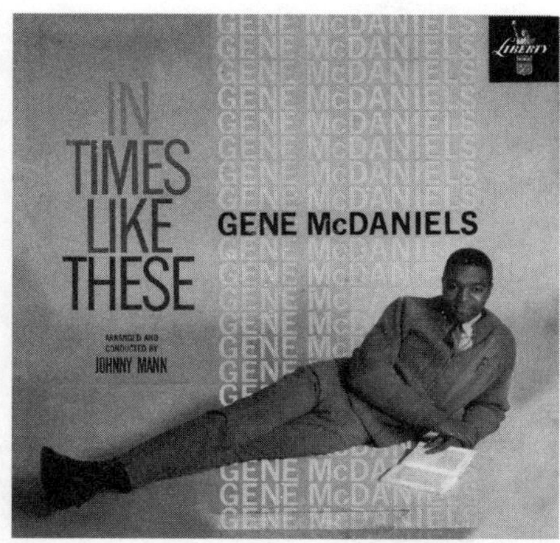

In Times Like These. Bacharach wrote the title tracks to four easy-listening albums by black vocalists in 1959. Gene McDaniels would seldom look this mellow on an album cover again.

"In Times Like These" (Burt Bacharach - Hal David)
First recorded by Gene McDaniels
Liberty 55231, released December 1959

Before this Kansas City baritone recorded semi-comical pop confections with trombones and "uh-huhs" from the Johnny Mann Singers, Gene McDaniels was Liberty's answer to Johnny Mathis and Roy Hamilton. Two albums of standards like "Mona Lisa" and "Love Is a Many Splendored Thing" came and went without registering a blip, including one with an incredible title track. "In Times Like These" is a sophisticated adult ballad similar in form to Mathis' "It's Not for Me to Say," from its tinkling piano phrases answering each vocal verse to its lyrics, which express an inability to control the fates, the world we live in and the start of an unshakable love affair.

Making full use of his interpretive skills and Bobby Short–like diction, McDaniels achieves his finest moment at the very end. After building up to a full-throated climax, he releases his beautiful falsetto like a flock of captured doves. Despite its substantial merits, neither the single nor the album of "In Times Like These" scored much chart action. Although it did receive considerable radio play, this didn't translate into sales. At least when McDaniels made the jump from teen market to adult contemporary, he already had two albums of previously issued adult easy-listening music in the vault. Liberty's budget label Sunset did the honors in 1967, releasing a sampling of his first two albums called *The Facts of Life*.

Gene McDaniels. The laid-back lad from the *In Times Like These* cover gives way to this strangling madman on a late-Sixties Sunset reissue.

Other Versions: *Film Score Orchestra • Stan Getz (1967) • Bud Shank with Chet Baker (1966)*

1959

Faithfully. Johnny in a chiaroscuro mood.

"Faithfully" (Burt Bacharach - Sydney Shaw)
Recorded by Johnny Mathis
From the album *Faithfully,* Columbia 8219
Released December 1959

Heavenly spent a lofty five weeks as a No. 1 album in the fall of 1959 and was eventually certified platinum by the RIAA. *Faithfully* was the speedy follow-up, and again Sydney Shaw and Burt Bacharach were tapped to write the adverbial title track. *Faithfully* almost repeated its predecessor's chart performance, rising to No. 2 but failing to overtake *The Sound Of Music* original cast album. It still managed a 63-week stay in the charts and also went gold that same year.

Although it sold markedly less than "Heavenly," *Faithfully's* title track provides a far more satisfying listening experience. While Mathis merely immersed himself in the choirboy bliss of the former song, here he sounds appreciably less pure, as if anesthetized by some powerful love narcotic. Several times during the song, especially on the word "connnnnnstantly," Mathis sounds as if he's free-falling with no worries of ever touching terra firma. Even the descending strings sound somewhat sinister, as if they're the same ones from "Heavenly" being played backwards and pulling the listener into hell's sinful flames.

"I think Mitch Miller let me come down to a Mathis session," recalls the composer of being in the studio when one or possibly both songs were recorded. Did either tune wind up sounding any closer to the way he originally envisioned it?

"No, not at all," laughs Bacharach. "But that's OK, because they were well-done arrangements." These were done under the orchestration of Glenn Osser.

SECTION TWO

ANY DAY NOW (1960-1962)

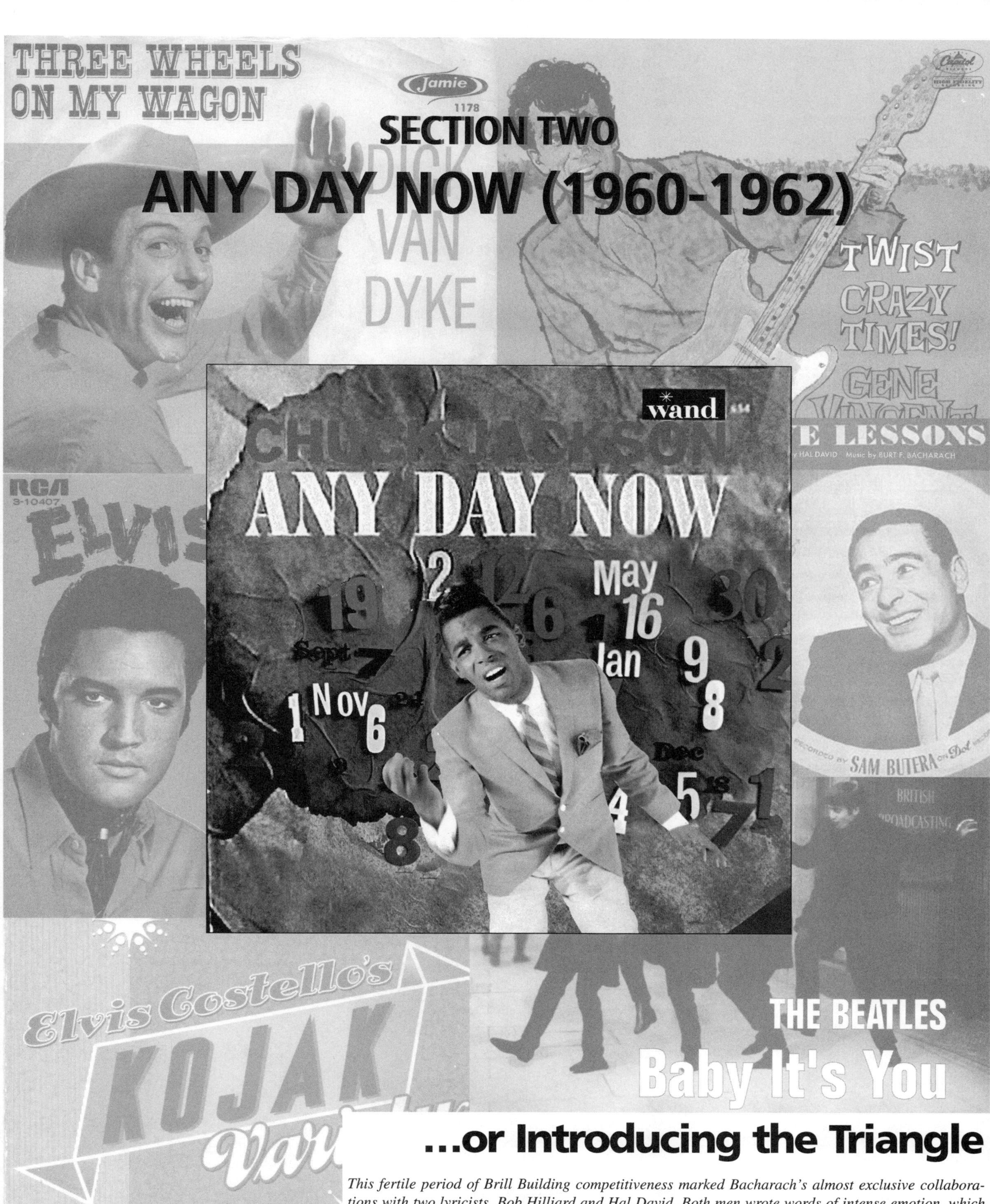

...or Introducing the Triangle

This fertile period of Brill Building competitiveness marked Bacharach's almost exclusive collaborations with two lyricists, Bob Hilliard and Hal David. Both men wrote words of intense emotion, which was finally being realized in the finished product now that Bacharach had assumed the role of producer and arranger. Bacharach also began working with more R&B artists and in the process discovered his sound—and Dionne Warwick.

Section Two: Any Day Now (1960–1962)

1. *"Crazy Times"* . . . . . *Gene Vincent*
2. *"A Girl Like You "* . . . . . *Larry Hall*
3. *"Your Lips Are Warmer Than Your Heart"* . . . . . *Rosemary June*
4. *"Two Hour Honeymoon"* . . . . . *Paul Hampton*
5. *"Creams"* . . . . . *Paul Hampton*
6. *"The Timeless Tide"* . . . . . *Joe Arthur*
7. *"We're Only Young Once (Yeh Yeh Yeh)"* . . . . . *The Avons*
8. *"Close"* . . . . . *Keely Smith*
9. *"You Belong in Someone Else's Arms"* . . . . . *Valerie Carr*
10. *"I Looked for You"* . . . . . *Charlie Gracie*
11. *"Long Ago Last Summer"* . . . . . *Diana Trask*
12. *"Indoor Sport"* . . . . . *Jo Stafford*
13. *"Boys Were Made for Girls* . . . . . *Everit Herter*
14. *"Ten Thousand Years Ago"* . . . . . *Rusty Draper*
15. *"I Could Make You Mine"* . . . . . *The Wanderers*
16. *"Take Me to Your Ladder (I'll See Your Leader Later)"* . . . . . *Buddy Clinton*
17. *"Joanie's Forever"* . . . . . *Buddy Clinton*
18. *"Three Wheels on My Wagon"* . . . . . *Dick Van Dyke*
19. *"One Part Dog, Nine Parts Cat"* . . . . . *Dick Van Dyke*
20. *"Come Completely to Me"* . . . . . *Steve Rossi*
21. *"Gotta Get a Girl"* . . . . . *Frankie Avalon*
22. *"And This Is Mine"* . . . . . *Connie Stevens*
23. *"Three Friends, Two Lovers"* . . . . . *The Turbans*
24. *"The Story Behind My Tears"* . . . . . *Kenny Lynch*
25. *"Out of My Continental Mind"* . . . . . *Lena Horne*
26. *"I'll Bring Along My Banjo"* . . . . . *Johnnie Ray*
27. *"Moon Guitar"* . . . . . *The Rangoons*
28. *"My Heart Is a Ball of String"* . . . . . *The Rangoons*
29. *"(Don't Go) Please Stay"* . . . . . *The Drifters*
30. *"Along Came Joe"* . . . . . *Merv Griffin*
31. *"Love In A Goldfish Bowl"* . . . . . *Tommy Sands*
32. *"Love Lessons"* . . . . . *Sam Butera*
33. *"Loneliness or Happiness"* . . . . . *The Drifters*
34. *"I Wake Up Cryin'"* . . . . . *Chuck Jackson)*
35. *"The Answer to Everything"* . . . . . *Del Shannon*
36. *"Deeply"* . . . . . *The Shepherd Sisters*
37. *"You're Telling Our Secrets"* . . . . . *Dee Clark*
38. *"Move It on the Backbeat"* . . . . . *Burt and the Backbeats*
39. *"Tower of Strength"* . . . . . Gene McDaniels
40. *"You're Following Me"* . . . . . *Perry Como*
41. *"The Breaking Point"* . . . . . *Chuck Jackson*
42. *"Somebody Else's Sweetheart"* . . . . . *The Wanderers*

43. *"The Miracle of St. Marie"* . . . . *The Four Coins*
44. *"Baby It's You"* . . . . *The Shirelles*
45. *"Windows of Heaven"* . . . . *The Four Coins*
46. *"Another Tear Falls"* . . . . *Gene McDaniels*
47. *"Mexican Divorce"* . . . . *The Drifters*
48. *"Waiting for Charlie to Come Home"* . . . . *Etta James*
49. *"Forever My Love"* . . . . *Jane Morgan*
50. *"For All Time"* . . . . *The Russells*
51. *"Wastin' Away for You"* . . . . *The Russells*
52. *"(The Man Who Shot) Liberty Valance"* . . . . *Gene Pitney*
53. *"Any Day Now (My Wild Beautiful Bird)"* . . . . *Chuck Jackson*
54. *"Too Late to Worry"* . . . . *Babs Tino*
55. *"Pick Up the Pieces"* . . . . *Jack Jones*
56. *"Forgive Me (For Giving You Such a Bad Time)"* . . . . *Babs Tino*
57. *"Feeling No Pain"* . . . . *Paul Evans*
58. *"The Hurtin' Kind"* . . . . *Lonnie Sattin*
59. *"Something Bad"* . . . . *Lonnie Sattin*

1960

Gene Vincent. Hoping they'd found their Elvis, Capitol released six Gene Vincent albums between 1956 and 1960. *Crazy Times* was the last of the line, and when it failed to sell in King-like quantities, they affixed the word "twist" to the cover, hoping they'd found their Chubby Checker.

"Crazy Times" (Burt Bacharach - Paul Hampton)
Recorded by Gene Vincent
From the album *Crazy Times,* Capitol 1342
Released February 1960

Bacharach could hardly have been thrilled with this assignment, his first-ever composition tailored for a *real live* rock star. Paul Hampton would seem to be the impetus behind this outing, written in the style of Fats Domino's "I'm Walking" and featuring a most un-Bacharachian one finger, three-note piano solo. It's probable that Bacharach again pitched in with these elemental lyrics: *"Crazy times, we'll have / Secretly / You and me / Ecstasy."* The verse melody is just as elemental, as it soon turns up in Hampton and Bacharach's worst-ever song, Steve Rossi's ludicrous "Come Completely to Me." Still, with Vincent's appealing and underrated voice, "Crazy Times" is a pleasant enough throwaway, and fellow Capitol recording artists the Eligibles (of "Faker Faker" fame) provide enthusiastic backgrounds.

Gene Vincent was indeed living crazy times in 1960. With his popularity steadily declining in the United States, the blue-jeaned bopper relocated permanently to England, where his records still sold in legend-worthy amounts. Unfortunately, during a British tour that followed the release of this album, Vincent was seriously injured in the same fatal automobile accident that claimed the life of his good friend Eddie Cochran. On that macabre note, the *Crazy Times* album contained a cautionary tale about a smoking, flaming wreck on the highway entitled "Why Don't You People Learn to Drive." (Sample eerie insight: "If you drive like crazy you'll be pushing up daisies.") Then again, if you really want eerie irony, didn't Vincent release an album just before his death in 1971 called *The Day the World Turned Blue*?

Larry Hall. Even if collectors were to come across an extremely warped 45 of "A Girl Like You," Larry Hall's vocals would still retain their distinct flat quality.

"A Girl Like You" (Burt Bacharach - Anne Pearson Croswell)
First recorded by Larry Hall
Strand 25013, flip side of "Rosemary"
Released March 1960

As you will see in subsequent entries, Bacharach never had much luck with teen idols whose vocal deficiencies were glaringly obvious to anyone not mooning over their "suitable for framing" photos. In a voice similar to Mark Dinning of "Teen Angel" fame but with no control whatsoever on the low end, Larry Hall all but ruins "A Girl Like You" with his precarious pitch at what should be the song's big finish. Unable to find his place after the key change, Hall begins oscillating between several wrong notes in the hope that one might be the correct one. None are.

Clearly, Hall's rendition was patterned after Frankie Avalon's "Venus," with its vigorously plucked harp and ethereal female vocalists ooh-ing up in heaven. This number's modest charms would be more keenly demonstrated when British pop star Adam Faith rescued it for his 1961 album *Adam* (retitled *England's Top Singer!* in the U.S.). Producer John Barry's arrangement ditched the "Venus" blueprint entirely and patterned the song after Buddy Holly's first string-accented single, "It Doesn't Matter Anymore." The song was not a hit, possibly because the lyric's renunciation of the monarchy *("Most any king would leave his throne and palace, too / For you")* reminded British loyalists of those damned Windsors.

Bacharach's first musical collaboration with a female lyricist would be his only one until the late Seventies, whereupon he experimented with Libby Titus, Sally Stevens and Carly Simon on the *Woman* album before hooking up with Carole Bayer Sager. Two years later, Anne Croswell would team with sometime Hal David partner Lee Pockriss to write songs for the show *Tovarich,* starring Vivian Leigh.

Other Versions: *Adam Faith (1961)*

Rosemary June. An early clue to a later direction. June gets in a Bacharachian moment on "Your Lips Are Warmer Than Your Heart" but would soon switch gears and unleash a double slab of virginal pop ("The Sound of Music" and "The Village of St. Bernadette") on an unsuspecting world.

"Your Lips Are Warmer Than Your Heart" (Burt F. Bacharach - Hal David)
Recorded by Rosemary June
United Artists 219, flip side of "Sunday Monday or Always"
Released April 1960

Good luck finding a copy of this, another understated and classy B-side in the vein of "It Seemed So Right Last Night," sung by session singer Rose Mary Jun, recording under a slightly altered stage name. Cleverly worded and wistfully arranged, it contrasts a cold heart to a warm kiss and a hard heart to a soft touch, while pizzicato strings simulate the expected falling teardrops. Miss June portrays a woman in the throes of a love affair, which seems like a casual fling to everyone but her. Even so, she prefers the relationship's imbalance of power to the loneliness she would feel if he left *("If I were to say we're through / It wouldn't bother you / Oh, but how lonely I would be").*

Like such upcoming Bacharach-David gems as "Anyone Who Had a Heart" and "Walk On By," this song wafts in on an air of uncertainty. The singer reveals some unbearable inner turmoil and fades out on the same note of resignation, the hurt continuing without resolve. When the intro is repeated at the end of the song and June sustains her final note over it, you have what can be categorized as a "Bacharach moment." Although addressed to an uncaring lover, the dialogue is probably being delivered in an empty room behind a closed door, as were so many of Dionne Warwick's later conversations with herself. With this song, Bacharach and David inch closer to perfecting those devastating confessionals meant for no one else to hear, except for lucky pop listeners.

Hal David must've been fond of "Your Lips Are Warmer Than Your Heart" as he copyrighted a song with that title in 1956, with music by Alex Alstone.

"Two Hour Honeymoon" b/w "Creams" (Burt F. Bacharach - Paul Hampton)
Recorded by Paul Hampton
Dot 16084, released April 1960

1960

Paul Hampton. Yes, Virginia, there is a Bacharach death disc. Historians may also refer to it as the first double-B-sided record because it also contained the excruciatingly annoying "Creams" on the flip.

Two of the strangest songs to turn up in the search for early Bacharachenalia make up this 45. Hampton and Bacharach solved the problem of bad lyrics and mediocre singing that plagued Paul Hampton's "Don't Unless You Love Me" and "Write Me" by allowing the singer/composer to talk his way through both songs. Perhaps Hampton saw himself as a better thespian than singer at this point, having already starred in the Moe Howard–produced *Senior Prom* in 1958.

Released two months after Mark Dinning's morbid death disc "Teen Angel" topped the nation's pop charts, "Two Hour Honeymoon" pushes the bad-taste envelope even further across the casket with its jarring car crash sound effects, screams and morose spoken-word passages. These would become more common pop devices after Shadow Morton fashioned the downcast "Leader of the Pack" for the Shangri-Las in late 1964.

"Two Hour Honeymoon" opens with the sounds of a speeding sports car and a startled male voice yelping when it careers off the road. After a few seconds of cricket chirping, a snazzy "Harlem Nocturne" sax serenade kicks in and Hampton momentarily regains consciousness. For a dying man, he sure sounds lucid, diagnosing himself as a goner and pleading with his soon-to-be-widowed bride not to move him and to just get on with her life. In between anguished cries of how unfair it is they only had a two-hour honeymoon, he concedes *"I guess you were right, honey. We were driving too fast."* Once Hampton expires for good, Bacharach—who arranged and conducted both sides here—stretches out for an instrumental coda that's interrupted only by the odd sirens.

Equally as curious is "Creams," where Hampton, not even bothering to rhyme this time, adopts the persona of a young boy angry with a girl won't share a box of chocolates. Its whimsical, woozy French-horn passages anticipate later Parisian pastiche work of Bacharach's, such as *Casino Royale*'s "Little French Boy."

"The Timeless Tide" (Burt Bacharach - Hal David)
Recorded by Joe Arthur
Seeco 6050, flip side of "When You Care Enough"
Released May 1960

Another 12/8 ballad sung by another crooner whose vital information has escaped this discographer. A keen guesser might hear the similarities between "The Timeless Tide" and Earl Grant's late 1958 Top 10 hit "The End"—parenthetically known as "(At) The End (Of the Rainbow)"—and pinpoint this song as being conceived a few months afterwards. Joe Arthur sounds like Andy Williams with a nervous disorder, reverently caressing each sappy syllable of what appear to be some of the most elemental and hackneyed lyrics imaginable from Hal David *("just like the timeless tide, my love is never-ending").* Unlike the timeless tide or the rainbow that stretches out to infinity, this interminably dull recording's longevity didn't transcend the second it was first slipped into a paper sleeve.

"We're Only Young Once (Yeh Yeh Yeh)" (Burt Bacharach - Robert Colby)
Recorded by the Avons
Columbia 4461, released in England, May 1960

London calling or Avons calling, take your pick. Having just scored a hit with a British-side cover of Paul Evans' "(Seven Little Girls) Sitting in the Back Seat" (with lyrics by upcoming Bacharach collaborator Bob Hilliard), the team of Valerie Murtagh, Elaine Murtagh and Ray Adams turned their attention to yet another Bacharach inanity of 1960, with its incessant "yeh yeh yeh" refrain anticipating Beatlemania but not kick-starting any such devotion for the Avons. England, enamored with the Bacharach name even when placed alongside a collaborator bent on inserting rockin' and rollin' terminology wherever possible, sent this song up to No. 45. The trio continued to cover other people's material, like Bobby Vee's "Rubber Ball," but oddly enough penned a No. 1 hit for the Shadows in 1963, "Dance On."

The Avons: This group's string of UK Top 50 hits appears to have never made the cross-continental trip. The were several other outfits releasing records under this name in the U.S.—a doo-wop group that recorded on Hull from 1956 to 1962 and other Avons turning up on R&B labels like Excello, Groove and Astra.

"You Belong in Someone Else's Arms" (Burt Bacharach - Bob Hilliard)
Recorded by Valerie Carr
Roulette 4254, flip side of "Oh Gee"
Released June 1960

Enter Bob Hilliard, Burt Bacharach's other frequent partner in the early Sixties. It has been suggested that Bacharach and David collaborated less frequently during the three years leading up to the momentous recording session of "Mexican Divorce" where Bacharach discovered Dionne Warwick, but such is not the case. For a time, Bacharach and Hilliard seemed to outpace Bacharach and David commercially, even though they ran pretty much neck and neck in the number of songs released. None of the Bacharach-David 1960–61 releases was a Top 40 qualifier. Chuck Jackson's "I Wake Up Crying" is remembered as being a hit largely for its No. 13 placement in the R&B listings, yet it only reached No. 59 on *Billboard*'s pop charts. In contrast, Bacharach and Hilliard scored a Top 20 and a Top 5 in 1961, while Bacharach also scored a Top 5 with Hal's brother, Mack David.

Like the David brothers, Hilliard had some impressive pre-Bacharach successes on his résumé. Few people realize that he co-wrote "In the Wee Small Hours of the Morning" for Frank Sinatra, "Bouquet of Roses" for Eddie Arnold, "Why Did I Tell You I Was Going to Shanghai" for Doris Day and "Moonlight Gambler" for Frankie Laine. In the following years his non-Bacharach collaborations would result in hits like Ruby and the Romantics' "Our Day Will Come" and Paul Evans' "(Seven Little Girls) Sitting in the Back Seat."

Hilliard's first collaborative effort with Bacharach was an undistinguished 12/8 ballad for Valerie Carr, who hit the Top 20 in 1958 with the teen ballad "When the Boys Talk about the Girls." Instead of starting out pleasing the youngsters and gradually gravitating toward the two-drink-minimum crowd, this New York singer tried having it both ways from the outset, with neither group getting enthusiastic enough about her to build

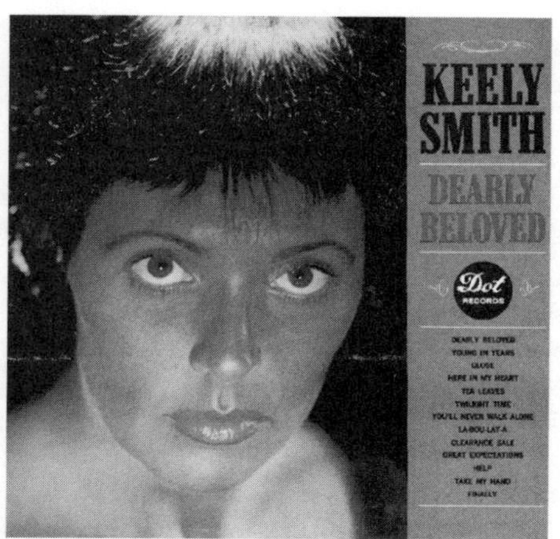

Keely Smith. A year after she recorded "Close" (found on the *Dearly Beloved* album), Keely divorced her swing partner Louis Prima on the grounds of "extreme mental cruelty." Hey, that's not funny!

any career momentum. Depending on the age of the listener, the creepy organ employed here sounds like it was piped in from a roller rink or the silent movie night at the Bijou. Carr's anguished alto is a tad too white-sounding for a black artist, yet her soulful voice would've been perfect for country music if the similarly toned Patsy Cline hadn't gotten there first.

This song soon fell prey to the England's answer to Caruso *and* Steve Rossi— David Whitfield, whose operatic bellowing turns a merely mediocre number into a noxious repellent.

Other Versions: *David Whitfield*

"Close" (Sydney Shaw - Burt Bacharach)
First recorded by Keely Smith
Dot 16089, flip side of "Tea Leaves"
Released June 1960

With her renown as the swinging foil to then-husband Louis Prima, Keely Smith seemed like a prime candidate to sing a song that summarizes "things in close proximity to one another," as a quizmaster might put it. For this exercise, lyricist Sydney Shaw trots out mostly tried-and-true similes for nearness ("like candle to a flame," "like honey to a bee," "like winter is to spring") that wouldn't seem out of place written in a graduation book.

Fortunately, Smith invests this lush ballad with enough gusto to transcend its clichéd lyrics, even inserting an exhausted gasp at the conclusion, as if she's blowing the bangs out of her eyes. For all that, Bacharach's melody and conductor George Greeley's arrangement are both fairly unmemorable—even more so on a phonetically sung 1966 version of "Close" by the Swedish vocal group Gals & Pals.

Other Versions: *Gals & Pals (1966)*

"I Looked for You" (Burt Bacharach - Hal David)
Recorded by Charlie Gracie
Roulette 4255, flip side of "The Race"
Released July 1960

Overseas, where memories are longer as far as early rock 'n' roll is concerned, the name Charlie Gracie is still revered. George Harrison called him "a brilliant guitarist." Paul McCartney included his hit "Fabulous" on his 1999 *Run Devil Run* album. Gracie was the second U.S. rocker to headline at the London Palladium, after Bill Haley, while in America he was just another *American Bandstand* regular, albeit one who had a No. 1 hit, "Butterfly," as did Andy Williams, depending on which chart you believe.

Gracie followed that up with another two Top 20s ("Ninety-Nine Ways" and "Fabulous") before going into litigation with his record label for non-payment of royalties. "When [Cameo] gave me the runaround, I took them to court and won a $50, 000 settlement," he recalls today. "As they say, I won the battle and lost the war. While I continued performing in the U.S. and in the UK, I found it very difficult to get my records played after the suit. I was never invited back on *American Bandstand*—I later found out that Dick Clark was a silent partner with Cameo."

Gracie signed with Roulette in 1960 to try to recapture his previous hit status. "The tune 'I Looked for You' was submitted to me with several other songs. I chose it! I thought it was a great song and I still do. At first I wasn't aware of the writer. I never met Burt and he was not in the studio, to my knowledge, when we cut it," Gracie states.

"I Looked for You" is a swinging sock-hop number that starts out in a minor key and goes major on the bridge (where a rat-a-tat-tat horn section blasts a spirited solo on the second go-round). Gracie plays the deserted boyfriend whose pleas to his hide-and-seek lover to return go unheeded despite his earnest protests of "Gimme a break-yeaaah!"

Charlie Gracie (circa 1957). Charlie today: "Burt and Hal became very successful, writing one great song after another. Perhaps I came along a little too early. But I feel grateful to have been a small part of their fabulous career!"

"By 1960, rock 'n' roll had softened in the U.S.," recalls Gracie. "Not so in the UK, where artists like myself, Eddie Cochran and Gene Vincent were still popular. A lot of the material I cut after Cameo on Coral and Roulette represented a softer, pop sound. I suppose 'I Looked for You' was a good example of this. Our problem was that it never got any airplay. If the disc got some exposure, I'm certain it would have gone Top 20 or 30."

At the same time most of the first wave of rock stars got killed or got religion, the teen market was being infiltrated by hack songwriters who were shut out of the first flush of rock. Suddenly they wanted those teenage millions and were prepared to make the least common denominator a little lower to get it. If some of Bacharach's 1960 efforts haven't exactly exonerated him of charges of down-market writing, "I Looked for You" proves he still had it in him to buck formulaic songwriting.

"Long Ago Last Summer" (Burt Bacharach - Hal David)
Recorded by Diana Trask
Columbia 41711, released July 1960

Most people remember Mitch Miller's Sing Along Chorus as a bunch of guys in bright-colored sweaters and bow ties who looked and sang like teamsters. But the Bearded One did employ female regulars like Leslie Uggams and Australian-born singer Diana Trask. After recording two albums and a handful of singles for her boss's label in the early Sixties, Trask found greater success as a country artist by the end of the decade.

Buried in Bacharach and David's ASCAP and copyright files is a song titled "Suddenly Last Summer," which began life as an exploitation song for the 1959 film version of Tennessee Williams' play of the same name. But someone wisely advised them that a movie dealing with such taboo topics as homosexuality, cannibalism and lobotomies would need no further exploiting, and the alternate title "Long Ago Last Summer" was substituted.

Sounding very much lobotomized by love, soprano Diana gushes gamely about coming face to face with completeness last summer, while Mitch's gang pull "doo doo doo" duty alongside the skipping strings. The song is very much a throwback to the "Magic Moments" period, but these sorts of Bacharach assignments were fast falling by the wayside, although there would still be Jane Morgan and Steve Rossi to contend with.

Sandy Stewart. Producer Don Costa made a few cha-cha-cha-changes to "Indoor Sport," but none of them qualifies as an improvement.

"Indoor Sport" (Burt Bacharach - Frederick K. Tobias)
Recorded by Jo Stafford
Columbia 41690, flip side of "Candy"
Released August 1960

Stafford and her arranger/husband Paul Weston had a sideline making comedy albums as Jonathan and Darlene Edwards, a fictitious duo of no fixed musical aptitude. Once the couple ended their long association with Columbia in 1960, they released a Mitch Miller lampoon called *Sing Along with Jonathan and Darlene*. Coincidence? Bah!

As mentioned earlier, Stafford did not appreciate the novelty songs Miller was supplying her with and cited Bacharach's "Underneath the Overpass" as a notable stinker in her career. If she had misgivings about the B-side of this, her final single for Columbia, it doesn't show in her performance. A humorous cha-cha-chá, it lists all the playing requirements for swimming, tennis, fishing, skiing, football, polo, bullfighting and boxing, as well as the indoor sport (nudge-nudge) that only requires "heart on fire, lips that can't wait" and "two arms that can hold you tight." It's one of a trio of Bacharach collaborations with Frederick Tobias from 1960 that also includes "Path of Pride" and "Two Figures on a Wedding Cake." Tobias would very shortly write hits like "The Brigade of Broken Hearts" for Paul Evans, "Born Too Late" for the Ponytails and "Blue River," which Elvis Presley recorded.

Petula Clark. Pet cut a French translation of "Indoor Sport" called "Le Tu Sais Quoi" that can be found on this Vogue EP as well as a 1994 RPM CD entitled *The Nixa Years, Volume I*. Clark and Jo Stafford also recorded competing versions of "Suddenly There's a Valley" in the Fifties.

Too clever to be buried on a contractually obligated B-side, the song was also given to singer Sandy Stewart that summer for A-side consideration on the newly formed United Artists label. The song begins with a marching-band fanfare and a whistle being blown, before Costa and the orchestra saunter in with lite flute jazz piffle instead of the more fetching Latin rhythm of the Stafford recording. Despite Stewart's sparkling efforts, the tune comes to resemble an early-Sixties jingle for a smooth-tasting cigarette.

Better results could be heard across the sea when Petula Clark cut a faithful French version of "Indoor Sport," with translation courtesy of Maurice Vidalin and Jacques Datin. Previously, Clark had issued a competing French version of Elvis Presley's "A Fool Such As I" and outsold Le Pelvis in Gay Paree. Vive la France!

Other Versions: *Petula Clark (French version, 1960) • Sandy Stewart (1960)*

"Boys Were Made for Girls" (Burt Bacharach - Hal David)
Recorded by Everit Herter
Capitol 4383, released August 1960

Imagine the limitless freedom Bacharach must've felt writing for Dionne Warwick's voice after having furnished songs for the unexpressive drones of Larry Hall and Everit Herter. This record smacks of another favor done. With the exception of the line "why was I created if I wasn't fated to fall in love with you," it seems like the usually thoughtful Hal David wanted to invest as little toil as possible in these proceedings. You also detect Bacharach's annoyance at having to write another "Venus" knockoff for another would-be Frankie Avalon by his insertion of an irritating cha-cha-chá riff composed of dissonant diminished chords careering drunkenly downward in half steps. Even a mambo middle eight pushed along by a cowbell doesn't bring this sour exercise to life.

Rusty Draper. Note the mistaken solo credit on this early Bacharach and Hilliard collaboration. Although it may seem like only yesterday, a teenaged Draper once worked at a Des Moines radio station with a sportscaster named Ronald Reagan, who actually *was* alive ten thousand years ago.

"Ten Thousand Years Ago" (Burt Bacharach - Bob Hilliard)
Recorded by Rusty Draper
Mercury 71706, flip side of "Jealous Heart"
Released August 1960

Judging by the jocular nature of some of the others titles in Hilliard's ASCAP files ("Typewriter Serenade," "Underwater Cha Cha Cha," "Frankenshteiner Polka"), it's no surprise his next collaboration with Bacharach would be a novelty record—Bacharach's first intentional one.

Nearly 20 years before Steve Martin's "King Tut," country/pop singer Rusty Draper got in touch with his inner Egyptian on "Ten Thousand Years Ago." While occult and paranormal subjects like flying saucers and witch doctors were par for the pop course at this time, songs dealing with reincarnation were not (and never were, unless you count Rodgers and Hart's "Where or When"). Our yelping archaeologist uncovers a mummy that looks remarkably like himself and wonders *"Was I alive ten thousand years ago? / Did I reside in Egypt? This I'd like to know."* By studying the hieroglyphics, he determines that the mummy was a womanizer just like him and was ordered killed by Cleopatra. The whooping vocals, lyrical content and snake-charming flute solo all indicate that this song was reincarnated from "Run Samson Run," Neil Sedaka's Top 20 hit of a few months before.

In answer to Draper's fadeout query "Do you think I'll come alive again ten thousand years from now?" the answer would seem to be: Not on the pop charts, Pharaoh! Draper had his last pop hit months before with a version of "Mule Skinner Blues" but lived on in the country-music market for many more years.

"I Could Make You Mine" (Burt Bacharach - Hal David)
First recorded by the Wanderers
Cub 9075, flip side of "I Need You More"
Released September 1960

In their book *Doo-Wop: The Forgotten Third of Rock 'n' Roll*, authors Anthony Gribin and Matthew Schiff write, "Doo-wop music had the unique distinction of fading from the public eye not once but twice." Its first rise they dub the "classical doo-wop" period, which began in the early Fifties and peaked around 1957. By 1960, the genre had shot its

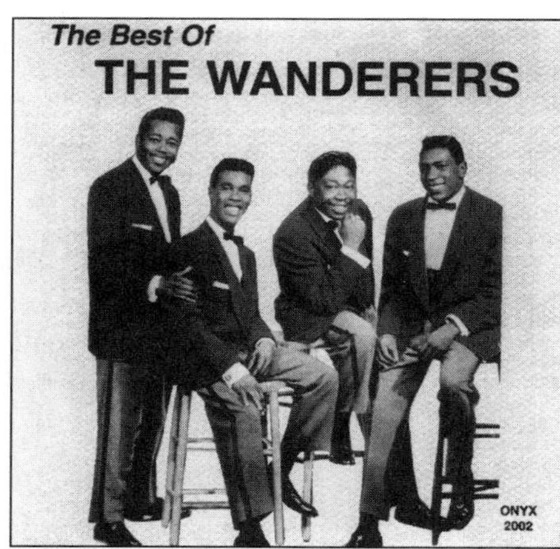

The Wanderers. Before the Drifters, Bacharach and David had the Wanderers. Their records are hopelessly out of print, so while we can't morally advocate the act of bootlegging, if you see this Onyx CD of dubious legality—snap it up! It too is out of print and almost as scarce as the group's original Cub 45s.

shooby-dooby-doo wad. Teens who grew up to songs with nonsense syllables had heard the C–A-minor–F-G chord progression one too many times and were now listening to folk music or jazz. Their younger siblings also wanted new sounds, and with the diminished exposure allotted black vocal groups on TV variety shows and dance programs, kids gravitated towards the new dance crazes and white teen idols these shows heavily promoted.

Then in 1961, a curious thing happened: rock experienced its first oldies revival. This brief second wind of popularity, dubbed "neo–doo-wop" by Gribin and Schiff, brought back elements of classical doo-wop, now bolstered by more sophisticated lyrics and musical arrangements. This suited songwriters like Bacharach and David just fine, since they were never enamored with early three-chord rock 'n' roll anyway.

If the Wanderers had recorded "I Could Make You Mine" in 1953 when they were on the Savoy label, the budget would've been too cheap to secure the soaring strings on display here, and the bass parts would've just been sung instead of played instrumentally. But even in a stripped-down voice-and-piano setting, the tune would've stood out. This New York quartet had both the classy elegance of the Platters and the comedic timing of the Coasters, plus a lead singer, Ray Pollard, whose Herculean octave leaps make this song and their next Bacharach-David outing, "Somebody Else's Sweetheart," most desirable lost treasures of the genre.

Of all the pre–Dionne Bacharach-David songs, this is one of only two the team thought enough of to rerecord with Warwick (for her *Anyone Who Had a Heart* album in 1964). In her less strenuous reading, she merely sounds rueful instead of devastated like Pollard. Yet in her sweet-voiced rendition you can hear where the writers of "It's Gonna Take a Miracle" (recorded in 1965 by the Royalettes and again in 1982 by Deniece Williams) got their inspiration.

It is interesting to note that Hal David employed the "triangle" song formula repeatedly once the team began working with black vocal groups. True, the triangle songs were very popular in doo-wop but it's also true that Bacharach-David songs were finally being accorded the soulfulness that countless white belters and black singers with diction coaches could never seem to manage.

Other Versions: *Dionne Warwick (1964)*

"Take Me to Your Ladder (I'll See Your Leader Later)" b/w "Joanie's Forever" (Burt Bacharach - Bob Hilliard)
Recorded by Buddy Clinton
Monroe 114, released November 1960

Bacharach's second pairing with Bob Hilliard combined flying-saucer rock 'n' roll à la "Purple People Eater" with the squealing girlie chorus of "Itsy Bitsy Teeny Weeny Yellow Polka Dot Bikini," a No. 1 smash for Brian Hyland just a few sunny months earlier. The most obvious tip-off was having the song break down and the girls demanding to know "What did he say? What did he say?" in the same manner and meter as "One, two, three, four, tell the people what she wore" from the Hyland hit.

The result—a cringe-inducing ditty where 20-foot-tall women living on the moon flutter about like dolphins when nerdy Buddy Clinton promises to use his spaceship's ladder to scale them. *"I'm kissing your shins when I'm on my toes,"* he sings with some confidence, since that the average moon man in this song is only three feet tall. As a hit single, "Take Me to Your Ladder" also fell short of the mark, bubbling under *Billboard*'s singles chart for one week and topping out at No. 115.

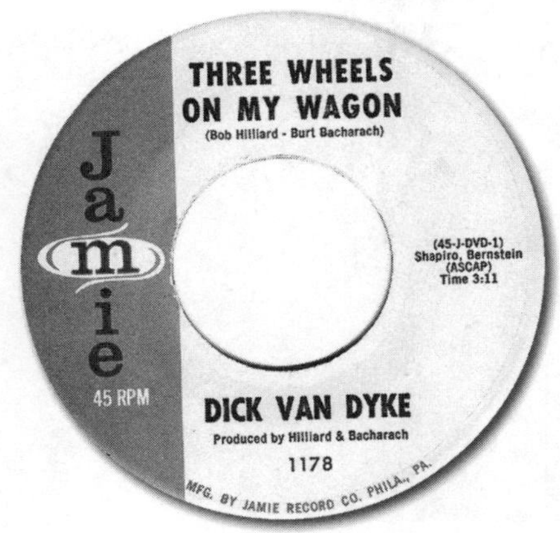

"Three Wheels on My Wagon." Bacharach's "pioneer" production?

One begins to feel as though Bacharach, tired of having no hits to show for all his hard work, was willing to try anything at this point: teen idols, novelty songs and the three-chord rock 'n' roll he found so abhorrent years before. His work in 1960 is arguably the crassest of his entire career, and the fact that this song charted higher than "I Can Make You Mine" or "Your Lips Are Warmer Than Your Heart" is proof that the pop audience was going through one of its frequent lapses in good judgment.

Novelties weren't the only thing on Bacharach and Hilliard's agenda, as evidenced by this 45's superior flip side. A Paul Anka–esque treatise on soda-shop betrayal, it has Clinton moaning the blues over Joanie, whose idea of forever is a Friday-to-Monday romance. The 20-foot female background vocalists of the previous cut are better utilized here, bathed in heavy reverb to resemble a lonesome roller-rink organ in space. Like Joanie's affections, which lasted less than a week, Buddy's notoriety was to endure considerably less than forever; today, Internet search engines turn up only Web sites devoted to President Bill Clinton's deceased dog.

"Three Wheels on My Wagon" (Bob Hilliard - Burt Bacharach)
First recorded by Dick Van Dyke
Jamie 1178, released January 1961

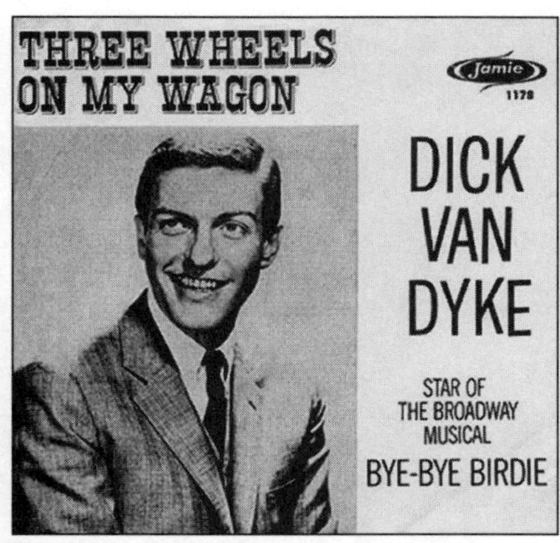

Dick Van Dyke. Despite the comedian's considerable gift for voices, he still failed to come up with anything as funny as Steve Rossi's singing.

Although the honor of "first Bacharach production" is frequently bestowed upon "Make It Easy on Yourself," the truth is that Bacharach was only credited as an arranger on that label. No, the first time he was officially listed as a producer on both the label and the sleeve was on this admittedly less prestigious release, which carried the rare "produced by Hilliard and Bacharach" credit on both sides. Having recently dabbled in the novelty song genre with Rusty Draper and Buddy Clinton, Hilliard and Bacharach fashioned both "Three Wheels on My Wagon" and "One Part Dog, Nine Parts Cat" to showcase the zany comedic voices of Dick Van Dyke, then starring in the Broadway musical *Bye Bye Birdie* and about to star in his own sitcom the following fall.

Bacharach and Hilliard again draw inspiration from a recent No. 1, in this case "Mr. Custer," Larry Verne's hit from the previous October. Van Dyke sings in a pinch-nosed voice like Verne's and drops the slight Southern accent in other places, much the way his cockney accent frequently disappears in *Mary Poppins*. Unlike the shaky-voiced Verne (who pleads, *"Please Mr. Custer, I don't wanna go"*), Van Dyke's "never-say

"Three Wheels on My Wagon." This 45 sported a different picture sleeve on its rerelease, meant to capitalize on Van Dyke's *Bye Bye Birdie* movie and Emmy Award–winning TV show.

die" pioneer seems unfazed about being attacked by wild Indians and begs off worrying about flaming arrows and the wheels on his wagon getting shot off by *"singin' a happy song."* Finally captured by Cherokees, he still manages to lead them in a spirited chorus of *"Higgety haggety hoggety hi!"* by song's end. Released on Jamie Records, the home of Duane Eddy, "Three Wheels" has a similar twangy guitar riff propelling it, as well as a sprightly banjo to make unhappiness a near impossibility.

Oddly enough, there is a sloppy tape edit that causes the start of the third verse to go momentarily out of beat. Somehow this escaped the finicky Bacharach and went uncorrected all the way to the pressing plant. Bacharach hadn't yet the clout he'd accrue by the end of the decade, where he could recall thousands of copies of "Raindrops Keep Falling on My Head" because he thought he'd chosen the wrong take.

In 1965, the New Christy Minstrels wagon-covered this song for their *Cowboys and Indians* album. NCM, as the kids might call them now, featured lead singer Barry McGuire, just one year away from coagulating about the "Eve of Destruction" and bodies floating in the Jordan River. Once hippies and flower power become the norm, singing about Indians in such a flippant manner would become politically incorrect.

Bacharach could be compelled to remember this number on occasion, if only as a punch line. When, on the 1973 TV show, *Opus No. 3—Burt Bacharach Special,* Peter Ustinov asked him if his first work (which he identified as "Three Wheels on My Wagon") was an overture or a chorale, Bacharach informed him, "actually, it was a bomb." And then there was the inexplicable June 23, 2001, appearance at the Fraze Pavilion, where a laughing Bacharach stuck the song in his pre-Dionne medley, insisting it was the first and probably last time he would ever sing it during a performance. No word on whether the folks in Kettering, Ohio charged the box office demanding a refund.

Other Versions: *Steve Downs • The New Christy Minstrels (1965)*

"One Part Dog, Nine Parts Cat" (Bob Hilliard - Burt Bacharach)
Recorded by Dick Van Dyke
Jamie 1178, flip side of "Three Wheels on My Wagon"
Released January 1961

In keeping with the western flavor of "Three Wheels," the reverse side has some leftover banjo, slide trombone and lonesome high-noon whistling. Sung in a voice that's one part Tweety Bird and two parts Aunt Blabby, Van Dyke tells of his schizophrenic pooch named *"Loo-see-fur,"* who thinks he's a cat. It's shamefully fun, with cheesy puns like *"dog-matically"* and *"con-fur-dentially."* After the success of Van Dyke's Emmy Award–winning show, Jamie Records reissued the single again to little fanfare. Had Van Dyke pushed to perform either side of this single on his television show, Nick at Night and VH1 would still be playing the video.

"Come Completely to Me" (Paul Hampton - Burt Bacharach)
Recorded by Steve Rossi
Columbia 41854, released January 1961

Picture a Mario Lanza wannabe trying to sing the Mystics' 1959 hit "Hushabye" and you have a vivid idea of why music lovers never developed an appreciation for the cheese-grating talents of Italian-American crooner Steve Rossi. Unable to score any chart hits, Rossi gave up on his shallow dream of being a Dean Martin–like demigod and settled for playing straight man to Marty Allen in the third-rate Martin and Lewis knock-off team of Allen and Rossi. Possibly one of the worst songs Bacharach's name was attached to, "Come Completely to Me" mercifully marks the end of the trail of appalling Paul Hampton collaborations, unless a published song called "Barracuda" turns up on an obscure B-side and bites us all in the ass.

Hal David continued writing with the Canadian composer and turned out some great songs in that combination. The Hampton-David team racked up 22 songs in all, including "Sea of Heartbreak" for Don Williams and "Donna Means Heartbreak" for Gene Pitney.

Steve Rossi. Here's Steverino, several years before partner Marty Allen's annoying catch phrase, "Hello dere," became a signal to viewers of *The Ed Sullivan Show* to turn down the sound until the Russian dancing bears came back on.

"Gotta Get a Girl" (Burt Bacharach - Hal David)
Recorded by Frankie Avalon
Chancellor 1077, flip side of "Who Else but You"
Released April 1961

After having twice rewritten "Venus" for Frankie Avalon wannabes like Everit Herter and Larry Hall, Bacharach and David finally got a shot at doing it for the real McCoy. While financially more rewarding, the end result couldn't be more artistically bankrupt. All the Venusian elements are in place on "Gotta Get a Girl"—the glockenspiel, the skipping beat played with brushes, the swirling strings, the pizzicato strings and those ethereal background vocals ooh-ing overhead while Frankie searches for that special girl who just might be you. All that's missing is Frankie calling out "Hey, Venus!" again.

David's lyrics couldn't be more banal if you woke him in the middle of the night with a flashlight and a legal pad *("Gotta get a girl, someone to talk with / I just gotta get a girl / someone to walk with")*. Only during the bridge, where Frankie gets to show off his lonely side, does any concentrated effort on either Bacharach's or David's part seem evident.

By 1962, with Avalon's attention increasingly focused on movies and Annette in a bikini, his recording efforts were meeting with declining bobbysoxer interest. Now only every fourth or eighth single reached the Top 30; the rest hovered in the lower regions of the Top 100. The topside to "Gotta Get a Girl" only got as far as No. 82.

"And This Is Mine" (Burt Bacharach - Hal David)
First recorded by Connie Stevens
Warner Bros. 5217, released May 1961

1961

Connie Stevens. When Connie left Edd "Kookie" Byrnes to pursue her solo recording career, Warner Brothers teamed him up with the "Voice of America" and future Pepsi Generation spokesperson, Joanie Sommers.

"Kookie, Kookie (Lend Me Your Comb)," a 1959 smash duet by *77 Sunset Strip* star Edd "Kookie" Byrnes and Connie Stevens, soon led the pretty Brooklyn girl to a Warner Brothers recording contract and a series of her own. Between 1959 and 1963, Stevens starred as Cricket Blake on *Hawaiian Eye* and had several hits without the aid of Kookie or his comb. This wasn't one of them, but it is sung with a lusty hush that makes you want to run to her in slow motion. You might want to reserve the opposite direction for your escape from Ginny Arnell.

Other Versions: *Ginny Arnell (1963)*

"Three Friends (Two Lovers)" (Burt Bacharach - Hal David)
Recorded by the Turbans
Roulette 4326, released 1961

This Philadelphia quartet did indeed wear turbans when they performed, which might qualify them as the first costume band if they ever cared to wage that argument. It had been five long years since the group's previous Top 40 hit, "When You Dance," and this Bacharach-David tune was a last-ditch attempt to upgrade the group's sound. When it failed to click with record buyers, the Turbans offered a remake of "When You Dance" that briefly "bubbled under" at No. 114 before officially calling it a day.

Definitely recorded on the cheap, "Three Friends" qualifies as a neo–doo-wop number by virtue of the plinky lead guitar way up front in the mix. Hal David again employs the love-triangle scenario for but adds the "good sport" angle that powered countless Bobbie Vee songs. The side of the triangle left alone with a broken heart after Billy and Janey pair up—in this case, lead Turban Al Banks—is a gracious loser who'll try not to cry, which makes us feel all the sorrier for him when three does not go into two.

"The Story Behind My Tears" (Burt Bacharach - Hal David)
Recorded by Kenny Lynch
HMV POP 900, flip side of "The Steady Kind"
Released May 1961 (UK only)

The story behind Kenny Lynch reads more like a series of footnotes. One of the few black vocalists recording in Britain during the early Sixties, Lynch racked up several Top 10 UK hits, jumping from string-attached Brill Building pop to Cliff Richard imitations to primitive Merseybeat. He went on to become more successful as a writer, penning the Small Faces first hit, "Sha-la-la-la-lee," as well as some notable album tracks for Dusty Springfield, the Swinging Blue Jeans and the Drifters. Yet none of these activities resulted in much name recognition in the States, where only the staunchest Beatlemaniac could be counted on knowing that Lynch was the first artist ever to cover a Lennon and McCartney tune ("Misery," though it wasn't a hit).

While Lynch wasn't the first British artist to record a Bacharach-David tune, he was the first British artist to have B&D write a song especially for him. For all that, the song, which appeared on Lynch's fourth single, wasn't terribly memorable. The title is an allusion to team's first hit, "The Story of My Life," and once again Hal David tells an exceptionally brief story, beginning at a dance and ending when someone runs off with his fiancée. The sound owes much to the slow-twistin' blues that Brook Benton was successfully selling at the time— lots of long-drawn-out phrasing, deep-dungeon bellowing, slip-note piano playing and a hyperactive string section. Gary Miller, hoping for another "Story of My Life," put out a rival version that also ended in tears and negligible sales.

When the Royal Albert Hall held a Bacharach–David tribute, "singer comedian entertainer and actor, Kenny Lynch O.B.E." opened the show. But he didn't bother with "The Story of My Tears." Instead he sang "Wives And Lovers," a song he is said to have witnessed Bacharach writing in London in 1963.

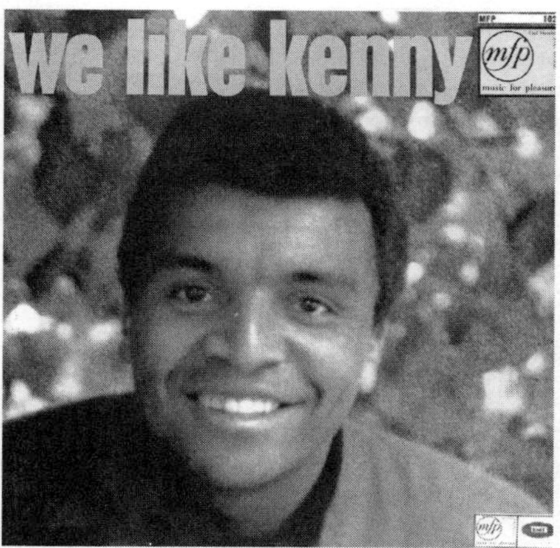

Kenny Lynch. People who memorize album covers for fun may remember Kenny Lynch as one of the celebrity jailbreakers invited to stand in the spotlight of Paul McCartney and Wings' 1973 album *Band on the Run.* Others may have found things like life more distracting.

Other Versions: *Gary Miller (1961)*

"Out of My Continental Mind" (Burt Bacharach - Sydney Shaw)
Recorded by Lena Horne
From the album Lena at the Sands, RCA Victor LPM-2364
Released June 1961

Very likely written to order as comic relief for Horne's nightclub act, "Out of My Continental Mind" is unlike any of the previous Bacharach–Sydney Shaw songs in that it's not a lush ballad but an up-tempo trifle in the style of "The Lady Is a Tramp." Actually this could almost be a "Lady Is a Tramp" answer record, with the trampy lady badgering her man with you-better-love-me-or-else sentiments.

Recorded live for her *Lena at the Sands* album, Horne goes from husky invocation to angry harangue in less than a few jazzy beats. Lyricist Shaw even loosens up enough here to rhyme "wow" with "pow"! His collaborations with Bacharach end here, but he would go on to pen other levity-driven numbers like the theme for "It's a Mad Mad Mad Mad World" and "Evil Spelled Backwards Means Live."

Lena Horne. Ms. Horne would later record covers of such Bacharach hits as "Wives and Lovers," "Message to Michael" and "What the World Needs Now Is Love." Didn't everybody?

Other Versions: *Ernestine Anderson • Claire Martin (1994)*

"I'll Bring Along My Banjo" (Burt Bacharach - Norman Gimbel)
Recorded by Johnnie Ray
United Artists 341, flip side of "How Many Nights, How Many Days"
Released June1961

Among the casual songwriting partners Bacharach hooked up with during his Famous Music days, Norman Gimbel is the only lyricist to work with the composer before *and* after his exclusive writing arrangement with Hal David. Gimbel co-wrote two inconsequential songs with Bacharach in 1961 ("I'll Bring Along My Banjo" and "Deeply") and later penned two ("Where Are You" and "When You Bring Your Sweet Love to

1961

The Rangoons. The first credited Bacharach-David production contained no lyrics—on either side of this Rangoons single. "Moon Guitar" elicited covers versions from other instrumentalists of the day, like Billy Vaughn and the 50 Guitars of Tommy ["Snuff"] Garrett.

Me") on Bacharach's 1977 album *Futures,* after his split with Hal. Among Gimbel's more famous works were the English translation lyrics for "The Girl from Ipanema" and Little Peggy March's "I Will Follow Him." Before making his re-acquaintance with Bacharach, he penned Roberta Flack's No. 1 "Killing Me Softly with His Song" and Jim Croce's first posthumous hit, "I Got a Name."

Johnnie Ray had a name, and a hand in inspiring Elvis Presley's vocal technique, but once the Hillbilly Cat was crowned King, the public sadly forgot Ray, the shameless shaman who waved his arms around like a drowning man and turned his back on the audience to simulate crying. This proved to be his only single on United Artists, as he hopscotched to Liberty, Decca and Groove before Mr. Sun finally set on his recording career. Easily the most maddeningly jolly song Bacharach ever reserved music for (*"I'll bring along my banjo and you bring along your songbook / And we'll sing-a-ling a-ling a-ling along, sing a happy song!"*), it's rendered even more virulent by Ray's buoyant shrieking. Deep into the bottle around this time, Ray must've required several gallons of Dutch courage to get through this number more than once.

"Moon Guitar" (Burt Bacharach - Hal David)
First recorded by the Rangoons
Laurie 3096, released June 1961

Back in the days when deejays needed a record they could interrupt when the station cut to the hourly news report, instrumentals were incredibly popular. Dozens of songs made it through the back door and onto radio station playlists this way. "Moon Guitar" didn't rocket up the charts, although it holds it own alongside instrumental rockers of the day like "Perfida" and "Penetration."

Yet another pre–"Make It Easy on Yourself" production, this one sports the first ever "produced by Bacharach and David" credit. No vocal version of this instrumental or its flip side has ever turned up. Like the Five Blobs, the Rangoons seem to be strictly a studio creation. Sounding like "The Blob" with its intermittently squeaky sax solos, "Moon Guitar" is mostly carried along by a riff played on the low strings of one guitar and the percolating dampened strings of another. There are also atmospheric harp-like electric guitars, probably recorded at half-speed to simulate mandolins in space at normal rpm. And there is that tingling sound again, which tells you it's still 1961 at the Brill Building and the Triangle Players Union looks after its own.

This is the only time Hal David received a credit for an instrumental. "Moon Guitar" was copyrighted under Bacharach's name alone, and unlike "Saturday Night in Tia Juana," no Hal David lyrics were ever written for it later on.

Other Versions: *Billy Vaughn • Tommy Garrett (1966)*

"My Heart Is a Ball of String" (Burt Bacharach - Hal David)
First recorded by the Rangoons
Laurie 3096, flip side of "Moon Guitar"
Released June 1961

Another instrumental, this one featuring a melancholy harmonica framed against a bed of exotic bachelor pad music and more speeded-up guitars. It's not hard to imagine Hal David scripting a tale of a feline devil stringing some poor heartsick fool along, and indeed there were copyrighted lyrics for this flip, but they were never issued.

The Cryin' Shames (1966). Don't confuse these Brits with the Cryan' Shames, an American group that had a hit with "Sugar and Spice" (a song first recorded by a British group, the Searchers). Their single "Please Stay" gives Bacharach fans the only chance to hear one of his songs produced the eerie Joe Meek way. The flip was a rocking parody of the Tom Jones hit, penned by the group and entitled "What's News Pussycat."

"(Don't Go) Please Stay" (Burt Bacharach - Bob Hilliard)
First recorded by the Drifters
Atlantic 2105 (*Billboard* pop #14, R&B #13)
Released June 1961

Bacharach, no longer able to stomach the meatball surgery producers were subjecting his songs to, took stringent self-defense measures to insure quality control over the final product. Henceforth the demos he'd send to A&R men and recording artists were more fleshed out than their voice-and-piano predecessors. A demo album of Bacharach songs that surfaced from this period featured Hammond organs and background vocals simulating the string parts, tambourines and either soulful or country-style lead vocals, depending on what the song required. If that weren't enough, once a song found its way to a recording artist, the composer planted himself in the recording studio to make sure they got it right. Although Bacharach often escaped getting a label check during this period, many of the artists he worked with have corroborated that he was de facto producer at these sessions.

Bacharach's move away from the strict confines of his Famous Music assignments led him to sympathetic songwriters-turned-independent-producers like Jerry Leiber and Mike Stoller at Atlantic and Luther Dixon at the fledgling Scepter Records. Working as an arranger for both R&B mavericks, Bacharach found himself surrounded by all the essential components of what would soon be his trademark sound—timpani, strings, triangles, trumpets and, of course, background singer Dionne Warwick.

The Drifters. "Please Stay" can be readily found on almost every Drifters collection. Of the five first-run Bacharach songs they recorded, it's the only one missing young Dionne Warwick on background vocals.

It also led him to further work with Bob Hilliard, whose R&B credentials were even more remote than his own. No matter. Everything the Drifters were cutting at this time had the Brazilian *baion* beat attached to it, which Bacharach was quite familiar with, having clocked numerous world tours conducting for Marlene Dietrich. The *baion* made its first appearance on a Drifters record with "There Goes My Baby," a finished master that Atlantic president Ahmet Ertegun sat on for two months because he felt the song sounded like two radio stations playing at the same time.

Considerably less chaotic-sounding than that record, "Please Stay" is a plaintive plea for love that is a cut above the standard pop begging of the day. Hilliard's second verse, with *"If I called out your name like a prayer in the night,"* transforms a disposable pop lyric into poetry.

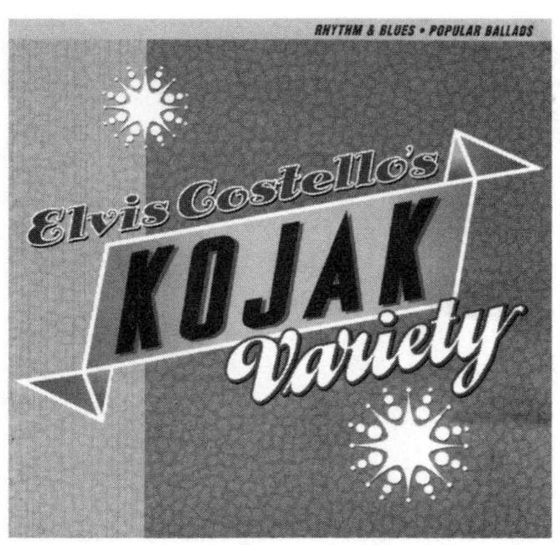

Elvis Costello (1994). With the princely budget Warner Brothers gave the singer to record the B-side of his hit "Veronica," Costello managed to bang out an entire album of cover versions in Barbados. The resulting *Kojak Variety,* which included a tranquil recitation of "Please Stay," appeared five years later.

Hilliard reserves his most colorful turns of phrase for the middle eight bars. *"Now I hang by a thread in the canyon of doom"* might come off as cartoon desperation worthy of the comical Coasters if Hilliard didn't balance that bit of heroics with the more earthbound *"you took me away from the rest of the world when you taught me to love you like this."* It helps that singer Rudy Lewis brings the same on-the-outside-looking-in longing that made "On Broadway," his debut single with the group, so memorable.

Many of the memorable cover versions eliminate the "don't go" prefix, such as Elvis Costello's 1994 reworking, which he claims to have learned off Zoot Money's version. Lou Johnson takes even more liberties on the Muscle Shoals treatment found on his 1969 album *Sweet Southern Soul*—he changes the "canyon of doom" to a valley!

Perhaps the most perplexing lyrical makeover comes from the UK and the Cryin' Shames' bizarre 1966 version, where whole verses are rewritten to accommodate singer Charlie Crane's lisp. Not surprisingly, it comes courtesy of eccentric British pop producer Joe Meek, whose macabre gifts for engineering and arranging around even his most talentless discoveries resulted in riveting recordings that are highly sought after by collectors today. One year away from committing suicide, Meek's ethereal production of "Please Stay" already feels posthumous.

Borrower's note: Early Bacharach watcher Bob Crewe thought enough of "Please Stay" to appropriate its pre-chorus to perform a similar function in the Four Seasons' 1964 recording of "Silence Is Golden." Also, the Drifters are listed again below as another cover version, since by 1976 it was probably an entirely alien set of Drifters pleading, "Don't go."

Other Versions: *The Chimetones • Elvis Costello (1994) • Cryin' Shames (1966) • Dave Clark Five (1968, UK only) • The Drifters (1976, rerecorded) • George Faith (1996) • Lou Johnson (1969) • Lulu (1970) • The Persuaders (1973) • Aaron Neville (1991) • Zoot Money's Big Roll Band (1965)*

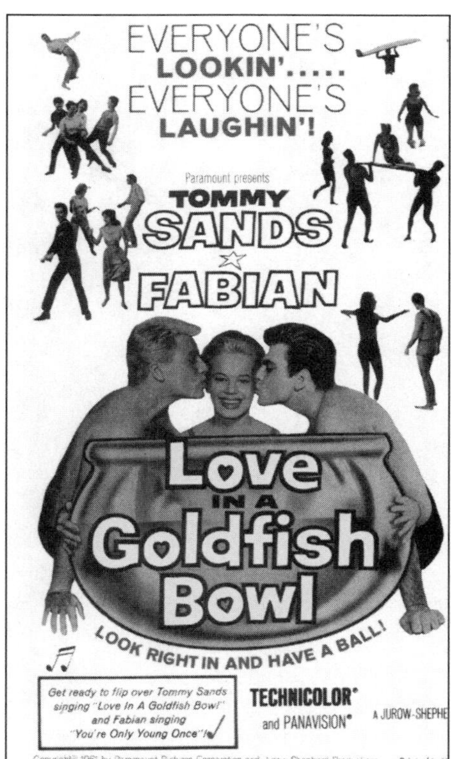

Tommy Sands. A year after doing laps in this soggy saga, Sands and Fabian reconvened in the all-star war epic *The Longest Day*; independently, they continued to make pop records that were largely ignored.

"Love in a Goldfish Bowl" (Burt Bacharach - Hal David)
Recorded by Tommy Sands
From the movie Love in a *Goldfish Bowl*
Capitol 4580, released June 1961

"Everyone's lookin'...everyone's laughin'"?? Chances are, if you've seen any movie about two teenagers up to crazy high jinks on a Hawaiian holiday, it probably wasn't this one. The two youths in question are Fabian and Tommy Sands, with Tommy's dark locks suspiciously bleached blond in order to provide that good-teen-idol/bad-teen-idol contrast. By 1961, Fabian hadn't seen the top reaches of a sales chart in two years. For Sands it had been four years—an eternity in the pop music business, especially by 1961 standards. But fresh from marrying Frank's kid Nancy Sinatra in 1960 and starring in *Sing Boy Sing* and Disney's *Babes in Toyland*, Sands was already something of a name in Hollywood, and thus received top billing and the title song to warble.

Blame for this brand of ersatz rock can be laid at the feet of Elvis Presley himself, who legitimized horn-riddled movie pop as far back as the *King Creole* soundtrack and was now making music every bit as annoying as his imitators. Another contributor to bad rock was the twist, especially hot on everyone's mind in 1961 and gaining popularity with jet setters like the Gabor sisters. "Love in a Goldfish Bowl" is the kind of doggerel middle-aged hipsters would swivel to if you poured enough martinis into them. Yet kids and adults alike managed to keep a safe distance from the dance floor whenever it played. Not even Tommy's injecting a few enthusiastic "yeahs" could stop the Sands slide to oblivion.

Merv Griffin. Hal David wrote English lyrics for "The Charanga," the not quite pachanga, not quite cha-cha-chá and not quite popular dance craze. A key track on the *Merv Griffin's Dance Party* album, the song came bundled with "Along Came Joe" on a 45 several months later.

"Along Came Joe" (Burt Bacharach - Hal David)
Recorded by Merv Griffin
Carlton 545, released June 1961

From the soulful to the doleful!

As Merv Griffin tells it in his autobiography, *From Where I Sit*, he was Bacharach's good friend and next-door neighbor in the mid-Fifties when the composer was still trying to establish himself in the songwriting world. He tells an amusing story that happened one summer when the two men shared a house in the Hamptons and Bacharach got a gig playing piano in a supper club. Every night he would get into heated arguments with drunken patrons whenever they would come over to the piano and sing along off-key with him. Bacharach's solution? Grab some planks and nails and build a fence around the stage!

Years later, Bacharach gifted Griffin with a love-triangle song that probably would've sounded bland even in a doo-wop setting. The future syndicated-talk-show host tries to inject plenty of bathos into the lyrics and, in an attempt to sound less wooden, rolls the letter *r* and winds up sounding like a dying buzz saw. He's simply too long in the tooth to be singing this Avalon-esque tearjerker. In October 1961, not long after the arrival and departure of "Joe," Merv made his move to national television, hosting a 55-minute daytime talk show on NBC.

Sam Butera. Louis Prima's *other* musical foil.

"Love Lessons" (Burt Bacharach - Hal David)
Recorded by Sam Butera and the Witnesses
Dot 16250, released July 1961

The "Big Horn" in Louis Prima's backup group, the Witnesses, Sam Butera gets to blast on his own here, with the boss man himself producing. Although most of Butera and the Witnesses' long-players for Dot and Capitol were instrumentals, at 45 rpm he was being groomed to sing, taking time out only for a few perfunctory horn blasts. Butera may not have had the greatest voice, but he does sound like he's having a lot of fun taking instruction from the luscious lips and fingertips of his baby doll/wife/mistress/whatever. Musically, the easygoing bop tune sounds similar to the Bert Kaempfert composition "L-O-V-E," a hit for Nat "King" Cole in 1964. Not a great record, but not a grating one, either.

1961

The Drifters. Manager George Treadwell owned the Drifters name, and to prove it, he fired the entire group in May 1958 and replaced them with the Crowns a week later. By the time this record was issued, three former Crowns still remained in the lineup.

"Loneliness or Happiness" (Burt Bacharach - Hal David)
Recorded by the Drifters
Atlantic 2117, flip side of "Sweets for My Sweet"
Released August 1961

The Bacharach demo of "Loneliness or Happiness" is religiously adhered to, from Rudy Lewis' faithful study of demo singer Lonnie Sattin's inflections to the minor fleshing out of Bacharach's original organ/timpani idea. Here the familiar *baion* beat is slowed to an almost funereal dirge, yet the recording never drags. The main innovation is the addition of background vocals by the Gospelaires, a New Jersey vocal group comprising Dionne and Dee Dee Warwick, their aunt Cissy Houston, Sylvia Shemwell and Myrna Smith. The Gospelaires, who evolved from the Drinkard Sisters, were often hired to either supplement, overshadow or completely replace the other Drifters, as they do on this recording. "Loneliness or Happiness" could almost be a Rudy Lewis solo recording, since none of the other Drifters sing on it.

As Bacharach recounts in Hal David's book *What the World Needs Now*, "We came into Jerry and Mike's office and there were these three girls, background singers, rehearsing for a Drifters' session. They sounded really great but Dionne had a very unique look—pigtails and sneakers, just a certain quality about her." After the session, he approached her about doing songwriting demos and used her on a studio date as early as Labor Day (for Burt and the Backbeats' "Move It on the Backbeat," released later that fall).

Dionne's voice is clearly audible on this track and would prominently find its way onto two more Drifters recordings of Bacharach origin in the ensuing year. This session also produced "Mexican Divorce," which would remain unreleased for another six months.

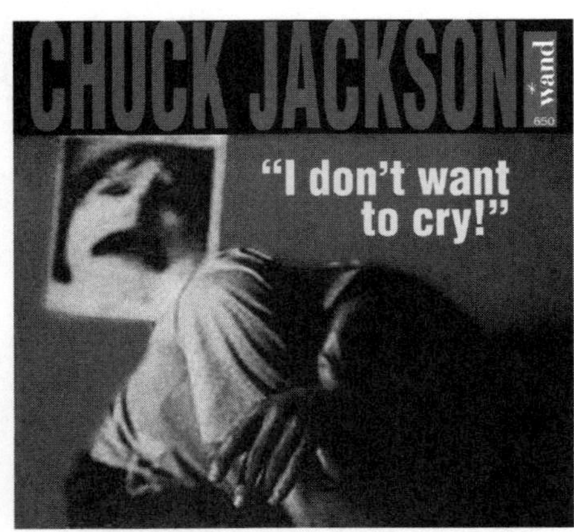

Chuck Jackson. Among those who idolized Jackson was Tom Jones, who once appeared on stage with Jackson and Dionne Warwick at the famed Apollo Theatre in Harlem. After being aghast at his Welsh ancestry, the silent audience was quickly won over. By way of tribute, Tom recorded seismic versions of Jackson's Bacharach hits "I Wake Up Crying" and "Any Day Now."

"I Wake Up Crying" (Hal David - Burt Bacharach)
First recorded by Chuck Jackson
Wand 110 (*Billboard* pop #59, R&B #13)
Released August 1961

Chuck Jackson was the first artist signed to Wand Records, a Scepter subsidiary created to showcase R&B acts somewhat grittier than the Shirelles and the Rocky Fellers. Both record labels had an unlikely owner—a Jewish housewife named Florence Greenberg who was looking for relief from her boring New Jersey suburban existence and thought the record business might provide it. After discovering the Shirelles and licensing their first single, "I Met Him on a Sunday," to Decca, she started up Scepter with the $4,000 she made from that maiden endeavor. The Scepterized Shirelles had a slow commercial start until producer Luther Dixon came on board to write material and produce for the girls.

A onetime singer with the Dell-Vikings, Jackson was encouraged to go solo by his idol, Jackie Wilson, who offered him a spot in his revue. It was in this context that Luther Dixon caught Jackson at the Apollo and offered him a contract with Scepter. Despite interest from RCA and Wilson's label, Brunswick, Jackson went with the smaller company after praying to God for a sign. That sign came when he went to Dixon's apartment and the pair co-wrote Jackson's first hit," I Don't Want to Cry."

Following the same lamenting path as that previous single, "I Wake Up Crying" evokes the nocturnal suffering of a man who can't find happiness in solitude. The heavy reverb on the timpani (reminiscent of "Warm and Tender") contrasts starkly with Jackson's vocals in the verses, recorded dryly to evoke that just-woke-up feeling when you're jolted back into reality by a lonely face staring you down in the mirror. As Jackson himself told *The R&B Page*, "the first time I heard it I knew it was a hit. I liked the melody. I liked the minor changes in it. As far as feeling, it was one of the greatest songs I've ever done."

Del Shannon. His *Live In London* album contains the preferable version of "The Answer to Everything."

Although the record is credited on the 45 label as "An Alpa Arrangement" (the "Al" being Alan Lorber and the "Pa" being session pianist Paul Griffin) and a Luther Dixon production, Bacharach's active role behind the piano at this session can't be underestimated. This was his first work at his soon-to-be home base, Scepter Records.

Other Versions: *Steve Alaimo (1963) • William Bell (1977) • Camille Bob & the Lollipops • Gene Chandler (1961) • Tom Jones (1967) • Jimmy Justice (1963) • Longines Symphonette Society (1970) • Warner Mack • Cliff Richard (1963) • Del Shannon (1961) • Smokin' Popes (2000) • Third World (1989)*

"The Answer to Everything" (Burt Bacharach - Bob Hilliard)
First recorded by Del Shannon
Big Top 3083, flip side to "So Long Baby"
Released September 1961

Among the first to cover "I Wake Up Crying" was Del Shannon, who also selected a Bacharach-Hilliard song, "The Answer to Everything," from the same batch of demos. Full-throated and at the top of his register, Shannon goes for the same notes as the unidentified woman on the demos, teetering on the verge of cracking. Arranged in the style of country great Jim Reeves' "He'll Have to Go," the finished recording of "The Answer to Everything" retains the demo's Floyd Cramer style of "slip note" piano playing and shuffling brush beat, while also adding the quiet marimbas found on many of Reeves' records. It's a mature sounding record for Shannon and quite a stylistic stretch from "So Long Baby," the rocking-with-a-kazoo A-side

"The Answer to Everything" remained in Shannon's live set up to 1973 and can be heard on his excellent *Live in England* album. Usurping the Jim Reeves feel for country rock, Del sounds more confident of the song's vocal requirements the second time around, and he attacks it with a David Allan Coe–like gusto.

Nancy Sinatra would give "The Answer to Everything" limited A-side exposure in early 1965. It was her eleventh flop 45 in a row for Daddy's Reprise label. In the liner notes for her Rhino collection *The Hit Years*, Nancy intimates that if it hadn't been for the lucky thirteenth single, "These Boots Are Made for Walking," she might have gotten dropped from the label. Yeah, right.

Other Versions: *Nancy Sinatra (1965)*

1961

Dee Clark. Here's one "where are they now?" you could probably do without reading. At the time of his death, this great singer was on his way to California to hawk his once-famous pipes on the syndicated talent-scout show *Star Search.*

Brigitte Bardot. Perhaps the strangest of Bacharach's 1961 releases was this piece of Brazilian parade music, with Joel Grey rolling his *r*'s and eyes in praise of "Brigitte Bardot."

"Deeply" (Burt Bacharach - Norman Gimbel)
Recorded by the Shepherd Sisters
United Artists 350, released September 1961

In the eat-'em-up world of early rock, the Shepherd Sisters were somehow allowed to cut 45s well after their 1957 Top 20 hit "Alone (Why Must I Be Alone)" slipped off to the golden-oldie netherworld. The frequently misspellings of Shepherd on their preceding singles ("Shepard," "Sheppard") were an indicator of just how bankable the group's name was it as it slid on and slipped off a near dozen record labels between 1956 and 1965. It sounds as if the McGuire Sisters were invited to record over a Drifters track for "Deeply," a Leiber-and-Stoller-produced *baion* ballad with furiously bowed violins that failed to leave much of an impression. Martha, Mary Lou, Gayle and Judy found their way into the Top 100 just one last time with "Don't Mention My Name," produced by Four Seasons producer Bob Crewe and written by the Four Seasons' Bob Gaudio. Its flip is an answer record to the Seasons' No. 1 hit "Big Girls Don't Cry" entitled "What Makes Little Girls Cry." Hint: it's boys.

"You're Telling Our Secrets" (Burt Bacharach - Hal David)
Recorded by Dee Clark
Vee-Jay 409, flip side of "Walk Away from Me"
Released October 1961

Similar in arrangement to Jerry Butler's Vee-Jay recording of "Moon River," this B-side could've been cut at the same session. Lyrically, Hal David brilliantly captures the jealousy of seeing a former lover with somebody new. Compounding this hurt is paranoia that the new couple's mating ritual entails reading his old love letters out loud and laughing at the passages where he begged her to stay. Even this severe form of self-persecution is preferable to the unspoken truth—that he's been completely forgotten by her and the new lovers are shagging away at this very moment.

This song seems to fade out a bit too prematurely to qualify as a bona fide classic: it almost demands Clark to get hysterical, as he does at the end of his biggest hit, "Raindrops." You can view "You're Telling Our Secrets" as a dry run for Butler's upcoming Bacharach and David smash "Make It Easy on Yourself," with Bacharach's guiding hand in the production department making all the difference.

"Move It on the Backbeat" (Burt Bacharach - Mack David)
First recorded by Burt & the Backbeats
Big Top 3087, released October 1961

Just a few short months before, Bacharach tapped young Marie Dionne Warrick to do some demo sessions for him. Ironically, the future voice of Bacharach and David would find herself cutting a Mack David lyric for the first and last time as part of this endeavor. In Adam White's liner notes for the Sequel CD reissue of Warwick's early Scepter albums, John Houston (Cissy Houston's husband) recalls, "Burt wanted to do a tune called 'Move It on the Backbeat and thought Dionne's voice was just what he was looking for. He called me on a big ole Labor Day to bring Dionne into New York."

The drive from New Jersey was worth it, at least for serendipity's sake, as it provides us the only opportunity of hearing Dionne Warwick and Bacharach singing together on a record (his voice is best audible in the second line of every verse). Bacharach had masqueraded behind a group alias before with the Five Blobs, but here was the first instance where he'd give himself a billing. No serious threat to the twist, the pony or the fly, "Move It on the Backbeat" is an unlikely dance-craze record that features dead stops, hesitations, tempo changes, marching rhythms, drum paradiddles and plenty of lip pressing on the dance floor. One wonders what would've happened if they actually had a huge hit on their hands with this record. Would a phony Burt & the Backbeats have been assembled for one of those grueling package tours? Would people have started calling Dionne Burtie?

Gene McDaniels. If he were a tower of strength, why, he'd be strangling you—JUST...LIKE...THIS!!!

Big Top single 3086, released just before "Move It on the Backbeat," was a brassy Brazilian march entitled "Brigitte Bardot." Roberto Seto sang the A-side, but the near-identical flip, produced and arranged by Burt Bacharach, was an English translation of sorts—it had Joel Grey singing "Brigitte Bardot" and saying "aaaaaaah!" like a lascivious Frenchman.

Yet there's no denying that Brazilian music was a heavy influence on the composer. Bacharach was an ardent admirer of Brazilian composers Antonio Carlos Jobim and Vinícius de Morais, who wrote the B-side, "A Felicidade."

"Tower of Strength" (Burt Bacharach - Bob Hilliard)
First recorded by Gene McDaniels
Liberty 55371 (*Billboard* pop #5, R&B #5)
Released October 1961

Bacharach and Hilliard were slowly gaining momentum. This was their second R&B hit in less than four months—Bacharach's biggest hit since "Magic Moments," five years before. It was also their highest-charting R&B hit until "Any Day Now" claimed that honor a few months later. "Tower of Strength" combined the comic elements of previous Hilliard prose such as "Ten Thousand Years Ago" and "Three Wheels on My Wagon" but informed by the same undercurrent of tragedy as on their breakthrough hit, the Drifters' "Please Stay."

Gene McDaniels followed up his Top 3 hit "A Hundred Pounds of Clay" with this song about a guy whose feet are like several hundred pounds of clay. Otherwise he'd walk out the door after telling his paramour he no longer wants, needs or loves her. Once he admits to himself that he will never be a tower of strength, he's reduced to shameful weeping, while a slide trombone mocks his weak-willed tears.

"I liked 'Tower of Strength' because of the humor and the trombone solo in front," recalls McDaniels in the notes to the Collectibles retrospective *A Hundred Pounds of Clay*. "You never heard a trombone solo to a song and there it was and it was a hit! It blew my mind!" McDaniels

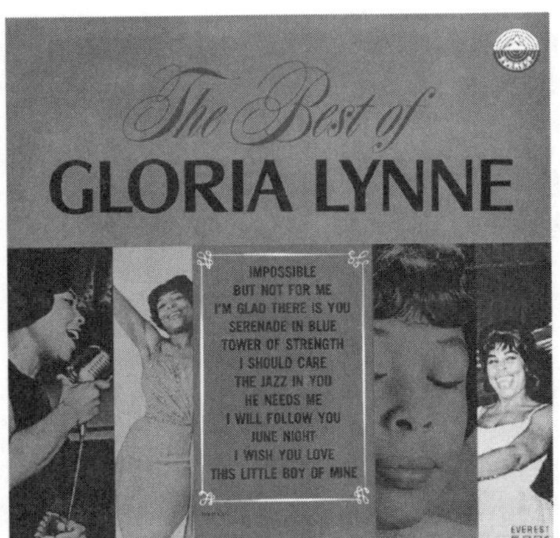

Gloria Lynne. Bacharach's only "answer" record. Don't look for this hit on any of her best-of CDs. In the LP format you'll find it only on this Everest compilation, appropriately titled *The Best of Gloria Lynne.*

clearly relishes growling the chorus instead of dispatching his usual eloquent phrasing, which will soon seem like a throwback to the Ink Spots when a new order of soul men takes over. Producer Tommy "Snuff" Garrett must've also loved this recording's arrangement, since it's cut from the same cheesecloth as McDaniels' previous hit as well as this single's follow-up, "Chip Chip." You'll recall that these were the days when a hit sound was furiously mined until the chart numbers went from single to triple digits.

Regardless of its Top 5 charting, Bacharach groused that its tempo sounded rushed. That complaint caused Bacharach and Hilliard to write a slower, bluesy answer disc, sung by jazz singer Gloria Lynne. Some familiar elements of the McDaniels recording remain, such as the loping backbeat and the pounding timpani, yet "(You Don't Have to Be a) Tower of Strength" (Everest 19420) really should be considered an altogether different song. First off, Lynne scat-sings in place of that slippery trombone. Then, instead of responding to the previous song from the viewpoint of a woman equally fed up with her powerless partner, Lynne is reassuring, building up her man by being submissive to his every whim if he'll only love her. Since there's nothing comical or humorous about this recording, it didn't connect with the same pop audience that chuckled at McDaniels. Lynne's record only reached No. 100 for one week.

Although not an answer record in the traditional sense, Italian pop sensation Andriano Celentano's foreign language version of "Tower of Strength" takes some liberties with the translation "Stai Lontano Da Me," which means "stay far away from me." After having loved and cried over his rotten *ragazza,* our Italian hero has found the necessary strength to tell her off and replaces McDaniels' bathetic weeping with diabolical laughter. If Bacharach thought the L.A. studio band on Garrett's arrangement of "Tower" was playing it too fast, Lord knows what he made of this rendition, raced through as if it were powered by a Ferrari engine.

Other Versions: *Audrey Arno ("Toute Ma Vie") • Casino Royale (1999) • Adriano Celentano - "Stai Lontana Da Me" (Italian, 1962), "Torre Poderosa" (Spanish, 1963) • Narvel Felts • Gloria Lynne - "You Don't Have to Be a Tower of Strength" (1961) • Mr. Bungle • Paul Raven (aka Gary Glitter) (1961) • Sue Richards (1975) • Frankie Vaughn (1961) • Jerry Williams (1974) • Billy Wade*

Perry Como. Although few record buyers were paying attention by then, Mr. C continued to cut Bacharach songs well into the Eighties. Check out his somnambulant stab at "That's What Friends Are For."

"You're Following Me" (Burt Bacharach - Bob Hilliard)
First recorded by Perry Como with the Ray Charles Singers
RCA 47-7962, (*Billboard* pop #92)
Released October 18, 1961

In 1960, Perry Como told the *Saturday Evening Post* "When I hear 'Hound Dog' I have to vomit a little, but in 1975 it will probably be a slightly ancient classic."

In 1961, with no Top 20 appearances since the "Magic Moments" era, Como wiped the vomit from his lips and embraced the new rockin' sounds with "You're Following Me." Someone must've spiked Como's Ovaltine with something potent on that particular session, causing him to sign off on uncommonly loud bass, drums, Scotty Moore-ish guitar leads and maniacal sha-da-das from background singers who sound like they were hijacked at gunpoint from a Bobby Rydell record.

While the authoritative finger snaps that open the song might make the Jets and Sharks jump into rumble stance, having Mr. C make like the Fonz with lines like *"When I've got the time I'll slip you a kiss"* must've had the kids doubling over with laughter. Still, the song is a lot more rocking than the substandard material Como's label mate Elvis was releasing with frightening regularity by this time. Hilliard's metaphysical lyrics were a cut above pop-norm clever—first having a girl follow Como around literally and later having just her memory trail him.

Peter Gordeno, another John Barry–produced hopeful, gave "You're Following Me" a try. Barry's dynamic production supplants the finger snaps with percussion and keeps the verses sparse just before exploding into James Bond bombast on the "eeeeeeeww come back bay-bay" release.

Other Versions: *Peter Gordeno*

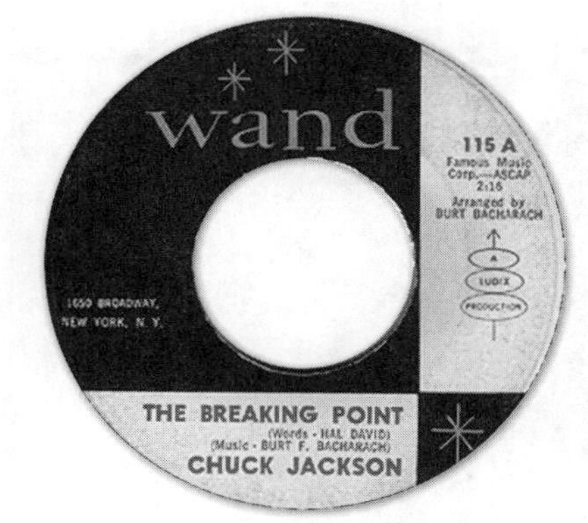

Chuck Jackson. He'd cut an answer record of sorts to "Raindrops" in 1970 called "Teardrops Keep Falling on My Heart" (V.I.P. 403).

"The Breaking Point" (Burt Bacharach - Hal David)
First recorded by Chuck Jackson,
Wand 115, released November 1961

Bacharach and David's most ferocious R&B track ever, "The Breaking Point," was a more than worthy follow-up to "I Wake Up Crying," which undeservedly failed to break into either the pop or R&B charts. Perhaps it was the whimsical references to mental illness that troubled programmers *("If you don't hurry back I'm gonna crack—up!")*. It contains the most insane nonsensical phrase yet uttered on a pop record: why da-doo-ron-ron when you can *"shagga dagga shagga dagga shick shick"*?

Jackson means every syllable he spits out; he must be at the breaking point because he's screaming himself hoarse at every chorus. And after threatening *"I'm gonna fade away shagga dagga / you know, you know I'm going to fade away, shagga-dagga-shagga-shagga"* for two minutes and twenty-two seconds—he actually does!

The Four Coins. This vocal quartet had no currency in 1961, yet they continued releasing records into 1967. They never forgot their roots, as they acknowledged on a 1965 album for Roulette, *Greek Songs Mama Never Taught Me.*

"The Miracle of St. Marie" (Burt Bacharach - Bob Hilliard)
Recorded by the Four Coins
Jubilee 5411, flip side of "Gee, Officer Krupke"
Released November 1961

With all the prime R&B Bacharach was cutting with Hal David and Bob Hilliard at this time, a return to the white pop stylings of the Four Coins seems like a pointless regression. Yet taken on its own, "The Miracle of St. Marie," with its soaring, Harry James–style trumpet solo, plus string charts, chiming bells and pounding kettle drums, sounds like it would've made a good theme for a TV hospital drama. But St. Marie isn't some medical center, it's a chapel by the sea where a prayer for love was answered. If the vocals were lifted off, we'd probably hear an instrumental that could've slotted nicely on one of Bacharach's early A&M albums. But Jubilee wasn't hedging any bets and put its money behind a *West Side Story* showstopper.

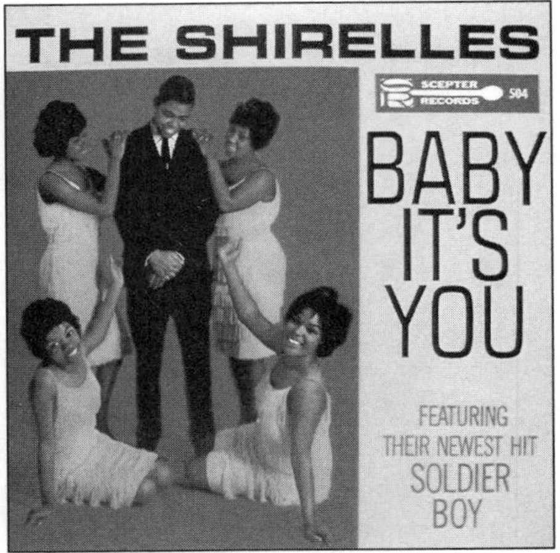

The Shirelles. When pop music's great appropriator, David Bowie, needed to write a theme for the spy movie *The Falcon and the Snowman,* he went back to the Shirelles' "Baby It's You" and ripped off its sha-la-la-la-las for "This Is Not America." Cheat! Cheat!

"Someone Else's Sweetheart" (Burt Bacharach - Hal David)
First recorded by the Wanderers
Cub 9099, flip side of "She Wears My Ring"
Released November 1961

As mentioned earlier, the Wanderers' ability to play it comical like the Coasters and elegant like the Platters was a trait that went underappreciated by all but the most rabid doo-wop aficionados. "Someone Else's Sweetheart" neatly showcases both qualities in high style. Ray Pollard's impassioned vocals over a track containing a head-pounding *baion* beat and chain-rattling tambourines. Once again Pollard is grappling with guilt over falling in love with another man's girl, causing him to leap from baritone lows to full-throated highs with a single bound like Buck Ram or Jackie Wilson. The other Wanderers do their bit by oohing and ahing majestically whenever they're not required to dooby-dooby-doo or emulate the bong of a church bell.

And for those fans of the obscure musical joke, it's one of many love-triangle songs where the steel triangle just happens to be tingling as a warning signal for three friends and two lovers everywhere.

Δ78
"Baby It's You" (Burt Bacharach - Mack David, Barney Williams)
First recorded by the Shirelles
Scepter 1227 (*Billboard* pop #8, R&B #3)
Released December 1961

Bacharach's songwriting demos from this period were carefully worked out exercises in minimalism. Generally there'd be a piano (sometimes with an organ suggesting string parts), background vocals, a generic lead vocal, a tambourine and a tom-tom drum subbing for the ever-popular timpani. All these components figured prominently on the Shirelles' released version of "Baby It's You," and with good reason: it's the original demo of a Burt Bacharach–Mack David composition once titled "I'll Cherish You," with Shirley Owens' lead vocal replacing the demo singer's.

The Beatles (1963). Bacharach and the Fab Four once played a show together—the 1963 Royal Command Performance where the boys informed the composer of "Baby It's You" that they had recently recorded it. No word if Marlene Dietrich took heed of Lennon's famous crowd-baiting remark and rattled her jewelry.

Producer Luther Dixon loved the demo but asked the composers if they could make the lyrics darker. Dixon contributed the "cheat, cheat" bit and accepted songwriting credit under his Barney Williams pseudonym. While Shirley Owens recorded over the demo's lead vocals, the original background vocals were retained, including the sha-la-la-la-loud contributions of a certain male vocalist (Burt Bacharach) in the opening moments. The combination of the echo and Owens' downcast reading—she utters *"What can I do, what can I do"* as if she's talking to herself—make for a very otherworldly recording whose reflective mood is only broken by the glass-shattering celestial organ solo in the middle eight.

The success of "Baby It's You" caught its creators by surprise, as it was the intended B-side to "The Things I Want to Hear (Pretty Words)," which was left dusted at No. 107 on the chart. It was Bacharach's first-ever chart triumph with a black female vocalist. The Shirelles had by this time proven themselves to be *the* ultimate girl group, having scored two songs in the Top 10 at the same time as well being as the first girl group in the rock era to reach No. 1. Two years after this issue, the girls received a prophetic honor when the Beatles—the group that virtually obliterated the girl group/Brill Building stranglehold on the charts—covered two Shirelles numbers for their Parlophone debut album, *Please Please Me*.

"I was in London doing the royal command performance with Dietrich—it was the first time I ever saw the Beatles," recalls Bacharach in a 2000 BBC radio interview. "One of them came up to me and said, 'Oh, we just recorded a song of yours, "Baby It's You."' I didn't know who these four guys were."

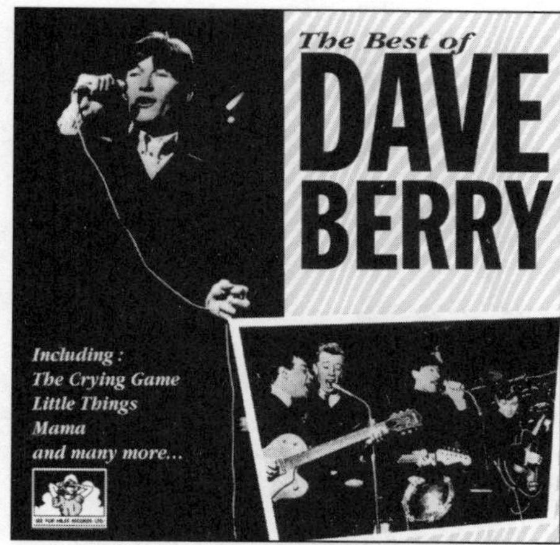

Dave Berry (1964). While no outstanding singer, England's Berry was the consummate performer, much revered for his vampirish stage movements and sleight-of-hand microphone-holding technique.

In Beatlemaniacal Britain, even the Fab Four's covers were worth plundering for their hit potential, as Dave "The Crying Game" Berry did with his whiny interpretation. "Baby It's You" was one of only two songs on the first Beatles album not to appear on a U.S. single in that first flush of Beatlemania. When a 1963 radio performance of "Baby It's You," taken from the group's 1995 *Live at the BBC* retrospective, reached No. 67, it marked the song's third appearance on the Hot 100.

The highest-charting version of the song was by a group called Smith, who reached No. 5 in the fall of 1969 on the strength of lead vocalist Gayle McCormick's Janis Joplinesque wails. No subsequent cover attempt, not even the exaggerated heaviosity of Sliver's glam-metal version, comes close.

Other Versions: *Shirley Alston (1976) • Dave Berry (1964) • The Beatles (1963) • Cilla Black (1965) • Petty Booka (2000) • Bradipos Four (2000) • Alan Caddy Orchestra (1972) • Carpenters (1970) • Casino Royale (1999) • Bruce Channel (1962) • Cherrelle (1991) • Elvis Costello & Nick Lowe (1984) • Desolation Angels (1989) • Dolly Mixture (1980) • Four Jewels • Gary & the Hornets • HiFi Ramblers (2000) • Chrissie Hynde - live version (1998) • Laima (1993) • The Last (1989) • Stacy Lattisaw & Johnny Gill (1983) • The Lettermen (1969) • Masqueraders (1975) • Metralhas • Curtis Mayfield • New World Orchestra • Bobby Rydell (1965) • Phil Seymour (1980) • Helen Shapiro • Michael Shelley (1998) • Sliver (1980) • Smith (1969)) • The Spaniels (1958) • Sterling (1980) • The Tempos (1966) • Pia Zadora (1982)*

Smith (1969). This San Fernando Valley group surpassed the Shirelles by making "Baby It's You" a Top 5 song in the fall of 1969. They were discovered by Del Shannon, who came up with the group's hard-rock arrangement.

"The Windows of Heaven" (Burt Bacharach - Hal David)
First recorded by the Four Coins
Jubilee 5419, flip side of "Come a Little Closer"
Released February 1962

"The Windows of Heaven" reeks of the same outdated odor as its predecessor, and with good reason: it had been lying around since 1959. It could've been cut at the same session as "The Miracle of St. Marie," with the same charts turned upside down on the music stands. While Hal David's lyrical metaphor, likening a woman's eyes to the windows of heaven, is lovely, the mood is undercut when all Four Coins blast in unison like foreign car horns in a traffic jam.

1962

"Another Tear Falls." This tune was published by Eleventh Floor Music, presumably a reference to the eleventh floor of the Brill Building, where Bacharach and David composed many of their great hits.

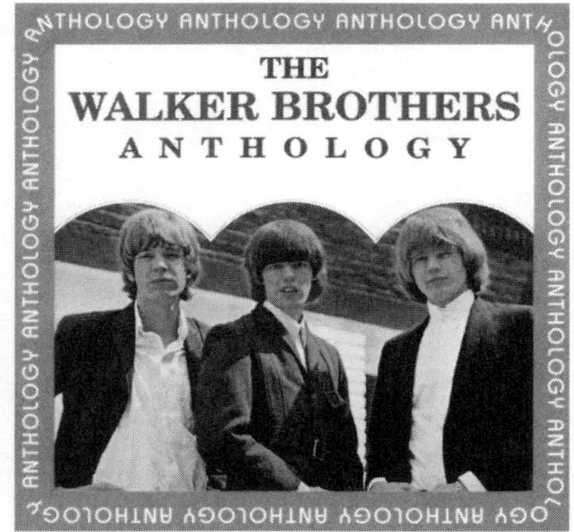

The Walker Brothers. Or Scott Engel, John Maus and Gary Leeds, for anyone who's already wasted precious time tracing the Walker family tree. Scott was actually discovered by crooner Eddie Fisher, but that whole Liz and Dick thing distracted him from promoting the young teen.

"Another Tear Falls" (Burt Bacharach - Hal David)
First recorded by Gene McDaniels
From the Columbia movie *Ring-A-Ding Rhythm*
Liberty 55405, flip side of "Chip Chip"
Released February 1962

Ring-A-Ding Rhythm, as it was known in the States, starred a multitude of pre–British Invasion American rock acts (Del Shannon, Gary "U.S." Bonds, Gene Vincent, Chubby Checker), some pre-Fab Britpop stars who would never invade the colonies (Helen Shapiro, John Leyton) and British trad-jazz performers who would be American one-hit wonders (Kenny Ball, "Mr." Acker Bilk).Originally released in England as *It's Trad, Dad,* this sharply scripted and photographed British pop movie marked the directorial debut of Richard Lester, who perfected his quick-cut technique here, just in time for the first two Beatles films, *A Hard Day's Night* and *Help!*

After such trivialities as Vincent's "Spaceship to Mars," Checker's "Lose Your Inhibition Twist" and Bonds' "Seven Day Weekend," it fell to Gene McDaniels to show those Britons that we Yanks have our serious side, and that a seven-day weekend can consist entirely of gloomy Sundays. Similar in its kettledrum drama to Ben E. King's "I Who Have Nothing," this mournful Bacharach-David ballad casts McDaniels as the jilted lover who always seems to relapse just at the point of recovery. Against a quiet bolero beat is a gradual swelling of strings and choral vocals, climaxing at each chorus with McDaniels crying, *"Now I know you are still in my heart; you are still here in my broken heart,"* only to start the whole sorrowful cycle again. McDaniels followed the histrionics of the original Bacharach demo very closely, although he reportedly didn't think the song was right for him.

As accomplished as McDaniels' version is, the Walker Brothers' 1965 "wall of sound"–alike remake cuts it to bits. Check out the way the doom-infused bells in the second verse add to the already-considerable anxiety. Lead singer Scott Walker ditches the final line, *"my love for you will never ever die,"* and repeats the more arresting *"you are still here in my broken heart"* before ringing the black curtain down. And to make an all-time low seem even lower, Walker has that peerless subterranean baritone that David Bowie would spend his entire career putting to greater financial gain. Strangely enough, this second export of a Bacharach-and-David did not consolidate the expatriate Walker Brothers' foothold in America—they remained a two-hit wonder, and Scott Walker a cult hero.

Other Versions: *Marv Johnson (1963) • Walker Brothers (1966) • Mark Wynter (1966)*

"Mexican Divorce" (Burt Bacharach - Bob Hilliard)
First recorded by the Drifters
Atlantic 2134, flip side of "When My Little Girl Is Smiling"
Released February 1962

The second travelogue in the Bacharach canon after "Saturday Night In Tia Juana" also crosses the Rio Grande, this time in more dramatic style. "Mexican Divorce" details an exotic excursion with a depressing motive behind it, namely the legal dismantling of a once-happy marriage. Released after sitting in the can since the previous July, the song once again features the background vocals of Dionne and Dee Dee Warrick and Cissy Houston assuming prominence over the other Drifters save for bass vocalist Elsberry Hobbs. This was the session where Bacharach first took notice of the young New Jerseyite Marie Dionne Warrick's stirring vocal quality and asked her to do some demo singing. Leiber and Stoller also noticed: they put Warwick's vocal so high up in the mix, this could almost be considered a duet with Rudy Lewis.

There are a lot of brilliant touches—the Latin guitars, the sliding strings and the pre-chorus where a piano chord initially sounds dissonant until it's repeated twice by the other Drifters singing a major note over it. All these features can be found on the original demo of "Mexican Divorce," which again was sung by Lonnie Sattin. Although "Please Stay" had charted high, none of Bacharach's subsequent Drifters offerings saw any A-side action. With the subject of divorce still touchy in 1962, this was relegated to a flip side, one of the Drifters' classiest ever.

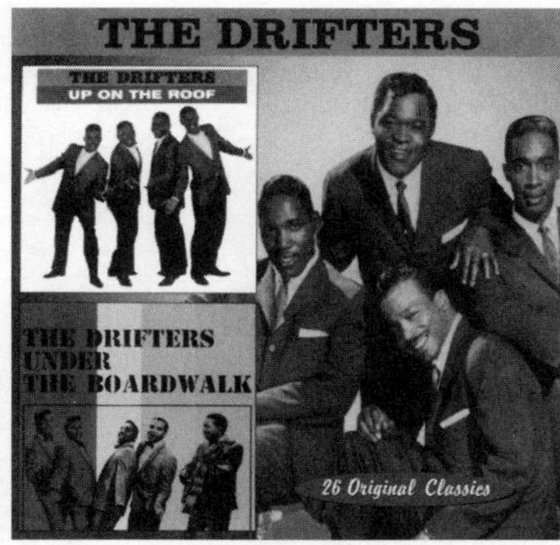

The Drifters. The Gospelaires' first professional recording session was singing behind Sam "The Man" Taylor on a song called "(Won't You) Deliver Me." They'd go on to do sessions with Dinah Washington, Brook Benton, Little Eva, Garnett Mimms and Ray Charles before tackling "Mexican Divorce" and "Loneliness or Happiness" for the Drifters in 1961.

Although no one could know it at the time, the Bacharach-Hilliard collaborations of the previous two years would abruptly come to an end after the back-to-back successes of "Any Day Now" and "Make It Easy on Yourself." This is one of Hilliard's finest lyrics, unfolding like a mini-drama in the vein of Leiber and Stoller, who produced the track. Bacharach thought enough of this song to make it the leadoff on his eponymous 1971 album on A&M Records, one of only two instances where he recorded a Bacharach-Hilliard tune under his own name.

Other Versions: *Burt Bacharach (1971) • Ry Cooder (1974) • Dobby Dobson • Nicolette Larson • (1978) • Sanchez - also "Mexican Divorce Dub" (1989) • Nat Stuckey (1969) • Jimmy Riley*

"Waiting for Charlie to Come Home" (Bacharach - Hilliard)
Recorded by Etta James
Argo 5409, flip side of "Something's Got a Hold of Me"
Released February 1962

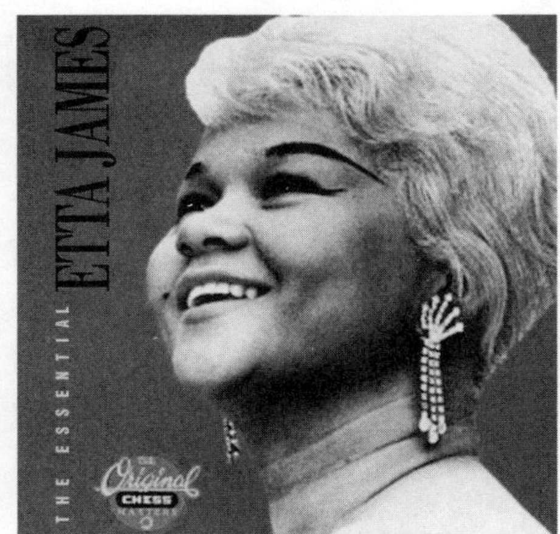

Etta James. The first Queen of Soul.

Chess Records had the foresight to crown Etta James Queen of Soul in an album title two years before Atlantic showed Aretha to the throne. Her performance on this B-side demonstrates why. No one had ever sung like Etta James before; not even her idols Dinah Washington and Billie Holiday ever roared with this much pent-up fury. An admitted on-again, off-again junkie throughout the Sixties and Seventies, Etta claims in her autobiography *All I Could Do Is Cry* that no matter how messed up on smack she was, it never affected her vocal performances. Having lived through such desperation, she could summon the pain at will.

On this definitive version of "Waiting for Charlie to Come Home," when Etta exhorts the listener to *"bring me his lips, his wild hungry arms,"* it sounds like she's the one with the wild hungry arms, in need of a fix *fast*! Riley Hampton's arrangement adheres closely to Bacharach's original demo, placing the swirling Hammond organ front and center and letting James growl over the loss of her happiness. And growl she does, adding mercurial screams during the verses that Janis Joplin would burn

Jane Morgan. This 1962 collection of torch songs was the first U.S. album to be produced and conducted in its entirety by Bacharach, who arranged all but three songs. The guest arranger was Peter Matz, Dietrich's previous musical director, who recommended Bacharach for that plum gig. Matz would later do the arrangements for Bacharach's numerous TV specials.

herself out emulating. The recording concludes with guitar flourish and a guttural moan from Etta that sounds as if she's found some fleeting solace in her endless night—until you start the record up again.

A different spelling made for a different reading when Jane Morgan included "Waiting for Charley to Come Home" as the closing number on her 1962 album of torch ballads, *What Now My Love*, released later in the year. Although Bacharach served as musical conductor and arranger on several Marlene Dietrich live recordings and one German-language studio album, *What Now My Love* was the first English-language album he would produce in its entirety on American soil. Burt and Jane get off some fine moments on the album, particularly her renditions of old-school standards like "Black Coffee," "It Never Entered My Mind" and "I'm a Fool to Want You." But when she lends her yearning voice to this ballad, the required desperation isn't quite there, and Bacharach's polite and somber orchestral setting is careful not to upstage her. You get the feeling she's just waiting for Charley to come home because he was supposed to bring some headache tablets.

Other Versions: *Jane Morgan (1962) • Nancy Wilson (1970)*

"For All Time" b/w "Wastin' Away for You"
(Burt Bacharach - Hal David)
Recorded by the Russells
ABC-Paramount 10319, released April 1962

If you think the double-sided brace of Bacharach-David tunes indicates a serious attempt to rocket the Russells to stardom, think again. Although both are first-run tunes, neither is first-rate. This qualifies more as a clearinghouse of B&D songs that didn't get past the demo stage. And yet "For All Time" does justify its inflated collector's price for being an early draft of "The Love of a Boy," with one Dionne Warrick singing the familiar flugelhorn parts and the verses. It sounds as if she was tapped to spread the gospel on what's otherwise a listless Paris Sisters recording. Her presence was not required on the B-side, a painfully perky piano thumper made even more wretched by the punctuating squeaks from a rubber toy. It's doubtful if this one-shot record provided either Bacharach or David with much pocket change. God help us if the Russells were a real girl group.

"Forever My Love" (Burt Bacharach - Hal David)
First recorded by Jane Morgan
From the Paramount Motion Picture *Forever My Love*
Kapp 450, flip side of "What Now My Love"
Released April 1962

"Forever My Love" was the theme of a Paramount motion picture of the same name about the emperor of Austria-Hungary, Franz Joseph, and his wife, Elizabeth, the empress of Austria and queen of Hungary. After stately trumpets usher us in, the recording leaps from 19th-century pomp to 20th-century pop, with tremolo guitars (the first of many appearances on Bacharach recordings) and Morgan wailing at the top of her range in a devotional not unlike the Angels' "Till." The song found its way into far more homes when Dionne Warwick's less-shrill rendition was included on *The Sensitive Sounds of Dionne Warwick* in 1965 and again on a second greatest-hits collection in 1969.

Other Versions: *Dionne Warwick (1965)*

"Forever My Love." Romy Schneider made her film debut as young Sissi, the future Empress Elizabeth of Austria. Romy would be an international star by the time she appeared in her next Bacharach-scored film, *What's New Pussycat?,* in 1965.

"(The Man Who Shot) Liberty Valance," (Burt Bacharach - Hal David)
First recorded by Gene Pitney
Musicor 1020 (*Billboard* pop #4)
Released April 1962

For those of you who haven't been keeping track, by 1962, Bacharach had penned six exploitation songs ("These Desperate Hours," "Hot Spell," "Country Music Holiday," "The Hangman," "That Kind of Woman" and "Who's Got the Action") and only four actual movie themes ("Sad Sack," "The Blob," "Love in a Goldfish Bowl" and "Forever My Love"). Most would lump "(The Man Who Shot) Liberty Valance" in the latter category. It was the first time that both a Bacharach movie song and the movie it was actually written for turned out to be huge hits. Yet they became popular independently of each other, and the sheet music confirms that the song was "inspired by" the motion picture.

There's still confusion over whether the song was ever intended for the film. Some say the movie's rushed release prevented its use. Others have said that director John Ford heard a demo recording featuring another singer and turned the song down flat. Once the tune was out of the running, it was offered to Gene Pitney, fresh from his first Top 20 hit and first movie theme, "Town Without Pity," a rare instance when the success of a song jump-started a movie that had already flopped. Paramount paid him "an immense amount of money," according to Pitney, to record "Liberty Valance." Although he thought the song was "corny," he recorded it anyway, as a career-building move.

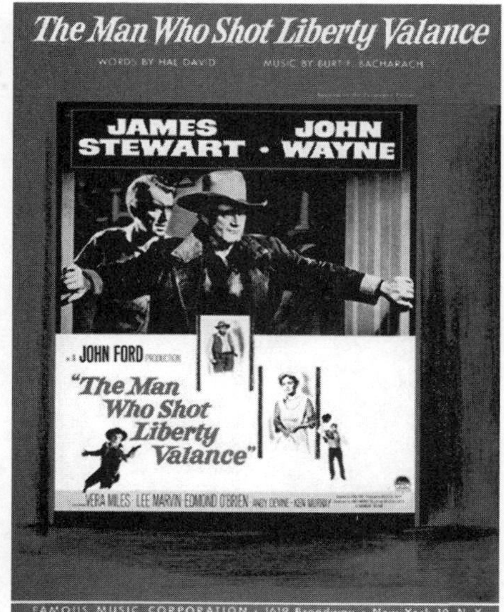

Liberty Valance. Jimmy Stewart played the tenderfoot who is believed to have shot Liberty Valance. But it turns out it was really the Duke—John Wayne—who did the honors. You weren't gonna see it for the first time any time soon, were you?

In a *Chicago Sun-Times* interview with writer Bob Greene, Pitney remembers finding out the song would not be in the film midway through the Bell Sound Studios session in New York. One of the orchestra members informed Pitney that the very film he was singing the theme to was playing down the street from the studio! "I knew he had to be mistaken," Pitney said. "How could the film have come out? We were recording the song for the movie. There was no question about that—Paramount Pictures was paying for the recording session. But the musician insisted...we went outside and looked, and sure enough, it was already in theaters."

Regardless of whether the song was originally intended for the film soundtrack, it virtually *is* the film, since it encapsulates the whole feel and story in less than three minutes. You have Gary Chester's drums simulating gunshots, a slightly sharp country fiddle for that authentic Wild West feel, the galloping beat on the verses and vivid Hal David lyrics. Maybe Ford thought the song gave too much of the movie away, but *you* try writing a song called "(The Man Who Shot) Liberty Valance" without giving

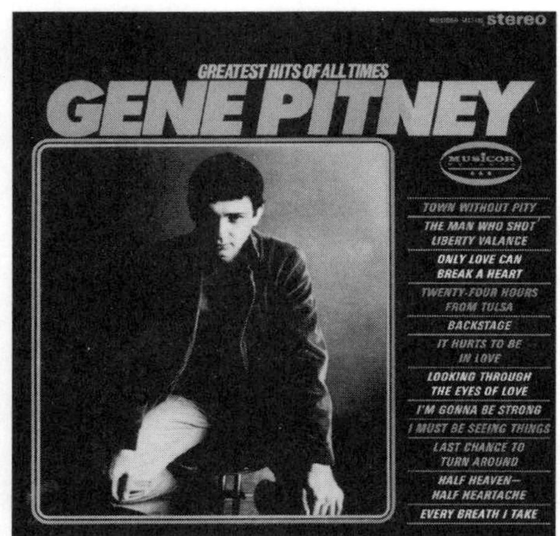

Greatest Hits of All Times. Pitney pisses off everyone from the Paleozoic Era on up with the presumptuous title of his 1966 compilation. Can he really be so big-headed as to think that future generations will never be able to come up with a tune that's better than "Half Heaven, Half Heartache"?

some background information on the guy or mentioning that fateful night he was shot.

Bacharach and David had taken an early interest in Pitney, and both men were in the control room watching the Phil Spector–produced session for the singer's "Every Breath I Take." It was an eventful session in more ways than one. Spector spent $13,000 to record only *one song.* And because Gene was suffering from a severe head cold, he resorted to using his glass-shattering falsetto for the first time that night. *"Aaah that night..."*

The pairing of Pitney with Bacharach and David was a fortuitous one. In Pitney, the songwriters finally found a teen idol who could actually sing. "Liberty Valance" gave Pitney his first Top 5 hit and a break from the barrage of lonely balladeer songs that would soon become his signature. Despite a winning performance, no one make any long-term connections between the song's tough-guy aura and Gene's wimpy image, especially when he revs up his vocals to build to the chorus, an effect that resembles a Mixmaster being set to "whip."

Note: the Pitney/Bacharach-David association began with a misunderstanding about a song that was intended for a film, and it would sadly end the same way when the wheeling and dealing of Pitney's manager/publisher Aaron Schroeder resulted in the song "Fool Killer" not being included in the film of the same name.

Other Versions: *Casino Royale (1999) • Fairmount Singers • Greg Kihn (1980) • Frankie Laine • Geoff Love • John Otway and Wild Willy Barrett (1980) • The Plaids - part of a "Bacharach at the Movies" medley • Regurgitator (1998) • The Royal Guardsmen • Elliott Sharp (1997) • Starlight Orchestra (aka Starshine Orchestra) (1995) • Susan & the Surftones (2000) • James Taylor (1985)*

"Any Day Now (My Wild Beautiful Bird)" (Burt Bacharach - Bob Hilliard)
First recorded by Chuck Jackson
Wand 122 (*Billboard* pop #23, R&B #2)
Released April 1962

With this song came some of the finest words Bob Hilliard ever sculpted to a Bacharach melody. At the prospect of seeing a cherished lover leave, Chuck Jackson successfully conveys such poetic embellishments as *"when the clock strikes go"* and *"the blue shadows will fall all over town"* with an even mix of dread and fury. But he almost didn't see his wild beautiful bird off. According to Jackson's account on the Web site *The R&B Page,* "the song was brought to Scepter Records and given to another person [Tommy Hunt]. Burt Bacharach and Bob Hilliard said, 'No, this song is for Chuck Jackson. If you don't do it on Chuck, we're gonna pull the song.' So they gave it to me."

Jackson remembers the sessions vividly: "When I recorded, I could hear the violins and the cellos and the horns and the rhythms and the girls and the fellas—everybody was there. Can you imagine all that energy in one room? So it's wonderful, the sound [you get] today, but those happenings in the studio can never be reproduced."

"Any Day Now" garnered more cover versions than any other Bacharach-Hilliard song. *Billboard* named it the top adult-contemporary single of 1982 when Ronnie Milsap's rerecording became a No. 1 country hit and a No. 14 on the Hot 100. Percy Sledge's cover version also made the Hot 100 in 1969, the same year Elvis Presley recorded it in Memphis. It was even redone by Bacharach that same year. By then, the sight of Bacharach's name next to Hal David's was so ingrained in everyone's mind that A&M wrongly credited "Any Day Now" to "Bacharach-David" on the cover of Burt's album *Make It Easy on Yourself.*

Chuck Jackson. No, Chuck isn't in the midst of a perplexing algebra equation—he's just in mute album-cover agony. This long-player would also include Bacharach and David's most ferocious R&B moment ever—"The Breaking Point."

The Italian pop groups I Corvi and Mal and the Primitives ("Mal" actually being British expatriate Paul Bradley Couling) managed to transmute "my wild beautiful bird" into "a little baby doll" (*bambolina*), but perhaps the oddest cover version of "Any Day Now" came courtesy of the Four Seasons. Previously, Frankie Valli and company had applied unnecessary Season-ing to half a dozen Bacharach-David songs (for their ill-conceived 1965 album *The 4 Seasons Sing Big Hits by Burt Bacharach/Hal David/Bob Dylan*). Later, in an attempt to put a happy ending to the lyric, the Seasons melded the song with the Edwin Hawkins Singers' gospel hit "Oh Happy Day." Sample call and response: when Frankie says "any day now, " the Seasons say, "oh happy day"; when Frankie says "when the clock strikes go," the Seasons say, "when Jesus walked." Let's call the whole thing off.

An even more curious version, because it isn't even titled "Any Day Now," can be found on Tommy Hunt compilations made long after Scepter went under. It's the same backing track with minor modifications and an entirely different set of lyrics! Entitled "Lover," this incarnation buries in the mix the distinctive Paul Griffin organ line, which makes its first appearance in the instrumental break. Heck, even the "wild beautiful bird" is missing.

"Lover" has long been believed to be an early draft of the song, but Bacharach maintains, "'Any Day Now was 'Any Day Now' from the get-go." The more likely explanation for this unreleased curio was that it came out of some late-night tinkering with the track by the honchos at Scepter. Originally they had wanted Hunt to cut the song, and this could be a test to see how he might fare doing it with some other dummy lyrics. If so, it fails miserably, since the melody never builds to anywhere near the heights of the Jackson version. Hunt sounds bored, and we only hear the distinctive organ line on the instrumental break and the fade. Scepter would try this same two-track hanky-panky again with the Isley Brothers and "Make It Easy on Yourself."

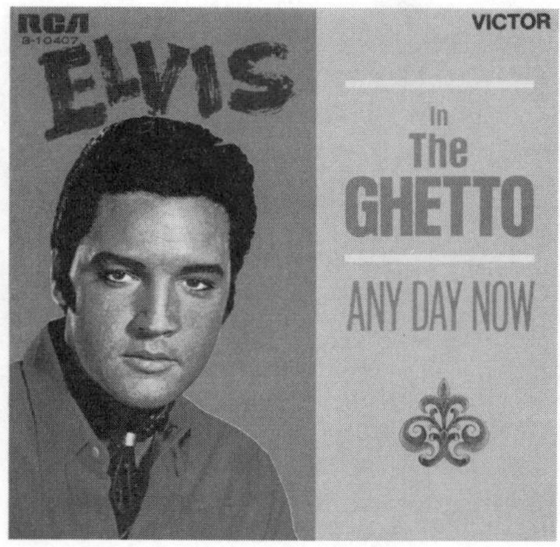

Elvis Presley. "Any Day Now" remains the lone Bacharach song to be recorded by the King.

Other Versions: *Gerald Alston (1990) • Burt Bacharach (1969) • James Brown (1969) • Carpenters - Bacharach medley (1973) • Casino Royale (1999) • I Corvi – "Bambolina" (1968) • Hank Crawford & Jimmy McGriff (1980) • Syd Dale • The Drifters • Don Gibson • Four Seasons - "Any Day Now/Oh Happy Day" medley (1970) • Mickey Gilley (1982) • Herbie Goins & the Nightmares – "Bambolina (Dimmi Ciao)" (1968) • Felix Hernandez (1997) • Susan Holiday (1962) • Ian & the Zodiacs • Tom Jones (1967) • Nick Kamen (1987) • Eddie Kendricks (1973) • Mal & the Primitives - "Bambolina" (1968) • Mel & Tim • Ronnie Milsap • Ben E. King • Peter & Gordon • Elvis Presley (1969) • Lou Rawls (1990) • Mitch Ryder & the Detroit Wheels (1966) • Sanchez (1992) • Dee Dee Sharp (1962) • Percy Sledge (1969) • Soft Cover • B.J. Thomas (1984) • Carla Thomas (1969) • Twisted Wheel • Oscar Toney Jr. (1967) • Scott Walker (1973) • Weeping Willows (1997)*

1962

Babs Tino. For those of you watching with black-and-white sets, her hair ribbon is vivid pink and her soul is boldly blue-eyed.

"Too Late to Worry" (Burt Bacharach - Hal David)
Recorded by Babs Tino
Kapp 458, released May 1962

The low-fi sound didn't become a sought-after aesthetic until the digital Nineties, but it's here in its full shoebox splendor on this Babs Tino single. Either the multitracks were bounced down too many times to accommodate strings, horns, timpani and the background singers or else this was another demo fleshed out with additional coloring for commercial purposes. One thing is certain: the overdubbed strings are a lot cleaner-sounding than Tino's echo-bathed vocals, not to mention the snare drum and the upright piano banging away throughout this catchy tune. It sounds like a casual take: you can hear an unused tambourine shifting in the song's opening verse.

Tino had previously issued a single on Cameo Records ("My Honeybun" b/w "Sweet Cakes") that pegged this female blue-eyed-soul singer as an ersatz Brenda Lee with a sweet tooth, as well as a previous Kapp single ("If Only for Tonight"). Bacharach and David thought enough of her kewpie-doll delivery to furnish her with four first-run tunes. While Tino's stylized pronunciation turns the word "worry" into "weary," the song would be completely translated from English by the singing talents of Ms. Sophia Loren, who recorded a French version entitled "Donne-Moi Ma Chance" (Barclay 60-362).

Other Versions: *Les Classels - "Donne-Moi Ma Chance" (1964) • Richard Anthony - "Donne-Moi Ma Chance" (1963) • Sophia Loren - "Donne-Moi Ma Chance" (1962) • Rosita Salvador - "Donne-Moi Ma Chance" (1963).*

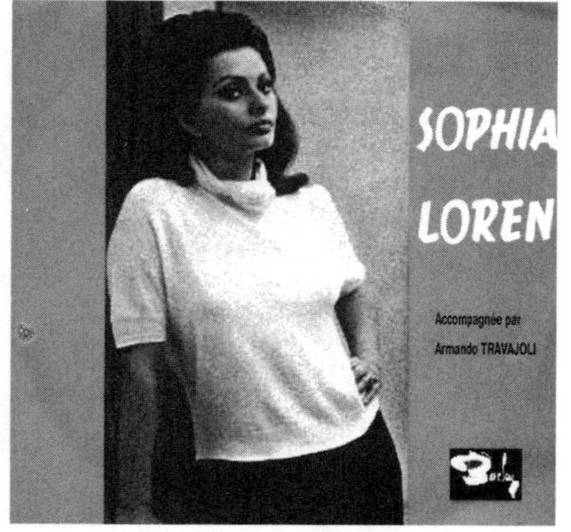

Sophia Loren. Insanely rare Belgian release, or *hebbedingetje*, as they say in the Netherlands. "Donne-Moi Ma Chance" was translated by André Salvet.

"Pick Up the Pieces" (Burt Bacharach - Bob Hilliard)
First recorded by Jack Jones
Kapp 461, flip side of "Gift of Love"
Released June 1962

Strangely enough, with all the R&B success they were enjoying at Atlantic Records, independent producers Jerry Leiber and Mike Stoller had a secret sideline producing "classy" nightclub material for people their own age. Hence this slow "ballin' the jack" number from Jack Jones, a jack in no danger of balling anytime soon, according to Hilliard's lyric. A classy post-breakup wallower, it's the first of two "Hilliard-Bacharach" numbers the team would write for Jones before Jack struck it lucky with everyone's favorite hausfrau makeover song, Bacharach-David's "Wives and Lovers."

"Forgive Me (For Giving You Such a Bad Time)"
(Burt Bacharach - Hal David)
Recorded by Babs Tino
Kapp 472 (*Billboard* pop #117)
Released June 1962

This potential smash for Babs, produced by Bacharach, briefly "bubbled under" in August 1962. Chuck Sagle's arrangement sticks closely to the Bacharach demo disc, which has background vocalists singing the pizzicato strings (and one male voice that sounds like Bacharach). "Forgive Me (For Giving You Such a Bad Time)" also has a unique structure, in that there is a long and a shortened variation of the verse. Tino gives a fetching Little Miss Dynamite performance every time out, so why wasn't this girl more famous?

Canadians for Bacharach. Our friends to the north were a tad more receptive to Bacharach material we Yanks overlooked. Not only was "Feelin' No Pain" a hit there, other U.S. low-charters such as "Saturday Sunshine" and "Blue Guitar" entered the Canadian Top 40 as well.

"Feelin' No Pain" (Burt Bacharach - Bob Hilliard)
First recorded by Paul Evans
Kapp 473, flip side of "A Picture of You"
Released June 1962

Before he became Bacharch's occasional songwriting partner, Bob Hilliard teamed up with Hal David's occasional songwriting partner Lee Pockriss, and the 1959 Top 10 novelty "(Seven Little Girls) Sitting in the Back Seat" was the result. It was the first hit for Paul Evans, who wrote such hits as "When" for the Kalin Twins and "Roses Are Red" for Bobby Vinton. Evans found himself hitless by the time he recorded this, his first single for Kapp Records. Its designated B-side carries the "produced by Hilliard and Bacharach" legend, and it's a waltz, Bacharach's first since Cathy Carr's "Presents from the Past" three-stepped into oblivion in 1956.

"Feelin' No Pain" finds Evans in love and singing in an over-the-top, inebriated manner while baby-doll background vocalists maniacally sing la-las behind him. It's Bacharach's first recorded use of a tack piano (an old-style saloon piano with tacks inserted into the felts), which would turn up on many later hits, such as the similarly lewd and lascivious waltz "What's New Pussycat?" in 1965. Bacharach's next waltz, Bobby Vee's "Anonymous Phone Call," would be a near carbon copy, retaining the identical brush rolls on the tom-tom but subtracting the drunk and disorderly singing.

While neither side of this Evans single infiltrated the Top 100 in the U.S., the record was flipped in Canada, and "Feelin' No Pain" crested at No. 23 in that country by August 1962.

"The Hurting Kind" (Burt Bacharach - Bob Hilliard)
"Something Bad" (Burt Bacharach - Hal David)
Recorded by Burt Bacharach, 1961–1962
Sung by Lonnie Sattin "For Professional Use Only"

Two comical Bacharach numbers included on an LP of Bacharach demos managed to escape a willing interpreter. "Something Bad" sounds like it was written with the Coasters or one of their numerous imitators in mind, as it has the singer grunting about the many suicidal feats he will undertake if his girl doesn't come back—from drowning to jumping off Pikes Peak to lying on train tracks until he is ground into hamburger meat. Two girl singers plus a pipsqueak male falsetto ask three times, "Whatcha gonna do?" To which Sattin and the singers reply, "something ba-aa-aa-aa-aa-aa-aad," like an off-centered record. Personally held suspicions that the cracking Mickey Mouse falsetto is none other than the "rumpled baritone" of Burt Bacharach have not been substantiated.

1962

Bacharach demos. Highly sought-after by collectors, these "professional use only" record albums contained commercially unavailable demonstration recordings of such hits as "Mexican Divorce" and "I Wake Up Crying," along with the familiar released versions of "Baby It's You" and "Any Day Now."

Bacharach demos. Although "Something Bad" never found a home, "A Sinner's Devotion" eventually did. The Shirelles and Tammy Montgomery both recorded versions, the latter finally seeing the light of day when Montgomery found fame as Tammi Terrell.

"The Hurting Kind" is arranged for one voice to jump into falsetto à la Lou Christie or Dee Clark. Lonnie Sattin again does the honors, turning castrato only when refuting jealous friends' assertions that his girl is a breaker of hearts and other susceptible organs. *("I don't believe it! No, I won't believe it! Woo-noo! Oh, noo!")*

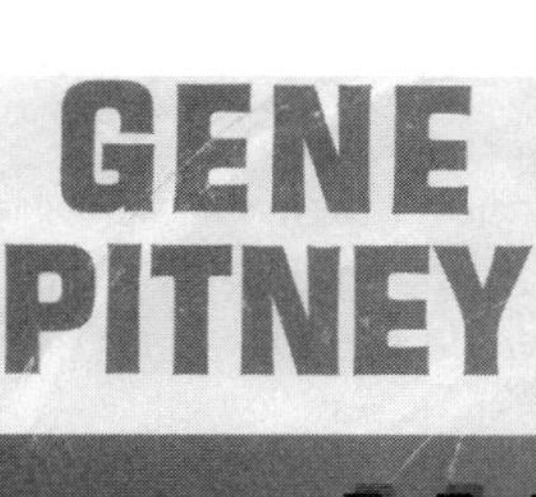

SECTION THREE

MAKE IT EASY ON YOURSELF (1962-1963)

...or Make Way for Dionne Warwick

In this section, Burt becomes a producer, Burt and Hal become an exclusive team, and Dionne becomes the prime interpreter of their songs. But there'd be other contenders, like Jerry Butler, Gene Pitney and Lou Johnson.

Section Three: Make it Easy On Yourself

1. *"Make It Easy on Yourself""* . . . . *Jerry Butler*
2. *"Dreamin' All the Time"* . . . . *Jack Jones*
3. *"The Love of a Boy"* . . . . *Timi Yuro*
4. *"Don't You Believe It"* . . . . *Andy Williams*
5. *"Only Love Can Break a Heart"* . . . . *Gene Pitney*
6. *"Little Betty Falling Star"* . . . . *Gene Pitney*
7. *"I Just Don't Know What to Do with Myself"* . . . . *Tommy Hunt*
8. *"It's Love That Really Counts (In the Long Run)"* . . . . *The Shirelles*
9. *"Wonderful to Be Young"* . . . . *Cliff Richard*
10. *"There Goes the Forgotten Man"* . . . . *Jimmy Radcliffe*
11. *"Keep Away from Other Girls"* . . . . *Helen Shapiro*
12. *"Don't Make Me Over"* . . . . *Dionne Warwick*
13. *"I Smiled Yesterday"* . . . . *Dionne Warwick*
14. *"Don't Envy Me"* . . . . *Joey Powers*
15. *"Anonymous Phone Call"* . . . . *Bobby Vee*
16. *"The Bell That Couldn't Jingle"* . . . . *Paul Evans*
17. *"Kleine Treue Nachtigall"* . . . . *Marlene Dietrich*
18. *"Message to Martha"* . . . . *Jerry Butler*
19. *"Call Off the Wedding (Without a Groom There Can't Be a Bride)"* . . . . *Babs Tino*
20. *"Rain from the Skies"* . . . . *Adam Wade*
21. *"Everyone Who's Been in Love with You"* . . . . *Marv Johnson*
22. *"This Empty Place"* . . . . *Dionne Warwick*
23. *"Wishin' and Hopin'"* . . . . *Dionne Warwick*
24. *"I Cry Alone"* . . . . *Dionne Warwick*
25. *"Let The Music Play"* . . . . *The Drifters*
26. *A Lifetime of Loneliness"* . . . . *Steve Alaimo*
27. *"Blue on Blue"* . . . . *Bobby Vinton*
28. *"True Love Never Runs Smooth"* . . . . *Don and Juan*
29. *"Be True to Yourself"* . . . . *Bobby Vee*
30. *"Saturday Sunshine"* . . . . *Burt Bacharach*
31. *"And So Goodbye My Love"* . . . . *Burt Bacharach*
32. *"That's the Way I'll Come To You"* . . . . *Jack Jones*
33. *"Please Make Him Love Me"* . . . . *Dionne Warwick*
34. *"If I Never Get to Love You"* . . . . *Lou Johnson*
35. *"Blue Guitar"* . . . . *Richard Chamberlain*
36. *"(They Long to Be) Close to You"* . . . . *Richard Chamberlain*
37. *"I Forgot What It Was Like"* . . . . *Ray Peterson*
38. *"Wives and Lovers"* . . . . *Jack Jones*
39. *"Reach Out for Me"* . . . . *Lou Johnson*
40. *"Magic Potion"* . . . . *Lou Johnson*
41. *"Twenty Four Hours from Tulsa"* . . . . *Gene Pitney*
42. *"Look in My Eyes Maria"* . . . . *Jay and the Americans*
43. *"Anyone Who Had a Heart"* . . . . *Dionne Warwick*
44. *"Who's Been Sleeping in My Bed?"* . . . . *Linda Scott*

“Make It Easy on Yourself” (Burt Bacharach - Hal David)
First recorded by Jerry Butler
Vee-Jay 451 (*Billboard* pop #20)
Released July 1962

“Make It Easy on Yourself.” Although the label says “Arranged by Burt Bacharach,” it's the start of many wonderful if uncredited productions.

Jerry Butler doesn't keep his customary Ice Man cool for very long here. Two lines in and he's reaching down into that deep voice and pulling out all the solemn suffering that makes this one of his best-loved hits. Significantly, the record that first fixated the hearts and minds of millions on the Bacharach-David sound was this ultimate love-triangle song. Its premise—a man nobly allows the love of his life to run to her new lover if his kisses and caress are harder to resist. *“Make it easy on yourself,”* he tells her, because if she sticks around, it'll be a two-way crying jag. Or maybe he's sending her off because he believes the opposite is true—that she won't shed a single tear over him and will only offer more words of consolation. Pop music doesn't get much more distraught than this.

It was Calvin Carter, A&R rep at Vee-Jay Records, who took a chance on letting Bacharach write the orchestration for Jerry Butler's “Make It Easy on Yourself” and, in a sense, letting him produce the session, because he thought the composer “felt the song better than anyone else did.” Although not credited in an official capacity beyond the “arranged by” label check, Bacharach often cites this important recording as the point in his career where he started producing and the world went from monochrome to color.

The demo session for this new composition was just as momentous, as it was the first to employ the services of session singer Maria Dionne Warrick, who became particularly enamored with the song. When Bacharach and David approached the gospel singer from East Orange, New Jersey, about considering a recording career as a solo artist (after two unsuccessful attempts at launching The Gospelaires as a secular group), she reportedly told the pair she was interested only if she could record “Make It Easy on Yourself.” Warwick was reportedly furious with Bacharach and David upon hearing Jerry Butler's recording, believing that they reneged on their promise to release it as her debut.

Butler's recent autobiography *Only the Strong Survive* reveals that the songwriters had indeed originally intended it to be Warwick's first single. “Burt and Hal offered me the song but not until Florence Goldberg turned it down,” writes Butler. “The way I remember it, Calvin played me a demo record. When it finished playing, I said ‘Man, it's a great song and the girl who's singing it, the arrangement and all, is a hit.’” Calvin said, ‘They're not going to put it out. The lady who owns the record company doesn't like the song.’” Warwick had to settle for her superb demo performance being belatedly issued “as is” on her first two Scepter albums.

Although the song seemed a sure-fire hit, the session was not without its difficulties. For one thing, Butler tended to lay back and sing behind the beat instead of dead on it. And there were other distractions. “Burt showed up at the studio with this knock-yourself-in-the-eye-gorgeous woman,” recalls Butler. “She had on this orange dress and was sporting one of those I-am-definitely-rich suntans. She looked absolutely fabulous.” Carter had to quip, “Hey Jerry, keep your mind on the song,

The Walker Brothers (1965). The Walker Brothers were neither Walkers nor brothers—discuss! This trio would soon return to the Bacharach-David folio for their third UK hit, "Another Tear Falls," while Scott Walker (né Engel) would go on to record "The Look of Love" and "The Windows of the World" during the course of his hugely successful (outside of the U.S.) solo career.

man," into the studio intercom to bring the singer back down to earth. "Everybody in the studio cracked up," recalls Butler. "I hadn't realized that I was staring at the woman, who Burt later introduced as Angie Dickinson, his soon-to-be wife."

The song became a Top 40 hit in the U.S. on two other occasions. In late 1965, it was the Walker Brothers—three American expatriates with a Righteous Brothers fixation—who had the biggest stateside hit with the song (peaking at a respectable No. 16). In the trio's adopted country of England, their convincing wall-of-sound replication of "Make It Easy on Yourself" became their first British chart-topper. And finally Dionne Warwick would reclaim the song with an astonishing 1970 live recording from the Garden State Arts Center, where Larry Wilcox's slowed-down arrangement allows her to explore all the emotional dynamics of her range.

As with "Any Day Now," a strange alternate version of "Make It Easy on Yourself" was recorded and left unissued by a Scepter/Wand recording artist. A 1962 Isley Brothers master entitled "Are You Lonely" remained in a vault until it landed on a British import CD in the early Nineties. While the lyrics of the verse are identical, the chorus finds Ronald Isley posing this question to a girl carrying a torch for someone who's discarded her: *"Are you happy by yourself / are you lonely by yourself / I hope it's true 'cause I'm so lonely too."* It's not until the last verse that we hear *"Make it easy for yourself / for I can't love nobody else."* If we believe Bacharach's assertion that the song was always "Make It Easy on Yourself" and no alternate lyrics existed, this may have been a Scepter experiment in album filler: name the song something else and consumers might not notice you're interchanging tracks with other Scepter artists until they get the record home. There is little doubt that this passionate version could've been a sizable hit for the Isleys, too, had "Twist and Shout" not come along around the same time and demanded their full attention.

Make it Easier on Yourself. The British pop band Ash sampled the opening flourish of the Walker Brothers' hit version for their new millennium UK chart-topper "Candy."

Taking into account Calvin Carter's suggestion that Bacharach felt the song better than anybody else, Burt deigned to record his own vocal version and draw attention to it by making "Make It Easy on Yourself" the title cut of his second A&M album. Critics have been less than generous about "the master's rumpled and earnest baritone," as *Los Angeles Times* writer Charles Champlin put it in the album's liner notes, but Bacharach's self-deprecating humor diffused any flack. As he quipped on one of his television specials, "I know people like my songs, because they buy the records even when I sing them." (Cue laugh track.)

Other Versions: *Ed Ames (1969) • Ash - "Candy" includes sample from Walker Brothers' "Make It Easy on Yourself" (2001) • Burt Bacharach (1969) • Terry Baxter (1971) • Tony Bennett (1970) • Cilla Black (1965) • Blackeyed Susans (1998) • Dennis Brown (1999) • Glen Campbell (1999) • Carpenters - Bacharach & David medley (1971) • Al DeLory (1971) • The Divine Comedy (1997) • Robbie Dupree (1997) • Bern Elliot and the Fenmen (1965) • Percy Faith (1966) • Arthur Fiedler & the Boston Pops (1972) • Film Score Orchestra • Connie Francis • Four Seasons (1965) • Claude François "Mais, n'essaie pas de me mentir" (1965) • Free 'n' Easy (1998) • Michael Henderson (1981) • Shauna Hicks - "A Bacharach Love Story" medley" 1998) • Ian and the Zodiacs • Idle (1998) • Impressions • Isley Brothers • Jack Jones (1972) • Kyoto Jazz Massive (1994) • Little Anthony and the Imperials (1964) • Kenny Lynch (1964) • Johnny Mathis (1972) • Anita*

Meyer (1989) • Rita Reys (1971, 1999) • RTE Concert Orchestra/Richard Hayman (1995) • Shirley and Johnny • Starlight Orchestra (1995) • Edwin Starr (2000) • Dakota Staton (1973) • Shoko Suzuki (1994) • Gary Tesca (1995) • Three Degrees (1973) • Jackie Trent (1967) • Sarah Vaughan (1966) • Walker Brothers (1965) • Dionne Warwick (1962, 1971) • Weeping Willows (1997)

"Dreamin' All the Time" (Burt Bacharach - Bob Hilliard)
Recorded by Jack Jones
Liberty 55469, flip side of "Poetry"
Released August 1962

Whistling along the middle-of-the road with another Bacharach-Hilliard ballad, we find Jack Jones "Dreaming All the Time." Producers Leiber and Stoller continued pitching the cabaret singer an odd mix of adult material with teen-idol overtones. This tastefully restrained country ballad features girl singers dreamily chiming along with the church bells while a double-tracked Jones semi-slurs lots of huggin', lovin', kissin', squeezin' and pleasin' action verbs. Unfortunately, it wasn't as successful as his subsequent city-boy butchering of country singer George Jones' hits "The Race Is On" and "Love Bug."

Jack Jones. Fans of deliciously bad rock cinema should seek out a gory horror film entitled *The Comeback*. Jack Jones plays Nick Cooper, a once-popular American singer who tries to jump-start his faltering career by recording an album in Britain—in the same house where his wife was hacked to death by a monster! Good idea if you're recording a Nick Cave album, bad idea if you're Jack Jones.

"The Love of a Boy" (Burt Bacharach - Hal David)
First recorded by Timi Yuro
Liberty 55469 (*Billboard* pop #44)
Released August 1962

If you were to prod fans to name a least-favorite Bacharach-David hit, "The Love of a Boy" would invariably figure in the Top 5. Generally, it's the females of the species who object to Hal David's lyrical suggestion that a girl's surest route to womanhood is "just one caress" of a boy. Not even Dionne Warwick's recording of the song (another Bacharach demo dispatched to flesh out her first long player) exonerates the number, as it contains the most Caucasian-sounding background vocalists on any of her recordings.

Opponents of "The Love of a Boy" are more familiar with Timi Yuro's ear-shattering version than Warwick's gentle reading. Yuro had already scored pathos-drenched Top 10 hits like "Hurt" and "What's the Matter Baby," in which she inserts laughing, crying and spoken asides that give the listener the feeling of being let behind a secret wall. If that weren't enough emotional wallop, Yuro's double-tracked vibrato sounds as if Jackie Wilson and Gene Pitney both sucked helium out of the same balloon.

Timi Yuro. Forward-thinking Liberty Records actually named Yuro's 1962 album *Soul!!* (the first exclamation point is theirs). Unfortunately, it has a cover picture that looks like Timi's about to scold a dog for jumping on the sofa.

Bacharach arranged the Yuro cut, adding the stuttering guitar and a false ending to his original demo idea. One reckons Otis Redding must have been listening carefully: his "I've Been Loving You Too Long" (released in the summer of 1965) seems to follow a chord progression nearly identical to the one on "Love of a Boy." It wouldn't be the first time Redding readily borrowed from a female Liberty recording artist: witness his conversion of Irma Thomas' "Ruler of My Heart" into "Pain in My Heart."

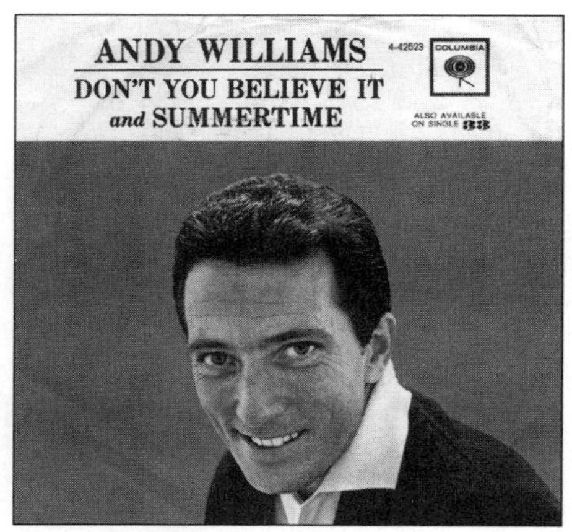

Andy Williams. His singing career was "criminally" overshadowed in the late Seventies when ex-wife and A&M recording artist Claudine Longet accidentally shot her ski-instructor boyfriend Spider Savitch to death. No firearms were necessary in the recording studio when Longet rendered lifeless such Bacharach classics as "Close to You" and "The Look of Love."

Andy Williams' Newest Hits. Andy's *mid-charting* hits is more like it: none of these "newest hits" climbed higher than a modest No. 24. But since Andy Williams albums are an inescapable commodity at thrift shops, this LP provides a convenient opportunity to purchase "Don't You Believe It," usually in mint condition, for about a quarter.

Critics of the song's lyrical content are best advised to seek out François Hardy's French version, "L'amour d'un Garçon," which obscures these Pygmalion tendencies and reveals the attractive melody in a far more pleasing fashion.

Attention, shoppers! Although listed below, Dusty Springfield's rendition, performed on BBC Radio, has not yet appeared on any officially released recordings but is worth seeking out.

Other Versions: *François Hardy (1963) • Julie Rogers (1964) • Dusty Springfield (1964) • Dionne Warwick (1964)*

"Don't You Believe It" (Burt Bacharach - Bob Hilliard)
First recorded by Andy Williams
Columbia 42523 (*Billboard* pop #39)
Released September 1962

Much had changed in the year and a half since Bacharach last landed a song on the Columbia label (Steve Rossi's ghastly "Come Completely to Me"). Mitch Miller, the label's powerful A&R man, whom the *New York Times* once dubbed "the bearded connoisseur of the echo chamber," was now focusing attention on his own recording career and enormously popular *Sing Along with Mitch* TV show. In the Fifties, under Miller's tutelage, Columbia released 14 Bacharach songs, with three apiece going to Johnny Mathis and Marty Robbins. The balance of the other Columbia recordings would be compromised efforts that the composer detested once he'd secured his artistic freedom.

With the back-to-back momentum of "Any Day Now" and "Make It Easy on Yourself," people were now paying closer attention to Bacharach's demos and arrangements. The demo for "Don't You Believe It" featured a female session singer (most likely Tina Robin, who performed similar duties for Goffin and King and later recorded for Mercury) and a plain country ballad accompaniment. The released Andy Williams version adds a few dreary background vocals ghosting up the choruses and a spoken word bridge. With the customary Columbia echo thrown in for atmosphere, it sounds as if he's delivering his *"I haven't changed, I still love you"* soliloquy from the inside of a lead-lined freezer.

This Top 40 offering was Williams' only scoop on a Bacharach song, but he would eventually cover a half dozen of the usual suspects, as well be among the brave few to rerecord "Don't Make Me Over" after Dionne Warwick put her stamp on it.

Other Versions: *Zack Laurence, Jefferson*

"Only Love Can Break a Heart" (Burt Bacharach - Hal David)
First recorded by Gene Pitney
Musicor 1022 (*Billboard* pop #2)
Released September 1962

Not many people remember Gene Pitney as a songwriter, but prior to his first Top 10 appearance as a singer, two of his compositions, "Hello Mary Lou" and "Rubber Ball," became huge hits for Ricky Nelson and Bobby Vee, respectively. Pitney also penned his first two singles, something he would never do again after the second one, "Louisiana Mama," failed to crack the Top 100. Pitney must have recognized that his voice was best suited to angst-ridden ballads and that even he could not surpass Bacharach and David in scribing them.

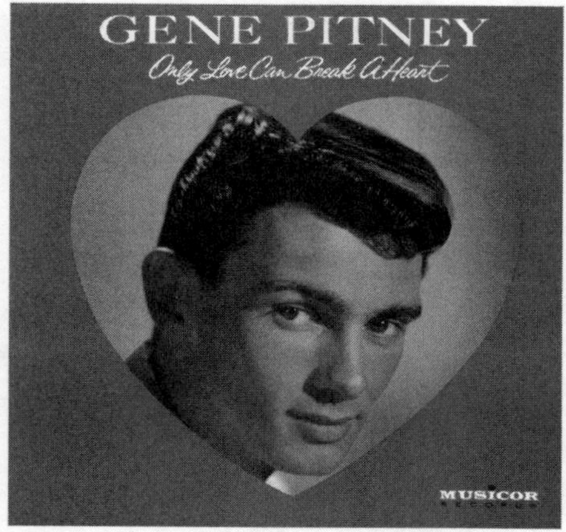

Gene Pitney. Few early pressings of the *Only Love Can Break a Heart* LP survived with its unique die-cut heart in unbroken mint condition. As to be expected, the vinyl inside is an embarrassment of crybaby riches such as "Cry My Eyes Out," "Donna Means Heartbreak" and the gospel weepie "Going To Church on Sunday." To stem the oncoming tide of tears, the album also includes "The Man Who Shot Liberty Valance."

With few exceptions, notably "Liberty Valance," Pitney's amazing string of hits was a joyless jamboree where "Only Love Can Break a Heart" was a way of life. Rarely was there a song where Pitney didn't sound as if he were seconds away from searing, skin-graft pain. Far from being a deterrent, this was the chief source of his appeal. And on the blockbuster "Only Love Can Break a Heart," he simmers in a kind of whining hurt, slurring his way to the top of each verse. Like Bacharach and David's other country ballad of the period, "Don't You Believe It," the song starts out with the chorus (a tag line, really), followed by a shortened verse consisting of two lines before the chorus returns.

The whistling that figured prominently in such early Bacharach-David favorites as "The Story of My Life" and "Magic Moments" momentarily returns. The big difference is that whenever someone puts his or her lips together and blows on a Bacharach-David record from here on out ("This Guy's in Love with You" and, especially, the unappreciated Dionne Warwick single "Odds and Ends"), it'll be the mark of isolation, resignation and uncertainty. Unlike many of the team's songs of 1961–62, there seems to be some hope of reconciliation, a hint of a happy ending, when Pitney's impressive whistle work duets nicely with the Bacharach-arranged horns on the fade.

The end result was both Pitney's and Bacharach-David's highest-charting song to date. It must have caused Pitney no small bemusement or grief that his closest shot at becoming a No. 1 recording artist was kept at No. 2 by the Crystals' recording of "He's a Rebel"—one of his own compositions!

Following the vinyl globetrotting excursions of Connie Francis and Paul Anka—two teen idols itching to ascend to the world of adult entertainment—Pitney went international, with three albums sung in Italian and one in Español. "Gino Italiano," as one LP dubbed him, recut this song as "Non Lasciamoci" (translation: "Let's not leave each other.")

As payback for being cheated out of a pop No. 1 in the Fifties, Sonny James hit upon a brilliant reverse strategy in the Sixties: he'd record countrified versions of proven pop hits like Petula Clark's "My Love" and the Seekers' "I'll Never Find Another You." By the early Seventies, he amassed 16 straight No. 1 country hits, a streak that was only broken when he decided to cover a Bacharach and David tune! James' unlucky retooling of the Gene Pitney hit failed to unseat three different country No.1's. Maybe the Southern Gentleman should've whistled on his version.

"Only Love Can Break a Heart" proved more fortunate for pop acts. Margaret Whiting and Bobby Vinton both managed the lower reaches of

1962

the pop Top 100 with their remakes, at a time when they weren't even expected to have hits anymore.

Dionne Warwick's strangely lukewarm version, cut during her Scepter days, was wisely kept in the vault until 1977, the year after Florence Greenberg sold the Scepter/Wand catalog to Springboard International and skimpy budget repackages of Dionne hits flooded the market. This track's appearance on a single gave the public the false illusion that the triumvirate of Warwick, Bacharach and David were all on good terms again. Nothing could be farther from the truth. It was also the title track of an album released on Musicor, Pitney's old label, containing previously released Scepter album tracks.

Other Versions: *Glen Campbell (2000) • Sonny James (1971) • Jody Miller (1966) • Bobby Vinton (1977) • Billy Wade • Dionne Warwick (1977) • Margaret Whiting (1967) • Timi Yuro (1975)*

George Hamilton. When the actor opened his mouth to sing in the 1965 Hank Williams biopic *Your Cheatin' Heart,* it was the voice of Hank Williams Jr. that came pouring out. Too bad Bocephus wasn't around to inject some much needed oomph into "Little Betty Falling Star."

"Little Betty Falling Star" (Burt Bacharach - Bob Hilliard)
First recorded by Gene Pitney
From the album *Only Love Can Break a Heart,* Musicor 2003
Released September 1962

Hiding out on Gene Pitney's *Only Love Can Break a Heart* album was this teen-angel tearjerker, where the brooding Pitney elevates his girl to a celestial body, only to have her fall from the sky and burn a hole in his heart. We never find out why she broke it off with him, but when he blurts out, "You made me cryyyy!" on the crescendo bridge, one surmises the off-putting wimp factor may have had something to do with it.

"Little Betty Falling Star" was no more macho when actor George Hamilton dusted off his questionable tonsils to sing it in 1963, on the flip of another Bacharach composition, "Don't Envy Me." Even with Bacharach producing and arranging, Hamilton's well-tanned version pales considerably beside Pitney's sincere attempt. In short, Hamilton sounds as if he's unwilling to try for any notes that might crease his skin.

The Cascades, who had a hit the previous year with "Rhythm of the Rain," were apparently still on the hunt for more things falling from the sky to warble about. They covered "Little Betty" for the 45 market, which did nothing to amend their one-hit-wonder status.

Other Versions: *The Cascades (1964) • George Hamilton (1963)*

Tommy Hunt. Four years after Hunt's version failed to penetrate the Top 100, Scepter sent Bacharach-David and Dionne Warwick back to the drawing board and—presto, another smash!

"I Just Don't Know What to Do with Myself" (Burt Bacharach - Hal David)
First recorded by Tommy Hunt
Scepter 1236 (*Billboard* pop #119, bubbled under for two weeks)
Released September 1962

Even if he hadn't recorded this Bacharach-David favorite, Pittsburgh-born vocalist Tommy Hunt's place in rock history would still be assured: he was one of the haunting "shoo-bop-shoo-bops" on the Flamingos' 1959 doo-wop classic "I Only Have Eyes for You." That song was a perfect marriage of the beautiful and the eerie, all bathed in a fog of echo. "I Just Don't Know What to Do with Myself" would seem to be the inverse of "I Only Have Eyes for You." Dryly recorded and stripped of all dreaminess, it finds Hunt a lonely man who only has eyes for someone who only has eyes for someone else.

Scepter producer Luther Dixon brought Hunt to the label as a solo act in 1961 and wrote "Human," a No. 5 R&B hit and a No. 48 pop hit. This proved Hunt's best-ever chart showing. Florence Greenberg never shared Dixon's enthusiasm for Hunt or his voice, which explains his relatively hitless tenure at Scepter. It hardly bodes well for your career when the president of your record company won't even allow you to set foot in her office. According to the liner notes in the boxed set *The Scepter Story*, it was Hunt's dating Beverly Lee of the Shirelles and a Mafia madam at the same time that brought out Greenberg's maternal instincts and caused her to stop promoting his records. Radio programmers might've held the record back, too, since the operatic highs and quiet lulls may have been a little too subtle for tiny transistor radios to transmit. For whatever reason, it never followed the similarly dynamic "Make It Easy on Yourself" up the charts.

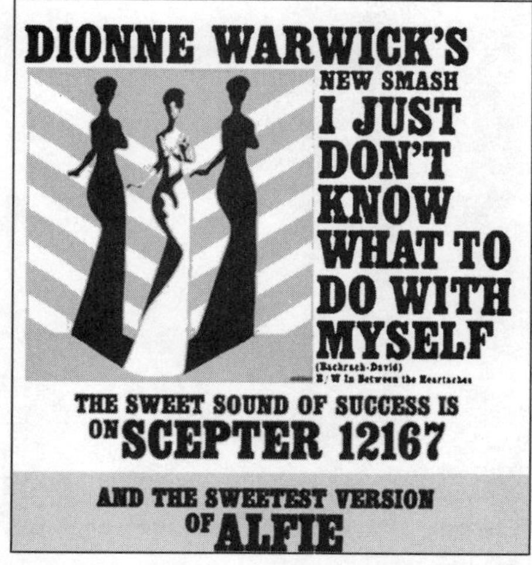

Dionne Warwick (1966). She secured the American hit version in the fall of 1966, 93 slots ahead of Tommy Hunt's peak position.

"To be given songs by Burt Bacharach was just such a joy," said Dusty Springfield in a 1992 interview for her video biography *Dusty Springfield: Full Circle.* "I flew in to New York from the Liverpool Empire [Theatre] to have dinner with him on the Sunday and flew back to do two shows in Liverpool the Monday night. I got 'I Just Don't Know What to Do with Myself' out of that." The song finally amassed worldwide attention with Springfield's explosive UK hit version in 1964. Unlike the Hunt version, with its slow builds and breakdowns, the Springfield recording accelerates upward and never looks back. By the fade, it sounds as if Springfield is in the throes of an emotional breakdown. It's her exclamations of *"I don't know what else to do! I'm still so crazy for you! No! No! No!"* that served as the model for Elvis Costello and the Attractions' *Live Stiffs* reenactment in 1978. Costello would, of course, redo the song again on tour with Bacharach in 1999, this time playing the "correct" chords.

***Live Stiffs* (1978).** On Costello's first tour, the "punk rock" singer was advised to hide his beloved George Jones cassette tapes on the tour bus because it might confuse the Bristish music press. Onstage, he proudly announced his adult-music roots by introducing a song by Burt Bacharach and Hal David for the safety-pin set's benefit. This sensational performance is included on the Rhino deluxe edition of *My Aim Is True.*

Dionne Warwick took a crack at the song in 1966, and her version reached the highest U.S. pop chart position at No. 26. According to an account of this session printed in a 1996 edition of *Mojo* magazine, the late summer sessions for the song proved problematic. Possibly wishing to avoid the bombast of the Dusty version, engineer Phil Ramone rode the faders to control Gary Chester's drum levels on the bridge, and the track didn't come to life until take ten, when a reluctant Bacharach slid behind the piano and led the 18 musicians to keepersville, earning a spontaneous burst of studio applause from the string section.

"I Just Don't Know What to Do with Myself" made one more Top 100 appearance in 1970 when a solo Gary Puckett, freed from the Civil War constraints of the Union Gap, gave it the "Bridge Over Troubled Water" treatment. At the same time, Cissy Houston's sensationally thumping up-tempo version failed to register with the soul market—a pity, since it's her finest-ever Bacharach recording.

Dionne Warwick. "I hate the song—but who's the girl?"

The last memorable version is Cameron Diaz's blackboard-scratching rendition in the 1997 box office smash *My Best Friend's Wedding.* Lord knows how many karaoke-bar massacres of the song have gone unreported since.

Other Versions: *Apollo 100 (1973) • Joan Baxter • Big Maybelle (1964) • Brook Benton • Joe Bourne (1993) • Lloyd Cole and Robert Quine (1997) • The Comets with Rosemary Scott • Elvis Costello & the Attractions (1978) • Elvis Costello and Steve Nieve (1996) • Floyd Cramer (1968) • The Dells (1972) • Cameron Diaz (1997) • The Earthmen (1998) • Chris Farlowe (1966) • Free'n' Easy (1998) • Isaac Hayes (1970) • Isaac Hayes and Dionne Warwick (1977) • Nicky Holland (1997) • Cissy Houston (1968)) • Chuck Jackson • Jill Jackson (1964) • London Film Orchestra (1988) • Joni Lyman (1965) • Mantovani • Anita Meyer (1989) • Smokey Robinson & the Miracles (1966) • Steve Newcomb Trio (2000) • Gary Puckett & the Union Gap • (1971) Linda Ronstadt (1993) • Demis Roussos (1977) • Helen Shapiro • Sheila - "Oui il faut croire" (1965) • Songrise Orchestra • Sonia (2000) • Sheila Southern (1968) • Dusty Springfield (1964) • The Stylistics (1991) • Ken Thorne & His Orchestra • Dionne Warwick (1966) • White Stripes (2002)*

"It's Love That Really Counts (In the Long Run)" (Burt Bacharach - Hal David)
First recorded by the Shirelles
Scepter 1237, flip side of "Stop the Music" (*Billboard* pop #102)
Released September 1962

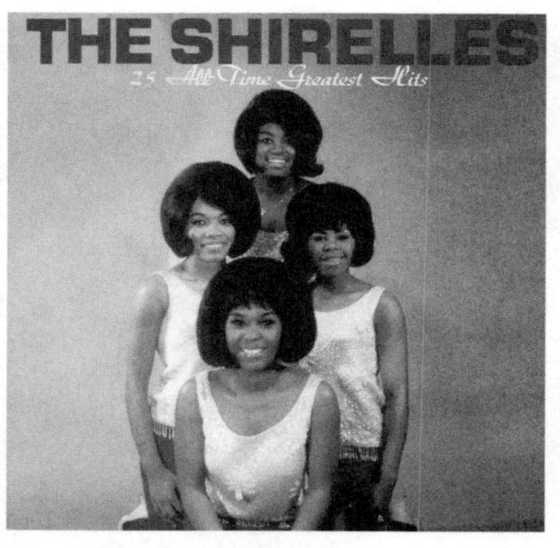

The Shirelles. Although they were the recipients of two great Bacharach hits, neither was intended for an A-side. The premier girl group recorded two other less readily available Bacharach songs, "Long Day, Short Night" and "A Sinner's Devotion.

Despite penning one of the Shirelles all-time biggest hits, Bacharach never actually got to work with the girls on a proper studio master, what with two of his demos being serviceable enough to be used as is. It's said that when Scepter founder Florence Greenberg first heard Dionne Warwick's voice on the demo of "It's Love That Really Counts," she remarked, "I hate the song—but who's the girl?" Dionne was soon signed and the song was tossed out on the flip side of a Shirelles 45 with the demo's backing track intact (the original demo version can be found on the *Presenting Dionne Warwick* LP).

Greenberg obviously misheard the potential of the song. Even with its low-priority placement; "It's Love That Really Counts" charted on its own and is better remembered now than its A-side. This Bacharach-David track seems to anticipate the Philly sound that producers like Thom Bell and Gamble and Huff would popularize in the late Sixties and early Seventies with falsetto-led male vocal groups like the Delfonics and the Stylistics. Husky-throated Shirley Owens' fragile voice reverts to falsetto the way a male singer would in order to reach those high notes. Compare and you'll see it's not a far stretch from "loo loo loo loo loo loo loo loo" to "La La Means I Love You."

While Hal David's lyrics stress that material things are of no importance to people in love, you hear a mournful sadness within Owens' shaking voice, as if the guy on the receiving end of these words is seriously depressed that he can't give his girl the things she pledges to disavow. The track's slow-grinding rhythm, with vibraslaps, provides a refreshing variation on the persistent Brazilian *baion* beat.

In Britain, where beat groups voraciously devoured both sides of American singles for potential cover material, the Merseybeats scored their first UK hit with an up-tempo revision of "It's Love That Really Counts," which reached No. 24. The group also scoured the flip side of Dionne Warwick's "This Empty Place" to arrive at another UK hit, "Wishin' and Hopin'," which reached No. 13. Thankfully, their appetite for Bacharach B-sides didn't extend to Dick Van Dyke singles.

Other Versions: *Barely Pink (1998) • The Exciters (1963) • The Merseybeats (1963) – "Nur uns're Liebe zahlt" (1964, 1986) • Dionne Warwick (1962)*

Cliff Richard. Offered up to American teen magazines as idol fodder in 1962, Richard was reduced to elder British statesman status by the time the Beatles invaded in 1964. By then, it may as well have been his *Wonderful to Be Young* co-star Robert Morley posing for the teen mags. He wouldn't crack the U.S. Top 10 until the bicentennial summer of '76.

"Wonderful to Be Young" (Burt Bacharach - Hal David)
Recorded by Cliff Richard with the Shadows
Dot 16399, released September 1962

Cliff Richard must've thought the word "wonderful" held supernatural powers for him: why else would it figure prominently in no less than three of his British releases (the albums *How Wonderful to Know, Aladdin & His Wonderful Lamp* and the Cliff Richard & the Shadows EP *Wonderful Life*)? When it was time to retitle his breakout UK film, *The Young Ones,* for American audiences, it was renamed (drum roll, please) *Wonderful to Be Young*—the celluloid tale of a young man bent on saving a youth center from his old man's wrecking ball.

By the time Americans got wind of him, the British equivalent to Elvis Presley was the British watered-down Elvis, making flaccid B-movies. *The Young Ones* was his *Blue Hawaii,* filmed in Technicolor and CinemaScope, both rarities in British-made films of the time. Paramount Pictures required a new title song for U.S. distribution, so Burt and Hal offered this skipping lightweight tune, similar to Bacharach's earlier "Dreaming All the Time." While nothing particularly wonderful ensues, the half-step drones in the melody give it a quasi-raga feel. Yankee youth, however, remained unconvinced.

"(There Goes) The Forgotten Man" (Burt Bacharach - Hal David)
First recorded by Jimmy Radcliffe
Musicor 1024, released September 1963

Jimmy Radcliffe was a staff writer for January Music, Musicor Records' music publishing company, as well as being Gene Pitney's recording manager and a much-sought-after session singer in his own right. He would often sing on Pitney's own demonstration discs for other artists. In a clear case of conflict of interest, Radcliffe may have snatched this song for himself before showing it to Pitney. Regardless of how he came to hear the song, he succeeds in making the inherent pain in the lyrics his own.

It matters little whether the opening pizzicato strings are there to signify footsteps or raindrops: it's a downpour of tears that he's trying to outrun. Because the "man ain't supposed to cry" ordinance was still being enforced in popular music, Radcliffe's painful transformation into a weeping puddle of testosterone is more jarring than any pathos distraught female singers could get away with.

The complete loss of identity one feels after a breakup is expertly nailed in Hal David's narrative and Radcliffe's performance. *"Ginny's gone and they pity me,"* he says of the onlookers who've chosen to stay friends with Ginny and forget about him. His sliding phrasing indeed sounds as if he's holding back tears, and no one sounds more damned than Radcliffe on the fadeout, where the enveloping echo and "walking all alone" refrain make this forgotten man seem as if he's shrinking as well.

Other Versions: *Gene McDaniels (1964)*

Helen Shapiro. Just how big was Helen Shapiro? The Fab Four were the opening act on her 1963 British tour. Lennon and McCartney even pitched a song to her that she never bothered to record. Instead, actor/singer Kenny Lynch recorded "Misery," making him the first artist ever to cover a Lennon-McCartney tune.

"Keep Away from Other Girls" (Burt Bacharach - Bob Hilliard)
First recorded by Helen Shapiro
Columbia (UK) 4908, released October 1962
Epic (U.S.) 9549, released November 1962

The female equivalent of Cliff Richard, Helen Shapiro was indeed very big stuff in the UK, with two British No. 1's by early 1963. Like Cliff, she was virtually unknown in America: her only U.S. hit, "Walkin' Back to Happiness," sat at No. 100 for all of one week in December 1961. The same thinking that governed Richard's U.S. campaign was also afoot in the Shapiro camp: get her in movies and show her off as an all-around entertainer. The young British songstress shook her beehive in two 1962 British rock films, *Play It Cool,* with Billy Fury, and *It's Trad, Dad,* Beatle-movie director Richard Lester's first film. Neither did much to bolster her name recognition here, but seeing as no British act had ever been more than a novelty to U.S. audiences before, this was not an unexpected outcome. The continental tide would turn very shortly.

Although not one of Shapiro's British chart-toppers, this swingin', twistin' Bacharach-Hilliard romp is a fine showcase for Shapiro, whose oddball voice most closely resembles Paul Anka with a severe head cold.

"Don't break my heart just to be smart," she warns the guy in the fancy restaurant who's always sporting *"a smile, a joke, and oh such a great big line!"* On the original demo it was "a smile, a smoke, and oh such a great big line," which simply would not do for a teen queen like Shapiro. But when Kapp recording artist Babs Tino recorded a Bacharach-produced version the following year, the ban on smoking was lifted. This song would be covered once more by Italian pop crooner Don Backy, who registered with a declaration of friendship called "Amico."

Other Versions: *Don Backy • Gisela Marell - "Ringe-ding-Don-Juan" • Babs Tino (1963)*

"Don't Make Me Over" (Burt Bacharach - Hal David)
First recorded by Dionne Warwick

Scepter 1239 (*Billboard* pop #21, R&B #5)
Released October 1962

When last we left young Maria Dionne Warrick, she was bitterly complaining to Burt and Hal that they were "giving away" her song to Jerry Butler. Until now, her only commercially available lead vocals were phantom studio appearances with Burt and the Backbeats almost a year before and the Russells the previous spring. When Bacharach and David tried to reassure her that there'd be other songs like "Make It Easy on Yourself," she hissed back, "Don't make me over, man." The two men returned to her with a song that would turn the defeated tone of "Make It Easy on Yourself" into a cry of defiance.

Dionne Warwick. A UK picture sleeve of the barely 21-year-old singer.

It's no exaggeration that this song would change the lives of all three participants forever. Who could've predicted that when they entered Bell Studios one rainy August night to record this song, they were off on a ten-year run that would be the most successful performer-songwriter pairing in the history of popular music? "When you want a Bacharach and David song recorded, you've got to come to the source," Warwick is often quoted as saying, and who can argue? She can pad her concerts with 30-minute Bacharach-David medleys and people can still rattle off numerous B&D hits she left out.

If Warwick's vocal prowess seems undervalued compared to that of today's overindulged divas, it's because she rarely showboats, preferring to glide through the most difficult passages without the slightest hint of strain. Warwick exerts far more lungpower on "Don't Make Me Over" than she would on subsequent hits—notice how she coos *"I'm begging you"* in an elegant, aching voice, just before lamming into you her list of demands: *"Accept me for what I a-ham!! Accept me for the things I do-hoo-hoo!"* "Don't Make Me Over" would pave the way for further female anthems like "You Don't Own Me," while also locking arms with other subliminal civil rights theme songs of the Sixties like "A Change Is Gonna Come" and "Dancing in the Streets."

Dionne Warwick. Here's a record label chock full of errors. First, Dionne Warrick's name was unwittingly changed to Dionne Warwick. Then Bacharach's first name is thrice misspelled. And surely they couldn't have meant for this to be the B-side. "Don't Make Me Over" indeed!

Bacharach recalls the emotional reaction of Scepter label head Florence Greenberg after first hearing it. "She cried, and not because she loved the record. Florence cried because of how much she didn't like it…needless to say we were taken aback by Florence's reaction." This marks the second time the opinionated Greenberg vetoed Bacharach's choice for Warwick's first 45. It's possible the label owner, who thus far had enjoyed hits only in the teen market, was worried that these songs were too adult and too downbeat. Or maybe it was the psychological stress of switching from 12/8 to 6/8 on a pop record. This dispute over the song's merits followed the single all the way to the pressing plant, where the side with "Don't Make Me Over" had a great big "B" stamped on it.

The opinionated Greenberg seemed determined to banish this song to flip-side Siberia, as she had with the Shirelles' "It's Love That Really Counts," but luckily this was the era where deejays were also opinionated and could flip a record over if they so desired. Greenberg learned to love "Don't Make Me Over" after it became a hit and tapped the same backing track as album filler for Scepter recording artist Tommy Hunt. Hearing Hunt instead of Warwick demanding acceptance makes his lackluster performance seem like trespassing. Barbara Jean English does a

Dionne Warwick. A French EP on Vogue, the same label where Petula Clark recorded competing versions of "Anyone Who Had a Heart" and "Don't Make Me Over." Clark's husband, Claude Wolff, even served as Vogue's public relations executive. Conflict of interest? Nah.

much better job with her *Soul Train*–era revisit. Although it's not the kind of makeover Isaac Hayes might subject the song to, she does add a brief but sassy spoken intro: *"Well, the long chase is over, so now that you've* got *me...don't make me oh-vuhhhh."*

Whether it was the energy crisis or just something in the water, it would appear that no one was able to figure out how to make an adult-contemporary album after 1972 that didn't suffer from laid-back-itis. Petula Clark and Jennifer Warnes both hit the snooze bar with their mellow renditions, the latter making it to No. 67 in 1980.

Almost every vocal version pales badly in comparison to the original, but you have to reach back to 1966 to find one as irritating as the Swinging Blue Jeans' singsong attempt, where "accept me for what I am" sounds like a whiny request to pass the biscuits at tea time. Amazingly, it reached the Top 30 in Britain, where no other Blue Jeans single would ever loiter again.

Other Versions: *Anita Kerr Singers (1969) • Terry Baxter (1971) • Brenda & the Tabulations (1970) • Burt Bacharach (1966) • Petula Clark • Lyn Collins (1974) • Neil Diamond (1993) • Dobbie Dobson • Barbara Jean English (1972) • Connie Francis (1968) • Lynden David Hall (2000) • Nancy Holloway - "T'en va pas comme ça" (1963) • Thelma Houston (1981) • Tommy Hunt (1962) • Les Surfs - "T'en va pas comme ça" • The Lettermen (1971) • Dee Dee Sharp (1963) • Shirley and Johnny (1969) • Swinging Blue Jeans (1966) • Sybil (1990) • Gary Tesca (1995)• Cal Tjader (1968) • Leslie Uggams • Ornella Vanoni - "Non dirmi niente" (1964) • Jennifer Warnes (1980) • Andy Williams (1963)*

I Smiled Yesterday" (Burt Bacharach - Hal David)
First recorded by Dionne Warwick
Scepter 1239, flip side of "Don't Make Me Over"
Released October 1962

Recorded during the same session as "Don't Make Me Over" and a Luther Dixon number called "Unlucky," "I Smiled Yesterday" was the designated A-side of Warwick's first Scepter single and would've made a worthy debut. Musically more exotic than "Don't Make Me Over," it perks along with a French-horn flourish that contradicts its *"I don't-wanna-cry-anymore-like-I-cried-today"* message.

Even more unconventional is the bridge, where Warwick sings *"Every day without you is a day that's gonna turn out wrong"* just seconds before she starts skipping like a broken record. By the Seventies, this familiar gimmick would be attempted by everyone from Bill Withers ("Ain't No Sunshine") to Squeeze ("If I Didn't Love You"), but it was uncharted territory in 1962, as unthinkable as intentionally inserting dead air on a single. Warwick and the drummer (presumably Gary Chester) lock in and stop so deliberately over and over that by the fourth "won't you," you're convinced her needle will be forever stuck in heartbreak. Possibly because of this innovative turn, no one else took a chance on recording it for fear of confounding deejays and losing valuable "needle time" on radio.

"Don't Envy Me" (Burt Bacharach - Hal David)
First recorded by Joey Powers
RCA 47-8119, released December 1962

It's hard to imagine any male singers that Bacharach and David were furnishing songs to at this time (Gene Pitney, Bobby Vinton, Jerry Butler) getting away with portraying the lonely-chick magnet this song outlines. Joey Powers' saving grace was that no one knew who the hell he was: even when he nabbed himself a Top 10 hit the following fall with "Midnight Mary," his record company photographed him for his first album in near darkness! Imagine Powers' personal shame, autographing an album cover where his face has all the detail of a used charcoal briquette. His recording of "Don't Envy Me" features a Hugo and Luigi production that borders on ska, with the orchestra honking where the saxophone would be. Powers sounds pleased with the swinging lifestyle the lyrics provide him with *("stay out late / lots of girls / life is great")* until he allows himself to think about the one girl he loves that got away and, well, you can imagine. His voice gets hysterical and cracks on the chorus, and the overdramatic bolero bridge pummels him into submission.

George Hamilton. Don't envy him because he tans so evenly. Envy him for recording a great Bacharach-David song, with the maestro himself producing and arranging.

Same time next year found actor George Hamilton covering the song with a sexier Bacharach arrangement but equally negligible chart results. Although it's hard to imagine the handsome movie star missing anything but a misplaced hand mirror, he tears into the song as if it's the role of a lifetime—a lady-killer who continues to live the fast life even though the only girl he loves is now safely away from his arms, lips and life. It almost reads like an old *Modern Screen* article: *"Lots of girls I can call / Lots of girls/ But still I'm lonely as I can be / So don't envy me...."*

Other Versions: *George Hamilton (1963)*

"Anonymous Phone Call" (Burt Bacharach - Hal David)
First recorded by Bobby Vee
Liberty 55521, flip side of "The Night Has a Thousand Eyes"
Released December 1962 (*Billboard* pop #110)

"[B-sides] were sort of like the musical equivalent to the prize at the bottom of the Cracker Jack box," writes Bobby Vee in the liner notes of his import double CD set *The Essential & Collectable Bobby Vee*. Such was the attention paid to flip sides by Vee and his fans that four of Vee's B's charted in the Top 100. "Anonymous Phone Call" just missed being the fifth, bubbling under for two weeks in January at No. 110. It was originally meant to be the A-side until deejays stated a preference, and *Billboard*'s prerelease review enthused that it had "a smart arrangement" that "could perk up teen ears." This waltz was the first of three Bacharach-David tunes earmarked for Bobby Vee.

Bobby Vee. While Vee recorded four Bacharach-David tunes, his all-time favorite composers appear to be Gerry Goffin and Carole King, whose Vee recordings number in the dozens.

Hal David's lyrics offer up a little parable on gossip and its detrimental effects on a relationship. The anonymous phone caller tips off Vee that his girl is a two-timer who's making a fool of him. Is it the other man she's going out with, *"some envious guy"* planting doubts in his head so that Vee will confront her and ruin everything? We never find out, but he does go to her after having a good cry in his room, demanding that she tell him it's all a lie. The conflict and the recording both end unresolved, with a few strums on an acoustic guitar that's slipped out of tune since the song was counted off.

Besides being one of the earliest attempts at blank verse by Hal David (a device only carried up to the chorus), "Anonymous Phone Call" can be cited as the first example of an artist copping Burt Bacharach's upturned phrasing, which sounds like he's asking a question: *"I said to myself? If I lost your love? My life would just end?"* As the composer's celebrity grows, more and more singers—like B.J. Thomas ("Raindrops Keep Falling on My Head," "Everybody's Out of Town") and Mark Lindsay ("Something Big")—adopt Bacharach's singing style under his vocal direction because it's a built-in hook of the song. It's also present on the version by UK singing star Frank Ifield, of "I Remember You" fame.

Other Versions: *Frank Ifield*

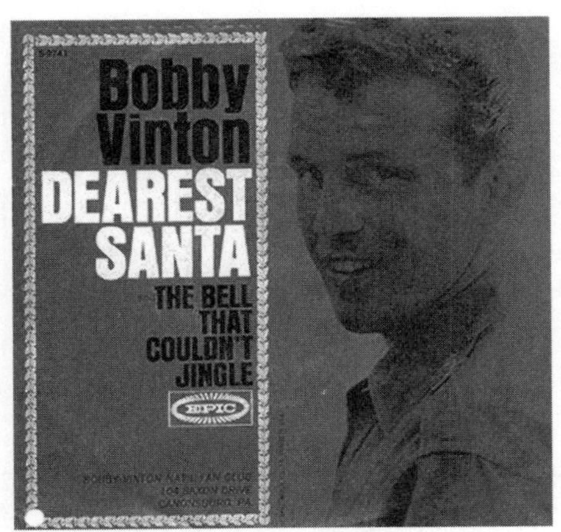

Bobby Vinton. After Vinton hit No. 1 with "Mr. Lonely", he released this holiday 45 before resuming his mission of recording as many songs with "lonely" in the title as possible.

The Bell That Couldn't Jingle" (Larry Kusik - Burt Bacharach)
First recorded by Paul Evans
Kapp 499, released December 1962

Because three reissues of Bobby Helms' perennial holiday favorite, "Jingle Bell Rock," had "The Bell That Couldn't Jingle" stowed away on the B-side, it's logical to assume that this country singer recorded Bacharach's first seasonal carol in 1957. Not so. Helms' version of "The Bell That Couldn't Jingle" first appeared on a 1965 rerecording of "Jingle Bell Rock" issued on Kapp. It certainly wasn't recorded in the Fifties, as a careful listen to the recording quality of both sides makes evident.

¡Something Festive! The BF Goodrich tire company put out a limited edition A&M Christmas album with Bacharach's own version of "Jingle" on it. A&M later rereleased it as *We Wish You a Merry Christmas*, upgrading Sergio Mendes' Brasil '66 to '77 and casting off forgotten names like We Five and Pete Jolly for later-to-be-forgotten names like Miguel Rios.

Three years prior to Helm's sleigh ride, New York singer-songwriter Paul Evans, who also recorded for Kapp, got first crack at the tune. Lyricist Larry Kusik (who would later write lyrics for "Love Theme from *Romeo and Juliet*") was hoping to create an evergreen Christmas character—like Rudolph the Red-Nosed Reindeer, Frosty the Snowman or the Little Drummer Boy—who returns to the special Christmas *Billboard* charts every Yuletide. With limited retail shelf life, it takes most Christmas records a few holiday seasons to build popularity with the public. "The Bell That Couldn't Jingle" did finally chart in 1964, when Bobby Vinton included the song on the reverse side of his "Dearest Santa" single and on his *A Very Merry Christmas* album. Vinton's producer, Bob Morgan, replicates Bacharach's arrangement from the Evans record, but Vinton's performance has the edge, mainly because he doesn't sound like he has a nervous tic every time the word "jingle" comes up.

If any singer could ferret out some underlying sadness in this deceptively cheerful holiday offering, it's Vinton, who hit No. 1 two weeks before Christmas 1964 with "Mr. Lonely." Here he turns the self-pity spotlight over to a little sleigh bell that is crying because it's too hollow and empty inside to give the customary jingle. Aware that a crying Christmas bell is bad for his image, Santa brings this matter to the attention of Jack Frost, who fixes the problem by freezing a teardrop and sticking it in the belly of said sad bell. Now it can jingle again and everyone is supposed to be jolly. Message? If you're blue on Christmas, never let anyone see ya sob. It's a message Hal David will take up in far more adult fashion on the pair of Christmas-related numbers written into the score for the musical *Promises, Promises.*

Bacharach issued his own version of "The Bell That Couldn't Jingle" as a seasonal single in 1968, with "What the World Needs Now Is Love" on the flip. The same year that found Herb Alpert first warbling on disc with "This Guy's in Love with You" also found the trumpeter unwrapping his vocal cords to sing this Bacharach carol on the Tijuana Brass's *Christmas Album.* It was plucked for Xmas-single consideration in 1970.

Other Versions: *Herb Alpert & the Tijuana Brass (1968) • Burt Bacharach (1968) • Bobby Helms (1965) • Anita Kerr Singers • Bobby Vinton (1964)*

Marlene Dietrich. Of Bacharach she once wrote: "No matter how many curtains open and close between me and the audience, his approval is what I'm seeking." He was her musical supervisor when this live album recorded in Rio de Janeiro.

"Kleine Treue Nachtigall" (Burt Bacharach - Hal David - Max Colpet)
Recorded by Marlene Dietrich
Barclay 856, released in Germany late 1962

"Message to Martha" (Burt Bacharach - Hal David)
First recorded in English by Jerry Butler
From the album *Giving Up on Love/Need to Belong,* Vee-Jay 1076
Released December 1963

This Bacharach-David classic went through four title changes before becoming a U.S. hit in 1966. Presumably offered to Jerry Butler as the team's follow-up to "Make It Easy on Yourself," "Message to Martha" instead languished in the can for a year until it was inconspicuously issued as an album cut in December 1963.

If Butler felt uncomfortable with the chorus's similarity to "Ring around the Rosy," he doesn't show it. The versatile singer sounds very much at home missing Martha in a setting that's both down-home folksy (an up-front banjo plucks out the melody) and urban (scratch rhythm guitar, triangle and the timpani pounding out the Brazilian *baion* beat once more).

Bacharach imported these identical Butler backing tracks to Germany for Marlene Dietrich's foreign language version. The German mix puts greater emphasis on the ghostly backing vocals and a more exotic string arrangement. In the Max Colpet translation, our Kentucky bluebird has morphed into a "small true nightingale" and Dietrich sings to it mournfully, like a woman longing for her freedom rather than pining for some fame-seeking lover. The small demands of the song are well suited to her near-conversational vocal style. Dietrich was said to have occasionally performed "Kleine Treue Nachtigall" live as well as tackling the far more taxing "Anyone Who Had a Heart" on occasion. To date, this 45 of "Kleine Treue Nachtigall" is the only known recording of Dietrich performing a Bacharach song, live or otherwise.

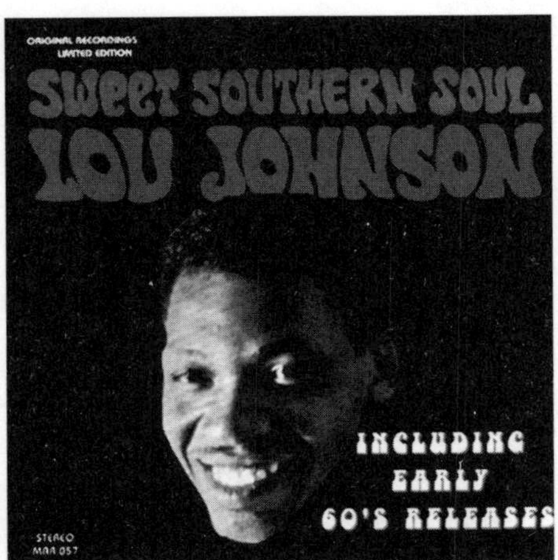

"A Message to Martha." Great Britain offered yet another title variation for Lou Johnson's 1964 recording, but it was Adam Faith who wound up with the UK hit.

From Butler we flash forward to the fall of 1964—and still no one's whistling "Message to Martha" in elevators! Bacharach, believing he could snag that elusive hit for "Martha," cut the song with Lou Johnson, substituting tack piano for banjo and giving props to the flyaway "Kentucky Bluebird" in the title. Inexplicably, it fared worse than Johnson's two previous Bacharach-David efforts, "Reach Out for Me" and "(There's) Always Something There to Remind Me," reaching No. 104 where the others had just missed the Top 40. Despite a heavy push overseas, Johnson again got scooped in the UK when Adam Faith's competing cover version overtook his own.

Dionne Warwick, who'd already made a bigger hit of Johnson's "Reach Out for Me" a year after he released it, wanted to record a female version of "Message to Martha" in 1966. Both Bacharach and David were against it, hearing it as a man's song despite the Dietrich version. David tried to discourage her, telling her that the only name that would work in place of "Martha" would be "Michael," a name he claimed he disliked. That was all Warwick needed to cut her own version, with the arranger for French singer Sacha Distel faithfully copying the Lou Johnson version. In his book *What the World Needs Now and Other Love Lyrics,* David admits being mistaken about the song's gender. "Dionne's vocal was so brilliant that it was obvious we had subconsciously written the song for her even while we thought we were writing it for a man....I don't mind being wrong if, in the final analysis, everything turns out all right."

James Brown also recorded the song as "Message to Michael," but before you start questioning Mr. Please Please Please's sexual preferences, remember that in 1964 he was in one of his periodic funks with longtime label King Records and simply started recording illegally for another company. After one single, King prevented Smash Records from issuing anything with the Godfather of Soul singing, screaming, hollering or even counting off songs. But there are a few Smash instrumental albums credited to James Brown and his Orchestra. But be forewarned: his Hammond organ workout on "Michael" barely sticks to the original tune outside of the chorus. Yep, papa's got a lotta nerve!

Other Versions: *Burt Bacharach (1968) • James Brown • Deacon Blue • Adam Faith (1964) • Gals & Pals (1967) • Lena Horne (1969) Lena Horne & Gabor Szabo (1970) • Chrissie Hynde • Ian & the Zodiacs • Jay & the Americans (1970) • Lou Johnson (1964) • Earl Klugh • Ellis Larkins • Ramsey Lewis • The Marvelettes (1967) • Barbara McNair • Christopher Scott • Soulful Strings • Cal Tjader (1968) • Dionne Warwick (1966)*

"Call Off the Wedding (Without a Groom There Can't Be a Bride)" (Burt Bacharach - Hal David)
First recorded by Babs Tino
Kapp 498, released January 1963

Episode three of the Babs Tino saga, in which our heroine's blue-eyed Italian soul finds an ethnic setting. It's no laughing matter finding out a week before the wedding that your rat of a fiancé is in love with someone new, but try to keep from smiling when listening to crybaby Babs run down her checklist of things to undo today. Compounding the song's pathos-driven comedic elements are the solemn but munchkin-like mutterings of the bridesmaids advising her to *"call off the wedding"* and *"cancel the flowers,"* while mandolins trill obliviously in the background as if nothing were wrong. Despite its sublime charms, the follow-up to "Forgive Me (For Giving You a Bad Time)" didn't even bubble under the Top 100 as its predecessor did. If filmmakers had been more up on their Bacharach history, this song could've made a great addition to the soundtrack of *My Best Friend's Wedding.*

After George Hamilton's "Don't Envy Me," this is the only other instance of a Bacharach-David song and a Bacharach-Hilliard song coexisting on the same seven-inch. "Keep Away from Other Girls" was hauled out of storage after Helen Shapiro failed to do much with it two months earlier.

Adam Wade. In 1976, long after the hits stopped coming, Wade became a game show quizmaster. Remember *Musical Chairs?* Didn't think so.

"Rain from the Skies" (Burt Bacharach - Hal David)
First recorded by Adam Wade
Epic 9566, flip side of "Don't Let Me Cross Over"
Released January 1963

No less an authority than *The Billboard Book of Top 40 Hits* states that "balladeer Adam Wade was a cross between Sam Cooke and Johnny Mathis, without the distinctive qualities of either." Indeed, when Wade goes up to the top of his range it sounds thin and shrill, adjectives you could never assign to Cooke or Mathis. Still, Wade turns in a fairly spirited performance of this obscure Bacharach-David morsel. While lyrically not much different from hundreds of other crying-in-the-rain ballads *("I don't know if it's rain from the skies or tears from my eyes"),* it impresses with its wandering verse, which never repeats one melodic phrase—evidence that Bacharach composed it in his head and not sitting at the piano.

The flugelhorn intro, soon to become a persistent Bacharach trademark, makes its earliest appearance here. Since Bacharach never gets a label credit for his later involvement on Bobby Vinton's "Blue on Blue," it was probably Epic's policy to just list the staff producer and arranger regardless of who did the work. What matters more is that that this sounds like a Bacharach production, one worth seeking out.

Apparently something of a Kingston classic, the song turns up on old-school reggae and second- and third-wave ska revival collections like *Reggae Rewind: Dem Ah Rush Me* and *Jamaica Ska Kore*, covered by the likes of Sly and Robbie, Dennis Brown, Sanchez, Barry Biggs and Delroy Wilson. The last rendition retains the flugelhorn line on slide trombone while bringing it into Rastafarian territory.

Meanwhile back in the States, an unknown lounge crooner named Peter Lemongello was moving tons of a heavily advertised TV album without anyone ever having heard of him. Yet Lemongello actually had made records years before. Several of his singles from the early Seventies left their forgettable mark, including a remake of "Rain from the Skies" that jettisons the poignant flugelhorn in favor of random blasts from a perfunctory brass section. Sounding very much like an Engelbert man in a Humperdinck land, Lemongello turns a bland eye on the phrasing, leaving it to the overexcited background vocalists to inject some much-needed soul into the proceedings. Of course, that never happens.

Other Versions: *Barry Biggs • Dennis Brown • Peter Lemongello • Delroy Wilson • Sanchez (1992) • Red Hot Reggae • Sly & Robbie (1981) • Delroy Wilson*

Marv Johnson. Bacharach's first collaboration with a Motown artist, as well as Leiber and Stoller's first production of one. Or executive production, as the case may be.

"Everyone Who's Been in Love with You" (Has Cried and Cried and Cried) (Burt Bacharach - Bob Hilliard)
Recorded by Marv Johnson
United Artists 556, flip side of "Keep Tellin' Yourself"
Released early 1963

Few Big Chillers recognize Marv Johnson as a Motown recording artist, since all his big hits—e.g., "You've Got What It Takes" and "I Love the Way You Love"—were on the United Artists label. Yet the first-ever Motown single was his recording of Berry Gordy's "Come to Me" (Tamla 101), a regional hit that was eventually picked up nationally and distributed by UA. By the time Johnson was actually on the Hitsville USA roster proper, the hits were no longer forthcoming.

While the Ellie Greenwich/Tony Powers/E. Glick–penned A-side bears a slight resemblance to "Any Day Now," the B-side marks one of the last times a new Bacharach-Hilliard composition turned up on 45. It also marks the first appearance of yet another Bacharach trademark—the strident-tack-piano-plus-skanking-rhythm that also found its way onto the concurrently released "This Empty Place." Johnson sings the sordid tale of a man who knew he was just the latest link in a long chain of fools but ignored the initial warning signs anyway. *"I mean nothing to you / But you mean everything to me,"* he begins, before getting more expansive in his suffering: *"Now my tears fall in the sea like big ocean waves against the rocks."* How's that for unhappy?

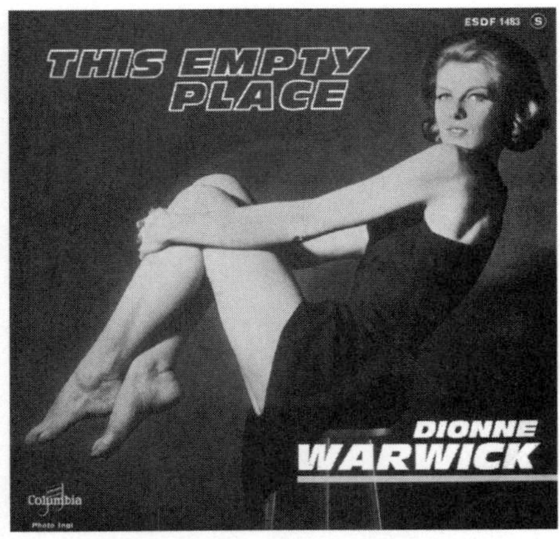

Dionne Warwick??? Back in the day, it was standard procedure to put young chickaroos on old bandleaders' album covers. But serving up this slice of Parisian cheesecake on a Dionne Warwick EP was more than a tad misleading. *Pour l'honte!*

"This Empty Place" (Burt Bacharach - Hal David)
First recorded by Dionne Warwick
Scepter 1247 (*Billboard* pop #84)
Released March 1963

Forgoing the "Don't Make Me Over" plea to be treated fairly in love, Warwick finds herself already on the outs with her lover on single number two. For this recording, Bacharach crafted a soulful, herky-jerky dance track built around minor-to-major chord changes. Against that, Hal David's lyrics chronicle the empty place that has taken permanent residence next to Warwick since her greatest love has gone. *"Sadness and tears, that's all you've left me / They're such bad, bad souvenirs,"* she remarks, sounding rather cool about her fate until she remembers what she once had. By song's end, she's pleading *"Come back, come back to me"* in double time in the hopes he'll return faster.

It's hard to fathom this superb single's disappointing chart showing after a Top 30 hit, yet "This Empty Place" was slightly ahead of the curve. A rhythmic precursor to "Walk On By," it also served as a blueprint for another early 1964 hit, Bob and Earl's ominous minor/major dance groove "Harlem Shuffle."

"This Empty Place" found delayed favor in the United Kingdom, where three British Invasion acts swooped down to cover it. While the Searchers' version would seem to hold the most promise, the Liverpudlians dispense with the double-time ending entirely, and Mike Pender lets his vocals dip and rise up whenever he says the words "place" and "space," which becomes annoying after the first time. The Fortunes manage to toss in the kitchen sink on their cluttered rendition, while the reverent Cilla Black stays faithful to the Warwick arrangement, save for her Ethel Merman belting.

Dionne Warwick. Her only Scepter-era picture sleeve in the U.S. was for "This Empty Place," the follow-up to "Don't Make Me Over". Thanks to Dusty Springfield, its B-side needs no introduction.

The Tangiers, a black vocal group who were Scepter's answer to the Delfonics, revived the song in 1969 and changed very little from Warwick's blueprint. The same can't be said for the version found on Stephanie Mills' 1975 album of Bacharach-David songs, *For the First Time.* There, "This Empty Place" gets a full-blown disco treatment by Kenny Asher; it's one of four songs on the album that Bacharach would have no hand in arranging. The most excessive version, however, remains Cissy Houston's. Despite being featured vocalist on Burt's 1972 album and background vocalist on countless Dionne sessions, she veers dynamically all over the place without the maestro around to reign things in. Her incredible pipes do the song no favors, and the arrangement has no choice but to break down in fits and starts to keep up with all the showboating.

Other Versions: *Cilla Black • The Fortunes (1965) • Cissy Houston • Roberta Mazzoni – "L'amore di Nessuno" • Stephanie Mills (1975) • The Searchers (1965) • The Tangiers (1969)*

"Wishin' and Hopin'" (Burt Bacharach - Hal David)
First recorded by Dionne Warwick
Scepter 1247, flip side of "This Empty Place"
Released March 1963

Dusty Springfield (1964). In England, her U.S., smash "Wishin' and Hopin'" was just track one side two of a between-album EP.

While Bacharach was still very much a behind-the-scenes man in the United States, the opposite held true in Great Britain, where he'd been a celebrity ever since 1958, when "Magic Moments" and "The Story of My Life" were back-to-back UK No. 1 hits. The bulk of the British Invaders were slipping at least one Bacharach-David tune in their repertoire without much prodding. Among the few who would work directly with the man himself was Dusty Springfield, who flew into New York in February 1964 specifically to meet with Bacharach and hear some songs for her next recording date. Bacharach told *Billboard* "Personalities" columnist Ren Grevatt, "We'll have them ready, in fact we hope to have six of them. She can pick out what she likes and we won't mind if she wants them all."

Today Bacharach can't recall if he presented her with any new songs at that first meeting. "I met Dusty initially taking her out to the Grammys in New York as my date. And I thought I tried to talk her into releasing 'Wishin' and Hopin',' because she had some ambivalence about it."

While Springfield's version is just two notes shy of being a note-for-note re-creation, it does exhibit some marked differences. Warwick's rendition sounds as if the singer is sharing a secret with the listener, while Springfield just throws open the shutters and blasts the advice to all

The Merseybeats (1964). Girls, they'll not only wear their hair just for you but they'll also do the things you like to do! Despite this earnest pledge, they remained in the minority of British rock bands that didn't chart in America in 1964–1966.

Stepford Wives and girlfriends within earshot: *"Wear your hair just for him, do the things* he *likes to do."* Ivor Raymonde's arrangement also has a slightly tougher edge to it, making the horns, background vocals, percussion and strings a little louder while throwing in an insistent chugging rhythm guitar instead of one that just chick-chick-chicks along.

Dusty's vaulting into the Top 10 with a virtual duplicate of "Wishin' and Hopin'" may have caused Dionne some grumblin' and cussin', but at least it didn't cost her any UK hits. Whether it was courtesy or insecurity, Dusty graciously never released competing 45s of American R&B hits in the mother country, unlike that Cilla Black girl. Plus, Dusty never failed to praise Dionne in interviews, ensuring that when Warwick appeared on Dusty's British TV show, no units of the catfight police had to be dispatched.

Despite its U.S. success, "Wishin' and Hopin'" remained a Dusty EP track in the UK, leaving the field open for Britbeat groups to explore its hit-single possibilities. For those listeners uncomfortable with the song's unenlightened, sexist message—that it's a woman's mission to groom and plan and scheme to ensnare a man's affection—might I suggest they meet the Merseybeats, four guys promising they'll wear their hair just for her—truly the prototype of the sensitive man! Even more eccentric was the version by the Eagles (the Bristol-based British group, not the Californians), who added a crazed whammy-bar guitar, ominous grand-piano stabs, a call-and-response intro *("You want to be hers!" "I wanna be hers")* and a "Please Please Me"–derived outro.

On to the foreign language versions. There are Dusty Springfield versions recorded for Germans *("Warten und Hoffen")* and Italians. Once again, the Italians mince no words: their translation is simply titled "Stupido Stupido"!!

Other Versions: *Terry Baxter & His Orchestra (1971) • Joe Bourne (1993) • Casino Royale (1999) • Petula Clark (2000) • Rita Coolidge (1981) • Ani DiFranco (1997) • The Eagles (UK) (1964) • 18th Century Corporation (1969) • Connie Francis (1968) • Gals & Pals (1967) • The Jody Grind (1990) • Brenda Lee • Londonderry Strings • Jenny Luna - "Stupido Stupido" • Marion Maerz "Warten und Hoffen" (1971) • The Merseybeats (1964, rerecorded 1986) • Vicki Randle (2000) • Christopher Scott (1970) • Nancy Sinatra (1967) • Sophie - "Tente Ta Chance" • Dusty Springfield (1964), also "Stupido Stupido" & "Warten und Hoffen" • Starlight Orchestra (1995) • Billy Strange (1965) • The Vandalias (1998)*

"I Cry Alone" (Hal David - Burt Bacharach)
First recorded by Dionne Warwick
From the album *Presenting Dionne Warwick,* Scepter 508
Released February 1963

In the liner notes to Rhino's *Hidden Gems* collection, Warwick insists this song had been written especially for Maxine Brown. The copyright date, 1960, bears this out: Bacharach and David must have been lobbying that far back to secure the follow-up to "All in My Mind," Brown's hit of that year. When Brown became a Wand recording artist in 1964, she recorded "I Cry Alone" using the identical instrumental track that appeared on the *Presenting Dionne Warwick* LP the previous year.

One of Bacharach and David's best torch songs, "I Cry Alone," captures all the hidden torment that someone newly out of love must hide from friends *("But when they talk about you / I make believe I never grieve")* and unleash only behind locked doors. While Brown's version is pretty impressive, Warwick's still has the edge. There's a sudden stop that occurs at one minute, 38 seconds, when Warwick inserts a wordless plea that would make any compassionate listener reach for a handkerchief.

Other Versions: *Maxine Brown (1964) • Vikki Carr - "No Llorar" • Betty Carter (1982) • Jackie Lee • Ruby & the Romantics (1964) • The Straight A's (1963)*

Presenting Dionne Warwick. Her first Scepter album was surprisingly cohesive, considering the grab-bag fashion in which it was assembled. It contained both sides of her first two singles, plus five Bacharach-David demos and three songs that also moonlighted as Shirelles album tracks ("Unlucky," "If You See Bill" and Zip-A-Dee-Doo-Dah"). The cover portrait is an out-of-focus stage shot, suspiciously tinted to make Dionne appear white.

"Make the Music Play" (Hal David - Burt Bacharach)
First recorded by Dionne Warwick
From the album *Presenting Dionne Warwick,* Scepter 508
Released February 1963

"Let the Music Play" (Hal David - Burt Bacharach)
First recorded by the Drifters
Atlantic 2182, flip side of "On Broadway"
Released March 1963

The question of which came first, the egg or the omelet, arises once again. Warwick's demo version of the song was released in advance of the Drifters' recording by a few weeks, but both versions were in the can the previous year. Bacharach's initial vision of the song was sufficiently altered by Jerry Leiber and Mike Stoller's production to merit its different title: Dionne's gentle request to "Make the Music Play" gives way to the Drifters' anguished life-or-death appeal to "Let the Music Play."

Leiber and Stoller improve upon an already fine song by injecting some key modulations, each upward step punctuated by a few kettledrum beats. The song neatly swirls upward like a spiral staircase, from which Drifter Rudy Lewis yells to the heavens to *"Keep the magic going / Keep the love light glowing / Or she may get away."* At least you hope he's yelling to the heavens—not even the dance band on the Titanic could endure this kind of pressure. Lewis, who had been a lead vocalist with the Clara Ward Singers before replacing Ben E. King in the Drifters, would eventually release a solo recording on Atlantic in 1963, but its failure insured that he would remain with the group until his sudden death the following year.

Other Versions: *Lana Cantrell • Lena Martell • Didi Noel (1966) • Rita Reys • Diana Ross & the Supremes (1968) • Leslie Uggams (1968)*

"A Lifetime of Loneliness" (Burt Bacharach - Hal David)
First recorded by Steve Alaimo
Checker 1042, released spring 1963

Teen heartthrob and future regular on Dick Clark's series *Where the Action Is*, Steve Alaimo was hot after turning Arthur Alexander's "Every Day I Have to Cry" into a regional hit (it peaked at No. 46 nationally). After releasing the predictable cash-in album *Every Day I Have to Cry* (which consisted entirely of songs with the word "cry" in the title), Alaimo was sufficiently prepped for "A Lifetime of Loneliness."

Steve Alaimo. Checker was normally the home for Chicago bluesmen and R&B singers, and Alaimo proved to be the only Dick Clark–sanctioned white teen idol at the label.

A slow, mournful ballad with an operatic middle of the kind Gene Pitney or Roy Orbison could be counted on turning in with regularity, it shows both Bacharach and David exhibiting a healthy appetite for bending the rules of popular songwriting. For Bacharach, it's constructing an unorthodox melody that is a series of sliding half-step descents. For David, it's taking the hoary prisoner-of-love motif *("You are the judge and I'm the prisoner")* but allowing the prisoner to turn the accusing finger elsewhere *("I believe when love is true / One hasn't got the right to turn to someone new / One hasn't got the right to break somebody's heart the way you've broken mine").* Clearly the innocent one here, he appeals to not only the judge but also to anyone who's ever been wronged in love after being faithful. One last plea for clemency *("I was born to love you / Come to my arms and rescue me")* and all is quiet in the courtroom.

The combination of naked self-analysis *("Without you darling, I'm such a lonely human being")* and the constant switching from major to minor notes may have hindered "A Lifetime of Loneliness" from ever finding mainstream acceptance, but Bacharach came closer two years later and three keys higher when he rescued this song with Jackie DeShannon's help. DeShannon's double-tracked performance, recorded at the same session that produced "What the World Needs Now Is Love," reveals a redolence of Gene Pitney that Bacharach and David must have already heard in her earlier recordings. It informed their decision to place "What the World Needs Now"—a song originally intended for Pitney—with DeShannon, following a dispute with Pitney's publisher.

Other Versions: *Jackie DeShannon (1965) • Tina Harvey*

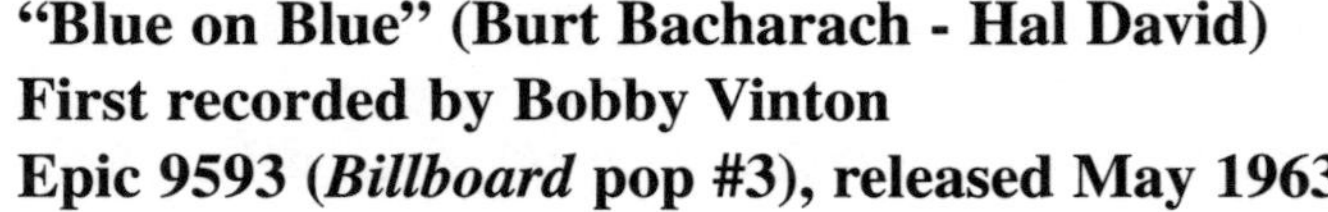

"Blue on Blue" (Burt Bacharach - Hal David)
First recorded by Bobby Vinton
Epic 9593 (*Billboard* pop #3), released May 1963

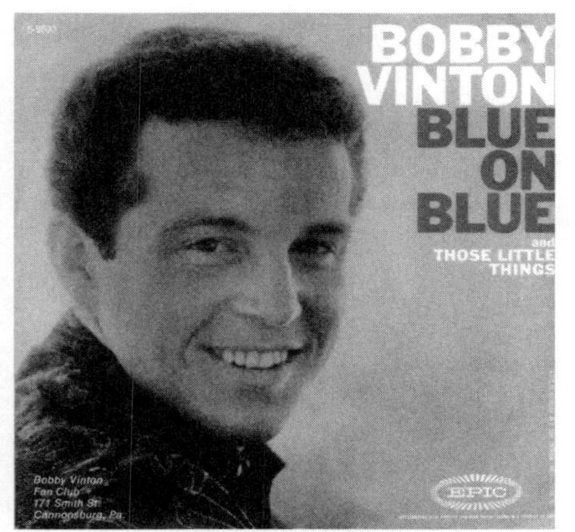

Bobby Vinton. Pictured here during his blue period. Epic issued "Blue On Blue" on blue vinyl, repeating the marketing strategy that worked so well with "Roses are Red."

There was no official announcement when Bacharach and David decided to become an exclusive songwriting team, but this 45 is as good a marking point as any, according to Hal David. "We worked off and on together for quite a few years and finally teamed up for keeps about a year and a half ago," he told *Billboard*'s Ren Grevatt in 1964. "Since then someone has been very good to us. It started with Bobby Vinton's 'Blue on Blue.'"

Consolidating the success of the similar "Only Love Can Break a Heart" the previous fall, the pair were back in the Top 5 again for the first time since "Magic Moments." Now, with the help of the Polish Prince, they were able to take the quasi-European mandolins-and-accordions feel of "Call Off the Wedding" and make it pay off.

If every recording artist has to have a gimmick, then Bobby Vinton's was recording songs that sounded old-fashioned on their day of issue. Vinton began his career as a trumpet player and bandleader, with his outfit serving as the touring band for one of Dick Clark's notoriously overworked "Caravan of Stars" packages in 1960. Signed at the time to Epic

Records as an instrumentalist, he cut two albums of Harry James–style big-band swing that failed to catch a break in a marketplace doing the twist. Wisely, Vinton switched to singing for his last contractually obligated single. "Roses Are Red (My Love)" shot up to No. 1 for four weeks in 1962, but when his next four singles failed to come close chartwise, Vinton went back to the color wheel in search of hits.

According to an account in *The Billboard Book of Number One Hits* by Fred Bronson, Bacharach personally pitched "Blue on Blue" to Vinton, who tried to secure some of the publishing rights. When Bacharach would not sign away any rights and left Vinton's office without a deal, Vinton chased after him. "Burt, I was kidding," he said. "That's a great song. I can't play games with you."

Although the production credit was Bob Morgan's, Bacharach played on the session and conducted from the piano. The song went to No. 3 and Vinton would follow it up with "Blue Velvet" and several other color-coordinated albums.

Other Versions: *Paul Anka (1963) • Burt Bacharach (1965) • Castaway Strings (1965) • Bobby Engemann • Percy Faith (1964) • Gals & Pals (1967) • Maureen McGovern (1991) • Dick Neelee • Royksopp - "So Easy" contains sample from Gals & Pals' "Blue on Blue" (1999) • Bobby Solo - "Blu e' Blu" (1963) • Bud Shank featuring Chet Baker (1965)*

"Blue on Blue." A sobbing, old-fashioned hit that even a grandmother could approve of. It's this octogenarian advantage that gave him a solid audience base that didn't rely solely on fickle teens during the British Invasion. Vinton was one of the few male singers who maintained a Top 10 presence throughout the Sixties.

"True Love Never Runs Smooth" (Burt Bacharach - Hal David)
First recorded by Don and Juan
Big Top 3145, released spring 1963

Which one was Don and which one was Juan may be a riddle for the ages, but there is no question that Roland Trone and Claude Johnson will live on in doo-wop infamy for posing the 1962 musical question "What's Your Name?" Bacharach and David's latest European paean to the gods of love takes the duo as far from their fabled street-corner sound as doo-wop ever dared to in its first golden era.

To ears accustomed to Gene Pitney's hit version, which followed later in the year, Don and Juan's severe seventh harmonies and extra grace notes on "True Love Never Runs Smooth" distract somewhat from the beautiful drama of Hal David's longing lyrics. Otherwise the mandolin arrangement is identical to Pitney's version, as are the la-la-la las.

Pitney's majestic take on the song makes for one of his most stirring sides ever, with the singer alternating between boldly belting out la-la-la las and commiserating about *"the heartaches and paaaaaain that we two may share."* Hal David beautifully captures the tug of war between inner completeness and outer distractions: "When the world outside my arms is pulling us apart / Press your lips to mine and hold me with your heart." And just to keep it Continental, Gino Italiano also cut the song in a Roman incarnation, "Resta Sempre Accanto A Me."

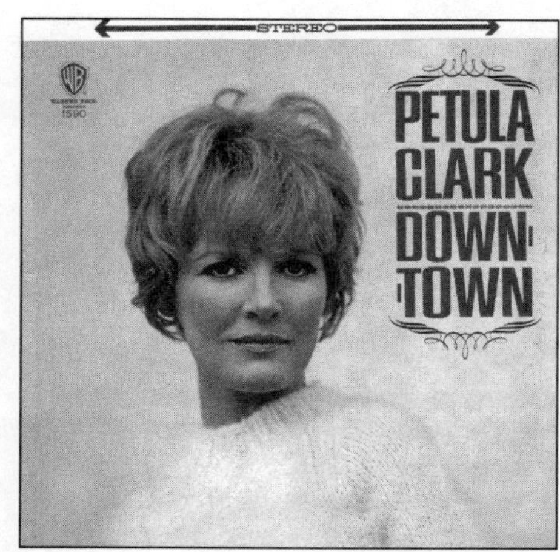

Petula Clark. Warner Brothers had a strange policy of keeping Pet's beauty mark from staring out at record buyers even though they could clearly see it on television and concert appearances. When it wasn't airbrushed out entirely, it was obscured by flowers or an upturned collar. One rear sleeve photo even eclipsed it with sheet music!

Petula Clark covered the song for a European single in 1964, backed by another Bacharach-David hit, "Saturday Sunshine," later installing it as the opening track on her first U.S. album. Producer Tony Hatch ditches the mandolins found on all other versions and furnishes a more rocking beat just so you'll remember you're in Swinging London, where all the lights are bright.

Other Versions: *The Caravelles - "In Gedanken Bin Ich Bei Dir"* • *Petula Clark (1964)* • *Gene Pitney - "Resta Sempre Accanto A Me" (1964)*

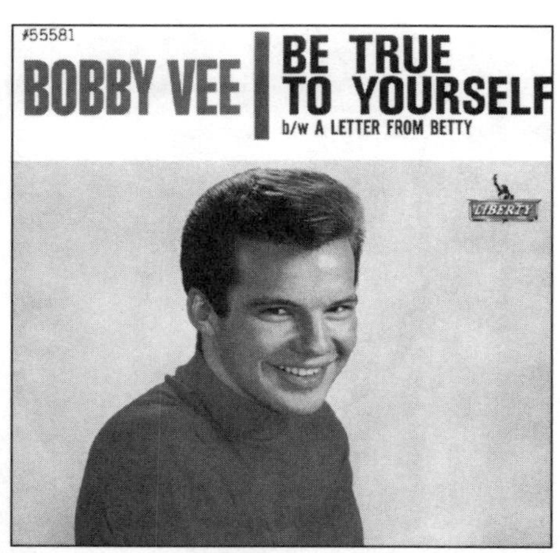

Bobby Vee. The ill-fated Winter Dance Party tour of 1959 that claimed the life of Buddy Holly, Richie Valens and the Big Bopper inadvertently gave Bobby Vee his first break. The tour's next scheduled stop after the fatal plane crash near Clear Lake, Iowa, was Fargo, North Dakota, where Vee and his group, the Shadows, filled in for the three perished rock stars. When Vee secured a deal with Liberty that same year, he cut a Buddy Holly tribute of sorts called "Suzie Baby," and in 1962 he cut an album with the original Crickets.

"Be True to Yourself" (Burt Bacharach - Hal David)
First recorded by Bobby Vee (with the Johnny Mann singers)
Liberty 55581 (*Billboard* pop #34)
Released June 1963

Liberty intended to launch a series of albums by its best-selling artists entitled *The Wonderful World of...*(insert name here), but due to poor sales the label cancelled the alphabetical series before it got to "V" and Vee. *The Wonderful World of Bobby Vee* was already in the can, so many of the album's standout tracks were issued as singles. These extracts proved to be some of Vee's best—"The Night Has a Thousand Eyes," "Charms" and "Be True to Yourself."

The credits on the record label read, "produced by Snuff Garrett" (the man who sped up "Tower of Strength") and "arranged and conducted by Ernie Freeman," but Vee recounts a different scenario in the liner notes of his self-titled disc in EMI's Legendary Masters Series. "Burt Bacharach pretty much took charge of that session. He played piano on it and I remember him wishing he had his horn player from New York with him." Whatever failings the composer heard in the West Coast horn player, the trademark flugelhorn intro still winds up sounding like pure Bacharach.

In this perky number, Vee tells his girl he has unshakable faith in her ability to resist the stray glances of some other guy. *"Be true to yourself and you'll always be true to me*," he advises, and because he manages to navigate a tricky key change, she probably does. "It was really on the edge of my range and it was all I could do to sing the song," says Vee. "Their songs were like that....Hal David is still one of my favorite lyricists. It's always surprised me that someone hasn't redone the song."

Saturday Sunshine. In 1973, the child-sung version of this song became the title track of "a special album of Burt performances," two of which ("Raindrops" and "One Less Bell to Answer") could be by Bert Kaempfert for all we know. They bear no resemblance to any A&M versions and are exceptionally bland. The Kapp LP was sponsored by Abbott Laboratories, former makers of Placidyl®, the drug of choice "if time is the criterion to inspire your confidence." Huh?

"Saturday Sunshine" (Burt Bacharach - Hal David)
First recorded by Burt Bacharach
Kapp 532 (*Billboard* pop #93)
Released July 1963

Imagine the reconditioning that casual record buyers were in for after plunking down money for the Kapp 45 of "Saturday Sunshine" and finding out that Burt Bacharach wasn't some squeaky preschooler.

Possibly a homage to the Cowboy Church Sunday School's 1955 hit "Open Up Your Heart (and Let the Sunshine In)" or else a marketing scheme to cut into the sale of Eddie Hodges singles, the child-sung "Saturday Sunshine" does remind one of "High Hopes," Hodges' optimistic duet with famous adult singer Frank Sinatra. While the sex of the child is hard to gauge, one thing is certain: enough people thought that children should be heard and not seen to keep it in the Top 100 for three weeks that summer, one of only two instances a Burt Bacharach single charted on *Billboard*'s Hot 100.

For those Scrooges allergic to the decibel range of singing children, an alternate, largely instrumental take without the kid can be found only on the 1997 U.S. compact disc edition of *Burt Bacharach Plays His Hits* (MCA).

Meanwhile in jolly old London, both Petula Clark and British comedian Bruce Forsyth imported "Sunshine" for *Top of the Pops* consideration in 1964. Johnny Mathis also turned his attention to the song at the end of his relatively hitless four-year stint at Mercury Records.

Other Versions: *Burt Bacharach (1963) • Petula Clark (1964) • Bruce Forsyth (1964) • Johnny Mathis (1967)*

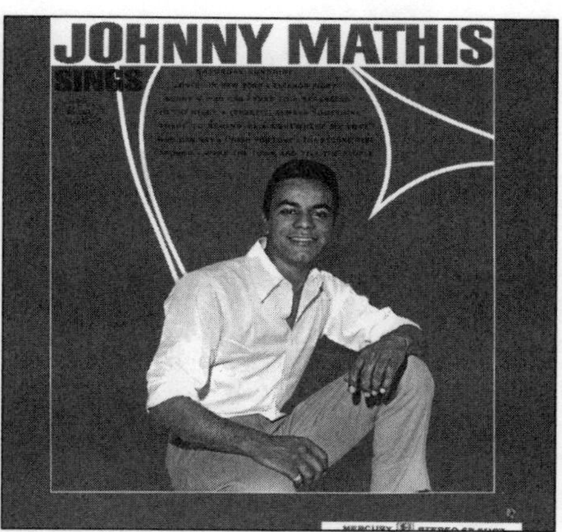

Johnny Mathis (1967). "Saturday Sunshine" was the last single Mathis released on Mercury Records. Once restored to Columbia Records' good graces in 1967, he would place at least one Bacharach song on a single every year until 1972. Really. We checked.

"And So Goodbye My Love" (Burt Bacharach - Hal David)
Recorded by Burt Bacharach
Kapp 532, flip side of "Saturday Sunshine"
Released July 1963

"And So Goodbye My Love" is largely instrumental except on the choruses, where a choir floats in singing, *"And so goodbye my love / Try not to cry my love,"* interspersed with occasional oohs. After the final crescendo, a coda is added—*"It's better to have loved and lost / If we have lost, at least we've loved"*—before the fade to black.

Barring his covers of "Searching Wind" and "Roseanne" (released on an obscure Cabot single in the mid-Fifties), this was the most Mancini-esque instrumental work Bacharach had done to date. Sounding very much like the sweeping closing credits for a touching love story, "And So Goodbye My Love" served as a dress rehearsal for the movie scores and orchestral albums soon to follow.

"And So Goodbye My Love." This is perhaps Hal David's most economical lyric, its 26-word total rivaling the simplicity of the Beatles' "The End," which tallies in at a comparatively excessive 29 words—plus a drum solo.

"That's the Way I'll Come to You" (Burt Bacharach - Hal David)
First recorded by Jack Jones
Kapp 534, flip side of "Love Is a Ticklish Affair"
Released summer 1963

This loping plea for instruction from a love partner *("Brave and unafraid or on bended knee / Tell me how you want me / Any way you want me, that's the way I'll come to you")* was originally furnished to Bobby Vee around the same time as "Be True to Yourself." With an abundance of finished masters left stranded in the Liberty vault in 1963 with the cancellation of that *Wonderful World of Bobby Vee* album, "That's the Way I'll Come to You" was never returned to until EMI dusted it off for *The Essential & Collectable Bobby Vee* in 1998. The recording sounds one or two steps away from completion, awaiting the reverb or double-tracked vocal that would give it the necessary Vee varnish. As it stands,

Marianne Faithfull. She has the distinction of having recorded both the Beatles' and the Rolling Stones' first string-laden recordings, "Yesterday" and "As Tears Go By," respectively.

Vee's rough lead vocal and the sly string buildup amply demonstrate the number's hit potential.

Taken at roughly the same slowpoke speed as "Pick Up the Pieces" and "Dreamin' All the Time," the song was well suited to Jack Jones' brand of croon. The high-cresting vocal demands of the song's ending force Jones to emote instead of just enunciating for a change. Less subtle than Vee's version but with the thicket of reverb applied to the vocals, this flip could've turned the tide for the hitless Jones a few months sooner than "Wives and Lovers," had it just been given some exposure. Only after he went full bore after hair-curler housewives did Jack Jones finally make a name for himself.

Other Versions: *Bobby Vee (1998)*

Please Make Him Love Me" (Burt Bacharach - Hal David)
First recorded by Dionne Warwick
Scepter 1253, flip side of "Make the Music Play" (*Billboard* pop #81)
Released July 1963

There's no doubt Hal David was raising the bar of literacy in pop music: not many 1963 hits started out with a line like *"Answer my fervent prayer."* It wasn't a highfalutin vocabulary that prevented "Please Make Him Love Me" from becoming a Bacharach-David standard as much as its odd descending melody, which leaves one with an uncomfortable plodding feeling.

"Please Make Him Love Me" has the distinction of being the first Dionne Warwick B-side to actually sound like one. Coupled with the coy "Make the Music Play," Warwick's third single was a meek letdown after the high standards set by the two previous seven-inchers. Even when Billy Joe Royal sound-alike Ray Lynn turned up the teen idol juice on his 1966 attempt, this plea for divine intervention also fell on deaf ears. Not even changing the "fervent prayer" to a "lonely" one helped.

Other Versions: *Ray Lynn (1966)*

"If I Never Get to Love You" (Burt Bacharach - Hal David)
First recorded by Lou Johnson
Big Top 3115, released August 1963

Vastly underrated by all but the most devout Northern-soul zealots, Lou Johnson is often referred to as the "male Dionne Warwick." Bacharach and David set aside superlative first-run material for him ("Always Something There to Remind Me" and "Reach Out for Me") that unfortunately found a larger audience only after the female Dionne Warwick covered them with identical arrangements. The same sort of bad luck followed Johnson to Great Britain, where his 45s were kept from the *Top of the Pops* by competing cover versions from the likes of Adam Faith and Sandie Shaw.

The first in Johnson's unsuccessful yet hardly unworthy series was "If I Never Get to Love You." A brisk bolero from its demo stage, it remained unchanged except for the exaggerated baby-voiced backgrounds on the instrumental break, which were substantially toned down on all subsequent versions.

In a voice capable of going from hoarse to smooth in an instant, Johnson resolutely runs down a list of things he will do to set his intended love's heart on fire. Both Lou and Gene Pitney are a near-match in their respective versions, and both barely contain their desperation, with Pitney practically growling after the full stop that launches into the bridge. Also on the growl is Timi Yuro, who attacks the song a key higher and a semitone or two faster, like a cardiac arrest candidate. This exciting and frenetic version was officially produced and arranged by Bacharach (his first such credit on a Liberty recording) and most likely was recorded at the same session as "The Love of a Boy."

Richard Chamberlain. How hot was TV's Dr. Kildare in 1963? Every 45 he released reached the Hot 100, including two B-sides. "Close to You" wasn't one of them, but his wooden version of "Hi-Lili Hi-Lo" was!

Marianne Faithfull's soft folk-rock version, found on her first album, floats past like a fluffy cloud—not unlike her first 1965 hit, "As Tears Go By." Over plucked harps, sonorous strings and male background vocalists, Faithfull's voice barely rises above a whisper until harsh harpsichord stabs and handclaps on the bridge necessitate a pinch more lungpower from the former convent girl turned Rolling Stones gal pal.

Other Versions: *Marianne Faithfull (1965) • Gene Pitney (1963) • Timi Yuro (1963)*

"Blue Guitar" (Burt Bacharach - Hal David)
First recorded by Richard Chamberlain
MGM 13170 (*Billboard* pop #42)
Released September 1963

Oddly enough, the second song in the Bacharach canon to spotlight a musical instrument favors the guitar over his customary piano. The first one, of course, was the wordless "Moon Guitar." Then the team came up with "Blue Guitar." Perhaps Hal David was avoiding the 88 keys in song because Tin Pan Alley had already churned out hundreds of "this ol' piano" rags. Or maybe he just needed a two-syllable word instead of three. Bacharach has often said in interviews that he likes to write his melodies away from the piano, so it's plausible he always heard the haunting "Blue Guitar" riff with the six-string in mind.

Richard Chamberlain. Both sides of the "Blue Guitar" single were tossed on as filler for the *Twilight of Honor* soundtrack, along with six (!) other John Green movie themes.

It's hard to believe the pair conceived any song with actor Richard Chamberlain in mind, but the TV star was still a viable chart commodity after scoring hits with the "Theme from *Dr. Kildare* (Three Stars Will Shine Tonight)" and covers of "Love Me Tender" and "All I Have to Do Is Dream." The novelty of Chamberlain bringing his bedside manner to transistor radios was already starting to wane when Bacharach was tapped to write and arrange both sides of his next single. Although not the greatest warbler in the world, Chamberlain, with his melancholy voice, was certainly light-years better than either substandard TV teen idols like Edd "Kookie" Byrnes or ridiculous TV operatic belters like Jim "Gomer Pyle" Nabors. Actually, the doc maintains a likeable quality throughout "Blue Guitar," but only if you can keep from thinking, "I wish it was Ricky

"Close to You." It's nice to know that Bacharach and David will live on in the cartoon world: that's where Marge Simpson bought a doorbell chime that wouldn't stop pounding out the opening notes of "Close to You."

Nelson singing this instead."

Other Versions: *Boots Randolph*

"(They Long to Be) Close to You" (Burt Bacharach - Hal David)
First recorded by Richard Chamberlain
MGM 13170, flip side of "Blue Guitar"
Released September 1963

Scratch out "likeable quality" for this one, unless you like singing as monotonous as an expired patient on a respirator. While it's not unusual to hear someone massacring this most lucrative Bacharach and David copyright, Richard Chamberlain had the dubious honor of ruining "Close to You" before anyone else got near it. Relatively few people have heard Chamberlain deliver his threat to sprinkle moondust in your hair with the same stiffness exhibited by his hair lacquer. In all fairness, Bacharach's strident piano arrangement gives Chamberlain little choice but to robotically follow every chord change on the bridge. Bacharach is just as exacting on the Dionne Warwick demo, which surfaced on the *Make Way for Dionne Warwick* album in September 1964.

"(They Long to Be) Close to You" came very close to becoming a throwaway despite having a lot going for it—an easy-to-sing melody (hence Chamberlain), clever Hal David lines about birds and stars going out of their way to be close to you, and let's not forget those two piano glissandos that approximate the sprinkling of starlight in your eyes of blue. Dusty Springfield eliminated those two flourishes on her superlative 1967 version (found on her fourth U.S. album, *The Look of Love,* and her third UK album, *Where Am I Going*), injecting the song with the same sultry sexiness that made "The Look of Love" such a revelation. It is believed that this Ivor Raymonde–arranged track was actually a leftover from her 1965 UK album *Everything's Coming Up Dusty*.

When Herb Alpert was searching for a B&D follow-up to his No. 1 hit "This Guy's in Love with You," Hal David sent Alpert the Dionne demo recording. The trumpeter passed on the tune (he couldn't imagine himself sprinkling moondust in anybody's hair) but foisted it upon newly signed A&M recording artists Karen and Richard Carpenter to record two years later. As it happens, the duo were performing at a benefit dinner after the premiere of *Hello Dolly* in December 1969 and Bacharach approached them about being the opening act for a benefit concert he was giving on February 27, 1970. Bacharach also requested that they perform a medley of his tunes—any ones they wanted. They arrived at eight titles, but "(They Long to Be) Close to You," the song Alpert recommended, wasn't one of them. By now Alpert was quite insistent that the duo record the song on their next album and reinstate those two piano glissandos missing from the Dusty version.

Richard Carpenter gave the song an updated Bacharach feel (bringing it up to the same jaunty tempo as "Raindrops Keep Falling on My Head" and "This Guy's in Love with You"), but the intro is all his own invention, as are the angelic block harmonies that drove the number up the charts. After three recorded attempts and the replacement of Karen on the drum stool by Hal Blaine (because Alpert felt that Karen wasn't really hitting hard enough), the siblings struck gold, making "Close to You" Bacharach and David's third and last No. 1.

As with "This Guy's in Love with You," the recording's chart-topper status opened up the floodgates for cover versions. Most singers religiously adhered to the Carpenters' hit rendition, the notable exception being Dionne Warwick, who returned to the song for her Warner Brothers debut album in 1972, with jazz pianist Bob James arranging. She omits the staccato singing at the end of the original bridge and that moondust/stardust sprinkling business, opting for the more casual *"and when all their work was done, well, there was no one else as wonderful as you."* Other deviating cover versions include Jerry Butler and Brenda Lee Eager's steamy duet, as well as the Longines Symphonette Society's bump-and-grind striptease rendition that probably livened up many dentist visits in the early Seventies.

The Longines Symphonette Society. Although no one can be sure what kind of society the Longines Symphonette was devising, it must have have something to do with the worship of cheese, as the ridiculous rendition of "Close to You" on this five-LP Bacharach-and-David set handily demonstrates.

Other Versions: *Yasuko Agawa (1996) • Ronnie Aldrich (1971) • Ed Ames (1969) • Lynn Anderson • Burt Bacharach (1971) • Barenaked Ladies (1998) • Billy Baxter (1998) • Cilla Black (1971) • Joe Bourne (1993) • B.T. Express (1976) • Jerry Butler & Brenda Lee Eager (1972) • Alan Caddy Orchestra (1972) • The Carpenters (1970) • Raffaella Carrà (1997) • Frank Chacksfield (1971) • Don Choi • Petula Clark (1971, 2000) • Richard Clayderman (1995) • Floyd Cramer (1970) • Perry Como (1970) • Ray Conniff (1970) • Cranberries (1994) • Hannah Cranna (1998) • The Dells (1972) • Sacha Distel - "Comme Moi" (1972) • EPO (1989) • Ethyl Meatplow (1993) • Ferrante & Teicher • Johnny Fiamma (of the Muppets) (1996) • Ella Fitzgerald • Free'n' Easy (1998) • Erroll Garner (1974) • Grant Geissman (1999) • Don Goldie (1977) • Ron Goodwin • Lou Green (2000) • Gwen Guthrie (1986) • Terry Hall (1997) • Lionel Hampton & Dinah Washington • Isaac Hayes (1970) • Shauna Hicks - "A Bacharach Love Story Medley" (1998) • Vince Hill (1971) • Wayne Horvitz (1997) • Engelbert Humperdinck • Manfred Krug - "Nah bei dir" (2000) • James Last (1972) • Liberace - "Medley" • Brenda Lee • The Lettermen (1970) • Claudine Longet (1971) • Longines Symphonette Society (1970) • Vera Lynn • Tony Mansell Singers (1970) • Johnny Mathis (1970) • Keff McCulloch (1996) • Anita Meyer (1989) • Sugar Minott • The Moments (1972) • Tony Mottola (1970) • Matt Monro (1970) • Steve Newcomb Trio (2000) • 101 Strings • Orquesta Sabor Tropical (1993) • Jose Padilla (1998) • Houston Person • Franck Pourcel • Renaissance (1970) • Rita Reys (1971) • Malcolm Roberts (1971) • Tommy Roe • Diana Ross (1971) • Royal Marines (1974) • RTE Concert Orchestra (1995) • Sanchez (1993) • Christopher Scott (1970) • George Shearing (1972) • The Simpsons (TV series) • Frank Sinatra (1971) • Jimmy Smith (1970) • David Snell (1972) • Dusty Springfield (TV Special 1967) • Starlight Orchestra (1995) • Jevetta Steele (1997) • Barbra Streisand & Burt Bacharach (1971) • Yume Suzuki (1997) • Synthesizer Rock Orchestra (1995) • Gabor Szabo (1970) • B.J. Thomas (1970) • McCoy Tyner (1997) • Jerry Vale (1969) • Sarah Vaughan • Squid Vicious (2000) • Wenche Myhre - "Solens Venn" (1970) • The Ventures (1974) • The Vocal Ballad Community • Ronnie Von (1977) • Dionne Warwick (1964, 1972, 2000) • Lawrence Welk (1970) • Andy Williams (1970)*

"I Forgot What It Was Like" (Burt Bacharach - Hal David)
First recorded by Ray Peterson
Dunes 2027, released summer 1963

Ray Peterson's trademark shaky voice (he suffered a bout of polio as a teenager) may have been an asset to the violent drama of "Tell Laura I Love Her" and "Give Us Your Blessing," two great teen-anguish anthems

1963

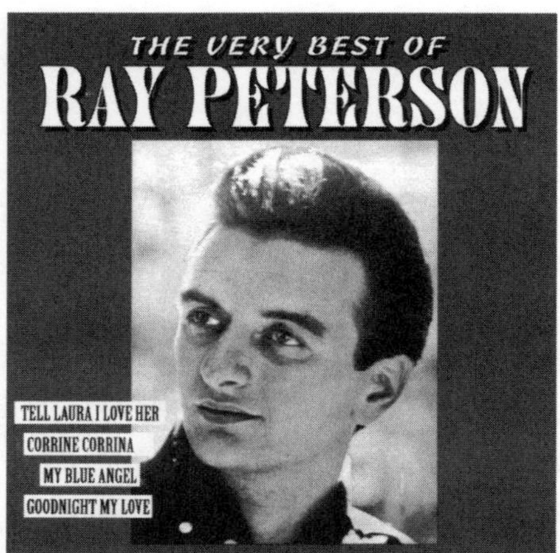

Ray Peterson. Like Gene Pitney, Peterson had an early brush with Phil Spector, who produced his Top 10 hit "Corrina, Corrina" in 1960. Something of a maverick, the Texas singer started his own record label, Dunes, once he started having hits.

that ended in flaming car wrecks. On everything else, he sounds a mite too overwrought. While anyone who had a heart could be expected to feel despondent over forgetting what it was like to be kissed and loved by a girl, Peterson just sounds like a guy being punctured with hot needles. Intended for Peterson, judging by the similarly shaky voice on the Bacharach demo, this released version sounds just as sparse and just as forgettable. A car wreck might've helped.

Other Versions: *Bobby Helms*

"Wives and Lovers" (Burt Bacharach - Hal David)
First recorded by Jack Jones
Kapp 551 (*Billboard* pop #14)
Released October 1963

Earlier installments of this discography haven't exactly been kind to Jack Jones, and we're not about to break a tradition here. For most styles of pop song, Jones is the worst kind of singer. He enunciates rather than emotes, reduces words to mere syllables and hits the notes square on the head like he's going down a shopping list. Refer to his hit renditions of "The Impossible Dream" and especially "Alfie" for further elucidation. Yet on "Wives and Lovers," Jones' insincerity actually works in the song's favor. If male chauvinist pigs needed a pledge drive song, they needn't have looked further than this king-of-the-castle anthem. And Jones sounds all too happy oinking the news—that a house is not a home, it's a sex slave camp where a breadwinner has a moral obligation to commit adultery if his wife sees him off to work with curlers in her hair.

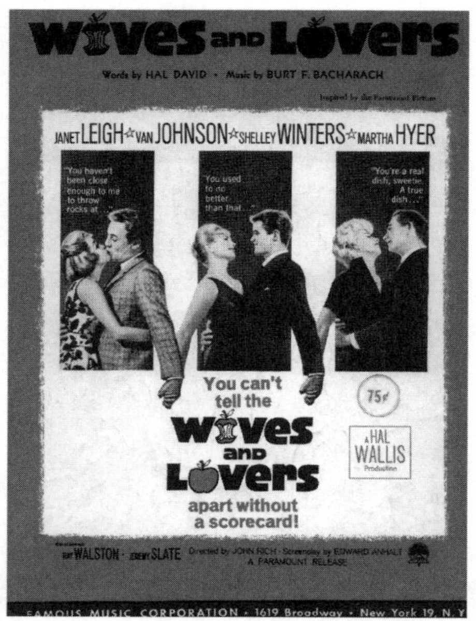

"Wives and Lovers." A Bacharach favorite among jazz musicians, it's been cut by everyone from Wes Montgomery to Stan Getz to Lena Horne. Duke Ellington and Ella Fitzgerald even cut a version together.

In defense of Hal David, who stayed home and greeted his working wife at the door when he was starting out as a songwriter, these lyrics weren't exploiting women so much as exploiting a Sixties cinematic sex romp that exploits women (and men, as skirt-chasing Neanderthals). And he all-too-perfectly captures the sleazeball allure of this otherwise forgotten film. In a major miscalculation, this exploitation song wasn't even added to later prints when it became a huge Grammy Award–winning hit—the first for Bacharach, and sweet vindication for all those times he was told by A&R men that audiences were not sophisticated enough to send a jazz waltz into the charts. Although Dave Brubeck's "Take Five" had made some inroads in 1960, this was the first time a jazz waltz in 5/4 with a vocal had any impact in the pop field.

At the time of issue, no one was offended by the song's sentiments. For the bulk of the Sixties, "Wives and Lovers" was a standard that every male vocalist appearing on *The Ed Sullivan Show* was required to lend a leer to. It's been recorded by quite a few, too, including Bacharach's old friends Steve Lawrence, Ed Ames and Andy Williams. Bacharach even reunited in the studio with his ex-boss Vic Damone to record a version. It was also the first of two Bacharach tunes covered by Angie Dickinson's Rat Pack pal, Frank Sinatra, who recorded it in dunderheaded 4/4 fashion. Enamored by its waltz time and playful melody, jazzy female vocalists like Nancy Wilson, Lena Horne and Ella Fitzgerald gave it a try. Ella's version, with Duke Ellington, is particularly delightful, her scat-singing overriding any bad taste lingering from the lyrics.

Dionne Warwick's playful rendition, which appears on her *Sensitive Sounds of Dionne Warwick* album in 1965, packs far more sizzle than the hit version. Bacharach would further explore the song's jazzy possibilities on two recorded instrumental versions. The first one, which appears on *Plays His Hits*, is not altogether different from the Dionne arrangement while the version that appears on his eponymous 1971 A&M album is a six-minute opus. Both steer clear of the verse lyric entirely, highlighting only the seductive *"time to get ready for love"* passage. Bacharach never performs a concert without featuring a snatch of this song, usually as part of a movie medley for people with short memories who assume it was actually in the film. It did belatedly wind up in a motion picture: Dionne Warwick's rendition is featured somewhat ironically in the1996 chick flick *The First Wives Club*.

It Might As Well Be 4/4. He's had more wives and lovers in one afternoon than you'll have in a lifetime. And he does everything *his* way. So watch what you say about his version of this Bacharach favorite: even from beyond the grave, he could have your legs broken!

Other Versions: *Ronnie Aldrich (1971 • Eric Alexander (1992) • Ed Ames (1969) • Apollo 100 (1973) • Burt Bacharach (1965, 1971) • Terry Baxter (1971) • Peter Beil (in German) • Joe Bourne (1993) • Casino Royale (1999) • Lee Castle & the Jimmy Dorsey Orchestra (1974) • Frank Chacksfield (1971) • Vic Damone • The Dells (1972) • Dave Douglas (1997) • Carl Doy • Johnny Dupont • Percy Faith (1964) • Arthur Fiedler & Boston Pops (1972) • Ella Fitzgerald & Duke Ellington (1966) • Kiley Gaffney (1998) • Gals & Pals (1967) • Stan Getz (1967) • Grant Geissman (1999) • Don Goldie (1977) • Dave Gordon Trio (1997) • Ron Goodwin • Grant Green (1964) • Tony Hatch Sound (1967) • Shauna Hicks - "A Bacharach Love Story Medley" 1998) • Red Holloway (1994) • Lena Horne (1966) • Dick Hyman (1963) • Kimiko Itoh (1997) • Thad Jones & Pepper Adams (1966) • Clifford Jordan & Ran Blake (1990) • King's Singers (1971) • Steve Lawrence (1966) • Jeanette Lindstrom (1995) • Julie London (1964) • Longines Symphonette Society (1970) • Kenny Lynch (2000) • Anni-Frid Lyngstad (Frida in ABBA) • Russell Malone (1991) • Marie McAuliffe (1998) • Wes Montgomery (1965) • Peter Nero (1968) • Steve Newcomb Trio (2000) • Orlando Philharmonic Orchestra (1995) • Dieter Reith (1967) • Rita Reys (1965) • Wallace Roney (1991) • Royal Marines (1974) • Richard Hayman & RTE Concert Orchestra (1995) • David Sanborn & George Duke (1998) • Christopher Scott (1970) • Frank Sinatra (1964) • Lonnie Liston Smith (1990) • Sheila Southern (1968) • Starlight Orchestra (1995) • Swing Out Sister (1992) • Dick Van Dyke with Enoch Light and His Orchestra and the Ray Charles Singers (1963) • Dionne Warwick (1965) • Andy Williams (1964) • Nancy Wilson (1964) • Monica Zetterlund (in Swedish) (1965)*

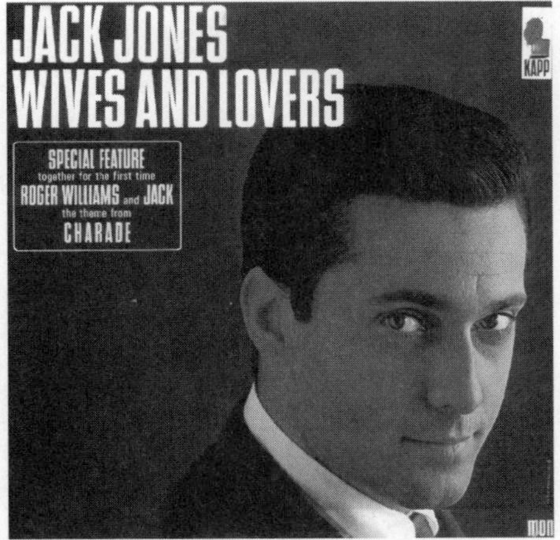

Jack Jones. Arguably this singer's best-remembered works were themes to cheesy productions. While this one rates a high *fromage* count, the "Love Boat Theme" remains Jones' most requested song. Of course, Bacharach and David didn't write "Love Boat" but on their ASCAP list of titles there is a "Love Bank" that's piqued our interest.

"Reach Out for Me" (Burt Bacharach - Hal David)
First recorded by Lou Johnson
Big Top 3153 (*Billboard* pop #74)
Released October 1963

In describing the Four Tops' "Reach Out (I'll Be There)," rock critic Dave Marsh wrote that Levi Stubbs sang the song like a guy trying to pull his buddy out of a fire. Lou Johnson summons that kind of urgency, tempered with moments of tenderness and reassurance on "Reach Out for Me," the second B&D-produced Johnson side lobbed at the listening public. Again Hal David breaks new pop ground: what other song has the singer pledging solidarity with someone so beleaguered by condescending people and untrue friends *("They make you feel that your heart will just never stop aching / And when you just can't accept the abuse you are taking...darling, reach out for me")*? Johnson's full-throated vocal leap in the song's final crescendo is breathtaking: it's amazing that he can blend so seamlessly with the female background vocalists.

The Searchers (1965). It's true: bands used to wrack their collective cranium trying to come up with names for their albums! In a quandary as to how to top such past triumphs as *It's the Searchers* and *This Is Us,* the lads deposited their cover of "Magic Potion" on the *Sounds Like the Searchers* album in the UK and *The New Searchers* LP in the States.

Substituting the urgency of the Johnson version with a soothing lead vocal, Dionne Warwick's 1964 cover version bested Johnson's chart performance by a considerable degree, peaking at No. 20. "Reach Out" later became the title track of Bacharach's first album for A&M in 1967, and Cissy Houston, who likely sang backgrounds for all three versions, turned in a fine rendition with the Sweet Inspirations in 1968.

Other Versions: *Burt Bacharach (1967) • The Carnival (1969) • Lyn Collins (1972) • Nicola Di Bari - "Ti Tendo Le Braccia" • 18th Century Corporation (1969) • Michael Henderson (1980) • Okazaki Hiroshi & His Stargazers (1966) • Brian Kennedy (2000) • Olivia Newton-John (1989) • Rock Academy String Quartette (1970) • Christopher Scott (1970) • Sweet Inspirations (1968) • David T. Walker (1967) • Walter Wanderley Set • Dionne Warwick (1964, 1998) • Nancy Wilson*

"Magic Potion" (Burt Bacharach - Hal David)
First recorded by Lou Johnson
Big Top 3153, flip side of "Reach Out for Me"
Released October 1963

In this gentle, less comical recast of the Clovers' "Love Potion No. 9," Johnson puts in a special order for "Magic Potion 309," which he hopes will win him the lovesick glances of not just any old girl but *the* girl, the *only* girl, the one he needs so desperately. *"I love her more than I can tell / So won't you weave your magic spell / Oh please, oh please, help me*," he begs the Gypsy, although the bossa nova beat takes some of the heat off his desperation.

It's possible that this excellent B-side may have split radio programmers, since an instrumental version of it turns up on the flip of his next single "Always Something There to Remind Me." Although it's the identical track, some sloppy touches are left showing. The vocal intro is deleted, with the last syllable of "desperate-leee" making it over to the other side of the splice. There's also background coughing, muttering and some swirling Jimmy Smith–ish Hammond organ from either Bacharach or Paul Griffin.

In England, Johnny Sandon and the Remo Four cut the obligatory competing cover version. Two years later, the Searchers had a belated U.S. hit with their 1963 recording of "Love Potion No. 9," so they turned their attention to "Magic Potion," although this obvious ploy was not exploited for 45 consideration on either side of the pond.

Other Versions: *The Kubas (1965) • Johnny Sandon & the Remo Four (1963) • The Searchers (1965)*

"Twenty Four Hours from Tulsa" (Burt Bacharach - Hal David)
First recorded by Gene Pitney
Musicor 1034 (*Billboard* pop #17)
Released October 1963

"Dearest darling, I had to write to say that I won't be home anymore."

So begins Hal David's mini-movie for small speakers. There have been other Dear John/Dear Joan letters set to music, but this is the first one where the person being dumped via the U.S. Postal Service isn't the person singing. On his way home, Pitney stops for the night and sees someone at a hotel; they get something to eat, they dance, they interlock, and all of a sudden Tulsa's his new forwarding address. The guilt he feels at the end is blatant, once his bravado over finding somebody new dies down and the realization that he can never go home again brings him the sense of dread on which the song expires, a distant piano mocking the opening notes Pitney sang "dearest" over.

Gene Pitney. You knew there was gonna be a version of "Twenty Four Hours from Tulsa" in Italian, didn't you? Sure you did! Gino Italiano made a special delivery overseas with "A poche ore da te."

Bacharach keeps the action moving musically and regionally. What starts out with Tijuana brass gives way to Dobro slide against the Brazilian *baion* beat, an arrangement that proved popular enough to be ripped off by Billy Joe Royal for his Top 5 hit "Down in the Boondocks." Later, wracked with guilt, Royal recorded a song called "Tulsa," but it's not even this song!

In a BBC radio interview that coincided with the Bacharach-David tribute concert at the Royal Albert Hall in 2000, Pitney said that this particular song was an important one for him. "It finally allowed me to make that jump outside the American market," he said. "I didn't have success in any other countries up until that point. Because 'Twenty Four Hours from Tulsa' was a country-and-western narrative type song and it came out right in the middle of the so-called British Invasion. So it was a whole different type of song. It was odd doing shows with a lot of the people who were successful at the time because this song didn't seem to fit anywhere, and yet it did."

As it happened, Pitney was in England to do a tour of the Mecca ballroom chain there in support of his single "Mecca." Brilliant idea, except that EMI wasn't interested in promoting a ballroom tour or a ballad singer. The tour was cancelled, so Pitney and his British publicist Andrew Loog Oldham, the Rolling Stones' manager/producer, decided to use every TV appearance and interview to promote "Tulsa," his latest single in America and a far better song than "Mecca" in his opinion.

Dusty Springfield. "Tulsa" was one of three Bacharach-David covers on Dusty's first U.S. album, named after her first two U.S. hits. The afterthought single of "Wishin' and Hopin'" would be more successful than either of them.

It made quite an impression on one British invader, Dusty Springfield, who included the song on her first long player (titled *A Girl Named Dusty* in the UK, *Stay Awhile* in the States). This version drew immediate attention, reputedly because it was the first time a female pop singer covered a man's tune without radically altering the lyrics. Although Dusty guarded her private life, she admitted in 1973 that her sexual Dutch door could swing either way. Yet it was probably her aggressive stance on "Tulsa"—picking up a strange guy at a hotel and sending her fiancé a cruel Dear John letter right when she was one time zone away from coming back to him—that endeared her to gay men. Or maybe it was her admission on *Dusty*'s liner notes that she hated "desperately masculine men."

Foes of lounge-lizard embellishments should avoid the smug Brian Foley version at all costs. In an attempt at bringing more gritty 1969 realism to the song, Foley speaks certain lines, unconcerned that it will throw off the meter when he continues singing. After singing *"I was only 24 hours from Tulsa,"* he exclaims *"it's truuuueee!!!"* in the same tone most people reserve for yelling "yahoo"! Inserting alternate words, ruining rhymes, Foley sounds as if he was strong-armed into doing the song and is bent on destroying any usable take. Feeling none of Pitney's pangs of guilt about never being able to go home again, he just feigns ignorance: *"I can never go home, y'know? She just made it happen. What can I say?"* Unless someone compiles a CD of the worst Bacharach covers, you're in no danger of ever hearing it.

Other Versions: *Apeman (2000) • Burt Bacharach (1965) • Joe Bourne & the Step in Time Orchestra (1993) • Claude François - "Maman Cherie" (1964) • Brian Conley (2000) • Brian Foley (1969) • Tommy Graham • Claire Hamill (1983) • Ian & Sylvia (1964) • Jay & the Americans (1965) • Marion Maerz - "Das Ende der Reise" (1971) • The Mariachi Brass featuring Chet Baker (1965) • Anita Meyer (1989) • Osten Warnebring - "Femton Minuter Fran Eslov" (1965) • The O'Kaysions (1969) • Showaddywaddy (1996) • Dusty Springfield (1964) • Chris Wilson (1998)*

Mademoiselle Petula. Dionne's sales in France were no doubt undercut by Petula Clark's French-language version of "Anyone Who Had a Heart" entitled "Ceux qui ont un coeur."

"Look in My Eyes Maria" (Burt Bacharach - Hal David) First recorded by Jay & the Americans United Artists 669, flip side of "Come Dance with Me" Released November 1963

Another Leiber and Stoller traipse through the Bacharach-David songbook and further proof that the *baion* beat, a constant throughout both teams' repertoire, was slowly being usurped by the bossa nova. At least the triangle players weren't left to starve. The surprise hook of the song is an insistent high C on the piano that follows the triangle and resonates like a plucked heartstring throughout

As on "Magic Potion," the easygoing Latin groove underscores the desperation of a singer pledging his life for the woman he loves. There might be some slight calculation on Hal David's part in using the name Maria, since Jay and the Americans rose to prominence singing to a chick named Maria when they covered "Tonight" from *West Side Story*. On this, only his third single replacing Jay Traynor, Jay (né David) Black tries to sound seductive and succeeds despite the Americans singing "loo loo loo loo" in the background like they're summoning an Italian waiter. "Look in My Eyes Maria" would've made a better A-side than "Come Dance with Me," a "Save the Last Dance for Me" sound-alike too blatant for Leiber and Stoller to cut with the Drifters. It could hardly have mattered which was the plug side, since the record debuted in the Top 100 on the worst radio week in history. After President Kennedy was assassinated, there was no music played on radio for four days.

Both John Andrea and Cliff Richard turn in solid performances of this criminally obscure number that are worth hunting for.

Other Versions: *John Andrea (1966) • Cliff Richard (1965)*

Dusty Springfield. Her affinity with blacks didn't stop with music. In 1964, she was deported from South Africa after refusing to perform for segregated audiences, long before apartheid was a cause célèbre. "I wasn't making any major statements," she told the British press. "I just thought it was morally the right thing to do."

"Anyone Who Had a Heart" (Burt Bacharach - Hal David)
First recorded by Dionne Warwick
Scepter 1262 (*Billboard* pop #8)
Released November 1963

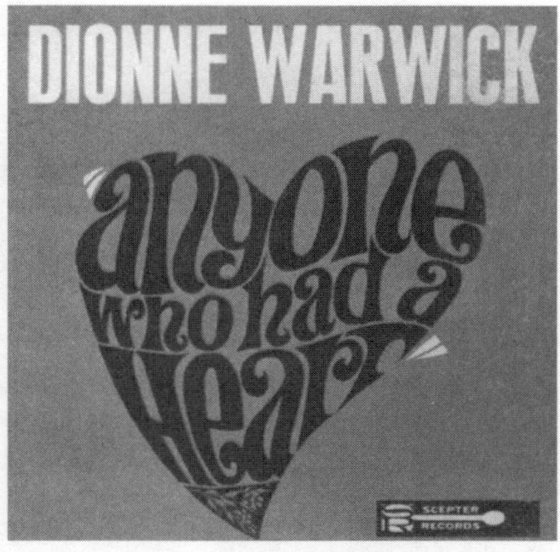

Anyone Who Had an Art Director. Some of the most grotesque album cover art of the Sixties can be blamed on the South, where some whites objected to black faces staring down from album covers. While the last LP cover tinted Dionne a Caucasian peach, this one kept her out of sight completely.

Cissy Houston recalls riding a bus en route to a Solomon Burke session in Manhattan when news came over a transistor radio that the president had been shot. In her 1998 biography, *How Sweet the Sound*, she writes, "As we watched the state funeral for John F. Kennedy, his little girl and John John saluting his coffin, I thought of the song we just cut with Dionne, 'Anyone Who Had a Heart.'" It's not hard to see why. The funereal pace, the soft pounding of the drums, the mournful sax solo and the oppressive sense of despair and helplessness in the lyric all command an outpouring of sympathy from the listener. The country was plunged into collective sorrow and couldn't bring itself to put such a dark song into the Top 40 until four days after the New Year.

Despite her expression of boundless love, Dionne is met with cruelty and indifference from her lover. She admonishes him, *"You couldn't really have a heart / then hurt me / like you hurt me and be so untrue,"* then quietly accepts his rejection with, *"What am I to do?"* Of course, the listener who does have a heart empathizes, giving this single an advantage over the earlier "Don't Make Me Over," where Dionne is telling her cad, *"Just love me with all my faults the way that I love you."* In this song Dionne has no faults except bad judgment—taking her tormentor back each time he returns.

The song, which introduced polyrhythms to pop radio, gave many a bandleader headaches with its long sequence of irregular bars. Bacharach was now calling the shots, and anyone covering this tune after it became a monster hit would grudgingly have to switch from 5/4 to 4/4 and 7/8 in order to replicate it.

While the time-signature changes may have driven Dionne's backup bands to distraction, it proved an even larger headache to Hal David, who revealed in a 2000 BBC interview with Johnny Walker that the rhyme was in the wrong place. "I had it almost the way I wanted it, and until we went into the recording studio, until that night, I was trying to change it. The song starts with *'Anyone who had a heart could look at me and know that I* love *you / Anyone who ever dreamed could look at me and know I dream* of *you.*' Well, the accent should not be 'dream *of* you.' The accent should be '*dream* of you.' But I had to have the accent on "of," because that's where the melody was. I tried to find a way to make the "of" do something, and I could never do it. And maybe it just wasn't able to be done. But I worked on that till it was recorded. Then it was gone. Had to let it go."

Dionne didn't fare too badly with that first draft, as it was her first Top 10 hit in the States. Warwick was hoping it would be the first 45 to do something overseas as well. "I had a little bit of a twinge going when Cilla Black decided to record 'Anyone Who Had a Heart,' because my recording was just getting ready to be released in Europe and she kind of covered it before mine had the opportunity to do what it was gonna do," Dionne said in an interview for the Dusty Springfield video biography *Full Circle.*

Cilla Black. When Brian Epstein first watched the Beatles play the Cavern Club, he made a second discovery, the club's hatcheck girl, Priscilla White. Cilla only cracked the U.S. Top 40 once with "You're My World," a song Dionne Warwick covered in 1968. And not a note-for-note copy, either.

Having no prior knowledge of Dionne's sensational recording, Brits naturally gravitated to the first version they heard. With the unstoppable Beatles combination of Brian Epstein's management and George Martin's production behind it, Cilla Black's carbon-copy version streaked passed Dionne all the way to No. 1. Black's recording has one very obvious deviation—the hysterical sopranos who screech behind her like a car alarm that's been set off on every chorus. Cilla's up-and-coming rival Dusty Springfield also recorded this tune, filing it away as filler on her first album. Sandie Shaw didn't actually get around to doing her version until 1982.

Although Dusty Springfield's note-for-note cover version contains the identical sax solo, there seems to have been an unspoken rule among everyone else to feature a different instrument for the musical break. Cilla Black had a piercing bassoon, Petula Clark a piercing organ; Gals & Pals featured guitar, the Four Seasons piano, and vibraphonist Cal Tjader had a vibraphone, natch!

Other Versions: *Sweet Pea Atkinson (1982) • Burt Bacharach (1965) • Shirley Bassey (1978) • Laurie Beechman (1990) • Cilla Black (1964, 1993) • Carola (2001) • Vikki Carr (1966) • Petula Clark - "Quelli Che Hanno Un Cuore," "Ceux Qui Ont Un Coeur," "Alles Ist Nun Vorbei"- "Tu No Tienes Corazon" • Tim Curry (1978) • Barbara Dickson (1985) • Percy Faith (1964) • The Four Seasons (1965) • Free 'n' Easy (1998) • Gals & Pals (1967) • Hub (1975) • Henry Kaiser (1990) • La Chanze (1998) • The Lettermen (1968) • Sandy Lynn - "Quelli Che Hanno Un Cuore" (1964) • Mantovani Orchestra • Maureen McGovern (1991) • Anita Meyer (1989) • Mina - "Quelli Che Hanno Un Cuore" (1968) • Martha Reeves & the Vandellas (1972) • The Orlons (1966) • Linda Ronstadt (1993) • Anne-Lie Ryde - "Ännu En Förlorad Dag" (1985) • Kim Salmon & the Surrealists (1998) • Sandie Shaw & B.E.F. (1982, 1988) • Smith & Mighty (1987, 1990) • Dusty Springfield (1964) • Starlight Orchestra (1995) • Nino Tempo (1991) • Gary Tesca (1995) • Cal Tjader (1969) • Luther Vandross (1986) • Ritchie Venus (2000) • Dionne Warwick and Burt Bacharach (2000) • Kai Winding (1965) • Wynonna Judd (1998)*

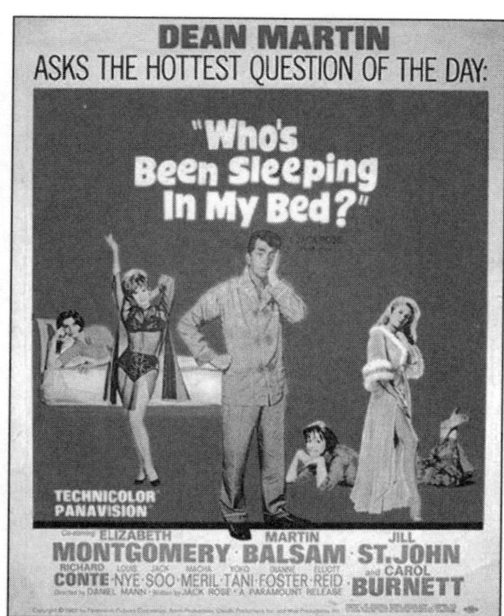

"Who's Been Sleeping in My Bed?" Is it an exploitation song if the single doesn't sell well and the movie bombs?

"Who's Been Sleeping in My Bed?" (Burt Bacharach - Hal David)
First recorded by Linda Scott
Congress 204 (*Billboard* pop #100)
Released December 1963

The kitten-voiced teen from Queens scored big when she confided "I've Told Ev'ry Little Star" in 1961. Soon after she waxed "Starlight, Starbright," "Count Every Star," "You Are My Lucky Star," "Little Star," "Land of Stars," "Catch a Falling Star"—are you sensing a pattern here? By late 1963, even the stars weren't listening to Linda Scott anymore and plans were afoot to turn Scott into an adult supper-club entertainer. The illusion of a girl group girl is still preserved on this exploitation song for a Dean Martin bedroom romp, which spent only one week on the last rung of the Top 100. Scott does her best to stay in denial, insisting that all the tears soaking her pillow nightly aren't hers. But this is 1963: you didn't think she was actually opening her bedroom door to strangers, did you?

SECTION FOUR

WHAT THE WORLD NEEDS NOW (1964-1965)

...or Trains and Boats and Planes

Burt spends a lot of time in London scoring his first film, What's New Pussycat?, *recording his first album and having massive chart hits under his own name overseas. More international cover versions of this material flourish. Burt and Hal are nominated for their first Oscar. We say hello Jackie D., goodbye Gene Pitney. And there is a fresh crop of singers competing with Dionne for new Bacharach-David songs.*

Section Four: What the World Needs Now (1964–1965)

1. *"To Wait for Love"* . . . . . *Jay and the Americans*
2. *"In the Land of Make Believe* . . . . . *The Drifters*
3. *"Lost Little Girl"* . . . . . *The Light Brothers*
4. *"Walk On By"* . . . . . *Dionne Warwick*
5. *"Any Old Time of the Day* . . . . . *Dionne Warwick*
6. *"From Rocking Horse to Rocking Chair* . . . . . *Paul Anka*
7. *"Errand of Mercy"* . . . . . *George Hamilton*
8. *"A House Is Not a Home* . . . . . *Brook Benton*
9. *"You'll Never Get to Heaven (If You Break My Heart)"* . . . . . *Dionne Warwick*
10. *"Me Japanese Boy I Love You"* . . . . . *Bobby Goldsboro*
11. *"Accept It"* . . . . . *Tony Orlando*
12. *"(There's) Always Something There to Remind Me"* . . . . . *Lou Johnson*
13. *"Long After Tonight Is All Over"* . . . . . *Jimmy Radcliffe*
14. *"The Last One to Be Loved"* . . . . . *Dionne Warwick*
15. *"How Many Days of Sadness"* . . . . . *Dionne Warwick*
16. *"Forever Yours I Remain"* . . . . . *Bobby Vinton*
17. *"Rome Will Never Leave You"* . . . . . *Richard Chamberlain*
18. *"Send Me No Flowers"* . . . . . *Doris Day*
19. *"Live Again"* . . . . . *Irma Thomas*
20. *"Say Goodbye"* . . . . . *Pat Boone*
21. *"Is There Another Way to Love You"* . . . . . *Dionne Warwick*
22. *"Don't Say I Didn't Tell You So"* . . . . . *Dionne Warwick*
23. *"Only the Strong, Only the Brave"* . . . . . *Dionne Warwick*
24. *"That's Not the Answer"* . . . . . *Dionne Warwick*
25. *"Fool Killer"* . . . . . *Gene Pitney*
26. *"Trains and Boats and Planes"* . . . . . *Burt Bacharach*
27. *"Don't Go Breaking My Heart"* . . . . . *Burt Bacharach*
28. *"What the World Needs Now Is Love"* . . . . . *Jackie DeShannon*
29. *"What's New Pussycat?"* . . . . . *Tom Jones*
30. *"Here I Am"* . . . . . *Dionne Warwick*
31. *"My Little Red Book"* . . . . . *Manfred Mann*
32. *What's New Pussycat? (Original Soundtrack LP)* . . . . . *Burt Bacharach*
33. *"Dance Mamma, Dance Pappa, Dance"* . . . . . *Joanne and the Streamliners*
34. *"London Life"* . . . . . *Anita Harris*
35. *"Everyone Needs Someone to Love"* . . . . . *Cliff Richard*
36. *"Through the Eye of a Needle"* . . . . . *Cliff Richard*
37. *"Looking with My Eyes, Seeing with My Heart"* . . . . . *Dionne Warwick*
38. *"I Fell in Love with Your Picture"* . . . . . *Freddie and the Dreamers*
39. *"Are You There (With Another Girl)"* . . . . . *Dionne Warwick*
40. *"If I Ever Make You Cry"* . . . . . *Dionne Warwick*
41. *"In Between the Heartaches"* . . . . . *Dionne Warwick*
42. *"Window Wishing"* . . . . . *Dionne Warwick*
43. *"Long Day, Short Night"* . . . . . *Dionne Warwick*
44. *"How Can I Hurt You"* . . . . . *Dionne Warwick*
45. *"More Time to Be with You"* . . . . . *Brook Benton*
46. *"Who's Got the Action"* . . . . . *Phil Colbert*

"To Wait for Love" (Hal David - Burt Bacharach)
First recorded by Jay and the Americans
United Artists 693, released January 1964

Few would argue that Tony Orlando's cover version of "To Wait for Love," released in September 1964, is not the definitive one, what with its Mediterranean lilt and active input from the composers. As the singer told Alec Cummings in the liner notes for *The Look of Love: The Burt Bacharach Collection*, "There's a little thing I do at the end of that song, 'fall in love today-yay-yay'...that was all Burt. Burt would sit at the piano, and he'd say 'No, man, I want you to say, "Yay-yay."' You'd never think that this classically trained, brilliant musician would worry about this little 'yay-yay.' I mean he really pushed on that."

Bacharach's insistence on a seemingly negligible tag may have been a reaction to a stiff campfire rendition recorded earlier by Jay and the Americans, who would never again be entrusted with a new Bacharach-David offering. Once producers Jerry Leiber and Mike Stoller saddle the song with a cowpoke arrangement that clumps along with one foot in the dung, the Americans have no recourse but to gang up behind Jay and glee-club the song to death.

Both Jay's and Tony's takes went largely unnoticed, yet millions of folks on both sides of the Atlantic who purchased Tom Jones' first hit single, "It's Not Unusual," probably played the flip side by mistake and liked what they heard. Recorded at the same historic November 1, 1964, session that produced Tom's signature song, Jones' sensuous and bombastic handling of "To Wait for Love" likely prompted Bacharach to think of the Welshman when it came time to cut the *What's New Pussycat?* theme. As on Petula Clark's version of "True Love Never Runs Smooth," the Mediterranean feel is supplanted by a Swinging London backbeat, provided here by the Ivy League, a Britpop combo.

Bacharach tried one last time in 1968 to give this excellent song its due, with Herb Alpert, but the trumpeter failed to get it any higher than No. 51 on the pop charts—this on the heels of a No. 1 hit, "This Guy's in Love with You"! Left without the inherent drama of that song's shy protagonist, we're left with a stately horn part and Alpert's monotone Chris Montez–style vocals.

The only evidence to support David's theory that it's a woman's lyric is Jackie DeShannon's cover version, recorded around the time of "Windows and Doors" and "Come and Get Me." Unfortunately, Bacharach had nothing to do with its arrangement (Arthur Wright does a limp Tony Hatch impersonation in an effort to make Jackie sound more downtown than Petula Clark), and the song wound up as filler on DeShannon's 1966 album, *Are You Ready for This?*

Other Versions: *Herb Alpert & the Tijuana Brass (1969) • Paul Anka (1964) • Frank Chacksfield (1971) • Jackie DeShannon (1966) • Sacha Distel - "Amour Perdu " (1972) • Ferrante & Teicher (1970) • Tom Jones (1965) • Tony Orlando (1964) • Ray Peterson • Royal Marines (1974) • Billy Vaughn Singers (1968)*

Jay and the Americans (1964). This vocal group became the primary outlet for material that producers Leiber and Stoller didn't think would be appropriate for the Coasters. The first album to feature the Americans' new Jay (Jay Black), *Come a Little Bit Closer,* had two first-run Bacharach-David compositions—"Look in My Eyes, Maria" and Jay's excruciating reading of "To Wait for Love."

Paul Anka (1965). File under "I'm so young yet I'm so old." Anka's popularity dipped considerably in America, where his single of "To Wait for Love" wasn't even released.

1964

"In The Land of Make Believe." A French EP with "You'll Never Get to Heaven" and two other selections.

"In the Land of Make Believe" (Burt Bacharach - Hal David)
First recorded by the Drifters
Atlantic 45 2216, flip side of "Vayo Con Dios"
Released early 1964

As happened with "Let the Music Play," the Drifters and Dionne Warwick both issued the same tune within weeks of each other, but this time the results couldn't be more different. Reportedly cut at the same session that produced "Walk On By" and "Anyone Who Had a Heart," Dionne's version of "In the Land of Make Believe" was no demo: it's a fully realized master that far outdistances the Drifters' rapidly antiquating sound and offers further proof that Bacharach had outlived his apprenticeship with Leiber and Stoller. Even with the addition of Hawaiian guitar, the Drifters sound like they're still loitering on Broadway, peering through the window of a travel agency after hours for a darkened glimpse of paradise. Rudy Moore's impressive vocal grows harsh and distorted as he ruminates over his paradise lost, but his passion is dissipated considerably by an unnamed Drifter's attempts to out-Caruso Mighty Mouse in the background. Here's a tune where the masking effects of the Gospelaires would've helped significantly.

Served up with a swirling string intro and pounding kettledrums at a hypnotically slow speed, Warwick's anguish is more torturous, too, because it's so private—a secret she's not even willing to share with herself. Unlike the accompaniment for the Drifters, who are outside looking into "yesterday in paradise," the Warwick instrumental track evokes the very Shangri-la that her self-deception allows her to wallow in. Particularly effective is her wordless gasp after uttering *"I need you so much"* two minutes into the song, which drives home both the pointlessness and the necessity of reliving each caress of a long-expired relationship.

Said to be one of Bacharach's own personal favorites, "The Land of Make Believe" anticipates his later work on the *Lost Horizon* score, as does Dusty Springfield's 1969 version, with its sitar/guitar underpinnings. Adding to her sexy performance is a "Ravel-inspired string arrangement" by Arif Mardin that sets it apart from the famous American Studios sound heard on the balance of the *Dusty in Memphis* album. The third single released from that much-loved long player, it reached no higher than No. 113.

In 1978, Steely Dan's Donald Fagen and Walter Becker produced an album for tenor saxophonists Pete Christlieb and Warne Marsh called *Apogee.* The Steely duo also contributed the song "Rapunzel," which they based on this Bacharach-David composition. "We heard the song on a Dionne Warwick record and thought it would be nice to blow on," Fagen told Robert Palmer in the liner notes for the album.

Other Versions: *Marie McAuliffe (1998) • Dusty Springfield (1969) • Swan Dive (1997) • Dionne Warwick (1964) • Leslie Uggams (1968)*

"Lost Little Girl" (Burt Bacharach - Hal David)
Recorded by the Light Brothers
ABC 10536, released winter 1964

Apparently, the charge of the Light Brothers was one of significantly low voltage. Few people have heard of them, and those who did couldn't be compelled to purchase their records. As far as we know, they recorded one single for Dot in the fall of 1961 and followed it up two years later with this truly obscure Bacharach-David cut. Sounding like an ambition-free Jan and Dean, the Light Brothers pine for a *"pretty little angel face"* who walked out the door, never to be seen again.

The Light Brothers. Proof positive that fear of the unknown is justified.

Even Beatlemania hadn't quashed audiences' morbid appetite for death discs, and this ballad has all the foreboding elements in place: an eerie soprano, someone leaving in a huff and a spoken-word passage from the poor lost girl herself: *"We quarreled and we said some things that I'm so sorry for."* Before he can stop her, she's out the door. No squealing tires ensue, there's no ascension into heavenly ranks, and all one's left with is a miserably anticlimactic death disc with a zero body count. That is, unless you count the career of the Light Brothers, which probably ended here—if such moments of minuscule importance can even be measured.

"Walk On By" (Burt Bacharach - Hal David)
First recorded by Dionne Warwick
Scepter 1274 (*Billboard* pop #6)
Released April 1964

Dionne Warwick's reputation as the queen of unrequited love songs is cemented with her landmark fifth single. Breaking from the pattern established by "Don't Make Me Over," "This Empty Place" and "Anyone Who Had a Heart," Warwick portrays a woman who will not plead for her lost lover, a woman who just wants to grieve in private. In her voice we hear the sadness, but we never get the cathartic climax of those previous singles. Warwick is able to walk the streets and refrain from bawling, until she sees the man who has forgotten her. Even her foolish pride, as personified by the carefree flugelhorn, isn't enough to stop her crying. The circular piano figure and the tick-tock woodblock in the chorus simulate the eternity it will take for her old lover to turn the corner and be completely out of the picture.

The Lady in Red. Yet another bold French EP, this time showing daring Dionne in scarlet hues. Scandalous!

Reportedly from the same session that produced her previous hit, "Walk On By" surpassed "Anyone Who Had a Heart" in terms of chart performance and number of recorded cover versions. Because both the overreaching vocal and the tricky time signature of the earlier tune aren't necessary components here, many less forceful singers and MOR orchestra leaders had a far easier time recording "Walk On By."

With this leeway, daring singers like Isaac Hayes were able to wrench 12 minutes of catharsis out of the tune, adding pleadings that would never roll out of Hal David's pen *("You put the hurt on me! You socked it to me, mama!… "There's no dust in my eyes, it ain't smoke that's making me cry").* Nonetheless, Bacharach heartily endorsed the Black

1964

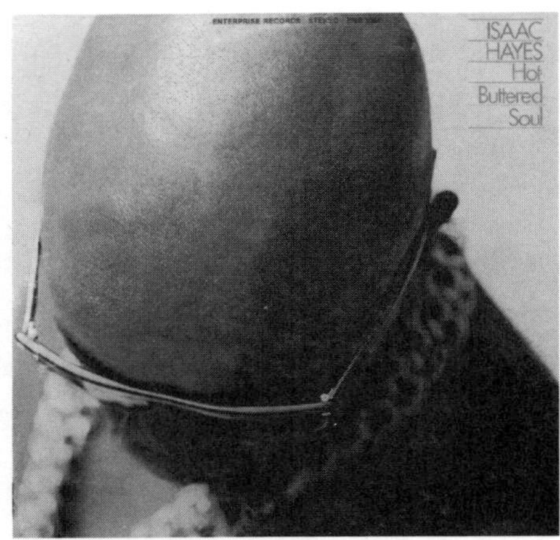

Isaac Hayes (1969). Over a quarter of his second album, *Hot Buttered Soul,* is devoted to elongating "Walk On By." Vanilla Fudge, also known to stretch material past the breaking point, had severely mellowed by the time of their 1984 reunion LP *Mystery.* Their bland CHR reading of "Walk On By" clocks in at a measly 4:57!

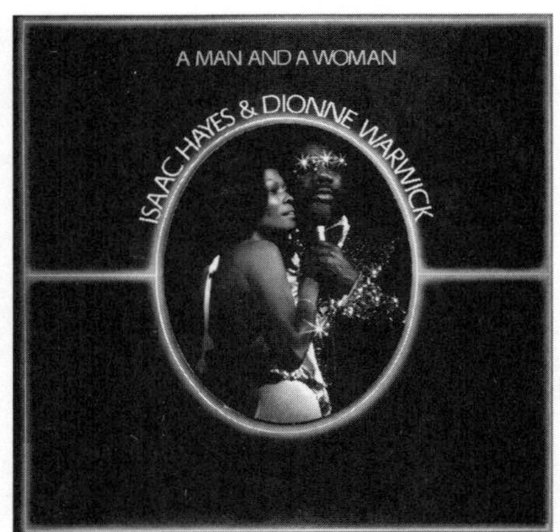

Ike and Dionne Revue? The pair toured together in 1977 and recorded this double-live album which reprises the "By The Time I Get To Phoenix/I Say A Little Prayer" medley Dionne performed with Glen Campbell on her 1969 TV special and they combine forces on "Walk On By." They also concoct a medley of—yikes—Captain and Tennille songs!

Moses' Olympian readings of the song and told him so when Hayes was a guest on Burt's 1972 special. Hayes would maintain a tradition of including a Bacharach-David tune on subsequent albums and later teamed up with Warwick for a 1977 live double album, *Hot! Live and Otherwise,* that would combine his versions of "Walk On By" and "I Just Don't Know What to Do with Myself" with Warwick's. Dionne sounds great doing Hayes' "Walk On By," albeit without handling the "sock it to me" asides.

Speaking of live embellishments, Warwick herself adds a chipper *"doncha dare stop"* on her 1967 *Live in Paris* version, a touch that Brenda and the Tabulations also used. The song was Warwick's first international smash; she rerecorded "Walk On By" in Italian ("Non Mi Pentiro") and German ("Geh Vorbei"), and did a slick easy-listening version on her 1999 album *Dionne Sings Dionne.*

Other Versions: *Afro-Blues Quintet (1966) • Richard Anthony -"Qui, Va Plus Loin" • Average White Band (1979) • Burt Bacharach (1965) • Bob Baldwin (1997) • Julius Wechter & the Baja Marimba Band (1965) • Terry Baxter (1971) • The Beach Boys (recorded 1968, released 1990) • George Benson (1967) • Joe Bourne (1993) • Brenda & the Tabulations (1967) • Les Brown & His Orchestra • Jonathan Butler (1987) • The Carnival (1969) • Bobby Caldwell (1995) • Dina Carroll (1989) • The Carpenters - "Bacharach and David Medley" (1971) • Casino Royale (1999) • Lee Castle & the Jimmy Dorsey Orchestra (1974) • Tony Cody (1972) • Cockeyed Ghost (1998) • Christopher Cross (1997) • D Train (1994) • Janet Lee Davis (1994) • The Dells (1972) • Carl Doy • Enoch Light (1969) • The Envoices (1980) • Fantasy Band (1994) • Donna Fargo • The 5th Dimension (1970) • Film Score Orchestra • The Four Freshmen • Four King Cousins • The Four Seasons (1965) • Connie Francis (1968) • Aretha Franklin (1964) • Free'n' Easy (1998) • Gabrielle (1997) • Gals & Pals (1967) • Jo Ann Garrett (1969) • Grant Geissman (1999) • Stan Getz (1967) • Marty Gold • Ron Goodwin • Tony Hatch Orchestra • Isaac Hayes (1969) • Hill-Wiltschinsky Guitar Duo (1996) • Okazaki Hiroshi & His Stargazers (1966) • Rhetta Hughes (1967) • Ike Isaacs (1967) • Ipso Facto (1992) • I-Tones (1992) • Jackson 5 - "Medley: Mama's Pearl / Walk On By / The Love You Save" (1971) • Jazz Crusaders (1966) • Jazz Jamaica - "Walk On By / You've Got It All Wrong" (1998) • The Jet Set (1999) • Lou Johnson • Anita Kerr Singers (1969) • Kindbergs (1998) • Rahsaan Roland Kirk (1965) • Kool & the Gang • Kramer (1997) • Ellis Larkins • The Lettermen (1964) • Little Anthony & the Imperials (1964) • The Lost (1965) • Jenny Luna ("Non mi pentirò") • Sandy Lynn (1964) • Melissa Manchester (1989) • Johnny Mathis • Jack McDuff (1966) • Mill Valley Taters (2000) • Mina (1981) • Sugar Minott (1981) • Smokey Robinson & the Miracles (1966, live 1969) • Missing Links • Peter Nero (1968) • New Direction (1969) • Steve Newcomb Trio (2000) • Laura Nyro (released 2001) • Outcasts (1966) • Pucho & His Latin Soul Brothers (1966) • Renaissance (1970) • Cliff Richard - live medley (1972) • Marianne Rosenberg - "Geh Vorbei" (1998) • The Mavis's (1998) • Mitch Ryder & the Detroit Wheels (1967) • Mongo Santamaria • Christopher Scott (1969) • Doc Severinsen (1966) • Helen Shapiro (1964) • The Simpsons (TV series) (1990) • Smith & Mighty (1988) • Sheila Southern (1968) • Starlight Orchestra (1995) • The Stranglers (1978) • Sonny Stitt (1966) • Gabor Szabo (1965) • Sybil (1990) • Gary Tesca (1995) • The Three Souls (1965) • Cal Tjader (1969) • Mel Tormé (1966) • Stanley Turrentine (1966) • Undisputed Truth (1973) • Vanilla Fudge (1984) • Dionne Warwick (rerecorded 1998) • We Five (1969) • Lenny White (1996) • Peter White (1962) • Brenton Wood • Timi Yuro*

"Any Old Time of the Day" (Burt Bacharach - Hal David)
First recorded by Dionne Warwick
Scepter 1274, flip side of "Walk On By"
Released April 1964

And again Florence Greenberg was backing the B-side! Although no one could dispute that the regal "Any Old Time of the Day" would've made a great follow-up to "Anyone Who Had a Heart," famed DJ and newly self-ordained "Fifth Beatle" Murray the K thought the A-side should be "Walk On By." Premiering both tracks on his radio program, he invited his listeners to vote for their preference. They sided with Murray, or Mr. the K., as the *New York Times* might call him.

If Warwick's detached cool on "Walk On By" is a necessary social disguise, "Any Old Time of the Day" finds the private Dionne giving round-the-clock consolation to a former lover who once decisively broke her heart. Dionne still carries that hurt around, but Hal David erases any trace of malice or rancor in her offer to come over any time of day: *"I'm not looking to try to get even, even though you've been unfair / I love you* [pause for drum roll] *much too much."*

The built-in conflict of Dionne comforting someone who has hurt her is mirrored in Bacharach's shifting from major to minor and back to major chords. Are selfless devotion and a fresh cup of coffee from an old friend enough to turn him back into her old lover? Will he see beyond his own hurt to hear her admission that *"even though you walked out of my life, you are my life, you are my love for always"*? Nah. Like Dionne, the song was thrown over for another, but it did have its ardent fans, particularly in Detroit, where it received considerable airplay.

Any fans out there who noticed commonalities between this track and Tony Hatch's "Call Me," recorded by Petula Clark and later a hit for Chris Montez, can go to the teacher's cupboard and give themselves a gold star.

Other Versions: *Dalida - "Questo amore e' per sempre" (1968) • Sue Raney (1966) • Sheila - "Chaque instant de chaque jour" • Franck Pourcel Orchestra (1966) • Stan Getz (1967) • Leslie Uggams (1968) • Earl Klugh (1989)*

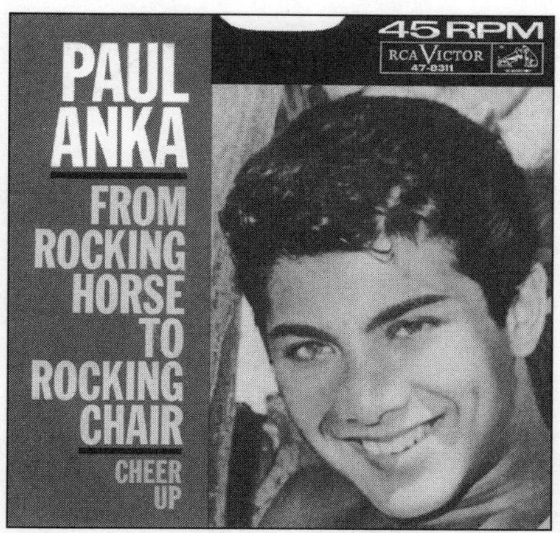

Paul Anka. Only two songwriters have written separately with both Burt Bacharach and Hal David, and both are named Paul: Paul Hampton and Paul Anka. The former "Puppy Love" idol wrote eight songs with Hal David and collaborated with Bacharach on the *Together* score in 1979.

"From Rocking Horse to Rocking Chair" (Burt Bacharach - Hal David)
Recorded by Paul Anka
RCA 47-8311, released January 31, 1964

With back-to-back Dionne Warwick Top 10s, the team of Bacharach and David was hotter than Hades at the start of 1964. What better duo to light a fire under the considerably cooled career of Paul Anka, who hadn't been a Top Tenor since "Dance On Little Girl" in 1961. Like most pre–British Invasion teen idols, Anka's career had been slowly moving toward that of an all-around adult entertainer in a tuxedo, appearing in posh nightclubs where requests for hits like "The Teen Commandments" would most definitely not be honored.

1964

Paul Anka. RCA may have signed the Canadian-born singer in part to keep him from competing with their real cash cow, Elvis Presley. The barrage of Anka hits did seem to ease up after Paul signed up with Lil' Nipper, and if the tape phasing at the top of "Rocking Horse" is any indicator, no one was paying much attention to the mastering. You can hear it digitally on BMG/Taragon's *The Essential RCA Rock and Roll Recordings (1962–1968).*

Trying to keep both kids and adults interested, David kindly chronicled a cradle-to -grave love affair that might've come off more than a little mawkish in lesser hands. Although it's hard to fathom a love between a three-year-old boy and a two-year-old girl that could last till their dentures soaked in side-by-side glasses, Bacharach's sweeping melody inspires us to overlook some of the sentimental improbabilities of the lyrics.

Early 1964 was no time to be getting sentimental on a pop record, what with the Beatles making every twenty-three-year-old American teen idol seem old and in the way. To demonstrate how industrious the industry was back then, Bacharach and David produced this recording on January 16 (two days before "I Want to Hold Your Hand" debuted on *Billboard*'s Hot 100). "Rocking Horse" was rush-released two weeks later, by which time the Fab Four had secured the No. 1 spot and held it with two more consecutive No. 1's until Louis Armstrong's version of "Hello Dolly" interceded in late spring. By that time the Beatles had secured all five of the Top 5 spots for one week, an unprecedented feat that probably won't be equaled anytime soon.

Shell-shocked by this Britannic turn of events, old-school teen idols went back to the drawing board to see if they could come up with something a little more Big Beat. Anka followed "Rocking Horse" with "My Baby's Coming Home, a herky-jerky rewrite of "When Johnny Comes Marching Home Again" that won him few hurrahs, although it did sneak up to No. 113 on the charts, the highest peak he'd have in the U.S. until 1968.

"Errand of Mercy" (Bob Hilliard - Burt Bacharach)
Recorded by George Hamilton
MGM 13215, flip side of "Does Goodnight Mean Goodbye"
Released spring 1964

In the days when it was customary to cut at least three songs per recording session, "Errand of Mercy" sounds like it was the last submission of the night, attempted only after Bacharach finished cutting both sides of actor George Hamilton's previous single. While not as catchy as "Don't Envy Me" or as cloying as "Little Betty Falling Star," this 1962 Bacharach-Hilliard holdout manages to captures Hamilton in a Lou Christie crybaby funk, but without the schizophrenic resolve.

A pathetic muted trumpet ushers in the song in the same comic manner the silly slide trombone does on Bacharach and Hilliard's earlier "Tower of Strength," leading one to believe this may have been an intended sequel that Gene McDaniels never followed up on. Hamilton tries to a stop a departing girl by pleading his case in the third person—*"a broken hearted boy who loves you so"* and whose world will crumble into a big, well-tanned pile of clay if you proceed to dump him.

In verse three we learn—surprise, surprise—that he's really that broken-hearted boy, poised to drop on both knees in just a moment! But the real surprise of the song is the discordant orchestral stabs Bacharach inserts and the uneasy pregnant pauses that linger afterwards. Hamilton's emoting reaches its zenith on the last three stops, when he yelps, *"Don't!*

Don't! walk away from me!" like a piteous traffic light. But even that idea was better utilized on "Walk On By."

Despite continued lack of chart success, the actor's exploitative recording career extended to include a 1966 album (*By George!*) and a 1971 single bereft of tears (the theme from Hamilton's *Evel Knievel* biopic).

A House Is Not a Home (1964). A movie house is not a home, and home is where most people sat out this Shelley Winters/Robert Taylor flick.

"A House Is Not a Home" (Burt Bacharach - Hal David)
First recorded by Brook Benton
Mercury 7203 (*Billboard* pop #75)
Released July 1964

Another year, another Shelley Winters B movie with a superlative Bacharach-David theme. Paramount, having learned its lesson with "Wives and Lovers," included Brook Benton's recording of "A House Is Not a Home" in its namesake film. While the young Ms. Winters began her career in the late Forties playing doe-eyed young girls who get murdered in really good films (*A Place in the Sun, A Double Life*), by the time her svelte figure rounded off to the nearest plus size in the early Sixties, she could be counted on to turn up in really crummy films, usually playing a weeping matron, a nagging spouse, a boozy whore or any combination of those three. As it happens, she's a matronly whore in this sanitized-for-your-protection biopic based on the life of famed New York madam Polly Adler.

Wisely, Hal David didn't point out that a brothel is not a house and a bed is still a bed even if it's paid for by the hour. Instead he constructed a somber facsimile of what those first minutes of loneliness are like after a loved one has vacated the premises, all because of something you did. You notice chairs and rooms being their old inanimate selves. You watch the shadows on the wall getting longer and keep imagining that someone's coming up the stairs to brighten things up again.

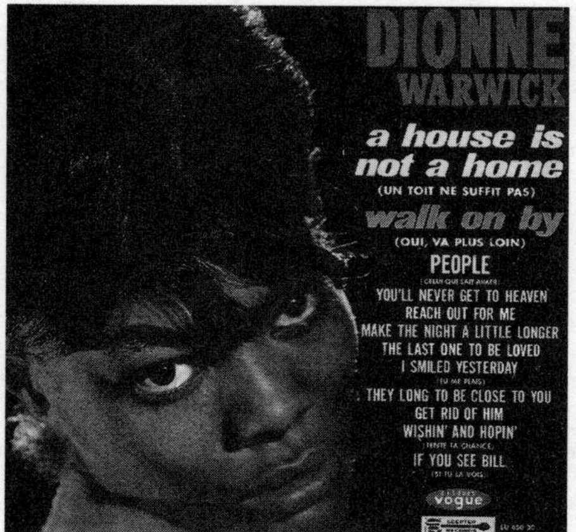

Dionne Warwick (1964). This French version of *Make Way for Dionne Warwick* had room for two extra songs and featured the hits "A House Is Not a Home" ("Un toit ne suffit pas") and "Walk On By" ("Oui va plus loin"). One of many French Dionne EP sleeves that is lit like an Ebony porno flick.

This last bit of pretend is skillfully expressed in what's usually considered the throwaway part of a song, the middle eight. David writes, *"Now and then I call your name and suddenly your face appears,"* and Bacharach provides an orchestral flourish that instantly dispels the gloom before reality checks back in for a lights-out call. Certainly nothing in the movie equals the cinematic sweep of this moment, a brilliant marriage of orchestration and words—this being one of the songs that came into the world lyrics first, based on a poem Hal David wrote about a former home of his in East Hills, Long Island. The house, designed by architect Sandford White, was not far from "Burt Bacharach's Rothman Inn," a restaurant his partner bought in the late sixties.

Structured very similarly to "Make It Easy on Yourself" (a shortened verse in a low key soaring several octaves above it on the chorus), it would seem to have been a natural choice for Jerry Butler. Ever eager to work with new people, however, Bacharach and David tapped Brook Benton, whose covers of older standards and duets with Dinah Washington made him seem like a better MOR choice for Oscar consideration. But wed to a stiff picture with future disaster-movie mascot Shelley Winters, the song wasn't even nominated.

1964

***Full Circle: The Life and Music of Dusty Springfield* (1997).** This fascinating career overview made two years before Springfield's death features the singer interviewed rather irreverently by comediennes Jennifer Saunders and Dawn French. Highlights include her duet with Burt Bacharach on "A House Is Not a Home" and the only surviving footage of Dusty and Jimi Hendrix performing "Mockingbird" on her BBC-TV variety series.

Dionne Warwick. In France, "A House is Not a Home" was clearly preferred over the designated A-side, a verdict many American deejays agreed with. Fans could hear her sing both songs in French for her not-exactly-live 1966 album *Dionne Warwick in Paris.*

Dionne Warwick fans, often eager to pit her in a grudge match against every other singer of a Bacharach tune, criticize Benton for his lagging-behind-the beat vocal style and for a flub that occurs at 1:39 into the song. After Benton sings, *"But it's just a crazy game,"* he's about to come back in early but then stops himself. Either that or it's a bad punch on the vocal track. But though you can go through the list of cover versions below and find more technically flawless performances, few are as heartfelt as this South Carolina man's recitation. The reason Benton's recording didn't set the charts ablaze might have had something to do with split airplay: Warwick's version was installed on the B-side of her latest single and charted only slightly higher than Benton's (No. 71 on *Billboard*'s Hot 100). Between the two versions, enough people heard it to warrant its now standard status.

This is perhaps the only Bacharach-David song whose original arrangement is adhered to in every recorded cover version. You won't find a reggae or hard-rock regurgitation: even *Switched on Bacharach* perpetrator Christopher Scott recorded two full albums of Bacharach-David moog-mangling without troubling this song. Its simple beauty makes it the perfect singers' showcase, except when they try to blow out all the windows of the house with their screeching (avoid Shirley Bassey's version on compact disc if you value the high end of your hearing). About the only truly eccentric rendition came from 'enry 'iggins' himself, Rex Harrison. Tenderly reciting the odd line as if wondering why a woman can't be more like a man, Rex winds up barking out the last chorus like he's about to fire the domestic help for drinking all the sherry.

Bacharach himself has two recorded versions—the largely instrumental model found on his 1965 *Hitmaker* album, which contains a different last verse for the chorale *("Please come back to me, I can't live with just a memory"),* and his first-ever lead vocal on a recording, found on the 1967 *Reach Out* album.

Bacharach can be seen and heard performing it with Dusty Springfield on one of her BBC-TV shows. Despite being encased in a ghastly pink dress and a poodle wig and surrounded by silver bubbles suspended from the studio ceiling, Dusty turns in a performance so moving that the composer bursts out singing the last chorus while passionately lurching at the keys like Ray Charles. To date it remains unreleased but can be enjoyed on an out-of-print Taragon video called *Full Circle: The Life and Music of Dusty Springfield.* About the nerve-racking experience of singing the song on live television with its composer, the late singer commented: "That took some courage. But you know you can rise to the occasion; when you think you can't do something, then you've just got to do it, 'cause it's just you and Burt Bacharach. And you'd better hit the notes. I was really proud of that...hate the hair, love the song."

Other Versions: *Monty Alexander (1969) • Gene Ammons • Burt Bacharach (1965) • Shirley Bassey (1964) • Laurie Beechman (1993) • Corry Brokken - "Ein Haus ist kein Zuhaus (1964) • Cher (1967) • Petula Clark (2000) • Anthony Coleman & the Selfhaters (1997) • Coombe Music • Perry Como (1970) • The Dells (1972) • Katja Ebstein - "Ein Haus ist kein Zuhaus" (1969) • Bill Evans Trio (1977) • Ella Fitzgerald (1970) • Georgie Fame (1970) • Film Score Orchestra • Dean Fraser • Grant Geissman (1999) • Stan Getz (1967) • Kellye Gray (1997) • Delores Hall (1979) • Beres Hammond & Derrick Lara (1995) • Rex Harrison (1978) • The Jet Set (1999) • Anita Kerr Singers (1967) • Ryo*

Kawasaki (1995) • Lainie Kazan (1968) • Steve Kuhn (1988) • Ellis Larkins • Ramsey Lewis (1983) • Longines Symphonette Society • Lulu (1969) • Marion Maerz - "Ein Haus ist kein Zuhaus" (1971) • Siw Malmqvist - "Ett Hus Är Inget Hem" (1971) • The Marbles (1969) • Marie McAuliffe (1998) • Jackie McLean (1988) • Peter Nero (1968) • Linda Purl (1998) • Nelson Rangell (1994) • Della Reese • Julie Rodgers (1965) • Rita Reys (1971) • Sonny Rollins (1974) • Joe Sample (1993) • Sheila Southern (1968) • Dusty Springfield with Burt Bacharach (TV show) (1968) • Mavis Staples (1970) • Dakota Staton (1972) • Barbra Streisand – medley (1971) • Les Surfs - "Un toit ne suffit pas" • The Three Souls (1965) • Mel Tormé with Rob McConnell & the Boss Brass (1986) • McCoy Tyner (1996) • Luther Vandross (1981, live 1989) • Sylvia Vrethammar • Dionne Warwick (1964) • Viola Wills (1994) • Stevie Wonder (1968)

"You'll Never Get to Heaven." The trademark Bacharach tack piano makes its first appearance on a Dionne record here.

"You'll Never Get to Heaven (If You Break My Heart)" (Burt Bacharach - Hal David)
First recorded by Dionne Warwick
Scepter 1282 (*Billboard* pop #34)
Released July 1964

After a flush of despondent Dionne singles, "You'll Never Get to Heaven" is a bright and deceptively cheery change of pace. Backed by a lively bossa nova beat, with tinkling chimes, harps and bells, Dionne teasingly informs her new lover that he faces eternal damnation if he breaks her heart. But the threat of being shut out of heaven only works if one is a mama's golden-rule-following girl like Dionne. Her bad beau, already hotly rumored to be a gadabout, can probably live with himself knowing he made the angels cry.

Having accepted Warwick as the queen of unrequited-love songs, the listening public seemed less willing to embrace a song where she gets the guy (on paper, at least) by song's end. That this quality 45 spent a mere three weeks in the Top 40 can be more easily attributed to the split airplay it met when numerous deejays flipped the record over for its despairing B-side, " A House Is Not a Home"—the first of Dionne's B-sides to chart in the Top 100. It's also the first of her singles with a faux-European flavor—accordions accorded equal prominence with the tack piano. Bacharach convinced Marlene Dietrich to give his discovery a slot on the tour in the fall of 1963. Once Dietrich introduced Warwick to Parisian audiences during her Olympia theater concert, she was immediately embraced by besotted French fans, who dubbed her "The Black Pearl." At the time of this single's issue, Warwick was off on a four-month European tour, for which she recorded her new single in French ("Tu n'iras pas au ciel") and German ("Ich warte jeden Tag").

The Stylistics (1972). It's a testament to the soaring falsetto of singer Russell Thompkins Jr. that he didn't need to transpose "You'll Never Get to Heaven" from its original key.

Philly-soul producer Thom Bell's love for the music of Bacharach and David was apparent to anyone who's ever played the Stylistics' "People Make the World Go Round" and Jackie DeShannon's "What the World Needs Now Is Love" back to back. Direct homage finally came when Bell and the Stylistics cut "You'll Never Get to Heaven" as the follow-up to "Break Up to Make Up" in the spring of 1974. It fared far better than Dionne's version, going to No. 23 on the pop charts and No. 8 on the R&B listings. Perhaps a wee too feminine for singer Russell Thompkins to carry off, the gentle la-la-las of the Dionne version have been replaced with minor-to-major orchestral drama and marimbas.

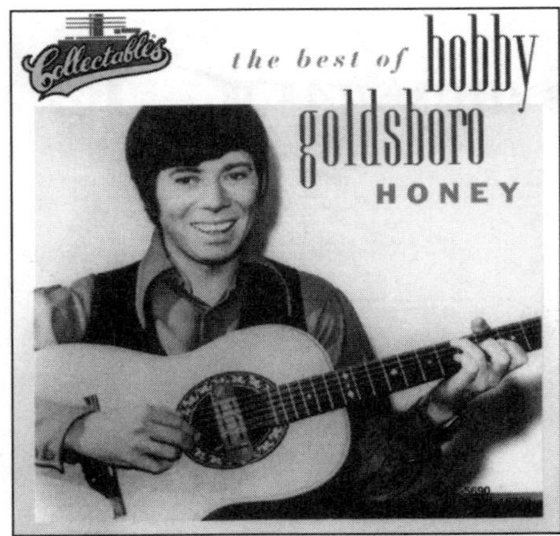

Bobby Goldsboro. "A lot of things I was writing [in 1965] were kind of influenced by Bacharach. They had a lot of chord changes and key changes. That's the kind of music I like," the singer says in the liner notes to his EMI collection *Honey: The Best of Bobby Goldsboro,* citing his 1965 ballads "If You Wait for Love" and "It Breaks My Heart" as two prime examples.

Tony Orlando. Before settling into Dawn, Tony sang lead for two other make-believe groups—Wind (who actually had a hit with a song called "Make Believe") and Cool Heat (Remember "Groovin' with Mr. Bloe"? No???).

Other Versions: *Shola Ama (2000) • Terry Baxter (1971) • Cilla Black (1969) • Joe Bourne (1993) • Frank Chacksfield (1971) • The Comets with Rosemary Scott • Aretha Franklin (1974) • Free 'n' Easy (1998• Ted Heath Orchestra • The Jet Set (1999) • Rahsaan Roland Kirk (1973) • Kiva (1998) • Les Surfs ("Tu n'iras pas au ciel") • New Direction (1969) • Sheila Southern - medley (1968) • Starlight Orchestra (1995) • The Stylistics (1972) • Gary Tesca • Cal Tjader (1969) • McCoy Tyner (1996) Dionne Warwick (rerecorded 2000)*

"Me Japanese Boy I Love You" (Burt Bacharach - Hal David)
First recorded by Bobby Goldsboro
United Artists 742 (*Billboard* pop #74)
Released July 1964

A former guitarist in Roy Orbison's backup band, Bobby Goldsboro had left the Candymen with his boss's encouragement when a song he'd written and recorded ("See the Funny Little Clown") looked like a potential hit. After Goldsboro's self-penned follow-up didn't follow through, Bacharach and David pitched him what seemed like a tailor-made song. While not quite "See the Funny Little Clown Goes to Japan," the arrangement merges an Oriental motif over a chord progression similar to the one on the earlier hit. Uniquely, no Japanese instrumentation is used—Goldsboro's 12-string acoustic guitar plays what would've been the koto line—and there are no Japanese words beyond "kimono." Any Asian exotica comes courtesy of the Old World gentility of the lyrics and a sentimental string arrangement.

Although it sounds like it was written in the style of Rodgers and Hammerstein's *Flower Drum Song*, "Me Japanese Boy I Love You" was not a movie theme. Its only tangible tie-in was the public's growing interest in Tokyo, the site of the upcoming winter Olympics. According to the singer's comments on EMI's *Best of Bobby Goldsboro* CD, the song's dashed commercial potential had something to do with the public's overriding interest in all things British. "I thought it was a great song. The record came out when the big British boom was in full blast over here. I think being such a slow soft ballad kind of got it lost in the shuffle. They were playing all the rockin' English stuff by then." Goldsboro also confirms that Bacharach produced the session, even though United Artists credited A&R man Jack Gold.

In today's politically correct climate, when Charlie Chan's flawed command of English grammar is considered a negative racial stereotype, people aren't exactly tripping over themselves to cover "Me Japanese Boy I Love You" although The Pizzicato Five proved they didn't have a problem with it back in Tokyo.

Other Versions: *Liz Damon & the Orient Express (1973) • Harpers Bizarre (1968) • Pizzicato Five*

"Accept It" (Burt Bacharach - Hal David)
First recorded by Tony Orlando
Epic 9715, flip side of "To Wait for Love"
Released August 1964

If American teen idols were yesterday's news in 1964, Tony Orlando was news from several weeks before last. Unable to vault any higher than a No. 83 chart placing since 1961, he clearly needed reinforcements. Forsaking the Gerry Goffin and Carole King team that gave Tony such early hits as "Halfway to Paradise," producer Bob Morgan summoned Bacharach and David in the hopes the duo could create the same chart magic with Orlando as they had with Bobby Vinton. Though they came through with a quality 45 on both sides, the public had already left Tony stranded "halfway to paradise." "Accept It" remains an obscure but worthy B-side, written in the smart-ass tradition of Bobby Vee songs like "Punish Her" that sound vicious and vindictive on first inspection but aren't really. Here Tony gives brotherly advice to a friend who's been rejected and replaced by another: *"Tear up all her pictures and burn them. There's no use in living in the past / Pack up all her gifts and return them / How long can a sad story last?"*

Sandie Shaw. Only Pye Records knows why they thought we'd rather have a pop-art sleeve than another sexy picture of shoeless Sandie.

One could only hope that Tony took some small comfort from Hal David's philosophical chorus, *"Accept it, accept it and don't feel dejected my friend...it's not the end"* In fact, it *was* the end for Orlando and Epic Records, although he would record one-shot singles for Atco and Cameo before returning to his 1960 *nom du disque,* Bertell Dache, and cut a final single on Diamond (with Carole King on backing vocals). He'd have a brief stint in studio-created groups like Wind and Cool Heat before settling into Dawn, then "Dawn featuring Tony Orlando," and finally "Tony Orlando and Dawn."

This song may or may not be the same "Accept It" recorded for Columbia in 1965 by the Bats, a Belfast garage band.

"(There's) Always Something There to Remind Me" (Burt Bacharach - Hal David)
First recorded by Lou Johnson
Big Hill 552 (*Billboard* pop #49)
Released August 1964

This bossa nova brought luckless Lou Johnson as close as he would ever get to a hit, and it charted significantly for Sandie Shaw, Dionne Warwick, R.B. Greaves and Naked Eyes in the Sixties, Seventies and Eighties. None of these other hit versions can match Johnson's for inconsolable regret or equal his torture when every place he happens to be reminds him of how much in love he was. Perhaps Johnson's raspy quality revealed more heartache than pop audiences were ready to hear. Contained at the end of his rendition is a sinister coda that appears on no other version, with Johnson emphatically stating over and over, "I'm never gonna love another baby," while encroaching dark strings stretch overhead like a black cloud and the background singers continue to shadooby, oblivious to his pain. The effect is chilling, like a man being condemned to death at the end of a perky pop song, Although some early cover versions (the Four Seasons, Lou Christie) hint at the original ending, even they stop short of going down that psychotic path. After Sandie Shaw had a hit with the song, hers was the model nearly everyone else followed.

Sandie Shaw (1964). Although Bacharach-David never wrote a song specifically for Sandie Shaw, she did procure several "Always Something There to Remind Me" soundalikes from other writers. The best was "Girl Don't Come," with its flugelhorn intro, light *baion* beat and despairing lyrics about being stood up for a date.

1964

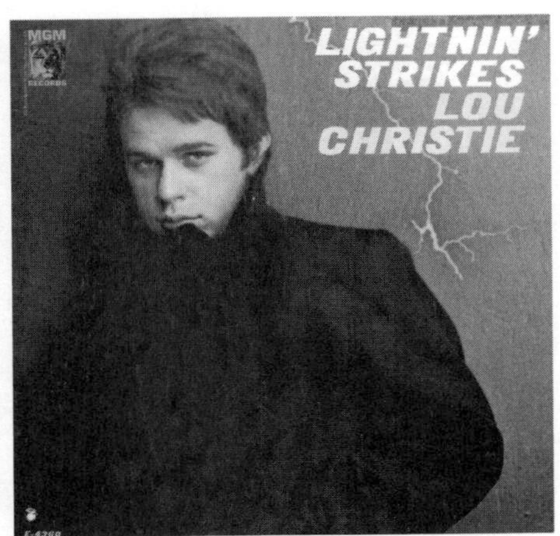

Lou Christie (1966). This album opens with Lou's version of "(There's) Always Something There to Remind Me," perhaps the most hurried version on record. It's as if he's racing to get to the end of the song before he involuntarily switches from his Jekyll midrange to his Hyde falsetto.

Prior to recording "(There's) Always Something There to Remind Me," Dagenham popstress Shaw was largely known for being incredibly photogenic and perpetually barefoot. Anxious to exploit the foot-fetish faction of the pop listening audience, Shaw's manager Eve Taylor went scouting for potential hit songs in America. Taylor imported the Bacharach-David song for her charge to premiere (barefoot, of course) on the popular Friday-night TV program *Ready Steady Go!* Rush-released in September 1964, Shaw's recording zoomed to No. 1 in the UK in three weeks time.

Oddly enough, the U.S. government is to blame for preventing Shaw's European hit from going any higher here. For reasons never disclosed, our bureaucrats decided on this moment to crack down the growing number of longhaired English rockers entering this country. Shaw and second-wave British Invaders like the Yardbirds, the Zombies, the Hullaballoos and the Nashville Teens were denied American work visas and could not appear on TV to promote their latest releases. Although the flap was a temporary one, tours had to be cancelled and Shaw's American label, Reprise, had to settle for a modest No. 52 placing.

"(There's) Always Something There to Remind Me," would achieve its greatest popularity in 1983, when the English synth duo Naked Eyes gave *"the city streets you used to walk along with me"* a mechanical, industrial clank. Despite the loud Yamaha DX7 bells and the incessant triggering of Linn drums, this recording would become a lite-rock radio staple once it became too dog-eared for modern-rock formats. Before splitting in 1984, Naked Eyes would score only one other significant modern-rock hit—ironically, a song entitled "Promises Promises" that has nothing to do with the Bacharach-David musical.

Other Versions: *Absolute Zeros (1998) • All Saints (1998) • Bel-Aires (1978) • Burt Bacharach (1965) • The Baja Marimba Band (1968) • Joe Bourne (1993) • Carpenters - medley (1971) • Casino Royale (1999) • Lou Christie (1966) • The Drifters (1973) • The Envoices (1980) • Percy Faith (1965) • Film Score Orchestra • The Four Seasons (1965) • Free'n' Easy (1998) • Jose Feliciano (1968) • Gals & Pals (1967) • Grant Geissman (1999) • R.B. Greaves (1969) • Buddy Greco (1969) • The Hippos (1999) • Don "Jake" Jacoby (1968) • Jay & the Americans• The Jet Set (1999) • Patti LaBelle & the Bluebelles (1967) • Peggy Lee (1970) • Lill Lindfors - "Alltid nat som far mig att minnas" (1967) • Longines Symphonette Society (1970) • Barbara Mason (1970) • Keff McCulloch (1996) • Anita Meyer (1989) • Eddy Mitchell - "(Il ya) Toujours un coin qui me rappelle" (1964, live 1984) • Naked Eyes (1983) • Peter Nero (1968) • New Direction - medley (1969) • Steve Newcomb Trio (2000) • Juice Newton (1997) • Sue Raney (1966) • Martha Reeves & the Vandellas (1968) • Rebecca's Empire (1998) • Renaissance (1970) • Rita Reys (1971) • Royal Marines (1974) • Steve Saxon (1977) • Leo Sayer (2000) • Christopher Scott (1970) • Sandie Shaw (1964), also German - "Einmal glücklich sein wie die andern" & Italian - "Guardavo il mondo con i tuoi occhi" • Dusty Springfield • Starlight Orchestra (1995) • Bjorn Skifs (1973) • Gary Tesca (1995) • Tin Tin Out featuring Espiritu (1995) • The Troggs • Stanley Turrentine (1968) • McCoy Tyner (1997) •Vodoo Court (2000) • Dionne Warwick (1967, rerecorded 1998) • Brian Whitman (2001) • Don Williams & the Pozo Seco Singers • Dick Zetterströms (1977)*

"Long after Tonight Is All Over" (Burt Bacharach - Hal David)
First recorded by Jimmy Radcliffe
Musicor 1042, released July, 1964

With nothing much to do on Saturday nights in the mining towns of northern England in the late Sixties, the popular pastime of playing obscure soul records in sweaty nightclubs somehow turned into an international record collecting obsession. Originally, deejays, tired of playing the popular soul records of the day, hunted for rare ones to feature. A deejay could make his reputation by snagging an acetate of an unreleased Motown song. And while this 45 by Jimmy Radcliffe actually charted in the UK Top 40, it's remained a personal favorite of Northern soul deejays to cap off an evening, which could end somewhere around 8 A.M.

Jimmy Radcliffe. Don't bother putting on your reading glasses, you won't find any of the following info on this label. The producer on this date was Bert Burns, the arranger was Burt Bacharach, and the recording manager was—Gene Pitney!

As was the case with Radcliffe's previous Bacharach-David recording, "There Goes the Forgotten Man," this tune was initially intended for Gene Pitney but found its way to his recording manager instead. Despite his energetic efforts, the record didn't chart in the U.S. With subsequent cover versions, Bacharach's arrangement took more of a "wall of sound" sheen. Dusty Springfield is at her Darlene Love-liest on her majestic retooling. Certainly worthy of single exposure, it remained a standout album track in the UK (*Everything's Coming Up Dusty*, released September 1965) and the U.S. (the *You Don't Have to Say You Love Me* LP, released 1966).

Irma Thomas' attempt, recorded August 6, 1965, at Western Studios in Hollywood, was even better—faster and filled with percussive woodblocks, triangles, furious drumming and a great husky vocal from this New Orleans belter. Sadly, it remained unreleased until EMI issued its *Best of Irma Thomas* CD in 1992. Julie Rogers' sensual attempt tries for a more contemporary feel—as contemporary as an adult could get in 1974. It's slower, with Rogers singing behind the beat and the studio musicians, particularly the bassist, overplaying as if they're getting paid by the note. It's still pretty impressive, proving that this is one Bacharach melody that leaves no room for sabotage.

Other Versions: *Dusty Springfield (1965) • Julie Rogers (1974) • Irma Thomas (recorded 1965, released 1992)*

Dusty Springfield (1965). No one flinched when pop idol Cliff Richard dubbed her "The White Negress" because her soulful voice could back up any hyperbole made on her behalf.

"The Last One to Be Loved" (Burt Bacharach - Hal David)
First recorded by Dionne Warwick
From the album *Make Way for Dionne Warwick,* Scepter 523
Released September 1964

After two albums, Scepter finally gave Dionne Warwick the star treatment. To make up for the out-of-focus, retouched-to-look-peachy photo on her debut cover and the total absence of photos on her second, there are now six pix of Dionne staring the record-buying public in the eye from behind shrink wrap. The album's title makes it clear: Dionne has arrived, in Pierre Cardin gowns no less. Not only can this young star take her R&B hits like "Walk On By" and "You'll Never Get to Heaven" into white-glove nightclubs like the Copacabana, but she also can take

Make Way for Dionne Warwick. In an era when three albums a year was the norm, Scepter Records had an easy solution to meeting the quota—just keep repeating songs! Owners of Dionne's first albums were treated to duplicates of her first two singles and their respective B-sides.

Broadway standards like "People" uptown and stop the show with it at the Apollo.

But things hadn't changed entirely. Scepter's annoying policy of padding each album with two songs from previous albums is still standard procedure, as is giving Shirelles backing tracks a third, fourth and fifth airing after Chuck Jackson, the Rocky Fellers and Tommy Hunt left their fingerprints all over them. Once you subtract the reruns, the Luther Dixon redux and the previously released single sides, you're left with only five new songs—Dionne's demo version of "(They Long to Be) Close to You," covers of "Land of Make Believe" and "Reach Out for Me," "People" and this, the only brand new Bacharach-David tune in the bunch. It's a touching song and performance, with Dionne finally finding love after being shortchanged at the receiving line for so long.

Whereas Dionne sounds mildly overanxious to be in love for the first time, Lou Johnson indeed sounds *"scared to death"* of being close to someone after so much downtime alone. After four Bacharach-David singles where love has eluded Lou, he finally gets the girl at the last possible moment—the B-side to "Kentucky Bluebird," released in October 1964. To say he's grateful would be downplaying it: he's practically frothing at the mouth at finally being kissed, caressed and blessed from above. He almost sounds psychotic, warning his new love *"If I hold you too tight and kiss your lips until you're out of breath / forgive me but I am so new at this."* Obviously, being alone all this time hasn't made him self-sufficient; as he delivers the last line, *"Without your love I know that I would [gasp] die."* What pressure that girl is in for!

Prior to this single, ending Lou Johnson's association with the Bacharach-David team, Bacharach produced and arranged a great recording of Lou singing "Ain't No Use" for a B-side that's worth hunting down (Big Hill 551).

Other Versions: *Burt Bacharach (1965) • Madeline Bell (1968) • Billie Davis • Lou Johnson (1964) • Gabor Szabo (1965)*

"How Many Days of Sadness" (Burt Bacharach - Hal David)
First recorded by Dionne Warwick
Scepter 1285, flip side of "Reach Out for Me"
Released October 1964

In the notes for *Hidden Gems*, Luther Vandross qualifies this as "easily one of my all-time favorite Dionne tracks," while Bacharach insists, "If the song had been an A-side, it might've done quite well."

This was Bacharach and David's first attempt at creating a standard gospel-style number for Dionne, with a faint hint of a string section behind the lurching piano and robust support from her fellow Gospelaires, sister Dee Dee and aunt Cissy Houston. Here Dionne summons the highest notes she's graced since "Don't Make Me Over" while questioning the lopsided ratio that allows her one day of gladness for every month of misery. Another distinguishing feature is the walls-of-Jericho trumpet solo, the like of which hasn't been heard on a Bacharach session since the Four

Aces' hymnal "Windows of Heaven" and "Miracle of St. Marie." Both producers and singer would venture further into the gospel realm on subsequent B-sides and Dionne's next long player.

"Forever Yours I Remain" (Burt Bacharach - Hal David)
Recorded by Bobby Vinton
From the album *Mr. Lonely,* Epic 24136
Released November 1964

Mr. Lonely? Certainly. But Mr. Bitter Twisted Freak? Who knew?

One doesn't expect vitriol or sarcasm from Bobby Vinton, yet this album cut proves that years of compounded blue-on-blue could turn even the Polish Prince postal, no matter how many accordions are on the session. Listen to how he accuses his tormenter in love of willfully and maliciously guffawing as she writes down the words *"forever yours I remain"* at the end of her letters—letters that appear to be the pathetic Vinton's only life source at this point. *"Oh, I'm glad I saved all of your letters, dear,"* he spews with mock happiness, stretching the word "dear" like a prosecutor closing in for the kill, *"they're all I live for / And as I read all of your love wuh-rrrrrds, I'm happy once more."* It's this same demented merriment that Vinton will bring to his 1964 Bacharach holiday single, "The Bell That Couldn't Jingle."

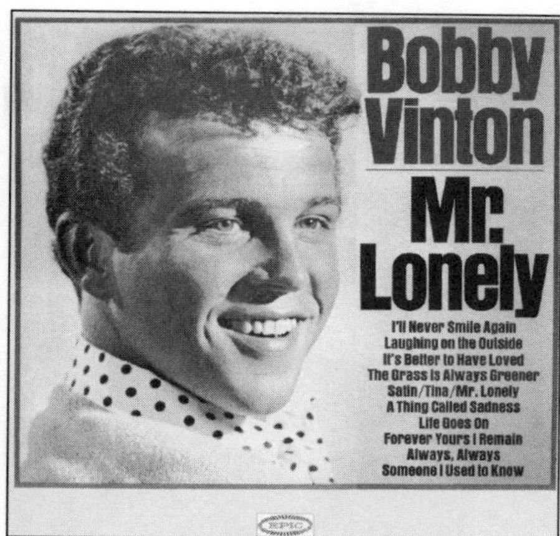

Bobby Vinton. While this album was being shipped to record emporiums, *Cashbox* had named Vinton "Best Male Vocalist of 1964" while *Billboard,* just to be different, called him "The Number One Most Popular Male Vocalist."

"Rome Will Never Leave You" (Burt Bacharach - Hal David)
Recorded by Richard Chamberlain
From the TV show *Dr. Kildare*
MGM 13285 (*Billboard* pop #99)
Released November 1964

Many a network television theme has pulled double duty as a pop hit, but this was perhaps the first instance where a song was commissioned for a specific episode of a prime-time drama. Generally, when a series goes to an exotic location with a special guest star in a two-part episode, it's a sure sign that the program is running out creative steam. Whatever the case was with the still-popular NBC TV series *Dr. Kildare*, the addition of *bellissima* eye candy like Bond girl numero due, Daniele Bianchi (dropping her *From Russia with Love* accent in fine when-in-Rome fashion), for a three-part Roman adventure couldn't have hurt ratings.

Too bad that in his fourth season as a pop recording artist, Chamberlain was as close to sleeping with the fishes as Luca Brasi. Not even the three weeks of prime-time promotion could drag this singing travel brochure any higher up the charts than No. 99. Although Bacharach and David had no trouble conjuring up the requisite Continental flavor on singles like "To Wait for Love" and "True Love Never Runs Smooth," Chamberlain's tedious tone makes the whole affair sound like a postcard from Snoresville. Arrivederci aroma!

Not heard since since the show's initial run, the song turned up again on a 1999 Universal Music/Hip-O CD entitled *The Reel Burt Bacharach.*

"Rome Will Never Leave You." Rome would never leave Richard Chamberlain, at least not the Vatican. That's where he would revisit for his second-most-popular TV role, that of Father Ralph in the miniseries *The Thornbirds.*

Send Me No Flowers. Is it a compliment to say this Bacharach and David tune holds its own alongside such other Doris Day movie themes as "Pillow Talk," "Move Over Darling" and "Please Don't Eat the Daisies?"

"Send Me No Flowers" (Burt Bacharach - Hal David)
Recorded by Doris Day
From the Universal movie *Send Me No Flowers*
Columbia 43153 (*Billboard* pop #134)
Released December 1964

Rock Hudson plays a hypochondriac who thinks he's dying, Tony Randall plays the guy Rock wants his wife to marry after he kicks the bucket, and Doris Day plays the gal who opens fire on the pair of them with a fully loaded Uzi and collects the insurance money. No, of course not!!! She plays the confused golden gal in the middle who sings the title song, a sugar-sweet confection that could've been a great Leslie Gore record if it wasn't Geritoled up with a MOR Mort Garson arrangement. Incredible as it seems, it's even less rocky on the version that plays over the credits.

"Live Again" (Burt Bacharach - Hal David)
Recorded by Irma Thomas
Imperial (unreleased), recorded January 20, 1965

The most criminal example of a Bacharach-David song not reaching its intended audience was the non-release of "Live Again." This Irma Thomas outtake, along with her shelved stab at "Long after Tonight Is All Over," embodies everything that was great about the girl-group genre—a walloping beat, a pounding piano, handclaps, finger snaps, guitars that go chick-chick, gorgeous background vocals, a lead vocal with more passion than polish and a heartache that can no longer be pretended away. Thomas resolves to have fun and paint the town red after the end of a love affair but finds herself unable to forget, regardless of how many people call her out to dance now. *"How long must I be-be with someone else when I love you?"* she wails, a tortured soul twisting her way through a party record.

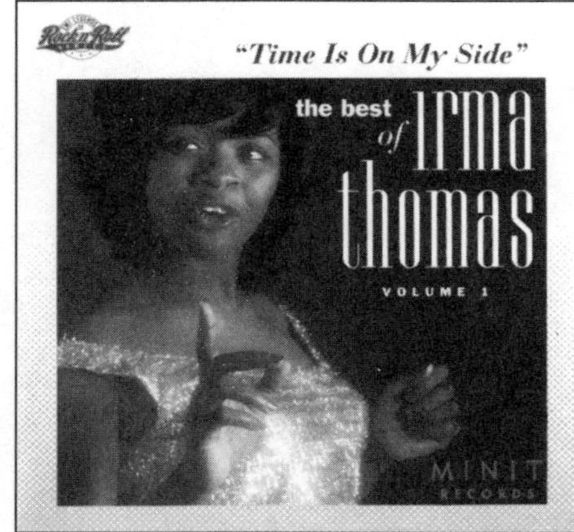

Irma Thomas. "I just had this gut feeling that my career was about to take off. I mean, I would've been up there with the Gladys Knights and Dionne Warwicks, because I was doing material equal to or better than the same stuff they were doing at that time."

How could this fantastic recording, and others of equal value, be allowed to collect dust for 27 years? In the liner notes to *Time Is on My Side: The Best of Irma Thomas*, the singer allows that bad management and poor personal judgment played an equal part. "[Those songs] were kept in the can because at the time when I did that stuff for Liberty and Imperial, there was a misunderstanding about me as an artist" the Soul Queen of New Orleans told writer Dawn Eden. "They thought I was going to be difficult to work with, when I really wasn't. I just wasn't getting good direction."

Produced by Jerry Ragovoy and recorded at Mirasound Studios in New York, "Live Again" rocks tougher than any Bacharach production at the time but the tack-piano arrangement is clearly Bacharach's touch. He would later revisit this life-of-the-party, out-on-the-town sound with a similar Jackie DeShannon track, "So Long Johnny."

Other Versions: *Jury Krytiuk Orchestra & Chorus*

"Say Goodbye" (Burt Bacharach - Hal David)
Recorded by Pat Boone
Dot 45-16707, flip side of "Baby Elephant Walk"
Released February 1965

It's hard to believe that Hal David, the guy who wrote so compassionately about former lovers unable to cope with being replaced on songs like "There Goes the Forgotten Man" and "Make It Easy on Yourself," could write a song as insensitive as "Say Goodbye." A negative image of David's future hit "To All the Girls I've Loved Before," it finds Pat Boone demanding that his girl tell all the boys she's loved before that their kissing services are no longer required: *"And even though they beg and they plead and they start to cry / You must say goodbye."* You find yourself rooting for Tim and Joe to jump Boone in a dark alley and beat him senseless for not only stealing their girl but also for changing the lyrics to "Tutti Frutti."

If Pat was trying to remedy his goody two-shoes image, it didn't work, especially since the plug side was a vocal version of Henry Mancini's "Baby Elephant Walk," announcing a lumbering new dance craze sure to invite instant public ridicule. And if the idea of Hal David using the word "groovy" in a lyric throws your universe off-center, tear this page out of the book and forget we ever had this discussion.

Pat Boone. Although Bacharach and David were writing together exclusively by 1963, the A-side of "Say Goodbye" was a Hal David–Henry Mancini collaboration that came in under the wire. Lyrics were added to the "Baby Elephant Talk" theme from the 1962 Howard Hawks film *Hatari*.

"Is There Another Way to Love You" (Burt Bacharach - Hal David)
Recorded by Dionne Warwick
Scepter 1294, flip side of "You Can Have Him"
Released February 1965

Motown, in an effort to get its artists into the ritzy supper-club circuit, had its vocal groups record more adult fare for the album market. But Motown would never endanger its bread and butter by releasing the Supremes' showstopping rendition of "Somewhere" (from *West Side Story*) as a 45. Scepter had more flexibility with its glitter girl because as a solo artist she was competing in a different arena, with people like Barbra Streisand and Tony Bennett. Besides commissioning an entire album of Dionne singing ballads and standards, Scepter released two non–B&D songs in rapid succession as singles. The first, Dionne's remake of Roy Hamilton's "You Can Have Her," is said to be one of her least favorite recordings of all time, as she has never performed it live. Recorded at Pye Studios in England, with the Breakaways substituting for Dee Dee Warwick and Cissy Houston, Bacharach's high-energy arrangement of "You Can Have Her" sounds more like a Broadway pit orchestra's translation of gospel music than the real thing as seamlessly captured on "How Many Days of Sadness."

The flip of "You Can Have Him" also has a show-tune feel: the furious piano triplets are reminiscent of the *Perry Mason* TV theme. Bacharach packs three meandering movements into the two minutes and 31 seconds of "Is There Another Way to Love You," and the song flows effortlessly until it's time to return to the triplet chorus. You can feel the band slowing down to keep from racing ahead of the changes. By the time

"Only the Strong, Only the Brave." The French manage to capture Dionne with her natural 'fro, while her hair would continue to be straightened on sleeves for years to come.

the song retards for the big finish, it sounds like a winded runner collapsing from exhaustion. It's one of the earliest examples of a Bacharach song where an ambitious structure threatens to overshadow Hal David's lyrics, which beg for guidance in alternate methods of demonstrating neediness and devotion. Clearly, the customary despairing and pleading to be wanted don't seem to be working for this adult contemporary.

Other Versions: *Tony Blackburn (1966)*

"Don't Say I Didn't Tell You So" (Burt Bacharach - Hal David)
First recorded by Dionne Warwick
Scepter 1298, flip side of "Who Can I Turn To?"
Released February 1965

The success of "People" as a concert showstopper insured that every album from here on would feature at least one Broadway standard. "Who Can I Turn To?" the Anthony Newley showstopper from *The Roar of the Greasepaint—The Smell of the Crowd* that had recently beeb a pop hit for Tony Bennett, proved marginally less successful this time around done by Dionne, although it surprisingly charted higher on the R&B listings than the up-tempo "You Can Have Him."

Providing familiar turf on the reverse side was this elegant redressing of "Walk On By," with spiteful wishes for comeuppance to an ex-lover. Dionne sweetly coos that he'll wish he was back with her after his new love puts him down. *"And she will do everything that you did to me / And she will cheat and tell you lies that you'll believe / While she's laughing up her sleeve / As you gave, you'll receive."* As if to demonstrate what sleeve-laughing sounds like, Dionne squawks along with a muted trumpet, clearly taking pleasure in some hard-won retribution after already having being wronged on countless other records.

In an attempt to update Petula Clark's sound after Tony Hatch stopped being her arranger, the singer was shipped off to American Studios in Memphis à la Dusty Springfield in 1970 and to Criteria Studio in Miami in 1971. The latter resulted in *Warm and Tender,* her final album for Warner Brothers, which featured some underwhelming soul excursions but a fine Arif Mardin arrangement of "Don't Say I Didn't Tell You So" sans squawking trumpets.

Other Versions: *Petula Clark (1971) • Herbie Mann*

The Sensitive Sounds of Dionne Warwick. The first Dionne album not relying on past hits didn't spawn any hits of its own but does contains such superlative performances as "How Many Days of Sadness," "Forever My Love" and "Wives and Lovers."

"Only the Strong, Only the Brave" b/w "That's Not the Answer" (Burt Bacharach - Hal David)
Recorded by Dionne Warwick
From the album *The Sensitive Sounds of Dionne Warwick,* Scepter 528
Released March 1965

Dionne Warwick's fourth album was a departure on several counts.

Meant to reel in the segment of the record buying public that snapped up Barbra Streisand albums but eschewed pop 45s, *The Sensitive Sounds of Dionne Warwick* seems purposefully devoid of hit singles. This album also marked the end of Scepter's practice of padding out Dionne's albums with previously released cuts, demos and stray Ludix Productions. For the first time, every note of a Dionne Warwick album was arranged and conducted by Burt Bacharach, and produced by Bacharach and David. Curiously, its grooves are populated with some of the team's least remembered songs, save for a sassy remake of "Wives and Lovers."

Together. Two of the ten songs on this Pitney-sings-Bacharach-and-David collection had nothing to do with either Bacharach or David. "Baton Rouge or Frisco" had lyrics by Larry Kusic of "The Bell That Couldn't Jingle" fame, while the George Tobin/Johnny Cymbal song "Somewhere in the Country" was Gene's most recent single. Why couldn't Pitney just cover "What the World Needs Now" like everyone else? Oh, the shame of it!

The previous three B-sides found their final resting place here, as did two songs that seemed to have escaped coverage by any other singers. Without a Shirelles outtake thrown into the mix this time around, "That's Not The Answer" is a gentle throwback to the ska-da-ska-da days of 1961, and Dionne soft inflections sound as if she's filling in for Shirley Owens on maternity leave again. There is a prominent but brief lead guitar line that one doesn't expect to hear on a Bacharach arrangement, a direct result of the composer recording the bulk of this album at Pye Studios in England and using British musicians instead of his usual crew.

"Only the Strong, Only the Brave" is yet another superb song, so typical of Bacharach-David and so untypical of everyone else. Who else would marry such a carefree melody with a deadly awareness of all the pain and heartache that lies in wait for people who love and dream *("When you reach out for a star, people pull you down)*? Hal David's positive message of "no pain, no gain" would turn up again in songs like "Alfie" and "In Between the Heartaches," while "Only the Strong, Only the Brave" would turn up again later the same year supporting the strong and brave 45 "Looking with My Eyes, Seeing with My Heart."

"Fool Killer" (Burt Bacharach - Hal David)
Recorded by Gene Pitney
From the album *Big Sixteen, Volume Two,* Musicor 3043
Released February 1965

Gene Pitney. Only two of Gene's *Big Sixteen, Volume Two* selections were hits of any size, but the album does contain two must-own Bacharach-David tracks, "Little Betty Falling Star" and the evocative "Fool Killer."

No other male singer enjoyed as much access to first-run Bacharach-David songs and shared as much chart success with the duo as did Gene Pitney. Who could've anticipated that "Fool Killer" would be the last time Pitney would work with Bacharach and David? A misunderstanding between the composers and Pitney's publisher/manager Aaron Schroeder ensued and the song never made it into the film of the same title. As Pitney comments in Rhino's *The Look of Love* collection, "Something went terribly wrong with 'Fool Killer.' I think it was proposed to Burt and Hal that the song was a done deal for the film and the film people were told it was a done deal with But and Hal...or something like that. The relationship between Bacharach and David and Schroeder soured. Because I was signed to Schroeder, this put a wedge in our relationship and things were never the same."

It's doubtful this dream-like parable about a runaway orphan who suspects that his giant friend is a mythical ax murderer would've seen as much chart action as "The Man Who Shot Liberty Valance," but surely it deserved a wider audience than just the Pitney fans who'd stick around

1965

Billy J. Kramer. In the Eighties, EMI released an album called *The Songs Lennon and McCartney Gave Away.* No one had more songs on it than Billy J—a whopping five. By the time "Trains and Boats and Planes" passed by, he was virtually Dakota-less.

for an album of leftover hits like *Gene Pitney's Big Sixteen, Volume Two.* Hal David's mysterious lyrics tell of a wandering boy wise beyond his years who is a lot like you but is later revealed to be the singer. The song is lyrically reminiscent of Nat "King" Cole's hit "Nature Boy," and the arrangement for "Fool Killer" makes similar use of the earlier tune's wandering flute, while Bacharach substitutes a shimmering tremolo guitar where the trance-inducing harp used to be. Pitney cited this as his favorite of the Bacharach-David tracks he cut, and if one follows the progression of the trio's work together, it's more than a trifle disappointing that publishing politics and pride killed off a winning combination so unlike the one the songwriting team enjoyed with Dionne Warwick.

It's widely known that Bacharach and David penned "Trains and Boats and Planes" and "What the World Needs Now" for Pitney, who was forced to find other avenues for his singing talent. In 1965, he would record several duet albums with country music stars (and Musicor recording artists) George Jones and Melba Montgomery, songs by the then-unknown Randy Newman and several foreign language albums. While his international popularity never flagged, Pitney's status as a hit-maker in the U.S. never fully recovered the loss of Bacharach and David's material.

"Trains and Boats and Planes" (Burt Bacharach - Hal David)
First recorded by Burt Bacharach
Kapp 657, flip side of "Don't Go Breaking My Heart"
Released May 1965

"Burt played me [a] song, and I listened to it and I don't know what I said to him after. I'm glad I don't remember, I said something like, 'Aah, it's all right but it's not one of your better ones.' Something like that. And the song was called 'Trains and Boats and Planes.' I must've had allergies like I've got today, that must be the thing that messed up my head," laughs Gene Pitney in a 2001 BBC radio interview aired prior to the Bacharach-David tribute concert at Albert Hall. "It's a wonderful song."

The travel motif of the song seemed to fit Bacharach's new jet-setting pace, as he began to spend most of his time in Europe—working, living with his new wife Angie Dickinson, conducting concerts with Marlene Dietrich and recording in England, the new Brill Building as far as the pop charts were concerned. He'd cut the bulk of *The Sensitive Sounds of Dionne Warwick* at Pye Studios in London the previous November when the singer was in the midst of a UK tour. In addition, Kapp Records wanted him to record an instrumental album of hits he'd written for other people. *Hit Maker!* contained two brand new songs not yet covered by anyone, which made them perfect candidates for a Burt Bacharach single. In England, where "Trains" was the designated A-side, Bacharach had a Top 4 hit, which pushed the British *Hit Maker!* album into the Top 5 as well.

The distorted electric piano that opens the song was not meant as homage to Ray Charles' "What'd I Say" but was one consequence of working in English recording studios, which Bacharach considered substandard. Although he imported engineer Phil Ramone to run the antiquated board, the rest of the personnel on the *Hit Maker!* sessions were British, including the three breathy vocalists—Barbara Moore, Gloria George and Margaret Stredder—who called themselves the Breakaways.

The British equivalent of the Blossoms, the Breakaways were the most frequently hired session singers in England at that time, doing everything from television work to ghosting behind the Jimi Hendrix Experience on that group's first single, "Hey Joe." Their dispassionate delivery blends perfectly with Hal David's haunted verses, which give all the responsibility for coming and going to the transportation and not the passengers. Like the elements in David's earliest hit, "The Four Winds and the Seven Seas," trains, boats and planes are capable of bringing back someone they took away, if the person left behind prays hard enough for their return.

Bacharach—*The Man!* The first reissue of *Hit Maker!* occurred in October 1965 with the addition of "What's New Pussycat?" and "My Little Red Book" and a title that differentiates the hit maker from...*The Man!* Bacharach's future co-writer would rehash this pompous title for his first hits collection *The Best of Elvis Costello—The Man.*

It's only at the bridge where we learn that the person so grievously missed on the other side of the world promised to return again and that his/her failure to do so must be the fault of some stubborn tug or passenger jet. When the song's bridge demands the kind of passion that would shatter the Breakaways' cool demeanor, an orchestral release ensues instead, which meant that most inadequate singers used this opportunity to sip at a beverage. There's a face-saving Merseybeat guitar solo on the competing disc by Billy J. Kramer, not the most talented of Brian Epstein's NEMS stable of artists. Usually he had to be triple-tracked before producer George Martin could announce, "That's a take," over the studio intercom.

Kramer discovered the song after his fellow Mancunians Four Just Men recorded the song but shelved it when they were dissatisfied with the results. Kramer's version topped out at No. 47 in the States, but no one would hear the *"You are from another part of the world"* bridge until Dionne Warwick covered it the following year, taking it as high as No. 22. As a rule, female singers like Alma Cogan, Joanie Sommers and Anita Harris follow Warwick's lead and tackle that tricky terrain, while male singers just watch it pass by.

Bacharach—The Woman. Kapp's second reissue of *Hit Maker!* came in 1969 with the same contents as *The Man!* and the addition of a lady in red on the cover. It was this edition that Austin Powers took with him in his 1967 time capsule.

Meanwhile on the other side of the Thames, Claude François' French translation, "Quand un bateau passe," would take the trains and the planes out of the equation completely, but the Royal Marines broke ranks and gave air and ground troops equal time!

Other Versions: *Apollo 100 (1973) • Chet Baker & the Carmel Strings (1966) • Les Baronics (2000) • Terry Baxter (1971) • Brass Band of the Japanese Air Defense Force • Jacqui Brookes (1984) • Joe Bourne (1993) • Caravelli • Frank Chacksfield (1971) • Alma Cogan (1965) • The Dells (1972) • Carl Doy • Dumb Earth (1998) • the Everly Brothers (1967) • Fleshquartet (Flaskkvartetten) - "Tag and Flyg and Bat" (1998) • Connie Francis (1968)• Claude François ("Quand un bateau passe" (1965) • Fred Frith (1997) • Gals & Pals (1966) • Stan Getz (1967) • Astrud Gilberto (1969) • Anita Harris • Hajime Iiyoshi - "Trains" • Tony Hatch Orchestra • The Jet Set (1999) • Dan Kibler (1998) • Billy J. Kramer & the Dakotas (1965, rerecorded 1986) • Marion Maerz - "Frag doch nur dein Herz " (1971) • Marie McAuliffe (1998) • Keff McCulloch (1996) • Missing Fortnight (1994) • Nana Mouskouri - "Wer hat das gewollt" • Mystic Moods Orchestra • New Direction - "Tribute medley" (1969) • Peter Nero (1968) • Vasso Ovale - "Treni, navi, aerrei" • Royal Marines (1974) • Sanchez • Christopher Scott (1970) • Wally Scott Chorale (1968) • The Shadows (1980) • Dinah Shore (1967) • Joanie Sommers (1967) • Sheila*

Southern (1968) • Starlight Orchestra (1995) • Starsound Orchestra • Billy Strange (1965) • Telstars (1965) • Gary Tesca (1995) • Caterina Valente - "Bacharach medley" (1971) • Dionne Warwick (1966) • Wrong Corpses (2000)

Burt Bacharach. The composer of "Trains and Boats and Planes" thought the song was "too country" for Dionne Warwick but she'd eventually have the biggest hit with it in America. In England, it was the composer's highest ever charting as a recording artist.

"Don't Go Breaking My Heart" (Burt Bacharach - Hal David)
First recorded by Burt Bacharach
Kapp 657, released March 1965

Contrast the popularity of "Trains and Boats and Planes" and the *Hit Maker!* album in England to the U.S., where Bacharach was still known as "Burt who?" The U.S. version of *Hit Maker!* sold roughly 5,000 copies, and the single of "Don't Go Breaking My Heart" didn't have any chart impact.

As we've already seen, so much of what came out of the Brill Building in the early Sixties was set to the *baion* beat, and Bacharach's burgeoning catalog was not exempt. But no one at 1619 Broadway had yet dared go *this* Brazilian, putting the kettledrums and strings away and bringing the nylon-stringed guitars way up in the mix. This relaxed samba was Bacharach's most Jobim-inspired meditation yet, with the tack piano thrown in to add Burt's distinctive signature. Once more the Breakaways are out front, softly insisting not to have their hearts broken but sounding more like beauties concerned with not getting their tanning session interrupted. Their Astrud-Gilberto-in-triplicate sound surely must've inspired Sergio Mendes circa 1965 to get Brasil '66 up and running: it's no small compliment to Bacharach's imagination that both Gilberto and Mendes quickly covered the song.

Dionne Warwick came to the tune a year later, sticking closely to the *Hit Maker!* cyanotype. Quite the reverse held true for Aretha Franklin, whose disco blowout of the song, included on her 1974 album *With Everything I Feel in Me*, is virtually unrecognizable from the original melody. Unlike her high-charting 1968 redo of "I Say a Little Prayer," this was one Aretha B-side that remained undisturbed on many jukeboxes.

Other Versions: *Yasuko Agawa (1996) • Herb Alpert & the Tijuana Brass (1966) • Terry Baxter (1971) • Caravelli • Syd Dale • Aretha Franklin (1974) • Astrud Gilberto (1969) • Tony Hatch Orchestra • Jack Jones • Marion Maerz - "Nimm nicht alles so schwer" (1971) • Johnny Mathis (1967) • Paul Mauriat (1976) • Sergio Mendes & Brasil '66 (1966) • Roger Nichols & the Small Circle of Friends (1968) • Marc Ribot Ensemble (1997) • Doc Severinsen (1966) • Shoko Suzuki (1994) • Dionne Warwick (1966) • The Wondermints (1998)*

Jackie DeShannon. Contracted to cut two sides with her, Bacharach and David came up with "What the World Needs Now Is Love" and "A Lifetime of Loneliness." The latter tune, intended as the B-side but instead issued as the follow-up single, rose to No. 66.

"What the World Needs Now Is Love" (Burt Bacharach - Hal David)
First recorded by Jackie DeShannon
Imperial 66110 (*Billboard* pop #7)
Released April 1965

"The unlimited vocal talent of Jackie DeShannon delivers the message as it was meant to be delivered." *Billboard* ad, 1965

On one memorable occasion, Dionne Warwick turned down a Bacharach-David tune and lived to regret it more than Gene Pitney regretted dismissing "Trains and Boats and Planes." Originally written for Gene but never shown to him, "What the World Needs Now" was presented to Dionne during the sessions for her *Sensitive Sounds* album, presumably in its original Pitney mode. After Warwick declined it for sounding "too country," it sat collecting dust for ten months until Jackie DeShannon took a shine to it.

As Bacharach recalled in a 2000 BBC radio interview: "I thought, wow, if Dionne doesn't like it, I don't think the song can be so good. And I put it in the drawer. When we were going to record Jackie DeShannon, Hal said, 'C'mon, play that song.' Jackie sang it in the studio—big hit! If Jackie hadn't walked in, if Hal hadn't said play that song, there may never have been a song called "What the World Needs Now Is Love." Maybe. Maybe not. But there's always a chance."

Jackie DeShannon. "What The World Needs Now Is Love" was actually not the singer's biggest hit. She wrote a universal love anthem called "Put a Little Love in Your Heart" that rose to No. 4 in the summer of '69.

It's doubtful that Hal David would've allowed "What the World Needs Now," the first of his "message" songs, to languish unheard forever. In his book of prose entitled *What the World Needs Now and Other Love Lyrics*, he states that this lyric had the longest gestation period of any of his songs. "I had thought of the idea at least two years before showing it to Burt. Then one day, I thought of 'Lord, we don't need another mountain,' and all at once I knew how the lyric should be written."

An account by Timi Yuro in David Freeland's 1999 book *Ladies of Soul* provides evidence that Bacharach hadn't let the song sit in a drawer before showing it to Jackie DeShannon. A few days after she opened at New York's prestigious Copa, Yuro says that Bacharach played her the song. "And I started singing it and he said 'No, I want you to sing [beats hands on the table to accent every word], "What...the...world...needs...now."' And I said 'Oh, go fuck yourself,' and I left his office. And I blew that song. It was out a few weeks later with Jackie DeShannon."

Arthur Fiedler. When the conductor of the Boston Pops depicts himself morphing into our blue earth and calls his album "What the World Needs Now Is Love," it can only really mean one thing—Come to Papa!

It probably helped that DeShannon was an accomplished hit composer in her own right (notably "Whenever You Walk in the Room" for the Searchers and "Come and Stay with Me" for Marianne Faithfull) and could look at the number as an objective peer. Once she became sufficiently enthused about its chances, Bacharach quickly booked a session at Bell Studios with the usual crew, including Cissy Houston on background vocals, and voila, the record was a monster! DeShannon's hesitant accents on "what the world" and her soulful woe-woahs on the chorus sounds as if she's genuinely empathetic about the corresponding lack of "love sweet love" in a world well stocked with mountains, wheat fields, oceans and meadows. Bacharach and David's first stab at a protest song is a gentle one: only the background-vocal-and-kettledrum buildup that starts at two minutes and 35 seconds conveys any sense of anger about the long wait for universal love. After that, the record ends as it began, with that sad little tuba riff, to remind listeners that if they continue to withhold love, the waiting might never end.

While DeShannon's recording never fails to move listeners' hearts, the well-over-100 cover versions (not counting the countless school marching band and karaoke massacres) seem to have drained all the

Tom Clay (1971). Clay's only previous record was a cash-in Beatles interview 45 where he received some pithy insults from John Lennon. Wonder if he asked him "What is prejudice?"

urgency out of the lyrics. Almost none can be classified as essential, and most can be filed under Dull (Johnny Mathis, Gals & Pals, Anita Kerr), Sanctimonious (Ed Ames) or Irreverent (Do you really need to hear Tiny Tim flailing it on a ukulele?). Even those artists who can usually be counted on for superlative Bacharach-David cover versions don't even try. Tom Jones' hip-swiveling version is just as unnecessary as Tony Bennett's hyped-up swing-band version. Another reason it's difficult to approach this anthem with fresh ears is that it has turned into Bacharach's signature song, the number the house band strikes up whenever he walks on stage to tumultuous applause, a song as synonymous with Bacharach's celebrity as it is with "love sweet love."

Perhaps the most blatant attempt to wring social significance out of the song came in 1971, when KGBS Los Angeles deejay Tom Clay created a six-minute-and-ten-second sound collage, superimposing sound bites of boot-camp drills, the Kennedy assassinations, Martin Luther King's "I Have a Dream" speech and Clay's quizzing of a preschooler on the subject of bigotry and prejudice over a schlocky Vegas medley of "What the World Needs Now" and Dion's "Abraham, Martin and John" (glibly sung by the Blackberries). This odd recording song was issued on MoWest, Motown's West Coast label, and its rise to No. 8 was thankfully blocked from going further by more reasonable pleas for social reform from the Detroit parent label, like Marvin Gaye's "Mercy Mercy Me" and Undisputed Truth's "Smiling Faces Sometimes."

With no small bit of resentment, Dionne Warwick watched her producers take the Dionne Warwick formula to Jackie DeShannon and have a huge hit with it. The version she'd record on her 1967 album *Here Where There Is Love* is cited by Hal David as his favorite of all the recorded versions, but coming as late as it did, it couldn't help but seem a lesser event, like the second man to walk on the moon. Dionne has performed the song ever since with a kind of implied ownership and would continue her association with the song in 1998. An outspoken opponent of the anti–love-sweet-love message of gangster rap, she voiced her objections in congressional hearings. With the help of her son, rap producer Damon Elliot, she organized a posse of rappers, including Big Daddy Kane, Bobby Brown and Coolio, to help her spread a more positive message of unity than West Coast vs. East Coast. The resulting single of "What the World Needs Now Is Love" by Dionne Warwick and the Hip Hop Nation United appeared to be a charity record à la "That's What Friends Are For" (the title of which is even invoked by one of the emcees) but this recording was only meant to raise awareness. At the very least, it got people like Big Daddy Kane to call Dionne "mom."

Forever his concert opener, the song would be reprised by Bacharach in two recorded versions. For the 1967 *Reach Out* album, it's fleshed out in choral and orchestral fashion, breaking momentarily into a jazz waltz. Thirty years later, his simple voice-and-piano rendition bookended a fine space-age bachelor pad/psychedelic version by the Posies, found on the first *Austin Powers* soundtrack.

Other Versions: *Barbara Acklin (1968) • Yasuko Agawa (1996) • Ronnie Aldrich (1971) • Ed Ames (1969) • Ray Anthony • Apollo 100 (1973) • Burt Bacharach (1967) • Burt Bacharach & the Posies (1997) • Nick Bariluk (1996) • Fontella Bass (1995) • Terry Baxter (1971) • Madeline Bell (1968) • Tony Bennett (1969) • Tony Bennett with the*

London Philharmonic Orchestra (1971) • Rita Bettis (1970) • Big Youth - "Hit the Road Jack" contains "What the World Needs Now" (1976) • Cilla Black (1968) • Joe Bourne (1993) • Karen Briggs (1996) • James Brown (1976) • James Brown & Vicki Anderson (1968) • Casino Royale (1999) • Lee Castle & the Jimmy Dorsey Orchestra (1974) • Frank Capp (1978) • The Chambers Brothers (1967) • Ray Charles Singers (1967) • Petula Clark (1974) • Tom Clay - "What the World Needs Now/Abraham, Martin & John" (1971) • Lynn Collins • Ray Conniff (1967) • Count Buffalo Big Band • Floyd Cramer • Sammy Davis Jr. & Burt Bacharach (TV, 1973) • Sammy Davis Jr. & Buddy Rich (1966) • Carl Doy • Katja Ebstein - "Soviel Liebe fehlt" (1970) • 18th Century Corporation (1969) • Enoch Light (1969) • Ferrante & Teicher (1969) • Johnny Fiamma (of the Muppets) (1997) • Arthur Fiedler & the Boston Pops (1969) • Film Score Orchestra • The Four Seasons (1965) • Connie Francis (1968) • Bill Frisell (1997) • Gals & Pals (1967) • Grant Geissman (1999) • Stan Getz (1967) • Ron Goodwin (1972) • Don Goldie (1977) • Dave Graney & the Dirty Three (1998) • Buddy Greco (1967) • Wayne Henderson (1969) • Lena Horne (1966) • Hullabaloo Singers & Orchestra • Ivory Joe Hunter • Sheila Hutchinson - Bacharach medley • Mahalia Jackson (1970) • The Jet Set (1999) • Samuel Jonathan Johnson (1978) • Pete Jolly (1969) • Jack Jones (1966) • Tom Jones (1970) • Anita Kerr Singers (1969) • John Klemmer Quartet (1968) • Ellis Larkins • Yank Lawson & Bob Haggart (1970) • Michele Lee (1967) • Lennon Sisters • Ramsey Lewis (1975) • J.C. Lodge (1997) • Johnny Mann Singers • Tony Mansell Singers (1970) • Mantovani Orchestra • Johnny Mathis (1966) • Peter Matz • Tommy McCook & the Supersonics • Keff McCulloch (1996) • Sergio Mendes & Brasil '66 (1969 • Anita Meyer (1989) • Mulgrew Miller (1988) • Mr. Bungle • Modern Barbershop Quartet (1974) • Rita Monico - "Quando tu vorrai" • Wes Montgomery (1966) • Peter Nero (1968) • New Christy Minstrels (1966) • Steve Newcomb Trio (2000) • New Direction - medley (1969) • Del Newman • Houston Person (1967) • Trudy Pitts (1967) • Duke Reid • Renaissance (1970) • Rita Reys (1969) • Rock Academy String Quartette (1970) • Diana Ross (1994) • Royal Marines (1974) • RTE Concert Orchestra/Richard Hayman (1995) • Ruby & the Romantics • Sceptres • SCLC Operation Breadbasket Orchestra & Choir (1970) • Christopher Scott (1969) • Shirley Scott (1966) • Doc Severinsen (1969) • Bud Shank with Chet Baker (1966) • George Shearing • Arthur Smith • Billie Jo Spears • Starlight Orchestra • Keith Textor Singers • Sheila Southern (1968) • Billy Strange (1965) • Les Surfs - "Quando tu vorrai, vorrai l'amor" • Diana Ross & the Supremes (1968) • Starlight Orchestra (1995) • Sweet Inspirations (1968) • Gary Tesca (1995) • Keith Textor Singers (1970) • Carla Thomas (1966) • Tiny Tim (1969) • Cal Tjader (1968) • Stanley Turrentine (1967) • McCoy Tyner (1996) • Leslie Uggams (1969) • Caterina Valente - medley (1971) • Louis Van Dyke Trio • Luther Vandross (1994, live medley 1998) • Sarah Vaughan (1966) • Sylvia Vrethammar - "Vad Varlden Behover Ar Karleken" (1969) • Dionne Warwick (1967) • Dionne Warwick & the Hip Hop Nation United (1998) • Lawrence Welk (1976) • Tony Joe White • Hugo Winterhalter • Klaus Wunderlich

Hip Hop Nation United (1998). It didn't stop gangsta rap, but it probably accelerated Coolio's relegation to the old-school section of the rap library faster than starring on a WB sitcom.

"What's New Pussycat?" (Burt Bacharach - Hal David)
First recorded by Tom Jones
From the United Artists movie *What's New Pussycat?*
Parrot 9765 (*Billboard* pop #3)
Released June 1965

Tom Jones. He changed his name and nose in search of fame! The rhinoplasty came later but it was just a formality, as tussles in the tough pubs and streets of Pontypridd, Wales, slowly worked away at Thomas Jones Woodward's noggin anyway!

Producer Charles K. Feldman (*A Streetcar Named Desire, The Seven Year Itch, Walk on the Wild Side*) was in London searching for a composer to score his next property, a comic screenplay by a writer new to films, Woody Allen. A chance encounter with Angie Dickinson at the Dorchester Hotel led to Feldman hiring Burt Bacharach for his first-ever film soundtrack. Bacharach's inexperience at film scoring caused him to

"What's New Pussycat?" The U.S. picture sleeve for Jones' 45 of this randy theme used a different Frank Frazetta design than the one that adorned the movie poster and soundtrack cover. It features a cartoon Peter O'Toole balancing himself on Capucine's and Romy Schneider's breasts while Woody Allen stands on Eddra Gale's face. Woah woah woah, indeed!

leave a lot of the work to the last minute. "When I finally got into it and learned what I was supposed to do, it was probably two and a half to three weeks. I was really under the gun because I was walking around the park wondering what I was gonna do because I didn't have a clue. Not a clue. I must've gone in with 40 different themes and recorded them, different sequences in the movie. I didn't know how to score a picture. And then afterwards Charlie Feldman fell in love with the title song and he took out all these pieces I'd written and stuck in instrumental versions of "What's New Pussycat?" Cop it from here, put it in there. I got really upset. I wanted to take my name off the picture. I was married to Angie at the time and she said, 'Don't be a fool, this picture's going to be a huge hit.' So I was glad I listened to her."

Originally the role of sex-addicted fashion magazine editor Michael James was to be played by Warren Beatty. Disgusted with Allen's script revisions that reduced his screen time, he backed out, but not before providing the film with its title. "What's new, pussycat?" was Beatty's stock phone greeting for his numerous female callers.

As for viable candidates to sing the hurdy-gurdy waltz Bacharach dreamed up, the composers didn't have to look very hard. They'd profited very handsomely from having "To Wait for Love" on the flip of "It's Not Unusual," a No. 1 hit in England with sales of 800,000 in just four weeks. Jones, teeming with volcanic sexuality, seemed the perfect choice to sing this sex maniac's theme. He, however, was less than thoroughly convinced this was a positive career move and told his manager, Gordon Mills, that it didn't seem right for him, that it sounded like "a Humpty Dumpty song." As Jones recounted in Colin MacFarlane's biography *Tom Jones: The Boy from Nowhere*, "My attitude wasn't wide enough then to see that it could be a direct contrast and a breakthrough. I thought it would be a miss." Bacharach allayed Jones' fears about the song and coached him through the midnight-to-4: 30-A.M. recording session. Jones came out of the experience claiming that the composer "had me singing better than I'd ever done before."

What's New, Pussycat? Jones, also a horse racing enthusiast, would name his first horse Walk on By in Bacharach's honor. Perhaps naming it Pussycat would only have confused the filly.

The public had no problems sending yet another Bacharach jazz waltz into *Billboard*'s Top 10. On July 27, "What the World Needs Now" peaked at No. 7, while the frisky "Pussycat" peaked at No. 2, just behind the Rolling Stones' sexually frustrated anthem "(I Can't Get No) Satisfaction." In an interview with the National Guard radio service, Bacharch commented, "A 3/4 thing—so what? Nobody said, '"What's New Pussycat?"—can you dance to it in discothèques?' They found a way if they wanted to move on the floor and it still turned into a giant hit."

Jones himself wouldn't have the same problem promoting "What's New Pussycat?" as he did with "It's Not Unusual." In a 1995 interview with this writer, Jones recalls "The pop programs [in England] used to come on in the afternoon at children's hour. I was on a show called *Blue Peter,* which sounds like a frozen dick. Parents wrote in and said I was too raunchy for children's hour." The BBC, which actually banned "It's Not Unusual," put up no resistance to "Pussycat," even with the "P" word. But, as Jones laughs in his rich Welsh bellow, "I don't think that term was used then."

The version Tom Jones growls in the film has a lengthier intro than the 13-second one on the soundtrack and single that ends with a shattered glass. The movie version also has a different vocal take. Subsequent reissues of the 45 lopped off the intro, as did some U.S. deejays, intent on keeping the song at 2:04 instead of an extravagant 2:20.

Bacharach rearranged the song in several ways for the score (see the entry for the *What's New Pussycat?* original soundtrack album), but he would also record another vocal version with Joel Grey and release it under his own name on the flip of his next Kapp single. Compared to Jones, Grey sounds like a meek little mouse, as did nearly everyone else who tried to follow the Welsh wonder. Oddly enough, another Kapp recording artist, the Do-Re-Mi Children's Chorus, would cover this lascivious-sounding number without even a word change, and no one batted an eye.

Woah Woah Woah-A-Go-Go? You really know you've got a hit song when the Chipmunks come gnawing at it. Although they turned some heads with their *Chipmunks a Go-Go* album, no one could've suspected they'd jump on the hippie bandwagon three years later, rerecording their classic "Christmas Song" with...Canned Heat?!!

Other notable cover versions include Bob Marley and the Wailers' 1966 ska take, which must've driven Bacharach crazy, since it retains the chords of the chorus for the verse (at least it had a tack piano). And for her first-ever Bacharach cover, Barbra Streisand sang a snippet of the song to a tiger during her *Color Me Barbra* TV special. Several foreign versions, like those by Richard Anthony, Gus Backus and Klaus Wunderlich, felt compelled to change the greeting to "Hallo Pussycat" or "Ciao Pussycat."

Despite largely unfavorable reviews, the movie became the biggest-grossing comedy up to that time. Woody Allen intensely disliked the way his script was changed through rampant ad-libbing by the actors and director Clive Donner, but he nonetheless promoted it diligently. On a *Tonight Show* appearance, he said he thought the best thing about the movie was the song and that he also wrote a song called "What's New Pussycat?" which he proceeded to sing to great comedic effect. United Artists liked the song but loved the box office receipts even more, well enough to order up *Pussycat, Pussycat, I Love You*, a similarly sex-crazed UK sequel, in 1970. This venture was not written by Woody Allen and did not feature anyone from the original film (it starred Ian McShane and John Gavin). The only spiritual link to the earlier film was an instrumental reprise of "What's New Pussycat?" Of course this Pussycat film tanked. Need you even ask?

As for Bacharach and David, "What's New Pussycat?" became the first of their four Academy Award–nominated songs (it lost to Johnny Mercer's "The Shadow of Your Smile" from *The Sandpipers*). Invited by Bacharach to attend the Oscar ceremony, Jones had to decline: The Voice was busy having his tonsils removed.

Other Versions: *Franco Ambrosetti (1988) • Richard Anthony -"Hello Pussycat" • Jan Astrom - medley (2001) • Burt Bacharach (1965) • Gus Backus - "Hallo, Pussy Cat" (1988) • Frank Bennett (1998) • Brass Band of the Japanese Air Defense Force • Bill Brown Singers (1966) • Camarata • Wendy Carlos • Casino Royale (1999) • Simon Chardiet (1997) • The Chipmunks • Floyd Cramer (1966) • Bobby Darin (1966) • The Do-Re-Mi Children's Chorus (1965) • Fishbone (1997) • The Four Seasons (1965) • The Flying Lizards (1985) • Grant Geissman (1999)• Jason Graae (1998) • Buddy Greco (1965) • Ernie Heckscher & the Fairmont Orchestra • Shelley Hirsch (1997) • Henry Jerome • Quincy Jones • Tom Jones (live, 1967) • Anita Kerr Singers (1967) • Andre*

1965

Kostelanetz • k.d. lang (1997) • Steve Lawrence (1966) • Living Brass (1969) • Bob Marley & the Wailers (1966) • Roy Meriwether (1966) • Mike Myers (live, 1998) • Orchester Ambros Seelos (1996) • The Pizzicato Five (1996) • Franck Pourcel (1966) • Rock Academy String Quartette (1970) • Royal Marines (1974) • Christopher Scott (1969) • The Simpsons (TV series) (1992) • Starlight Orchestra (1995) • Billy Strange (1965) • Barbra Streisand – medley (1966) • Tiki Tones (2000) • Klaus Wunderlich - "Hallo Pussy-cat" (1965)

Here I Am. Future generations will never quite understand what was so great about 8-tracks. They were skimpy with song information, had no packaging to speak of, sounded lousy, jumbled the song order of the original album and sometimes broke up long songs into two different programs (separated by irritating clicks). But hey, that's the price you had to pay for wanting to hear "In Between the Heartaches" in your truck.

"Here I Am" (Burt Bacharach - Hal David)
First recorded by Dionne Warwick
From the United Artists movie *What's New Pussycat?*
Scepter 12104, released June 1965

A forerunner to "The Look of Love," this seductive surrender to love is the first Dionne Warwick single without the presence of implied infidelity looming over it. *"You'll always be the one thing I'm certain of / Here I am / And here I'll always stay / Close to you,"* she coos, and for once it seems like she's found someone worthy of such devotion.

In this movie, however, every man walking erect is both a scoundrel and a cheat except for Woody Allen's character, only because he's a nebbish incapable of such deception. Director Clive Donner loved the song and features the vocal version three times during the film, although the subdued audio quality makes it seem as if it's playing on a stereo in the next room. When Bacharach scored his next Charles Feldman film, "The Look of Love" sounded as if Dusty Springfield was in your lap singing it.

Initially, the song serves as Romy Schneider's theme, seemingly cued up to play whenever she emerges from the shower with a towel. We hear it again during Peter O'Toole's tryst with uni-monikered actress Capucine and again when parachute woman Ursula Andress falls out of the sky and into his convertible. "Here I Am" also appears in several instrumental incarnations, including two comical inversions not featured on the original soundtrack recording. These are used during scenes where O'Toole is locked out of Schneider's apartment and begs his pussycat's forgiveness.

Audiences still had a hard time recognizing Dionne Warwick without the heartache, sadness and tears in 1965; this gem of a song became her third straight single to miss the Top 40. Nonetheless, it became the title track of her fifth LP, released three months after it had peaked at No. 65 on the Hot 100. It's strangely unpopular as far as beautiful Bacharach-David songs go, its paltry number of cover versions no indicator of its unassailable quality.

dionne warwick
here i am

"Here I Am." A UK picture sleeve. Beach Boy Brian Wilson likened Dionne's singing on this track to "the voice of God." The few of us who've never heard the Almighty say "I'll be what you want me to be" will just have to take his word for it.

Other Versions: *Burt Bacharach - "Medley: Marriage French Style/Here I Am" (1965) • Gals & Pals (1966) • Gary McFarland (1965) • Diana Ross (1977) • Sheila Southern (1968)*

"My Little Red Book" (Burt Bacharach - Hal David)
First recorded by Manfred Mann
From the United Artists movie *What's New Pussycat?*
Ascot 2184 (*Billboard* pop #124)
Released July 1965

My Little Red Book. All three vocal performances from the *What's New Pussycat?* soundtrack were title tracks for the respective artists' albums. Manfred Mann's, which sold in negligible quantities, is by far the hardest to find today.

Despite being an opponent of early rock 'n' roll, Bacharach had nothing but praise for the Beatles in interviews during this time, firstly for having the good taste to cover one of his tunes right off the bat and secondly for raising the stakes of Top 40 beyond the three-chord rock that stymied him all during the Fifties. Less apparent is the sly way in which he incorporated some of their sound into his own music (sing "Can't Buy Me Love" in waltz time and "What the World Needs Now" in 4/4 to flesh out that theory). Until now, he'd never had hands-on experience working with a British beat group, and it probably helped that he picked the jazziest combo in the bunch. Led by South African–born pianist Manfred Mann, this British quintet of the same name incorporated jazzy instrumental breaks into its R&B-derived pop. It probably also helped that they were signed to a United Artists subsidiary in the States and could be gotten for cheap.

With the rushed work schedule Bacharach had to adhere to, it's doubtful there's anything "Mann-made" about the movie version beyond Paul Jones' edgy vocals. Inserted in the discotheque scene, where Peter O'Toole and Paula Prentiss shake things up, is a bare-bones version of the song, obscured with crowd noises and handclaps. There is no background chorus, organ or tambourine on the track, and the song has yet to acquire the distinctive flute riff that probably came courtesy of Mike Vickers, the band's multi-instrumentalist. This film version, which ultimately surfaced on Rykodisc's *What's New Pussycat?* CD, closely resembles the one Bacharach released as a Kapp single soon after. Former doo-wopper (Hollywood Flames, Five Willows) and future Broadway star (*Purdie*) Tony Middleton did the vocal honors, giving a more over-the-top reading than even Paul Jones dared to.

"My Little Red Book" (1966). Love's malevolent garage version made the song a hit, much to Bacharach's chagrin.

Most likely, Bacharach returned to the studio with the Manfreds after the film was done to re-cut the song again. By all accounts, his first session with a self-contained, independent group—not used to taking direction like the session men in New York and Los Angeles—was rife with tension. Mann objected that the chords were "too strident," forcing Bacharach to deposit himself behind the piano and pound both it and Mann into submission. A great single, it reached far more ears on the soundtrack album (which reached No. 14 on *Billboard*'s album chart) than it did as a stand-alone item.

Hal David's unfailing ability to encapsulate an entire movie in one song is realized again here. The Michael James character, unable to curb his appetite for other women, goes through a bevy of beauties, despite knowing that he only has true love for one girl. That this playboy's proverbial little black book is red only indicates that his carnal intentions are not honorable. Or else he's old enough to remember Perry Como's pre-rock tune "In My Little Red Book" and shouldn't be anywhere near a discotheque at his age.

1965

What's New Pussycat? One of the first but certainly not last various-artist soundtracks.

Arthur Lee became enamored with the song at a movie house, but rather than shell out money for the single or soundtrack, he simply ran the song down to his group, Love, the way he remembered it—or misremembered it. As Lee recounted in the *Love Story* boxed set, "I couldn't play guitar that well [at the time], so I made it more of a rock thing with a tambourine." Love's translation soared all the way to No. 52 nationally, much to the chagrin of Bacharach, who bemoaned the loss of most of the song's original chords. Since it was the hit version, most hard-rock and punk acts covering the tune just followed Love's streamlined arrangement. Lee may have further incurred Bacharach's irritation by naming a song on Love's third album "A House Is Not a Motel."

Other Versions: *Burt Bacharach (1965) • The Bad Seeds • The Barracudas (1981) • Toni Basil (1981) • Episode Six (1966) • Gals & Pals (1966) • Grant Geissman • Melba Joyce (1998) • Greg Kihn (1986) • Arthur Lee & Shack • The Litter • Longines Symphonette Society (1970) • Love (1966) • The Nomads • Ted Nugent (1986) • Rising Storm • The Rockin' Berries (1965) • Rumour (1980) • Sounds Incorporated (1966) • The Standells (1966) • Cal Tjader (1969) • Mel Tormé (1966) • The Ugly Ducklings • UK Subs • The Zakary Thaks*

***What's New Pussycat?* (Original Soundtrack LP)**
Original score composed by Burt Bacharach, lyrics by Hal David
United Artists 5117 (*Billboard* album chart #14)
Released July 1965

"What's New Pussycat?" • "School for Anatomy/Bookworm" (medley) • "High Temperature, Low Resistance" • "Downhill and Shady" • "Stripping Isn't Really Sexy, Is It?" • "Marriage, French Style/Here I Am" (medley) • "Here I Am" • "Marriage French Style" • "My Little Red Book" • "Pussy Cats on Parade" • "A Walk on the Wild Wharf" • "Chateau Chantel" • "Catch As Catch Can"

Whatever the other 40 themes were that Bacharach originally worked out for the film, his output on the soundtrack amounts to 10 brief instrumentals, besides the three vocal numbers. The most frequently used instrumental, "High Temperature, Low Resistance" appears in the film over a dozen times, while the snazzy "Stripping Isn't Really Sexy, Is It?" is only heard in a 12-second snippet, when Woody Allen and Romy Schneider go to the strip club after the crowds have filed out. "Downhill and Shady" affords Bacharach the rare opportunity of stretching out in both Merseybeat and blues styles—the former containing the most driving bass line on any Bacharch recording. "Marriage, French Style" appears in part of a mellow medley with "Here I Am" and as a raucous tarantella. "Pussy Cats on Parade" is used in the film's dream sequence, reprising both the title song and "My Little Red Book." "A Walk on the Wild Wharf" is a tip of the hat to producer Charles Feldman's 1962 film *Walk on the Wild Side,* which also starred his mistress, Capucine (its title song, written by Mack David and Elmer Bernstein, was also nominated for an Academy Award). "Chateau Chantel," a baroque instrumental that again reprises "Pussycat" as a slow waltz, resembles Bacharach's later work on *Butch Cassidy*. "Catch As Catch Can," which plays under the film's final chase scene on go-carts, combines a gospel-organ groove with a tack-piano Charleston romp straight out of a Keystone Kops film.

The soundtrack album's strong chart action provided Bacharach with his first taste of solo success. This was a peak year for movie music. Between *Roustabout, Help, Goldfinger* and a pair of record-breaking Julie Andrews musicals, original soundtracks occupied the No. 1 position on *Billboard*'s album charts for 29 weeks in 1965.

Other Versions: *The Waistcoats - "Downhill and Shady" (2000)*

The Easy Project II: House of Loungecore. Anita Harris was loungecore before loungecore was cool. This 1996 collection of British easy-listening, soundtrack music and space-age pop provides the cheapest avenue to obtain "London Life." Harris would also cut a fine rendition of "Trains and Boats and Planes."

"Dance Mamma, Dance Pappa, Dance" (Burt Bacharach - Hal David)
Recorded by Joanne and the Streamliners
United Artists 912, released summer 1965

Thanks to its parent movie company, United Artists Records had a steady stream of soundtracks as well as an abundance of international music on its roster. UA catered particularly to an Italian-American audience, putting out albums by comedian Pat Cooper, instrumentalists of Italian descent like Al Caiola and Ferrante & Teicher, and singer Jimmy Rosselli, who, some Italians will swear to you with Fatima fervor, was ten times the singer Sinatra was. Therefore it seemed like a reasonable request to break out the tarantella from the *What's New Pussycat?* score and give it lyrics so Aunt Millie and Uncle Nunzio could sing along. "Marriage, French Style" became "Dance Mamma, Dance Pappa, Dance," a wildly enthusiastic interpretation of what Romy Schneider's parents must be thinking in the scene when their happy daughter and afraid-to-commit future son-in-law take them out dancing.

The over-enunciation by "Joanne" (actually British jingle singer Rosemary Squires) sounds as if she's trying too hard to pass her citizenship test: this record probably would've sold more copies had it been sung in Italian. "Dance Mamma, Dance Pappa, Dance" didn't become a wedding staple or even a chart hit but did spawn French, Italian and German cover versions before going away quietly. If there's a grandmother out there somewhere with a working Victrola insisting that this be played at an engagement party, chances are her name's Joanne.

Other Versions: *Lill-Babs - "Nu vill jag dansa hela da'n" • Karin Kent - "Dans je de hele nacht met mij?" • De Sjonnies - "Dans je de hele nacht met mij?" (1995)*

The Sound of Bacharach. The cover shows Bacharach in what looks like various stages of bullet catching, but the contents make up the first various-artist compilation devoted to Bacharach songs, which was issued in England by Pye Records to tie in with his 1965 Granada TV Special of the same name. The 2001 West Side CD expands the original album to 27 tracks with the inclusion of B.J. Thomas, the Isley Brothers, The Tangeers, Tammi Terrell and Big Maybelle.

"London Life" (Burt Bacharach - Hal David)
Recorded by Anita Harris
Pye 7N15971, released fall 1965

This UK-only single was Bacharach and David's love letter to London, capturing the city at its swinging peak with, of all people, a children's TV-show host, Anita Harris. Sounding very much like a husky, congested Petula Clark, Harris waxes romantic about a downtown that's got it all—rain, cold and thunder! Both singer and song are dynamically all over the place, the moderate-to-rushing orchestration neatly approximating the continual London drizzle that becomes a downpour in mere seconds.

Cliff Richard. Although he was a lost cause on this country's record buyers, his popularity continued in all other foreign territories, including Canada, which released this album. Cliff's U.S. label said *no mas* after his *Cliff Richard in Spain* album failed, and it would be 11 years before Cliff would get another U.S. long player, the humbly titled *I'm Nearly Famous.*

The most thrilling passage comes at the bridge, with Hal David giving some insight as to why Bacharach is working in Old Piccadilly: *"While Paris sleeps / London just keeps right on swinging / And all the songs that the world is singing / You will find they all are born in London, England."* That last note is stretched out with Streisand-like bravura as the crescendo slowly dips to a romantic calm. While no one doubts a rain-drenched London has its romantic plusses *("In this cold umbrella weather / Boys and girls all keep warm together"),* it's perhaps a bit of a stretch of David's imagination to insist that *"London made love its seventh wonder."*

"Everyone Needs Someone to Love" (Burt Bacharach - Hal David)
First recorded by Cliff Richard
From the album *Love Is Forever,* Columbia SX1769
Released in the UK November 1965

By mid-1965 a second wave of British acts began washing up on American shores, but there was still no room in the lifeboat for old sailors like Cliff Richard. Fair enough, since the former proponent of real rock like "Move It" was turning out housewife pop guaranteed to deter teens. Nonetheless Epic, the American affiliate of Cliff's label, was still willing to release occasional product and fly Richard to the States to cut some sides with producer Bob Morgan. Epic passed on issuing the ballad-laden *Love Is Forever* in America, having given up any hope of establishing him as an adult-contemporary artist. Except for a soundtrack album on Uni, he'd have no more long players in this country until Elton John took up his cause and signed him to his label, the Rocket Record Company, in 1976.

The album's opening track, "Everyone Needs Someone to Love," was a classy if lightweight loping number most notable for hopping in half steps at the top of each verse and then dropping down three half steps at the end of the song. With its hop-along feel and relaxed sax that hark back to "Only Love Can Break a Heart," this seems like another prospective Gene Pitney number cast adrift. Richard turns in a likeable enough performance, but deservedly obscure RCA recording artist Nick Palmer obliterates any charm the song had with a rest-home sing-along version.

Other Versions: *Nick Palmer (1969)*

"Through the Eye of a Needle" (Burt Bacharach - Hal David)
First recorded by Cliff Richard
Epic 9866, flip side of "Wind Me Up (and Let Me Go)"
Released November 1965

With the success of "What the World Needs Now Is Love," it seems foolhardy to have squandered this stylish Bacharach-David ballad on a B-side. Hal David stresses the importance of keeping a lover's spat in proper scale: *"Through the eye of a needle an elephant seems very small / and through the eye of a needle, a mountain's not so very tall / look at our great big quarrel / Through the eye of a needle, please won't you hurry back to me my love."*

This track, also from the *Love Is Forever* LP, works because of its subtle pleasures—Richard's smooth lower register, the understated sweet female backgrounds and a sympathetic orchestration. Even when you remove all of these elements and stick in the high-register pleadings of yet another obscure singer, Columbia recording artist and future Archies vocalist Donna Marie, you've still got a nice set of chord changes and sage lyrics that actually bring the word "hate" into an adult-contemporary track *("I can't believe one mistake could really make your love for me turn into hate"),* a rare occurrence even now, when there's a lot more of it to go around.

Other Versions: *Donna Marie (1967)*

Cliff Richard. Whoever heard of a Cliff without any rock? Despite a guest appearance by the Shadows on one cut from *Love Is Forever,* Richard would rather be alone singing ballads in 1965.

"(Here I Go Again) Looking with My Eyes, Seeing with My Heart" (Burt Bacharach - Hal David)
Recorded by Dionne Warwick
Scepter 12111, released September 1965

A writer for *Creem* magazine once likened the strange experience of hearing Queen's "Bohemian Rhapsody" for the first time to "watching color TV before it was invented." That's probably an apt description for this bold progression into the future for Dionne Warwick. Being the voice of Bacharach-David carries with it certain indelible responsibilities, not least of which is being the only person uniquely qualified to tackle the team's toughest constructions. No question, Bacharach and David were pulling out all the stops this time around—signature changes, strange internal rhymes, the bass and background vocals droning on root notes different than the other instrumentation and a melodic nod to Duke Ellington's "Take the 'A' Train." It's hard to imagine anyone else singing this song without calling a huddle with the vocal coach.

Dionne rides the wild mood shifts as if she's being carried on a conveyor belt through the world of tomorrow. When she closes her eyes, her heart sees someone who loves her, and all the lies disappear. But when she opens them, she's filled with fears of abandonment. If successful commercial pop is based the audience's familiarity of a song through constant repetition, few casual listeners stuck around for the requisite seven or eight plays necessary to anticipate what's going to happen next on this least celebrated yet most adventurous of Dionne's Bacharach-David A-sides.

Freddie and the Dreamers. Meant to be taken to heart but not taken seriously. What other group would simultaneously drop their trousers to sing "Short Shorts" in boxers?

"I Fell in Love with Your Picture" (Burt Bacharach - Hal David)
Recorded by Freddie and the Dreamers
From the album *Fun Lovin',* Mercury LP 21061
Released December 1965

In the spring of 1965, a full year after every Liverpool group and their uncle had scooped up at least three U.S. chart hits, the States indeed seem ready for Freddie. His quintet's two year-old British hit "I'm Telling You Now" belatedly reached No. 1 here, a fortunate bit of timing since Britain was concurrently ready to drop Freddie and the Dreamers like a

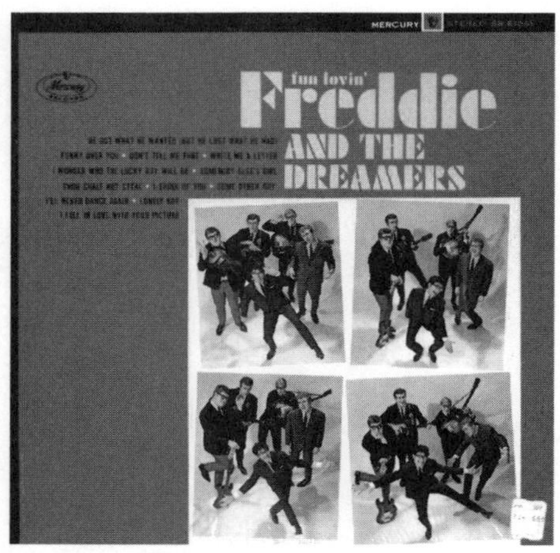

Freddie and the Dreamers. Getting in some last-minute poses for their fifth and final U.S. LP. Amazingly, all their American albums were issued in 1965! Mercury Records saw the wisdom in passing on their Freddie and the *Dreamers in Disneyland* LP and their children's concept album, *Oliver in the Overworld,* for American audiences. Look, if you knew all this stuff, it wouldn't be trivia.

lead tea bag. Perhaps the motherland was anticipating the irreparable damage the "Freddie" dance might wreak on its "Swinging London" tourism.

No sooner had this neo-vaudevillian and his band of goons leaped and high-kicked their way across the stages of *Hullaballoo, Shindig* and *The Ed Sullivan Show* than they met a new Manchester rival waiting for them on American soil. Yes, Herman's Hermits, whose toothy lead singer, Peter Noone, had two things going for him: (1) he reminded many of a young John F. Kennedy and (2) he didn't goose-step like Freddie and the Dreamers. *Ich bin ein Berliner,* indeed! In no time at all the Hermits scored two No. 1's with English music-hall pastiches not unlike "I Fell in Love with Your Picture." One reckons the only reason it's Freddie and the Dreamers mooning over a photo of a friend's sister is that Herman's people said no.

The background singers seem to be having fun with their parts, which sound as if they're telling Freddie to "shaddap" every time he talks about his Kodachrome cutie. But it may as well have been the listening public shutting Freddie up. The track, which has a jarring tape edit at 1:36 that undermines its sing-along potential, wound up on the last of Freddie's U.S. albums and didn't see release in Britain until November 1967, on the *King Freddie and His Dreaming Knights* album. Freddie's people must have been sleeping on the job.

"Are You There (With Another Girl)" (Burt Bacharach - Hal David)
First recorded by Dionne Warwick
Scepter 12122 (*Billboard* pop #39)
Released December 1965

"Are You There with Another Girl"? Yet another brilliant Bacharach-David mini-drama finds Dionne in denial again.

Finally, a song that restored Dionne Warwick to the Top 40 after four consecutive singles failed to impress the charts. "Looking with My Eyes" had proven a mite too progressive for most pop listeners, a kind of "wall of sound" record that didn't emphasize the beat and wasn't swathed in reverb or echo but felt as if all the action was taking place in a far-off distance. The team went back to the drawing board and came up with a single that continued to take risks while retaining all the familiar elements of the earlier Dionne hits.

Bacharach reprises the *baion* beat and chick-chick guitar but factors in all kinds of new coloring (droning strings, a strange fret-sliding guitar figure that sounds like the purr of a puma, an orchestral crescendo), while Hal David brings back the tried-and-true love-triangle song and all its rage-inducing trappings (the two silhouettes dancing on the window shade, the laughter coming from inside her boyfriend's room and the romantic music playing).

Dionne, true to form, is in a state of denial. Refusing to believe that her lover would break his promises, she allows the anger to slowly build inside her delicate frame. This mounting rage is mirrored by the orchestral crescendo that occurs twice, just as it would two years later on the Beatles' "A Day in the Life." When George Martin instructed a 40-piece orchestra to swell from lowest note to highest, the impressive cacophony stood apart from the rest of the song. Bacharach had the same idea, but he integrated it into the body of the song and its narrative. The effect isn't so much mind-blowing as it is "My God, that girl is going to blow her stack!"

Perhaps the most brilliant synchronicity of music and lyrics is when the piano and background vocals evoke the music that Dionne hears coming from the radio. *"Oom pah pah, pity the girl"* it gently mocks, as does all happy music when the listener is anxious and on the receiving end of a betrayal. It's Dionne's cousin Myrna who sings the part, with instruction from Bacharach to emulate a whistle.

Bacharach and David had now been producing for a few years but were finding themselves having to compete for chart space with a whole new breed of rock producer: people like Phil Spector, Brian Wilson, Holland-Dozier-Holland and the Beatles with George Martin were all trying to outdo one another with their sound paintings. With this single, Bacharach and David not only met the challenge but made an impact on some peers as well. Brian Wilson cited Bacharach as being a direct influence on his masterwork, *Pet Sounds*, particularly the instrumental "Let's Go Away for Awhile," where traces of "Are You There with Another Girl" are hiding in the shadows.

Other Versions: *Farah Alvin (1998) • Burt Bacharach (1968) • Terry Baxter (1971) • Bill Bentley • The Buckinghams (1968) • Carnation (1994) • Deacon Blue (1990) •18th Century Corporation (1969) • Percy Faith (1966) • Okazaki Hiroshi & His Stargazers • Anita Kerr Singers (1969) • Johnny Mann Singers • Marie McAuliffe (1998) • Maureen McGovern (1991) • Rock Academy String Quartette (1970) • Mari Wilson (1983)*

"Are You There with Another Girl." Against such formidable competition as the Beach Boys and the Mamas and the Papas for Best Performance by A Vocal Group in 1966, the winner was…the Anita Kerr Singers! The same Ms. Kerr-age of justice took place in 1965 when the Kerr Singers' equally obscure *We Dig Mancini* demolished the Beatles' *Help!* in this same category. Could the fact that Ms. Kerr was the vice president of the Nashville chapter of NARAS have had anything to do with the voting? Nah!

"If I Ever Make You Cry" (Burt Bacharach - Hal David)
Recorded by Dionne Warwick
Scepter 12111, flip side of "Are You There (With Another Girl)"
Released December 1965

Hopelessly romantic and achingly beautiful, it could very easily make you cry. The second of Dionne Warwick's torchy gospel-inspired B-sides was cut from the same cloth as "How Many Days of Sadness"—prominent piano, trumpet solo and tremolo guitar. But here's a torch song with a difference: Dionne wishes only the worst punishments imaginable for herself if she ever makes her beau sob. *"Long as I live, may the world turn away from me…may my dreams never come to be….May I never see the sun appear and may I go through life and never hear a tender voice say I love you."* Did anyone say mea culpa?

"In Between the Heartaches" (Burt Bacharach - Hal David)
First recorded by Dionne Warwick
From the album *Here I Am,* Scepter 531
Released December 1965

"Here I Am" lets us peek at a private moment of tenderness between two lovers. "In Between the Heartaches" does the same thing, but only as

"In Between the Heartaches." Hal David wrote this song to illustrate how some couples stay together during the hard times, making it somewhat more optimistic than the after-the-fact A-side. Exceptional versions by Stan Getz and Marie McAuliffe can be found, but avoid Dionne's lukewarm remake.

a matter of defense. Friends only see how Dionne's lover mistreats her, not how he holds her and tells her he loves her when they're alone. While Hal David may have written it as a positive treatise on what goes on when no one else is around that makes the hard times a little better, the ominous drum breaks that underscore her insistent *"I know you love me"* and the dissonant chording behind *"all of the heartaches and the sadness and the tears"* seem to indicate there will be plenty more hard times to follow.

A hard-to-find album released by the Venture Music Group called *Dionne Warwick & Friends* contains seven unreleased tracks she recorded in the early Seventies with producer Tony Camillo. Five were written by Jim Weatherly and would eventually be recorded by Gladys Knight and the Pips. The remaining two are remakes of "Don't Say I Didn't Tell You So" and "In Between the Heartaches." While the originals sound timeless, these remakes sound superficial, dated and cheap in a way that only Seventies byproducts can.

Other Versions: *Terry Baxter (1971) • Stan Getz (1967) • Anita Kerr Singers (1967) • Marie McAuliffe (1998)*

"Window Wishing" (Burt Bacharach - Hal David)
First recorded by Dionne Warwick
From the album *Here I Am,* Scepter 531
Released December 1965

The cheerful melody belies the pool of tears collecting on the windowsill. In a tale that's a bit like "Walk On By" for shut-ins, Dionne watches her old boyfriend strolling passed with someone new and declares, *"Without your love I can't go out and face this world."* But what would a great Bacharach-David track be without a smidgen of self-deception? Our window wisher is also an excellent phone sitter, determined that her wishin' and hopin' will result in him calling to say, *"let's give love one more try."* In the days before answering machines, voice mail, cell phones, and e-mail, options were extremely limited: *"if I'm not there when you call, I will die."* If someone ever does call, it'll be the landlady saying she smells gas.

Other Versions: *Terry Baxter (1971) • Alet Oury (1998)*

"Long Day, Short Night" (Burt Bacharach - Hal David)
First recorded by Dionne Warwick
From the album *Here I Am,* Scepter 531
Released December 1965

Bacharach moves it on the bluebeat! The United States' working knowledge of ska music in the mid-Sixties was limited to Millie Small's 1964 hit "My Boy Lollipop" and the guitar break on the Beatles' "I Call Your Name," recorded that same year. Bacharach must have heard early reggae music in his travels, and he used the upstroke guitar rhythm with unison violins to make another fine Shirelles track, this one about making a night of premarital bliss last a little longer. For whatever reason, their version wound up shelved until it landed on a 1987 *Lost and Found* compilation. The waste not, want not powers that be at Scepter again substituted Dionne's voice for Shirley Owens'; by this time a Dionne album track was a bigger priority than the former top female group in the country. The departure of Luther Dixon from Scepter/Wand left the trio without a father figure, and when the girls turned twenty-one and didn't get the "trust fund" money that was supposedly set aside for them, they sued their mother figure, Florence Greenberg. Unable to sign with another label, they continued a downward slide at Scepter that ended with "Hippie Walk" in 1968.

Other Versions: *The Shirelles*

Brook Benton. When his 1970 hit "Rainy Night in Georgia" reached No. 4, it joined "Raindrops Keep Falling on My Head," "Who'll Stop the Rain" and "Kentucky Rain" in an unusually wet Top 20.

"How Can I Hurt You" (Burt Bacharach - Hal David)
First recorded by Dionne Warwick
From the album *Here I Am,* Scepter 531
Released December 1965

This time Bacharach really got a background singer to imitate a panpipe for what turns out to be a strange mixed marriage of a classy ballad and a loony polka. The song sounds like it was excised from a musical comedy, with Dionne telling a reluctant lover *"Trust me! Trust me!"* as he's running away from her. An unlikely candidate for a potential Dionne track, it sounds like it could either have been a *What's New Pussycat?* reject or an attempt by the producers to add some much-needed whimsy to an album dense with longing ballads.

Other Versions: *Lana Cantrell (1967)*

"More Time to Be with You" (Burt Bacharach - Bob Hilliard)
Recorded by Brook Benton
From the album *Mother Nature, Father Time,* RCA LPM-3526
Released late 1965

This long-lost Bacharch-Hilliard composition had circulated "for professional use only" as early as 1961, on a demo that featured roller-rink organ, squawking sax and singer Lonnie Sattin wrenching the hell out of it as if it were finished master. Usually a demo singer will just flesh out the song as generically as possible, but Sattin's scenery-chewing on the bridge is about the only point of interest on what is one of Bacharach's conservative early attempts at writing a bluesy R&B number. Nothing was heard from it again until Brook Benton needed a twelfth song to fill out his first album for RCA Victor, one that marked his reunion with Clyde Otis, the producer and co-writer of his many hits. The hype on the rear sleeve of the *Mother Nature, Father Time* album promises "Brook Benton—the way YOU like to hear him," which means lots of slip-note piano, swooping strings and resonant, laid-back phrasing.

Although not much slower than the demo version, Ray Ellis' arrangement drops the song down a few keys, and Benton's word-stretching and long, slow drags of breath make it seem like it's moving at half the speed. A good third of the words get changed around, too, with our frisky friend demanding more time for teasing, squeezing and loving

1965

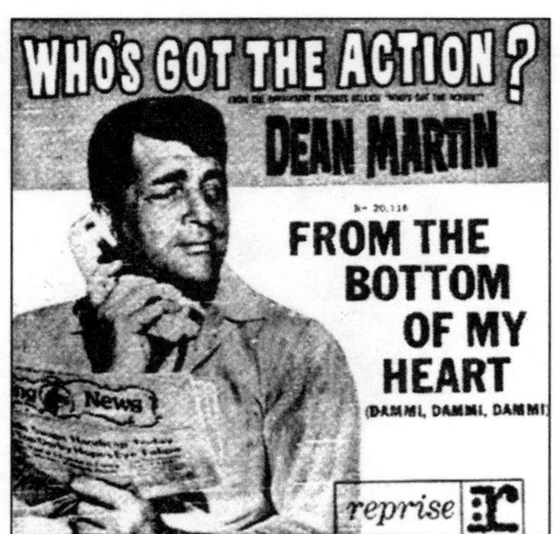

Dean Martin. The Rat Packer sings a different tune with the same title in his 1962 film. The version Phil Colbert sings is the second Bacharach "exploitation" theme for a Dino film. He'd finally secure a Dean Martin title song in 1973 with "Something Big," although the singing honors went to ex-Raider Mark Lindsay.

instead of the "more time for singing, more time for dancing" Hilliard originally required. The song ends somewhat haphazardly, with the string section playing a snatch of Young and Heymann's "When I Fall in Love" while Benton holds a low F note over it.

Although results may differ on the mono version, the stereo mix is a sloppy dub that leaves more time for distortion and more time for spotting microphone pops.

"Who's Got the Action?" (Burt Bacharach - Bob Hilliard)
Recorded by Phil Colbert
Phillips 40313, released fall 1965

With so many artists revisiting old Bacharach-David tunes for hit potential, yet another unheard Bacharch-Hilliard tune from the misty past rears its head. Although Dean Martin starred and sang a song called "Who's Got the Action?" in his Paramount film of the same name, it's not this one. Most likely this was written and rejected by Martin or Paramount, which explains its low-priority placement with a hitless blue-eyed soul singer like Phil Colbert all these years later. Northern-soul collectors take notice!

SECTION FIVE
THE LOOK OF LOVE (1966-1967)

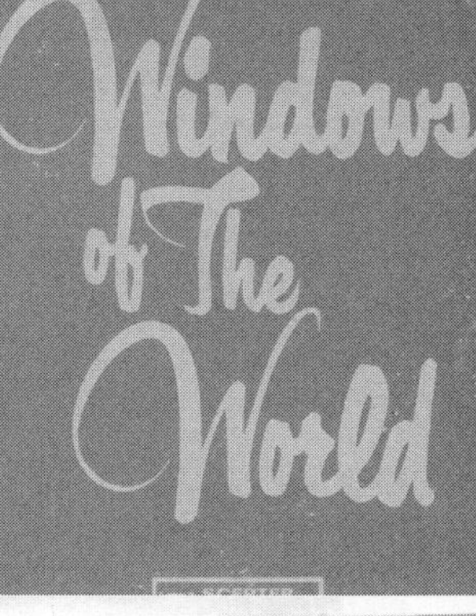

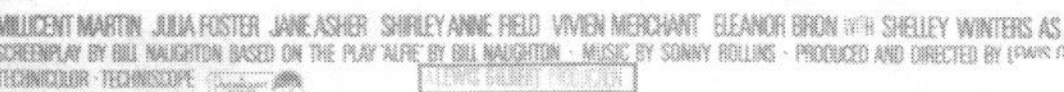

...or On TV and in the Movies

Very few songs from the '66–'67 period are without a movie or TV tie-in. Burt spends a lot of time in London writing film music and scoring chart hits under his own name. He and Hal David write a made-for-TV rock musical, On the Flip Side, *that is the first of its kind. It serves as the trial run for the Tony-winning* Promises, Promises. *Then there are two movie scores, three stand-alone movie themes and two more Oscar-nominated songs.*

Section Five: The Look of Love (1966–1967)

1. *"Alfie" .... Cilla Black*
2. *"Made in Paris" .... Trini Lopez*
3. *"Promise Her Anything" .... Tom Jones*
4. *"Here Where There Is Love" .... Dionne Warwick*
5. *"Come And Get Me" .... Jackie DeShannon*
6. *"Cross Town Bus" .... Gals & Pals*
7. *"Windows and Doors" .... Jackie DeShannon*
8. *"So Long Johnny" .... Jackie DeShannon*
9. *"After the Fox" .... Peter Sellers and the Hollies*
10. *After the Fox (Original Soundtrack LP) .... Burt Bacharach*
11. *"Making a Movie in Sevalio" .... Burt Bacharach*
12. *"Another Night" .... Dionne Warwick*
13. *"Go with Love" .... Dionne Warwick*
14. *"They Don't Give Medals (To Yesterdays Heroes)" .... Rick Nelson*
15. *"W.E.E.P." .... On the Flip Side cast*
16. *"Take a Broken Heart" .... Rick Nelson*
17. *"It Doesn't Matter Anymore" .... Rick Nelson*
18. *"Fender Mender" .... The Celestials*
19. *"Try To See It My Way" .... Joanie Sommers (and Rick Nelson)*
20. *"They're Gonna Love It" .... Donna Jean Young*
21. *"Juanita's Place" .... Burt Bacharach*
22. *"Nikki" .... Burt Bacharach*
23. *"The Beginning of Loneliness" .... Dionne Warwick*
24. *"One Less Bell to Answer" .... Keely Smith*
25. *"Bond Street" .... Burt Bacharach*
26. *"Casino Royale" .... Herb Alpert & The Tijuana Brass*
27. *Casino Royale (Original Soundtrack LP) .... Burt Bacharach*
28. *"Money Penny Goes for Broke" .... Burt Bacharach*
29. *"The Look of Love .... Dusty Springfield*
30. *"Let the Love Come Through" .... Roland Shaw*
31. *"The Windows of the World .... Dionne Warwick*
32. *"Walk Little Dolly" .... Dionne Warwick*
33. *"I Say a Little Prayer" .... Dionne Warwick*
34. *"A Sinner's Devotion" .... Tammi Terrell*
35. *"Lisa" .... Burt Bacharach*
36. *"Love Was Here Before the Stars" .... Brian Foley*
37. *"Do You Know the Way to San Jose .... Dionne Warwick*
38. *"Let Me Be Lonely" .... Dionne Warwick*
39. *"As Long As There's an Apple Tree" .... Dionne Warwick*
40. *"Where Would I Go" .... Dionne Warwick*
41. *"Walking Backwards Down the Road" .... Dionne Warwick*
42. *"This Guy's In Love with You" .... Herb Alpert*
43. *"Who Is Gonna Love Me?" .... Dionne Warwick*
44. *"He Who Loves .... Jerry Vale*
45. *"Don't Count the Days" .... Marilyn Michaels*

"Alfie" (Burt Bacharach - Hal David)
First recorded by Cilla Black
Parlophone R 5427 (UK pop #9)
Released January 1966
Capitol 5674 (U.S. *Billboard* pop #95)
Released August 1966

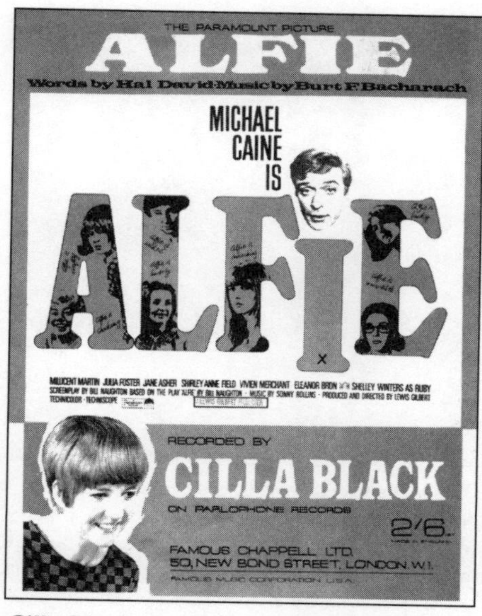

Cilla Black. Her manager Brian Epstein was furious when Cher's version was inserted into the American prints of *Alfie,* robbing Cilla of the chance for an American breakthrough hit.

(From the movie *Alfie,* U.S. version only)
Recorded by Cher
Imperial 66192 (*Billboard* pop #32)
Released July 1966

Perhaps the most important song in the Bacharach-David catalog, "Alfie" is certainly the one its composers seem proudest of in interviews. Bacharach went so far as naming it his No. 1 favorite on TNT's *One Amazing Night* television special, and it's one of the few songs he sings in concert. Yet the team almost passed on title song of the Michael Caine movie when Ed Wolpin of Paramount suggested it. "Writing a song about a girl with a beautiful name can be exciting. Writing a song about a man called 'Alfie' didn't seem too exciting at the time," Hal David explained in his book *What the World Needs Now.* Bacharach and David relented only under the condition that if they didn't come up with anything they liked, they wouldn't even show it to Wolpin.

While Bacharach flew to California to see a rough cut of the film, David stayed behind in New York to read the script and write the lyrics. "Burt called me to tell me how much he liked the movie," remembered David. "He assured me that it was completely faithful to the script. With that assurance I went to work on the lyric…I must say I was happy with the way the song worked. It did what we set out to do—put a button on the picture. In other words, it summed up the story of *Alfie.*"

The story concerned a cocksure Cockney who felt very little for his numerous female conquests beyond his enjoyment of their flesh. Gradually he comes to realize the error of his ways, but David chooses to mark the transformation of one of Alfie's disillusioned partners, now at the point of self-examination. At a time where even the use of the word "God" in a pop song was considered taboo (the same month "Alfie" appeared, so did the Beach Boys' "God Only Knows"), David goes so far as to acknowledge the existence of atheists *("As sure as I believe, there's a heaven above, Alfie / I know there's something much more / Something even nonbelievers can believe in")* and gives them something reasonable to hope for *("When you walk, let your heart lead the way, and you'll find love any day").*

Cher. Wondering "What's it all about?" is Cher, on the album that featured the hit "Alfie." She would also record "A House Is Not a Home" six years before splitting from hubby Sonny.

Having the singer pose the big questions that haven't yet occurred to Alfie forces the listener in effect to become Alfie for a few minutes and to contemplate issues of kindness, cruelty and higher beliefs. It is for this reason that people have such an emotional response to this song. Hearing *"without the love you've missed you're nothing"* at a particularly vulnerable time can be devastating to one's psyche. This is one song people have been known to pull over to the side of the road and weep unashamedly to when it comes on the car radio.

Dee Dee Warwick. She recorded "Alfie" with Dusty Springfield's producer Johnny Franz and arranger Peter Knight. "I couldn't believe what they had there for me—this forty piece orchestra and full chorus," Dee Dee told David Nathan in the notes for her *I Want to Be with You: The Mercury/Blue Rock Sessions* collection. "The whole session just blew me away."

That is, depending on who is singing it. With over 100 recorded cover versions, there are plenty of non-contenders, from the perpetually tear-shedding Vicki Carr to the tuxedo-tarnishing Jack Jones. Although Dionne Warwick had been offered as Bacharach and David's choice to sing the theme, the British distributors wanted Cilla Black, the onetime usurper of "Anyone Who Had a Heart." Yet, as she reveals on the BBC documentary *This Is Now*, she, too, was reluctant to do the song, based on its nag-worthy title. "I got this demo from Brian Epstein, my manager. And I listened to this demo of some fella singing 'Alfie,' and I actually said to Brian 'I can't do this.' For a start—*'Alfie'??* You call your dog Alfie! I mean, I'm sorry—can't it be Tarquin or something like that?"

The documentary footage shows Bacharach working with George Martin for the first time at Abbey Road's massive Studio One, with the Beatles' producer overseeing things from the control booth while Bacharach conducts from the piano. At one point, Cilla jokes in the control room about this becoming an all-nighter, which it very well became. "I don't think she knew what hit her," Bacharach admits. "We must have done 28 or 29 takes with her. Had it up early, but I kept going. Can we get it a little better? Can we get one more? Just some magic." When Black appeared on Bacharach's 1972 *Close to You* TV special, she recalls racking up a total of 18 takes before magically going back to the third one. She then performed the song with Bacharach in a more pleasing legato fashion than the 1966 recording. It must also be noted that she also sang it in a lower key—and with a different nose!

Dionne Warwick's facility with the melody didn't come quite so easily to Cilla. "When I start the song in that soft voice, it was awfully difficult to get all that energy up, literally from my boots to get up to that high note." This audible struggle mars Black's recording of "Alfie," with her Ethel Merman belting sounding less like an explanation of love's fickle ways and more like she's ordering poor Alf to take out the trash.

What's It All About, Shelley? Shelley Winters, the star of *A House Is Not a Home*, was one of Michael Caine's numerous female companions in the film but the only one to share an Italian picture sleeve.

The film's director, Lewis Gilbert, apparently didn't care for the song and simply went with jazz saxophonist Sonny Rollins' instrumental score, which had its own "Alfie's Theme," leading to much head scratching among purchasers of the original soundtrack album. United Artists, the studio that distributed the film in the U.S., was determined to get some additional promotional mileage through Top 40 radio. Imperial Records, a subsidiary of UA's record branch, had Cher under contract and asked her to sing it for the American prints of the film. While the future Mrs. Bono turns in a vocal performance even nonbelievers can believe in, she had the marital misfortune of having to compete for listener attention with Sonny's Italian replica of the "wall of sound," as the bridge shifts into a blustering bolero that robs the lyrics of its reassuring intent. However one feels about the recording, this political maneuvering did insure the song's Oscar eligibility, Bacharach's second nomination in as many years. Insert your boos and hisses here for the voting acumen of the academy: they actually preferred John Barry's love-among-the-lions anthem "Born Free."

When *Alfie* the movie made its U.S. premiere on August 24, 1966, at the New Embassy and Coronet Theaters in New York, six versions of the song had already been released on 45 (by Cher, Cilla, Tony Martin, Jack Jones, Joanie Sommers, Carmen McCrae and Billy Vaughn). Jerry

Butler's rendition was one that didn't make it to a single, and with good reason. In his biography *Only the Strong Survive*, Butler voices his displeasure with the funky Latin-jazz arrangement that producer Luchi DeJesus laid out for *Soul Artistry*, Butler's first album on Mercury Records. "Knowing Burt Bacharach and the way he approached his music, I don't think he was the least bit pleased with what Luchi had done to his song. I wasn't."

Another recently signed Mercury recording artist, Dee Dee Warwick, was persuaded to record a version while in London for a *Ready Steady Go* appearance. Cilla's version was already a UK hit, but Dee Dee Warwick claims she learned the song from the same original Bacharach-David demo Black was given. With imaginative if slightly over-lush orchestration by arranger Peter Knight and a sultry performance from Dee Dee, the chances for her "Alfie" becoming a U.S. hit were already remote in light of all the other versions. Mercury waited a bit too long, eventually slipping it out in America after that other Warwick scored a big hit with it. "Dionne didn't even consider doing it before," said Dee Dee, "In fact, she even says that hers was the 42nd version ever recorded. But she forgets to mention that my version provided her with a great demo." And a very different demo, too, since the song ends with the name Alfie repeated twice and the orchestra and choir floating away like a question mark without returning to the first chord.

Vanessa Williams. Her version of "Alfie" was a Japanese-only release.

It was only when Dionne's *Here Where There Is Love* album came up one song short that Scepter A&R man Steve Tyrell suggested they record the song, with Bacharach varying the arrangement slightly. Unlike her version of "What the World Needs Now" on the same album, Dionne owns this song within the first few bars, allegedly turning in the definitive cry-along version in one take. Deejays pounced on the album cut, forcing its release as a single the following summer.

"One of Burt and Hal's best was 'Alfie,'" says Gene Pitney, one of the few singers who didn't cover the song, in a 2000 BBC interview. "It took a long time to get to the point where the music that Burt was writing was accepted in the pop listener's ear. My own thinking is that it changed was when 'Alfie' came out. The movie was successful, of course, and the song was very successful. It needed the film to hammer home the unusual sevenths, rhythms, and time changes that Burt likes to use."

The only instrumental cover version of a Bacharach-David song to chart in the Top 100 (*Billboard* pop No. 66) was Eivets Rednow's harmonica version, released in the fall of 1968. The identity of this mysterious harmonica man was evident to anyone with ears for talent and a talent for spelling names backwards. *Billboard* rightly surmised, "It must be Stevie Wonder…it's his instrumental harmonica showstopper from his live performance." Still, Motown felt it necessary to dole out flagrant hints on the album cover when the disc was rereleased in the Eighties.

Other Versions: *Ronnie Aldrich (1971) • Lorez Alexandria (1995) • Burt Bacharach (1967) • Nick Bariluk (1996) • Joey Baron (1997) • Terry Baxter (1971) • Tony Bennett (1969) • Cher (1966) • Joe Bourne (1993) • Barbara Brown • Count Buffalo Big Band • Jerry Butler (1966) • Charlie Byrd • Al Caiola • Bobby Caldwell (1981) • Vikki Carr (1969) • Mel Carter (1966) • Lee Castle & the Jimmy Dorsey Orchestra (1974) • Frank Chacksfield (1971) • Ray Charles Singers • Randy Crawford (2000) • Carl Doy (1998)*

1966

Promise Her Anything. This hokey comedy was written by William Peter Blatty, who'd later pen a real head-turning screenplay, *The Excorcist.*

• The Delfonics (1968) • The Dells (1972) • Peter Duchin (1970) • 18th Century Corporation (1969) • Duke Ellington • Enoch Light • Bill Evans (1967, 1969) • Everything but the Girl (1986) • Percy Faith (1967) • Fantastic Strings • Maynard Ferguson (1968) • Ferrante & Teicher • Film Score Orchestra • Arthur Fiedler & the Boston Pops (1972) • Ella Fitzgerald • Free'n' Easy (1998) • Fred Fried (1996) • Don Friedman - Medley (1978) • Linda Depinquertaine-Gauthier (1993) • Grant Geissman (1999) • Stan Getz (1967) • Ron Goodwin (1972) • Leo Green - medley (2000) • Don Goldie (1977) • Great Guitars (Charlie Byrd, Herb Ellis, Barney Kessel) (1979) • Philip Green & His Pops Concert Orchestra (1995) • Tony Hatch Orchestra (1971) • Wayne Henderson (1992) • Terumasa Hino (1993) • John Holt (1974) • Dick Hyman (1969) • Willis Jackson (1967) • Lex Jasper (1975) • Sumudu Jayatilaka (2000) • The Jet Set (1999) • Harold Johnson Sextet (1967) • Jack Jones (1966) • Katja (1973) • Anita Kerr Singers (1969) • Rahsaan Roland Kirk (1967) • Andre Kostelanetz • Cleo Laine (1987) • Ellis Larkins • Yank Lawson & Bob Haggart (1970) • Gary LeMel (1994) • Liberace • Living Strings • London Pops Orchestra • Ramsey Lewis (1968) • Mantovani • George Martin • Tony Martin • Johnny Mathis (1970) • Marie McAuliffe (1998) • Keff McCulloch (1996) • Carmen McRae • Roy Meriwether • Midnight String Quartet (1967) • Mina (1971) • Matt Monro • Nanette • Peter Nero (1968) • Steve Newcomb Trio (2000) • New Direction - medley (1969) • Michelle Nicastro (1998) • Orchestra of Aries • Jaco Pastorius (1991) • Art Pepper • Frank Portolese (1995) • Pucho & His Latin Soul Brothers (1966) • Boots Randolph (1976) • Karl Ratzer (1994) • Dianne Reeves (1997) • Renaissance (1970) • Rita Reys (1971) • Buddy Rich (1968) • Nelson Riddle (1968) • Sonia Rosa • Royal Marines (1974) • RTE Concert Orchestra/Richard Hayman (1995) • Vanessa Rubin (1994) • San Remo Golden Strings (1968) • Christopher Scott (1969) • Renato Sellani (1993) • Roland Shaw Orchestra (1968) • Rosana (1997) • Don Shirley (1971) • Johnny "Hammond" Smith (1967) • Joanie Sommers (1966) • Soulful Strings (1967) • Sheila Southern (1968) • Starlight Orchestra (1995) • Barbra Streisand (1969, 2000) • Ed Sullivan Chorus • Sweet Inspirations (1968) • Buddy Terry (1967) • Gary Tesca (1995) • McCoy Tyner (1997) • Caterina Valente - medley (1971) • Sarah Vaughan (1967) • Lena Valaitis (1976) • Sylvia Vrethammar (1969) • Dee Dee Warwick (1968) • Dionne Warwick (1967, live 1982) • Frank Wess (1994) • Andy Williams • Roger Williams (1968) • Vanessa Williams (1997) • Nancy Wilson (1967) • Stevie Wonder (1968) • George Young (1970) • Young Gyants • Monica Zetterlund (1967)

"Made in Paris" (Burt Bacharach - Hal David)
Recorded by Trini Lopez
From the movie *Made in Paris*
Reprise 0435 (*Billboard* pop #113)
Released January 1966

Dallas-born Latino Trini Lopez put the Los Angeles nightclub PJ's on the map—just think what he could do for the City of Light. As our Parisian love guide, Lopez assures us that every girl with a French birth certificate is in search of *l'amour.* Linguistic problems? Don't sweat it. Sings Trini: *"If you don't know how to speak French, she'll understand,"* on account of the love being made in Paris every night. *"Find your dream! Find your love! I've got mine! Go get yours!"* That's a direct from order from Monsieur Lopez.

Odd that this snappy song's raison d'être, a fluffy Ann-Margaret/Louis Jordan vehicle of the same name, should summon more rocking sounds out of Bacharach than we'd been accustomed to hearing. In keeping with Lopez's *Live at PJ's* recorded sound, rhythm guitar and loudly cracking drums are brought to the fore, augmented by tack piano and decisive strings. In short, there's nothing French about Bacharach's arrangement or Lopez's performance. Typically, when Trini gets overly excited during the instrumental break he yells "Huhh! Haaah! Huuuuuh!" as if he's whipping a team of Alaskan huskies. At least he doesn't squeal uncontrollably like a pig here, the way he did on his hit "Lemon Tree."

A-Tom-ic Jones. The U.S. version of this album contained "Promise Her Anything" but didn't feature this eye-searing sleeve. Parrot, Jones' American label, thought having Tom swiveling in front of an A-bomb blast was in bad taste. Hell, we dropped the dang thing on Hiroshima: *that* was bad taste!

"Promise Her Anything" (Burt Bacharach - Hal David)
First recorded by Tom Jones
From the Seven Arts movie *Promise Her Anything*
Parrot 9809 (*Billboard* pop #74)
Released February 1966

For a short while anyway, it seemed as if Bacharach was willing to take on the guitar rock of the British boom, even turning in a 4/4 rocker. This movie theme is based around a circular guitar riff, the calling card of so many recent British imports (the Yardbirds' "Heart Full of Soul," the Kinks' "Tired of Waiting for You," the Rolling Stones' "The Last Time," the Searchers' "When You Walk in the Room"). But it's the Beatles' 1965 singles that provide the main source of inspiration. Compare the fadeout of "Promise Her Anything" to that of "I Feel Fine" and you'll hear Bacharach substituting for John Lennon's closing "ooohs" with droning brass, clinging to an A note much the same way the bass does during the verses of "Ticket to Ride."

The Warren Beatty/Leslie Caron farce for which this was written strives to create a bohemian Greenwich Village sex farce with family values: the presence of a baby throughout the movie insures that nothing too promiscuous ever really happens. Tom provides the sex, while Hal David's lyrics instill the traditional sentiments—*"you can promise her the moon when the sun is bright and promise her the sun when you're out at night"*—but all she really wants is your love. She'd even trade rubies and diamonds for a plain gold wedding band bought on the installment plan. The man whose fans once called him "Tiger Tom" gives this an even more ferocious reading than "What's New Pussycat?" practically growling out the words "night" and "bright" on the bridge before subsiding into a consolatory "just love will do." That's Jones appeal: he's a man who can sound like he's trying to seduce you and pick a fight in the same breath.

Promise Her Anything. The soundtrack has no Bacharach involvement beyond the title song, showcased in two instrumental versions arranged by John Keating. The balance of the album is Lynn Murray's anonymous score.

Jones' newly launched recording career was already going through something of a lull—a small indication of how overworked rock stars were in the Sixties. Several of his recent U.S. and UK singles failed to sell in quantities comparable to the first two. "Promise Her Anything" got lost in the shuffle, it being Jones' third movie theme in less than six months (he also turned in a typically explosive "Thunderball" for the James Bond people). The song didn't rear its head in Great Britain until it was pasted on the B-side of "Green, Green Grass of Home" in October 1966. By then, Jones was already shedding his initial teen audience for a less fickle adult female fan base, one that just wanted to act like teens in his presence.

Other Versions: *Bobby Byrne & His Orchestra (1966) • Gladhands (1998) • Living Brass (1968) • Marty Paich (1966) • Mike Melvoin (1966)*

1966

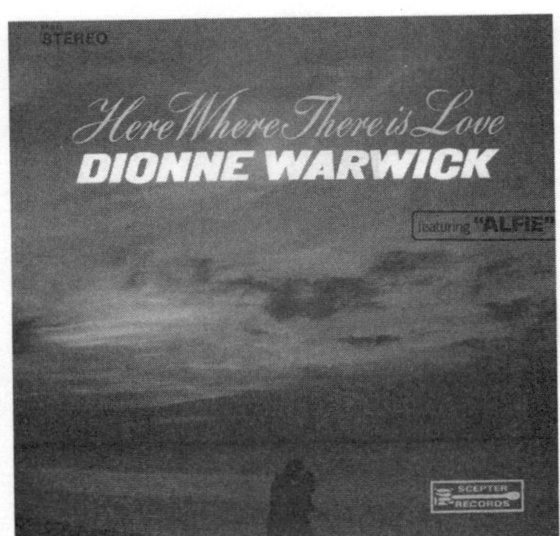

Here Where There Is "Alfie." Including "Alfie" was an afterthought, as this cover art clearly illustrates. The long delay Scepter took to release the track as a single aided in making this Dionne's first gold album.

"Here Where There Is Love" (Burt Bacharach - Hal David)
First recorded by Dionne Warwick
Scepter 12133, flip side of "Message to Michael"
Released March 1966

Having missed out on what could've been the biggest hit of her career by turning down "What the World Needs Now Is Love," Dionne was understandably disgruntled. Whether she lost her temper with Bacharach and David, à la her "Don't make me over, man" incident, is uncertain, but it does seem that "Here Where There Is Love" is the team's first attempt to fashion a similar waltz with humanitarian leanings for her *("for no man is an island and we need love")*. Like the earlier song, its melody is based on Bacharach's upturned phrasing *("Here? Where there is love—you're? Not alone")*. Starting with just Dionne singing softly to a piano, the song gradually builds up to a cymbal-crashing crescendo, with full support from her background stalwarts. Meant to be her next A-side, the record was flipped over in favor of "Message to Michael," a song Bacharach and David didn't even want Dionne to record. Not giving up on the song, it would become the title track of Warwick's sixth album in December 1966. On the strength of the single "Alfie," this would become her first album to enter the Top 40 and the first to go gold.

Other Versions: *Terry Baxter (1971)*

"Come and Get Me" (Burt Bacharach - Hal David)
First recorded by Jackie DeShannon
Imperial 66171 (*Billboard* pop #83)
Released April 1966

Jackie DeShannon (1969). Anyone looking to collect Jackie's Sixties Bacharach-David recordings can find them all on this budget reissue LP. She'd later record two songs with Bacharach on the soundtrack for the 1979 film *Together.*

One can imagine that the continental hopscotch back and forth from America to England took its toll on the songwriting team. Hal David used his jet-lagged melancholia for song fodder, and if "London Life" was his love letter to England, this is its Piccadilly polar opposite. The earlier song's conviction that "London made love its seventh wonder" has been worn away by endless gray skies and fog. While the lyrics never implicate London directly, the music and even the high haunt count in the reverb evoke the place where it was recorded, the Swinging London of Petula Clark's "Downtown," only this time as seen on depressants.

"Come and Get Me" displays resemblances to "Trains and Boats and Planes" beyond foggy reverb and the vocal reappearance of the Breakaways. Both songs have the singer getting left behind for greener pastures. Both have the singer reconciled with the fact that something bigger than their relationship has caused a lover to flee. And both songs have the singer stumped as to where that lover could be. The only clear difference in the narrative is that DeShannon knows the place she's been left to wallow in is one campfire short of a living hell: *"I know what life has done to you / Things haven't been to much fun for you.... This town isn't the town for you / You have to be where the skies are blue / And here the skies are gray."*

The oddest feature of this song is how the chorus stubbornly refuses to settle down and provide the listener with some security. Instead, DeShannon's pleading climaxes in an entirely different key. Even odder is how the song seems to just fade away on the melancholy verse instead of returning to the customary chorus before the end. It's still a great record, but you can see why its uneasy feeling prevented it from becoming a hit.

Singer Lisa Shane's arranger tacked on the forced orchestral ending, utilizing the same subtlety as someone yelling out "ta-da" at the end of a magic trick. Her hysterical regurgitation of the song is unnecessarily transposed several keys higher than human ears should be allowed to hear.

Other Versions: *Lisa Shane (1966) • Susan Maughan (1966)*

Gals & Pals. One only wonders if the cries of "Who the hell are Gals & Pals?" will drown out the people who are screaming "I'd like to meet their wardrobe coordinator."

"Cross Town Bus" (Burt Bacharach - Hal David)
First recorded by Gals & Pals
From the album *Sing Somethin' for Everyone,* Fontana LP 27557
Released spring 1966

Although Bacharach-David tribute albums would seemingly number in the hundreds by the early Seventies, in the mid-Sixties the field lay barren. Frankie Valli and the Four Seasons took the initiative in late 1965 by concocting a semi-tribute album to Bacharach and David, devoting half a side to the team's work while handing the other half over to Bob Dylan. Oddly enough, Fontana Records issued the very first album to cover Bacharach's music exclusively but completely ignored this very obvious selling point by titling the collection *Gals & Pals Sing Somethin' for Everyone.*

***The 4 Seasons Sing Big Hits by Burt Bacharach... Hal David... Bob Dylan* (1965).** One of the first tribute albums to Burt and Hal had to split needle time with Bob Dylan. It contains the only known version of "What's New, Pussycat?" with actual kitty sound effects and the only pinch-nosed rendition of "Don't Think Twice, It's All Right." Why babe, why babe?

Yes, the first band to go all the way with Burt and Hal, as it were, was this Swedish sextet and forerunner of the ABBA school of phonetic American singing. Bacharach first heard Gals & Pals in Stockholm while on tour with Marlene Dietrich in 1963, and one imagines that his publisher furnished them with some prospective songs. Aside from the usual selections were two songs that even their composer forgot about—"Close" (the song he and Sydney Shaw wrote for Keely Smith) and "Crosstown Bus," which dated back to 1960 and was published by Arch Music, Aaron Schroeder's publishing company. Schroeder handled Bacharach songs recorded by Gene Pitney, Jimmy Radcliffe and the Shirelles, and "Crosstown Bus" would've been a fine choice for Radcliffe: its driving beat, deep brass blasts to simulate a car horn and jazzy middle eight could've combined to make it another classic slice of lost Northern soul.

Instead, all we have to gauge this song about meeting a girl and falling in love on mass transit is this outdated chorus-style arrangement. The group's head Pal, Lars Bagge, did the vocal arrangement, which achieves maximum irritation levels when the Gals & Pals call-and-response the word "anything" eight times, climbing octaves every other time. One can hardly believe Bacharach's liner note gushing about this being "delightful to the ear" and a "highly flattering handling of my music." Thank your maker that hysterically high girl vocals punctuating every other line like Chihuahuas yapping at the end of a tenement corridor are no longer in vogue.

1966

Longines Symphonette Society (1971). Why do birds suddenly appear on an album cover? Look no further than the title track. This album of Bacharach and David faves has the only cover version of "Windows and Doors" we found. We also found an error in the liner notes: the team of Bacharach and David won almost every coveted statuette but never an Emmy, although the *Sound of Bacharach* special won three for its director, musical director, and editor.

"Windows and Doors" (Burt Bacharach - Hal David)
First recorded by Jackie DeShannon
Imperial 66196 (*Billboard* pop #108)
Released July 1966

After two despairing singles, Bacharach and David return Jackie DeShannon to the gentle social relevance of "What the World Needs Now." Instead of not needing another mountain or river, Jackie's rejecting the need for more ceilings and floors. *"If we have each other,"* she concludes, *"that's all we need."* Although fully bundled with strings, timpani and the Breakaways (fortified with a male voice or two), this made-in-London recording also has a prominently finger-picked acoustic guitar, which anticipates the laid-back singer-songwriter sound that would become inescapable in the early Seventies, as well as sounding like a distant cousin to Jill O'Hara's version of "I'll Never Fall in Love Again."

Other Versions: *Longines Symphonette Society (1970)*

"So Long Johnny" (Burt Bacharach - Hal David)
First recorded by Jackie DeShannon
Imperial 66196, flip side of "Windows and Doors"
Released July 1966

If Jackie DeShannon was Bacharach and David's female Gene Pitney, this was her "Twenty Four Hours from Tulsa"—with a twist. Instead of kissing off with the customary "Dear Johnny" letter, she assures Johnny she's only going away for a short while to break it off with her old beau. Yeah, right! She's practically stifling a laugh while making him promise he'll wait for her. The only time she sounds passionate about anything is when she refers back to her old lover, and it guarantees that Johnny will be spending a lot of time waiting by windows and doors and staring at ceilings and floors before he puts two and two together. Certainly the pessimistic chromatic descent Bacharach inserts behind every "so looooong John-nny" should've tipped him off.

"After the Fox" (Burt Bacharach - Hal David)
First recorded by Peter Sellers and the Hollies
From the United Artists movie *After the Fox*
United Artists 50079, released September 1966

"You caught the 'Pussycat'...now chase the Fox!" trumpeted the ads for *After the Fox,* United Artists' first blatant attempt at following up what was then the top-grossing comedy of all time. Once again a former television writer and playwright (Neil Simon) was given a shot at his first screenplay. Once again Peter Sellers was enlisted to star. And once again Bacharach was chosen to score the film and write the title song with Hal David. But whose idea was it to have Sellers participate in the recording of it? Maybe it was the former *Goon Show* star himself, keen on building up his pop movie-theme repertoire after his comical reworkings of the Beatles' "A Hard Day's Night" and "Help!" Sellers leaves the singing to the Hollies, answering Alan Clarke's and Graham Nash's various queries of "Where is the gold?" and "Why do you steal?" in the voice of Aldo

Vanucci, aka "the Fox." Bacharach registers a vocal presence, too: it's Burt making the open high-hat sound he introduced back in 1956 on his first movie song, "I Cry More."

After the Fox. The 1998 Ryko CD adds seven bits of incidental dialogue from the film and an enhanced CD-ROM clip of the scene where Victor Mature first meets Peter Sellers, but no musical outtakes.

While the production credit went to Sellers' and the Hollies' respective producers (George Martin and Ron Richards, former EMI A&R men and, after 1965, partners in Associated Independent Recordings, Limited), Bacharach was once again running the show from his piano. Apparently, he was just as demanding an arranger with the Hollies as he was with Manfred Mann. This would be the last instance where Bacharach produced a self-contained group until the *Night Shift* soundtrack in 1982, but the winning results he achieved here makes you wish he'd been a little easier on the hired help.

Other Versions: *Burt Bacharach (1966)* • *Ferrante & Teicher* • *Losers Lounge (1995)* • *Magistrates (1968)* • *Oranj Symphonette (1998)* • *The Pied Pipers*

After the Fox (Original Soundtrack LP)
Recorded by Burt Bacharach
United Artists 5148, released September 1966

"After the Fox" - Peter Sellers and the Hollies • "Making a Movie in Sevalio" • "Gold, Gold Who's Got the Gold" • "World of Make-Believe" • "Italian Fuzz" • "The Fox in Sevalio" • "Wheeler Dealer" • "Tourist Trap" • "After the Fox" (instrumental) • "Hot Gold" • "The Via Veneto" • "Making a Movie in Sevalio" • "Love x 2" • "Ukeatalia" • "Visiting Day" • "Bird Bath" • "Grotta Rosa"

Although a markedly funnier film than *What's New Pussycat?*, *After The Fox* fell far short of the mark commercially. Unlike the earlier soundtrack, this LP was not highlighted by three star vocal performances but rather two stars crammed onto one infectious theme that didn't chart. Yet in place of hits, the score contains plenty of whimsical character studies, the star's happy-go-lucky title theme, the bumbling Italian police's menacing search music ("Italian Fuzz"), the simple yet easily deceived people of Sevalio ("Making a Movie in Sevalio") and a slinky, exotic love interest ("Love x 2"). There's no character in the film sinister enough to correspond with "Wheeler Dealer," a brief but sluggish number that Bacharach scores so that the horn section sounds like a 45 playing at 33 rpm. It went unused on screen, as did "Grotta Rosa," one of several Italian dance pastiches that make up the balance of the score.

Bacharach, whose Hammond B3 work is usually reserved for demos, gets in several Jimmy Smith organ runs here on "Italian Fuzz," which also features his unlikely first use of guitar distortion. Another modern touch is the jumbled juxtaposition of neo-vaudeville clarinet, belly dancing music, sliding Hindu strings and harpsichord stabs that makes "Love x 2" seem like a precursor to English psychedelia. Like *Pussycat*, *After the Fox* climaxed with a chase scene, marked by "Foxtrot," which sounds similar to the later "Bond Street" from *Casino Royale* but with more Sevalio seasoning. Although given the name "Foxtrot" on the single, it's actually the same recording as "Gold, Gold Who's Got the Gold" from the soundtrack. And it actually is a foxtrot, one that breaks down and substitutes a Latin beat for a few bars.

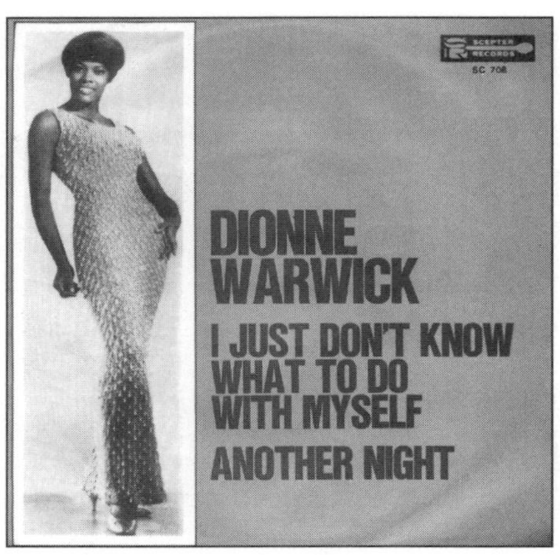

"Another Night." And another one of the more underappreciated Bacharach-David works, made near-famous by Dionne Warwick.

The film opened to unenthusiastic notices, and everything connected to it correspondingly disappeared. Eventually *After the Fox* would find a belated audience on television and video. First-time screenwriter Neil Simon learned some valuable lessons in filmmaking, which he shared in his autobiography, *Rewrites*: "Never collaborate with a writer who doesn't speak a word of your language; never work with a director who speaks *half* your language and is doing a picture strictly for the money; and never work on a film that can be doomed to failure because a woman in a purple dress walked on the set." He would, however, work with Bacharach and David again on the musical *Promises, Promises*.

"Making a Movie in Sevalio"
From the *After the Fox* soundtrack LP
United Artists 5148, released September 1966

Although this score didn't produce the bumper crop of cover versions that *What's New Pussycat?* did, the *After the Fox* theme did catch the ear of many soundtrack-savvy space-age-bachelor-pad music groups that sprang up in the Nineties. Although credited as containing the title song, Space Ponch's "Tati Suite: After the Fox/Traffic/Playtime" (found on the *World Shopping with Space Ponch* CD) actually excerpts "Making a Movie in Sevalio." So there.

Other Versions: *Space Ponch (2000)*

"Another Night" (Burt Bacharach - Hal David)
First recorded by Dionne Warwick
Scepter 12181 (*Billboard* pop #49)
Released December 1966

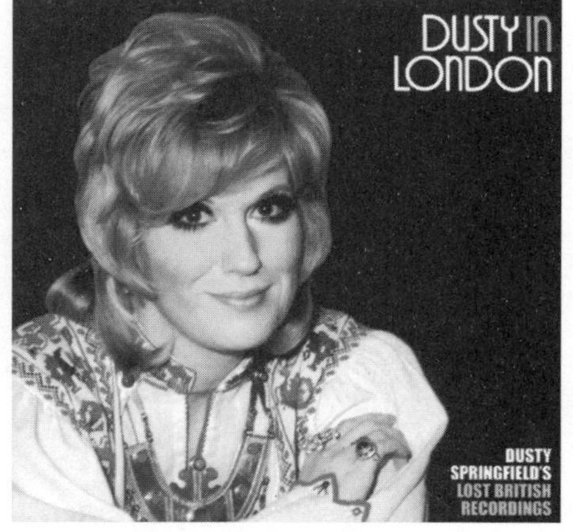

Dusty In London (1999). The balance of two UK Springfield albums that slipped through the cracks for American audiences can be heard on this Rhino collection.

While Dionne Warwick is universally acknowledged as the prime interpreter of Bacharach-David songs, 1966 proved to be the year she became their prime reinterpreter. "I Just Don't Know What to Do with Myself," "Message to Michael" and "Trains and Boats and Planes" all became Top 40 hits for the first time while simultaneously rejuvenating Dionne's career with higher chart positions than she'd seen since early 1964. Because she could sing anything the team put in front of her, they generally gave her their most daring and difficult vocal challenges. Yet the majority of 45 buyers stayed away from "Are You There with Another Girl," "Looking with My Eyes" and "Here I Am."

After these dense productions, Bacharach's arrangements for Dionne took a more open-air approach. There's nothing especially daring about "Another Night," her gentlest use of the *baion* beat since "You'll Never Get to Heaven." What first sounds like a light marimba in the background is actually a piano pounding low in the mix, and the horns are kept to a compressed cluster until the fade-out, when they're allowed to blow free.

The soft samba verses find a mellow Dionne once again left alone to air her disappointments. Because Hal David structures the verses like the popular you-show-me-and-I'll-show-you joke that would later be the staple of hundreds of *Laugh-In* blackouts *("Find me a rose that never fades and dies and I'll show you a man that never ever cheats and lies"),* her current woes seem like a laughable trifles. Naturally, by the jazzy shuffle chorus, she's a textbook desperation doll, crying that the louse she loves abandons her night after night but his permanent absence would presage the loss of her life.

Springfield's nearly identical rendition, placed on her late 1968 UK album *Dusty Definitely,* met with even more obscurity. By then Springfield had begun her association with Atlantic Records in the U.S., while continuing to record for Philips in foreign territories. Atlantic was only interested in her work with American producers. This album and many quality Johnny Franz/Dusty Springfield productions fell through the cracks for all but the most dedicated import-bin inspectors. A pity, since this rhythmic ballad eventually snuck out on Atlantic under the auspices of Aretha Franklin.

The Warwick recording of "Another Night," or seven seconds of it anyway, enjoyed a revival when Japanese Bacharach lovers the Pizzicato Five sampled it for their Swinging Sixties ode to "Twiggy Twiggy."

Other Versions: *The Pizzicato Five - sample in "Twiggy Twiggy" (1994) • Dusty Springfield (1968)*

***Go with Love* (1970).** Scepter Records made two special double-album sets exclusively for members of the Columbia House record club. This one collected tracks from *The Sensitive Sounds, Here Where There Is Love, Valley of the Dolls* and *I'll Never Fall in Love Again*, trimming what many consider the filler (non Bacharach-David cuts).

"Go with Love" (Burt Bacharach - Hal David)
First recorded by Dionne Warwick
Scepter 12181, flip side of "Another Night"
Released December 1966

Another spectacular flip so charged with emotion it's a wonder the hurt doesn't bleed through while the other side is playing. What guy could even make it halfway up the driveway without hearing Dionne and the orchestra explode, *"Go with love! When you leave me you go with love!"* and *"If it takes my life through, I will wait for you!"* and not turn around? Few of Hal David's end-of-relationship lyrics are as generous to the leaver as "Go with Love": the inevitability of parting is ever present, with the hope of inevitable reconciliation just two steps behind. Here is one of the few instances where you hear the usually effortless Dionne venture past her extensive comfort zone to hit notes somewhere out of the stratosphere, only to return to a hushed sigh seconds later. In a word, breathtaking.

Do You Know the Way to San Remo. Many collectors believe "Dedicato all'amore" is an Italian translation of "Go With Love," but it's actually a similar-sounding Italian hit Dionne performed at the San Remo Song Festival in 1967. Licensed by Scepter, this unique non-Bacharach song and production appears only on this rare souvenir 45. Cher was also in the *casa* that year, singing the equally rare "Ma piano."

"Go With Love" is the kind of passionate ballad that Italian audiences go *pazzo* for. So it's no surprise that Warwick was asked to perform "Dedicato all'amore," the Peppino Di Capri hit that sounds remarkably similar to "Go With Love," at San Remo, the famous popular songwriting festival held in Italy every year since 1907. The rules require that a foreign artist as well as an Italian one perform each nominnated song. Even if the song had won top honors in 1967, it would've been thoroughly overshadowed by the actions of young Italian singer Luigi Tenco. When his song "Ciao amore ciao" didn't make it into the finals, he killed himself! His lover, French singer Dalida, also performed the song and also attempted suicide two months later but was rescued. Now that's going with love!

Other Versions: *Barbara Acklin (1969) • Terry Baxter (1971)*

1966

Ben E. King. His early expulsion from the Drifters meant that he missed out on those great Bacharach-David and Bacharach-Hilliard songs. He made up for lost time with a speedy cover of "They Don't Give Medals to Yesterday's Heroes."

"They Don't Give Medals (to Yesterdays Heroes)" (Burt Bacharach - Hal David)
First recorded by Rick Nelson
From the *On the Flip Side* TV soundtrack
Decca 32055, released December 1966

Revisionists have offered *On the Flip Side* as a candidate for the first rock opera, but there's far too much script and too few songs to qualify in that regard. It is, however, Bacharach and David's first stab at writing a musical, an hour-long one for television to play between Singer Sewing Machine and Alka-Seltzer commercial interruptions. Since the show was rehearsed and filmed in New York in five exhausting weeks, it's easy to see why its co-star Joanie Sommers is sketchy about certain production details. She does recall: "The whole ensemble worked very well together, all things considered. It was fun to do. I'd do it again in a minute. Burt and Hal were there off and on, checking things out. They were definitely around."

Sommers knew Hal David, who wrote her first and biggest hit, "Johnnie Get Angry," but this was her first time meeting Bacharach. "Of course I was in awe of Burt. I remember sitting next to him at the piano on the seat going crazy while he was trying to show me what he wanted from the songs," she giggles. "I thought he was outrageously good-looking. All the tunes were fun to do. The things with Ricky were sweet. He was just a wonderful person to be around." *On the Flip Side* was Rick Nelson's first TV project since the cancellation of the network's *Adventures of Ozzie and Harriet*, which he had starred in since its early days on radio. As Rick was still under contract to ABC, the network tried to find a suitable vehicle for the singer and built this show around him to air on the short-lived *ABC Stage '67,* a program with a flexible format that encompassed variety shows, documentaries and dramas with international stars.

The former teen idol could not have felt great about portraying Carlos O'Connor, a rock star who was washed up at 25. Rick was 27 and hadn't seen a Top 40 hit since the Beatles eclipsed any American singer that smacked of "before." Throughout this rock parable, Carlos O'Connor is constantly being told by his handlers that "these days you've gotta be in a group" and "you're so solitary," pop truisms Nelson must've heard ad nauseam in real life from record execs at a loss to explain the absence of Rick Nelson hits. Oddly enough, Nelson would not have another hit until 1972, when he billed himself with a group, the Stone Canyon Band.

Although Carlos O'Connor's career is going down the toilet, the character is a likeable optimist who feels his rotten luck is going to change any day now. The one moment of self-pity he allows himself is when he sings a brief intro with an acoustic guitar, which doesn't appear on the final recording. The omission is a wise move, since no pop singer would've wanted to cover a song that starts: *"They should've seen me when I was 20 / You never heard such applause / But now I'm 25 / And hardly anyone knows I'm alive / There's no use in looking back 'cause they don't give medals."*

It's a nice old-fashioned tip of the hat to pre-rock songwriting, when every song had to have a wonderful stripped-down intro to set it up. Along with "Take a Broken Heart," "They Don't Give Medals" makes fine use of blank verse, which would come into heavy pop use in the coming years with the Beatles' "I Am the Walrus" and nearly all of Simon and Garfunkel's *Bookends* album ("Save the Life of My Child," "America," "Mrs. Robinson"). "They Don't Give Medals eventually rhymes, but it takes three different melody lines to get there, so it may as well be blank verse.

Nelson maintains his near-conversational style of singing until hitting the "yesterday is over" chorus at the very top of his range, something his oldies never allowed for. In fact he sounds a great deal like Glen Campbell singing a Jimmy Webb song here. It couldn't have helped Nelson's yesterday's-hero status when Ben E. King and Walter Jackson rushed out competing versions. Not wanting to give up on the song, Bacharach and David produced Chuck Jackson doing a forceful version in early 1967 that didn't see release until 20 years later on his *A Powerful Soul* album. They tried it yet again on Dionne Warwick, who sang it several octaves higher than the male vocalists, and on Lainie Kazan, whose somber version moves at a slower, syllable-stretching speed.

Other Versions: *Terry Baxter (1971) • Lainie Kazan (1968) • Chuck Jackson (recorded 1967, released 1987) • Walter Jackson (1967) • Ben E. King (1966) • Peter Matz (1967) • Lou Rawls • Dionne Warwick (1970)*

***Lainie Is Love* (1968).** Who's Lainie Kazan? You kids amaze me. She was the understudy for Barbra Streisand in *Funny Girl* and a popular nightclub entertainer in the late Sixties, but all you need concern yourself with is that she recorded four B&D tunes on the *Lainie Is Love* album, including an overwrought "They Don't Give Medals." Despite Rex Reed's fawning liner notes, she doesn't improve on any of them, no matter how much "the light plays with her hair."

"W.E.E.P." (Burt Bacharach - Hal David)
From the *On the Flip Side* TV special, unreleased

Although it's not actually a song, the team had this brief AM radio station ID jingle copyrighted. *"W.E.E.P., the station with a smile! Just listen to W.E.E.P. a while, W.E.E.P., W.E.E.P., W.E.E.P. and smile!"* Murray Roman played "one of the Swell Fellas," Hairy Harry, a typically frenetic '60s DJ based on WMCA's "Home of the Good Guys" and WABC personality Harry Harrison.

"Take a Broken Heart" (Burt Bacharach - Hal David)
First recorded by Rick Nelson
From the *On the Flip Side* TV soundtrack
Decca 32055, flip side to "They Don't Give Medals
Released December 1966

Nearly every Hal David lyric written for Nelson in this score has him singing from the viewpoint of Carlos O'Connor, a stubborn loner who knows what's best for him. Here's the exception, a vulnerable precursor to "This Guy's in Love with You" where Nelson begs forgiveness for his foolishness—*"Take my arms, take my lips, take my tears away and love me / Come back to my arms / Believe me, if you leave me I will die*—followed by some lonesome whistling. Beautifully sung by Nelson, it's a fine choice to make former Carlos O'Connor fans swoon for him all over again. The television broadcast featured two other versions of the song not found on the soundtrack LP. One has Nelson performing it with the Celestials, an overblown production where the Celestials repeat every

***What the World Needs Now* (1997).** While an album of Bacharach covers with Jack Davis cover art sounds intriguing, it's marred by artists who can't sing very well and can't seem to pull off these songs as anything but pop-culture kitsch. One of the few exceptions is the BMX Bandits' straightforward handling of "It Doesn't Matter Anymore."

word Carlos sings, to the headache-inducing chime of cathedral bells. This is the one that sends Don Prospect, the show's wicked send up of Phil Spector, salivating. The second version has Nelson performing it solo on acoustic guitar. Unfortunately, life didn't imitate art, and this wonderful song was callously forgotten.

Possibly owing to licensing conflicts, Columbia's loan of Joanie Sommers to Decca Records for the cast album somehow prevented her from releasing her solo number in the show, "Try to See It My Way," as a Joanie Sommers single. Instead, Columbia released "It Doesn't Matter Anymore" backed with "Take a Broken Heart" (Columbia 43950), two songs she didn't perform on the Decca soundtrack. Despite the 45's listing in *Goldmine* price guides, Sommers, interviewed especially for this book, doesn't recall ever recording this hard-to-find pair of Bacharach-David tunes. "I was with Columbia but not for a very long time. If I did [those songs], they didn't do very much with it," she laughs.

Other Versions: *Joanie Sommers (1966)*

"It Doesn't Matter Anymore" (Burt Bacharach - Hal David)
First recorded by Rick Nelson
From the *On the Flip Side* TV soundtrack LP, Decca 4826
Broadcast December 7, 1966, released March 1967

Nothing released in conjunction with *On the Flip Side* provided either Nelson or Joanie Sommers with that elusive chart smash. Both singers released singles to coincide with the December 7 telecast, which was trounced in the ratings by *I Spy* and *The Danny Kaye Show*. By the time the cast album appeared the following March, even the few people who caught the show could be excused for not remembering it.

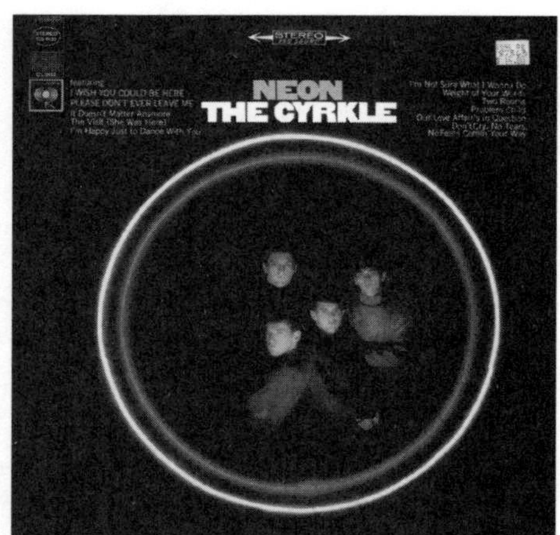

The Cyrkle (1967). Beatles manager Brian Epstein discovered this Pennsylvania pop group and had them opening for the Fabs on their last U.S. tour. This album, released the following year, contained their cover of "It Doesn't Matter Anymore," which would've worked if they hadn't changed the arrangement, just to be different.

"It Doesn't Matter Anymore" kicks off the cast album smartly but is barely heard during the teleplay: it's in the opening scene blaring through a transistor radio underneath dialogue. Peter Matz's use of brass throughout the score is more extroverted than anything Bacharach previously allowed on one of his sessions, and he applies mighty Jericho horn blasts to usher in Carlos O'Connor like pop royalty. In the show, this modern-sounding number is supposed to represent one of O'Connor's golden oldies. Hal David's unsentimental lyric, expressing O'Connor's cavalier indifference after being burned once before, shows the influence Bob Dylan had on contemporary popular music: *"There's no use crying, no use telling me you're sorry now / It doesn't matter anymore / I know, I took you back before / But I'm all through forgivin' you."* There's an intriguing bit of dissonance between the "no use crying" melody and the climbing horn chart that's all but lost in the Cyrkle's soft-rock cover version, which has a jazzy Vince Guaraldi–style piano as the prominent lead instrument. And the "Red Rubber Ball" boys sing it behind the beat.

Other Versions: *BMX Bandits (1998) • The Cyrkle (1967) • Guy Haines (1997) • Joanie Sommers (1966)*

"Fender Mender" (Burt Bacharach - Hal David)
Recorded by the Celestials
From the *On the Flip Side* TV soundtrack LP, Decca 4826
Broadcast December 7, 1966, released March 1967

Fender Mender. B&W promotional still circulated by ABC-TV for *On the Flip Side*, starring Joanie Sommers, which aired in color on December 7, 1966.

In the CD reissue notes for the Byrds' *Younger Than Yesterday*, Chris Hillman revealed that he and Roger McGuinn wrote "So You Want to Be a Rock and Roll Star" after getting incensed over watching the manufactured Monkees climb to the top of the charts two weeks after their TV series premiered. If the Monkees were a carbon copy of the Beatles, the Celestials are a spiritual carbon copy of the Monkees, portrayed by actors who aren't even playing what look like real instruments.

On the Flip Side is one of the rare exceptions where Hal David allowed trendy references to creep into the lyric—"They're Gonna Love It" makes references to Sixties fashions like miniskirts, while "Fender Mender" pays verbal homage to the Fab Four ("I wanna do the things the Beatles do," shriek the Celestials, with "yeah yeahs" inserted in case someone missed the point). The actors are scripted to spout hip doggerel with word like "groovy" and "gear," but thankfully they never have to sing it. Even David's nod to the electric guitar in the title *("Fender mender, fix my guitar; I wanna be a real big record star")* is a cautious step in rock referencing without using the dreaded words "rock 'n' roll." David's sons played in rock bands at the time, but he never thought of his own writing as part of that genre. Unlike his peers, who would gladly make fools of themselves to get a hit with the youth market (witness Bob Hilliard's "Ringo for President" or Jack Wolf's "My Boyfriend Has a Beatle Haircut"), David wisely chose to maintain a respectable distance.

Just as the Beatles were sparing with their use of the Moog because they didn't want to be gimmicky, so too does arranger Peter Matz make conservative use of what was then a modern touch—a fuzz bass line. Throughout, it's maintained at a low volume: even when it's isolated on the breakdowns, it doesn't even come close to competing with the horns. Bacharach himself would demonstrate this tasteful restraint again the following year with Herb Alpert's "Casino Royale." Still, when you listen to the session drummer pummeling the floor toms en route to the chorus, you realize that underneath this 5th Dimension–foreshadowing track, you can hear a hard-rocker that one could see the Move sledgehammering home.

"Try to See It My Way" (Burt Bacharach - Hal David)
First recorded by Joanie Sommers (and Rick Nelson)
From the *On the Flip Side* TV soundtrack LP, Decca 4826
Broadcast December 7, 1966, released March 1967

"I sing better by myself. I don't want your magical gimmicks," Carlos O'Connor rails at Angie, his angel muse, before she launches into her solo in the show, which takes its title from the first line in the Beatles' "We Can Work It Out" and similarly criticizes the stubbornness of the other partner in seeing a solution. The song is repeated more gently as a duet later in the story, with Carlos and Angie going head-to-head:

Terry Baxter (1971). If not for this four-album treasury of orchestral and choral cover versions available only through Columbia House, obscure *On the Flip Side* tunes like "Try to See It My Way" and "They Don't Give Medals"—as well as ignored Dionne B-sides like "Go with Love,""Walk Little Dolly" and "Here Where There Is Love"—might've escaped muzak lovers' attention banks. Too bad Baxter didn't yield to "Fender Mender."

Sommers: "There you go heading fall."

Nelson: "Must you be a know-it-all?"

Sommers: "Don't you know you can't go wrong if you do it my way?"

Nelson: "Angie, please let me do it my way, I know what's best for me."

Anyone reading deeper into the naming of O'Connor's muse might wonder if that other Angie held similar powers over Bacharach's composing abilities, but Angie Dickinson denies inspiring him. She told radio commentator Fred Robbins in 1968: "The only credit I take is that I haven't stopped his genius from flowing through. Because he's really wonderful. He's his own best judge. I hear the songs [being written] through two walls and two doors. I only hear them when Hal and Burt have finished and happen to have time and say, 'Hey, you want to hear the new song?' and play it for me. I don't get in on any ground floor."

Whatever prevented "Try to See It My Way" from coming out as a Joanie Sommers single, Little Peggy March, the youngest female singer to have a No. 1 hit ("I Will Follow Him") was quick to cover it. March, who stopped being "Little" around the time she stopped having hits, sang this showstopper sotto voce and double-tracked on the flip sides of two singles—"Fool, Fool, Fool (Look in the Mirror)" in 1966 and "Purple Hat," her next-to-last RCA 45, in 1969

Other Versions: *Terry Baxter (1971) • Little Peggy March (1966) • Jackie Trent & Tony Hatch • Leslie Uggams*

Rick Nelson. One of his rarest LPs, yet most discographies don't even list this as a Rick Nelson album. A four-disc boxed-set retrospective on the singer released in 1999 doesn't include even one song from it. But that doesn't mean you should stop looking for it. Where else can you get the complete works of the Celestials?

"They're Gonna Love It" (Burt Bacharach - Hal David)
Recorded by Donna Jean Young
From the *On the Flip Side* TV soundtrack, Decca 4826
Broadcast December 7, 1966, released March 1967

Broadway scores typically contain several "situational" songs that move the story along but don't have a life outside the show. *Flip Side* arguably had two such numbers: Bacharach and David certainly wouldn't have written "Fender Mender" for Jackie DeShannon, nor could Dionne Warwick have been expected to sing this song in a semi–Betty Boop voice while ghastly housewife voices holler back. Character actress Donna Jean Young played Juanita, whose boutique promoted fashions too bold for straight people to wear. *"Oh no, not even if it's free,"* women jeer at her, despite Juanita's assuring them, *"Don't worry, they're gonna love it."* Although working in trendy territory *("It isn't very hard to become a mod"),* Hal David does get in some good old-fashioned yuks, like *"There's a miniskirt that hardly covers your thighs / If you just pull your tummy in I'm sure it's just your size."*

"Juanita's Place" (Burt Bacharach - Hal David)
First recorded by Burt Bacharach
Liberty 55934, flip side of "Nikki"
Released December 1966

Three versions of this hyperactive *On the Flip Side* number exist on vinyl, with two appearing on the cast album. The one called "Juanita's Place Montage" features both the Celestials and Donna Jean Young and clocks in at 4:48, with several jarring tape edits as it goes from marimba to mambo to salsa. Meant to be the big dance sequence any self-respecting musical must contain, the TV segment shows the Celestials and Young on film, cavorting on New York mass transit, dancing in front of Madison Square Garden and busking before a few Broadway theaters in an effort to drum up interest for their "happening." The Celestials reprise the number more sedately the second time, singing an additional verse and a coda not found in the "Montage": *"So come along and you'll find love inside / True love cannot find those who hide."* We see love-seeking teens dancing to the song at Juanita's Place only once in the show, with choreography that has more in common with domestic violence.

Bacharach's own version, found on the flip side of "Nikki," gives an indication of how he might've conducted the show's score differently. Although considerably slower, this take has louder, more propulsive drumming, jangling guitars, vibes and a more lethal fuzz bass. Unlike the A-side, Bacharach would never recut "Juanita" or any other song connected with *Flip Side*, save for "They Don't Give Medals." Generally his own harshest critic, Bacharach appraised his first musical in a recent issue of *Pulse!* magazine: "I don't think it was very good."

"Nikki." A very public display of affection from the intensely private Bacharach—in a trade ad, no less! His paternal single would be a one-off for Liberty Records.

Other Versions: *The Celestials (1967)* • *The Celestials & Donna Jean Young (1967)*

"Nikki" (Burt Bacharach - Hal David)
First recorded by Burt Bacharach
Liberty 55934, released December 1966

"One of the best reasons I ever had for writing something was six years ago when my someone very important stepped into my life…my daughter Nikki had just been born," Bacharach recalls on his 1972 TV special *Bacharach and Associates*. Leah Nikki Bacharach's struggle to stay alive—she was born three months premature, weighing just one pound, 10 ounces—and the painful separation her parents endured while she was fighting in an incubator is a subtext that few could pick up on while casually listening to Ed Ames sing Hal David's sympathetic lyrics. It could just as easily pass for yet another song about lovers whom fate has destined to be unhappy until they're reunited. *("Nikki, it's you / Nikki, where can you be / It's you, no one but you for me / I've been so lonely since you went away / I won't spend a happy day till you're back in my arms")*. Despite Ames' earnest reading and Terry Baxter assigning an Ed Ames sound-alike to sing his version, most people preferred not to hear the words ever again.

***When the Snow Is on the Roses* (1967).** Clearly Ed Ames has brought this bonnie lass here under false pretences, as there is neither snow nor roses anywhere on this sleeve. Thrift shoppers are advised not to pay more than 50 cents for the privilege of hearing "Nikki" with vocals.

In the year between his *Hitmaker* sessions and this one-shot single for Liberty Records, Bacharach flexed his arranging muscles with two film scores and was now ready to put out a single that didn't rely on background vocals to carry the melody at least part of the way. It's fun to listen to the melodic tag team of flugelhorn and trumpets banter back and forth, joined by faint choral vocals and strings that float in like a light whistle. This arrangement is adhered to religiously on Bacharach's 1971 version, with only a fuller stereo sound to differentiate it.

1967

Session guitarist Vincent Bell recorded his version in 1970, shortly after "Nikki" was adopted as the theme for ABC's *Movie of the Week*, in an orchestral version never made commercially available. Bell was popular for his "water sound" guitar, which makes one of its earliest appearances on Dionne Warwick's "The Beginning of Loneliness" and would figure prominently in Top 5 hits like "Can't Take My Eyes off You" by Frankie Valli and "Theme from Midnight Cowboy" by Ferrante and Teicher. Bell also played the electric sitar on B.J. Thomas' "Hooked on a Feeling."

Other Versions: *Ed Ames (1967) • Terry Baxter (1971) • Vincent Bell (1970)*

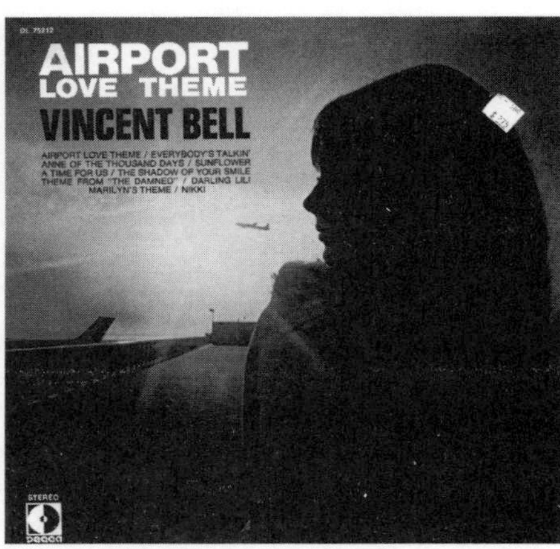

Vincent Bell (1970). A theme album of theme songs, including "Nikki," better known as the *ABC Movie of the Week* theme. Guitarist Bell's "water sound" was a gimmick that got old pretty quickly—it ended with this album —but collectors are advised to seek out his single of "The Ballad of John and Yoko" and his 1967 Decca album *Pop Goes the Electric Sitar!* Bell unpacked his guitar sitar sound on "Feel The Joy" for the *Lost Horizon* sessions.

"The Beginning of Loneliness" (Burt Bacharach - Hal David)
Recorded by Dionne Warwick
Scepter 12187, flip side of "Alfie" (*Billboard* pop #79)
Released March 1967

Initially this power ballad was the designated A-side, but deejays and the public preferred hearing Dionne redo familiar Bacharach-David fare for the third consecutive time. Once Vincent Bell's water guitar, simulating raindrops, provides the count-off, Dionne traces her loneliness from the doorbell that doesn't ring to the empty chair no one's sitting in anymore. The pleasurable set of chord changes in the verse quietly looks around for somewhere to go, and the song rather predictably escalates into bombastic orchestral firepower and cracking drums, making these proceedings feel more like a Little Anthony and the Imperials blowout. Providing more than ample support for "Alfie," "The Beginning of Loneliness" would make one more scheduled stop on the next Dionne album and end there.

The 5th Dimension (1970). They were the Versatiles when they were discovered by Johnny Rivers, who insisted they change their name and record for his Soul City label. There they cut many songs by Rivers' other discovery, songwriter Jimmy Webb.

"One Less Bell to Answer" (Burt Bacharach - Hal David)
First recorded by Keely Smith
Atlantic 2429, released spring 1967

Hal David has stated in numerous interviews that Angie Dickinson was the inspiration behind the title. While hosting a dinner party, she asked if one of the early arrivals could open the door for any incoming guests. "That will be one less bell to answer," she replied and David immediately seized on it as one more metaphor for abandonment.

According to an exchange between Barbra Streisand and Bacharach on his 1971 Singer-sponsored special, she was sent a copy of the song but was indecisive about the ending. Its first recorded appearance was by Keely Smith, but this now-classic torch ballad would not fully reach its potential until the 5th Dimension's 1970 hit version. For one thing, Keely's version begins with the first two notes of the song repeated twice to simulate door chimes. Like Richard Carpenter's revision of "Close to You," "One Less Bell to Answer" is greatly improved by an added intro, courtesy of producer Bones Howe and his co-arrangers, Bob Alcivar and Bill Holman. And although Keely Smith sings the song expertly, it seems incomplete without Marilyn McCoo's nervous obsessing about her diminished egg-frying chores. Maybe she knows something we don't:

when the group and producer Howe premiered the song on the Robert Wagner TV series *It Takes a Thief*, the song's last chord activated an explosive device!

Prior to 1970, the 5th Dimension recorded for Johnny Rivers' Soul City label, until Larry Utall's Bell Records bought out their contract. After a pair of stiff singles from their *Portrait* album, Utall insisted that "One Less Bell to Answer" be released next. The group and producer Bones Howe didn't want the song out as a single: it was practically a Marilyn McCoo solo record. At Utall's insistance, dub copies were sent to a New Orleans radio station, and within a few days they had enough requests to justify releasing it as a single.

Barbra Streisand (1971). In attempt to look hip and with it for the post-Woodstock crowd, Babs instead foreshadows her Yentl look of 1983.

Barbra Streisand got over her indifference to the song's ending when she coupled it with that other domestic desertion anthem "A House Is Not a Home," found on her *Barbra Joan Streisand* album and dutifully performed on the Bacharach TV special. Around the same time, Bacharach revived the song for his third A&M album, with Cissy Houston intermittently adding the necessary anguish. The most satisfying post-hit version would be Dionne's cover, onto which arranger Bob James adds an altogether different intro and we have the pleasure of hearing her sing the title in two different octaves. Dionne didn't record the tune earlier because she didn't feel it suited her; she revealed to writer David Nathan that it was only included on her Warner debut as filler.

Other Versions: *Burt Bacharach (1971) • Shirley Bassey • Terry Baxter (1971) • Joe Bourne • Reuben Brown Trio with Richie Cole • Vikki Carr • Sheryl Crow • Lenny Dee • 5th Dimension (1970) • Sheila Hutchinson - medley • Stanley Jordan • Gladys Knight • Andre Kostelanetz • Marie McAuliffe (1998) • Christiane Noll • Rita Reys • Dinah Shore • Lucie Silvas (2000) • Starlight Orchestra • Barbra Streisand - medley, with "A House Is Not a Home" • Gary Tesca • McCoy Tyner • Dionne Warwick (1972) • The Wilders*

"Bond Street" aka "Home James, Don't Spare the Horses" (Burt Bacharach)
First recorded by Burt Bacharach
A&M 845, flip side of "Alfie"
Released March 1967

This galloping instrumental has earned a permanent spot in the movie-medley segment of Burt's concerts: it's the number that has wives nudging their husbands and whispering, "What's this one from?" Although renamed "Bond Street" on Bacharach's *Reach Out* album, it began life as the "Home James, Don't Spare the Horses" on the soundtrack. Its enduring popularity with Bacharach and other recording artists might lead one to believe that the wrong song may have been chosen for the title theme.

"Bond Street." A *Cashbox* ad for Bacharach's debut A& M single, which sported a catchier title than "Home James, Don't Spare the Horses."

Other Versions: *Terry Baxter (1971) • Brass Band of the Japanese Air Defense Force • Casino Royale (1999) • Enoch Light (1969) • Arthur Fiedler & the Boston Pops (1972) • Les 5-4-3-2-1 with K-taro Takanami (1994) • Rock Academy String Quartette (1970) • RTE Concert Orchestra/Richard Hayman (1995) • Sala Especial (1999) • Susan & the Surftones (2000) • Yuri Tashiro*

1967

Herb Alpert & the Tijuana Brass. The Mexicali-flavored instrumentalists released 12 albums between 1963 and 1969, all of which went gold. Five held down the No. 1 slot. And all of them occupied the Top 40 for months at a time.

"Casino Royale" aka "Have No Fear, Bond Is Here" (Burt Bacharach - Hal David)
First recorded by Herb Alpert & the Tijuana Brass
From the Columbia motion picture *Casino Royale*
A&M 850 (*Billboard* pop #27)
Released April 1967

"Burt Bacharach did [a Bond theme] for *Casino Royale*. I turned it down. I just didn't like the song. Herbie Alpert wound up doing an instrumental trumpet thing on it. It was terrible. Even the instrumental wasn't any good."

The person not so enamored of the theme was none other than Johnny Rivers, who told me as much in a 2001 interview. While the Secret Agent Man would seem a logical choice to do a Bond theme, neither the song nor the movie was typical of the Bond series, as they were spoofs. *Casino Royale* was based on Ian Fleming's novel of the same name, but seeing as it was filtered through seven screenwriters and five directors—with seven actors, not including the chimp portraying James Bond—any resemblance to characters shaken or stirred is purely coincidental. Given the silly mission, a menacing spy theme à la John Barry didn't seem in the cards. Instead, Bacharach wrote a playful romp with furious double trumpets.

Stuck without his first choice to sing the theme, Bacharach tapped Herb Alpert and the Tijuana Brass to tackle it instrumentally. This was a shrewd move, since Alpert's albums were outselling everyone else's in 1967, save the Beatles and the Monkees. What started out in 1962 as Alpert playing multitracked mariachi parts abetted by a few studio musicians had now grown into an actual touring group. Bacharach sat in on his trademark tack piano at Gold Star Studios and pounded away with Herb's seven-piece band. For the movie mix, the fuzz bass and tambourines seem considerably more in-your-face than they turned out to be in the final studio mix. Although this was the height of the psychedelic era, there was no reason to freak out millions of adult contemporaries for whom "copping some Herb" meant something entirely different.

Over the film's closing credits, you can hear a vocal version of the song, delivered with blustering bravado by an unidentified singer who sounds more like an overworked butler than Tom Jones. Bacharach's exclusion of this recorded version from the soundtrack album seems to indicate his dissatisfaction with the end result. However, the song works far better having mousy female voices oohing and aaahing over 007, as the Harry Roche Constellation's recording of "Have No Fear, Bond Is Here" demonstrates: *"They've got us on the run / With knives! And guns! / We're fighting for our lives / Never fear, look who's here."* And you can hear a similar-sounding version by the band Casino Royale, who include it as a hidden "Track-a-rach" on their *Back to Bacharach* CD. They preface with "Dream on James, You're Winning," before going into "Have No Fear, Bond Is Here."

Other Versions: *Terry Baxter & His Orchestra • Big Ray & the Futuras (2000) • Casino Royale - "Have No Fear, Bond Is Here" • 18th Century Corporation (1969) • The Jet Set (1999) • Peter Nero • Floyd Cramer • Living Guitars • Frank Pourcel (1968)*

• *Harry Roche Constellation - "Have No Fear, Bond Is Here" (1967)* • *Doc Severinsen* • *Starlight Orchestra (1998)* • *Roland Shaw Orchestra (1968)* • *Torero Band (1969)*

Casino Royale (Original Soundtrack LP)
Recorded by Burt Bacharach
Colgems 5005, released April 1967 (_Billboard_ pop #22)

"Casino Royale Theme" (main title) - Herb Alpert & the Tijuana Brass • "The Look of Love" - Dusty Springfield • "Money Penny Goes for Broke" • "Le Chiffre's Torture of the Mind" • "Home James, Don't Spare the Horses" • "Sir James' Trip to Find Mata" • "The Look of Love" (instrumental) • "Hi There Miss Goodthighs" • "Little French Boy" • "Flying Saucers - First Stop Berlin" • "The Venerable Sir James Bond" • "Dream On James, You're Winning" • "The Big Cowboys and Indians Fight at Casino Royale - Casino Royale Theme" (reprise)

Casino Royale. Stereo nuts would spend to upwards of $100 for a mint copy of this album just to demonstrate the superiority of their turntable equipment. That devotion didn't transfer to the compact disc.

Following his success with the score of *The Graduate*, Paul Simon turned down director John Schlessinger's invitation to compose music for *Midnight Cowboy* because he didn't want to be seen as "Dustin Hoffman's songwriter." One hardly thinks of Burt Bacharach as Peter Sellers' songwriter, yet here he is scoring his third consecutive Sellers picture. For some strange reason, Sellers tries playing Bond straight in a movie that could've really used more laughs. Maybe that's why he stayed away from the recording studio this time around.

In terms of musical objectives, this score isn't altogether different from *What's New Pussycat?* or *After the Fox.* Both offer several instrumentals for a seductress to, well, move seductively to, both have a love theme and both included some boisterous pastiches to make the chaotic mess that's filling up the screen seem somehow funnier than it actually is. Although the film is visually stunning (especially those scenes in which bountiful female pulchritude is on display), the laughs are in short supply and the solution seems to be just blow some things up, spray the cast with laughing gas, stick in some big-name cameos who wink at the camera like zany idiots, and hope no one will notice. That the movie's climax—with cowboys and Indians parachuting through the glass ceiling of Casino Royale and doing the frug—seemed like a funny idea to somebody indicates the lack of lucid minds at work here. Given that to work with, Bacharach dutifully scored music that Indians parachuting through the ceiling could conceivably frug to. Asked to orchestrate a scene for "Le Chiffre's Torture of the Mind," Bacharach responded with torturous bagpipe music.

Casino Royale. When Bacharach approached Alpert about doing this theme together, it began a professional association with A&M Records that would last until the *Arthur2* soundtrack in 1988.

Besides straight cover versions and the recycling of "Home James, Don't Spare the Horses" into "Bond Street," two tunes found unique life after *Casino Royale*: "Flying Saucers - First Stop Berlin" morphed into "Let the Love Come Through," while the clarinet whimsy of "Little French Boy" later found use on a Cracker Jack commercial.

For those who enjoy multiple ironies, Bacharach's first Oscar-losing song, "What's New Pussycat?," is alluded to twice in the film. It comes wafting out of an uncovered manhole the first time, and it's mangled as a slow marching-band dirge during the cowboys-and-Indians finale. The

Cal Tjader Sounds Out Burt Bacharach (1968). Not only does this vibraphonist's tribute to Bacharach and David contain a great version of "Money Penny Goes for Broke," but it's also the only such LP to have the complete endorsement of Bacharach's onetime next-door neighbor Merv Griffin.

oddest inside musical joke occurs in an early scene at Bond's estate, which is patrolled by a pack of roving lions. Over these visuals, Bacharach plays a brief snippet of "Born Free," the John Barry/Don Black song that beat "Alfie" out of the Academy Award for best song the previous year.

"Money Penny Goes for Broke" (Burt Bacharach)
Recorded by Burt Bacharach
From the *Casino Royale* soundtrack LP
Colgems 5005 (*Billboard* pop #22)
Released April 1967

If you took the "Casino Royale" theme, with its dual trumpet flourishes, and "The Look of Love," with its scraper, and put them in a blender, you'd come out with something like this alluring music-to slink-around-office-furniture-to. It became the unlikely opening track of a Bacharach tribute album by xylophonist Cal Tjader.

Other Versions: *Cal Tjader (1968)*

The Look of Love (Burt Bacharach - Hal David)
First recorded by Dusty Springfield
Philips 40465, flip side of "Give Me Time" (*Billboard* pop #22)
Released July 1967

Once again, the only component of a Charles K. Feldman enterprise worthy of Oscar consideration is a classic Bacharach-David song. *Casino Royale*'s love theme differed from its *What's New Pussycat?* counterpart in that *Pussycat*'s "Here I Am" was sung by the about-to-be seduced. In "The Look of Love," the singer is the aggressor, about to put the moves on as soon as the Dubonnet is sufficiently chilled. Only the Almighty could calculate how many a love child was spawned from knee-to-knee encounters to this recording. This must come as no small comfort to its composer, for whom "so many nights like this" meant threading a Moviola machine for the millionth time and accentuating Ursula Andress' every move with a bar of music.

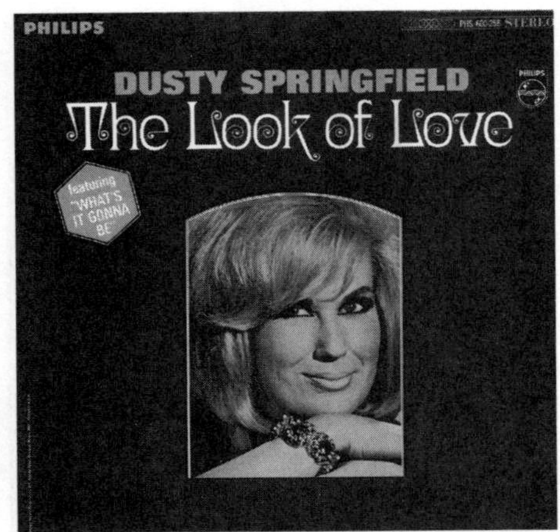

Dusty Springfield. U.S. record companies had an annoying compulsion to plaster reverb on any records coming out of England, believing they'd somehow sound better coming out of American car radios that way. Anyone who bought Dusty's *Look of Love* album on Philips heard her bathed in a sea of echo, which went uncorrected on Mercury's slapdash 1999 compact-disc transfer.

Previously, Bacharach had pitched already-released songs to Dusty Springfield, but never before had he worked with the singer in a recording studio. The *Casino Royale* soundtrack afforded him the perfect opportunity, but the sessions proved to be one of his most difficult collaborations, for an entirely different set of reasons. "That was a trip," he admits somewhat cautiously on her video biography, *Full Circle*, "simply because I'm a perfectionist. And she's a perfectionist, but much harder on herself than I think I am on myself." Sadly, their one-on-one collaboration would not resume beyond this recording and a duet of "A House Is Not a Home" on her TV show. If they ever attempted an entire album, Bacharach believes that "we probably would've killed each other in the studio, probably just destroy one another. On a playback I remember that she wound up going in another the studio by herself in the control room just to hear herself. She didn't want anyone around. She didn't want me around. So I stayed in the control room. [But] I thought it was great, just what we wanted for the picture."

Dusty's perfectionism prevented her from hearing that greatness in her performance, and it took another version of "The Look of Love," produced with Johnny Franz, before she was satisfied. This would become the hit version most people remember, although it was initially relegated to the B-side of "Give Me Time," another translated-from-Italian ballad ("L'amore se ne va") à la "You Don't Have to Say You Love Me" ("Io che non vivo senza te"). Any deejay with sense would've flipped this rehash over in favor of the song with a timely movie tie-in, and luckily one in Seattle did just that. Once it became a hit there, it broke in California and worked its way east. By mid-October it was in the Top 40.

Sergio Mendes & Brasil '66 (1968). Bacharach & David's first three Academy Award nominations all lost out to animal songs—first "The Shadow of Your Smile" (also known as "Love Theme from the Sandpiper"), then "Born Free" and finally "Talk to the Animals."

Opinions differ sharply between Bacharach and Springfield devotees as to which recorded version is the more effective. Audiophiles who spent hundreds of dollars for a clean vinyl copy of the *Casino Royale* soundtrack prefer this version for its dry, in-your-lap vocals and the closeness with which the sax solo was miked. Also, the movie version had a slightly more aggressive delivery from Dusty and an extended sax-and-horn coda that's pay-dirt Bacharach. Naturally Dusty has the last word on her remake, which has sustained strings and just a hint of reverb. Known to sometimes record her vocals one syllable at a time, she achieves a vulnerability with her phrasing here that she apparently had a hard time capturing with the song's composer present.

Sergio Mendes and Brasil '66's more ostentatious version the following year proved an even bigger hit, soaring all the way to No. 4. The group would perform the song on the 1968 Academy Awards show, but the third Oscar-nominated song for Bacharach and David suffered an unconscionable loss to the already-forgotten "Talk to the Animals" from *Doctor Dolittle*. "The Look of Love" would be featured in two films within two years, *The Boys in the Band* and *Mad Monster Party*, the latter a stop-action puppet movie with Paul Frees singing the Dusty hit in the voice of Boris Karloff!

"The Look of Love" proved to be one of the elite group of Bacharach-David songs that artists could only ruin by making a concentrated effort. All the elements are there, and all an artist needed to do was to color inside the black lines. Of special note are the rock versions—a BBC recording by the Zombies, whose lead vocalist, Colin Blunstone, achieves the same husky tonality as Dusty Springfield, and a surprisingly tasteful interpretation by Vanilla Fudge, who usually stretch a song mercilessly on a rack before calling it a day. Here they demonstrate an elegant, almost spooky restraint.

"The Look of Love." Truly Philips meant for this song not to be the plug side.

Other Versions: *Barbara Acklin (1968) • Yasuko Agawa (1996) • Ronnie Aldrich (1971) • Herb Alpert & Lani Hall (1999) • Ed Ames (1969) • Chet Atkins (1969) • Burt Bacharach (1967) • Baja Marimba Band (1967) • Anita Baker (1994) • Shirley Bassey (1971) • Martyn Bates • Terry Baxter (1971) • Laurie Beechman (1993) • Tony Bennett (1968) • Jeri Brown (1994) • Willie Bobo (1968) • Joe Bourne (1993) • Casino Royale (1999) • Blue Velvet (2000) • Lee Castle & the Jimmy Dorsey Orchestra (1974) • Frank Chacksfield (1971) • Cosmonauti (2000) • King Curtis • Vic Damone • Michael Davis (1995) • Deacon Blue (1990) • Neil Diamond • Delfonics (1968) • Linda Di Franco • Carl Doy • Either/Orchestra (1986) • Lars Ekstrom (1997) • El Chicano (1970) • Percy Faith (1968) • Ferrante & Teicher (1969) • Arthur Fiedler & the Boston Pops • (1972)*

1967

"The Look of Love." There were no labor laws in place as far as LP work was concerned. Scepter released *five* Dionne Warwick albums in 1967: *Here Where There Is Love, The Magic of Believing, On Stage and in the Movies* and *Windows of the World*, as well as *Dionne Warwick's Golden Hits, Part 1. On Stage* contained Dionne's take on "The Look of Love."

Film Score Orchestra • The Foundations • The Four Tops (1969) • Connie Francis (1968) • Free'n' Easy (1998) • Paul Frees (as the voice of Boris Karloff) (1970) • Tommy Garrett (1969) • Grant Geissman (1999) • Stan Getz • Don Goldie (1977) • Eydie Gorme • Buddy Greco (1976) • Rune Gustafsson (1969) • Scott Hamilton (1993) • Hampton Hawes • Isaac Hayes (1970) • Susanna Hoffs (1997) • Yuka Honda & Sean Lennon (1997) • Shirley Horn (1996) •The Impressions (1968) • Milt Jackson (1995) • Ahmad Jamal (1968) • Lainie Kazan (1968) • Anita Kerr Singers (1968) • Barney Kessel (1968) • Andre Kostelanetz (1968) • Gladys Knight & the Pips (1968) • Diana Krall (2001) • Jane Krakowski (1998) • Michele Lee (1968) • The Lettermen (1968) • Linda Lewis (2000) • Ramsey Lewis • Claudine Longet (1967) • Alan Lorber Orchestra (1967) • Michelle Malone & Karyn Folmar Malone (2000) • Jon Lucien (1997) • Tony Mansell Singers (1971) • Mireille Mathieu • Johnny Mathis • Billy May & His Orchestra (1997) • Tina May • Marie McAuliffe (1998) • Keff McCulloch (1996) • Carmen McRae • Sergio Mendes & Brasil '66 (1968, live 1972) • The Meters (recorded 1970, released 1999) • Midnight String Quartet (1967) • Liza Minelli (1968) • The Moments (live 1972) • Greg Morris • Nanette • Peter Nero (1968) • Steve Newcomb Trio (2000) • 101 Strings • Tex Perkins & Lisa Miller (1998) • Bill Plummer (1968) • Queen Samantha • Boots Randolph (1969) • Renaissance • Cliff Richard - live medley (1972) • Rita Reys (1969) • Howard Roberts • Christopher Scott (1969) • Marilyn Scott (1998) • Doc Severinsen (1967) • Roland Shaw & His Orchestra (1968) • RTE Concert Orchestra/Richard Hayman (1995) • Nina Simone (1967) • The Simpsons (TV series, 1991) • Soul Bossa Trio (1994) • Sounds of Our Times • Sheila Southern (1968) • Victor Sylvester Orchestra • Gabor Szabo (1968) • Bill Tarmey • Gary Tesca (1995) • The Three Sounds (1968) • Dusty Springfield & Mireille Mathieu (1968 TV special) • Tokyo Ska Paradise Orchestra (1993) • Stanley Turrentine (1968) • McCoy Tyner (1996) • Caterina Valente • Vanilla Fudge (1968) • Billy Vaughn (1968) • Jerry Vale (1968) • David T. Walker (1967) • Scott Walker (1969) • Shani Wallis (1967) • Dionne Warwick (1967, rerecorded 2000) • Grover Washington Jr. (1987) • Tony Joe White (1968) • Wild Bunch (Massive Attack) (1986) • Andy Williams (1967) • Pat Williams (1968) • Roger Williams • Bobby Womack (1973) • Zip Code Rapists • The Zombies (1967)

"Let the Love Come Through" aka "Flying Saucer—First Stop Berlin" (Burt Bacharach - Hal David)
First recorded by Roland Shaw
From the album *World of Spy Thrillers*
Decca SPA 213, released 1967

British bandleader Roland Shaw recorded some generic orchestral albums for Decca before hitting on a winning formula—anthologizing James Bond movie music for people who didn't wish to buy each successive soundtrack. With the series updated every few years to include new music, Shaw amassed a nice collection of albums with bikini-and-bazooka babes on the covers, easily spotted in the sea of droll Mantovani-and-his-baton sleeves.

People who bought his 1967 spy maestro work probably scratched their heads wondering why they'd seen all the Bond films but never heard this song. They *did:* less than two minutes worth of "Let the Love Come Through" was featured without words as part of "Flying Saucer—First Stop Berlin" from *Casino Royale*. Whether it's a rejected love theme or a lyrical afterthought, it provides Bacharach fans a fine excuse to seek out a Roland Shaw recording. Sung by a double-tracked coquette, it's got pretty bare-boned instrumentation, with piano, chunky rhythm guitar and, dare I say it, funky brushwork on the drums. Once again, Hal David is forced into a hip corner by pseudo-psychedelic music, but he extricates himself in stylish fashion: *"I know that you know where it's at tonight, let the love come through / It's right here in my arms when I hold you tight, let the love come through / There is nothing to be afraid of / Our emotions are what we are made of, darling."* The groove is actually very similar to Paul Simon's psychedelic gripe "Fakin' It," which came out days before the Summer of Love officially kicked off.

Too good a song to waste, "Let the Love Come Through" was recorded again by Australian singer Janice Slater the following year (Spin EK-1984, produced by Robert Iredale).

Other Versions: *Janice Slater (1968)*

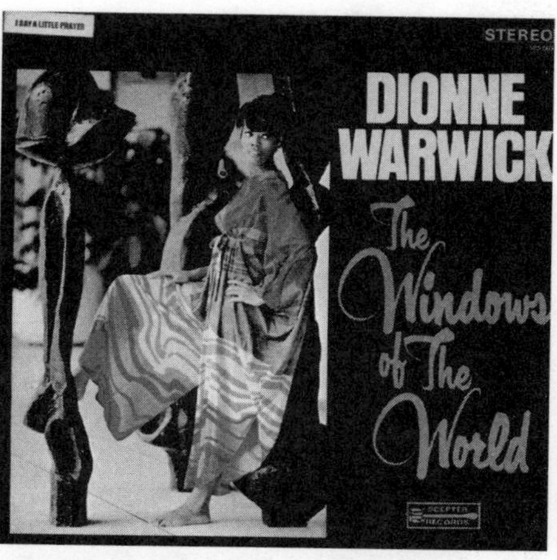

"The Windows of the World." This message song inspired several other impeccable versions by Isaac Hayes, Scott Walker, the Pretenders and Stan Getz.

"The Windows of the World" (Burt Bacharach - Hal David)
First recorded by Dionne Warwick
Scepter 12196 (*Billboard* pop #32)
Released July 1967

This is the first overtly political salvo from Bacharach-David, with specific lyrical references to the unpopular war Americans were embroiled in at the time *("When boys turn into men they start to wonder when their country will call,…When men cannot be friends their quarrel often ends when some have to die").* Bacharach also provided musical cues—the pizzicato strings softly playing like an Asian koto and finger cymbals that suggest both a Vietnamese rice paddy and a window covered with rain. The war was weighing heavily on Hal David's mind, as he had two sons, one eligible for the draft. His gentle wisdom stood in stark contrast to more vocal anti-war sentiments on the pop charts, and while the song's subtlety may have prevented audiences from hearing its message, it did succeed in taking that message to places it never would've been voiced otherwise, like on a Jack Jones or Anita Kerr record.

Other Versions: *Terry Baxter (1971) • Burt Bacharach (1967) • Fabulous Planktones (2000) • Free Design (1968) • Stan Getz (1967) • Isaac Hayes (1972, live 1977) • The Jet Set (1999) • Pete Jolly (1968) • Jack Jones • Lainie Kazan (1968) • Anita Kerr Singers (1969) • Longines Symphonette Society (1970) • Keff McCulloch (1996) • New Direction - medley (1969) • The Pretenders (1988) • Rita Reys (1971) • Jimmie Rodgers (1969) • McCoy Tyner (1996) • Luther Vandross - live medley (1998) • Caterina Valente - medley (1971) • David T. Walker (1976) • Scott Walker (1968)*

"Walk Little Dolly" (Burt Bacharach - Hal David)
First recorded by Dionne Warwick
Scepter 12196, flip side of "The Windows of the World"
Released July 1967

"When I'm hurt, I revert back to my doll," Dionne confesses in yet another post-breakup mini-drama, one that locates her in a locked room again, afraid to face the world. Trying to find strength and resolve by reliving childhood innocence, she sings some words of encouragement to her dolly that work for a few bars, until she comes back to the depressing conclusion that *"It is only in real life that a girl has to cry."* Some terrif-

ic little-dolly singing from Dionne and Cissy Houston make this yet another essential B-side.

Other Versions: *Terry Baxter (1971)*

"I Say a Little Prayer." After the single sold 700,000 copies, Scepter flipped the single back over and made "Theme from Valley of the Dolls" an even bigger hit. Contrary to what most people think, Bacharach and David didn't write that song—André and Dory Previn did. And Pat Williams arranged the song, with Bacharach conducting.

Billboard
August 10, 1968

Aretha Franklin. This song was responsible for yet another double-sided hit.

"I Say a Little Prayer" (Burt Bacharach - Hal David)
First recorded by Dionne Warwick
Scepter 12203 (*Billboard* pop #4)
Released October 1967

The Windows of the World album contained only one never-before-heard Bacharach-David song, and it was one Bacharach didn't wish to be released as a single. Ever the perfectionist, he believed the arrangement was too rushed, and he grew to dislike it. As with "Alfie," deejays across the country took to playing an album track until its momentum couldn't be denied. "That's the great thing about the record business, that you can be that wrong. You can believe in a song that's a hit and not believe in a song that's an even bigger hit," Bacharach told the National Guard radio several months after this became Warwick's biggest Bacharach-David hit. While Bacharach was at a loss trying to explain the uncertain science of what makes a hit, the listening public was bypassing his first choices on an almost continual basis. But they only ignored the B-side for a few months, eventually making "Theme from the Valley of the Dolls" Dionne's biggest Sixties-era hit (*Billboard* pop No. 2) and the double-sided hit single her first gold record.

To gauge what Bacharach meant by the tempo being rushed, listen to the slightly slower velocity he used for his instrumental of "I Say a Little Prayer" on the *Reach Out* album. It's quite telling that the demonstration recording furnished by his publishing company features Aretha Franklin's later rendition, which is also a tad slower.

To any human ear not attached to the Bacharach mind, the Dionne version sounds quite perfect, thank you—its swift tempo ideal for suggesting someone's morning workaday preparation rituals. If Bacharach thought the antiwar message of "The Windows of the World" was too subtle, what could he have thought of "I Say a Little Prayer"? One could pass through an entire lifetime without knowing that Hal David wrote the lyrics as a message to send out to our boys in Vietnam. *"To live without you would only mean heartbreak for me"* adds the essential tension that any great love song needs, although the tension is eased somewhat by the freewheeling way Dionne chases the horn part in the instrumental break.

When Aretha Franklin covered "Respect," its composer, Otis Redding, joked that "that girl stole that song away from me" and turned it into her signature anthem. If it's possible to go the voice of Bacharach-David one better, we must demur to the Queen of Soul, who was absolutely unstoppable in 1968. No matter that "I Say a Little Prayer" was a Top 5 hit just six months earlier, Aretha had only to open her mouth in a recording studio and the song became hers. Reportedly, Aretha and the Sweet Inspirations were just fooling around with the number during rehearsals when they stumbled on a good thing. Placed on the rear side of her single "The House That Jack Built," it became so popular that Atlantic was forced to deem the pairing a double A-sided 45.

When several male entertainers sauntered up to cover the tune, they had some trouble getting out *"The moment I wake up / before I put on my makeup."* Glen Campbell skirted the issue by turning the song into a duet with Anne Murray just so he wouldn't have to sing the line. Ed Ames warbled what seems like the official male version: *"The moment I get up / before I can shave and set up."* Johnny Mathis mixed up the two versions thusly: *"The moment I wake up / before I shave and set up."* Would it have killed him to come up with a rhyme? The Reverend Al Green, whose little prayer carries more weight than the others, kept the original lyric, unashamed to admit wearing makeup. Ditto for the cast of *My Best Friend's Wedding,* led by Julia Robert's gay confidant in the film, played by Rupert Everett. The wedding singer, played by Andy Marvel, comes up with another variation for males *("The moment I wake up, before* you *put on* your *makeup"),* while reggae artist Diana King, in the same movie, temporarily misplaces her pronouns on the verses *("The moment* me *wake up, before* me *put on* me *makeup"),* only to conform on the chorus.

***My Best Friend's Wedding* (1997).** Three versions of "I Say a Little Prayer" are featured in this film, none sung by Dionne Warwick. "Who's Dionne Warwick?" a boy in the wedding party asks. The singer couldn't have been happy with being referenced as a Psychic Network star, Whitney Houston's aunt and, according to Rupert Everett's tall tale, a crazy guy in a mental ward named Jerry.

Other Versions: *Akira Ishikawa Trio • Ed Ames (1969) • Julius Wechter & the Baja Marimba Band • Burt Bacharach • Terry Baxter (1971) • Tony Bennett • Mary Black • Bomb the Bass (1988) • Booker T & the MG's • Perry Botkin Jr. & His Orchestra • Joe Bourne (1993) • Ray Bryant (1968) • Glen Campbell & Anne Murray - "By the Time I Get to Phoenix/I Say a Little Prayer" medley (1971) • Raffaella Carra • Casino Royale • Lee Castle & the Jimmy Dorsey Orchestra (1974) • City of Westminster String Band (1970) • Ray Conniff (1968) • Skeeter Davis • Carl Doy • Martha Dove (1968) • 18th Century Corporation (1969) • Percy Faith • 5th Dimension • Film Score Orchestra • Connie Francis • Aretha Franklin • Free'n' Easy (1998) • Gloria Gaynor • Grant Geissman (1999) • Gene (1998) • Ron Goodwin • Al Green (1991) • Anita Harris • Tony Hatch Orchestra • Isaac Hayes & Dionne Warwick - "By the Time I Get to Phoenix/I Say a Little Prayer" medley 1977) • Woody Herman (1968) • Shauna Hicks • Holy Groove (1997) • Ahmad Jamal (1968) • Anita Kerr Singers (1969) • Diana King (1997) • Jonathan King • Rahsaan Roland Kirk (1968) • Earl Klugh (1991) • Ellis Larkins • Jackie Leven (1994) • Tony Mansell Singers (1970) • Johnny Mathis • Russell Malone • Andy Marvel (1997) • Hiroshi Matsumoto (1970) • Paul Mauriat • Marie McAuliffe • Sergio Mendes (1968) • Anita Meyer (1989) • Missing Fortnight • Willie Mitchell • Wes Montgomery • Carl Myrén - "Sen drömmer jag en stund om dig" (1984) • Lady Nelson & the Lords (1968) • Larry Page Orchestra • Cast of My Best Friend's Wedding (1997) • Mitch Rasor • Martha Reeves & the Vandellas (1968) • Renaissance • RTE Concert Orchestra • Christopher Scott (1969) • Bud Shank with Chet Baker (1967) • Helen Shapiro • Sound of Our Times • Starlight Orchestra • Shoko Suzuki • Swan Dive • Cal Tjader (1968) • Caterina Valente (1971) • Reuben Wilson*

"A Sinner's Devotion" (Burt F. Bacharach - Bob Hilliard)
Recorded by Tammi Terrell
From the Chuck Jackson and Tammi Terrell album *The Early Show,* Wand WD 682
Released November 1967

When Tammi Terrell paired off with Marvin Gaye for a series of highly successful Motown duets, the chemistry was so potent that everyone was convinced the love that fueled "Ain't No Mountain High Enough" and "Your Precious Love" was genuine. So what better time for Scepter to make use of all those Tammy Montgomery recordings in their vault? But the crafty powers that be decided that the recent defection of

Chuck Jackson and Tammi Terrell. Despite the "graphic" togetherness, they never sang a note together on Wand Records or Motown, where they both found new homes in 1967.

Chuck Jackson to Motown Records should not go unpunished, so they slapped six of his old cuts onto side two of the album and deceptively packaged it so that it looked like a collection of duets. To quote Marvin and Tammi, this truly "ain't nothing like the real thing, baby."

Among the unissued Terrell titles was this old Bacharach- Hilliard piano-and-tambourine dirge, which had been originally recorded and left unused by the Shirelles. The Shirelles were no strangers to the proverbial one-night-stand dilemma, as "Will You Still Love Me Tomorrow" attested, and this was an obvious attempt by Hilliard to have them tramp that passion ground again—"tramp" being the operative word. This time, there is a compounded awareness of being an adulteress as well as a loose woman, as the sinner in question belongs to someone else. Currently, no Shirelles-only track has surfaced, so we turn our attention to Tammi-with-a-"y," sounding quite ready to give in to the tempting combination of exciting lips and serious moonlight until the very last moment, when she declares: *"The price is too tall / Mustn't listen to your call / For a sinner's devotion is no devotion at all."* All that's missing is the sound of the sinner zipping up his pants.

Although the production is credited to Luther Dixon, it doesn't sound any different than the Bacharach demo that had been circulating since 1961. Which means that Shirley Owens again replaced the demo singer on the track and that she in turn was taped over by Terrell. It's the Shirelles' "ska-da-da, ska da dee dee" background vocals you hear coming out of the right speaker. And on your left you can hear a badly recorded Tammy, with several microphone pops that kept this from ever becoming her third Scepter single. The recording would have taken place sometime before 1962, when she left Scepter to record as Tana Montgomery on James Brown's Try Me label.

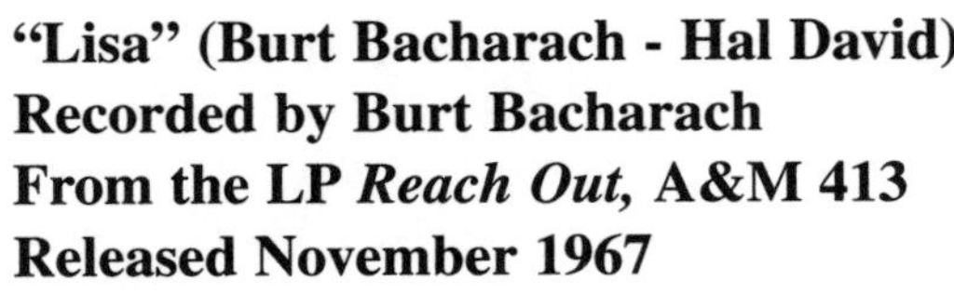

"Lisa" (Burt Bacharach - Hal David)
Recorded by Burt Bacharach
From the LP *Reach Out,* A&M 413
Released November 1967

Burt Bacharach. Unlike *Hitmaker,* which yielded no U.S. hits, the title track of Bacharach's first A&M album, *Reach Out,* reached No. 8 on Billboard's adult-contemporary chart.

Reach Out, Bacharach's first long player for A&M, followed the *Hitmaker* formula of intermingling instrumental versions of proven Bacharach-David hits with one or two new numbers. This album had only one premiere composition, and it seemed more like a stylistic throwback to the pre-Dionne days of "And So Goodbye My Love" than something new. Sung by a chorus so Mancini-esque that Moon River probably sent a search party out for them, "Lisa," the way Hal David describes her, could almost be Holly Golightly—lovely and alluring and alone. Few songs have ever dealt with the intimidation men feel in the presence of a beautiful woman, especially when wealth and fame also set her apart. *"Some men are afraid to reach for a star / so you must be worshipped from afar / How can anyone so beautiful be so unloved?"*

Though it was the second song to take its name from Bacharach first child, Leah Nikki, its title was changed to "Lisa" to avoid confusion with Roy Orbison's similarly dreamy 1962 hit "Leah."

Other Versions: *Jorgen Ingmann*

"Love Was Here Before the Stars" (Burt Bacharach - Hal David)
First recorded by Brian Foley
Kapp 861, released fall 1967

Generally when people speak of psychedelic music, they're referring to pretentious, navel-gazing lyrics or cheap gimmicky instrumentation. This record had neither, but it does have an eerie, unsettling quality that one could associate with many other records that came out that year. Even when everyone was expounding on peace and love and good vibrations, there was a sense of foreboding, as if everyone already knew that the hippie movement and its dependence on mind-altering drugs was a spiritual dead end. "Strawberry Fields Forever," "White Rabbit," "We Love You," "Twelve Thirty" and anything by Pink Floyd echoed this emptiness musically: even pop hits like "Ode to Billie Joe" and "Pretty Ballerina" had sinister string arrangements that would've been unthinkable two years before.

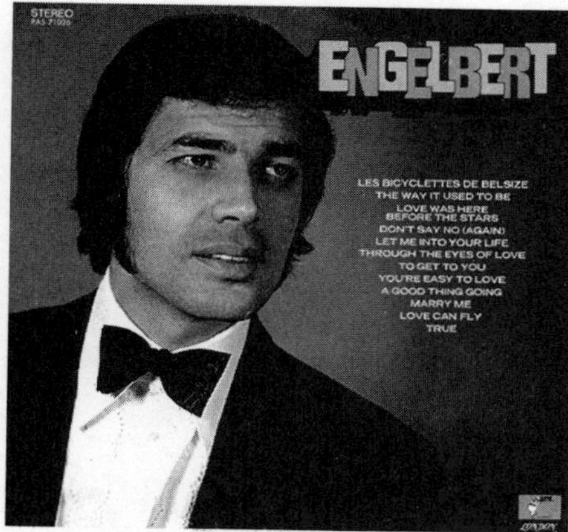

***Engelbert* (1969).** Emphatically on a first name basis with the record-buying public by the time of his fourth album, he was made out to be a rival of Tom Jones by the press. The once-friendly pair was managed by the same man, the late Gordon Mills. Later, feeling that Mills was devoting more time to Tom, Engelbert split and the rivalry became real.

Imagine being lost in a dark forest at night with no sense of direction and you get an idea of the ominous orchestral tension at the outset of this song. Brian Foley discourages you from following the stars, whether in a scoutmaster or astrologer sense, instead asking you to put your trust in him because "love's a weakness that makes you strong." Then he launches into a tortuous melody, perhaps the dreariest chorus Bacharach has ever devised. One can defend Burt's decision to introduce a bold, progressive direction to pop ballads, but it hardly made sense to launch a would-be teen idol with this intricate bit of composing. The record requires multiple plays before one is comfortable enough singing it in the shower, a luxury its relative gloominess doesn't afford it. The air of danger built into Gary Sherman's arrangement was thoroughly fumigated out before Engelbert Humperdinck recorded "Love Was Here Before the Stars" for one of his ballad-laden albums.

Other Versions: *Engelbert Humperdinck (1969)*

"Do You Know the Way to San Jose" (Burt Bacharach - Hal David)
First recorded by Dionne Warwick
From the LP *Valley of the Dolls*
Scepter 12216 (*Billboard* pop #10)
Released April 1968

"Sometimes I'd write against the mood. For instance, 'Do You Know the Way to San Jose' is bright and rhythmic, and because of that you'd think it was instinctively happy. But it wasn't to me."

In fact, Hal David's tale of someone heading back to San Jose after their dreams of fame and fortune went bust can be downright depressing, depending on which lines you're reading between. Although Dionne waxes nostalgic for the breathing space and friends back home, she also must abandon the aspirations that have sustained her this long *("With a dream in your heart you're never alone / But dreams turn into dust and blow away / And there you are without a friend / You pack your car and ride away")*. Now all she has are friends and breathing space.

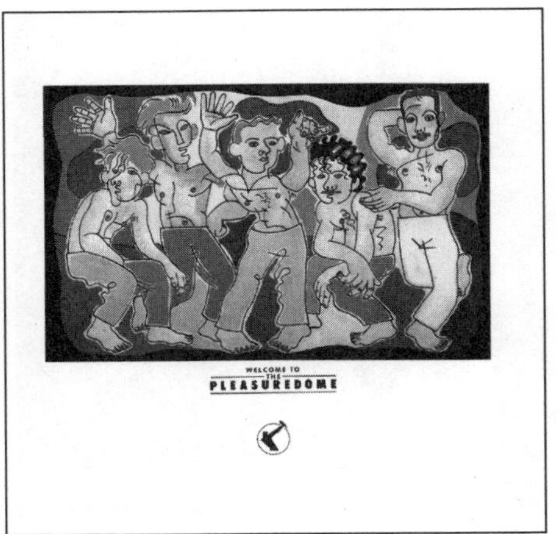

Do You Know the Way to the Pleasuredome? Enormously popular in Britain in 1984 with the success of the controversial dance hit "Relax," the Frankies released a double album that contained a third side of cover songs, including their take on Bacharach-David's first Grammy winner which they retitled, "San Jose (The Way)".

Despite the song's cynical view of the star-making machinery *("All the stars that never were are parking cars and pumping gas")*, Gary Chester's loudly recorded bass drum keeps Dionne's denouement deceptively bouncy. Initially nonplussed about recording the song that became her most popular up-tempo hit and won her first Grammy, Dionne had a change of heart after visiting San Jose. About the city where Hal David was stationed during his navy stint, she told Alec Cumming, "It's a beautiful little city. I was made an honorary citizen. I'm accused of putting it on the map and overpopulating it."

"San Jose" would turn out to be the last of her singles recorded at Bell Studios on West 54th, where "Don't Make Me Over" had started the ball rolling years before. For her last three Scepter albums, she would work at engineer Phil Ramone's A&R Studios on Seventh Avenue.

Other Versions: *The Avalanches (1998) • Ed Ames • Burt Bacharach (1969) • Julius Wechter & the Baja Marimba Band • Terry Baxter (1971) • Bossa Rio • Joe Bourne • The Carpenters (1971) • Casino Royale • Lee Castle & the Jimmy Dorsey Orchestra (1974) • Ray Conniff • Floyd Cramer • Xavier Cugat & His Orchestra • Carl Doy (1998) • Neil Diamond (1993) • Percy Faith • Arthur Fiedler & the Boston Pops • 5th Dimension • Film Score Orchestra • Connie Francis (1968) • Frankie Goes to Hollywood (1984) • Free'n' Easy (1998) • Ron Goodwin • Robert Goulet • Ray Hamilton (1996) • Richard "Groove" Holmes (1970) • Sheila Hutchinson - medley: • Anita Kerr Singers • Yank Lawson & Bob Haggart • Ramsey Lewis (1968) • Johnny Mann Singers • Tony Mansell Singers (1970) • Marie McAuliffe (1998) • Jane McDonald • Medeski, Martin & Wood (1997) • Buddy Merrill • Tony Mottola • Mystic Moods Orchestra (1979) • Jack Nathan Orchestra (1968) • Peter Nero (1968) • 101 Strings (1994) • Paper Dolls (1968) • Boots Randolph • Renaissance • Rita Reys • RTE Concert Orchestra (1995) • Christopher Scott • George Shearing • Sheila Southern • Starlite Orchestra • Diana Ross & the Supremes (1968) • Gary Tesca (1995) • Bobby Timmons • Jerry Vale • Lawrence Welk • White Shark • Yazz (2000)*

"Let Me Be Lonely" (Burt Bacharach - Hal David)
First recorded by Dionne Warwick
From the LP *Valley of the Dolls*
Scepter 12216, flip side of "Do You Know The Way to San Jose" (*Billboard* R&B #71)
Released April 1968

Once again, Dionne reserves the gospel truth for the reverse side of a single. The recent flipping of all her singles insured that this superb performance would not go unnoticed. Around this time, criticism was starting to creep in that Dionne's records were becoming "too white," that she exuded more virtuoso technique than soul and that most of the passion was built into the songwriting of Bacharach and David. Her singing on "Let Me Be Lonely" makes mincemeat out of that statement: here she must travel to the very top of her range to even approximate the strain and struggle that soul aficionados seem to require from a sister. Sounding very much like it could've been recorded at American Studios in Memphis, this B-side charted well enough on the R&B list to influence her decision to record her next album, *Soulful,* at American with producer Chips Moman. That album's lack of Bacharach-David involvement was a message to her critics that she was capable of supplying passion without the team writing it into the script for her.

Other Versions: *Terry Baxter (1971) • Lee Castle & the Jimmy Dorsey Orchestra • 5th Dimension (1973)*

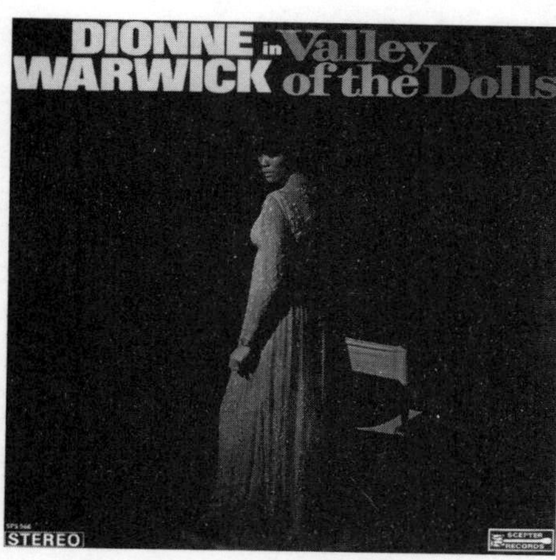

"Do You Know the Way to San Jose?" Or in Spanish, "¿Conoces El Camino Hacia San Jose?" In any language, it was the team's first Grammy winner.

"As Long As There's an Apple Tree" (Burt Bacharach - Hal David)
First recorded by Dionne Warwick
From the LP *Valley of the Dolls,* Scepter 568
Released March 1968

Although capable of writing the direst of self-damnations, Hal David was also a source of bottomless optimism. If the windows of the world are covered with rain, he can see it as angel's tears. Here he lists love among the constant and enduring things in the universe, along with birds flying, babies crying and roses blooming: *"Love that's faithful and true will go on forever / As long as there's an apple tree/ There'll be apple pie/ As long as there's a you and me/ Love can never die."*

Uncharacteristically for Bacharach, there is a tape splice connecting the instrumental break to a tricky multiple-key-change ending, suggesting that either the change was flubbed or the superfluous last verse was snipped out to ensure the album would clock in under 25 minutes per side.

Other Versions: *Film Score Orchestra*

"Where Would I Go" (Burt Bacharach - Hal David)
First recorded by Dionne Warwick
From the LP *Valley of the Dolls,* Scepter 568
Released March 1968

What would've made a spectacular single winds up as added incentive for Dionne's *Valley of the Dolls* album. Part Bacharach, part Motown, with a heavy dash of "What Becomes of the Broken Hearted," it's a dynamic mix of regal flugelhorns, descending strings and furious triplets from Gary Chester's open snare. Hal David sizes up the problem right out of the gate *("Why must I need someone who can't be true / How can I take you back and love you")* and predicts the losing outcome in fairly dramatic fashion *("For the rest of your life I will be by your side / When a fool falls in love there is no place to hide / Where would I go?").*

Other Versions: *Barbara Acklin (1969)*

"Walking Backwards Down the Road" (Burt Bacharach - Hal David)
First recorded by Dionne Warwick
From the LP *Valley of the Dolls,* Scepter 568
Released March 1968

Musically speaking, "Walking Backwards Down the Road," the *Valley* album's low-key finale, is "The Windows of the World" devoid of any political content. Dionne is leaving town, and her novel mode of

"This Guy/Girl's in Love with You." (1970). Something of a soul standard, it's been covered by Aretha Franklin, Al Green, James Brown, Lynn Collins, Marva Whitney, Smokey Robinson and the Miracles, and Diana Ross and the Supremes with the Temptations.

backwards transportation allows her to take in all the sights one last time. Unlike the leavers in most songs, she has nothing pulling her somewhere else: her departure is based on an inability to go to parties and movies without running into her ex and someone new. At least Dionne's defection is preferable to her usual custom of staying locked in her room for the rest of her life. And leaving a note wishing him well is a mark of personal growth any psychologist would applaud. Had this song come a year later, it wouldn't be hard to imagine B.J. Thomas applying the same playful yet melancholy approach he brought to "Raindrops Keep Falling on My Head."

"Walking Backwards" was covered by one other lady on the move, Liz Damon. Her Orient Express was a Hawaiian lounge act made up of four guys in leisure suits and three girls in bridesmaid outfits who managed to score a Top 40 hit in 1970 with something called "1900 Yesterday." Fans of lounge camp are encouraged to seek out their later albums, which are bundled with lavish gatefold advertising from Cartan Tours. Why didn't Kathie Lee Gifford think of that?

Other Versions: *Liz Damon's Orient Express (1971)*

"This Guy's in Love with You" (Burt Bacharach - Hal David)
Recorded by Herb Alpert
A&M 929 (*Billboard* pop #1)
Released May 1968

Herb Alpert. Some 50 songs were submitted for Alpert to sing on his 1968 TV special. This was the only one he chose to sing to his then-wife Sharon. Alpert later married Brasil '66 lead singer Lani Hall.

As Herb Alpert prepared for his CBS-TV special on April 22, 1968, he had two coups already sewn up—advance orders of over a million for his tenth album with the Tijuana Brass and $100,000 worth of sponsorship. What he didn't have was a song with which to serenade his wife, Sharon, on the program, something he could walk along a California beach and croon without breaking a sweat.

As Alpert told A&E's *Biography*, "There's a question I ask all great songwriters that I've been privileged to be around: 'Is there a song you've written that's tucked away in a drawer someplace that you had a good feeling for but for some reason never surfaced? I asked Burt that question and he pulled out "This Girl's in Love with You."

The melody is an anomaly for Bacharach in that it sounds like it only has five notes. And there isn't a three-syllable word hidden in its simple lyrics. No wonder everyone with a five-note range rushed to record it. So who was "This Girl's in Love with You" originally intended for? A good bet would be Dusty Springfield, whose own version came out later that same year in the UK on the *Dusty...Definitely* album. The hushed singing style she employed on "The Look of Love" was utilized for her recording of "This Girl's in Love with You," but she sounds far too laid-back during the *"I need your love / I want your love"* section, as does the orchestra. This under-realized version must have predated Alpert's, since it's missing so many elements of the hit arrangement.

Who could've predicted a Herb Alpert song that starts with an electric Wurlitzer, harmonica and strings and doesn't get wind of a trumpet until two minutes have passed? Anyone hearing the trumpeter bleat out those words in a monotone with a massive orchestra firing on all cylinders, and how vulnerable he sounds when they all drop out of the sonic picture, would have to agree with Noel Gallagher's assessment that this is "the best love song ever."

Initially, the song was not meant to be a single, but the volume of calls the television stations received the day after the broadcast convinced Alpert otherwise. Rush-released, it went to No. 1 six weeks later, a first for Bacharach and David in the U.S. and the first No. 1 for Alpert and A&M Records. And like many of B&D's Top 5 hits, it contains whistling. The advice Darius Milhaud gave young Bacharach about a good melody is still well remembered.

"This Guy's in Love with You." The first No. 1 single for A&M Records, it ranked eighth for the year 1968. Before that, the label's biggest hit was We Five's "You Were on My Mind," which ranked 18th for the year 1965.

Amazingly, the song had enough staying power to become a Top 10 hit six months later when Dionne Warwick released it as a single. It also served as the title track of Aretha Franklin's 1970 album, released around the time Aretha's troubled marriage to husband/manager Ronnie White unraveled and she began missing concert dates. When her Las Vegas engagement was canceled after only a few performances, the singer took a year off from performing and recorded an album chock full of cover songs, including "This Girl's in Love with You." Canadian journalist Ritchie Yorke, who was at the session, recalls, "She sang, her hands clenched in fists in front of her. One forgot about the Herb Alpert version within four bars." Also in 1970, Bacharach and David cut a fabulous version with B.J. Thomas, who demonstrates what the song sounds like when eight, nine or ten notes are applied.

A hit in both genders, it was a natural for male-female duets, as demonstrated by James Brown and Lyn Collins, and the Supremes and Temptations. It even held a special power over cross-dressing Kevin Rowland, former lead singer of Dexy's Midnight Runners. Rowland, returning after an 11-year absence due to drug addiction and fallen fortunes, released an album of cover versions that was greeted with bewilderment and scarce sales. Although he could've gone the easy route, he chose to overreach and complete the embarrassment.

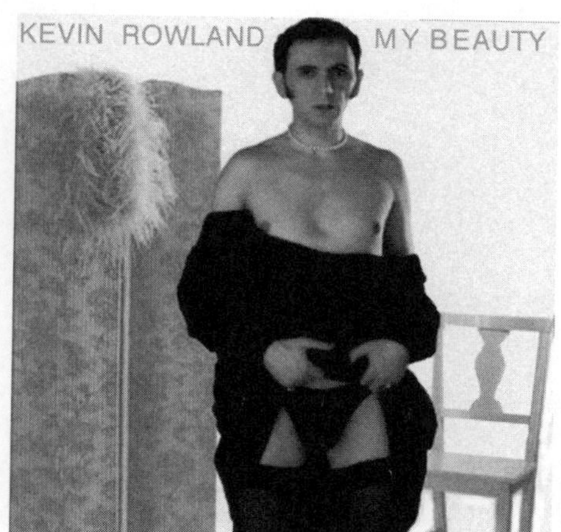

Kevin Rowland (1999). If a picture is worth a thousand words, two of them would have to be "oh my."

If one pinpoints the composer's reemergence as a pop icon with Oasis' placement of a Bacharach poster on the cover of the band's debut album, *Definitely Maybe,* the first concrete evidence of an influence in Noel Gallagher's largely Beatle-derived catalog is a song called "Half a World Away." In the BBC documentary *This Is Now*, Gallagher readily admits having nicked it from the ultimate love song: "I must say it took me nearly two years to work out that song. We adopted the key, swapped the chords, put some words on top, and I'm surprised he hasn't sued." Quite the reverse: Bacharach invited Gallagher to perform "This Guy's in Love with You" with him on the Royal Festival Hall stage in 1996.

Other Versions: *Barbara Acklin (1969) • Cliff Adams Singers (2000) • Yasuko Agawa (1996) • Ronnie Aldrich (1971) • Ed Ames (1971) • Apollo 100 (1973) • Dorothy Ashby (1969) • Chet Atkins with Arthur Fiedler & the Boston Pops (1969) • Roy Ayers • Burt Bacharach (1969) • Terry Baxter (1971) • Rita Bettis (1970) • Acker Bilk • Cilla Black & Burt Bacharach - Bacharach TV special (1972) • Willie Bobo (1968) • Booker T & the MG's (1969) • Joe Bourne (1993) • James Brown & Lyn Collins (1972) • Magnus Carlson - "A Musical Tribute to Burt Bacharach Medley" (2001) • Vikki Carr (1969) • Paul Carrack (2000) • Lee Castle & the Jimmy Dorsey Orchestra • Frank Chacksfield (1971) • Gene Chandler • Petula Clark (1968, live 1972) • Tom Clay (1971) • Richard*

1968

Oasis (1998). *The Masterplan* collected all the group's stray B-sides that never made it over to America. It included the "This Guy's in Love with You" soundalike "Half a World Away" (reportedly Paul Weller's favorite Oasis track) and "Going Nowhere," a song with Bacharach-inspired horns.

Clayderman (1997) • Harry Connick Jr. (1996) • Ray Conniff (1968) • Alan Copeland Singers • Count Buffalo Big Band • Lenny Dee • The Dells (1972) • Robert Crenshaw (2000) • Sacha Distel (1968) • The Dramatics (live 1973) • Carl Doy • 18th Century Corporation (1969) • Percy Faith • Faith No More (1998) • Georgie Fame (1970) • Fantastic Strings • Fastball (1997) • Ferrante & Teicher (1970) • Arthur Fiedler & the Boston Pops (1972) • Film Score Orchestra • Ella Fitzgerald (1970) • Four Tops (1969) • Connie Francis (1968) • Aretha Franklin (1970) • Free'n' Easy (1998) • Noel Gallagher with Burt Bacharach - live at Royal Festival Hall (1996) • Tommy Garrett (1969) • Don Goldie (1977) • Ron Goodwin • Eydie Gorme • Grenadine (1994) • Terry Hall (1994) • Tony Hatch Orchestra • Richard Hayman/RTE Concert Orchestra (1995) • Hampton Hawes • Ted Heath Orchestra • Jorgen Ingmann • Harry James • The Jet Set (1999) • Etta Jones (1997) • Salena Jones • Bob Jung & His Orchestra (1969) • Bert Kaempfert • Barney Kessel (1969) • Guy Klucevsek (1997) • Manfred Krug - "Schau her zu mir" (2000) • Ellis Larkins • Brenda Lee • Leonardo's Bride (1998) • The Lettermen (1968) • Enoch Light Singers (1968) • London Viola Sound (1995) • Joe Loss (1971) • Charlie Mangold (1997) • Johnny Mann Singers • Tony Mansell Singers (1971) • Hank Marvin (1969) • Johnny Mathis • Keff McCulloch (1996) • Roy Meriwether (1969) • Smokey Robinson & the Miracles (1970) • Alan Moorhouse Orchestra • Tony Mottola (1968) • Wenche Myhre - medley (1970) • Peter Nero (1968) • Steve Newcomb Trio (2000) • Peter Nordahl (2002) • Nose Riders (2000) • Des O'Conner • Donny Osmond (1973) • Fausto Papetti (1996) • Arthur Prysock (1986) • H.B. Radke & the Jet City Swingers (1999) • Rita Reys (1971) • Kevin Rowland • Royal Marines (1974) • Jimmy Ruffin (1970) • Christopher Scott (1969) • Vonda Shepard (1997) • Bobby Sherman (1969) • Jimmy Smith (1968) • Johnny "Hammond" Smith (1969) • Sheila Southern (1968) • Dusty Springfield (1968) • Nat Stuckey (1968) • Sud (2000) • Diana Ross & the Supremes & the Temptations (1968) • B.J. Thomas (1970) • Svante Thuresson - "Du ser en man" (1968) • Stanley Turrentine (1968) • The Unifics (1968) • Jerry Vale (1968) • Billy Vaughn (1968) • Bobby Vinton • Dionne Warwick (1969) • Marva Whitney (1971) • Roger Williams • Klaus Wunderlich

"Who Is Gonna Love Me?" (Burt Bacharach - Hal David)
First recorded by Dionne Warwick
Scepter 12226, flip side of "(There's) Always Something There to Remind Me"
Released August 1968

Bacharach and David prematurely return to the waltz idiom to come up with a fairly nondescript pop ballad that covers ground already trodden for "Here Where There Is Love." Anything of interest here will be improved upon with the exquisite "Odds and Ends."

Other Versions: *Terry Baxter (1971) • Alfie Davison (1993) • Film Score Orchestra • Peter Nero (1968) • Sounds of Our Times • Billy Vaughn Singers (1968)*

"He Who Loves" (Burt Bacharach - Hal David)
First recorded by Lenny Welch
Mercury 72811, flip side of "Tennessee Waltz"
Released summer 1968

"He who loves stands very high / High enough to touch a sunbeam." Shortly after this pronouncement we're up, up with Lenny, painting rainbows and flying around like bluebirds. This could've been easily cited as a drug song by *Newsweek,* which ran a cover story about covert drug messages in pop music and cited "Puff the Magic Dragon" as its smoking gun. Lyrically, it shows solidarity with what the beautiful, gentle people were expressing on Haight and Ashbury, but the music couldn't sound more middle-of-the-road if you painted a yellow line through it. And after yelpin' Lenny Welch, this peaceful paean was recorded by the Mob's favorite hit man, Jerry Vale, in whose tonsils even the most familiar songs sound like a foreign horn on a domestic car. The trick is to give him a song so anticlimactic he never gets to those wretched highs. Such a song is the forgettable "He Who Loves," most likely knocked off while B&D furiously worked on *Promises, Promises.*

Jerry Vale (1969). This singer enjoyed a revival of sorts when a TV album called *The Mob's Greatest Hits* became an offer many record buyers couldn't refuse.

As mentioned before with "As Long As There's an Apple Tree," Hal David was capable of boundless optimism, manifested here in lines like *"Smile at the people who haven't been kind to you / Show them what love can mean in this world."* Yet one couldn't help but feeling that a touch of the sap was seeping into David's lyrics, in proportion to the width of his silk ties. The treacle count would get almost unbearable in parts of *Lost Horizon,* but in the secular pop world, he was counterbalancing it with some of the grittiest and despairing stanzas he ever penned.

Other Versions: *Jerry Vale (1969)*

"Don't Count the Days" (Burt Bacharach - Hal David)
First recorded by Marilyn Michaels
ABC 11098, flip side of "MacArthur Park"
Released fall 1968

Most people know Marilyn Michaels as a impressionist of celebrities like Zsa Zsa Gabor, Judy Garland and, of course, Barbra Streisand, whom she understudied for during the Broadway run of *Funny Girl.* Several attempts were made to launch her as a singing star in her own right, but one wonders why ABC Records, whose Dunhill label had already scored a gargantuan hit with "MacArthur Park," would release a cover version less than six months later. At seven-plus minutes, the original clocked in quite enough airtime, and people still needed a rest from it by the time Michael's version came up. The song didn't become a hit again until the Four Tops remade it in 1971 and Donna Summers discoed it up in 1978.

Marilyn Michaels. Years before recording this obscure Bacharach-David composition, Michaels recorded an answer disc to Ray Peterson's "Tell Laura I Lover Her"—"Tell Tommy I Miss Him."

"Don't Count the Days" had a better shot at hitdom—even subpar Bacharach-David would've sounded fresher. Forgoing calendars, Marilyn's method of tear counting is a more accurate method of marking the passage of time, especially when she's already spent what seems like a lifetime crying since her love has gone. As for Michael's own voice, it's a pleasing cross between Dusty Springfield, Liza Minelli and La

Dionne Warwick. Just for the record, Dionne has never recorded "Blue on Blue" or "The Man Who Shot Liberty Valance."

Streisand when falsetto is dispatched. Compared to her frantic version, Lawrence Welk stalwarts Sandi and Salli seem as if they were dosed with Sominex.

Other Versions: *Sandi & Salli (1969)*

SECTION SIX
PROMISES, PROMISES (1968-1970)

...or Accolades, Accolades!

From the time that Promises, Promises *premiered on Broadway on December 8, 1968, to Bacharach's being dubbed "The Music Man 1970" on the June 22 cover of* Newsweek, *the composer was on a streak where everything he touched turned to gold. On March 11, he received two Grammys for best score from an original cast show album and best score written for a motion picture. Three days later, two Emmys were awarded to the "Sound of Burt Bacharach" installment of* The Kraft Music Hall. *On April 7, Bacharach left the Dorothy Chandler Pavilion with two Oscars, one for the* Butch Cassidy *soundtrack and one for best song. On May 22, he received gold certification for the* Butch Cassidy *soundtrack, and by the fall, all his A&M albums had gone gold. In this period he and Hal David enjoyed two No. 1 singles, with many older compositions, like "One Less Bell to Answer," "Walk On By" and "Baby It's You," finding sudden interest. It didn't seem like there was any peak in sight. Does it ever?*

Section Six: Promises, Promises (1968–1970)

1. *"Promises, Promises"* .... *Dionne Warwick*
2. *"Whoever You Are, I Love You"* .... *Dionne Warwick*
3. *"Wanting Things"* .... *Dionne Warwick*
4. *"What Am I Doing Here"* .... *Rose Marie Jun*
5. *"Half As Big As Life"* .... *Jerry Orbach*
6. *"You'll Think of Someone"* .... *Jerry Orbach and Jill O'Hara*
7. *"Upstairs"* .... *Jerry Orbach*
8. *"She Likes Basketball"* .... *Jerry Orbach*
9. *"Let's Pretend We're Grownup* .... *Rose Marie*
10. *"A Young Pretty Girl Like You* .... *Jerry Orbach and A. Larry Haines*
11. *"Tick Tock Goes the Clock"* .... *Rose Marie Jun*
12. *"Christmas Day"* .... *Edward Winter, Kay Oslin, Rita O'Connor, et al.*
13. *"Knowing When to Leave"* .... *Jill O'Hara*
14. *"Overture"* .... *Original Broadway Cast and Orchestra*
15. *"Hot Food"* .... *deleted song from original score*
16. *"Loyal, Resourceful and Cooperative"* .... *deleted song from original score*
17. *"A Stork of Luck"* .... *deleted song from original score*
18. *"The Grapes of Roth"* .... *Original Broadway Cast and Orchestra*
19. *"Turkey Lurkey Time"* .... *Donna McKechnie, Margo Sappington, Baayork Lee*
20. *"Where Can You Take a Girl?"* .... *Paul Reed, Norman Shelly, et al.*
21. *"A Fact Can Be a Beautiful Thing"* .... *Jerry Orbach and Marian Mercer*
22. *"I'll Never Fall in Love Again"* .... *Jerry Orbach and Jill O'Hara*
23. *"Our Little Secret"* .... *Jerry Orbach and Edward Winter*
24. *"Dream Sweet Dreamer"* .... *Dionne Warwick*
25. *"The April Fools"* .... *Dionne Warwick*
26. *"Pacific Coast Highway"* .... *Burt Bacharach*
27. *"She's Gone Away"* .... *Burt Bacharach*
28. *"Odds and Ends (Of a Beautiful Love Affair)"* .... *Dionne Warwick*
29. *"I'm a Better Man (For Having Loved You)"* .... *Engelbert Humperdinck*
30. *"Raindrops Keep Falling on My Head"* .... *B.J. Thomas*
31. *"Come Touch the Sun" aka "Not Goin' Home Anymore"* .... *Burt Bacharach*
32. *"The Sundance Kid"* .... *Burt Bacharach*
33. *"On a Bicycle Built for Joy"* .... *Burt Bacharach*
34. *"The Old Fun City (N.Y. Sequence)"* .... *Burt Bacharach*
35. *"South American Getaway"* .... *Burt Bacharach*
36. *"Let Me Go to Him"* .... *Dionne Warwick*
37. *"Loneliness Remembers (What Happiness Forgets)"* .... *Dionne Warwick*
38. *"Everybody's Out of Town"* .... *B.J. Thomas*
39. *"Where There's a Heartache (There Must Be a Heart)"* .... *The Sandpipers*
40. *"Paper Maché"* .... *Dionne Warwick*
41. *"The Wine Is Young"* .... *Dionne Warwick*
42. *"Send My Picture to Scranton PA"* .... *B.J. Thomas*
43. *"The Green Grass Starts to Grow"* .... *Dionne Warwick*
44. *"Check Out Time"* .... *Dionne Warwick*
45. *"Walk the Way You Talk"* .... *Dionne Warwick*
46. *"How Does a Man Become a Puppet"* .... *Ed Ames*
47. *"All Kinds of People"* .... *Burt Bacharach*
48. *"And the People Were With Her (Suite for Orchestra)"* .... *Burt Bacharach*
49. *"Freefall"* .... *Burt Bacharach*
50. *"Hasbrook Heights"* .... *Burt Bacharach*
51. *"Ten Times Forever More"* .... *Johnny Mathis*
52. *"My Rock and Foundation"* .... *Peggy Lee*
53. *"Who Gets the Guy?"* .... *Dionne Warwick*
54. *"Long Ago Tomorrow"* .... *B.J. Thomas*
55. *"Something Big"* .... *Mark Lindsay*

"Promises, Promises" (Burt Bacharach - Hal David)
First recorded by Dionne Warwick
From the Broadway musical *Promises, Promises*
Scepter 12231 (*Billboard* pop #19)
Released October 1968

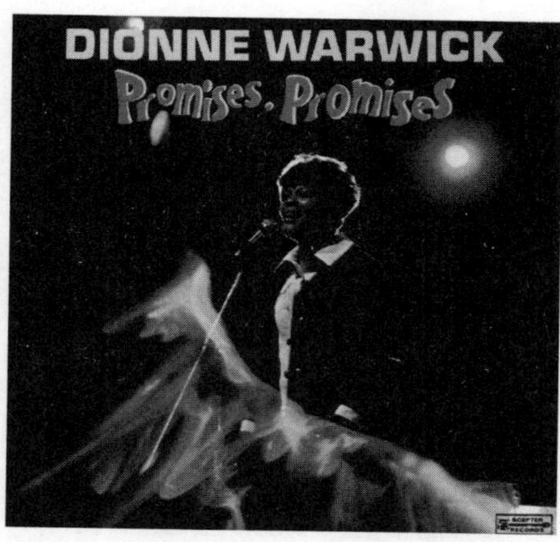

Promises, Promises. Easily the most hideous album cover ever to escape the Scepter art department. It's taken this writer over 30 years to figure out what the hell that strange thing that's about to envelop Dionne is. It's (drumroll please) Bacharach's conducting hand!

When playwright Neil Simon met producer David Merrick for lunch, it was to tell him he was *not* interested in writing a musical. But before Simon even touched his fettuccine, the cunning Merrick got him to reveal that if he *were* interested in doing a musical, he'd like to do an adaptation of Billy Wilder's *The Apartment*, the Academy Award winner for best picture in 1960. Pressed further to name his ideal choice of composers, Simon suggested Bacharach and David, who'd scored his first screenplay, *After the Fox*. Of course, that's when Merrick sprung the trap and asked him whether he'd be interested doing in a musical adaptation of *The Apartment* if he could secure the rights and get Bacharach and David to agree. Happily, the answer was yes.

Three weeks later, bicoastal writing sessions for *Promises, Promises* commenced between Simon and Hal David in New York and Bacharach in Los Angeles. For this project, all the songs were written lyrics first, as they needed to make sense in connection with Neil Simon's dialogue. Eleven titles were copyrighted on February 8, with 11 more new titles added and subtracted to the score before New York rehearsals on September 4. Among the first set of songs was "Promises, Promises"; it was Simon who came up with the title to illustrate the Faustian bargain young accountant C.C. Baxter makes with horny, adulterous executives to lend his apartment out in exchange for promotion consideration.

"Promises, Promises" turned out to be the show's most troublesome number. Composed in the style of Jules Styne's "Don't Rain on My Parade," its rapid-fire melody left many singers short of breath. Even after studying Bacharach's sparse piano-and-voice demo recording with Rose Marie Jun and Kenny Karen, Jerry Orbach still had some unanswered questions. It was Dionne Warwick's recording of "Promises, Promises" that proved the ideal vocal guide for the show's male lead. In a sense she was enlisted to become a Bacharach–David demo singer once more, but this time the recording was being issued as her new single. This also served Bacharach's aim of previewing some songs for the show before opening night. Orbach attended this recording session at A&R Studios and reportedly asked Warwick, "How the hell do you sing this?"

***Promises, Promises* Shubert Theatre Playbill.** The initial show logo didn't have the swinging, key-holdin' bikini girls but rather this simple depiction of a girl getting dumped on her ass. It was used as late as January 1970 and was used for the British production as well.

If musicians at the Apollo had a tough time understanding the arrangement for "Anyone Who Had a Heart," imagine the pit musicians' bewilderment at seeing a song with a verse that goes from 3/4 to a bar of 4/4 to a bar of 6/4 and switches from 3/4 to 3/8 to 4/8, with the trumpet players having to come in one beat later!

In a *Playbill* interview made before the Washington previews, Bacharach pointed out the difference between Jonathan Tunick's stage arrangement for the show and what he was able to achieve for Warwick in the recording studio. "On Dionne's recording of 'Promises' there are three guitars and two percussion players all playing different rhythm patterns. I wouldn't even try to do that for the theater. That's too intricate to

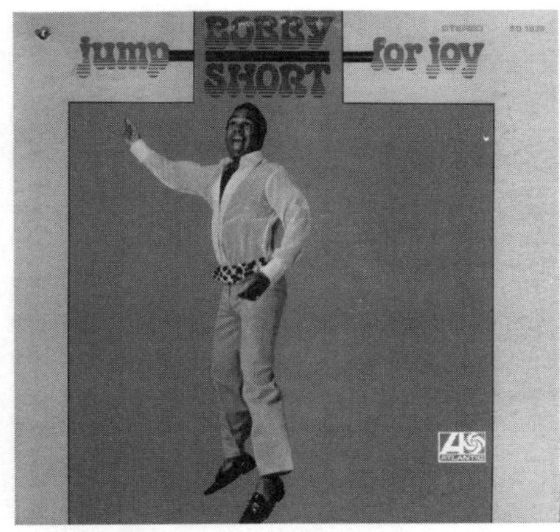

Bobby Short (1969). In defiance of Randy Newman's edict about short people having no reason to live, Bobby's had a steady gig as the Cafe Carlyle's resident pianist since 1968, the year *Promises, Promises* opened at the Shubert Theatre. Short's version of "Whoever You Are, I Love You" features just Bobby and his 88 keys.

be sure of every single performance." Even with reduced rhythmic thrust, the Orbach recording is still pretty radical for Broadway: this is perhaps the only time a Broadway cast album features songs that fade out!

Other Versions: *Herb Alpert & the Tijuana Brass (1974) • Burt Bacharach (1969) • Terry Baxter (1971) • Liz Callaway - medley (1995) • Johnny Dorelli & Catherine Spaak (Italian production* Promesse, Promesse *(1970) • 18th Century Corporation (1969) • Percy Faith (1969) • Arthur Fiedler & the Boston Pops (1972) • Connie Francis (1968) • Erik Friedlander & Chimera (1997) • Shauna Hicks - "A Bacharach Love Story Medley" (1998) • Al Hirt (1969) • Jazz Crusaders (1969) • The Jet Set (1999) • Rose Marie Jun & Kenny Karen with Burt Bacharach - demo (1968) • The Lennon Sisters • Longines Symphonette Society • Marie McAuliffe (1998) • Steve Newcomb Trio (2000) • Jerry Orbach (1969) • Tony Roberts (1969) • Christopher Scott (1970) • Dinah Shore • Martin Short (1997) • Starlight Orchestra (1995) • Jerry Vale (1969) • Billy Vaughn (1969)*

"Whoever You Are, I Love You" (Burt Bacharach - Hal David)
First recorded by Dionne Warwick
From the Broadway musical *Promises, Promises*
Scepter 12231, flip side of "Promises, Promises" (*Billboard* pop #19)
Released October 1968

"With the songs that we write and the records that we make, I know that we have a problem," Bacharach confessed to reporter Fred Robbins at the *Promises, Promises* opening night party. "We get a breakthrough after five or six plays, it takes five or six times around for the guys in the business to get with it. And then they say, 'Hey, it's got it. Boy, I love it. It left me with nothing the first time I heard it.' You get in the theater and you do the same thing and they say, 'Hey, I don't like it at all.' But I don't have the benefit of five or six plays. It would've been marvelous if we could've done the soundtrack album, put it out on the market a month and a half. People would've heard it in New York, would've heard the title song and be exposed to five or six of the songs and wouldn't be hearing them for the first time in the theater. With 90 percent of the stuff Hal David and I write, you've got to hear it."

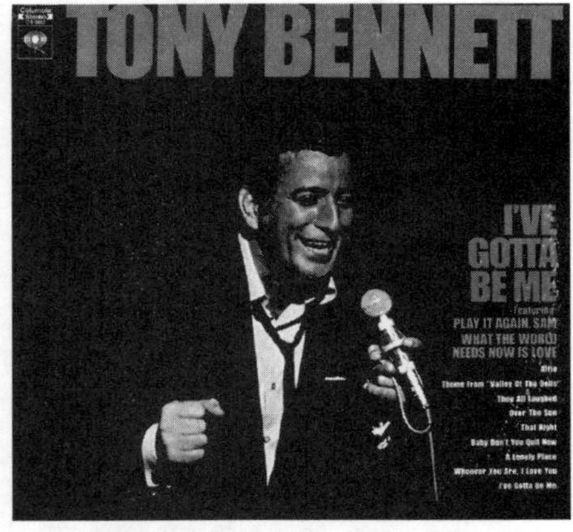

Tony Bennett. By 1969, adult singers, once Columbia Records' bread and butter, were being pressured into either recording the new sounds the kids were digging or sitting out the Age of Aquarius on some crummy vanity label. Bennett stood his ground and would only record what he considered to be "good songs." One of Bennett's finest albums of this period, *I've Gotta Be Me,* rounded up three of the usual Bacharach suspects, a jazzy "What the World Needs Now," a faithful "Alfie" and a breathtaking "Whoever You Are, I Love You."

Ideally, Dionne's *Promises, Promises* album might've contained more songs from the show than a mere three, but seeing as four songs were dropped after the Boston tryouts, it made sense to only feature songs that were definitely going to be in the show. One of the showstoppers was "Whoever You Are, I Love You," a torch ballad where the female lead (Fran Kubelik, played by Jill O'Hara) attempts suicide after her lover (Jeff D. Sheldrake, played by Edward Winter) abandons her so that he can spend Christmas Eve with his wife and family. Although the lyrics express the heartbreak she endures in not knowing what to expect from a man who alternately treats her with tenderness and cruelty, her ingestion of the vial of sleeping pills that she discovers in Baxter's apartment is only alluded to in the song's haunting piano coda, which rendered Dionne's superlative recording of the song a little too desolate to make the "Promises, Promises" single a double-sided hit. But the song coaxed some dramatic performances from Tony Bennett, Johnny Mathis and especially Bobby Short, whose high tenor and vibrato comes closest to matching Jill O'Hara's emotional torment.

Other Versions: *Burt Bacharach (1969) • Terry Baxter (1971) • Tony Bennett (1969) • Betty Buckley (1969) • Susan Egan (1998) • Enoch Light (1968) • Rose Marie Jun with Burt Bacharach - demo (1968) • Hildegard Knef - "Warum lügst du mich immer an" (1980) Longines Symphonette Society (1970) • Johnny Mathis • Gordon MacRae (1969) • Jill O'Hara (1969) • Bobby Short (1970) • Catherine Spaak - "Chiunque tu sia ti ama" (1970)*

"Wanting Things" (Burt Bacharach - Hal David)
First recorded by Dionne Warwick
From the album *Promises, Promises,* Scepter LP 571
Released December 1968

"Wanting Things." Connie Francis was the first artist to cover songs from *Promises, Promises*— the title song and "Wanting Things." She was also one of the first acts to be dropped from MGM Records when President Mike Curb decided to clean house of all artists who "promote and exploit hard drugs through music." Amazingly, Eric Burdon was allowed to stay on!

The three pivotal characters in the show reveal their inner struggles through song; not coincidentally, their three songs are the first to premiere on Dionne Warwick's *Promises, Promises* album. Hal David takes the unusual step of giving the "heavy" of the story, J.D. Sheldrake, a song that makes him almost sympathetic to the audience. Sheldrake's problem is not too different from C.C. Baxter's, except that Sheldrake has the ability to get whatever he wants instantly and doesn't value anything he possesses. Edward Winter is able to breathe some humanity into his character, but confessing vulnerability behind closed doors changes nothing: he remains a sniveling bastard for all of Act Two.

The Italian production awarded this number to Johnny Dorelli, who plays the Chuck Baxter character, leaving the J.D. Sheldrake role an unsung one. Producers Garinei and Giovannini structured their shows around big stars while keeping the secondary roles minor. And when in Rome, "Wanting Things" translates into "learning to live without what I do not have," which almost sounds like a Morrissey title.

Other Versions: *Burt Bacharach (1969) • James Congdon - London cast (1969) • Johnny Dorelli - Italian production (1970) • Connie Francis (1968) • Astrud Gilberto (1971) • Kenny Karen with Burt Bacharach – demo (1968) • Siw Malmkvist - "Kanske var sommaren varm" (1970) • The Pointer Sisters (1975) • Mathilde Santing (1987) • Edward Winter (1968)*

"What Am I Doing Here" (Burt Bacharach - Hal David)
Demo recorded by Rose Marie Jun with Burt Bacharach, 1968
From the Slider Music CD *Broadway First Takes, Vol. 2*
Released September 26, 2000

This downbeat sob song was dropped from *Promises, Promises* prior to rehearsals, since Jill O'Hara needed something up-tempo to sing, and having a depressing ballad where she first meets Sheldrake at the Chinese restaurant really put the brakes on the show. Hal David took the general idea of not knowing how to extricate oneself from a bad situation and removed the more tragic implications of the earlier song *("It's hard to face the truth after living such a beautiful lie"),* and Bacharach fabricated the more contemporary sounding "Knowing When to Leave."

"What Am I Doing Here?" (1994). Broadway star Liz Callaway (*Cats, Miss Saigon*) performs this never-before-heard song on the now out-of-print CD *Lost in Boston II*. Also featured are songs cut out of *I Do, I Do, Fiddler on the Roof, On the Town* and *The Fantastiks.*

In 2000, Slider Music released a series of CDs consisting of Broadway show demos. *Broadway First Takes, Vol. 2* contains ten *Promises, Promises* demos, including three songs cut from the show. The source of these rare acetates is session singer Rose Marie Jun (aka Rosemary June), whom you'll remember as having cut the should've-known-better Bacharach-David ballad "Your Lips Are Warmer Than Your Heart" back in 1962. She gives the song her all, but despite some terrific lines, it suffers in comparison to the more fully realized dirge of regret "Whoever You Are, I Love You," which Jun also recorded with Bacharach. "What Am I Doing Here" was one of two excised *Promises, Promises* numbers resurrected as part of Varèse Sarabande's *Lost in Boston* series; Liz Callaway's rendition appears on *Lost in Boston II.*

Other Versions: *Liz Callaway (1994)*

"Half As Big As Life" (Burt Bacharach - Hal David)
First recorded by Jerry Orbach
From the original cast album *Promises, Promises,* United Artists UAS 9902
Released December 1968

"Promises, Promises," Chuck Baxter's victory song, comes at the end of the show, so it was necessary to construct a "before" song for comparison's sake. "Half As Big As Life" is written in the same splashy manner as the title song and finds Chuck wanting things like stature and respect. Two weeks into rehearsals, Neil Simon began sizing up Jerry Orbach and decided that this veteran of several Broadway and off-Broadway musicals was too grim and unlikable for the role. Simon wanted to replace him with another actor, but once Merrick attended a rehearsal, Orbach transformed, and the matter was happily dropped. The public agreed, and Orbach went on to win a Tony for best musical actor.

This is one of a handful of songs that seems not to have inspired cover versions, possibly because the griping lyrics about being five feet tall and not much to look at don't appeal to most vain singers. The Italians take the height thing quite literally in their translation, roughly "I am a half heel."

Other Versions: *Johnny Dorelli - Italian production (1970) • London cast/orchestra (1969) • Martin Short (1997)*

"You'll Think of Someone" (Burt Bacharach - Hal David)
First recorded by Jerry Orbach and Jill O'Hara
From the original cast album *Promises, Promises,* United Artists UAS 9902
Released December 1968

Of the writing process, Bacharach said that he and Hal David "tried not to sound like we were writing show songs. Maybe we get into trouble doing it that way, I dunno." This almost vaudevillian number is one of the exceptions. You can just about picture Jill O'Hara twirling a parasol as she runs down a list of hobbies that require a partner. Meanwhile, Orbach is jockeying to be that elusive someone who'll be her doubles partner, only to back down at the end of each chorus. She doesn't hear a word he says, but in the anything-to-be-different Italian production, Catherine Spaak actually reacts to what Johnny Dorelli is saying.

In its demo form, this duet brings together two old Bacharach alumni, Rose Marie Jun and Bernie Knee (aka Nee) of *The Blob* fame. Each were paid 20 to 25 dollars per recording for the demo sessions conducted on June 7 and 26 at Associated Recording Studios in New York.

Other Versions: *Betty Buckley & Tony Roberts - London cast (1969) • Ronnie Carroll & Aimi MacDonald (1969) • Johnny Dorelli & Catherine Spaak - Italian production (1970) • Rose Marie Jun & Bernie Nee with Burt Bacharach - demo (1968) • Martin Short & Kerry O'Malley (1997)*

Promises, Promises. Liza Minelli and Alan Alda were the original choices for the roles of C.C. Baxter and Fran Kubelik, but both stars turned down producer David Merrick.

"Upstairs" (Burt Bacharach - Hal David)
First recorded by Jerry Orbach
From the original cast album *Promises, Promises,* United Artists UAS 9902
Released December 1968

Written and performed in Bacharach's own manner of singing, this situational song finds Baxter explaining the loan-out of his $86.50-a-month brownstone apartment to Mr. Kirkeby every Wednesday night. The Bacharach demo has an additional verse concerning Mr. Dobitch that was lopped off early in the game. The verse about Mr. Eichelberger's claim on Baxter's apartment on Thursday nights was added later, and again the brief verse is reprised at the end of Scene Two.

When the show was brought back as part of a revival series at New York's City Center, it went from being a modern-day story to a period piece. Chuck Baxter's two-flights-up apartment held fast at $86.50 a month: you can't ask for better rent control than that.

Other Versions: *Ronnie Carroll (1969) • Johnny Dorelli - Italian production (1970) • Jazz Crusaders (1969) • Kenny Karen with Burt Bacharach - demo (1968) • Tony Roberts - London cast (1969) • Martin Short (1997)*

"She Likes Basketball" (Burt Bacharach - Hal David)
First recorded by Jerry Orbach
From the original cast album *Promises, Promises,* United Artists UAS 9902
Released December 1968

"Basketball? I love it. I was going to play in college...but I stopped growing in high school."
—Chuck Baxter to Mr. Sheldrake, Scene Four of *Promises, Promises*

In Bacharach's youth, his desire to be an athlete far outweighed his

Broadway First Take, Vol. 2. Session singer Rose Mary Jun saved acetates from all the shows she did demos for, which led to this exciting series of CDs from Slider Music. Included are ten of the songs the backers of *Promises, Promises* heard before reaching for their checkbooks.

desire to practice piano, but his small physical stature in high school prevented him from pursuing the matter further. In 1957, he was able to combine his love for sports and music by touring North African army bases as musical conductor for the Harlem Globetrotters. "I brought my sneakers because I hoped that Abe Saperstein, the owner, would let me into at least one game," Bacharach told *Newsweek* in 1970. "Saperstein used to say to me, 'Bacharach, I may have you suit up tonight' and I'd say 'Just one shot, Abe, please.' It never happened."

Who could ever have thought that 11 years later he'd have the opportunity to write a song about basketball, let alone a waltz? The odd contrast of ballroom dance with fast-paced street sport made for Bacharach's most playful use of triple time since "What's New Pussycat?" although you could never picture Tom Jones bragging about his jump shot.

Other Versions: *Ronnie Carroll (1969) • Johnny Dorelli - Italian production (1970) • Guy Haines (2000) • Kenny Karen with Burt Bacharch - demo (1968) • Tony Roberts (1969) • Martin Short (1997)*

"Let's Pretend We're Grownup" (Burt Bacharach - Hal David)
Demo recorded by Rose Marie Jun with Burt Bacharach, 1968
From the Slider Music CD *Broadway First Take, Vol. 2*
Released September 26, 2000

In the early draft of *Promises, Promises,* this was the number the gals from accounts receivable, mimeograph and petty cash cooked up to perform at the office Christmas party, presumably dressed up as little girls mooning over boys in the same immature manner executives chase women around desks. *("Let's pretend we're grownup up and make a fuss and try to do to them what they would do to us / Gotta grab 'em and pinch and chase 'em and really kiss 'em").* The girls rev through a strenuous cancan melody *("Mo-ther won't ap-prove go-ing out with older men, but then again most mothers aren't in the groove")* and conclude with an obligatory holiday wish *("Let's pretend we're grownup and learn to live / It's Christmas time, we all should give").* Such heavy moralizing from the Christmas party committee! It's little wonder that this song was scrapped for the more subtle "Turkey Lurkey Time."

"A Young Pretty Girl Like You." Post-overdose publicity still with Jerry Orbach, Jill O'Hara and A. Larry Haines.

"A Young Pretty Girl Like You" (Burt Bacharach - Hal David)
First recorded by Jerry Orbach and A. Larry Haines
From the original cast album *Promises, Promises,* United Artists UAS 9902
Released December 1968

Here's a festive rag to lighten the mood after Dr. Dreyfuss and Baxter have spent the night helping Miss Kubelik walk off the aftereffects of an overdose of sleeping pills. At one point Orbach lurches into a fake cowboy accent to cheer up his "purty" suicidal houseguest. And it's the first of five songs snipped out of the Italian production. Maybe Varèse Sarabande should've put out a *Lost in Italia* CD.

Other Versions: *Kenny Karen with Burt Bacharach – demo (1968) • Tony Roberts & Jack Kruschen (1969) • Martin Short & Dick Latessa (1997)*

"Tick Tock Goes the Clock" (Burt Bacharach - Hal David)
Demo recorded by Rose Marie Jun with Burt Bacharach, 1968
From the Slider Music CD *Broadway First Take, Vol. 2*
Released September 26, 2000

Said to be Hal David's favorite song written for *Promises, Promises,* "Tick Tock Goes the Clock" was dropped after the tryouts at Boston's Colonial Theatre. Since the demos had already gone out to prospective cover artists, this old-maid anthem might've had a life if the perennially despondent Vikki Carr or the Lennon Sisters had pounced on it. Thirty years on the biological clock passed before it was dusted off for the first volume of Varèse Sarabande's *Lost in Boston* series, but the best version still remains the 1968 demo found on *Broadway First Take, Vol. 2,* where Bacharach sings the horn parts in a charmingly flat way.

Johnny Mathis (1969). It took two years for Johnny's first classic Christmas album to go gold and 28 years to go platinum. By that time, this second Christmas collection was unavailable, but it did reach gold status in 1979, ten years after its release.

Other Versions: *Judy Malloy & Debbie Pavelka (1997)*

"Christmas Day" (Burt Bacharach - Hal David)
First recorded by Edward Winter, Kay Oslin, Rita O'Connor, Julane Stites and Neil Jones
From the original cast album *Promises, Promises,* United Artists UAS 9902
Released December 1968

Bacharach and David's first-ever Christmas song occupies a curious place in *Promises, Promises*. It's the only number not to be performed in its entirety during the show and, like "The Grapes of Roth," isn't even listed in the playbill. Transitional music of sorts, it marks the beginning and end of Baxter's phone conversation with Mr. Sheldrake like a moralistic dial tone. As for its chances of becoming a holiday staple, its depressed tone and the children's chorus borrowing of "It's Raining, It's Pouring" (the official schoolyard taunting melody also known as "Nyeah, Nyeah, Nyeah, Nyeah, Nyeah,") conspired to give it even less Yuletide recognition than "The Bell That Couldn't Jingle."

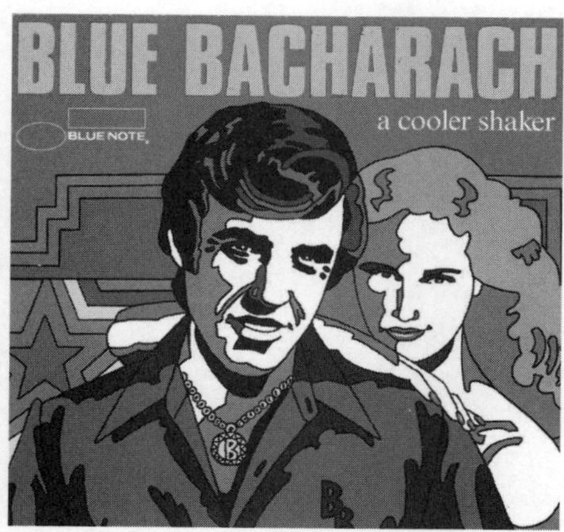

Blue Bacharach A Cooler Shaker. In addition to containing the Ernie Watts Quintete's jazzy interpretation of "Knowing Where To Leave," this 1999 retrospective of Capitol/Blue Note jazzy Bacharach favorites has recipes on how to mix the perfect Manhattan, Martini, On the Rocks and Whiskey Sour!

Other Versions: *Toni Eden, Eula Parker, Jackie Lee, Barbara Moore (1969) • Ensemble with Burt Bacharach (demo - 1968) • Robert Goulet (1968) • Jack Jones (1969) • Johnny Mathis (1969)*

"Knowing When to Leave" (Burt Bacharach - Hal David)
First recorded by Jill O'Hara
From the original cast album *Promises, Promises,* United Artists UAS 9902
Released December 1968

Strange as it may seem, most of the songs initially written for the

Sue Raney (1969). This jazz vocalist was a regular on Ray Anthony's television program before the age of 18. Raney's recording of "Knowing When to Leave" was an attempt to establish her as a pop singer. The flip side of this single was a cover of a Monkees tune, "Early Morning Blues and Greens."

show's female cast were cast aside, and this up-tempo number was one of the first replacements. Like the title song, it's quite a mouthful; one can hear Jill O'Hara gasping for air with what sounds like four choruses all railroaded together before concluding in a dramatic heave. Without the built-in drama of the married man in the Chinese restaurant calling his wife on the pay phone, Dionne Warwick's rendition of this showstopper sounds cool and collected, as if she's casually pushing a shopping cart down the frozen-food aisle. Michelle Lee offers a slower but similarly composed version that actually made it to No. 32 on the adult-contemporary chart during the show's opening month.

Other Versions: *Arthur Brooks Ensemble • Burt Bacharach (1969) • Joe Bourne • Betty Buckley - London cast (1969) • Liz Callaway - medley (1995) • Vikki Carr (1973) • The Carpenters - Bacharach/David medley (1971) • Enoch Light (1969) • Eydie Gorme • Michelle Lee (1968) • Aimi MacDonald (1969) • Gordon MacRae (1969) • Hugo Montenegro (1968) •Sue Raney (1969) • Helen Reddy (1998) • Mike Sammes Singers • Catherine Spaak - "L'Ora Dell'Addio" • Dionne Warwick • Ernie Watts Quintet (1969) • Julius Wechter & the Baja Marimba Band*

"Overture" (Burt Bacharach - Hal David)
First recorded by the original Broadway cast and orchestra
From the original cast album *Promises, Promises,* United Artists UAS 9902
Released December 1968

After opening with a few horn blasts of "Whoever You Are," the overture vamps a bit before launching into "Knowing When to Leave," switching into "Turkey Lurkey Time," following with "She Likes Basketball" and concluding with "Promises, Promises." One of the few bars of music in the "Overture" that was not a part of the show later became the bridge of "Loneliness Remembers What Happiness Forgets."

Known for their predisposition to speeding, the Italians raced through the "Overture," managing to shave almost 20 seconds off the Americans' running time.

Other Versions: *Italian cast/orchestra (1970) • London cast/orchestra (1969)*

"Hot Food" (Burt Bacharach - Hal David)
"Loyal, Resourceful and Cooperative" (Burt Bacharach - Hal David)
"A Stork of Luck" (Burt Bacharach - Hal David)

This trio of songs emerged after the early demos were recorded; they were deleted from *Promises, Promises,* along with "Tick Tock Goes the Clock," following the Colonial Theatre tryouts in Boston, The four executives in the dining room sent back "Hot Food" in favor of "Where Can You Take a Girl?," while "Our Little Secret" aced out "Loyal, Resourceful and Cooperative" by the time the show reached Washington. Little is known about "A Stork of Luck." It may be a transitional step between "Let's Pretend We're Grownup" and "Turkey Lurkey Time"; possibly it's an alternate title for either "The Grapes of Roth" or a song copyrighted in April 1969 called "Wouldn't That Be a Stroke of Luck?"

Other songs written during this period that may have been intended for the show include "In the Right Kind of Light" and "Phone Calls." The only other song B&D registered with the copyright office in 1968 was the revised title and arrangement for "This Guy's in Love with You."

Dorelli! Spaak! Songwise, the Italian production of *Promises, Promises* was a two-star affair except for Bice Valori, who sang on the Chuck & Marge duet "Natale dura giorno solamente." Note the diminished importance of the key in this cover design. Or even the title of the show.

"The Grapes of Roth" (Burt Bacharach - Hal David)
First recorded by the orchestra and chorus of *Promises, Promises*
From the original cast album *Promises, Promises,* United Artists UAS 9902
Released December 1968

One of Bacharach's unique innovations on the Broadway stage—one he wasn't sure would be accepted by the Great White Way—was his use of voices as instruments, often blended with horns. The technique was never better showcased than in this brief piece of transitional music, where the chorus is compelled to squawk like chickens. More fowl play ensues with Act One's closer.

Other Versions: *London cast/orchestra (1969)*

"Turkey Lurkey Time" (Burt Bacharach - Hal David)
First recorded by Donna McKechnie, Margo Sappington and Baayork Lee
From the original cast album *Promises, Promises,* United Artists UAS 9902
Released December 1968

Rock musicians are used to banging out material on the road to record once touring is over, but having to write on the run—and to have the material ready for performance the same night—was a new experience for Bacharach and David. Scripted somewhere between the Boston and Washington previews of *Promises, Promises,* "Turkey Lurkey Time" was a less heavy-handed way to sing about adulterous males at the office than "Let's Pretend We're Grown Up," and its comical use of voices and horns to sound like gobblers made it an ideal dance number to cap off Act One. Producer David Merrick reportedly didn't care for this number at all but changed his opinion after John Kenneth Galbraith, who attended a Washington show with Jacqueline Kennedy Onassis, said he loved it.

Other Versions: *Debbie Shapiro Gravitte • Donna McKechnie, Miranda Willis & Susi Pink (1969) • Italian production* Promesse, Promesse *(1970)*

1968

Dirty Old Men. Paul Reed, Norman Shelly, Vince O'Brien and Dick O'Neill in the Broadway production, performing "Where Can You Take a Girl?"

"Where Can You Take a Girl?" (Burt Bacharach - Hal David)
First recorded by Paul Reed, Norman Shelly, Vince O'Brien and Dick O'Neill
From the original cast album *Promises, Promises,* United Artists UAS 9902
Released December 1968

Could it be the Italians didn't see anything particularly funny about making love in a baby carriage, a kiddy car, a rowboat or rooftops? Or was it the depiction of married men as browbeaten mice who are allowed only "one night out" that spurred them to delete this song from the show? Hal David's gift as a humorist served him well on this number, where four middle-aged lotharios plead for a reasonable place to pin down the office girl of their choice "for 60 minutes or 40 minutes, more or less." Not really 60-minute men, they downsize their happiness requirements two lines later to just 20 minutes *("We can be fast!")* . These are the real husbands behind "Wives and Lovers"—balding, clutching perverts who look nothing like Jack Jones, who spend most of their overtime trying to con secretaries into a U-Haul trailer because their fear of curlers prevents them from finding love at home.

Other Versions: *Ronnie Carroll, Jay Denver, Ivor Dean, Don Fellows - London production (1969) • Paul Reed, Norman Shelly, Vince O'Brien and Dick O'Neill (1969)*

"A Fact Can Be a Beautiful Thing" (Burt Bacharach - Hal David)
First recorded by Jerry Orbach and Marian Mercer
From the original cast album *Promises, Promises,* United Artists UAS 9902
Released December 1968

Although this song was not recognized as a *Promises, Promises* showstopper, both principals in Act Two's opening scene won Tonys for their slurring participation, with Marian Mercer's stage time as the flirty and soused Marge MacDougall barely totaling over ten minutes. Similarly, when Christine Baranski (who also played a great drunk on the TV series *Cybil*) reprised the role of Marge in 1997, she generated some of the easiest laughs when she was trying to not look easy. Hal David's underlying theme of abandonment and drowning the holiday blues with depressants is rather grim *("Not a time to be alone with memories / Christmas is supposed to be a happy holiday.... What's gone is gone and don't you ever doubt it")*, yet he offers our amorous barflies hope that things are looking up, even at rock bottom *("Forget about the past and think about the present / The present's very pleasant").*

Si vede la differenza! The Italian version of "A Fact Can Be a Beautiful Thing" highlights the holiday in its title, *"Natale dura un giorno solamente,"* as "Christmas Day" was also cut from that production. This number also includes an extended instrumental section that allows drunkards Chuck and Marge a chance to dance.

Other Versions: *Johnny Dorelli & Bice Valori ("Natale dura un giorno solamente" - Italian production (1970) • Ronnie Carroll & Patricia Whitmore (1969) • Tony Roberts & Kelly Britt (1969) • Martin Short & Christine Baranski (1997)*

"I'll Never Fall in Love Again" (Burt Bacharach - Hal David)
First recorded by Jerry Orbach and Jill O'Hara
From the original cast album *Promises, Promises,* United Artists UAS 9902
Released December 1968

Although Hal David recalls the whole project as a joy from beginning to end, there were some hairy moments, particularly involving the show's volatile producer David Merrick. In the warts-and-all Merrick biography *The Abominable Showman*, there is an account of him chewing out the novice Broadway composers in New Haven, as witnessed by the show's costume designer Robin Moore. Merrick was alleged to have to have snarled, "You people cannot write theater music. If I don't have a new song Friday night—and it doesn't stop the show—I'm getting new composers."

Tony Roberts and Melissa Hart, performing the showstopper "I'll Never Fall in Love Again" in the Canadian production of *Promises, Promises*. Roberts resumed the role of Chuck Baxter immediately after leaving the London cast.

Adding to his troubles, Bacharach contracted pneumonia during the New Haven run and had to be hospitalized. Merrick continued his harangue regardless, insinuating that Bacharach wasn't actually sick and even threatening at one point to bring in Leonard Bernstein. Would this showstopping song have happened without Merrick's blustering? Probably. Bacharach was able to set Hal David's lyric up on his piano and knock the song out mere hours before that night's performance. But would David have thought to work "pneumonia" into the lyric and rhyme it with "he'll never phone ya" had Bacharach not gotten so deathly sick? Probably not.

The hit version with flugelhorn is what we remember best, yet the song stopped the show as a gently fingerpicked acoustic duet (no reason to use the word "unplugged," is there?), with understated orchestration sneaking in midway through. Among the answers most given to the question "What do you get when you fall in love?" our survey says "lies, pain, sorrow" and "a guy with a pin to burst your bubble." Less popular answers include "a heart that's shattered," since that verse is omitted when singing the song the Warwick way. The Carpenters came up with a verse not even included in the show version: *"You get enough tears to fill an ocean / That's what you get for your devotion."*

Ella Fitzgerald (1969). Dionne was reluctant to record "I'll Never Fall in Love Again" until after Ella's version finished its chart run. It appeared on *Ella,* the Richard Perry–produced Reprise album that also has the Divine Miss F swinging through the Beatles' "Savoy Truffle" and "Got To Get You into My Life," plus three Smokey Robinson hits, two Randy Newmans, a Harry Nilsson and an Eddie Floyd. The results are really not as jarring as one might think.

Although not noted for her singing ability, Angie Dickinson was the first person to perform the song on television. Gently pressured to perform one of her husband's tunes by Greg Garrison, producer of *The Dean Martin Show*, her reaction was "My God, he'd kill me. He knows what kind of singer I am." After mentioning that her husband was in Boston, where a great little number for the Broadway-bound show had just been added, Garrison suggested she try doing that one. After Dickinson reluctantly cleared it with her husband, he reluctantly ran over the chord changes with the show's musical supervisor. According to Dickinson, her finicky husband was so irritated by the resulting performance that she never even watched the show when it aired. Years later, she viewed her one and only public performance of a Bacharach–David song on videotape and declared to Garrison, "I had to call that son of a bitch and tell him he made a nervous wreck out of me all these years. It was damned good!"

1968

"I'll Never Fall in Love Again." Bacharach and Elvis Costello performed the *Promises, Promises* showstopper in the second Austin Powers movie, *The Spy Who Shagged Me*. Too bad Mini-Me didn't tackle "Half As Big As Life."

Although he wouldn't repeat his Broadway experience anytime soon, Bacharach did rerecord this showstopper twice. On his second A&M album, it was performed with unnamed session singers, becoming a No. 18 adult contemporary hit in mid-1969. More recently he remade the song for a cameo appearance with Elvis Costello in the second Austin Powers movie, *The Spy Who Shagged Me*. When asked in *GQ* magazine how the time-traveling secret agent could stumble upon a white haired Bacharach and a middle-aged Costello on Carnaby Street in 1969, Mike Myers likened it to the wristwatches that turn up on Roman soldiers in Cecil B. De Mille movie epics.

Other Versions: *Johnny Adams • Yasuko Agawa (1996) • Chet Atkins (1969) • Burt Bacharach (1969) • Balsam Boys - "Jag tanker aldrig mer blir kar" (2001) • Shirley Bassey (1969, live 1970) • Terry Baxter (1971) • Joe Bourne (1993) • Dennis Brown (1969) • Ruth Brown • Betty Buckley & Tony Roberts (1969) • Charlie Byrd • The Carpenters (1970) • Mary Chapin Carpenter (1997) • Casino Royale (1999) • Frank Chacksfield (1971) • Floyd Cramer • Elvis Costello & Burt Bacharach (1999) • Bing Crosby (1975) • Deacon Blue (1990) • Arthur Fiedler & the Boston Pops (1972) • Angie Dickinson (1968) • 5th Dimension (1970) • Sandy Duncan (1972) • Film Score Orchestra • Ella Fitzgerald (1969, live 1970) • Grant Geissman (1999) • Bobbie Gentry (1969) • Free'n' Easy (1998) • Don Goldie (1977) • Grant Green (1970) • Guitars Unlimited • Guy Haines (1998) • Emmylou Harris (1968) • Isaac Hayes (1970) • Ted Heath Orchestra • Florence Henderson • Sheila Hutchinson - medley (1997) • The Jet Set (1999) • Bibi Johns - "Die Liebe ist für mich vorbei" (1969) • Jack Jones (1970) • Brian Kennedy (2000) • Colin Keyes (1995) • Andre Kostelanetz (1970) • Lynette Koyana (2000) • Mark Lindsay (1970) • Mantovani (1970) • Johnny Mathis (1969) • Keff McCulloch (1996) • Akira Miyazawa (1970) • Tony Mottola (1969) • Wenche Myhre - "Vill aldrig mer bli kär igen" (1969) • Orquesta Sabor Tropical (1993) • Patti Page • Fausto Papetti (1996) • Franck Pourcel (1969) • Renaissance (1970) • Martin Short & Kerry O'Malley (1997) • Christopher Scott (1970) • Royal Marines (1974) • RTE Concert Orchestra/Richard Hayman (1995) • Splitsville (1998) • Starlight Orchestra (1995) • Gary Tesca (1995) • Viktoria Tolstoy – "Musical Tribute to Burt Bacharach" (2001) • Sugar Townes • Jerry Vale • Dionne Warwick (1969, rerecorded 2000) • The Whitlams (1998) • Klaus Wunderlich • Caterina Valente - medley (1970) • Bobby Vinton*

"Our Little Secret" (Burt Bacharach - Hal David)
First recorded by Jerry Orbach and Edward Winter
From the original cast album *Promises, Promises,* United Artists UAS 9902
Released December 1968

Baxter and Sheldrake exchange mischievous whistles on this silly duet, which premiered in Washington. Bacharach told *Playbill*, "After this change, we'll freeze the show. This song is a replacement for one that I supremely disliked, so that makes me feel better." He must've really hated "Loyal, Resourceful and Cooperative," because it's the only one of the show's songs copyrighted in February 1968 that hasn't turned up on a demo acetate. Maybe Rose Mary Jun was ordered to break hers!

At the opening night party for *Promises, Promises*, David Merrick obviously revised his uncharitable opinion of Bacharach, declaring that he was "the first original composer since Gershwin" and that his music was more emotional than Strauss's. More importantly, he added, "Young people understand it." The press and public agreed, and the show ran for 1,281 performances, earning Tony Awards for Jerry Orbach and Marian Mercer and a Grammy for Bacharach and David.

You can hear the reluctance to take on another Broadway show in Bacharach's candid and exhausted responses to reporter Fred Robbins' questions at that same triumphant opening night party. "I'd like to get away to the desert with my wife and my baby. Forget about it, whether the show's a smash or not. I'm very tired and enervated by it all," he sighed. "My memories of the time out on the road are not good. I got sick on the road. I got pneumonia and wound up in the hospital. It colors your memory of the experience. You've got to rewrite when you are out on the road. Not a very happy time. Not a very exciting time." And he missed the autonomy of the recording studio. "With a musical, there are five or six people involved. We all try to please each other. If someone says 'Hey, I don't like that ending,' you respect what they say."

Opening Night Premiere Album. United Artists released this rare, promotional-only LP, which captures the Schubert Theater opening-night excitement and the on-the-spot reactions of Pearl Bailey, Herb Alpert, Cab Calloway, Milton Berle, Burt's parents, Angie Dickenson, David Merrick, Neil Simon and a very tired Burt Bacharach. Curiously, there's no interview from Hal David preserved for posterity, but we do learn that Carol Channing's favorite tune is "Upstairs."

Despite the deafening cries that he had something to contribute to the Broadway stage, Bacharach felt that over a year of his life was enough of a contribution. "If you're making a record, as soon as you have it right, it's on tape. In the theater, it's right tonight but tomorrow's another story. The trumpet player's lip may be bad, the tempos could be off, the singer may have a cold…it's nerve wrecking but you have to adjust." Bacharach's ultimate contributions were in making the reproduction of the music in the theater as close as possible to the recording experience at Bell or A&R Studios. At his insistence, the innovative decision was made to relocate the orchestra pit and conductor offstage and have an engineer control the sounds and balances through amplification. And Bacharach handpicked the rhythm section so that the songs would have a more contemporary feel than most of what had been heard on Broadway at the time.

Following *Promises, Promises* and *Hair,* which premiered the same year, Broadway updated its antiquated sound amplification and moved further away from the traditional musicals of yesteryear. With no forthcoming Bacharach–David shows, the Great White Way looked to rock musicals like *Godspell, Jesus Christ Superstar* and *Beatlemania* for less traditional fare

Other Versions: *Tony Roberts & James Congdon - London production (1969) • Martin Short & Terrence Mann (1997)*

"Dream Sweet Dreamer." Dionne's only non-LP B-side in the Scepter era.

"Dream Sweet Dreamer" (Burt Bacharach - Hal David)
Recorded by Dionne Warwick
Scepter 12241, flip side of "This Girl's in Love with You" (*Billboard* pop & R&B #7)
Released January 1969

It's hard to hear *"Dream me a world made of peace and love / This is my dream, make it come true"* and not think that Hal David wrote a beautiful eulogy to Martin Luther King, assassinated just nine months previously. After a turbulent year like 1968, one could hardly ask for a more appropriate hope than *"Dream me a year where we hear no more*

April Fools, Indeed! To those who bought the original soundtrack album expecting to hear the Dionne hit recording, it's performed "especially for this album" by the Percy Faith Orchestra and Chorus! Also not included on the soundtrack is a party sing-along of "I Say a Little Prayer" that predates *My Best Friend's Wedding*'s similar blowout by 24 years!

goodbyes / And build me a life filled with faith, hope and compassion / And fill it with people that trust other people." Yet the song was written in 1967, in the same burst of utopian awareness that produced "I Say a Little Prayer" and "The Windows of the World." "Dream Sweet Dreamer" got considerably less attention than either of those, earning the distinction of being the only Warwick non-album B-side of the Scepter years, a perfectly perverse waste of a gorgeous track at a time when unwarranted filler like "I Got Love" and "Up Up and Away" were taking up residence on Warwick albums.

Dionne has also said in interviews that she asked Burt and Hal to come up with a song for her firstborn son, Damon Elliot, who was born in March 1969. The team responded with this thoughtful lullaby, complete with a recorder flute beginning and nonsensical "bee-by-o" baby talk syllables that fill out the verses. The baby talk was meant to emphasize the piano line; Hal David found no actual words that better fit that interval and kept it in. If you could look up "bee-by-o" in the Hal David dictionary, it would say "See 'ba-da–da dah,'" found in their next children's song, "The World Is a Circle."

"The April Fools" (Burt Bacharach - Hal David)
First recorded by Dionne Warwick
From the Cinema Center film *The April Fools*
Scepter 12249, released May 1969 (*Billboard* pop #37)

With Dionne's last single ("This Girl's in Love with You"), her record-buying public again proved that they vigilantly exercised the option of hearing her sing time-proven Bacharach-David hits before stamping a great big DEFINITIVE sticker on them. Unfortunately, these remakes tended to overshadow the team's newer material. Coming off a Top 10 single, "The April Fools" should've reached more ears than its No. 37 chart position indicates. The film starred Jack Lemmon and Catherine Deneuve as two people unhappily married, but not to each other. As the designated April fools, seemingly mad with April love, they are entering a potentially volatile domestic situation by flying off to Paris and abandoning their spouses and alleged good life. This is the danger hinted at in Hal David's lyric, but it's counteracted by the security of two people who love each other in equal measure.

Aretha Franklin identified strongly with the lyric: not only did she record an equally intense version for her *Young, Gifted and Black* album, she quoted the lyrics liberally in the text of her autobiography when describing meeting the man of her dreams, Dennis Edwards from the Temptations: *"Are we just April fools who can't see all the danger around us / If we are just April fools, I don't care / True love has found us now."*

Marvin Hamlisch, three years away from his Oscar-winning breakthrough work on *The Sting*, scored *The April Fools* utilizing Bacharach's theme throughout.

Other Versions: *Yasuko Agawa (1996) • Ronnie Aldrich (1971) • Burt Bacharach • Cilla Black (1970) • The Cozy Corners (1994) • Enoch Light (1970) • Percy Faith (1969) • Ferrante & Teicher • Aretha Franklin (1972) • Marvin Hamlisch (1969) • Earl Klugh*

(1977) • Living Voices (1970) • Ray Price (1970) • RTE Concert Orchestra/Richard Hayman (1995) • Christopher Scott (1969) • Vanessa Williams (1997)

"Pacific Coast Highway" (Burt Bacharach)
Recorded by Burt Bacharach
A&M 1064, flip side of "I'll Never Fall in Love Again"
Released May 1969

After the opening of *Promises, Promises*, Bacharach took a month to unwind in Palm Springs with Angie and Nikki. Upon his return, his agenda included writing the *April Fools* theme and compiling songs for a second A&M album. *Make It Easy on Yourself* contained five numbers from the Broadway smash, four past hits and two brand new instrumentals, the first of which sounded as if Bacharach were subconsciously scoring his own vacation. After starting off with what sounds like "I Say a Little Prayer," Bacharach picks up the ocarina revival where the Troggs' "Wild Thing" left off. The flutelike instrument's wavering pitch suggests bleary-eyed early morning consciousness giving way to an alert and caffeinated midday rush carrying through to evening, when a star-studded sky competes with city lights for reflection space along the bay. Compelling background music for housewives who don't get out of the domicile enough.

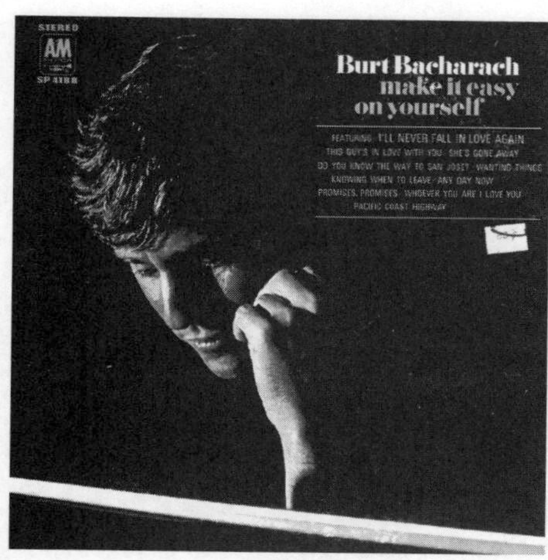

Make It Easy On Yourself (1969). Check out Bacharach's post *Promises Promises* album for the fleshed out treatment the five show songs got here. The show's arrangements had to be drastically simplified for Broadway pit musicians to pull off night after night.

"She's Gone Away" (Burt Bacharach)
Recorded by Burt Bacharach
From *Make It Easy on Yourself*, A&M LP 4188
Released May 1969

Unlike "Pacific Coast Highway," this instrumental eventually did require the services of Hal David when the chord changes in the verses became the basis for Ed Ames' "How Does a Man Become a Puppet" in 1971.

"Odds and Ends (Of a Beautiful Love Affair)" (Burt Bacharach - Hal David)
First recorded by Dionne Warwick
Scepter 12256 (*Billboard* pop #43)
Released July 1969

If you remember staring at the red, black and white Scepter label spinning around on a battery-operated phonograph player, it's a safe bet you also clocked countless hours in front of the television set. One of the most popular commercials of the early Seventies was for Colt 45 malt liquor. Generally, a well-dressed man would find himself inappropriately seated in the center of a bullfighting arena or some other dangerous non-spectator area. Even after the bull charges him, he merely dusts himself off and smiles at the beery beverage he's not allowed to consume on television. The easygoing whistling of that Colt 45 jingle is quite similar to "Odds and Ends," another of Bacharach and David's unjustly ignored classics.

"Odds and Ends." The only two Scepter A-sides never to appear on a Scepter album were "Who Gets the Guy?" and "Odds and Ends."

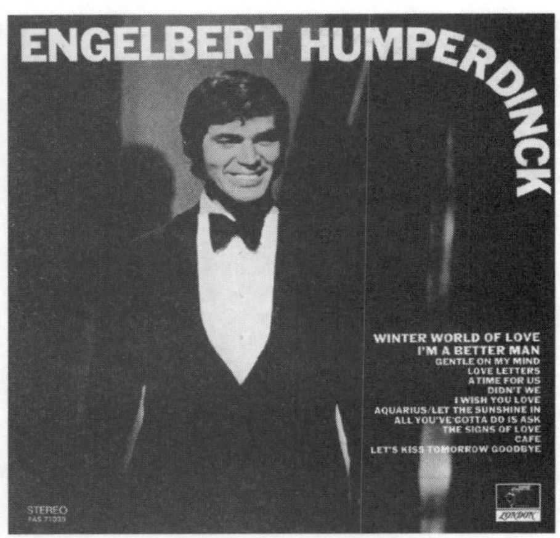

Engelbert Humperdinck. After Tom Jones' ABC-TV variety show became a hit, the network gave one to Engelbert. Unlike Tom, however, he didn't have a set design that spelled out his first name in 20-foot letters. There was no TV screen manufactured in 1970 wide enough to accommodate E-N-G-E-L-B-E-R-T!

Like our malt liquor-holic, Dionne seems unusually unfazed about having the domestic rug yanked out from under her. She seems more amazed that her partner in this once beautiful love affair was able to remove every trace of their years together from their apartment: *"Nothing was left to show that we were once so happy there / Just an empty tube of toothpaste and a half-filled cup of coffee / Odds and ends of a beautiful love affair."*

Only a hint of heartache remains once that cheerful whistling returns. One can almost imagine singing the lyrics of "Magic Moments" over this track and getting the same pick-me-up. Terry Baxter's choral cover version comes very close indeed to matching Perry Como and the Ray Charles Singers for wide-eyed innocence. Yet it's a very different world from the 1950s, with people living together and splitting up without it ever becoming a legal matter—or in this case, a crying matter: this odds-and-ends guy didn't even wait for the first teardrop to fall before turning the latch on the door.

Other Versions: *Ronnie Aldrich (1971) • Terry Baxter (1971) • Sacha Distel - "Ce qui reste d'un grand amour" (1972) • Marion Maerz - "Einsame Träume" (1971) • Johnny Mathis (1970) • Penny and Her Friends • Billy Vaughn (1969)*

"I'm A Better Man (For Having Loved You)" (Burt Bacharach - Hal David)
First recorded by Engelbert Humperdinck
Parrot 40040 (*Billboard* pop #38)
Released August 1969

A Better Mantovani for Having Loved You (1969). Sure, anyone can cover Bacharach-David songs, but it takes 100 strings sawing away in unison to really impress music lovers. This is one of the rare album covers where Mantovani's trusty baton cannot be seen. But it's there: people can flip the cover over to reveal the full Manty!

Once the two "medallion men" in Gordon Mills' MAM management empire, Tom Jones and Engelbert Humperdinck were poles apart stylistically. "When the press compared Humperdinck and myself, I couldn't see it," said Jones. "He's a balladeer. I consider myself more of a rhythm and blues singer." No Joe Tex covers for Humperdinck, a "Quando Quando Quando" man all the way. Clearly, this was the Anti-Tom.

This perception was certainly shared by the public, who never sent anything but schmaltz, schmaltz and more schmaltz into the Top 40 whenever Engie was at the microphone. Interestingly enough, Bacharach and David never scripted a ballad for Jones but did find one suitable for Der Humper (all right, we'll stop with the nicknames now). As schmaltz goes, "I'm a Better Man" is top-notch, carried along by a classy circular piano figure similar to the one on his previous hit, "The Way It Used to Be." What blue-haired lady could resist a handsome devotee with mutton-chop sideburns promising he'll gift-wrap the moon and stars just to illustrate his devotion? Yet nearly 30-odd records crowded it out of the Top 5, where his biggest hit, "Release Me," once crested. Humperdinck was persuaded to record four more Bacharach and David tunes in the next two years, including the obscure but likewise romantic "Love Was Here Before the Stars," which turned up on his next album, simply titled *Engelbert*.

Other Versions: *Terry Baxter (1971) • Alan Caddy Orchestra (1970) • Film Score Orchestra • Mantovani (1969) • Al Martino (1970) • David McAlmont (1998) • Singers And Chorus of Manhattan (1977)*

"Raindrops Keep Falling on My Head" (Burt Bacharach - Hal David)
First recorded by B.J. Thomas
From the 20th Century Fox film *Butch Cassidy and the Sundance Kid*
Scepter 12265 (*Billboard* pop #1)
Released November 1969

Thanks to the invention of the DVD, we now have a wealth of information at our fingertips about the making of the film *Butch Cassidy and the Sundance Kid*. Wanna see signed contracts? Interoffice memos at 20th Century Fox? Facts about the bull? It's all here, but if your interest begins and ends with the Oscar-winning score, you'll learn that the famous bicycle scene as originally written had no music scheduled behind it!

A week before production, director George Roy Hill and screenwriter William Goldman decided to insert three musical sequences into the picture. They felt that the schoolteacher Etta Place (played by Katherine Ross) didn't have enough screen time and that there weren't any dialogue scenes in the picture to establish her relationship with Butch (Paul Newman) or the symbiotic three-way relationship among Butch, Etta and Sundance (Robert Redford). A July 23, 1968, memo from studio head Richard Zanuck to Paul Newman agreed: "I like the idea of the musical interludes as long as they are not carried to excess. To be really effective, I think they should be used sparingly, as to go overboard would, in my opinion, detract from the flow of the story. Rod McKuen might be an excellent choice for this type of thing." In a word—yikes!

At the suggestion of Paul Newman, Bacharach met with Hill and was shown a rough-cut of the film. According to Newman's recollections: "George was never satisfied with that [bicycle] scene until we got...Simon and Garfunkel's '59th Street Bridge Song,' I think it was, and he actually edited the film to that. We have this pastiche of little bits of music and classics that George put together when he ran the picture the first time for Burt Bacharach. And it was so eclectic that it freed Bacharach up to do something more modern in the scoring of the picture than he might have otherwise."

By May 1969, Bacharach had been contracted to write the background score and to write two songs for the film with Hal David. Even with the Simon and Garfunkel temporary track, Bacharach wasn't altogether sure that Hill wanted a vocal number in the bicycle sequence. "I just kept watching that scene over and over on my Moviola machine and I got this theme; I thought maybe it could be a song," Bacharach remembers. "I didn't know how oppositional George would be about a song there. He was a little bit. But Hal David and myself wrote it, and I explained to him that it would go as far as it could go—become an instrumental, takeoff, variations and departures on the melody. And he kind of went into it, I don't think 100 percent. But I think he did get to see and appreciate it. It was a dangerous call on George's part and my part. It could've been very disruptive in that picture. But it worked."

Adds David: "It was such a happy-go-lucky scene in the sunshine, and there was Butch Cassidy on the bike having a great old time, and

Bull Run. Let's take this time to honor the unsung hero of the bicycle sequence, Bill the Bull, whose balls were squirted with something they called "high life" to make him charge. Said director George Roy Hill, "Bill's forte was that he didn't turn ugly afterwards."

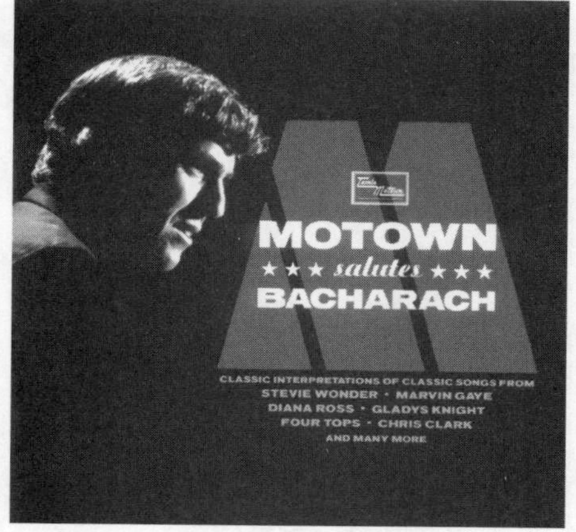

Motown Salutes Bacharach. There's plenty of schmaltzy cover versions of "Raindrops Keep Falling On My Head" but few soulful ones. An exception is Levi Stubbs' and the Four Tops' over-the-top 1970 reading, conveniently located on this 2002 Universal UK collection of Motown Bacharach covers.

Raindrops Keep Messin' with My Head. In our continuing efforts to discourage you from getting a life, let us note that first pressing of this LP has a fold-open Unipak cover and came out with a muddy mix. This batch can be identified by the matrix numbers SPS-580 A-1B/SPS-580 B-1A scratched in the runout groove area. The second pressing has a clearer mix; its matrix numbers are SPS-580 A-1C/SPS-580 B-1C.

Song of the Year? Bacharach and David had two 1969 Grammy song-of-the-year nominations for "Raindrops" and "I'll Never Fall in Love Again" but got beat out by a song with a considerably shorter shelf life, Joe South's "Games People Play."

everyone knew watching the film that Butch Cassidy was a guy in all sorts of trouble. Things always went wrong with him; raindrops kept falling on his head. Looking at the scene and trying to tell the story of Butch Cassidy is what we accomplished. Burt wrote this kind of happy-go-lucky tune with this wonderful melody, in my opinion, and then a lyric which went against that melody and I think caught what the scene was about, and that accomplished the success of the song."

"Raindrops" is a rare example of Bacharach supplying a dummy title that remained in the final draft. Despite the complete absence of precipitation in the scene, nothing else fit the metering quite as well. "I wrote the first lyric, which probably took me a couple of days, and then tried another turn at it," Hal David recalls on the DVD. "I wound up with two lyrics called 'Raindrops Keep Fallin' on My Head,' and I took what I thought was the best out of each and glued it together. We played the song for George at Burt's house in Beverly Hills. He liked it immediately and there wasn't anything to sell. He heard it, liked it and said, 'That's it.' B.J. Thomas turned out to be a wonderful choice."

Time proved B.J. the best man for the job, but he was far from the first choice. The song was offered to him as a last resort after both Ray Stevens and Eddy Arnold turned it down and time was running out. It was Scepter A&R man Steve Tyrell who suggested using Thomas. Warwick has also claimed credit for bringing Thomas to Bacharach's attention. Then there is this business about Bob Dylan being approached to do the song. Thomas revealed his thoughts on this subject in *The Billboard Book of Number One Hits*. "Burt had originally composed the melody to fit Bob Dylan. In subsequent years Burt has denied it, but this is what I understood at the time. Burt really admired Bob Dylan and the way he phrased. When Bob, for whatever reasons, didn't do it, I was his second choice. What's funny is that I actually had laryngitis and was barely able to eke out the thing for the soundtrack." Although Thomas' doctor advised him not to use his voice for two weeks, he relented and gave the singer medication that lubricated his throat for roughly five passes at the song.

Bacharach's upturned phrasing was a good deal like Dylan's, and he rehearsed Thomas to get a more polished version of it. When Thomas turned up in California with a sore throat, he succeeded in sounding exactly like Bacharach, although a 20th Century Fox executive at the session thought B.J. was trying to emulate Paul Newman! The hoarse version of "Raindrops" appears in the film and as part of "A Bicycle Built for Joy" on the soundtrack, but the more familiar hit version was recorded two weeks later at A&R Studios in New York, with the perky horn tag added to the fade. Even after recording the song twice, Bacharach wound up stopping the pressing plant when the single was being manufactured. In a 1980 interview he explained, "I had been torn between two takes—one that sounded comfortable, one that had a lot of energy. I went with the comfortable. But what I would up doing was making an edit right in the middle of the song and picking up the fast one in the break. That's how it was finally released." Additionally, Bacharach recorded a harpsichord, French horn and ukulele-driven instrumental version of "Raindrops" for the soundtrack that was not used in the film.

Bacharach and David closed out the Sixties with their all-time biggest hit and only Academy Award–winning song sitting at No. 1 for four weeks. Like the team's other No. 1 hit "This Guy's in Love With You," "Raindrops" sounds like it has about four or five notes in it, which meant everybody could sing it, from Japanese punk minimalists Shonen Knife to the cast of *Monty Python's Flying Circus*. The song is excerpted three times in the second *Python* season, which first aired in the fall of 1970. In Show 17, *The Buzz Aldrin Show* (Series 2, Show 9), Graham Chapman portrays Police Constable Pan-Am and sings the tune while under the delusion that he is an airplane. Chapman sings it again while playing a waitress in Show 18, *Live from the Grill-o-Mat* (Series 2, Show 7). And for something completely different, Show 19 (*School Prizes*, Series 2, Show 8) concluded with an "Election Night Special," where an independent Very Silly Party candidate's extremely long name contains—you guessed it—a sung snippet of "Raindrops Keep Falling on My Head."

Raindrops Keep Fallin' on My Hedgehog. The Python troupe worked pop hits of the day into their offbeat series, but the Bacharach-David hit made it into more shows than either "Don't Sleep in the Subway" or "Yummy Yummy Yummy (I've Got Love in My Tummy)."

Other Versions: *Ronnie Aldrich (1971) • Ed Ames (1969) • Robert Audy (1994) • Roy Ayers (1970) • Burt Bacharach (1969) • Terry Baxter (1971) • Big Ben Banjo Band with the Mike Sammes Singers - medley • Acker Bilk • Yami Bolo (1997) • Fred Bongusto - "Gocce di pioggia du di me" • Joe Bourne (1993) • Dennis Brown (1969) • Heidi Bruhl - "Regen fällt heute auf die Welt" (1970) • Buffalo Bob (1971) • Vikki Carr • Raffaella Carra (1997) • Frank Chacksfield (1971) • Chelsea Strings (1995) • Perry Como (1970) • Cordrazine (1998) • Ray Conniff (1970) • Russ Conway • Floyd Cramer • Ray Davies & the Button Down Brass Band (1969) • Sammy Davis Jr. (1973) • Deadbolt (2000) • The Dells (1972) • Sacha Distel - "Toute la pluie tombe sur moi" (1970) • Craig Douglas (1969) • Enoch Light (1970) • Percy Faith (1969) • Fantastic Strings • Johnny Farnham (1969) • Ferrante & Teicher • Arthur Fiedler & the Boston Pops (1972) • Film Score Orchestra • Mickey Finn & Big Tiny Little (1987) • Ella Fitzgerald (1970)) • Ben Folds Five (1998) • Pete Fountain (1970) • Four Tops (1970) • Free Design (1970) • Free'n' Easy (1998) • Paul Frees & the Poster People (1970) • Bobbie Gentry (1970) • Anders Glenmark - medley (2001) • Don Goldie (1977) • Ron Goodwin • Robert Goulet • Leo Green (2000) • Las Guitarras del Renacimiento (1993) • Guitars Unlimited (1970)• Johnny Hartman (1975) • Tony Hatch Orchestra • Ted Heath Orchestra • Engelbert Humperdinck • Ferlin Husky • Sheila Hutchinson - medley (1997) • The Jet Set (1999) • JPJ Quartet • Bert Kaempfert (1970) • Andre Kostelanetz (1970) • Manfred Krug - "Wenn´s regnet" (2000) • Peggy Lee (1970) • Raymond Lefevre (1972) • The Lettermen • Liberace - medley • Living Strings • London Pops Orchestra • Jacques Loussier Trio • Siw Malmkvist ("Regnet det bara oser ner") • Henry Mancini (1970) • Manic Street Preachers (1995) • Mantovani • Dean Martin (1970) • Al Martino (1970) • Barbara Mason (1970) • Johnny Mathis (1970) • Paul Mauriat (1970) • Keff McCulloch (1996) • Mercury Rev (1999) • Buddy Merrill • Roger Moore & Burt Bacharach (1972) • Tony Mottola (1973) • Mummy the Peepshow (2000) • Wenche Myhre - medley (1970) • Peter Nero • 101 Strings (1971) • Orquesta Sabor Tropical (1993) • Wynn Osborne • Patti Page • The Plaids - "Bacharach at the Movies" medley (1998) • Franck Pourcel (1973) • Patty Pravo - "Gocce di pioggia su di me" (1970) • Boots Randolph (1970) • Renaissance (1970) • Rita Reys (1971) • Chris Roberts (1971) • Rockin' Jukebox (1969) • Jimmy Roselli (1974) • RTE Concert Orchestra/Richard Hayman (1995) • Lalo Schifrin (1998) • Christopher Scott (1970) • Shonen Knife (1998) • The Simpsons - TV series (1993, 1995) • Starlight Orchestra (1995) • Gary Tesca (1995) • Keith Textor Singers (1970) • Mel Tormé (1970) • Trio Mocoto - "Gotas de chuva na minha cuica" (1973) • Caterina Valente - "Wenn ich die Regentropfen seh" (1970) • Billy Vaughn (1970) • The Ventures (1970) • Dionne Warwick (1969) • Lawrence Welk (1970) • Gerhard Wendtland - "Wenn ich die Regentropfen seh" (1970) • Dottie West • Roger Whittaker (1996) • Andy Williams (1969) • Roger Williams • Roger Williams and Liberace - "Bacharach medley" • Hugo Winterhalter • Klaus Wunderlich (1973)*

1969

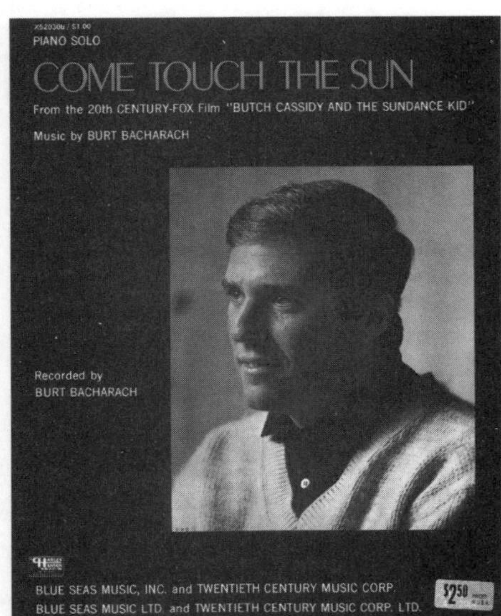

Butch Cassidy and the Sundance Kid. It won in the two musical Oscar categories—best score and best song—and didn't do to shabbily come Grammy time, winning in the best original score category.

"Come Touch the Sun" aka "Not Goin' Home Anymore" (Burt Bacharach)
First recorded by Burt Bacharach
From the Soundtrack LP *Butch Cassidy and the Sundance Kid,* A&M 4227
Released December 1969

Even with three musical interludes, the film uses less than 12 minutes of music from the soundtrack album, including a minimal version of this number, used in the opening credits, that's never been commercially available. Director George Roy Hill preferred not to run music under dialogue scenes but allowed the sad, quiet accordion reprise of "Come Touch the Sun" entitled "Not Goin' Home Anymore" (cut 3 on the soundtrack) to play during the campfire scene when Etta decides to leave (it's unofficially known as "Etta's Theme" as well). The version actually titled "Come Touch the Sun," which was released as a single (A&M 1153), was not used in the film. Hal David was slated to write a second song for the film, and although a vocal version of this song was scripted, it wasn't recorded until the following summer, under the title "Where There's a Heartache."

"The Sundance Kid" (Burt Bacharach)
Recorded by Burt Bacharach
From the Soundtrack LP *Butch Cassidy and the Sundance Kid,* A&M 4227
Released December 1969

Named in honor of the character played by Robert Redford, who in real life was less than charitable about his buddy Butch's theme, calling "Raindrops" a "dumb song" in a *TV Guide* interview. Then again, Redford is the same music lover who told Randy Newman, "I don't like the sound of trumpets," when the composer was scoring *The Natural*. To which Newman replied "What the hell do you want me to use—kazoos?"

This tack-piano-propelled opening track was nowhere to be found in the movie, but it ultimately made itself useful on the *Butch Cassidy* DVD, where it's looped to play forever unless you select a feature from the menu screen.

Other Versions: *Peter Duchin (1970)*

Oscar-Winning Composer. What were an Oscar-winning score and best song worth in 1969? Bacharach received $35,000, plus 50 cents publishing, for writing the score. Hal David received $5,000 per song for the two songs required.

"On a Bicycle Built for Joy" (Burt Bacharach - Hal David)
Recorded by Burt Bacharach
From the Soundtrack LP *Butch Cassidy and the Sundance Kid,* A&M 4227
Released December 1969

Bookended by the sore-throated version of "Raindrops" is the first of the three musical interludes. "On a Bicycle Built for Joy" is a lively circus big-top fanfare that plays while Paul Newman shows his prowess as a stunt cyclist. Most of these perilous moves were ad-libbed by the actor on the morning of the shoot, since the double originally hired to do some two-wheeled trick hadn't come up with anything worthwhile.

Whose Month Is It Anyway? To illustrate the scarcity of fresh marketing ideas, A&M named March "Burt Bacharach Month" in flagrant disregard of Scepter's "March Is Dionne Warwick Month" campaign established three years earlier.

"The Old Fun City (N.Y. Sequence)" (Burt Bacharach)
Recorded by Burt Bacharach
From the Soundtrack LP *Butch Cassidy and the Sundance Kid,* A&M 4227
Released December 1969

Used to accompany the montage of sepia photos of Butch, Sundance and Emma traveling through New York on the way to Bolivia and living the high life in plain sight of the law, this semi-Charleston is the only number in the score one can accuse Bacharach of plagiarizing from himself, as it bears more than a scandalous resemblance to "Little French Boy" from the *Casino Royale* soundtrack. The tail end of it contains the accordion version of "Not Goin' Home Anymore."

Originally this segment was to be done in live action at the Fox studio, where a grandiose New York street set was built for the *Hello Dolly* movie, but seeing as Hill's movie was scheduled to open before the Streisand musical, Zanuck didn't want them showing the street first!

Other Versions: *Hal Serra*

"South American Getaway" (Burt Bacharach)
Recorded by Burt Bacharach
From the Soundtrack LP *Butch Cassidy and the Sundance Kid,* A&M 4227
Released December 1969

The Bolivia bank-robbing montage is the last musical interlude. The filmmaker's bold decision to forego a traditional Western score in favor of a semi-modern soundtrack goes hand in hand with the contemporary demeanor of the main characters, which film critic John Simon dismissed as "a mere exercise in smart alecky device mongering." Incorporating jazz waltzes, slow sambas and modern Brazilian pop in the Bolivia bank-robbing scenes establishes the location and the mood without detracting too much from the period-piece ambiance. Bacharach continues his dexterous use of voices as instruments, as first featured in *Promises, Promises,* besides paying tribute to the music of South America. The song itself received a bizarre tribute of sorts when it was arranged not for voices but for 12 cellists.

Soulful. The first Dionne album with zero involvement from Bacharach-David was produced by Dionne and American Studios' enginneer Chips Moman. These Memphis sessions contained Dionne's versions of contemporary hits like "People Got to Be Free," "You've Lost That Lovin' Feeling" and "Hey Jude."

Other Versions: *The 12 Cellists of Berlin Philharmonic (2000)*

"Let Me Go to Him" (Burt Bacharach - Hal David)
First recorded by Dionne Warwick
Scepter 12276 (*Billboard* pop #32)
Released March 1970

Following the success of "I'll Never Fall in Love Again," this little lite-gospel single got lost in the shuffle. Perhaps Warwick's version of "Knowing When to Leave" would've been a better choice for the general public, who always seemed to be a couple of songs behind the Bacharach-David-Dionne triumvirate. Finally having someone to run to after a crumbling love affair, Dionne haltingly sings the overlapping words that Hal David marks his partner's time changes with *("He...loves...me...you never have...to...you, I'm only a plaything"),* and the cymbal-crashing chorus puts a bit of Broadway splash on what might've been a straight gospel number a few years before. This number features Bacharach's most recent calling card—the extended instrumental coda à la "The Look of Love," executed by a baroque string quartet with plenty of vibrato.

Other Versions: *Jury Krytiuk Orchestra & Chorus • Pete Moore (1970)*

"Loneliness Remembers." The recording session for this song was filmed for the *Kraft Music Hall* special "An Evening with Burt Bacharach."

"Loneliness Remembers (What Happiness Forgets)" (Burt Bacharach - Hal David)
First recorded by Dionne Warwick
Scepter 12276, flip side of "Let Me Go to Him"
Released March 1970

Forgoing prime-time promotion for Dionne's latest single, Bacharach instead showcased its flip side on his Emmy-winning 1970 *Kraft Music Hall* special. Here, staged especially for the cameras, we have a fly-on-the-wall opportunity to see Bacharach walking Warwick through "Loneliness Remembers What Happiness Forgets" for the first time at A&R Studios. Although it's a somewhat skewered version of what actually goes on (for one thing, there's no Hal David anywhere in sight; for another, how's she gonna tell him she doesn't like the song on national television?), it's a fascinating segment, completely different from the scripted banter and canned applause that precedes it. Bacharach kids her that this new song is not a crazy time-signature song, it's only the piano that is playing in different tempos. He describes "Loneliness" as "a cross-Brazilian thing," and she keeps assuring him that she indeed loves the number. "It's groovy," she giggles as she chews her gum and nails the song cold, with just a casual glance at sheet music and a bit of direction from the composer. In turn, we get to see Bacharach at the piano, fleshing out what would eventually be the finished production.

The intriguing title alone could make Smokey Robinson bolt from his chair, but Hal David explains it with internal rhymes: *"I had to lose you to recall that life's not really all sunshine and laughter."* The second section of the song turns perky à la "Do You Know the Way to San Jose," with the world spinning faster when Dionne remembers how *"We were the talk of the town / Ask anybody around / They'll let you know."* Her exhilaration grinds to a halt in the last three chords of the song: *"first came the pleasure, then came...all...the...pain,"* which is punctuated by the same flugelhorn that launched the song so cheerfully, now sounding profoundly sad.

Only two cover versions have surfaced. For some strange reason, Terry Baxter and his Orchestra and Chorus race through the song in a vain effort to illustrate that *"when you fall in love too fast / The sunshine does-*

n't last forever." And there's the Stephanie Mills version, one of two Dionne remakes on her 1975 Bacharach-David-produced album *For the First Time. "We were the talk of the town"* is no longer an abiding concern: that lyric is removed, as well as the final fatal horn blast. The song fades somewhat more cheerfully with some new Hal David lines: *"Love was a flower that bloomed in vain / First came the pleasure then came…all the…pain and the sorrow that brought the rain."*

Other Versions: *Terry Baxter (1971) • Stephanie Mills (1975)*

Everybody's out of Town. The bulk of B.J.'s albums were Chip Moman tracks produced at Memphis' American Studios. They contrasted greatly with the songs Bacharach recorded at A&R Studios, like the title track and "Send My Picture to Scranton PA."

"Everybody's out of Town" (Burt Bacharach - Hal David)
First recorded by B.J. Thomas
Scepter 12277 (*Billboard* pop #26)
Released March 1970

Coming after the enormously successful "Raindrops," this release must have seemed like the proverbial bunt instead of a grand slam at the time it was issued. In retrospect it's a pretty progressive choice, grafting social commentary and quasi-psychedelic touches onto the old-fashioned clop-along of the former hit. The guy whose feet are too big for his bed has even bigger concerns: he's the last man on earth! Like a one-man Sgt. Pepper's Lonely Hearts Club, Thomas surveys the evacuated cities; he no longer has to wait in line at the movies or suffer any further pollution. The moral of this Hal David *Twilight Zone* episode? To get rid of all this world's problems, you'll have to eliminate all the people that inhabit it. A far cry from "What the World Needs Now," it's a message song people likely weren't comfortable with, especially with somber trombones and French hornists exhaling as if they're blowing out their livers trying to play "A Day in the Life" forwards and backwards. Or it's possible the song reminded people of a record they purchased en masse a few months prior—Peggy Lee's jaunty yet disheartened "Is That All There Is?"

Other Versions: *Terry Baxter (1971) • Film Score Orchestra • Rex Harrison & Burt Bacharach (1972) • Pete Moore (1970) • Christopher Scott (1970)*

The Sandpipers (1970). The title song of this LP was from the movie *The Sterile Cuckoo,* two adjectives that adequately describe the nutty castrato versions of "The Long and Winding Road," Beethoven's "Ode to Joy" and "Where There's a Heartache" contained within.

"Where There's a Heartache (There Must Be a Heart)"
(Burt Bacharach - Hal David)
First Recorded by the Sandpipers
From the album *Come Saturday Morning,* A&M SP4262
Released spring 1970

Talk about putting off afterthoughts! It took a Grammy and an Oscar win for best musical score before someone put the rush on getting out a vocal version of "Come Touch the Sun" from *Butch Cassidy and the Sundance Kid.* If these lyrics were written for inclusion in the score, it's no wonder they weren't used in the film. It's sentimental where the film was wisecracking and sounds as if Hal David was trying to pen prose that wouldn't have sounded out of place on a late-19th-century song folio. If so, the effect is completely lost when put in a contemporary lite-rock setting.

"Paper Maché." Hal David takes on suburbia, consumerism and tasty treats for the kids on this smart 1969 single.

"Where There's a Heartache" had the misfortune of attracting some of the dullest recording acts this side of Thomas Edison. First to doom these verses to obscurity were the Sandpipers, one of several A&M recording acts who went through their entire career singing like they didn't want to wake the baby in the next room. Then came Pat Boone's treacle treatment, with a Don Costa arrangement that skidded just short of having a kiddie choir singing along. There are two worthwhile versions: Van McCoy, one-time Scepter A&R man and future proponent of "The Hustle," has a suitably old-fashioned arrangement, with autoharp, a gorgeous soprano voice and a unique added bridge—*"Forgive me, I'm sorry I made you cry"*; Astrid Gilberto softly cooed the tune on her 1970 CTI album *Astrid Gilberto with Stanley Turrentine.*

Other Versions: *Ronnie Aldrich (1971) • Pat Boone (1971) • Carnival • Astrud Gilberto (1971) • Van McCoy • Oliver*

"Paper Maché" (Burt Bacharach - Hal David)
First recorded by Dionne Warwick
From the album *I'll Never Fall in Love Again,* Scepter 581
First released April 1970
Also Scepter single 12285 (*Billboard* pop #43), released June 1970

Two tracks that premiered a few months previously on Dionne's *I'll Never Fall In Love Again* album were siphoned off to make up her next single. "Paper Maché" is a mild indictment of consumerism, scarcely months into what would become the Me Decade: *"Can we be living in a world made of paper maché / Everything is clean and so neat / Anything that's wrong can be just swept away / Spray it with cologne and the whole world smells sweet."* Of course, Bacharach and David explored Madison Avenue's empty promises with "They're Gonna Love It" from *On the Flip Side,* which was also punctuated with marimba, only here the sound is dampened to sound like soda pop set to go flat. Not the sort of recording you could expect to hear blaring out of car radios or even piped into greeting card stores. Suburbanites put the Carpenters version of "Close to You" on their shopping lists instead: that record was well into its four-week stay at No. 1 while "Paper Maché" slid down from its peak position of No. 43.

Other Versions: *Ronnie Aldrich (1971) • Frank Chacksfield (1971) • Ferrante & Teicher (1970) • Rita Reys • Christopher Scott (1970)*

"The Wine Is Young" (Burt Bacharach - Hal David)
First recorded by Dionne Warwick
From the album *I'll Never Fall in Love Again,* Scepter 581
First released April 1970
Also Scepter 12285, flip side of "Paper Maché," released June 1970

"I'd bring you back if I knew how / But our world's all over now."

The recent outburst of message songs hadn't dulled Hal David's penchant for penning exceptionally piercing torch songs. An appropriate opening track for an album called *I'll Never Fall in Love Again*, "The Wine Is Young" finds every part of Dionne's body aching to relive dashed dreams. For two and a half minutes, the world of then never seemed more attractive *("Each night the moon used to wait for us before it would shine")* and the world of now so inconsolable *("the wine is young, our dreams are old")*. For those keeping track, Dionne names this obscure number "one of my all-time favorites I recorded back then" on the 2001 Rhino compilation *Love Songs*.

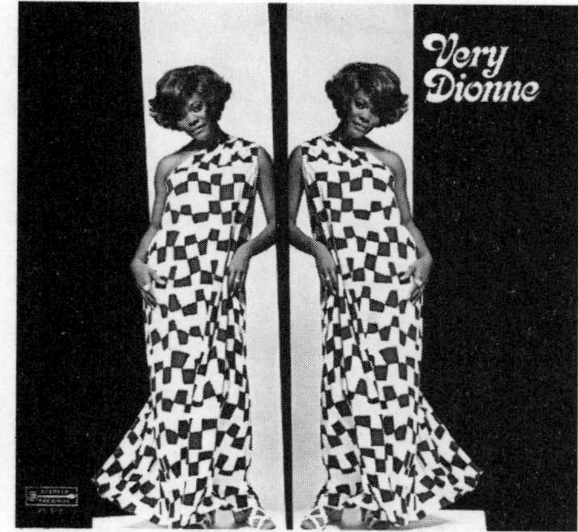

Very Dionne. Dionne's very last Scepter studio album showed signs of repeating herself, and not just on the cover. Here she rerecords the first demo she did with Bacharach and David—"Make It Easy on Yourself."

"Send My Picture to Scranton PA" (Burt Bacharach - Hal David)
First recorded by B.J. Thomas
Scepter 12283, flip side of "I Just Can't Help Believing"
Released July 1970

One can easily picture this local-boy-makes-good story kicking off a Seventies sitcom, complete with a drive past the "You Are Now Entering Pennsylvania" highway sign. While Memphis producer Chips Moman was simultaneously producing B.J. with sitar-guitars and thumping bass, Bacharach preferred keeping the singer in tuba and tack-piano territory. This production is significantly more modern sounding, not unlike the bridge of "Everybody's out of Town."

Hal David took a liking to B.J. and tailor-made this Scranton, Pennsylvania, success story for the guy from Hugo, Oklahoma. Although the protagonist of the song has every reason to be resentful about the faculty at his old school who ignored him and never tried to understand what was wrong with him, rancor never enters into the picture. Instead, he sees his achievement as a catalyst for enacting change in what should be a place of higher learning: *"Maybe now they'll give kids a helping hand / I was the guy they cast aside, so I went out and really tried / Now they can point to me with pride."* A stylish support side for the A-side that restored B.J. to the Top 10.

The Love Machine. This soundtrack, with music scored by Artie Butler, contained only two Dionne vocals produced by Burt and Hal, "Amanda" and "He's Moving On (Theme From *The Love Machine*)." But it's more notable for being the being the last Scepter LP with any new material and the first Scepter LP to carry the extra "e" at the end of "Warwick."

"The Green Grass Starts to Grow" (Burt Bacharach - Hal David)
First recorded by Dionne Warwick
From the album *Very Dionne,* Scepter LP 587 (*Billboard* LP #37)
Released November 1970

Dionne is thrust in the same tuba and tack-piano musical setting that served B.J. Thomas so well on the last few Bacharach-David produced sides. Of course, this quasi-seasonal tune (it mentions snow and jingles Christmas bells on the fade) wasn't a huge hit. Her mellowest single to date, it left people with the impression that she may have strayed too far outside the realms of R&B and that the green grass is growing somewhere in the middle of the road.

Other Versions: *Terry Baxter (1971) • Frank Chacksfield (1971) • Percy Faith (1971)*

1970

"Walk the Way You Talk." One of Bacharach's finest bossa novas, it was later done on Sergio Mendes and Brasil '66's debut on Bell Records, *Love Music.*

"Check Out Time" (Burt Bacharach - Hal David)
First recorded by Dionne Warwick
From the album *Very Dionne,* Scepter LP 587
Released November 1970

In contrast to the suburban modesty of the *Very Dionne* album's first single, the opening track is like a blast of dynamite, a one-woman mini-drama where Dionne goes off on a tear, holing up in an old motel to escape a loveless relationship that's inching towards the altar. Everything comes to a head in the breakdown just after the bridge: *"Because to be his wife* (insert Gary Chester drum flam!) *Well, that would be* (and a roll please...) *just giving up on life."* This spur-of-the-moment defection has forced her to face the truth—that she has not known any real love in her life and has no plan B but to keep running until it finds her. It's a great piece, the first and only time Bacharach and David gave their "voice" something callous to sing *("I just hope he doesn't follow me"),* but in doing so they scripted a character the singer found little empathy for. "I thought it just didn't fit my personality," Dionne told Alec Cummings in *The Look of Love*'s liner notes. "It wasn't someone I could identify with." It hardly sounds as if she's punching a clock on "Check Out Time," a better showcase for her acting abilities than *Slaves* or the Psychic Network ever were.

"Walk the Way You Talk" (Burt Bacharach - Hal David)
First recorded by Dionne Warwick
From the album *Very Dionne,* Scepter LP 587
Released November 1970

In the world of Bacharach and David, an aural contradiction rears its head once again. While Bacharach constructs a breezy Brazilian samba that just makes you want to kick back, Hal David is chiding you for being a person guilty of inaction, of just being talk and not walk. Even your grandmother never gave you a sage piece of advice like *"There's nothing that's so bad that leaving it alone just doesn't make it worse,"* let alone threw in extra words to keep up with the beat. Again, Sergio Mendes paid the pair the ultimate compliment by covering it, but Astrud Gilberto stayed off the case. Why?

Other Versions: *Burt Bacharach (1973) • Sergio Mendes (1973)*

"How Does a Man Become a Puppet?" One of the most valuable Ed Ames collectors' items (if there even *are* Ed Ames collectors) fetches $50 if in mint condition with a picture sleeve. It's Ames' 1964 presidential campaign recording for LBJ, called "Hello Lyndon." It's also the only known release on the Hello Lyndon label.

"How Does a Man Become a Puppet" (Burt Bacharach - Hal David)
Recorded by Ed Ames
From the LP *Ed Ames Sings the Songs of Bacharach and David,* RCA 4453
Released late 1970

In a 1968 interview for National Guard radio, Bacharach told Skitch Henderson that a once-popular style of singing had disappeared at that point: "I feel it affects more the male singers...it's hurt them more than it's hurt the big-belting girls. Shirley Bassey will still have a hit record.

Vicki Carr will still have hits if the material is right. The big male voices don't seem to strike it rich today [as far as recording]. Bob Goulet goes in and does a Broadway show and it's magnificent, it's an absolute joy to hear him on stage. But records, it's something else."

Bacharach never gave up on booming male voices throughout the rock era, and just about the only booming baritone claiming any Top 20 victory in 1967 and 1968 was Ed Ames. Of course weekly TV exposure on the *Daniel Boone* series as the pioneer's Indian friend Mingo couldn't have hurt his record sales. Once he left the cast, the hits slowed to a standstill. His last album for RCA was an entire album devoted to the most repeated Bacharach-David hits save one, the only known U.S. recording of "How Does a Man Become a Puppet," which was cobbled together largely from the instrumental "She's Gone Away" on Bacharach's second A&M album. Unlike Ames' earlier recording of "Nikki," this melody works better with words. It sounds as if it could've been a *Promises, Promises* outtake for either Mr. Sheldrake *("How does a man become a puppet / A puppet with strings, attachments and things that bind you")* or the newly promoted C.C. Baxter *("I found success has brought so much less than I sought and I just get moved back and forth")*. And Ames belts it out before capping it off sotto voce: *"If there's such a thing as a man that's free / Why can't it be me?"* This from a guy who proudly sang "It's a Man's World" only a few albums ago!

"All Kinds of People." Dionne's last single for Scepter was a medley of this number and the Diana Ross hit "Reach Out and Touch Somebody's Hand."

Other Versions: *Malcolm Roberts (1970)*

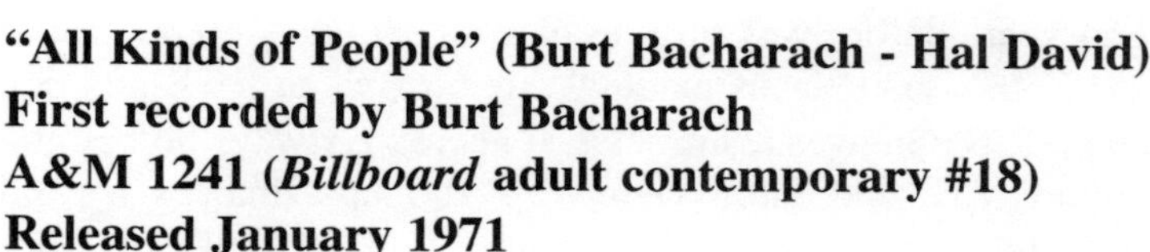

"All Kinds of People" (Burt Bacharach - Hal David)
First recorded by Burt Bacharach
A&M 1241 (*Billboard* adult contemporary #18)
Released January 1971

It should be noted that with "What the World Needs Now," Bacharach and David beat everyone to the marketplace with an everybody-should-love-one-another message song. And they did it with more subtlety than the Youngbloods, the Rascals, the Plastic Ono Band, Spanky and Our Gang, and Ray Stevens subsequently did. Yet "All Kinds of People" has more in common with "Give Peace a Chance," a slogan song that starts in an "A" section and never leaves it, than the earlier jazz waltz. Hal David writes a plea to unite the tall and small, the light and dark, the young and old. Cissy Houston, by now a solo recording artist in her own right, handles the lead vocals, while a choir of high- and low-voiced people join in, eventually inviting the don't-know-the-words people to sing the all-inclusive "ba ba ba ba ba."

Gente De Todos Los Tipos. This Spanish sleeve photo was taken from Burt 1971 Singer TV Special where he performed "All Kinds of People."

Bacharach had high hopes for this universal song, premiering it on his March 14 special sponsored by Singer, the "Golden Touch and Sew" people. The record sold enough to make it a No. 18 adult contemporary hit, but its inability to even dent the pop Top 100 at the same time is an indicator that radio and retailers had already begun catering to one kind of people to the exclusion of all others.

When a set of belligerent tonsils like John Rowles' tackles the tune, the results feel uncomfortably preachy. Jerry Butler's stripped-down

1971

Burt Bacharach. His eponymous album, also known by fans as the "Green Album," the "White Sweater Album" or the cumbersome "'Close to You/One Less Bell to Answer' Album."

gospel version builds gradually, with the singer advising everyone to "try to communicate with each other" before fading out into what sounds like the squeals of kids playing in a schoolyard. Dionne Warwick recorded the song in a medley with Ashford and Simpson's "Reach Out and Touch Somebody's Hand." After Dionne left for Warner Brothers, this unreleased track was released on the *From Within* compilation and as her final Scepter single in 1973.

Other Versions: *Burt Bacharach (1971) • Terry Baxter (1971) • Jerry Butler • The 5th Dimension (1973) • John Rowles • Marion Maerz - "Auf dieser Erde" (1971 • Dionne Warwick*

"And the People Were with Her (Suite for Orchestra)" (Burt Bacharach)
Recorded by Burt Bacharach
From the album *Burt Bacharach,* A&M 3501
Released January 1971

Bacharach's eponymous album came on the heels of two Top 10 hits, "Close to You" and "One Less Bell to Answer," both remakes of songs written several years previously. Burt included his own pair of remakes as well as another attempt at "Nikki," an ignored 1967 single that was now a popular TV theme for the *ABC Movie of the Week.*

In the prior 15 months, it seemed as if everything Bacharach had touched several years before was turning to gold. Smith scored a Top 5 with "Baby It's You," Isaac Hayes made "Walk on By" an R&B and pop hit all over again, R.B. Greaves resurrected "(There's) Always Something There to Remind Me" and there were Top 100 appearances by old favorites like "I Just Don't Know What to Do with Myself" by Gary Puckett and "In the Land of Make Believe" by Dusty Springfield. Even the Bacharach-Hilliard standard "Any Day Now" found new life with Percy Sledge and Elvis Presley. Like the proverbial dividends from the world's most successful chain letter, Bacharach's hard work was paying off in spades. He was a star in his own right when work for his fourth A&M album commenced: the previous year's Oscar, Tony, Grammy and even Emmy success (director and editor awards were given for one of his *Kraft Music Hall* specials), and the cover of *Newsweek,* all saw to that.

Burt Bacharach. His eponymous yellow mini-album, also known by fans as the "'Close To You/One Less Bell to Answer' eponymous yellow mini-album." Not commercially available, it was manufactured for jukebox use by Little LP's Unlimited of Northfield, Illinois.

For the first time, Bacharach's own recording career became a priority: witness the presence of four brand new titles, including this standalone suite, the first extended Bacharach instrumental that didn't owe its existence to a few feet of film or a staged musical. Section A of the suite is an overture, section B goes into a pianissimo middle section, and section C explores section A again, with varying degrees of dynamics.

"Freefall" (Burt Bacharach)
First recorded by Burt Bacharach
From the album *Burt Bacharach,* A&M 3501
Released January 1971

Music to ski by! This second instrumental is unusual in that its main theme consists of quiet guitar figures doubled by what sounds like a plucked harp.

Other Versions: *Zeena Parkins (1997)*

"Hasbrook Heights" (Burt Bacharach - Hal David)
First recorded by Burt Bacharach
From the album *Burt Bacharach,* A&M 3501
Released January 1971

Although the lyrics are credited to Hal David, it's hard to imagine a second party was involved in plotting Burt's personable invitation to come to his house, kick one's shoes off and start having a good time. It's filled with the kind of assurances that anyone who isn't a professional lyricist offers when playing host: *"Just phone me /I'll come and get you"* and off-the-cuff jokes like *"Bring along your swimsuit, that's how we get dressed up."* The key word here is casual, with a ukulele opening so similar to "Raindrops Keep Falling on My Head" that it would seem to indicate a desire not to have to work too hard on what's supposed to feel like a week's vacation every day. Even sophisticated rhyming schemes are dispensed with for the duration of your stay: *"Throw some things in a grip / Take the early train / It's a beautiful trip / Don't forget the name / Hasbrook Heights."*

Remembering the spelling might be another matter, as Burt lived in a place called Hasbrouck Heights, New Jersey, another reason one suspects Bacharach had a hand in the lyric writing. With Bacharach's busy tour and TV appearances making it tougher to schedule songwriting sessions with Hal David, it's very possible that Bacharach came up with enough dummy words that sounded good or wrote the entire verse by his lonesome and gave it the umbrella credit. Certainly David is talented enough to tailor his lyrics to the person singing, and this is the first time he's done it for his songwriting partner.

Regardless of who wrote the verses, Dionne Warwick tackles them with a friendly grin on the final track of her first Warner Brothers album, *Dionne.* Most of the casual charm of the original is gussied away by arranger Bob James, rendering it less like "Raindrops" and more like "San Jose."

Other Versions: *Dionne Warwick (1972)*

"Ten Times Forever More" (Burt Bacharach - Hal David)
First recorded by Johnny Mathis
From the album *Love Story,* Columbia 45323
Released early 1971

A year after Mathis compiled a whole album's worth of Bacharach covers, he was furnished with his first newly designated Bacharach-David song since 1957's "Warm and Tender." Sharing common melodic qualities with "Where There's a Heartache," this slight and unmemorable ballad finds Mathis wondering if "Ten Times Forever More" is a shorter wait for love to end than until "The Twelfth of Never."

"Ten Times Forever More." A Bacharach-David B-side in 1971? This weak song was the support side of an old Goffin-King song entitled "I Was There."

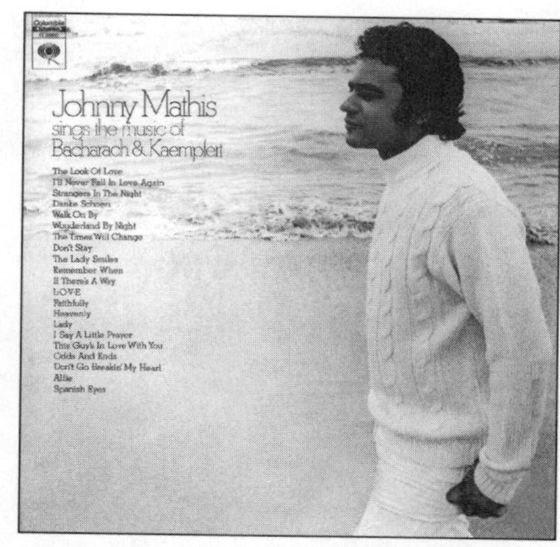

Johnny Mathis (1971). This double album pays tribute to Burt and Bert—Bert Kaempfert. A compilation, it goes back to "Heavenly" and "Faithfully" but rightly assumes that everyone and his auntie already owns a copy of *Johnny's Greatest Hits* and leaves off "Warm and Tender."

Peggy Lee. Leiber and Stoller brought her back to the charts with the hit "Is That All There Is?" From there, she worked with other star producers like Snuff Garrett and Paul McCartney.

Bacharach's exacting quality control, so persistent since he started producing to protect his songs, is now beginning to erode, since the composer's schedule no longer allows overseeing such extracurricular recording sessions. Produced by Jack Gold and arranged by Perry Botkin Jr., this recording seems to recede from memory even before the fade out.

"My Rock and Foundation" (Burt Bacharach - Hal David)
First recorded by Peggy Lee
From the album *Where Did They Go?,* Capitol ST-810
Released early 1971

Produced by Snuff Garrett (the man behind "Tower of Strength"), arranged by former Eligible Al Capps (remember "Faker Faker"?) and engineered by trusty Bacharach associate Phil Ramone, this recording is yet another undistinguished Bacharach-David effort. The problem lies not so much with the song as with the miscasting. Fresh from winning a Grammy for the cynical and downbeat "Is That All There Is?," Lee fails to convince on material cut from such a chipper bolt, even with a slightly melancholy string arrangement. Probably one of those songs Dionne didn't like enough to preserve.

"Who Gets the Guy?" (Burt Bacharach - Hal David)
First recorded by Dionne Warwick
Scepter 12309 (*Billboard* pop #57)
Released March 1971

Even if forensic investigation proves that this song is "This Guy's in Love with You" speeded up in a blender, with a dash of "Raindrops Keep Falling on My Head" for the bridge, it still wouldn't detract from the enjoyment of hearing Dionne wondering what her audience usually does, i.e., whether she's gonna get the guy by song's end. *"When the picture's over, will it be all over?"* she asks, and of course we never find out if she walks out of the theater a single act or not. But we get a clue to just go with the flow of the song: *"I'll just keep listening if the music is happy or sad / Because if it's happy that's how I'll be, and if it's sad, well, that's too bad for me."*

A poignant close to the Scepter era, it was preceded by one last official single for the label—an Artie Butler/Mark Lindsay song ("Amanda") from *The Love Machine* soundtrack, produced by Bacharach and David.

Other Versions: *Guy Klucevsek - "Who Gets the Guy?/This Guy's in Love with You" medley*

"Long Ago Tomorrow" (Burt Bacharach - Hal David)
First recorded by B.J. Thomas
Scepter 12335 (*Billboard* pop #61)
Released October 1971

This unforgettable title theme to a long-ago-forgotten British film is arguably among the finest Bacharach-David productions. The composers finally cast B.J. Thomas in a setting as soulful as his voice, posing another intriguing series of Hal David predictions: *"Maybe I'll be the things I dream and not the things I see / Maybe I'll get to change the world before it changes me / And maybe my life will always be just as happy as it seems."* Suddenly there's an exhilarating buildup to a chorus that leaves you floating in a beautiful, unexpected new key before settling in a wash of liquid bass, triangle, harpsichord and swampy Fender Rhodes. Also prominent here is the Bacharach false ending, which takes the song out on the verse instead of repeating the chorus one last time.

Unlike more recent Bacharach-David movie themes, the song is dispensed over the opening credits and never heard again during the picture. That makes some sense, seeing as the theme's lyrics hold out optimism for the future that is immediately squashed when a sudden illness paralyzes a cocky soccer player (played by Malcolm McDowell). In a church-run rest home he meets another paraplegic (played by Nannette Newman), whom he falls in love with but who unfortunately dies before they can roll slowly into the sunset together. Killing off the girl with the Movie Disease worked with Ali McGraw in *Love Story* but not here, where we're only left with an overabundance of sorrow and self-pity by film's end.

Unlike the previous B.J. movie theme, "Long Ago Tomorrow" met with zero Oscar nominations. "You win some, you lose some," Bacharach told the Associated Press. He was, however, nominated with co-arranger Pat Williams for a 1971 best-arrangement-accompanied-by-a-vocal Grammy but lost to Paul McCartney's "Uncle Albert/Admiral Halsey."

Other Versions: *Erlon Chaves*

"Long Ago Tommorrow." The song was later added to the American version of the film. The original English film was called *Raging Moon.*

"Something Big" (Burt Bacharach - Hal David)
From the Cinema Center film *Something Big*
First recorded by Mark Lindsay
Columbia 45506, released December 1971

In case you haven't noticed, covering a Bacharach song is the best way of getting the composer's attention. If he likes the cover, chances are vastly increased that your name will come up when he's brainstorming for someone to voice an untried new composition. Mark Lindsay, the lead singer of Paul Revere and the Raiders, covered "I'll Never Fall in Love Again" on his first solo album, *Arizona,* and was just what the maestro ordered for this Dean Martin comedy-western theme. The sound and tone are decidedly modern, with Hal David philosophy served on the chuck wagon: *"After taking, take up giving / Something big is what I'm living for."* Listeners who noticed that the Raiders' middle-period hits slavishly copied Mick Jagger and Company's *Aftermath/Between the Buttons* sound will delight in hearing Lindsay, one of rock's great underrated lead vocalists, deliver the song's opening confessional: *"Like the grain of sand that wants to be a rolling stone."*

Like B.J. Thomas, Lindsay proved an apt pupil, falling naturally into Bacharach's unique style of phrasing. John D'Andrea's arrangement is

"Something Big." Dean Martin was an avid Western buff and this is one of his last films, if you don't count *Cannonball Run* and *Cannonball Run II.* And really, why would you?

slightly more rocking than the one Bacharach would pencil out for himself when he recorded a vocal version on the *Living Together* album. As with his previous Cinema Center Films assignment, *The April Fools*, Bacharach handed the film-scoring chores over to Marvin Hamlisch, future husband and songwriting partner of Bacharach's future wife and songwriting partner, Carole Bayer Sager.

When last we heard "Something Big," a UK gas company was using the song on its commercials!

Other Versions: *Burt Bacharach (1973) • Jim O'Rourke (1999)*

SECTION SEVEN
THE LOST HORIZON (1972-1979)

...or No One Remembers My Name

As of this writing, no one else has ever attempted "the disaster musical." Some tried dancing around the drama-musical in the Eighties with the surreal Pennies from Heaven *and* Cop Rock, *but only after a generation of moviegoers and TV watchers had forgotten all about* Lost Horizon. *So thorough was the carnage left behind by this film that it ripped apart the world's most successful songwriting team. Dionne added an e at the end of her name that might as well have stood for estrangement, since Burt and Hal's inability to work together made it a three-way split. After Bacharach hid out and stopped writing for a year, he temporarily reunited with Hal David for a Stephanie Mills album, forged tentative new songwriting collaborations with Bobby Russell, Paul Anka, Libby Titus and poet James Kavanaugh and recorded his best-ever solo albums—all career moves that went unnoticed after his celebrity dimmed. But Bacharach would be back.*

Section Seven: The Lost Horizon (1972–1979)

"I Just Have to Breathe" .... *Dionne Warwicke*
"The Balance of Nature" .... *Dionne Warwicke*
"If You Never Say Goodbye" .... *Dionne Warwicke*
"Be Aware" .... *Dionne Warwicke*
"Lost Horizon" .... *Shawn Phillips*
"Share the Joy" .... *Andrea Willis*
"The World Is a Circle" .... *Diana Lee and Bobby Van*
"Living Together, Growing Together" .... *James Sigheta and Shangri-La Chorus*
"I Might Frighten Her Away" .... *Jerry Hutman and Diana Lee*
"The Things I Will Not Miss" .... *Sally Kellerman and Andrea Willis*
"If I Could Go Back" .... *Jerry Hutman*
"Where Knowledge Ends (Faith Begins)" .... *Diana Lee*
"Question Me an Answer" .... *Bobby Van*
"I Come to You" .... *Peter Finch, Jerry Hutman, Diana Lee*
"Reflections" .... *Sally Kellerman*
Lost Horizon (Original Soundtrack LP) .... *Burt Bacharach*
"Monterey Peninsula" .... *Burt Bacharach*
"Seconds" .... *Gladys Knight and the Pips*
"I Took My Strength from You" .... *Stephanie Mills*
"No One Remembers My Name" .... *Stephanie Mills*
"Living on Plastic" .... *Stephanie Mills*
"If You Can Learn How to Cry" .... *Stephanie Mills*
"I See You for the First Time" .... *Stephanie Mills*
"All the Way to Paradise" .... *Stephanie Mills*
"Please Let Go" .... *Stephanie Mills*
"Charlie" .... *Bobby Vinton*
"Us" .... *Tom Jones*
"Where Are You" .... *Burt Bacharach*
"When You Bring Your Sweet Love to Me" .... *Burt Bacharach*
"Another Spring Will Rise" .... *Burt Bacharach*
"Futures" .... *Burt Bacharach*
"Time and Tenderness" .... *Burt Bacharach*
"We Should've Met Sooner" .... *Burt Bacharach*
"The Young Grow Younger Every Day" .... *Burt Bacharach*
Woman .... *Burt Bacharach and the Houston Symphony*
"I Don't Need You Anymore" .... *Jackie DeShannon*
"Find Love" .... *Jackie DeShannon*
Together? (Original Soundtrack LP) .... *Burt Bacharach*

"I Just Have to Breathe" (Burt Bacharach - Hal David)
First recorded by Dionne Warwicke
From the album *Dionne,* Warner Bros. 2585
Released January 1972

"In this world where nothing stays the same / Stay with me."

One thing Bacharach could always pride himself on was his music's ability to appeal to both young and old listeners. By 1971, this knack was getting progressively more difficult to exercise, with hard rock, soft rock, soul, adult contemporary, country and bubblegum all pulling Top 40 audiences into new, isolated areas. Dionne Warwick's signing with Warner Brothers may have seemed an ideal move, since they were a company driven by album sales. But their output was mostly albums for the underground FM radio market: AM singles were flukes that either happened on their own or not at all. While Dionne sold a respectable number of albums, it was because there were hit singles on those albums, and now she wasn't getting the airplay she'd enjoyed before 1970. Penalized by the FM stations for being only a singer when singer-songwriters were all the rage, she also was a tough fit on AM stations where "Paper Maché" and "The Green Grass Starts to Grow" seemed a tad incongruous sharing a format with "Knock Three Times," "One Bad Apple" and "Chick-a-Boom."

"The Balance of Nature." Dionne upset the Balance of Nature when she added an e to her last name, which stayed on for four of her six Warner Brothers albums.

Dionne, her first Warner Brothers album, should've been a grand slam. Instead it was a harbinger of declining sales and diminishing interest. Her first album of all-new material since *The Sensitive Sounds of Dionne Warwick* not to reach the Top 40, it spawned only one single (the Mort Shuman–Jacques Brel composition "If We Only Have Love," which reached No. 84).

The ever-changing world of "I Just Have to Breathe" was mirrored by the team's changing relationships to that world. Dionne Warwicke purchased a vowel for the end of her name on the advice of her astrologer, Linda Goodman, for vibratory purposes. Bacharach, now arguably a bigger star than his discovery, was finding less time to write and arrange her records. As his fame grew, it was eclipsing the contribution of Hal David, who was valiantly struggling to find pure and true things to write about in a world that would just as soon call out for "I Gotcha." A sad lullaby in the mold of "Dream Sweet Dreamer," with "Golden Slumbers" bombast in the center, "I Just Have to Breathe" is yet another classic Bacharach-David tune that slipped under the radar. It has it all—a beautifully poignant arrangement, emotion-packed lyrics that never turn to sap and an effortless vocal that glides across several dynamic shifts without any noticeable turbulence.

Other Versions: *Teish O'Day (2000)*

"The Balance of Nature" (Burt Bacharach - Hal David)
First recorded by Dionne Warwicke
From the album *Dionne,* Warner Bros. 2585
Released January 1972

1972

Dionne. Warwick(e) released two albums with this name. *Dionne,* her first Warner Brothers album, did middling business and was followed by several costly lawsuits. But *Dionne,* her first Arista album, was her only platinum album and spawned the hit "I'll Never Love This Way Again," which won her a Grammy for best female pop vocal performance.

The ukulele has seemingly replaced the tack piano as Bacharach's signature instrument of choice, while the thoughtful harmonica of "That's What Friends Are For" makes its first appearance on a Bacharach session. A more somber version of "As Long As There's An Apple Tree," "The Balance of Nature" suggests that as long as birds suddenly appear in twos and deer continue coupling up, there will always be humans searching for love.

If Bacharach's voice sounds more confident than ever before on his recording of this song (found on the *Living Together* LP), it's partially because he, too, has paired off and is singing each chorus with an unnamed female session vocalist for the first time since "Baby It's You."

Other Versions: *Anita Kerr Singers (1973) • Burt Bacharach (1974)*

"If You Never Say Goodbye" (Burt Bacharach - Hal David)
First recorded by Dionne Warwicke
From the album *Dionne,* Warner Bros. 2585
Released January 1972

After the two somewhat-subdued ballads that kick off the *Dionne* album, the third track switches to the allegro setting and winds up being the most Bacharachesque number on the record. Combining antiquated touches like a slippery slide trombone and an unusually compressed and distorted guitar playing a riff that sounds like the one from "Everybody's Talking," this track injects some much-needed levity into the proceedings. Via Dionne Warwicke, Hal David advocates the importance of compromise over collapse: *"If you never say goodbye / Nothing ever ends / As long as we still can talk we can make amends."*

Other Versions: *Erlon Chavez ("If You Never Say Goodbye/Cafe Regio" medley)*

"Be Aware" (Burt Bacharach - Hal David)
First recorded by Dionne Warwicke
From the album *Dionne,* Warner Bros. 2585
Released January 1972

On the March 14, 1971, *Singer Presents Burt Bacharach* TV special, the composer has an intimate duet with Barbra Streisand where they sing "Close to You" inches away from each other's faces. Afterward, Barbra reveals that she is nervous about what's coming up next—performing the song he and Hal David wrote especially for her, with Bacharach playing piano and conducting a 40-piece orchestra. The song is "Be Aware," a passionate plea for the underprivileged in the face of forgetful prosperity *("When there is so much / should anyone be hungry?")* that ends with a chilling and discordant orchestral coda. While Streisand's version of "One Less Bell to Answer/A House Is Not a Home" (also performed on the special) turns up on her next album come September, and the "Close to You" duet was one of the unreleased nuggets on her *Just for the Record* boxed set in 1997, "Be Aware" has yet to be made commercially available.

The song was the last of the four new Bacharach-David songs on *Dionne*, its arrangement the same as the one on the special, minus the sinister freak-out at the end. An outstanding version by Laura Nyro came to light in 1994; it begins with a piano intro much like the one Sergio Mendes fashioned for the Brazil '66 version of "The Look of Love." That leaves only Anita Kerr's sterilized version, which takes a complacent stand against complacency. Beware!

Other Versions: *Anita Kerr Singers (1973) • Laura Nyro (1994) • Barbra Streisand & Burt Bacharach – TV special (1971)*

Shawn Phillips. The lilting voice behind *Lost Horizon*'s theme continues to perform and save lives as an EMS officer.

"Lost Horizon" (Burt Bacharach - Hal David)
First recorded by Shawn Phillips
From the album *Lost Horizon (Original Soundtrack),* Bell 1300
Also A&M single 1305 (*Billboard* pop #63)
Released December 1972

Bacharach and David's first musical had been an unnoticed TV special that was completed and forgotten within six weeks. Their second was a Broadway smash that took over a year to create, from the writing to the out-of-town tryouts to opening night. Their third was a movie musical—perhaps one of the most hated in celluloid history. Bacharach may have galvanized the stagnant Broadway musical with *Promises, Promises*, but not even Jesus Christ with a top hat and cane could save movie musicals from imminent extinction. If *Star!,* a $14 million Robert Wise production starring Julie Andrews, could take in only $4 million just three years after *The Sound of Music*, what hope did *Lost Horizon* have, with a Julie Andrews sound-alike dubbing in vocals for Liv Ullman?

The elephantine budgets required and the minimal returns collected for recent musicals like *Hello Dolly!, The Boyfriend, Chitty Chitty Bang Bang* and Ross Hunter's own *Thoroughly Modern Millie* should've given the director pause. But fresh from his success with the disaster movie *Airport,* he came away with the idea of remaking Frank Capra's 1937 film about Shangri-La as a *disaster musical*. And he succeeded magnificently. The first half-hour supplies the necessary thrills—an escape from war-torn India, a plane hijacking, the left engine blowing out, a crash landing in the Himalayas, an attempted suicide—all coming to pass without a single ditty or singing nun aboard the plane. Once the songs start coming fast and furious, they're hard to take with a straight face.

***Lost Horizon* (1956).** From Shangri-La, the first ill-fated musical play based on James Hilton's novel *Lost Horizon*. Other songs in the Harry Warren-Jerome Lawrence-Robert E. Lawrence score include the title song, "A Man in the Dark," "I'm Just a Little Bit Confused," "Love Is What I Never Knew," "The World Outside" and "Om Mani Padme Hum."

But before we are cinematically thrust into a world of turmoil and bedlam, where the guns will be pounding in our ears, the title tune, sung above the opening credits, sets the peaceful mood of Shangri-La magnificently. Shawn Phillips was an interesting choice to record the title song. A&M Records' resident pacifist was a gifted singer-songwriter who possessed an earnest voice and longer hair than Karen Carpenter. As Phillips remembers it: "I was given a recording of the song. It was just a recording of Bacharach singing with a piano. And I learned it as best I could. A couple of weeks later I was in the recording studio, Hal David was there, and I do remember there was a bit of a fiasco. Burt thought the song with just voice and piano was absolutely magical. And Ross Hunter came in

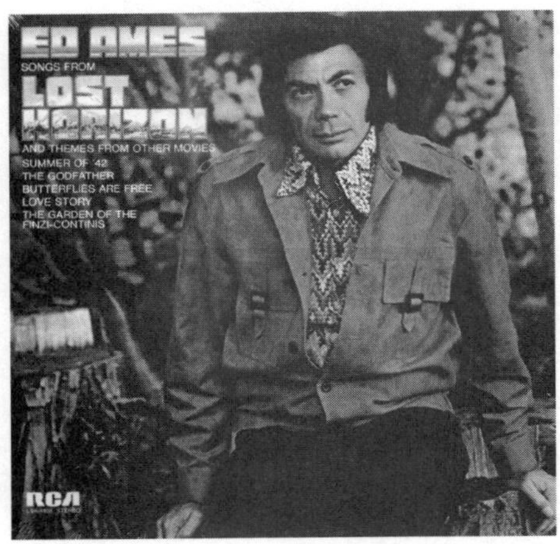

Lost Horizon. Ed Ames, fresh from delivering his previous album for RCA, *Ed Ames Sings the Songs of Bacharach-David,* recorded an album of selections from *Lost Horizon*, even releasing the title song as a single, with "Question Me an Answer" on the flip.

and said, 'Absolutely not! This is an enormous production. It must have an orchestra.' And they got into a big hassle with it. I'm told he got so upset that Hal David left the control room."

Hunter got his orchestrated theme, opening the song with explosive flourishes and cymbal crashes before Phillips comes in with guitar and woodwinds. If Bacharach felt the antiwar "Windows of the World" was too subtle, this theme spells it out in giant letters and strange internal rhymes: *"There's a lost horizon / Waiting to be found / There's a lost horizon where the sound of guns doesn't pound in your ears."*

Bacharach himself does a fine job of singing the song on his 1974 album *Living Together*, where his phrasing is quite close to Shawn Phillips and there are several intriguing tempo changes that make the song seem more like a suite.

Not reliant on hit singles, Phillips' career continued relatively unscarred by the film's dashed fortunes. It also didn't hurt that his song comes at the very beginning of the film, before people realized it was about to nosedive. But the singer is one of the few participants who still rushes to its defense. "I saw the movie before it opened and I thought it was just great," he laughs. "It was supposed to be an enormous success but it didn't happen. Then again I'm so gullible. What do I know?" That this fine song never made it onto any of his albums or greatest-hits collections is neither a revisionist bid for damage control nor an oversight. "That's something to do with the rights, and it would cost me a fortune to put it on one of my albums," says Phillips. "That's one of those anomalies: I sang it but I have to pay to put it on a CD."

Most of the cover versions were orchestra-only affairs, but Ed Ames, fresh from delivering his last album for RCA, *Ed Ames Sings the Songs of Bacharach-David*, recorded an album of selections from *Lost Horizon,* even releasing this as a single with "Question Me an Answer" on the flip. And once again the mysterious Erlon Chavez shoves this Bacharach-David anthem of peace into a medley with another contemporary hit, "Killing Me Softly with His Song." The High Lama might have a thing or two to say about that!

Other Versions: *Ronnie Aldrich • Ed Ames (1973) • Burt Bacharach (1973) • Fred Bongusto - "Orizzonte perduto" • Erlon Chavez "Lost Horizon/Killing Me Softly" - medley • Arthur Fiedler & the Boston Pops (1973) Film Score Orchestra • Dennis Lopez Liquid Latin Sound (1973) • Werner Müller • 101 Strings (1973) • RTE Concert Orchestra/Richard Hayman (1995)*

"Share the Joy" (Burt Bacharach - Hal David)
First recorded by Andrea Willis
From the album *Lost Horizon (Original Soundtrack),* Bell 1300
Released December 1972

Certainly not your typical movie-musical fare, "Share the Joy" is tastefully presented as part of Chang's after-dinner entertainment. In keeping with the High Lama's one simple rule—"be kind"—no songs were given to George Kennedy to sing, and the other principal actors who could not carry a tune from their trailer to the set were assigned a ghost singer. In the case of beautiful Olivia Hussey, she only mouths the opening and closing lines: the vocals were later supplied by a session singer.

Andrea Willis, who'd later lay down background vocals for Joan Baez, Paul Butterfield, Neil Diamond and Keith Moon, has a voice similar to Renaissance's Annie Haslam, and this minor-key Tibetan meditation with spinet electric harpsichord, finger cymbals and tastefully recessed sitar is the sort of number you could expect an art-rock band to deliver with half the desired restraint. In a typical drama, this number would've been offered as a token musical interlude, and it's consumed as such by the viewer. But little does that unsuspecting viewer know that nearly a dozen instances of characters suddenly bursting into song was going to slow the action down to an afternoon nap.

Other Versions: *Burt Bacharach (1973) • 101 Strings (1973)*

101 Strings. Really going out on a limb, 101 Strings recorded six *Lost Horizon* songs but then padded this record out with three songs that no one's ever heard of. Kooky!

"The World Is a Circle" (Burt Bacharach - Hal David)
First recorded by Diana Lee and Bobby Van
From the album *Lost Horizon (Original Soundtrack),* Bell 1300
Released December 1972

The only song from the soundtrack that had a Shangri-La-like extended life in Bacharach concerts, "The World Is a Circle" has snuck into his "Movie Medley" and stayed there in place of the theme song, which unfortunately carried the stigma of the film's title. On Bacharach's April 23, 1972, ABC-TV special, *Close to You*, we see footage of Bacharach teaching it to the children's chorus. There he explains that the orchestral arrangement, which starts with just a tuba and grows as the children themselves grow, with more voices gradually brought in for the crescendo. He must have handpicked these children: one sounds identical to that squeaky-voiced kid on "Saturday Sunshine."

A harmless children's song on its own, it has a noxious effect in this movie, following all that melodrama. Plus we have to stomach Liv Ullman, the protagonist of such Ingmar Bergman classics as *Scenes from a Marriage*, *Face to Face* and *Cries and Whispers,* suddenly transformed into a counterfeit Fräulein Maria.

Other Versions: *Ed Ames (1973) • Burt Bacharach (1973) • Film Score Orchestra • 101 Strings (1973) • Franck Pourcel • Royal Marines (1974) • The Sandpipers*

"Living Together, Growing Together" (Burt Bacharach - Hal David)
First recorded by James Sigheta and the Shangri-La Chorus
From the album *Lost Horizon (Original Soundtrack),* Bell 1300
Released December 1972

This song marks the point in the movie where most viewers throw up their hands and ask to leave the room. If we believe Chang's words to suicidal Sally that "virtue lies in avoiding excess," this song and the "Festival of the Family" sequence it appears in seem too excessive (and far too

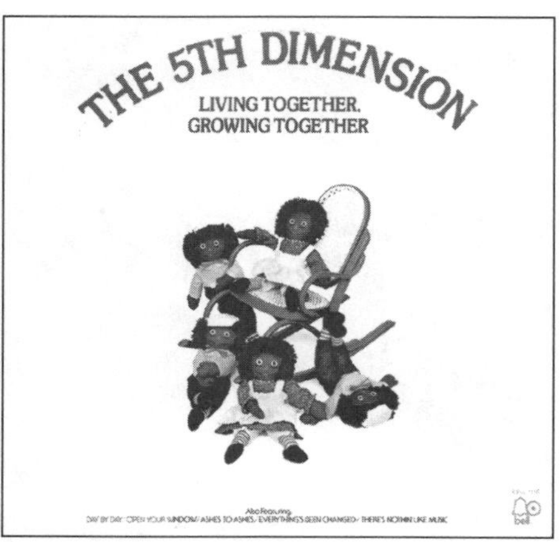

***Living Together* (1973).** This album featured a solo spot for Florence LaRue, who sings the Bacharach-David oldie "Let Me Be Lonely." Strangely, the group worked on a choral version of the spiritual "Nobody Knows the Trouble I've Seen" on the *Burt Bacharach in Shangri-La* special that was quite good and is otherwise unavailable.

Western) to ring true. Thankfully, the Shangri-La chorus just marches stoically through it without busting any significant moves. Trapped inside such a wooden framework, Hal David's sincere words can't help but sound preachy or worse, like something warbled on a typical *Sesame Street* broadcast day sponsored by the numbers one, two and three, which, according to Hal David, make up a family.

Since Bell Records was a part of Columbia Pictures, the label had hit-bound hopes for "Living Together" and strongly persuaded (i.e., forced) the 5th Dimension to record the song. The group's first single in many a moon not to feature a solo vocal by Marilyn McCoo turned out to be their last-ever Top 40 hit (*Billboard* No. 32). For the *Burt Bacharach in Shangri-La* TV special, the 5th Dimension dance and sing "Living Together" on the actual set of *Lost Horizon*. Watching this segment, one is suddenly gripped by the realization that there were no black people in Shangri-La, not even ones with singing voices as vanilla as the 5th Dimension. (In all fairness, there is one squeaky-voiced mulatto kid that sings "woah" in "The World Is a Circle" and one mean-looking dude at the front of the Festival of the Family procession who probably went on to be an extra in *Slaughter's Big Ripoff*.)

Most prints of the film omit an exciting tribal dance that would've livened up this all-too-sedated sequence. Also edited out were several reprises of "Living Together," none of which were restored on the Pioneer laserdisc of the movie.

Other Versions: *Ed Ames (1973) • Tony Bennett • Mike Curb Congregation • Ferrante & Teicher • 5th Dimension (1972) • 101 Strings (1973)*

Living Together. Burt's sixth solo album contains his best and last vocal performances on record. For those who can't take the 5th (Dimension, that is), Bacharach's own version of the title track features a more soulful and less saccharine vocal treatment.

"I Might Frighten Her Away" (Burt Bacharach - Hal David)
First recorded by Jerry Hutman and Diana Lee
From the album *Lost Horizon (Original Soundtrack)*, Bell 1300
Released December 1972

The first of two duets between the real-life husband-and-wife team of Jerry Hutman and Diana Lee, substituting for actors Peter Finch and Liv Ullmann. A not-altogether-obvious attempt at re-creating the acoustic intimacy of "I'll Never Fall in Love Again" without any of its humor, this number shows the two principals grazing in the grass, smiling at one another and singing without ever moving their lips. This duet of the mind temporarily solves the problem of lip synchronization, but once audiences know these people are not the true possessors of these voices, they'll cease to care. And it's not as if Peter Finch is some great eye candy for the ladies: he waddles through this movie with the grace of a taxidermic penguin.

That shouldn't stop you from enjoying the recording. Hutman and Lee sound close enough to Finch and Ullmann (or at least to their speaking voices) to make a convincing forgery. Bacharach makes an even stronger sales pitch on his *Living Together* album, adding a Harry James–ish trumpet coda that takes the song out on the verse, as he did with "Long Ago Tomorrow." Although on this album Cissy Houston and

Tony Middleton sing the movie's other duet, "I Come to You," Bacharach gives "I Might Frighten Her Away" over to anonymous white voices, much the way his early demos geared certain songs to pop and R&B singers.

Other Versions: *Burt Bacharach (1974) • Herb Alpert & the Tijuana Brass (1974)*

Herb Alpert (1974). Envious of his labelmate Sergio Mendes' ability to change his band's name every ten years or so, he rechristened his horn-heavy combo the TJB. Fans of ELO, ELP, NRBQ, NKOTB and TSOP were initially impressed.

"The Things I Will Not Miss" (Burt Bacharach - Hal David)
First recorded by Sally Kellerman and Andrea Willis
From the album *Lost Horizon (Original Soundtrack)*, Bell 1300
Released December 1972

Had *Lost Horizon* been a stage musical, this number would certainly have met the criteria for a showstopper. Sally Kellerman and Olivia Hussey good-naturedly muse about switching places. Hussey's character Maria wants to leave Shangri-La, complaining of too much sunshine, open spaces and time for contemplation, while Sally insists the list of things she will not miss includes noise, crowds, work and rain. Bacharach's arrangement underscores all of Maria's lines with quiet orchestration, while Kellerman's every word is accompanied by cacophonous sitars and clashing chord voicings.

A 2002 rereleased version of the *Diana and Marvin* album reveals that these two Motown greats actually recorded a version of "The Things I Will Not Miss" that was taken out of the final running order. This song about opposites who agree to disagree perhaps struck too close to home, seeing as Ross and Gaye clashed throughout the making of the album and were photographed back-to-back on the cover to keep them from snarling at one another.

Other Versions: *Burt Bacharach (1973) • Film Score Orchestra • Diana Ross & Marvin Gaye (recorded 1973, released 2002)*

Diana & Marvin & Marijuana. Marvin turned down the diva's polite requests that he refrain from smoking dope in the studio. From then on, they recorded all their loving duets separately, but listeners never caught on.

"If I Could Go Back" (Burt Bacharach - Hal David)
First recorded by Jerry Hutman
From the album *Lost Horizon (Original Soundtrack)*, Bell 1300
Released December 1972

Director Ross Hunter should've known that you don't cast George Kennedy in a project and expect it not to be a disaster movie. And you don't give the best song in the movie to the guy who played Howard "I'm Mad as Hell and I'm Not Going to Take It Anymore" Beale. Sadly, the ideal man for the job became apparent when it was too late to do anything about it.

It was as if Bacharach was using his TV specials as high-budget screen tests for great English actors. Nine months before the film opened, Rex Harrison was a guest on his *Close to You* special. Granted, Harrison was a bit too old for the part and talked his way through this yet-unheard

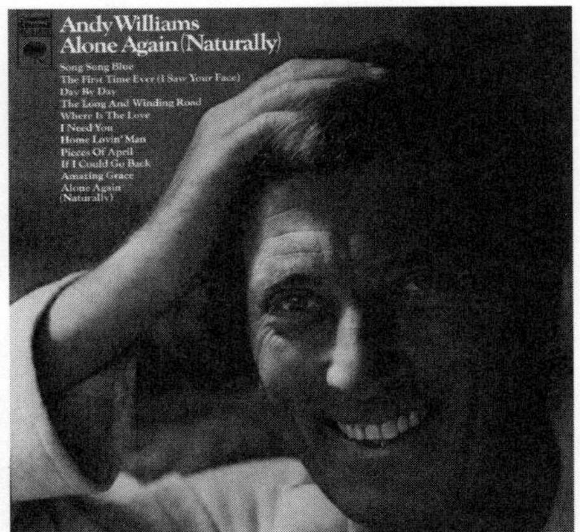

"Alone Again Naturally." By law, every adult contemporary singer had to cut Gilbert O'Sullivan's suicidal weeper. Too bad the same didn't hold true for "If I Could Go Back," which adorns this album.

song, but he did have an undeniable presence. Then came the *Burt Bacharach in Shangri-La* TV special aired just after the film opened, which guest-starred actor turned cake-out-in-the-rain pop star Richard Harris. His riveting performance of "If I Could Go Back" on the *Lost Horizon* set shows what a wasted opportunity casting Peter Finch was. Bringing Camelot to Shangri-La would've raised this movie's stature significantly and added weight to the role of Richard Conway. Instead what we are left with is a better-than-average *Fantasy Island* two-part episode with a bunch of songs shoveled in.

Casting singers as actors would've been an equally frivolous operation, but at least Andy Williams' recorded performance exudes more expressive torment than Finch's furrowed brow. Any references to Shangri-La are excised to make the song less monastic, and producer Artie Butler adds a distant dog barking that sounds right out of Pink Floyd's *Animals,* while Williams returns to the chilly spoken word of "Don't You Believe It."

Previously, Bacharach had the luxury of writing to already-shot footage he could run over and over until the music matched the visuals. Now the music had to be laid down in advance, and if the visuals fell flat, he was stuck with it. This point still leaves a bitter taste in Bacharach's mouth. "It doesn't matter if Peter Finch sings 'If I Could Go Back,' which is really a damn good song. That song by itself has a lot of heart," he says. "But you saw it in the movie and you don't give a fuck if he goes back or not."

Other Versions: *Tony Bennett (1973) • Richard Harris - TV special (1973) • Rex Harrison - TV special (1972) • Dorothy Squires • Andy Williams (1972)*

"Where Knowledge Ends (Faith Begins)" (Burt Bacharach - Hal David)
First recorded by Diana Lee
From the album *Lost Horizon (Original Soundtrack),* Bell 1300
Released December 1972

In direct response to Richard Conway's question *"How do I know this part of my real life / If there's no pain, can I be sure I feel life?"* Cathy cuts through his doubt with this plea to *"look inside yourself, that is where the truth always lies*." If we were to draw *Sound of Music* analogies, this pretty ballad would be the moment that the Mother Superior tells Fräulein Maria to climb every mountain and ford every stream.

Other Versions: *Film Score Orchestra*

"Question Me an Answer" (Burt Bacharach - Hal David)
First recorded by Bobby Van
From the album *Lost Horizon (Original Soundtrack),* Bell 1300
Released December 1972

The only actor in the *Lost Horizon* cast whose résumé qualifies him to sing and dance in a movie musical, Bobby Van appeared in such early-Fifties MGM romps as *Small Town Girl, Kiss Me Kate* and the Esther Williams naval aquatic ballet *Skirts Ahoy!* This solo number gives Van, the son of vaudevillian parents, the chance to work in pratfalls and some old soft-shoe. Van's effervescent personality provides a welcome respite to the solemnity occupying the screen the rest of the time. With this song he explains what turned out to be the rules for playing TV's favorite game show, *Jeopardy: "I will answer with a question, clear and bright! Even though your question may be wrong, my answer will be right!"* Van offered this explanation of the Hal David lyric on the *Burt Bacharach in Shangri-La* special: "Questions aren't important, it's the answers that are important in life. Once you can come up with the right answers, the questions will take care of themselves." Van copies Bacharach's inflections "clear and bright" as well.

With the movie musical officially pronounced dead once *Lost Horizon* was threaded into theater projectors, Van would boost his career in television as a frequent game show host and celebrity participant before his untimely death in 1980 at age 50.

Other Versions: *Ed Ames (1973) • 101 Strings (1973)*

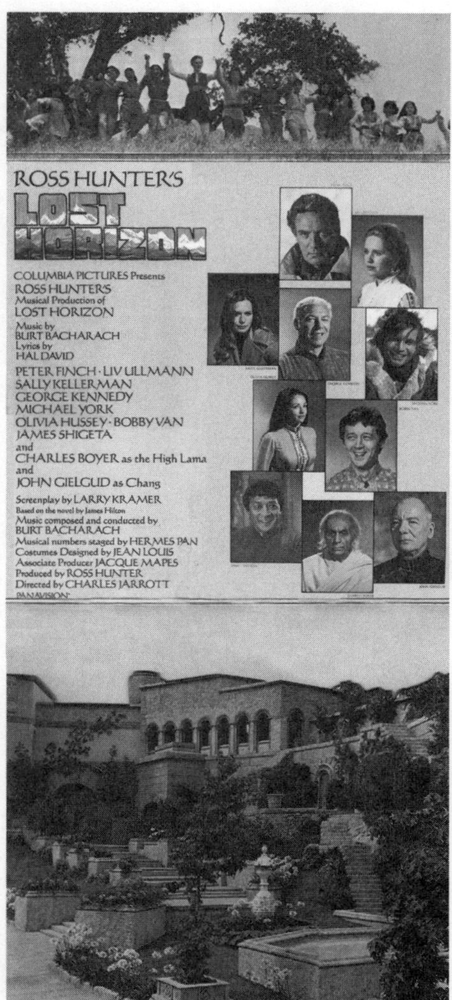

Die Cut or Cut Out? Wonder how many trees in Shangri-La had to be chopped down to accommodate this lovely but extravagant gatefold sleeve? The bottom scenery is actually a die-cut, behind which the record slots in a blue-sky dust sleeve. As the *Lost Horizon* soundtrack became an immediate staple of cut-out bins, a budget cover was never manufactured.

"I Come to You" (Burt Bacharach - Hal David)
First recorded by Peter Finch, Jerry Hutman and Diana Lee
From the album *Lost Horizon (Original Soundtrack)*, Bell 1300
Released December 1972

This is the second Hutman and Lee duet—or should we say trio, since Finch recites the opening verse until Hutman's off-screen voice takes over. As with much of the cast album, this pretty ballad is better serviced by Bacharach's 1974 version, which brings back Tony Middleton, who recorded the splendid vocal on Bacharach's 1965 Kapp single of "My Little Red Book," and Cissy Houston, always a welcome presence on a Bacharach recording. Another compelling argument against Shangri-La's non-black status!

Other Versions: *Burt Bacharach, with vocals by Cissy Houston & Tony Middleton (1974) • 101 Strings (1973)*

"Reflections" (Burt Bacharach - Hal David)
First recorded by Sally Kellerman
From the album *Lost Horizon (Original Soundtrack)*, Bell 1300
Released December 1972

A perfectly fine song ruined by the godless sight of Sally Kellerman twisting by the lake for George Kennedy. Despite such cringe-worthy moments, *Newsweek* (which had crowned Bacharach "The Music Man 1970" only two year earlier) complained of the film, "It can't even be

1972

George Kennedy. One of the stars of *Lost Horizon* told *TV Guide* in 1976, "How could you have known going in with all that talent that it wouldn't work? When they ran it on TV, I just got drunk. I couldn't watch it."

Three Friends, Three Plaintiffs. Somebody knows something the other two do not on the rear cover of the 1972 *Dionne* album. The trio would never be this together until 1993!

enjoyed as camp." Bacharach and David were too accomplished to turn in any work that could be considered substandard, but their excellence is greatly diminished in the context of such a problematic film. The film does have its avid fans, who go as far as hoping that one day *Lost Horizon* will be salvaged or revived as a stage musical. Bacharach, who rarely completes any sentence about *Lost Horizon* without punctuating it with the word "disaster," puts the kibosh on that almost immediately: "You can't think that way because there ain't no chance that that's gonna happen."

Other Versions: *Ed Ames (1973) • Burt Bacharach (1974) • Film Score Orchestra • 101 Strings (1973)*

Lost Horizon Incidental Music (Burt Bacharach)
Lost Horizon Laserdisc
Pioneer Special Edition PSE 92-25
Recorded 1972, Released 1992

"Introduction/The Lost Horizon" • "Refueling in the Desert" • "The Hijacking" • "The Crash" • "Himalayan Trek" • "The Rescue Party" • "Arrival in Shangri-La/Sally Attempts Suicide" • "Sally and To-Leen/Richard Meets Catherine" • "Dinner with Chang" • "The Truce Is Over" • Valley of the Blue Moon" • "The High Lama" • "George and Maria" • "Conway and Chang Tour Shangri-La" • "The Waterway" • "Return to High Lama" • "Funeral Procession" • "Mystery of Maria/The Departure" • "The Avalanche" • "The Truth Revealed/Richard Recovered" • "End Title"

In exploring any possibilities of a show-biz curse, let's examine the toll this movie's failure exacted on its participants. Certainly none of the actors faced too much downtime. George Kennedy would survive bigger disasters, including *Airport 1975, Airport 1977* and *Earthquake*. Sally Kellermen continued to make movies and found a lucrative sideline doing voiceovers. Peter Finch would win a posthumous Oscar for *Network*, and Liv Ullmann would continue to make foreign and American films.

The real impact was felt by the names above and below the title—*Lost Horizon's* director and its composers. This turned out to be Ross Hunter's last feature film: he would only direct made-for-TV movies from here on, but at least he could dart in and out of supermarkets unnoticed. Bacharach, being the most celebrated and visible of the three, took the hardest hit—people could recognize him at Del Mar racetrack, after all—and he bore the brunt of this very public failure. Unjustly so, since one listen to the soundtrack proves that these songs work perfectly fine without the visuals.

Hal David also put a lot of his heart and soul into these songs, but it was Bacharach who appeared in TV specials talking about Shangri-La and the philosophy behind the music—Bacharach, who had to put in an extra year of work producing a whole album's worth of incidental music that couldn't compel most viewers enough to care about these characters. These disproportionate duties made Bacharach resentful of his partner. "I got upset with Hal because I had to work and teach Sally Kellerman how to sing," he said in his 2002 installment of A&E's *Biography.* "This is the role I picked for myself. I'm the musician, so I'm gonna protect my song. I guess it's OK to work that hard if you win something in the end. But it was a disaster."

After two years of exhausting work and nothing but poor notices to show for it, the two men no longer felt like writing together. Sure, they'd had dozens of flop songs before: the first two chapters of this book bear that out. But those songs thudded like the proverbial tree falling in a deserted forest. These songs were openly criticized like no other work they'd done before. Knocking the score was par for the course if you were already down in the mud soiling the movie. Pauline Kael wrote, "The narrative has no energy, and the pauses for the pedagogic songs are so awkward that you feel the director's wheelchair needs oiling." Just as *Magical Mystery Tour* gave the Beatles' critics an open opportunity to land a blow, this ill-fated project gave disgruntled anti-bodies who might have heard "Close to You" in one too many elevators a chance to air their petty grievances.

Burt Bacharach. Before "live at Budokan" was a common contractual obligation item, there was Burt's *Live in Japan* album, recorded in 1971, with a standard song selection that didn't extend beyond the *Butch Cassidy* soundtrack. *Live in Japan* was reissued for Europe as *In Concert.* Americans were pacified with a *Greatest Hits* package.

And after operating autonomously in the recording studio since 1963, Bacharach found himself waging war with a powerful movie studio and director over his music, a battle he subsequently lost. Bacharach explains: "The whole experience was pretty bad because I kept fighting for the way the music should sound and they wound up banning me from the dubbing stage and the mixing stage. It should've been thrilling, because that's the way it was on tape. But it came out sounding compressed."

In 1992, all the movie's music was digitally remastered for the Pioneer Special Edition Laserdisc, which has since gone out of print. It contains a music-only right channel that allows you to hear all the music backgrounds sans dialogue. To date, the Laserdisc remains the only commercially available outlet for Bacharach's incidental orchestral score.

"Monterey Peninsula" (Burt Bacharach)
From the album *Living Together,* A&M 3527
Released December 1973

"After *Lost Horizon,*" Bacharach sighs, "it was just 'I wanna get away from everybody, live down on the beach.' And that's what I did."

"Monterey Peninsula," like "Pacific Coast Highway" before it, serves as chill-out music after a particularly arduous project. But while Bacharach could bask in critical and commercial acclaim during his post-*Promises, Promises* vacation, the world after *Lost Horizon* was considerably less carefree. This instrumental represents the only new material on his fifth A&M album, the first not to contain any blockbuster hits. It had the title song, a middling Top 40 hit, plus three other low-charting Top 100 movie themes, two under-appreciated Dionne Warwick album tracks and four more *Lost Horizon* retreads.

People were still covering old Bacharach-David hits but at a less furious clip than two years earlier. Perhaps the most successful example was the Stylistics' "You'll Never Get to Heaven (If You Break My Heart)" (*Billboard* pop No. 23). The year 1973 had seen "The Windows of the

1974

Tour Program. The only way anyone was going to see Bacharach and Warwick together again without a judge present in 1974 was when Bacharach played the Warwick Theatre in Connecticut.

World" revived by Isaac Hayes and "All Kinds of People" get the 5th Dimension treatment. But there would be no new Bacharach-David songs in 1974. And judging by the finality of the headlines announcing the team's acrimonious split, there didn't seem to be a chance for a reunion anytime soon. Although privy to bad vibes between Burt and Hal at the end of the Scepter years, Dionne only found out about the split by reading it in the papers. Although they had been contracted to write and produce her next Warner Brothers album, neither man was in any condition to write or produce anything. Faced with being sued by Warner president Mo Ostin for failure to deliver a second Warwick-Bacharach-David album, Dionne was forced to sue both men for $5.5 million. They settled out of court, with Bacharach not speaking to Warwick until he called her up to sing "Finders of Lost Loves" in 1985.

"Seconds" (Neil Simon - Burt Bacharach)
First recorded by Gladys Knight and the Pips
From the album *I Feel a Song,* Buddah 5612
Released November 1974

Bacharach's public take on the Hal David split, circa 1977: "There was a period there where we not only did not write together, we did not speak. That was the period after *Lost Horizon*. There's no big story, just one of those things. I wondered if he'd feel better writing with someone else, and I questioned whether I would feel better writing with someone else myself."

No one would've predicted that someone else would be Doc Simon, but when a proposed movie version of *Promises, Promises* came up on the boards, Bacharach and David were several months into their silent treatment. While nothing came ever of the filmed adaptation, Bacharach and Simon did manage to write "Seconds." Neil Simon does a fairly accurate approximation of what Hal David might have done, namely having fun with the double-meaning title, e.g., *"I've got more now than seconds....All the men I've met since then were seconds."* Bacharach produced and arranged the Gladys Knight version, but the listing of his name second in the writing credits indicates that the music man was still nurturing a powerful desire not to be seen.

This was his only new work in a year of water treading. In January, he starred in a special that featured not a single new song. A&M Records released a predictable *Greatest Hits* gathering, while a face-saving *Burt Bacharach Live in Japan* album, recorded in 1971 (and also titled *In Concert* in Europe), kept the same old songs in circulation overseas, with polite bursts of applause at the end of them.

Other Versions: *Burt Bacharach (1977)*

"Seconds." *I Feel a Song* won best R&B album honors at the 1974 Grammys.

"I Took My Strength from You" (Burt Bacharach - Hal David)
First recorded by Stephanie Mills
From the album *For the First Time,* Motown 2531
Released December 1975

Most accounts of the Bacharach and David split tend to gloss over the fact that in 1975 the pair did reunite to write and produce an entire album for Motown recording artist and elfin star of *The Wiz*, Stephanie Mills. What could have made both men put aside their acrimonious differences in the flurry of lawsuits and write songs together? Surely the need to prove to themselves and the public that they'd not lost the fabled magic touch after the *Lost Horizon* fiasco was weighing heavily on them. More urgent motivation occurred on October 26, 1974, when Dionne Warwick went to No. 1 for the first time with "Then Came You," a bouncy duet with the Spinners. That their former "voice" was making it without them, performing a song arranged and produced by Thom Bell, the last man to chart significantly with a Bacharach-David song ("You'll Never Get to Heaven" by the Stylistics, which peaked at No. 23 on the pop charts and No. 8 on the R&B listings in the spring of 1973), was reason enough not to go quietly into the night.

Joshie Armstead. Maybe she should've recorded "We Should've Met Sooner," since the former Ikette also recorded countless backup sessions at Scepter for Chuck Jackson and Maxine Brown and co-wrote the Ray Charles hit "Let's Go Get Stoned" with Nicholas Ashford and Valerie Simpson.

Helping history repeat itself, the team selected the 18-year old Mills to be their de facto Dionne, a shrewd judgment considering the easy way she maneuvered around the album's two covers of former Dionne evergreens, "This Empty Place" and "Loneliness Remembers What Happiness Forgets." And even though Dionne had been their voice for all those years, they'd never constructed an album filled top to bottom with their originals. Nor were they ever credited on the front cover, "Produced by Hal David and Burt Bacharach," the reversed order a consolatory gesture to the lyricist's under-appreciated work in the control room. Despite the album title's proclamation, this was actually the young singer's second album—she had debuted the previous year with *Movin' in the Right Direction* on ABC.

For the First Time finds Bacharach in a curious transitional phase—willing to try new musical things like a grinding funk ballad but then tracking a signature tack piano over it. But his reprise of a big gospel chorus and Hal David's equally big-hearted lyrics didn't quite repeat the success of Dionne's first record. Not willing to give up on "I Took My Strength from You," Bacharach looked around for another unknown voice. It was Angie Dickinson who first heard Joshie Armstead in a CARE commercial on her car radio and told her husband he ought to find that girl. A few phone calls later, they found the session singer in New York. The first of her four vocal contributions to Bacharach's 1977 *Futures* album, Armstead's "I Took My Strength" is lighter in feel than the Stephanie Mills version—a simple matter of using a cross stick instead of a straight snare hit. The latter version also contains the standard David Sanborn sax solo that sterilized countless records in the late Seventies.

Other Versions: *Burt Bacharach (1977) • Eyvind Kang (1997) • Sylvester*

"I Took My Strength from You." The most recent Bacharach-David copyright on John Zorn's double-CD tribute, *Great Jewish Music: Burt Bacharach,* where it's performed by Eyvind Kang.

"No One Remembers My Name" (Burt Bacharach - Hal David)
First recorded by Stephanie Mills
From the album *For the First Time,* Motown 2531
Released December 1975

No one called it a comeback when Bacharach and David hit with

1975

Call Her Miss Dorothy. Stephanie Mills was prevented from reprising her starring role in the Broadway smash *The Wiz* on the silver screen when Diana Ross decided it should be her next movie part. Apparently it was preferable for all parties involved to just let the movie sink than tell Miss Ross she was too old to play Dorothy.

"Make It Easy on Yourself" after the five-year drought of hits that preceded "Magic Moments," but there were few who paid close attention to the ongoing careers of songwriters in those days. Besides, the pair hadn't stopped writing together. The two-year period of relative silence from Bacharach-David following *Lost Horizon* was quite different. In their absence, disco had pushed many of the great R&B voices that used to record Bacharach-David tunes off the radio. So putting out a song called "No One Remembers My Name" when your name is colder than the frozen tundra outside of Shangri-La is almost begging for that connection to be made.

In the *Self-Portrait* interview disc A&M used to promote *Futures*, Bacharach spends a great deal of time talking about career ups and downs and personal insecurities before discussing the motive behind this track: "Hal caught a particular thing that happens to a lot of people. You go back into a neighborhood you once lived in. The people are different, everything's changed, and you don't recognize things that used to exist. That's happened to many of us in life." In this success story with a twist, Mills portrays someone who has made a name for herself returning to her hometown and finding no one there to share the joy with. The people to whom her success would have meant something have all moved on: *"I came back to show them I really made my dreams came true / I'm dying to tell them but there's no one to tell it to / They just rush passed me / And now I know the past is just a memory."* With an air of finality, she decides, *"I belong where people smile back at me / That's the only place for me,"* even if it's a place that no longer exists.

Mills uses her acting skills to give this character some spunk, while on Bacharach's *Futures* album, session sirens Melissa Mackay, Sally Stevens and Marti McCall give the tune a pretty but generic sheen.

Other Versions: *Burt Bacharach (1977)*

"Living on Plastic," "If You Can Learn How to Cry," "I See You for the First Time," "All the Way to Paradise," "Please Let Go" (Burt Bacharach - Hal David)
Recorded by Stephanie Mills
From the album *For the First Time,* Motown 2531
Released December 1975

The largest bombardment of new Bacharach-David originals on one album produced a meager number of cover versions, with six songs appearing here for the first and last time. "Living on Plastic" is the most uncharacteristic of the batch, a wry observation from Hal David on what goes on in the minds and hearts of the unemployed. It sounds as if David is identifying with his estranged partner, hiding out on the beach trying to figure out what he wanted to do in music. *"Here come the surf boys / Guess I'll stop and get some sun / Just bake until I'm done / Maybe tomorrow I'll have to go to work again / But I can wait till then."* Mills gets by on charge accounts and a solid belief that the gods are watching over her. If you substitute royalties from round pieces of vinyl for her plastic credit cards, this story is fair assessment of Bacharach and David's extended hiatus.

Record dynasties being what they are, Bacharach and David never got to write for Motown recording artists during that company's boom period. This project made up for the lost time, with Mills approaching the coquettish charm of Supremes-era Diana Ross on material Ross would have likely cut in her later solo career. This lite thumper is perhaps the closest Bacharach and David would come to fabricating a disco hit for their files.

It's as if Hal and Burt are still writing songs with Dionne's voice in mind when they came up with "If You Can Learn to Cry." Mills handles its gradual buildups with Warwick's straightforwardness; the chorus's melodic similarities to the bridge of "This Empty Place" may be the reason why that old Dionne chestnut was dusted off and included on this album. Another non-Bacharach arrangement, the solo section of "If You Can Learn to Cry" combines real horns with synthetic ones.

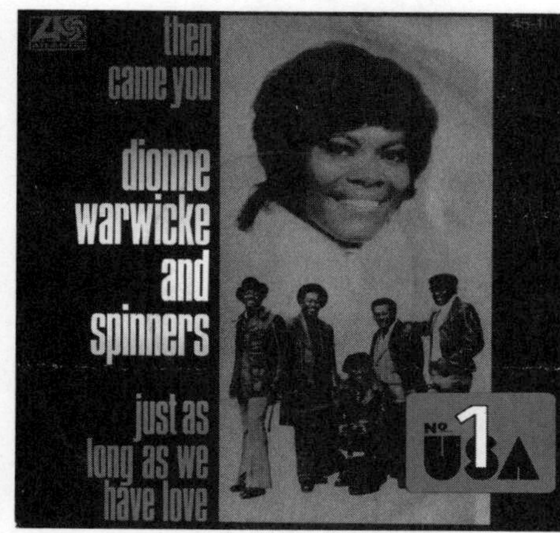

Dionne Warwicke. Nothing Dionne recorded for Warner Brothers ever disturbed the Top 40. Her hitless streak of 45s was interrupted by a No. 1 hit duet with the Spinners, which came out on Atlantic. Despite the presence of her first chart-topper, Warner's cash-in album *Then Came You* fared no better than any of their other Dionne LPs.

After its most credible dance-floor nominee breezes by, the album slowly winds down with intelligent ballads more typical of an older adult-contemporary artist than Mills, who would soon become known for funkier fare. None of these songs indicates diminished strength on either man's part: each tune has stock Bacharach touches (the clarinet opening on "The Way I Feel about You," the whistle-pitched organ that becomes the main hook of "Please Let Go"), and David's considerate word-smithing is as potent as ever. The change seems to be that the audience has moved on in their absence. Adult listeners had gotten more sedentary and less interested in hearing new music, while the R&B crowd was showing a consistent preference for rump-moving songs over heart-tugging ones that told a story or expressed emotional turmoil. The failure of this album to connect with either faction proved that this unfortunate cycle was still ongoing.

Despite Bacharach's comments on the 1977 *Self-Portrait* interview disc that the two men were speaking again and looking to write another musical or movie score, the truth was that they would continue a mostly litigious relationship for the next four years, writing only three unrecorded songs in 1978. By the following year, they settled their publishing dispute out of court, but they didn't reconvene to write together until 1989, just as Bacharach's marriage to Carole Bayer Sager was coming undone.

"Charlie" (Burt Bacharach – Bobby Russell)
First recorded by Bobby Vinton
From the album *Heart of Hearts,* ABC ABCD 891,
Released June 1975

Bacharach hadn't furnished the Polish Prince with a new song since 1964. Unlike most of his male vocal contemporaries, Vinton still had the occasional hit, usually some nauseating polka. Traumatically programmed on the *Heart of Hearts* album before "Beer Barrel Polka" and "Polka Pose," "Charlie" is one of only two songs Bacharach wrote with Bobby Russell. It's just the sort of shameless tearjerker you'd expect from the guy who extorted tears from radio listeners with Bobby Goldsboro's "Honey."

Waiting for Charlie to Come Home...and Die! Easily the sappiest song in Burt's discography. In an unrelated story, Charlie was Dionne Warwick's nickname for Bacharach.

Russell tries to blame this story on some observant old men in the park. They tell of a car wash attendant named Charlie who works every day except Sunday. That's the day he takes the only love in life—his 10-year old daughter from a previous marriage—to the park, where they wave at the old men and he buys her a single red rose. One Saturday night, Charlie complains of pains and closes the car wash early, and if you guessed that he goes to bed and never wakes up, help yourself to a complimentary handkerchief. But while Charlie the car wash attendant is finally out of his misery, "Charlie" the song grows even more maudlin. Vinton gets a catch in his voice over the poor little girl who's *"dressed and ready for her daddy just like every Sunday but he didn't show up / Now she goes to the park every Sunday alone."* You were about to guess that she still waves to the old men at the park and buys a single red rose for Charlie's grave, weren't you? God, you're good.

"Charlie" comes back from the dead to make a final appearance on the 1977 *Burt Bacharach in Concert* special, and this pap is slightly more tolerable sung by a pretty woman than it is by a polka pusher.

Other Versions: *Burt Bacharach with Sally Stevens - TV special (1977)*

"Us" (Burt Bacharach – Bobby Russell)
First recorded by Tom Jones
From the album *Memories Don't Leave Like People Do,* Parrot PAS 71068
Released October 1975

The only song Bacharach and David penned specifically with Tom Jones in mind, "Promise Her Anything" was a caricature of his lascivious stage persona. Despite his excellent readings of Chuck Jackson songs, they never gave Jones the torturous, hurt-in-love songs they might offer to Gene Pitney or Lou Johnson. But this rather theatrical breakup opus changed all that: it's another Bacharach and Bobby Russell story song, and Jones confidently sells every line like a snake oil vending machine. At first tempestuous towards his ex *("Where's the glue that could be mending us? Are you* ashamed *of us?"),* he calms into a conversational slur *("Where's the love that we made, that gave our kids to us? / By the way, heard today, the neighbors know...baay-beee")* with some gobbledygook lines that Russell should've run Wite-Out over *("Once we were sheltered safe inside the circle of content, we spent it all to feel").* In comparison, the Joshie Armstead–sung version on Bacharach's *Futures* only veers from overwrought to uncomfortably shrill.

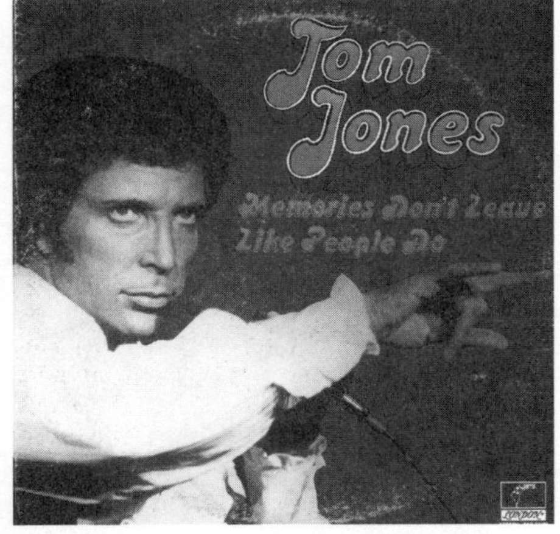

Where's the Glue That Could Be Mending Us? That's the musical question Tom Jones asks in the Bacharach-Russell heartbreaker "Us." Perhaps a more burning question is, What does Tom's hand gesture mean, and does it have anything to do with not fetching him a moist towelette?

"Where Are You" (Burt Bacharach - Norman Gimbel)
Recorded by Burt Bacharach
From the album *Futures,* A&M 4622
Released April 1977

One of Bacharach's more infrequent songwriting partners in 1961 was Norman Gimbel. With two rampantly terrible songs already under their belts ("I'll Bring Along My Banjo" and "Deeply"), this was one reunion few were clamoring for. Nonetheless, the two associates doubled their catalog with two more songs in 1976, both infinitely better than what came before. Although "Where Are You" has a full set of lyrics, Joshie Armstead's near-hysterical vibrato doesn't launch into them until two minutes into the song, giving the classical strings a chance to intermingle with modern jazz. There are a lot of things you're not accustomed to hearing on a Bacharach album—extreme anxiety in the lead vocal, improvised solos from star session players, and a tricky arrangement that allows synth strings to chase around the real ones. Challenging tracks like this are a perfect antithesis to the easy-listening tag that's been unimaginatively stenciled across Bacharach's work since his first A&M recordings.

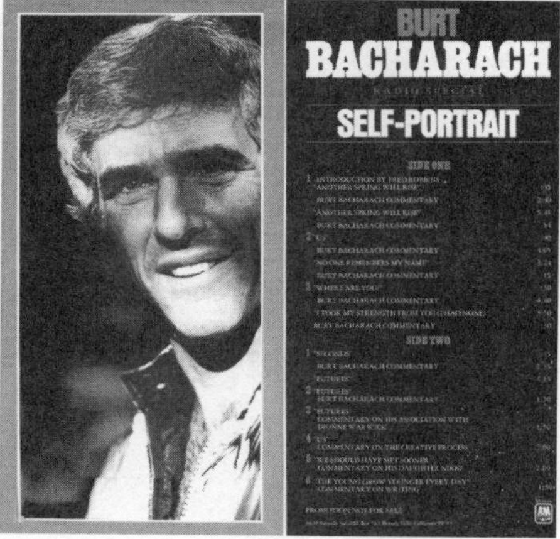

Self-Portrait. This A&M promotional disc for radio broadcast contains no interviewer, just Bacharach talking in stream-of-consciousness. Between selections from *Futures*, he shares his thoughts on the split with Hal and Dionne ("We had a terrific run of ten years"), the process of writing, and his dry periods ("I may have written all the best music I'm capable or writing. I don't think you just go on endlessly").

Other Versions: *Marie McAuliffe (1998)*

"When You Bring Your Sweet Love to Me" (Burt Bacharach-Norman Gimbel)
"Another Spring Will Rise," "Futures" and "Time and Tenderness" (Burt Bacharach)
"We Should've Met Sooner" and "The Young Grow Younger Every Day" (Burt Bacharach - James Kavanaugh)
Recorded by Burt Bacharach
From the album *Futures,* A&M 4622, released April 1977

Futures is perhaps Bacharach's best marriage of his jazz and classical muses. Consisting of music he'd written over the previous three years, following his *Lost Horizon* bust, it finds him taking bold strides in new directions with nearly every track. Barring the two songs previously ignored on the Stephanie Mills album and repeats of "Us" and "Seconds," most of the music of *Futures* was made specifically for a Burt Bacharach album. He notes the various departures on the *Self-Portrait* radio special: "The continuing link in the album is that the music is all composed by the same person. I find the album to be all over the place, not necessarily in a bad way. Instead of a consistency that everything goes from one track into another very smoothly, there are many changes that the album puts you through…and that's sort of deliberate. There's certain jazz influences that I got into on this album, having had those roots in jazz when I first cared about music. Featured soloists, there a lot of freewheeling players—that's something I've never done on an album."

"Another change is that I don't sing a note in the album. I think that's OK. I think the majority of people will be happy with that," he laughs. "There are some people who say, 'Why don't you record an album just singing the whole album?' I mean, we wouldn't sell 10 albums. I have no illusions about my singing. I decided to leave the singing to other people."

And Who Said Ex-Priests Weren't Funny? James Kavanaugh has collections of romantic as well as humorous poems. Among his collections are *Celibates, Will You Be My Friend* and *A Modern Priest Looks at His Outdated Church.*

Two songs on the album feature the gruff voice of a young singer recording for A&M at the time. Jaime Anders becomes the surrogate Bacharach voice on this record, and "When You Bring Your Sweet Love to Me" is the track Bacharach himself would've probably once have elected to sing for himself. In his efforts to show us California piece by piece, he now brings us Hollywood by night *("Looking down on tinsel town where shiny cars like fireflies make neon tubes of all the streets below").*

Anders weighs in again with "We Should've Met Sooner," one of two Bacharach collaborations with the San Francisco priest-turned-poet

1979

Futures. Bacharach and David attempted to write together again after this LP but copyrighted only three songs in 1978 before splitting up again. "Looking Back over My Shoulder," "You Learn to Love by Loving" and "Everybody Knows the Way to Bethlehem" remain unrecorded.

James Kavanaugh. His words on this album are the polar opposite of those of Hal David, who strives to mask the art of writing in his compositions, to write in a way that makes you think the song and the lyrics wrote themselves. Kavanaugh only sounds conversational if you live next door to a priest-turned-poet, but he does register some interesting blank verse, wishing he had made your acquaintance *"before mortgages and children / To hold you and chain you / To smother you with demands / Before the wind was out of your hair."*

Peter Yarrow guests on the second Kavanaugh track, "The Young Grow Younger Every Day." In a bit of irony, the former first name in Peter, Paul and Mary pled guilty in 1970 to "taking immoral liberties" with a 14-year-old girl in Washington, D.C., unable to distinguish how young a groupie actually was. This mellow bit of programming, not dissimilar to "I Might Frighten Her Away," precedes the thrilling instrumental "Another Spring Will Rise" and contributes its title in the lyric "Another spring will rise to silence death."

In another first, Bacharach previewed this new material on the road with Anthony Newley the previous December, and it was registered with ASCAP as "Last Ride." Says Bacharach, "It didn't have a title at the time. I asked the audience what they felt, and they would write very interesting titles, what it conveyed to them. I feel there's a lot of hope…that you do win at the end of this piece. It's very hard to put into words or have somebody write a lyric. I think Kavanaugh could do it if we ever do wind up with words going into it. It feels instrumental. It's the most piano playing that I've done on any of the albums."

Futures contains his most satisfying instrumental pieces, including the title track released as a single in August, 1977. In an era when instrumentals seem to be finding their way to No. 1 again ("The Theme from S.W.A.T.," "A Fifth of Beethoven," "Star Wars Theme/Cantina Band"), it's odd that more people didn't lock into his fine mix of swampy Fender Rhodes, speeding trumpets and tornado strings. Bacharach gets in some of his most animated live piano playing on the *Burt Bacharach in Concert* special when he performs "Futures" and "Another Spring Will Rise."

Woman. Her agent promised her a Roxy Music album cover if she did this Bacharach guy's record first. Bacharach attempted to write three other songs with Libby Titus for this album, but "A Single Girl," "Chicago Farewell" and "Amnesia: The Inderal Song" went no further than the Library of Congress. He would also attempt to write with Carole Bayer Sager in the same period, but their three-hour session produced no song.

Woman
Recorded by Burt Bacharach and the Houston Symphony
A&M 3709, released June 1979

"Summer of '77" • "Woman" • "Magdelena" • "New York Lady" (Burt Bacharach) • "There Is Time" (Burt Bacharach - Sally Stevens) • "Riverboat" (Burt Bacharach - Libby Titus) • "The Dancing Fool" (Burt Bacharach - Anthony Newley) • "I Live in the Woods" (Burt Bacharach - Carly Simon - Libby Titus)

"I wrote something for the Houston Symphony," Bacharach recalls in the *This Is Now* BBC documentary, "and it wasn't necessarily successful. But it was something that was very exciting to do. It wasn't successful at all. Very expensive failure. What happened was that it was all live, everyone playing at the same time. If there was a mistake, that's it. You were saddled with it. I dreamt about that whole process for two months afterwards. Every night it was the same dream. Always the panic. Always the fear I wasn't gonna get it done."

"I never had that," he laughs. "Once, about a lady, I dreamt every night for two weeks." But this was no lady. This was *Woman,* the album.

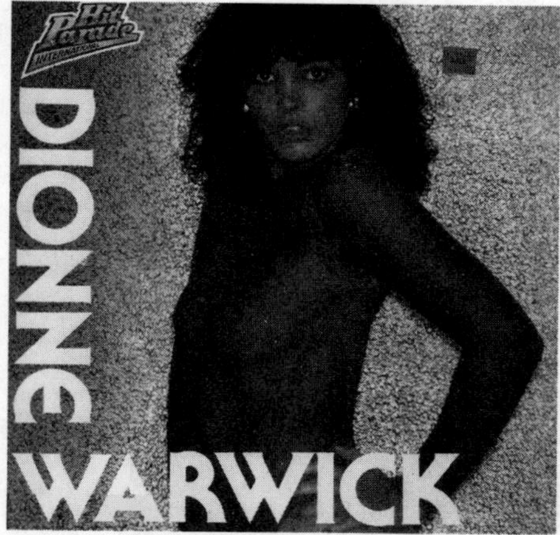

Love at First Sight, Too. Of course, we know this cutie in the see-through body suit isn't the First Lady of Song—it's just the Italians' strange distribution of soft porn via record shops.

What turned this long player into a recurring nightmare was Bacharach's decision to record it entirely in one four–hour session at Houston's Jones Hall on November 2, 1978. This can be viewed as a reaction to *Futures'* three-year song gestation period and the one year that he took to record and remix it to try to get everything perfect. Having loosened up enough to let soloists improvise on *Futures*, was he now going to allow for imperfections? Or was he already bemoaning the loss of spontaneity in the multitrack recording process, where 24 tracks made it too easy to go in and record all the parts separately? Even in the Bell Studios days, they'd only undertake three songs in an evening's session, with a break for dinner. This project required cutting five extended instrumentals, clocking in at an average of six minutes, plus three vocal tracks, with three different sets of singers, in less time than he even allowed himself to record the brisk *What's New Pussycat?* score. One wonders what musical blemishes, if any, Bacharach still hears when listening to the album now.

Having already articulated a wish to do extended works as far back as "And the People Were with Her," Bacharach reiterated that desire on the *Self-Portrait* radio special: "They don't have to be terribly serious and heavy, but they will fuse all the musical elements that I feel. I think one must grow. You can't force yourself to grow. I think its natural progression. You can't push growth any more than you can retreat and write the way that you wrote once upon a time."

Bacharach really deserves credit for pursuing serious composition once more at a time when the world was badgering him to churn out hits again. In a 1995 *GQ* magazine interview with writer David Toop, he revealed a wish to follow through on the neoclassical composing of his early musical education. "It was a very peak time in my life when Leopold Stokowski came with a commission, a grand, for me to write something for the New American Symphony Orchestra. I turned it down. I think it hurt my mother a lot. It was something in retrospect I should have done. But I didn't."

Another thread Bacharach picked up and discarded early in his career was songwriting with the opposite sex. To date, he had only done a threesome with Margery Wolpin and Hal David for "Tell the Truth and Shame the Devil"; then there was "A Girl Like You" with Anne Pearson Croswell and an unrecorded song or two with Anita Jones. "I think, for me, I always shied away from writing with a woman. Maybe that scared me. Maybe that's too much like my mother. Maybe [a woman's] power would be too strong, and I don't need to be in a room with someone who would call in any of this stuff that made it into a mother-son relationship."

On *Woman,* Bacharach's only genuine concept album, every note is sung by a woman, every song is about a woman, and every lyric is written by a woman—sometimes two. Libby Titus revives the woman-waiting-for-her-sailor-man theme of "With Open Arms," which, you'll recall, was the first hit Bacharach ever had with a female singer. But unlike Jane

Amo Non Amo. Bacharach's music supplanted the original Italian film's score, written and performed by the Italian progressive "horror rock" group Goblin.

Morgan, the gal awaiting on the "Riverboat" isn't as desperately reliant on seaman per se. Titus collaborates lyrically with Carly Simon on "I Live in the Woods," a character sketch of a mysterious divorced single mother who's gossiped about by the town folk. The men are drawn to Carly's strange idiosyncrasies, but the women think she's dangerous—about the same reaction husbands and wives would have to picking up a risqué Carly Simon album cover. Sally Stevens, a background singer on *Futures* and Bacharach's live show, pens the minimal words to "There Is Time," which she sings in a wraithlike soprano.

But it's the instrumentals that are the real impetus behind the project and that deliver the most sizzle. "Summer of '77" packs all the anticipation of the *Promises, Promises* overture, while the cinemascopic "Woman" affords us a few minutes alone with the album's most dangerous femme fatale—musically replicated by strings that go off like sirens, aggressive percussion that evokes a spinning wheel of fortune and guitar chicks straight out of Bell Studios circa 1964. Although Anthony Newley wrote lyrics to "The Dancing Fool," Bacharach preferred to keep it as an instrumental.

Most of the album's commercial hopes were pinned on the uptown "New York Lady," which came out as a single and a rare (for Bacharach, anyway) disco 12-incher. More funk-fusion than disco, it might've made the same inroads that A&M label mates Chuck Mangione or Herb Alpert made if the sax melody line were a tad easier to hum. Had Burt not taken his teacher Darius Milhaud's advice all those years ago and not pursued melodies people could whistle, *Woman* might have been considered a successful jazz album, without having commercial expectations thrust upon it. It may be harder to write a three-minute pop song that becomes a standard than a seven-minute piece, but it's even harder writing a string of seven-minute pieces for people who just want to hear "Do You Know the Way to San Jose?"

Along with *Futures, Woman* remains to be rediscovered by future fans as one of Bacharach's most adventurous albums, the only one written as a complete piece from start to finish. It's also the last album to date released under his name, barring soundtracks and endless repackages of the past.

"I Don't Need You Anymore" b/w "Find Love" (Burt Bacharach - Paul Anka)
Recorded by Jackie DeShannon
From the Compagnia Europea Cinematografica/Titanus/Valerio De Paolis-Gianni Bozzacchi movie *Together?*
RCA 11902 (*Billboard* pop #86)
Released January 1979

"I'm dying to do another picture," said Bacharach in 1977, "but I want to be in love with the picture that I do. I don't want to write a score that just services the picture. I get too involved with the picture. I see it too many times and I'm spoiled after a picture like *Butch Cassidy* and spoiled in another way with a picture like *Lost Horizon.*"

Perhaps Bacharach saw this Armenia Balducci–directed movie when it was *Amo Non Amo* (aka *I Love You, I Love You Not*), filmed in English and dubbed in Italian—which spared him from hearing such inane sexual gripes as "That wasn't a blowjob, that was a hand job," "Who are you to tell me who I can or can't sleep with," "You think all men are a pile of shit" and, of course, the ever-popular "Fuck your barman!" Maybe after watching Ursula Andress countless nights through his Moviola, Bacharach relished the idea of scoring a sexy foreign film that wasn't a comedy. But if anyone gave anyone head in this movie, it would be an incessantly talking one. These songs are too well intentioned to be in such a cranial carnal film, filled with filibusterin' fornicators who mount the sexual revolution soapbox whenever one of their selfish needs isn't being met.

Together Again! This wasn't the first Jackie Bisset film to feature a Bacharach score: remember, she made her film debut as Miss Giovanni Goodthighs in *Casino Royale*.

Consider the sorry placement of the hopeful "Find Love" in a scene where Jacqueline Bisset sneaks some afternoon delight with Terence Stamp while her boyfriend is on a dingy screwing his old girlfriend. It's one thing to hear Jackie DeShannon in "What the World Needs Now" waltz time again, singing *"When two people meet and they care and get together, together you'll find love too."* It's another thing to see four people acting like what the world actually needs now is a quickie, preferably out of sight of the coast guard.

Paul Anka, who had previously contributed music to a handful of songs written with Hal David, was the closest of any of Bacharach's post-Hal collaborators to complying with the gentle lyricist's directive to craft songs as if they came out fully formed. Anka provides couplets that occasionally wax poetic, but he never pours on the polish like James Kavanaugh or pushes the pathos envelope like Bobby Russell. That a line like *"I'll leave my memories in the hall before they reach my heart"* could've slotted into the ultimate vacate-the-premises anthem, "A House Is Not a Home," is high praise indeed. This is DeShannon's last Top 100 appearance, and judging by the dismal performance of the film, it pushed up the charts strictly on its own merits.

Together? (Original Soundtrack LP)
RCA 3541, released January 1979

"I Don't Need You Any More" (Burt Bacharach - Paul Anka) • "I Think I'm Gonna Fall in Love" (Burt Bacharach - Paul Anka) • "In Tune" (Burt Bacharach - Libby Titus) • "If We Ever Get Out of Here" (Burt Bacharach) • "On the Beach" (Burt Bacharach) • "I've Got My Mind Made Up" (Burt Bacharach - Paul Anka) • "Find Love" (Burt Bacharach - Paul Anka) • "Luisa" (Burt Bacharach)

The deficient box office receipts for the film *Together?* killed any chance of Bacharach's last really satisfying movie soundtrack having much commercial impact. It's also the last one conceived with real orchestration: from here on out it's the digital sterility of the *Arthur* movies, *Night Shift* and the more recent *Isn't She Great*.

While the majority of *Together?*'s adult contemporary supergroup may have seen better days commercially, special guest Michael McDonald was everywhere you looked in the late Seventies and early

1979

"Sexual Liberation Only Goes So Far..." At a $59.95 list price, it doesn't go far enough.

Eighties, and usually in the upper regions of the charts. Although it seemed unlikely that the former Steely Dan keyboardist would be accepted as the new voice of the Doobie Brothers after Tom Johnson's departure in 1975, the public took to this blue-eyed soulster with surprising speed.

As Mike McDonald, he had recorded some singles for Bell Records in 1972, but neither the Doobies nor Warner Brothers were anxious for him to resume that solo career after the Doobies' late 1978 *Minute by Minute* album was on its way to going platinum the first time, thanks to the No. 1 single "What a Fool Believes." Because of restrictions, "I've Got My Mind Made Up" was never released as a single. A damn shame, since McDonald's outstanding vocal is even better than the one his future chart-topper "On My Own." That's mainly because it doesn't have to compete with Patti LaBelle for air space: an unlisted background female vocalist chimes in to soften his husky eruptions, much the way Odia Coates accompanied Anka's on his 1974–75 Top 20 hits. When providing lyrics for someone else, Anka refrains from the graphic your-hair-in-my-mouth imagery that he's used ever since "You're Having My Baby" pushed so many reams of adult contemporary envelopes.

Another Anka collaboration, "Think I'm Gonna Fall in Love," contains no words beyond the title, sung at the end in much the same way "Gonna Fly Now" comes in at the end of Bill Conti's "Theme from *Rocky*." Bacharach also continued the writing combination he formed with Libby Titus on *Woman*. Her sly and sensual vocals on the slow-cooking "In Tune" pointed to what might have been a viable collaboration had Carole Bayer Sager not come along to stir the soup.

SECTION EIGHT
THAT'S WHAT FRIENDS ARE FOR (1980-1991)

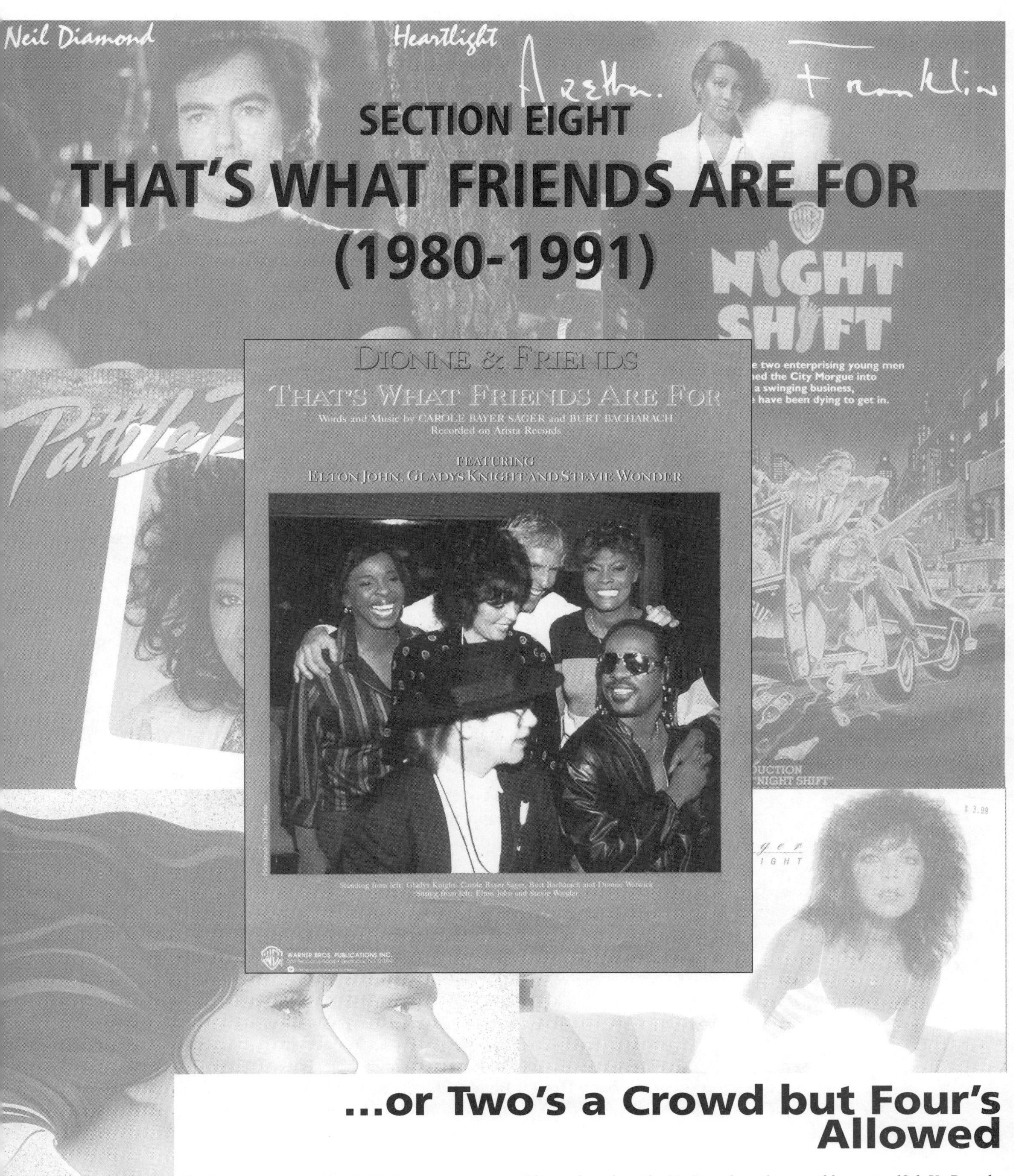

...or Two's a Crowd but Four's Allowed

Whether you're ready for the Eighties or not, we're making a leap from the Me Decade to the arguably more selfish Us Decade. The turnaround is more than a little jarring. Your ears must sonically adjust from Burt's lush, intricate orchestrations, where he obsessed over every triangle part, to crass Yamaha DX7 patches of the Fender Rhodes that dated records to the week they were issued. Join us as we count how many Carole Bayer Sager lyrics feature the word "hey" in them, reunite with Dionne, learn Neil Diamond's work habits and how many names can be crammed into parentheses, and watch Bacharach and Sager equal the number of No. 1 hits and Oscars that Bacharach and David collected in their heyday.

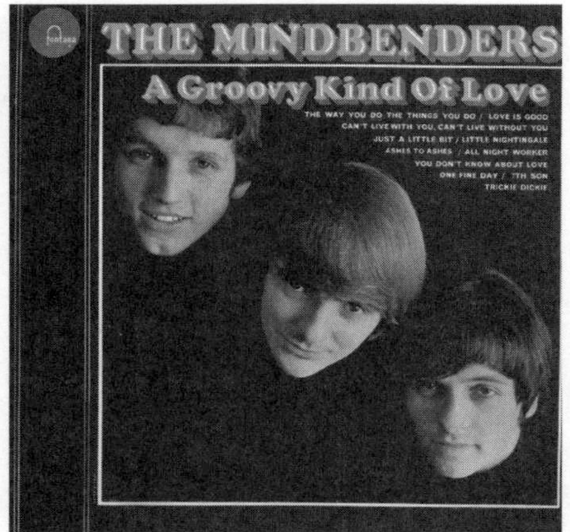

The Mindbenders. The Wayne Fontana-less Mindbenders made Sager's "Groovy Kind of Love" a Top 3 hit and shortly afterward performed her Leslie Gore hit "Off and Running" in the film *To Sir with Love*.

Some

Bayer Sager

Background...

Few people would credit daytime talk-show maverick Mike Douglas with playing two pivotal roles in Burt Bacharach's career, but the one-time singer for Kay Kaiser's band was there for a pair of milestones. He claims in his 1999 autobiography, *I'll Be Right Back,* to have encouraged Burt to sing one of his songs for the first time on national television. "He didn't laugh it off or go shy on me, just nodded reflectively. I think he'd been waiting for someone to suggest that for a long time," Douglas writes. Apparently Douglas forgot to mention in his memoirs that it was his show that ultimately brought Bacharach and Carole Bayer Sager together. She was a guest on his November 29, 1979, program the week Bacharach co-hosted.

"I went on to sing a song," Sager recalls for the *This Is Now* documentary, "and after the show he said, 'Would you like to have dinner with me one night?' and 'Would you like to write a song with me one day?' To this day, I never really figured out which he said first, because I think that would be a key as to what happened with our marriage."This concern sounds very much like the one raised by Sonia Walsk, her fictionalized self from the Neil Simon musical *They're Playing Our Song,* loosely based on Sager and her ex-husband Marvin Hamlisch.

Unlike Bacharach, Sager wrote with multiple partners throughout her career. As Carole Bayer, she began working as a songwriter for Screen Gems Publishing. Its magnate, Don Kirshner, who struck gold with another teenage songwriter name Carole, signed the High School of Music and Art graduate in the mid-Sixties. Some of Bayer's earliest credits were on singles by Leslie Gore, a girlfriend of hers from summer camp. Gore almost recorded Bayer's first hit, "A Groovy Kind of Love," cowritten with Toni Wine, but Gore's producer, Shelby Singleton, wanted Bayer to omit the word "groovy." Bayer was very upset by this suggestion, and it wound up being the Mindbenders who took the song all the way to No. 2 that spring.

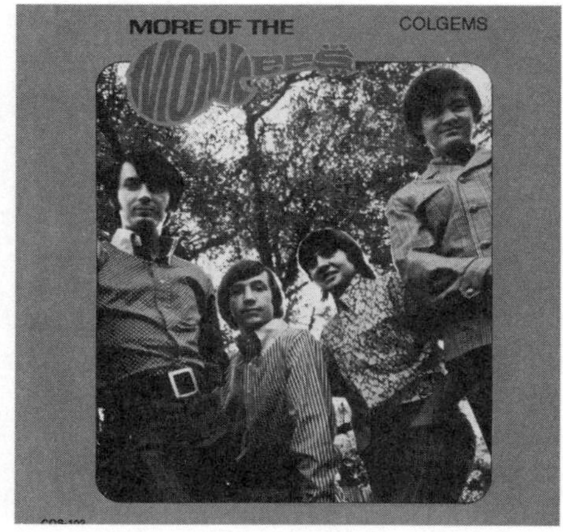

More of the Monkees. Sager landed three songs, all sung by Davy Jones, on various Monkees albums. "When Love Comes Knocking at Your Door" cowritten and produced with Neil Sedaka, made it onto this, the Monkees' biggest-selling album. Two subsequent Sager cowrites wound up on *The Birds, The Bees and the Monkees* ("We Were Made For Each Other") and *Instant Replay* ("The Girl I Left Behind Me").

Bayer later teamed with Neil Sedaka to write songs for the Monkees and with Peter Allen to write for Bobby Sherman ("Jennifer"), but her biggest hits would be scripted for adults. Sager returned to the Top 10 in 1975 with her Melissa Manchester collaboration "Midnight Blue," which was also No. 1 on the adult contemporary chart. Manchester rerecorded a song Allen and Sager wrote for the Moments, "Don't Cry Out Loud," and made that a Top 10 hit. Sager finally captured the top spot with Leo Sayer's rendition of "When I Need You," a song she wrote with Albert Hammond for one of his albums. She was nominated for a 1977 Oscar for "Nobody Does It Better," the theme from *The Spy Who Loved Me* (and a No. 2 hit for Carly Simon), which she wrote with husband Marvin Hamlisch.

While Sager was enjoying career highs, the climate was decidedly colder for Bacharach. In the years following *Lost Horizon*, he'd recorded three solo albums for A&M, each less successful than the one that preceded it. The final two found him pursuing jazz and long-form composition, diversions he found personally satisfying but commercially frustrating. Ditto for a Stephanie Mills album and a soundtrack to a dud foreign film. To someone used to having his songs incessantly covered, the lack of street-level response to his newer work must have been maddening.

As Sager recalls, "We'd go somewhere and people would say, 'Hey, Burt, don't you write anymore?' or 'What are you writing, why don't we hear any songs of yours anymore?' And to me the absurdity of it was, here was this man whose contribution to music was phenomenal. If he never wrote another song after 'Alfie,' 'Do You Know the Way to San Jose,' 'What the World Needs Now Is Love,' 'A House Is Not a Home,' 'Message to Michael,' et cetera, et cetera, he had already done it."

It's got to be intimidating for any songwriter to compete with the run of hits Bacharach enjoyed with Warwick and Hal David. Even to this day, his interviews find the composer ruminating over these reasonable doubts—that maybe that he's not the arranger he once was, that maybe the best he can do doesn't equal the best of what he's already done. Sager took it upon herself to help the Music Man of 1970 find a way to get to 1980, and it's to her credit that she was able to restore him to radio's good graces. That it happened with some of the blandest Bacharach music imaginable cannot be blamed on her lyrics but rather her approach to songwriting, which tends to favor multiple input from partners diluting the music for one-third of the credit. Certainly the songs the couple cowrote with Neil Diamond, Christopher Cross and Peter Allen tend to favor those writers' musical styles over Bacharach's own unique design. And of course, being married to your songwriting partner requires a great deal of diplomacy.

Think of how much compromising you have to do with the missus just to buy living-room furniture and you have some idea how hemmed in Burt must've been at those ivories. Only three songs from their entire 11-year partnership are represented in Rhino's 3-CD career Bacharach retrospective, *The Look of Love*. All three were No. 1 hits, but it's as if the beautiful, adventurous soul who was driven to write such universal masterpieces of longing as "Twenty Four Hours from Tulsa," "Are You There with Another Girl" and "Alfie" has been forever anesthetized in the dentist chair and forced to write songs Christopher Cross wouldn't mind recording. With the advent of MIDI programming, Bacharach becomes further distracted to come up with arrangements that rival his passionate orchestrations of yesteryear. Many wondered if he would ever scale those heights again.

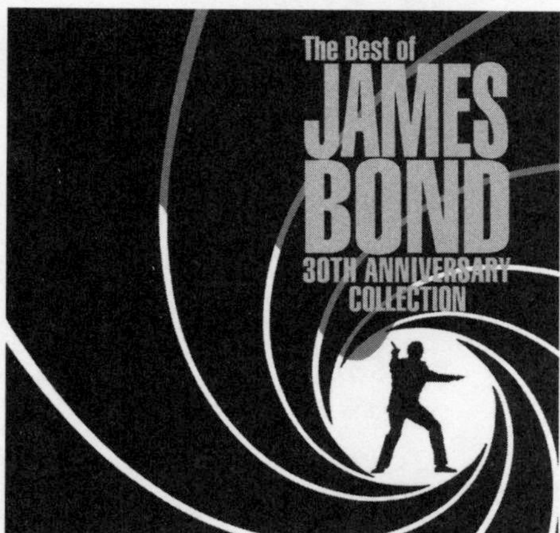

Hamlisch & Sager. They won a Tony for their score to Neil Simon's *They're Playing Our Song* and an Oscar nomination for "Nobody Does It Better," the sexy Bond love theme sung by Carly Simon in *The Spy Who Loved Me*.

Section Eight: That's What Friends Are For (1980–1991)

1. *"Where Did the Time Go"* .... *The Pointer Sisters*
2. *"Love Too Good to Last"* .... *The Pointer Sisters*
3. *"Stronger Than Before"* .... *Carole Bayer Sager*
4. *"You Don't Know Me"* .... *Carole Bayer Sager*
5. *"I Won't Break"* .... *Carole Bayer Sager*
6. *"Somebody's Been Lying"* .... *Carole Bayer Sager*
7. *Stronger Than Before ("Just Friends" "Tell Her," "Wild Again," "Easy to Love Again," "Sometimes Late at Night")* .... *Carole Bayer Sager*
8. *"Truth and Honesty"* .... *Aretha Franklin*
9. *"Arthur's Theme" (Best That You Can Do)"* .... *Christopher Cross*
10. *"Fool Me Again"* .... *Nicolette Larson*
11. *"It's Only Love"* .... *Stephen Bishop*
12. *"Money"* .... *Burt Bacharach*
13. *"Poor Rich Boy"* .... *Ambrosia*
14. *"Touch"* .... *Burt Bacharach*
15. *"Moving Pictures"* .... *Burt Bacharach*
16. *"Making Love"* .... *Roberta Flack*
17. *"Night Shift"* .... *Quarterflash*
18. *"Street Talk"* .... *Burt Bacharach*
19. *"Girls Know How"* .... *Al Jarreau*
20. *"That's What Friends Are For"* .... *Rod Stewart*
21. *"Heartlight"* .... *Neil Diamond*
22. *"I'm Guilty"* .... *Neil Diamond*
23. *"Front Page Story"* .... *Neil Diamond*
24. *"Hurricane (Swept Away)"* .... *Neil Diamond*
25. *"In Ensenada"* .... *Neil Diamond*
26. *"Lost among the Stars"* .... *Neil Diamond*
27. *"Our Lovely Days"* .... *Nancy Wilson*
28. *"Heart Strings"* .... *David Foster*
29. *"Blame It on Me"* .... *Peabo Bryson and Roberta Flack*
30. *"Maybe"* .... *Peabo Bryson and Roberta Flack*
31. *"Time"* .... *Melissa Manchester*
32. *"A Chance for Heaven"* .... *Christopher Cross*
33. *"Crazy"* .... *Neil Diamond*
34. *"Sleep with Me Tonight"* .... *Neil Diamond*
35. *"Turn Around"* .... *Neil Diamond*
36. *"Finder of Lost Loves"* .... *Dionne Warwick with Glenn Jones*
37. *"Extravagant Gestures"* .... *Dionne Warwick*
38. *"How Long?"* .... *Dionne Warwick*
39. *"Stay Devoted"* .... *Dionne Warwick*
40. *"On My Own"* .... *Patti LaBelle and Michael McDonald*
41. *"I'll See You on the Radio (Laura)"* .... *Neil Diamond*
42. *"Me Beside You"* .... *Neil Diamond*
43. *"Love Always"* .... *El Debarge*
44. *"Love Will Show Us How"* .... *Glenn Jones*
45. *"They Don't Make Them Like They Used To"* .... *Kenny Rogers*
46. *"Love Power"* .... *Dionne Warwick and Jeffrey Osborne*
47. *"In a World Such As This"* .... *Dionne Warwick*
48. *"Heartbreak of Love"* .... *Dionne Warwick and Bonnie Pointer*
49. *"In My Reality"* .... *Natalie Cole*
50. *"Split Decision"* .... *Natalie Cole*
51. *"Over You"* .... *Ray Parker Jr. with Natalie Cole*
52. *"Perfect Lovers"* .... *Ray Parker Jr.*

53. *"Overnight Success"* . . . . *.Gladys Knight and the Pips*
54. *"Love Is Fire (Love Is Ice)"* . . . . *.Gladys Knight and the Pips*
55. *"Everchanging Times"* . . . . *.Siedah Garrett*
56. *"Love Is My Decision"* . . . . *.Chris de Burgh*
57. *"The Best of Times"* . . . . *.Burt Bacharach*
58. *"Love Theme from Arthur"* . . . . *.Burt Bacharach*
59. *"One More Time Around"* . . . . *.Barbra Streisand*
60. *"Love Light"* . . . . *.Barbra Streisand*
61. *"You and Me for Always"* . . . . *.Barbra Streisand*
62. *"Need a Little Faith"* . . . . *.Patti LaBelle*
63. *"Why Can't We Be Together"* . . . . *.June Pointer*
64. *"Take Good Care of You and Me"* . . . . *.Dionne Warwick and Jeffrey Osborne,*
65. *"Love Hurts"* . . . . *.Burt Bacharach*

1980

The Pointer Sisters. Although Perry is accused of being the archetypal slick producer, his polished constructions provided multiple hits for Nilsson, Leo Sayer, Ringo Starr and Carly Simon. This was the Pointer Sisters' third album under Perry's direction, and Bacharach and Sager's contributions to it could be categorized as "quiet storm" selections—sophisticated urban ballads crafted for seductive purposes only.

"Where Did the Time Go" (Burt Bacharach - Carole Bayer Sager)
First recorded by the Pointer Sisters
From the album *Special Things,* Planet P-9
Released June 1980

Once Bacharach and Sager forged their personal and professional relationship, they first began calling the names in Sager's Rolodex. Case in point—Richard Perry, who produced Sager's first No. 1 hit, Leo Sayer's "When I Need You," and brought a Sager-Allen song to Frank Sinatra's epic *Trilogy* album. Bacharach, too, had some fleeting connection with Perry, who produced Ella Fitzgerald's reading of "I'll Never Fall in Love Again" and Barbra Streisand's medley "A House Is Not a Home/One Less Bell to Answer" in 1971.

As we'll see later, the compositions that the couple wrote without an intervening third party were generally their best. This recording of "Where Did the Time Go" had the added bonus of Bacharach playing acoustic piano and conducting a real string section, although with layered multitrack recording now the norm, there would be no need to instruct the violin players at the same time he was tickling the ivories. This same add-and-subtract dynamic would find Trevor Lawrence orchestrating the horns at a later date, something that would have been unthinkable in the cost-conscious days at Bell and A&R Studios.

Nothing signifies the start of a new era more than having one of Bacharach and Sager's earliest songs open with the word "hey." Not a word that Hal David used too often but one that cropped up in many of the Seventies' biggest No. 1 ballads, e.g., "You Light Up My Life" and "Touch Me in the Morning." It's an overly familiar greeting that writers previously shied away from for fear of coming off too forward in a song, like a pickup artist at a singles bar. You can find a glossary of sexual positions in the way someone says 'hey,' but here its use is purely droll, addressing a love mate like he's a total stranger *("hey...you...where did the time go?").* The song was a great choice for a summer single, but not after the *Special Things* album ran out of promotional steam the following summer.

Phyllis Hyman. Unable to cope with the vicious cycle of alcohol, weight gain, financial loss and depression, this talented singer took her own life on June 30, 1995, only hours before she was scheduled to perform at the famed Apollo Theatre. *I Refuse to Be Lonely,* posthumously released later that year, was her last stab at outrunning her demons.

"Love Too Good to Last" (Burt Bacharach - Carole Bayer Sager - Peter Allen)
First recorded by the Pointer Sisters
From the album *Special Things,* Planet P-9
Released June 1980

Sager had kept up her other writing partnerships while married to Marvin Hamlisch and continued to do so in 1980, with Bacharach now thrown into the mix. Peter Allen was one of her oldest associates: both were staff writers at Metromedia Records, where the Australian song-and-dance man was also signed as a recording artist. Allen's proficiency at writing both words and music blurs the line of certainty as to who wrote what here. Knowing how exacting Bacharach had been in the past about the integrity of his melodies and arrangements, the fact that he began writing with Sager in a third-wheel capacity suggests either an attempt on his part to loosen up or ongoing insecurity that perhaps it was his input that was keeping him out of the charts. If one were to speculate, the verses here sound more like Allen, and the choruses (especially the Pointers' impeccable unison vocal arrangements) seem to carry the Bacharach touch. Structurally, the whole thing sounds like a good emulation of the sort of soul ballad Earth, Wind & Fire was cooking up at the time.

Singer Phyllis Hyman would revive the tune the following summer, and the Pointer Sisters' version, which really does capture *"the best of love gone bad,"* would be pulled out of storage for reuse on the *Night Shift* soundtrack.

Other Versions: *Phyllis Hyman (1981)*

"Stronger Than Before" 2. On the same album where Chaka Khan covered "Stronger Than Before," she also plumbed "I Feel for You," an obscure Prince song from his debut album. In 1998 the Purple One would write and produce an entire album for her called *Come 2 My House*.

"Stronger Than Before" (Burt Bacharach - Carole Bayer Sager - Bruce Roberts)
First recorded by Carole Bayer Sager
Boardwalk 02054 (*Billboard* pop #30)
Released April 1981

In an earlier threesome with Bruce Roberts and Bette Midler, Sager penned her first charting single as a recording artist, "You're Movin' Out Today." Roberts, the co-author of such hits as "The Main Event/Fight" and "No More Tears (Enough Is Enough)" for Barbra Streisand, joined up with the Bacharachs (and arranger David Foster) to come up with this Top 30 hit, Sager's highest charting record as a performer.

Bacharach alumni Sacha Distel and Dionne Warwick each covered the song individually in 1985, but the most interesting interpretation comes via Chaka Khan. Even with a production drenched in echo, backwards emulators, DX7 patches and drum programs that all conspire to scream out "1984," Khan can't be overshadowed. She's the only vocalist who dares to tackles both the reasonably registered lead vocals and the siren-pitched background wails.

Other Versions: *Sacha Distel (1985) • Joyce Kennedy (1984) • Chaka Khan (1984) • Keff McCulloch (1996) •Dionne Warwick (1985)*

"You Don't Know Me" (Carole Bayer Sager - Burt Bacharach)
First recorded by Carole Bayer Sager
Boardwalk 02054, flip side of "Stronger Than Before"
Released April 1981

The heart-wrencher of the *Sometimes Late at Night* album finds Bacharach and Sager working unobstructed at the get-go—just piano, a lonesome flugelhorn and a vocal box marked "fragile." Sager aches out every syllable in the process of putting away a love that's outlived its usefulness. Despite the tragic circumstances, Sager has the moxie to play games, if only to demonstrate just how much you don't know her: *("If you loved me, even now / would you watch while I leave you? / Maybe you would / maybe I'll still be here / trying to let go").* It's a masterpiece of emotional unraveling on a par with "Whoever You Are (I Love You)" and a fine close for the album, which reprises the title song for the big woe finish.

Steve Lawrence. Without even consulting Eydie, Steve chose the *Greatest 20th Century Songs*! They include "New York, New York," "She's Out of My Life" and two songs Sager and Peter Allen had a hand in, "I Won't Break" and "I'd Rather Leave While I'm in Love." What? No "Pretty Blue Eyes"?

Neil Diamond's reading of "You Don't Know Me" is possibly his most emotionally naked recording since "I Am, I Said," complete with his cracking vocals twice in the beginning. Recorded for the *Heartlight* album in 1982, it was stupidly passed over in deference to the other six Bacharach-Sager songs with a Diamond cowriting credit. Nonetheless, it wound up making a nice chunk of change for its composers as the non-LP B-side of "Heartlight."

Other Versions: *Neil Diamond (1982)*

"I Won't Break" (Carole Bayer Sager - Burt Bacharach - Peter Allen)
First recorded by Carole Bayer Sager
From the album *Sometimes Late at Night,* Boardwalk 37069
Released April 1981

Few figures better typify the gluttonous sins of the record industry in the disco era than Casablanca Records' honcho Neil Bogart. His knack for overspending, overpromoting and overpressing albums may have worked for hit acts like Donna Summer, the Village People, Parliament, Cher and Kiss, but it failed to catapult the nearly 100 other dead–weight acts he'd also signed to the roster, like Cindy and Roy, Bugs Tomorrow, Group with No Name, Mizz and the Joel Diamond Experience. Factor in the mounds of drugs reportedly ingested by even the lowliest of Casablanca employees, and the $10 million Polygram Records shelled out for the label seems like highway robbery.

Once Bogart was ousted as president in 1980, he immediately set up another independent label, Boardwalk. At the same time David Geffen was snapping up superstars like Elton John, Joni Mitchell, Cher, Peter Gabriel and John Lennon for his namesake label, Bogart and Boardwalk went after what was left—commercially challenged acts like Harry Chapin, Joan Jett, Ringo Starr and Carole Bayer Sager. Although she'd previously recorded two albums for Elektra that garnered high critical marks but insignificant sales, Sager turned out to be the dark horse that gave the fledgling label its first Top 30 hit.

"You Don't Know Me." A song sung indescribably blue. Wanna hear Neil "with a cry in his voice?" Check out this non-LP B-side of "Heartlight."

On the *Sometimes Late at Night* sleeve, Neil Bogart and his wife Joyce are credited with conceptualizing the album. It wasn't a unique idea to run all the songs together in a seamless suite, as the Bogarts had already done that with every Donna Summer album to encourage continuous dancing. On Sager's breakup-at-dawn album, it's done so that the torch can be passed from song to song like a relay race.

"I Won't Break" beautifully captures the initial shock when Sager's partner drops the bombshell that he's leaving. *"Well I guess that love is blind / I thought we were doing fine,"* she trembles, before putting on a brave face to make it easy on her deserter *("I won't break so you don't have to worry")*. Sager used the same hushed, scared little-girl voice throughout most of this album, but Bacharach's production makes such effective use of background vocalists Richard Page and Steve George that one has to listen like an audio specialist to realize that the wordless wail to *"turn the radio up loud"* isn't actually her.

Other Versions: *Steve Lawrence (1981)*

Neil Bogart. In tribute to her former record boss, Carole Bayer Sager cofounded the Neil Bogart Memorial Fund with his widow, Joyce, in 1983. The president and owner of Casablanca Records and Filmworks died of lymphoma at age 39.

"Somebody's Been Lying" (Carole Bayer Sager - Burt Bacharach)
First recorded by Carole Bayer Sager
From the album *Sometimes Late at Night,* Boardwalk 37069
Released April 1981

Sager's sensitive version employs little more than a twelve-string guitar and the near-whispered vocal she employs throughout her nocturnal concept album *Sometimes Late at Night.* But this song gains more significance in the ornate rendition released by the Carpenters in June 1981.

Significantly, the artists who had prospered recording Bacharach's music were scarcely to be found on the radio in those peak disco days, except for Dionne Warwick, who was enjoying her biggest year ever at Arista under the auspices of Clive Davis and producer Barry Manilow. Two professional associations Bacharach did renew were the Carpenters and Aretha Franklin: each had a huge hit with a previously recorded Bacharach-David song.

The Carpenters. Sixteen years after *Made in America* appeared in place of the Phil Ramone–produced Karen Carpenter solo album, A&M finally released the fiasco. In anyone else's hands, a disco song entitled "My Body Keeps Changing My Mind" would've remained merely innocuous. Coming from someone with a fatal eating disorder, it's positively chilling. Initially, the cause of death was listed as a heart attack, but it was anorexia nervosa that killed Karen on February 4, 1983.

But much had changed since the Carpenters gave Bacharach his last No. 1 with "Close to You." Battle-scarred from overwork since 1975, the duo suffered professional and personal setbacks in the ensuing years. Richard Carpenter's painkiller addiction and Karen's anorexia nervosa were both red flags that the duo needed to take time off and deal with their personal tribulations. While Richard recovered in a clinic for much of 1978, Karen threw herself into a solo album produced by Phil Ramone that was ultimately shelved, largely at the behest of her brother and A&M Records, who felt a disco Karen Carpenter might wound the franchise even more seriously than covering a Klaatu tune did. The resulting Carpenters album, *Made in America,* didn't make the Top 40 album charts, but "Touch Me When We're Dancing," a song about dancing that's not a dance track, temporarily restored them to the Top 20. The slightly danceable next single wasn't as fortunate (*Billboard* pop No. 71), and this appeared on its B-side.

During the Carpenters' first golden era, a song like "Somebody's Been Lying" would've been unthinkable: there seemed to be an unspoken rule that if anyone was going to break Karen's heart, it might as well be Karen herself. "Rainy Days and Mondays," "Superstar," "It's Gonna Take Some Time This Time" and "Goodbye to Love" all present the protagonist being harder on herself than any outside force, offering hindsight evidence that everyone overlooked of the silent insecurities destroying the singer. With a song like "Somebody's Been Lying," we're clearly given a villainous lover to hiss at *("He's making fun of me and laughing at my*

Carole Bayer Sager. Her records were not merely demonstration discs for people to pluck songs from the Bayer Sager songbook. The chart placings for her singles "You're Moving Out Today" and "Stronger Than Before" proved that record buyers liked her singing, too.

Bacharach on Marriage and Working Together. "It puts a severe degree of difficulty [on the relationship]. You're in a recording studio all day and you come home; instead of arguing about something that's a real personal thing, it's 'the drums should be playing a backbeat with the snare, not the cross stick.'"

dreams"), and the built-in heartache in Karen's calm low register is all the sales pitch this song requires. Richard, back at full strength, outdoes himself with a stylish orchestral arrangement in the vein of Nelson Riddle or Gordon Jenkins and an a cappella section where the double-tracked siblings sound like the Four Freshmen!

Other Versions: *The Carpenters (1981)*

Stronger Than Before - Carole Bayer Sager
Boardwalk 02054, released April 1981

"Prologue" (Sager - Peter Allen) • "I Won't Break" (Sager - Bacharach - Peter Allen) • "Just Friends" (Sager - Bacharach) • "Tell Her" • (Sager - Bacharach - Peter Allen) • "Somebody's Been Lying" (Sager - Bacharach) • "On the Way to the Sky" (Sager - Neil Diamond) • "You and Me (We Wanted It All)" (Sager - Peter Allen) • "Wild Again" (Sager - Bacharach) • "Easy to Love Again" (Sager - Bacharach) • "Stronger Than Before" (Sager - Bacharach - Bruce Roberts) • "You Don't Know Me" (Sager - Bacharach) • "Sometimes Late at Night" (Sager - Bacharach)

Critics flat-out dismiss the Bacharach-Sager years in the rush to praise Bacharach-David's output, but this superlative album proves that they weren't listening carefully enough. True, the team produced its share of pablum (don't worry, we'll get to it), but what other pop music that came off the conveyor belts in the Eighties doesn't sound expendable now? One listen to *Sometimes Late at Night* blows any Bacharach-Sager dismissals out of the water, as it captures everything the pair did well. Sager's confessional lyrics are at their sharpest; Bacharach's arrangements, particularly the segues between the songs that preview the next track, are as passionate as his best instrumental work on A&M. And if Sager's vocal range is just as limited as her husband's, it's a triumph of skilled production that one never notices it, especially in the album's more dynamic passages.

The album's concept is actually two concepts, side one being the "hey, you're leaving me" suite and side two the "hey, before things get worse, I'm leaving you" movement. The "Prologue" that starts off the album is actually a verse of "You and Me (We Wanted It All)," which also closes side one. This leads directly into "I Won't Break," where Sager is given the bad news that she'll be eating frozen dinners for one from now on. Strings carry us along into the album's next single, "Just Friends," the only session ever to feature Bacharach and the self-anointed King of Pop sharing production credits. Ten years after their first Motown hit, Michael Jackson and his brothers were finally allowed to produce and write their own material, since Epic Records was ready to drop them after two mildly successfully albums. The world was still a couple of years away from being blown away by the creative growth he'd demonstrate with *Thriller,* and Sager was among the first people to recognize Michael's multi-talents. Her patronage is still vital to Jackson, who gave Sager a one-page dedication for making possible his 2001 album, *Invincible*.

Although Bacharach handles the string arrangement, the hookiest qualities of "Just Friends" belong to Jackson, who does all the background vocals. As on his future duet with Seidah Garrett, the two voices sound like one voice in certain sections, with Michael's falsetto handling the "la da da da" high parts. Horn and piano neatly dovetail into "Tell Her," side one's lone up-tempo number. Here, Sager plays the other woman urging her man to dump the crying chick back home. There's even an a cappella girl-group handclapping demonstration that recalls her early days writing for Leslie Gore. The remainder of side one includes "Somebody's Been Lying" and two non-Bacharach titles—"On the Way to the Sky," the title track of the Neil Diamond album released that same year, and "You and Me (We Wanted It All)," which Sager wrote with Peter Allen in 1979 for Frank Sinatra's *Trilogy* album.

Aretha Franklin. What a difference a few years make. Steely Dan's 1980 hit "Hey Nineteen" makes the point that that nobody under 20 seems to know who the Queen of Soul is anymore. By 1985, Scritti Politti was praying like Aretha Franklin!

Except for "Stronger Than Before," side two consists entirely of songs Bacharach and Sager penned without a collaborator. The title track finds the uncertainty of the relationship carried over from side one without a musical segue. "Wild Again" and "Easy to Love Again" make full use of background singer Richard Page's similarity to Michael McDonald; both songs feature the kind of slick but humdrum guitar solo that would soon be an inescapable presence on Bacharach sessions all the way up to "This House Is Empty Now." After these less riveting moments, the album picks up steam with the single and the "You Don't Know Me/Stronger Than Before (Reprise)" finale.

Bacharach's photographic presence on the back cover of *Sometimes Late at Night* breaks a two-year disappearance, and there was every indication he would follow it up with an instrumental album of his latest songs, as he is still credited as appearing "through the courtesy of A&M Records." That acknowledgment is absent from the *Arthur* soundtrack later that year but then shows up once more on Neil Diamond's *Heartlight* album in 1982. As of this writing, Bacharach yet to release another album under his own name without a movie tie-in. Despite one Top 30 single, Sager's career as a recording artist ended here, presumably because she preferred not to have her husband producing her. Today Bacharach admits, "I think she went along with me and she's not a big singer, and maybe I swamped her a little bit with orchestration and the demands, vocally, I was looking to make with her."

"Truth and Honesty" (Peter Allen - Burt Bacharach - Carole Bayer Sager)
First recorded by Aretha Franklin
From the album *Love All the Hurt Away,* Arista 9552
Released July 1981

Hard to believe that neither the Carpenters nor Aretha Franklin was ever furnished with a new, tailor-made Bacharach-David tune. Aretha had just signed with Clive Davis' Arista Records, the clear successor to A&M as the mellow adult-pop label of choice. As for cracking the R&B market, Arista wasn't any more certain than Atlantic Records what to do with the Queen of Soul while disco was still king. So they reunited her with old friends like producer Arif Mardin and an all-star background choir (Cissy Houston, Darlene Love, Myrna Smith and Linda Lawrence) and furnished her with happy dance drivel like this. Except for the sustained minor chord that leads into the verse, there's very little in this routine disco-gospel number that sounds even vaguely like Bacharach's handiwork. Sager overworks a good analogy—*"nothing up my sleeve except my heart"*—by repeating hand, heart and cards-on-the-table similes. This track follows a cover of "It's My Turn," Sager and Michael Masser's hit for Diana Ross; the seamless segue between songs is done in the tasteful manner of Sager's third album.

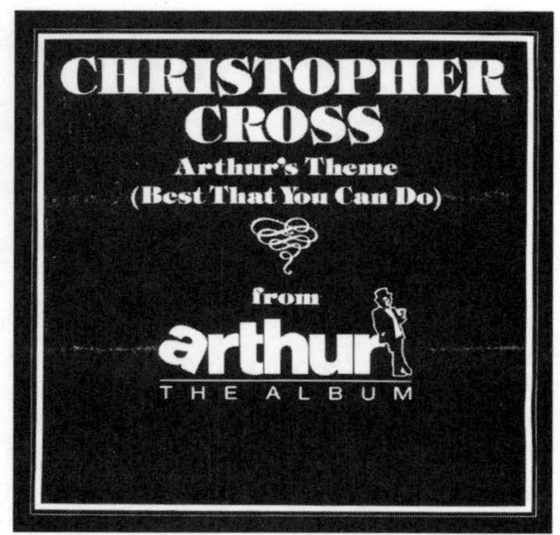

Arthur on 45. Shouldn't this have been called "Arthur: the Single"?

"Arthur's Theme" (Best That You Can Do)" (Bacharach - Sager - Christopher Cross - Peter Allen)
First recorded by Christopher Cross
From the Orion motion picture *Arthur*
Warner Bros. 49787, released August 1981

When four people go up to accept Academy Awards for "Arthur's Theme," the question of how many people it takes to screw in a light bulb comes to mind. Surely it didn't take four people working furiously to come up with this laid-back song, but it's likely the lack of noticeable struggle in this easygoing record that attracted buyers to it in the first place. What we do know is that Peter Allen and Carole Bayer Sager had an unpublished song called "When You Get Caught between the Moon and New York City" that was picked apart for its famous chorus. The rest of the lyrics are an awkward attempt to work drunk little Arthur into the verses, and the dreaded word "hey" is tapped twice to fill in the blanks *("hey, what have I found?"* and *"hey, what does it mean?")*

Opinions differ sharply on the somnambulant merits of Christopher Cross, whose gutless singing makes Chris Montez seem like Otis Redding by comparison. Unfathomably big at the time, Cross won five Grammys in 1981 for just the sort of subpar singing he displays here; listen to how the end of each line seems to get swallowed up before completion, like a shy pupil who answers the teacher's queries with his chin on his chest.

Regardless of who sang, it was an important assignment for Bacharach, whose agent reportedly had to do some heavy lobbying to get the score. This may seem incredible unless you're familiar with the what-has-he-done-lately mentality that governs our entertainment industry. Here's the man that wrote "Alfie," for Chrissakes! And while "Arthur" is no "Alfie," writing a No. 1 hit for a successful movie went a long way toward repairing his tarnished image as the guy who scored *Lost Horizon*. Finally Bacharach could point to a success without Hal David or Dionne Warwick to validate his continued work ethic. But to be so heavily rewarded for disposable pop like "Best That You Can Do" signaled only a tapering off of risk taking and more songwriting by committee.

Christopher Cross. It's hard to believe that poorly made pre-recorded cassettes were outselling vinyl in the Walkman age. But it was in their faulty shells that the first bonus cuts originated. Before CDs, only the cassette release of *Another Page* featured the smash title tune from the movie *Arthur.*

On March 29, 1982, Christopher Cross performed the theme at the Dorothy Chandler Pavilion, and after much piss taking of all the nominees by presenter Bette Midler, she announced the foursome for best-song honors. "When I met Carole maybe I wasn't writing music that was so accessible at the time," began Bacharach in his halting acceptance speech. "But meeting Carole, she has a very good sense of a positive direction to go. And she put the blinkers on the horse. I feel like I'm writing much better being with Carole."

Five days after winning the Oscar for "Arthur," Bacharach and Sager were married in Beverly Hills at the home of Boardwalk Records president Neil Bogart. The only people present to witness the ceremony besides the Bogarts were Mr. and Mrs. Neil Diamond. Diamond had already written several songs with the newlyweds for his upcoming album.

Other Versions: *Alden David & Peter Triggvi • Ronnie Aldrich • Peter Allen • Burt Bacharach (1981) • Shirley Bassey (1995) • Acker Bilk • Christopher Cross – live (1998) • Erich Kunzel & the Cincinnati Pops Orchestra • Peter Duchin • Ernestine • Art Ferrante (1991) • Earl Klugh with Hiroki Miyano (1983) • The Jet Set (1999) • London Pops Orchestra • Keff McCulloch (1996) • Fausto Papetti (1990) • Georgio Parreira • RTE Concert Orchestra/Richard Hayman (1995) • Starlight Orchestra (1995) • Starsound Orchestra • Mel Tormé • The Ventures (1991) • Roger Williams (1982)*

Stephen Bishop. He not only sings themes from movies, he appears in them! Look for the bespectacled soft-pop star in *The Blues Brothers, Animal House, Someone to Love, Twilight Zone* and *Kentucky Fried Movie.*

"Fool Me Again" (Burt Bacharach - Carole Bayer Sager)
First recorded by Nicolette Larson
From the Orion motion picture *Arthur*
Warner Bros. 49820, released September 1981

Most people recall Nicolette Larson as a background singer who moved to the foreground with "Lotta Love," a song she found on a cassette lying on the floor of Neil Young's car. Subsequent Larson albums and singles failed to reach the Top 10, including this inexplicable chart miss. All the ingredients for an irresistible L.A. lite-rock classic are in place, with Andrew Gold providing production, piano, percussion, plush background vocals and a pseudo–George Harrison slide guitar underneath Jim Horn's sax solo. Larson, also a background vocalist for Linda Ronstadt and Emmylou Harris, sounds almost like an effortless blend between the two singers, combining the former's high range and the latter's husky earnestness. A gorgeous melody from Bacharach with yearning Sager lyrics to match, "Fool Me Again" is easily the preeminent track in the film. It's also the only one of the soundtrack's vocal turns that doesn't have a companion instrumental version on side two.

Larson found later success as a country singer and was still highly respected in the industry when she passed away in December 1997 from complications from a cerebral edema. Two months later she was honored with an all-star memorial concert, featuring many of the artists her background vocals appreciably supported.

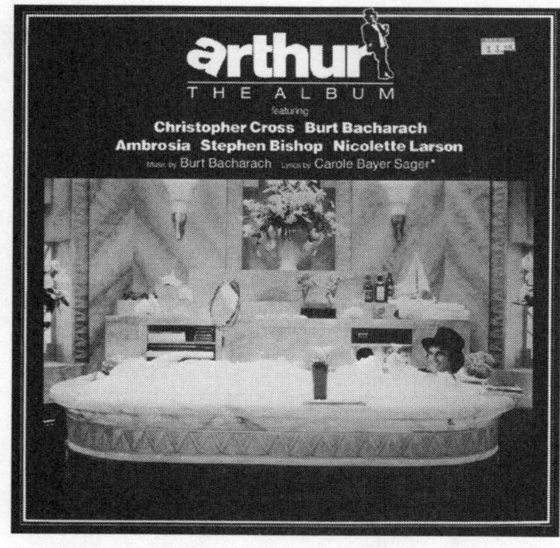

The Best That You Can Do. The soundtrack to the Warner Brothers–distributed *Arthur* couldn't have been more in-house, as it featured four Warner recording acts, each doing a song not found elsewhere in Warner's LP catalog. And Bacharach recorded the entire orchestral score at the Warner Brothers Recording Studio.

"It's Only Love" (Burt Bacharach - Stephen Bishop - Carole Bayer Sager)
Recorded by Stephen Bishop
From the original soundtrack *Arthur the Album,* Warner Bros. 3582
Released September 1981

Stephen Bishop was still a few years away from being synonymous with movie themes. Prior to *Arthur,* "Bish" penned the themes for *Animal House, Roadie* and *The China Syndrome*, but he'd soon sing the Oscar-

Quarterflash. The flip of some singles of "Night Shift" contains an instrumental version that's not the unreleased Bacharach incidental music but just the Quarterflash version with no Rindy Ross vocals.

nominated *Tootsie* theme "It Might Be You" and pen the No. 1 theme to *White Nights*, "Separate Lives," also nominated for an Academy Award. "It's Only Love," the film's mandatory love theme, would probably have been nominated also had it not been overshadowed by "Arthur's Theme." Warner Brothers saw no wisdom in issuing this relaxed ballad on a seven-inch until 1984, and then only on the B-side of a Bishop theme for another Dudley Moore movie, *Unfaithfully Yours.* "It's Only Love" reappeared as an instrumental theme in *Arthur 2* under the name "Love Theme from Arthur," with neither Bishop nor Sager credited, illustrating that the melody was entirely his own.

Other Versions: *Burt Bacharach (1981, 1988)*

"Money" (Burt Bacharach)
Recorded by Burt Bacharach
"Poor Rich Boy" (Burt Bacharach - David Pack - Joseph Puerta)
Recorded by Ambrosia
From the original soundtrack *Arthur the Album*, Warner Bros. 3582
Released September 1981

This song's pounding beat is reminiscent of "My Little Red Book," and with good reason: it's one of the rare occasions Bacharach collaborated with a rock band, and one with prog-rock tendencies at that. The difference here is that Ambrosia's David Pack and Joe Puerta wrote the lyrics to a preexisting movie instrumental (titled "Money" on side two), and the finicky Bacharach, who drove Manfred Mann to distraction with piano instruction, is nowhere to be found in the studio. It's Ambrosia's own arrangement, punching quite harder than the almost vaudevillian version Bacharach originally tendered. It's also a departure from the gentle rock ballads like "Biggest Part of Me" and "How Much I Feel" that Ambrosia had recently become popular for. Both versions of the tune contain squiggly synthesizer sounds, marking Bacharach's first flagrant use of the Robert Moog invention. Judging by his choice of settings, it sounds like he may actually have enjoyed listening to those *Switched-On Bacharach* albums!

"Touch" (Burt Bacharach)
"Moving Pictures" (Burt Bacharach - John Phillips)
Recorded by Burt Bacharach
From the original soundtrack *Arthur the Album*, Warner Bros. 3582
Released September 1981

Although three of *Arthur*'s four vocal numbers were also featured as background incidentals (with *Sometimes Late at Night* session singers Richard Page and Steve George often singing the horn parts), there were two unique instrumentals. The slinky, Herbie Mann-ish "Touch" might've been released as a Bacharach single if he was still an active solo artist on A&M. Flutist John Phillips (who also plays sax and oboe on the score) carries the main minor-key melody along and is given a cowriting credit for "Moving Pictures." It's great hearing Bacharach on tack piano again—the melody almost resembles something off the *Butch Cassidy* soundtrack until the urban sax jolts you away from such thoughts. The album closes with Bacharach's bland Muzak version of "Arthur's Theme," which sounds like heavily tranquilized Herb Alpert. Hearing it, you can't help but feel as if you're being put on hold.

Night Shift. Ron Howard's second big-screen directorial effort turned out to be a popular small-screen movie. Among the people who first watched it on television was Dionne Warwick!

"Making Love" (Burt Bacharach - Carole Bayer Sager - Bruce Roberts)
First recorded by Roberta Flack,
From the 20th Century Fox/Indie Production Company film *Making Love*
Atlantic 4005, (*Billboard* pop #13, R&B #29)
Released February 1982

Roberta Flack's big break came when a 1969 recording of "The First Time Ever I Saw Your Face" was used in the 1971 Clint Eastwood stalker flick *Play Misty for Me* and became a hit in 1972. Got that? A decade later "Making Love" returned Flack to the silver screen, killing moviegoers softly with this theme, which wouldn't have seemed out of place on *Sometimes Late at Night*. The film story concerns a happily married woman who discovers her husband is gay. Sager writes sensitively from the point of view of a woman finding her composure and realizing that the end of sexual relations doesn't necessarily spell the end of love *("There's more to love than making love")*. But the accumulating reverb on the sad closing line *("and I'll remember you")* shows that parting can't always be painless.

Other Versions: *Anita Meyer (1989)*

"Night Shift" (Burt Bacharach - Carole Bayer Sager - Marvin Ross)
Recorded by Quarterflash
From the Warner Brothers movie *Night Shift*
Warner Bros. 29932 (*Billboard* pop #60)
Released July 1982

Bacharach and Sager's work on the *Night Shift* soundtrack represents the zenith and nadir of their affiliation. It brought them their most rewarded copyright in "That's What Friends Are For" and their most loathsome one, namely the theme to this early Ron Howard directorial effort. Clearly the tradition of witty songs about prostitution that started with Cole Porter's "Love for Sale" was not being upheld here. Bacharach and Sager are just punching the clock along with Marvin Ross, the dubious brain behind the lite-rock outfit Quarterflash. The group scored several thrill-free singles, including "Harden My Heart," "Find Another Fool" and one other selection with heart in the title. One suspects their chief appeal was having a sexy female singer and sax player rolled into one—Marvin's wife, Rindy Ross. No surprise that this track sounds more like Quarterflash than Bacharach, especially when you've got Rindy blowing sax solos so generic they must look like a bar code when you notate them.

1982

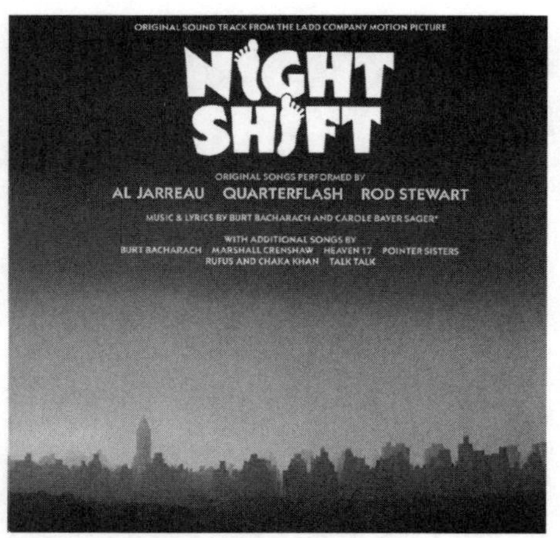

Night Shift. Despite all the stars enlisted on this soundtrack, the Warner Brothers art department chose to give some sooty city smog the spotlight. Also note the curious diminished billing for Oscar winners Burt Bacharach and Carole Bayer Sager.

The subject of this black comedy—two morgue attendants running a prostitution ring—is grist for some of Sager's crassest lyrics yet *("They call you Cat's Eye down on the corner, they call you Mr. Flash / They got some ladies who never see the light").* But even lowest common denominator wasn't working here; by now audiences were getting wise to the fact that Rindy's sexy video come-ons only amounted to excessive pouting, and fans only sent this dry hump midway up the Top 100.

"Street Talk" (Burt Bacharach - Carole Bayer Sager)
Recorded by Burt Bacharach
From the soundtrack of *Night Shift,* Warner Bros. 23701
Released July 1982

Night Shift continued Bacharach's soundtrack modus operandi of having at least three artists do as many vocal selections, but virtually no incidental Bacharach backgrounds used in the film are included on this album beyond the instrumental of "That's What Friends Are For." That Sager was credited on a stand-alone instrumental probably meant this track originally had lyrics that never got used, maybe because Sayer's street talk on the *Night Shift* theme sounded like imaginings from a high-rise apartment vantage point. Instead, "Street Talk" played out like a silent movie, making you almost wish that Bacharach had been furnished with a blaxploitation film or a buddy/action movie at some point in his career: this moves along like one of *Shaft's* calmer incidentals.

"Girls Know How" (Burt Bacharach - Carole Bayer Sager - David Foster)
Recorded by Al Jarreau
From the soundtrack of *Night Shift,* Warner Bros. 23701
Released July 1982

If you put up a wanted poster for an adult-contemporary co-conspirator, David Foster's name would top the list of usual suspects. "Love, Look What You've Done to Me," "You're the Inspiration," "After the Love Has Gone" "St. Elmo's Fire (Man in Motion)" and "Hard to Say I'm Sorry" are just a few of the AC staples Foster had a hand in writing. As a producer and arranger, he's aided and abetted Alice Cooper, Air Supply, All 4 One, the Corrs, Kenny Rogers, Lionel Richie, Whitney Houston, Celine Dion, Madonna, Mariah Carey, Toni Braxton, Patti LaBelle, Andrea Bocelli, Brandy, Paul McCartney, Frank Sinatra, Barbra Streisand—just stop us when you're tired of hitting big names and commas.

Foster was as ubiquitous in the Eighties and Nineties as Bacharach was in the Sixties, but one can also argue that this Canadian wunderkind achieved his notoriety without ever forging a signature sound that the public could easily identify and just as easily tire of. His work is as unfailingly radio-friendly as it is artistically unchallenging, a broad approach to record making perfect for accommodating the expansive range of non-specific vocal talents available to record them. George Benson, Luther Vandross or even former folkie Kenny Loggins could've been deputized at the mike while Al Jarreau was in the loo on "Girls Know How" and no one would've been the wiser. But Bacharach, you'll remember, could do better.

"That's What Friends Are For" (Burt Bacharach - Carole Bayer Sager)
Recorded by Rod Stewart
From the soundtrack of *Night Shift,* Warner Bros. 23701 (*Billboard* pop #4, R&B #1)
Released July 1982

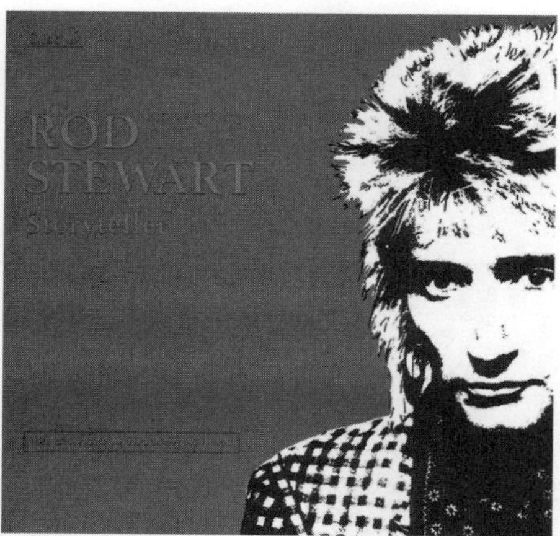

Rod Stewart. Writer Greil Marcus once said of Stewart, "Rarely has anyone betrayed his talent so completely." That's no comment on his recording of "That's What Friends Are For." Just liked the quote.

Bacharach and Sager's most successful song was originally written with no intention beyond providing Henry Winkler, Shelley Long and Michael Keaton a song to jaywalk in the moonlight to. In its original version, the song was a modest charmer sung by Rod Stewart, who enjoyed the performance, judging by the satisfied "yeah" he inserts before the whistling synthesizer break. Breaking with Bacharach soundtrack tradition, Stewart produced the session himself. Sager revealed in *The Billboard Book of Number One Hits* that "Burt and I were not very happy with the record. The record company didn't want to consider it as a single for Rod because they thought it was too soft. The song quietly slipped into oblivion."

There are conflicting accounts of whose idea it was to have Dionne Warwick rerecord the song and who thought to donate the resulting royalties to the American Foundation for AIDS Research. Dionne claims to have fallen asleep in front of the television when she half heard the tune rolling over the *Night Shift* closing credits. Sager recalls that it was included among the songs they played for the singer at the start of her *Friends* album. It was Warwick's idea to invite her friend Stevie Wonder, fresh from working with her on the *Lady in Red* soundtrack, to cut a vocal to the track at a later date and Sager's idea to invite her friend Elizabeth Taylor to Stevie's session. It was decided after Wonder's performance that this would make an ideal candidate for a charity record and that it might be fun to add more "friends."

"That's What Friends Are For." Most of the all-star charity 45s of the Eighties sound more like pledge drives than songs. This one is distinguished by its lack of ya-gotta-lend-a-helping-hand self-righteousness that might've dogged it if amFar had been its primary impetus.

With the song's conversion from the "Night Shift Love Theme" into an amfAR anthem, anything that could be construed as a sex/love angle was taken out of the second verse. The new lyrics gave Wonder the ironic declaration *"Well, you came and opened me and now there's so much more I see"* and afforded Elton John yet another video opportunity to raise his eyebrows, clutch his arms and wrench the word "heart" out of his mouth. The two men had also just worked together when Wonder played harmonica on John's 1983 hit "Guess That's Why They Call It the Blues"; between them they had already notched six No. 1 duets. Warwick's last pseudo-duet (can you consider it a duet if four Spinners are boogalooing behind Phillipe Wynne?) had resulted in a No. 1 hit, yet her only other singing partners on record had been Sacha Distel and Isaac Hayes, who'd done live recordings with her. Gladys Knight, as far as the public knew, had only sung with the Pips, but she nearly reduces this to a "Gladys Knight and…" recording when her extraordinary voice kicks the whole media event into high gear. Dionne returns for the last half-minute of the record to remind everyone it's her session. There is a sense of closure in Warwick finally getting to No. 1 with a Bacharach melody, even if it had to be on a playing field as crowded as this one.

1982

"That's What Friends Are For." Burt and Carole make a rare sheet-music appearance. This photo was taken during the music-video shoot: all four friends tracked their vocals on separate sessions.

In the *This Is Now* documentary, Sager points up the inherent differences in her own and her ex-husband's approaches to writing, a clear indication of why they ultimately stopped working as a team. The two hit a deadlock on the first two syllables of the song, namely the "And I" prefix. "I got so pissed off, it's just a little eighth note, sixteenth note," she laughingly complained. "What does that matter? But I think that's part of his brilliance is that those sixteenth notes, that thing that most people I've ever written with would just say, 'Fine,' he was so precise about. It was so important to him, he could sit in his music room and spend an hour on whether he did or didn't write that sixteenth note.... But he was right, and that's why the song starts with 'And I...'."

It apparently worked with the record buying public, who simultaneously sent this to the top of the pop and R&B charts, the first such occurrence in Bacharach's career. Amazingly, Bacharach and Sager would repeat this feat six months later.

Other Versions: *Burt Bacharach (1982) • Joanie Bartels (1997) • Shirley Bassey (1991) • Cilla Black & Cliff Richard (1993) • Joe Bourne (1993) • Tom Browne (1994) • Carola - "A Musical Tribute to Burt Bacharach" medley (2001) • Columbia Ballroom Orchestra (1984) • Perry Como (1987) • Ray Conniff (1986) • Alden David & Peter Triggvi • Carl Doy • Bill Easley (1996) • The Jet Set (1999) • Peter Land (1996) • Patrick Lindner - "Wenn man Freunde hat" (1999) • Keff McCulloch (1996) • Anita Meyer (1989) • Mantovani Orchestra • Paul Mauriat (1986) • Orchestra Manhattan (1987) • Brendan Power • Helen Reddy (1998) • Royal Dragoon Guards • RTE Concert Orchestra/Richard Hayman (1995) • Starlight Orchestra (1995) • The Swarbriggs • Gary Tesca (1995) • Greg Vail (1996) • Dionne Warwick & Friends (1985)*

"Heartlight" (Burt Bacharach - Carole Bayer Sager - Neil Diamond)
First recorded by Neil Diamond
Columbia 03219 (*Billboard* pop #5, AC #1)
Released September 1982

On July 4, 1982, Neil Diamond joined the newlywed Bacharachs in New York to catch a showing of *E.T. the Extraterrestrial.* Inspired by the film's heartwarming story of a displaced alien longing for home, the trio wrote "Heartlight." But exploitation songs were no longer the welcome promotional tool they were in the Famous Music days, and Universal Studios was none too thrilled about the team's nod to the little guy with the chest night-light. As a result, the studio extracted $25,000 for copyright infringement from the writers. MCA Records, owned by Universal, had just issued its own Michael Jackson–narrated *Story of E.T.* album with the Alan and Marilyn Bergman song "Somewhere in the Dark," and suddenly someone else is riding across the moon with Elliott's outer-space friend. Perhaps MCA Records was just getting even with Diamond, who defected from its roster when he signed with Columbia in 1972. No one would've been the wiser about the song's inspiration had it not become such a big hit and had Diamond not posed in *People* magazine with E.T., flashing the No. 1 sign.

Other Versions: *Neil Diamond (live1987, 1995) • Anita Meyer (1989)*

"I'm Guilty," "Front Page Story," "Hurricane (Swept Away)," "In Ensenada," "Lost among the Stars" (Burt Bacharach - Carole Bayer Sager - Neil Diamond)
Recorded by Neil Diamond
From the album *Heartlight,* Columbia QC 38359 (*Billboard* LP #9)
Released November 1982

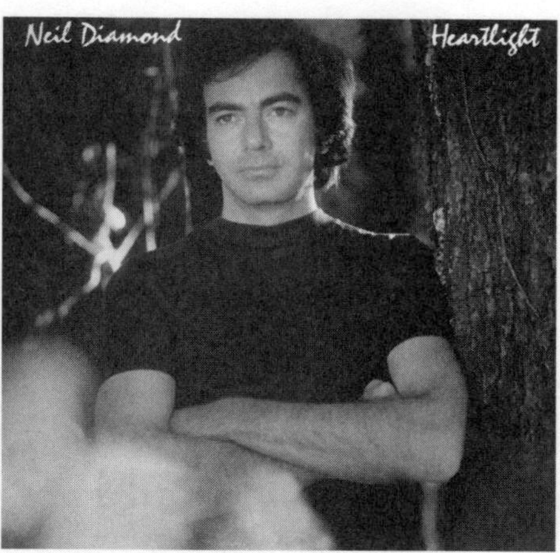

Neil Diamond. Despite the E.T. tie-in, it wasn't the kids who sent "Heartlight" the top of the pop charts, it was the adult contemporaries who bent to Neil.

Diamond's first album following his cinematic debut in *The Jazz Singer* found him adopting the excessive expenditures of a major motion picture production. Six studios were engaged concurrently—two for overdubs, two for mixing, one for recording and one for the sole purpose of working with writer/arranger/producer Michael Masser on what wound up being a solitary track on the album.

In the biography *Neil Diamond: Solitary Star*, writer Richard Wiseman interviewed Diamond's recording engineer Ron Hitchcock about the making of the *Heartlight* album and the problems Hitchcock encountered serving three masters in six studios. After he mixed "Front Page Story," Hitchcock recalled, Bacharach and Sager walked in and instantly vetoed it. "It turns out that Burt Bacharach had his engineers, his people, his trip. He's a very strong producer, a very strong writer, and he knows what he wants, how and when he wants it.…And I got thrown to the lions, quite frankly." Before the song was wrapped up, two of Diamond's engineers and two of Bacharach's had taken a crack at mixing the song.

Besides grappling with the "two very serious egos" of Bacharach and Diamond, Hitchcock also had Sager to contend with. "She's not pleasant to work with," he griped. "Once Neil and Burt decided they liked something, she would always dislike it and throw a real kink into it." Yet once work was over they all became jovial again, as if it were a particularly grueling but enjoyable tennis match.

It's a particularly grueling set of songs to slog through, nearly all listless Fender Rhodes-riddled ballads. On "In Ensenada," Diamond demonstrates an annoying nasal likeness to Dana Carvey's Grumpy Old Man character, and the tepid tempos throughout might even coax cantankerous listeners to cane their turntables. It's dismal going when "Love among the Stars," a pastiche of "Trains and Boats and Planes," turns out to be the uptempo song in the bunch. Knowing Bacharach's aversion to reprising the past, this nod to Burt's former life had to be Diamond's idea. Neither follow-up single to the title track did much to turn on anyone's "heartlight"; even the mixed-to-perfection "Front Page Story" only managed to do 65 before decelerating in reverse.

The trio's next collaboration, a racehorse Bacharach and Sager purchased and named Heartlight No. One, offered some hope for the future. The Eclipse Award–winning three-year-old filly won her first race after a Diamond serenade in the stable. This ritual continued for as long as the horse kept up her winning streak.

1983

David Foster. The original release of this album didn't include Foster's instrumental version of "Hard to Say I'm Sorry" but instead featured a vocal duet by David Foster and Vicki Moss entitled "Love at Second Sight." That song was later covered by Dionne Warwick on her album *Friends*.

"Our Lovely Days" (Burt Bacharach - F. Audat)
Recorded by Nancy Wilson
From the 12-inch EP *Your Eyes,* Nippon Columbia (Japan release only)
Released January 1983

This is the second of only three Bacharach extracurricular collaborations without Carole Bayer Sager during their decade-plus marriage. Disenchanted with the record business in the United States, jazz singer Nancy Wilson complained in the pages of *Jet* magazine that "I can't sing for a splice in the middle," adding, "When they stopped recording live, they started doing things you can't reproduce live." With that, her U.S. discography stopped cold in 1982 and didn't resume until she recorded for Columbia in 1987. In that gap are several hard-to-find Japanese-only releases, with Wilson captured live in a Tokyo studio sans mixing-board trickery. This move would win her the respect accorded to purist male singers like Tony Bennett and Mel Tormé, but without the corresponding media hoopla.

"Heart Strings" (Burt Bacharach - David Foster)
Recorded by David Foster
From the album *The Best of Me,* Mobile Fidelty MFSL 1-123
Released early 1983

From "Heartlight" we turn to "Heart Strings," an instrumental found on the first-ever David Foster album, which Foster cheekily titled *The Best of Me* after a song he co-wrote with Richard Marx. It was originally released on Mobile Fidelity, an audiophile label that specialized in albums pressed on high quality 90- and 110-gram vinyl for people who enjoy yelling "hold it on its sides" at their spouses. For the first two minutes it's just synthetic and acoustic piano dancing around each other peaceably, until a rhythm section intervenes.

Following somewhat in Bacharach's *Hitmaker* footsteps, Foster included some of his better-known compositions written for other artists on this debut, which is currently available on a Japanese import (Sound Design P33S20015). With the later addition of lyrics, this instrumental would become "Love Will Show Us How," which only served to demonstrate how melodically similar it is to "That's What Friends Are For."

"Blame It on Me" (Burt Bacharach - Carole Bayer Sager)
First recorded by Peabo Bryson and Roberta Flack
From the album *Born to Love,* Capitol 12284
Released July 1983

It must have been difficult for Roberta Flack to carry on with her 1980 tour only months after her great friend and singing partner Donny Hathaway committed suicide. Yet she developed some chemistry with her touring co-headliner Peabo Bryson, captured for posterity on the *Live and*

More album. When Flack was ready to undertake some new duets, Bryson was the obvious choice to help her sing the Gerry Goffin-Michael Masser song "Tonight, I Celebrate My Love." That became a Top 20 hit and continued to enjoy popularity when it became Bo and Hope's theme song on the long-running TV soap opera *Days of Our Lives*.

When the logical duet cash-in album followed, it contained two Bacharach-Sager contributions, with "Blame It on Me" programmed directly after "Tonight, I Celebrate My Love." Sager is quick to point out that unlike the preceding hit, it's "not a night for celebration," since both leaving lovers are blaming themselves for being the wrong person for the other one. Sager kicks off the breakup with the comical opening salvo *"due to certain circumstances,"* as if anticipating a lover's mad rush to the box office to demand his or her money back. This Bacharach production combines a quiet-storm groove with fat mechanical tom-toms that occasionally sound like microphone pops, a welcome departure from the sterile sounds he was entangled with through much of the Eighties.

Nancy Wilson. Primarily a jazz singer, she made overtures to the pop world in the Sixties with hits like "How Glad I Am," and "Face It Girl, It's Over." It was then that she recorded four Bacharach tunes: "Alfie," "Reach Out for Me," "Wives and Lovers" and "Waiting for Charlie to Come."

"Maybe" (Burt Bacharach - Carole Bayer Sager - Marvin Hamlisch)

First recorded by Peabo Bryson and Roberta Flack
From the MGM film *A Romantic Comedy*
From the album *Born to Love,* Capitol 12284
Released July 1983

If you can find a record written by a woman, her ex-husband and her future ex-husband—*buy it!* In the well-adjusted world of adult contemporary music, these unlikely forces converged when Marvin Hamlisch was working on a score for *A Romantic Comedy.* Sager continued to work with Marvin Hamlisch on soundtracks after their divorce papers were filed, and Bacharach and Hamlisch worked together indirectly when the latter did the orchestral score on *Something Big* and *The April Fools*, both of which had Bacharach-David title songs. Bacharach also provided the ending to the Hamlisch-arranged "You And Me (We Wanted It All)" on *Sometimes Late at Night*.

On "Maybe," Sager takes a mature and novel approach for a romantic ballad, choosing truth and honesty over romantic fire. Bryson and Flack are reconciling lovers willing to lower expectations below pre-courtship levels to make the relationship work again. To contradict Jimmy Van Heusen and Sammy Cahn, love might not be lovelier the second time around in the absence of falling stars, candles and guitars, but at least it will be more believable. Sager's future ex-husbands pull off some impressive musical sleight of hand of their own: the chorus modulates a half-step higher than the verses. When the second verse kicks in, Peabo's in a higher register, and from this elevated observation deck you can see the string section mounting an assault. Try getting your Barry Manilow records to do that.

Other Versions: *Keff McCulloch (1996)*

1983

Melissa Manchester. Sager co-wrote two of her biggest hits, "Midnight Blue" and "Don't Cry Out Loud." Manchester also sang one of the *National Lampoon's* best musical parodies, a swipe at Les Crane's 1971 hit "Desiderata" entitled "Deteriorata." It's found on the 1972 *Radio Dinner* LP.

"Time" (Melissa Manchester - Burt Bacharach - Carole Bayer Sager)
Recorded by Melissa Manchester
From the album *Emergency,* Arista AL 8094
Released fall 1983

Scoring an up-tempo hit like "You Should See How She Talks about Her" gave Melissa Manchester the idea of reinventing herself as a synth-pop queen—a gutsy move which showed off her great rock voice in dramatic style but bewildered her old fans while accruing few new converts. When neither single from *Emergency* placed in the Hot 100, Arista quietly showed Manchester the door with a request not to cry out loud. "Time," the final cut on her last Arista album, was one of the album's few AOR holdouts, dappled with a shower of glacial DX7 sounds to distinguish it from her older predictable ballads.

"A Chance for Heaven" (Swimming Theme from the Official Music of the XXIIIrd Olympiad Los Angeles 1984)" (Burt Bacharach - Carole Sager - Christopher Cross)
First recorded by Christopher Cross
Columbia 38-04492 (*Billboard* pop #76)
Released June 1984

Olympic tie-ins are the most brazenly brainless of product endorsements: do we actually need to have an Official™ Potato Chip of the Olympic Games? We do, however, need official Olympiad music for athletes to train and excel to. With the impact of the 1982 Vangelis movie hit "Chariots of Fire" and the accompanying cinematic re-creation of the 1924 Olympics, the pressure was on to come up with more of the same sort of muscular, win-at-all-cost anthems. While this rush of whooshing synthesizers can send ABC's Olympic correspondent Jim McKay's frozen feet a-tapping, the rest of us might get sidelined by the ludicrous lyrical belief that victory is *"a gift from the angels,"* as if bad people never won anything. Worse, Cross keeps harping about *"one more mountain to climb"* on what's supposed to be a swimming theme. Why couldn't he have just rewritten "Sailing" three times as fast?

Other Versions: *Paul Mauriat (1984)*

Star-Crossed Chris. Had this record become a hit, it would've been the most cumbersome Top 40 title since "Jeremiah Peabody's Poly Unsaturated Quick Dissolving Fast Acting Pleasant Tasting Green and Purple Pills."

"Crazy" (Burt Bacharach - Carole Bayer Sager - Neil Diamond)
First recorded by Neil Diamond
From the album *Primitive,* Columbia QC 39199 (*Billboard* LP #35)
Released August 1984

Despite the close contact with E.T. last time around, the songs on the ensuing *Heartlight* album could've used some serious lightening up. And seeing all the differences of opinion each writer encountered during the mixing stage, it was a good idea to have someone with objective ears in the studio. Enter producer Richard Perry to inject a little oomph into the proceedings. To make up for inducing raging sleep last time around, the trio of writers came up with "Crazy," a surprisingly infectious dance trance that sounds as if Diamond accidentally walked into a Howard Jones session and was having too much fun to leave.

If Diamond sounded like a party animal for a change, Bacharach's matched his enthusiasm with ringing Yamaha sequences and a fat digital bass. Although Bacharach is credited with arranging, David Foster gets credit for synthesizer arranging and conducting on the other side of the dust sleeve and is more likely responsible for this track's kick. Of course, no modern rock station worth its weight in Depeche Mode promotional items would've kept the needle on the wax once Diamond's agitated baritone started getting crazy with the vivacious girl singers, so it was never released as a single. Two ballads were lifted off *Primitive* for the 45 market before "Crazy" was pasted onto the flip of the third single, "You Make It Feel Like Christmas," which people had roughly 32 shopping days to buy and file away for another year.

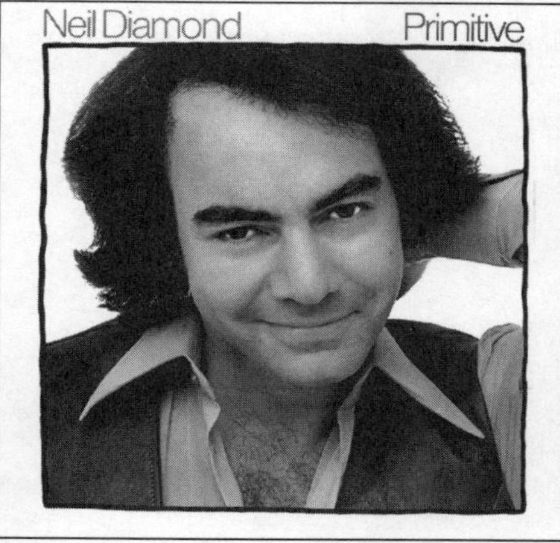

Primitive. CBS requested that Neil replace four of the songs on the original draft of this album. They were "Hit Man," "Act Like a Man," Positive Vibrations" and a song he must've penned with Bacharach in mind, "What Was It Like For You, Marlene?"

"Sleep with Me Tonight" (Burt Bacharach - Carole Bayer Sager - Neil Diamond)
First recorded by Neil Diamond
From the album *Primitive,* Columbia QC 39199 (*Billboard* LP #35)
Released August 1984

"Sleep with Me Tonight" was more atypical Neil Diamond, begging forgiveness for not bringing flowers and asking if he can spend the night forever. And he had a decent shot: there was more pulse coursing through this tune than through any of the lifeless *Heartlight* ballads, thanks to a combination of congas and celestial synthesizer chimes that sound like close encounters of the Burt kind. Reprising the "Heartlight" formula, a big, rousing chorus was added to keep the blue-haired ladies in the audience happy. But less of them heard it than would've in previous years, thanks to the internecine battles between Diamond and Columbia following his temporary defection to Capitol for the soundtrack of *The Jazz Singer*. Relations were strained even further after Diamond cancelled a two-record live set that Columbia had scheduled for the 1983 Christmas shopping season.

So when Diamond handed *Primitive* in to Columbia president Walter Yetnikoff, the album was forwarded back with a request to remove four below-average compositions and replace them with new ones. Diamond, badly stung by this constructive criticism, filed a lawsuit on March 1, 1984, to force Columbia into releasing the album as is. The label filed a countersuit on March 9 and was prepared to call Bacharach, Sager, Perry, Diamond's manager and band, the studio engineers and Diamond himself, as well as to subpoena any document related to the creation of the songs on the album. By the end of April, Diamond dropped his suit and Columbia installed executive producer Denny Diante to supervise the completion of the album. In its original form, the *Primitive* album contained "Sleep with Me Tonight" and "Crazy," both of which got face-lifts because of what Diante cited as dated production values. But despite the producer's objection that the title was a played-out theme, it remained unchanged.

Other Versions: *Patti LaBelle (1986)*

Finder of Lost Loves. It was Bacharach's only commissioned TV theme and the title track of a quickly disappearing Dionne Warwick album. The balance of this long player consisted of, yawn, more Barry Manilow productions.

"Turn Around" (Burt Bacharach - Carole Bayer Sager - Neil Diamond)
Recorded by Neil Diamond
Columbia 04541 (*Billboard* pop #62)
Released August 1984

The four songs ejected from *Primitive* never surfaced on another LP, so it's hard to say whether Columbia was just nitpicking, but the completed album was a vast improvement over *Heartlight*. One of the tracks added at the behest of producer Denny Diante was "Turn Around," singled out from a bunch of writing demos as having the most potential. Yet another ballad in the lurching tradition of "September Morn," "Love on the Rocks" and "Heartlight," it has Diamond demanding *"you loved me once before, please love me once again."* This play-it-safe first volley from the album proved a strategic mistake, as *Primitive* contained some of Diamond's most vital up-tempo writing and singing since *Beautiful Noise*. Blame can also be laid at the feet of Columbia's promotion department, which failed to get behind the album with the same blazing support they'd demonstrated in the past.

Producer Diante notes in Rich Wiseman's book *Solitary Star* that Bacharach's perfectionism made the session for "Turn Around" rather turbulent. "I remember Neil inverted a note. We were on the third chorus on the way out and Neil, instead of going 'da DA' went 'DA da.' And of course Burt had a fit: *'That's not right!'*...I have so many punch–ins on 'Turn Around,' on words, inverted melodies." Neil obediently complied with everyone's suggestions, and the songs on *Primitive* are a marked improvement over the collaborations on *Heartlight*, an indication that Bacharach's take-charge stance was making much of the difference.

"Finder of Lost Loves." This 1999 release gives Bacharach fans nearly a half-dozen tracks never issued on compact disc any other time. You can also get this "lost" theme on *The Best of Glenn Jones*, but then you'll have to suffer us laughing and pointing at you.

"Finder of Lost Loves" aka "Find Love" (Burt Bacharach - Carole Bayer Sager)
Recorded by Dionne Warwick with Glenn Jones
Arista 9281 (*Billboard* R&B #47)
Released January 1985

Riding high on the success of *The Love Boat* and *Fantasy Island*, TV producer Aaron Spelling put both ideas in a blender to come up with a third series with equal pinches of love and fantasy. That series was *Finder of Lost Loves*, starring Tony Franciosa as part Cupid, part detective Cary Maxwell, who reunites lovers who somehow couldn't make it work without the help of Maxwell's team of romance enablers and Oscar, a highly sophisticated computer bank that does most of the "finding" legwork. No computers were necessary when the star-crossed Bacharach and Warwick were reunited after 13 years of estrangement. It was Spelling who first suggested contacting Warwick and Sager who urged her husband on.

When Bacharach made the cold call, he was greeted with a querulous "Burt who?" After Bacharach said, "It's me, Charlie," her old nickname for him, the years of icy separation melted away.

While a Warwick-Bacharach reunion was big news, the absence of Hal David kept it from being a front-page story. It wasn't much of a recording either: a pretty melody expertly transported by Warwick eventually gets driven into the cold earth once former gospel singer Glenn Jones rides in on the most ho-hum key changes this side of the Copacabana. In the end, it's not all that different from the many predictable Barry Manilow–produced paeans Dionne had already recorded for Arista. And Bacharach and Sager don't help matters, okaying yet another passionless, paid-by-the-hour guitar solo. Despite one season of prime-time exposure and the media hype of a reunion, this theme didn't entice the pop people, although R&B listeners seemed more willing to snuggle up to it. Spelling's Midas touch was becoming tarnished, as *Finders of Lost Loves* went into hiding after summer reruns were dutifully screened.

Extravagant Gestures. The melancholy finale to Dionne's *Friends* album is also the title of Sager's enjoyably funny novel about the fictitious best-selling author Katie Fielding. The book name-drops real-life luminaries from Phil Donahue and Halston to Sager's pal Liz Taylor. She dedicates it to Burt, "for making my life so much more."

"Extravagant Gestures" (Burt Bacharach - Carole Bayer Sager)
"How Long?" (Burt Bacharach - Carole Bayer Sager)
Recorded by Dionne Warwick
From the album *Friends,* Arista 8398 (*Billboard* LP #12)
Released December 1985

While Dionne Warwick never became the recognized voice of Bacharach-Sager the way she was with Bacharach-David, here the threesome attempt the kinds of songs the bygone team excelled at—songs of romantic despondency and songs with a burning concern for humanity. "Extravagant Gestures" finds Dionne once again acting noble about being the one getting left behind *("when someone goes away, someone has to stay")* and not too proud to weep about it, either *("planes still make me cry")*. Unlike her traveling ex-companion, the song doesn't go anywhere, and her promise of no "extravagant gestures" rings all too true. However, the song's simple virtues are preferable to the empty bluster of "Finder of Lost Loves. "How Long" is a brooding meditation on the general state of affairs that's a little bit of "What the World Needs Now," a little bit of "Windows of the World" and a great deal of Marvin Gaye's "What's Going On"; in fact, the song's middle eight can be classified as a direct lift.

Friends. To date, Dionne's last Top 40 album.

"Stay Devoted" (Burt Bacharach - Carole Bayer Sager)
Recorded by Dionne Warwick
From the album *Friends,* Arista 8398 (*Billboard* LP #12)
Released December 1985

An agreeable mellow funk ballad, the kind the Pointer Sisters did on "He's So Shy," right down to the playful keyboard line in the chorus.

Other Versions: *Anita Meyer (1989)*

1986

Patti LaBelle (1985). The *Winner in You* album that contained her smash hit of "On My Own" with Michael McDonald also housed a rousing solo stab at "Sleep with Me Tonight."

"On My Own" (Burt Bacharach - Carole Bayer Sager)
Recorded by Patti LaBelle and Michael McDonald
MCA 52770 (*Billboard* pop #1, R&B #1)
Released March 1986

Bacharach had the title first and became enraptured with the melancholy three notes that buttressed them. Sager was less committed initially and thought the progression sounded Polynesian, but she wrote irreverent lyrics to it, including the line *"Now we're up to talking divorce and we weren't even married."* The song was supplied to Patti LaBelle for her *Winner in You* album. Producer Richard Perry recorded a version but was ultimately unsatisfied, and when Bacharach and Sager tried their hand at it, they still thought it was missing something.

That something turned out to be blue-eyed soul man Michael McDonald, everyone's favorite duet partner. His cameo was fleshed out to a second lead vocal for a unique duet in which the two principals are truly on their own: there's not one line in the song the two sing in unison until the last dying seconds of the fadeout. But this isn't like Sinatra's *Duets* album, where everyone's phoning in his parts. McDonald may have only sung to LaBelle's taped voice, but he's committed to the song, playing it out thematically like one of two lovers separated bicoastally, which he and LaBelle were. Even after being spliced into a video together, even after the song went to No. 1, they still hadn't met. The first time the "On My Own" pair converged, it was for an appearance on *The Tonight Show*.

In the vocal cutting contest, it's McDonald who commands the verses (where LaBelle contorts her voice and often comes off cartoonish) and McDonald who gets to invoke the infamous Bayer-Sager "hey" midway through the number. This time it's not a seductive "hey," it's more of a what-the-fuck-are-you-trying-to-prove "hey." Two No. 1 hits on the pop and R&B charts in less than six months is Bacharach's best-ever statistical achievement. But if you examine them carefully for innovative new ideas, both "That's What Friends Are For" and "On My Own" employ musical elements like harmonica and Michael McDonald that Bacharach had already used on the *Together* soundtrack, combined with the popular celebrity-pairing format, which is still capable of generating reams of press today if a novel enough combination that doesn't involve Willie Nelson or Julio Iglesias is struck.

Other Versions: *Sheena Easton (2000) • The Jet Set (1999) • Lalah Hathaway (1997) • Reba McEntire (1995) • Des O'Connor (1985) • Starlight Orchestra (1995)*

"On My Own"? Quick-cut videos on MTV shortened people's attention span for hearing one person sing a song all the way through. Initially approached to guest on two Bacharach-Sager tracks for Patti LaBelle's *The Winner in You* album, McDonald passed on "Sleep with Me Tonight" but agreed to make a brief cameo on this record. It was eventually fleshed out to a full-length duet and a costarring video.

"I'll See You on the Radio (Laura)" and "Me Beside You" (Burt Bacharach - Carole Bayer Sager - Neil Diamond)
Recorded by Neil Diamond
From the album *Headed for the Future,* Columbia 40368 (*Billboard* LP #20)
Released May 1986

After all the bruised egos engendered during the *Primtive* debacle, Columbia and Neil Diamond decided to make nice again with *Headed for the Future*. The album received a massive promotional push and coincided with a CBS-TV special. Diamond decided to go contemporary on every track, teaming up with Stevie Wonder, Bryan Adams and Maurice White of Earth, Wind & Fire. In another departure, Diamond abandoned his practice of using pre-*Jazz Singer* photos on the covers of his albums. This move was applauded by fans who wanted Neil to grow old along with them, but for those who weren't paying close attention, it gave the impression that Diamond had aged overnight, like bad cheese.

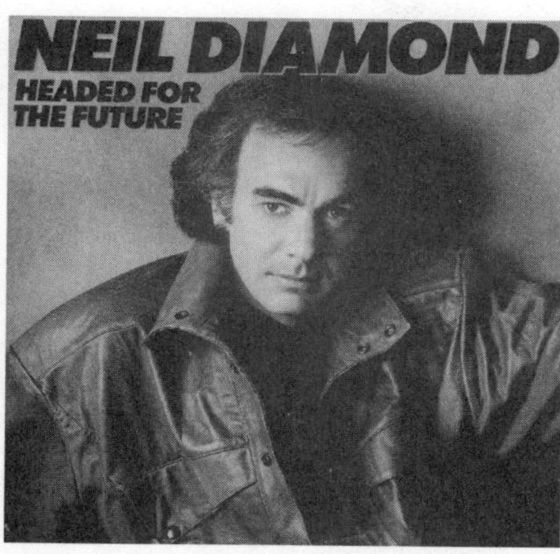

The Story of My Life. That was the title of this album in an earlier, more autobiographical incarnation. Columbia deemed the results not commercial enough and sent Diamond back to the drawing board to write some more upbeat songs. Although it fit the upbeat criteria, the Bacharach-David classic "Story of My Life" was never in consideration for either album.

Fortunately, bad cheese would not be an apt description for Diamond and the Bacharachs' latest round of songs. They seemed to have hit their stride on the previous album and steered clear of the geriatric sound that fossilized Diamond on "Heartlight." In a slow R&B groove, Diamond kicks himself because someone else got the girl on "Me Beside You." Sager gets in a few wry observations *("Saying it's kind of funny, baby, but it's the kind of funny that can break your heart")*, while Bacharach proves he can elicit heart pangs with his synthesized strings when the words are up to the task.

"I'll See You on the Radio (Laura)" finds a summer affair between two married people kept alive whenever the radio plays summer songs in lite-rotation through autumn. A plausibly au courant production with female backgrounds acting out the part of the radio, the song seems to lapse into monotony when a payoff bridge fails to materialize.

"Love Always" (Burt Bacharach - Carole Bayer Sager - Bruce Roberts)
Recorded by El DeBarge
Gordy 1857 (*Billboard* pop #43, R&B #7)
Released July 1986

Motown signed up the talented DeBarge family in hopes that it had another Jackson 5 on its hands. In the rush to produce another superstar of *Thriller* proportions, the label pushed El DeBarge into the solo spotlight in 1985, second-billing the family ("El DeBarge with DeBarge") before leaving them completely rudderless. El's sweet Michael Jackson tenor was the major selling point behind such ballads as "All This Love" and "Who's Holding Donna Now," but one misses his siblings' block harmonies on "Love Always," a by-the-numbers long-distance dedication unimaginatively produced and arranged by the Bacharachs.

El DeBarge. Although he left the group in 1985, the only way to obtain his solo hits on compact disc is to buy them is bundled on anthologies of the whole DeBarge family. Who says you can't go home again?

"Love Will Show Us How" (Burt Bacharach - Michael Jay Miltenberg - David Foster)
Recorded by Glenn Jones
From the album *Take It from Me,* RCA AFL1-5807
Released July 1986

Guesting on the Dionne-Burt reunion made Glenn Jones, onetime gospel singer and Norman Connors acolyte, something of an intimate friend. Thus the cupboard was opened, and Jones was served up a reheated Bacharach-Foster number, "Heart Strings," from Foster's first album, with afterthought lyrics by Michael Miltenberg.

1986

Dionne Warwick & Jeffrey Osborne. Another year, another duet.

"They Don't Make Them Like They Used To" (Burt Bacharach - Carole Bayer Sager)
Recorded by Kenny Rogers
From the Touchstone motion picture *Tough Guys*
RCA 5016, released October 1986

Ladies and gentlemen, I give you the star of stage, screen and rotisseries, Mr. Kenny Rogers, onetime leader of the rock group First Edition and later the Cosmo of cosmopolitan country music. His dalliances with Lionel Richie, Kim Carnes, Gladys Knight & the Pips, the Bee Gees, James Ingram, Richard Marx, David Foster and Sheena Easton all served to ease country music audiences out of the cornfields and into the lite-pop morass that envelops Nashville now. It was only a matter of time before Bacharach and Sager would get around to penning him a groggy valentine.

One year after his appearance on USA for Africa's "We Are the World," Rogers was already receding into the background of the pop music landscape. Recording a musical placebo like this didn't help.

"Love Power" (Burt Bacharach - Carole Bayer Sager)
Recorded by Dionne Warwick and Jeffrey Osborne
"In a World Such As This" (Burt Bacharach - Carole Bayer Sager - Bruce Roberts)
Recorded by Dionne Warwick
Arista 9567 (*Billboard* pop #12, R&B #5)
Released June 1987

"Saw a psychic in L.A. just the other day"

When Sager penned those really soothsayin'-something lyrics, little could she have known the affiliation Dionne Warwick would have with the Psychic Friends Network, an association that diminished the goodwill she'd earned from three decades of peerless singing. Warwick's last public brush with a psychic—when Linda Goodman advised her to add an *e* to her name—was nothing short of cataclysmic, and her stint as a psychic spokesperson would make her a *Tonight Show* punch line. No psychic apparently warned her about that looming disaster, but this harmless single yielded some immediate benefits, like restoring Dionne to the Top 20 after solo follow-ups to "That's What Friends Are For" did spotty business. There was no hiding her dependence on "friends," psychic or otherwise: every other single was now a double-billed affair.

Besides Jeffrey Osborne, the star power behind "Love Power" includes David Foster on synthesizer and Kenny G doing an alto saxophone solo. Going against type, Warwick stays in contralto territory for the entire chorus, while Osborne handles all the skyward vocal acrobatics. Most people would have a hard time distinguishing who is who when Warwick plumbs the depths of her lower range. Reportedly, Warwick sight-read the song and captured it in one take; the appealing raspiness of her vocal hints that she jumped into the song stone cold, without a warm-up exercise.

Dionne also swings low for "In a World Such As This," whose similarities to the top side make it seem like an earlier draft of "Love Power" without the power. Structured as a duet for the *Reservations for Two* album, this was probably one of those songs where the scheduled copilot failed to show up and anonymous background vocalists were enlisted instead. In latter-day Dionne songs such as this, there seems to be a missive to put forth some affirmative life message, a be-all-you-can-be philosophy no doubt inspired by the uplifting effects of her psychic networking behind the scenes. But it led her away from those wrist-slashing hits of yore, like "I Just Don't Know What to Do with Myself" and "Anyone Who Had a Heart," that we remember better today than these positive platitudes.

Reservations for Two. "The Album of Her Lifetime" but not the last time Dionne and Friends would gang up on us. Can someone get this woman to sing in an isolation booth?

"Heartbreak of Love" (Burt Bacharach - Carole Bayer Sager - Diane Warren)
Recorded by Dionne Warwick and Bonnie Pointer
From the album *Reservations for Two,* Arista AL-8446
Released June 1987

Most people would consider Carole Bayer Sager a prolific songwriter, but even her catalog pales compared to the 800-plus songs Diane Warren has written, and that's probably a conservative estimate. Unlike Sager, Warren isn't reliant on a partner for the musical settings and has come up with some of her biggest hits solitaire-style, such as Celine Dion's "Because You Loved Me, " Whitney Houston's "You Were Loved," Toni Braxton's "Un-Break My Heart" and Aerosmith's "I Don't Want to Miss a Thing." As she was almost as inexorable a pop presence as David Foster, her writing with the Bacharachs would seem a forgone eventuality.

By 1987, three of the four Pointer Sisters had recorded solo albums. Sister Bonnie joins Dionne for one of those why-do-lovers-break-each-other's-hearts conversations, to which the only suitable response is a world-weary "I know, I know." Pleasant urban-adult fodder, livened by some spirited singing and a chirpy bridge.

Natalie Cole. Some speculate the real reason she recorded *Unforgettable* was that after naming her albums *Inseparable, Unpredictable, Thankful, Live, I'm Ready, Dangerous* and *Everlasting,* that was the only adjective left untapped.

"In My Reality" and "Split Decision" (Burt Bacharach - Carole Bayer Sager)
Recorded by Natalie Cole
From the album *Everlasting,* EMI Manhattan 53051
Released June 1987

This album found the daughter of Nat "King" Cole on a career upswing after years of substance abuse and spotty live appearances had caused Capitol Records to drop her. After a brief stint at Epic and Atlantic's Modern subsidiary, she returned on Capitol's lower priority EMI-Manhattan subsidiary with *Everlasting*. The album became her first million seller since 1979, with several dance hits that crossed over into pop. These two first-class Bacharach-Sager breakup numbers weren't among them, but each provided the album with some comfortable rest spots. "In My Reality" is a swinging jazz-lounge number that has Sager raising the same East Coast versus West Coast questions that gangster-

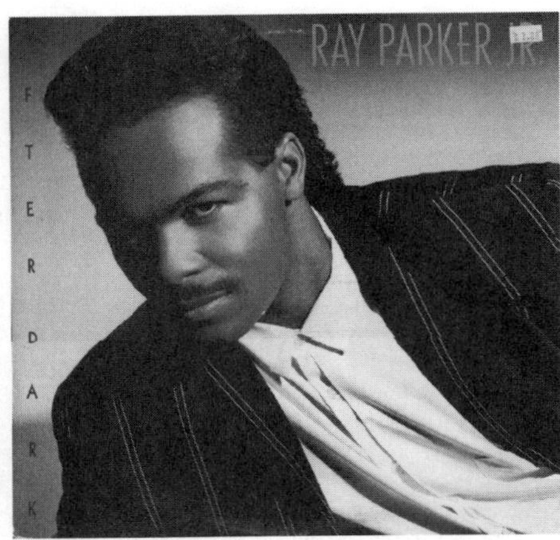

Ray Parker Jr. The former Raydio star got the opportunity to sue Huey Lewis over "Ghostbusters" in March 2001 when he accused Lewis of violating a confidentiality agreement by talking about the settlement on VH1's *Behind the Music*.

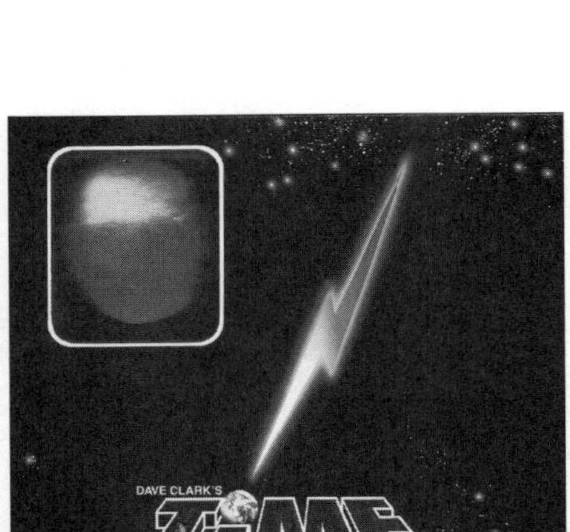

Dave Clark's Time - The Musical. Although they did not appear in the London that ran from 1986 to 1988 and starred Sir Cliff Richard and Sir Laurence Olivier in his last stage appearance, Dionne Warwick and Burt Bacharach make a joint appearance on the celebrity-studded double album that followed the show's opening. Other celebrities included Stevie Wonder, Julian Lennon, and Freddie Mercury.

rappers feel the need to settle with bullets. Cole requires only the *"need to feel to the heat of the street"* and to be away from Hollywood, where reality is just a word people use to pitch gritty police scripts. "Split Decision" has a nimble melody that percolates with the bass line, but you might want to set your watch during the predictable sax solo.

"Over You" (Burt Bacharach - Carole Bayer Sager - Ray Parker Jr.)
Recorded by Ray Parker Jr. with Natalie Cole
"Perfect Lovers" (Burt Bacharach - Carole Bayer Sager – Nathan East)
Recorded by Ray Parker Jr.
From the album *After Dark,* Geffen 9 24124-2
Released July 1987

Ray Parker Jr.'s hit-making career was blemished in 1984 when he was sued for ripping off Huey Lewis' No. 1 song "I Want a New Drug" to come up with *his* only No. 1, the *Ghostbusters* theme. The real scandal here wasn't that director Ivan Reitman first approached Lewis to do the theme but that the dozing public bought the same record twice. This collective amnesia should've helped them take "Over You" to heart. It sounds like millions of other forgettable songs, but its failure to crack the Top 100 meant that no litigious songwriters got any bright ideas. It's pretty unflattering for all involved that Parker's duet with Cole doesn't come alive until the two deviate from the script and Natalie starts singing another former No. 1 hit, the Staple Singers' "Let's Do It Again."

"Perfect Lovers" is a slight improvement, thanks largely to a keyboard-generated steel-drum solo where the pitch-control wheel is liberally jerked. One comes away with the overall impression that Bacharach may have been listening to a lot of Sade when this track was conceived.

"Overnight Success" (Burt Bacharach - Carole Bayer Sager)
First recorded by Gladys Knight and the Pips
From the album *All Our Love,* MCA 42004
Released December 1987

Gladys Knight had been singing with her brother Merald ("Bubba") Knight and various combinations of cousins since the age of 12, when the group, then simply billed as the Pips, cut "Every Beat of My Heart" for the Huntom label. Except for a three-year stint in the late Seventies, when legal problems prevented them from recording as a group, they remained a constant pop presence. This album marked the end of the road for the retiring Pips, which gave MCA a perfect marketing angle to jump-start the public's craving for the legendary group it had taken for granted.

"Overnight Success," the last track on the last album, provides a thoughtful farewell to a group that began each show with a prayer to stay humble. There is subtle career advice to showbiz up-and-comers *("Just believe in what you're doing and try not to expect overnight success," "Some will last, some will burn out too fast"* and *"I've worked hard for my respect")* ; Sager even alludes to her husband's career washout, *Lost*

Horizon (*"the world is still a circle"* and the High Lama-ish reminder to *"just treat every person fairly"*), to keep him humble. MCA went for the dance floor with the album's two singles instead of highlighting this heartstring-tugger. Big mistake: this should've been the Pips' "Long and Winding Road"—or their "Someday We'll Be Together," as they *did* reunite for their Rock and Roll Hall of Fame induction ceremony in 1996.

Other Versions: *Anita Meyer (1989) • Anita Pointer (1987)*

Gladys Knight and the Pips. Knight performed her first-ever solo concert at Bally's in Las Vegas on March 30, 1989, 40 years after first getting up to sing at Mount Moriah Baptist Church at age four.

"Love Is Fire (Love Is Ice)" (Burt Bacharach - Carole Bayer Sager)
First recorded by Gladys Knight and the Pips
From the album *All Our Love,* MCA 42004
Released December 1987

Yet another fine Bacharach-Sager song about trial separations, but this one concerns a couple who were never married to begin with. The chorus has several catch phrases battling for title status—*"come back baby," "flashback"* and the *"love is fire, love is ice"* tag. Also confusing matters is the repetition of *"these are everchanging times,"* which might mean either that Sager was hot on that title and was trying it out in a few songs or that she was already cross-promoting for the *Baby Boom* theme song.

"Everchanging Times" (Burt Bacharach - Carole Bayer Sager - William Conti Jr.)
Recorded by Siedah Garrett
From the MGM/UA motion picture *Baby Boom*
Qwest 28163, released October 1987

Quincy Jones' discovery Siedah Garrett scored a major singer-songwriter coup by singing and writing on *Bad*, Michael Jackson's follow-up to the biggest-selling album of all time, *Thriller.* Garrett cowrote "Man in the Mirror" with Glen Ballard and stepped in to sing "I Just Can't Stop Loving You" after Barbra Streisand and Whitney Houston both turned down the invitation to sing it with Michael.

Garrett was contracted to sing this theme for the movie *Baby Boom,* an assignment that brought the Bacharachs together with Bill Conti Jr., the writer of the *Rocky* theme and the James Bond ballad "For Your Eyes Only." Yet for all this star power, the Siedah recording is an off-the-rack performance of what seemed like an off-the-rack song until it became an astonishingly good duet between the Queen of Soul and Michael McDonald. Chuck Negron, late of Three Dog Night, surpassed their efforts with a more pulsing drum loop arrangement, swirling synth strings and Three Dog three-part harmony. Having survived years of drug abuse and 36 unsuccessful rehab stints before coming back to performing music in 1994, Negron invests the line "every day I keep forgetting what's mind" with new meaning Sager couldn't have possibly imagined.

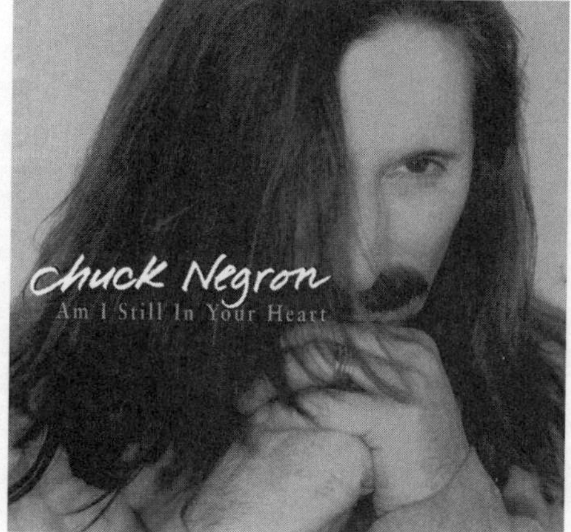

"Ever Changing Times." Chuck Negron chronicled his years of drug addiction and recovery in an autobiography entitled *Three Dog Nightmare,* published in 1999.

Other Versions: *Aretha Franklin & Michael McDonald (1991) • Chuck Negron (1995)*

1988

Arthur 2: On the Rocks. *Arthur I* was among the top-grossing films of 1981, with a domestic take of around $84 million, while this second coming petered out at around $14 million.

"Love Is My Decision" (Burt Bacharach - Carole Bayer Sager - Chris de Burgh)
Recorded by Chris de Burgh
"The Best of Times" and "Love Theme from Arthur" (Burt Bacharach)
Recorded by Burt Bacharach
From the soundtrack album *Arthur 2: On the Rocks,* A&M 3916
Released July 1988

Seeing Arthur panhandling in the movie ads should've tipped off moviegoers to downsize their expectations for *Arthur 2: On the Rocks*. That also goes for Bacharach's paltry score, which amounted to one vocal theme, an instrumental reprise from the last film and an inconsequential end-credit instrumental to subliminally evict people from the theater. The slapdash assembly of the *Night Shift* soundtrack is evident once again here, with the balance of the movie-souvenir album made up of previously released selections from A&M acts like Kylie Minogue, Brenda Russell and Orchestral Maneuvers in the Dark, all heard a millisecond or less in the film.

You knew *Arthur 2* was in trouble when director Bud Yorkin resurrected Oscar winner John Gielgud to make a cameo appearance, even though his character died in the first *Arthur*. No Lazarus spells were used on Christopher Cross, whose name had gotten considerably colder since the last movie; instead, a new golden boy named Chris (de Burgh, who'd scored a Top 3 hit with "The Lady in Red" the previous year) was enlisted to sing and take a songwriting credit. Sager desperately invokes the moon and New York City in the lyrics but this time without having to give Peter Allen any credit. Not that he'd want to take one for the unremarkable "Love Is My Decision," which installs a big choir towards the end to give the track some artificial propulsion.

Barbra Streisand. This was her 34th or 38th album, depending on whether you want to count greatest-hits collections or soundtracks. Nearly every album had a movie or TV special tie-in. The title track was from the Broadway musical *Goya*, and it was sung with another movie tie-in, Don Johnson.

"One More Time Around" (Burt Bacharach - Carole Bayer Sager - Tom Keane)
"Love Light" and "You and Me for Always" (Burt Bacharach - Carole Bayer Sager)
Recorded by Barbra Streisand
From the album *Till I Loved You,* Columbia 40880
Released October 1988

Till I Loved You ignored the multi-platinum success Streisand's *The Broadway Album* and returned to the scattershot approach of her 1984 pop album *Emotion*, using a different producer on virtually every cut in hopes that one might hit on something. This album contained the already-forgotten theme from the previous year's flipped-out Streisand chick flick *Nuts,* plus the title song, a laughable duet with her then-boyfriend Don Johnson that even he couldn't keep a straight face through. There's also a trio of Bacharach-Sager songs that might otherwise have gone to Neil Diamond, except that his 1988 album *The Best Years of Our Lives* was shaping up to be mostly songs he wrote with David Foster.

Songs like "One More Time Around" and "You and Me for Always" tend to overstay their welcome after Streisand has had a chance to hit every note in her astonishing range: it's here that the seeds of the intolerable Celine Dion are sown. Sager packs each song with relationship-counseling messages about giving love another chance and learning to trust and love again, maybe as a hint to Babs' then-current poster boy Don Johnson to behave or you won't be posing with Streisand on any more dust sleeves. As life never imitates art, by the time fans first pulled the shrink-wrap off this record, their romance had cooled, and all the singer had to show for it by Christmas was another platinum album.

June Pointer. Her best remembered Sisterless moment occurred in 1987, when the youngest Pointer played second fiddle to actor Bruce Willis on his Top 10 cover of "Respect Yourself." Already in a career slump when June's second solo album escaped attention, the Pointer Sisters returned with their nostalgia roots exposed in a 1995 revival of *Ain't Misbehavin'*.

"Need a Little Faith," (Burt Bacharach - Carole Bayer Sager)
Recorded by Patti LaBelle
From the album *Be Yourself,* MCA 6292
Released June 1989

As with most of her recordings, Patti's patented over-the-top eruptions at the end make it worth a listen, although this track has simpler built-in pleasures—affecting lines like *"I can't let go so I hold on too tight"* and an exquisite melody that allows LaBelle some agile octave jumping in the verses. But it all leads up to a chorus so routine it could be in latter-day Disney animated feature.

"Why Can't We Be Together" (Burt Bacharach - Carole Bayer Sager - Bruce Roberts)
Recorded by June Pointer
From the album *June Pointer,* Columbia 44315
Released 1989

With the Pointer Sisters/Richard Perry hit formula having exhausted itself several years earlier, it seemed like a sensible time for June Pointer to release a second solo effort. Carole Bayer Sager executive produces here, while every knob twiddler from Narada Michael Walden to Kashif gets a shot at pitching a hit June's way. A likeable up-tempo ballad that seems to have Pointer Sisters written all over it, it instead deputises one Phil Perry for what sounds like a reheated Peaches and Herb duet. This session raises an interesting query: if the Bacharachs are producing and Sager is also executive producing, does this mean Sager has veto power over Burt for the first time in their professional relationship? In later years, Bacharach admitted that Sager's desire for equal involvement in the music led to many disagreements, which then led to professional and personal estrangement. A far cry from asking Hal David if he thinks the triangle is helping a song.

1989

Dionne Warwick. Her 11 years at Arista had enough hits and misses to fill one album, but just remember that Scepter needed two albums just to accommodate the years 1962 through1969!

Love Hurts. Hey, all you couch potatoes looking for something to do, find the two minutes of Bacharach music hidden in this film. Go on. We'll wait.

"Take Good Care of You and Me" (Burt Bacharach - Carole Bayer Sager - Gerald Goffin)
Recorded by Dionne Warwick and Jeffrey Osborne, From the album *Greatest Hits 1979–1990,* Arista 8540
Released fall 1989

This troublesome Warwick best-of compilation drives home the point that Dionne may have gone to her friends once too often to prop up her Arista releases. This collection should've been called *Dionne & Friends' Greatest Hits,* since Elton John, Gladys Knight, Stevie Wonder, Jeffrey Osborne, Luther Vandross, Johnny Mathis and the Spinners occupy half of the album. And though the record jumps the gun with the optimistic 1990 in the title, three of its duets hadn't even been released yet, much less been preserved as hits. No outlandish guesses as to why this one didn't pass muster. See if you can remember even a note of it as soon as the CD whirls to a halt.

"Take Good Care of You and Me" pulled double duty as one of 13 other previously released male-female duets on *Friends for Life: Men and Women United in Harmony*, a benefit album to raise money for prostate- and breast-cancer research. This is the first of two recorded songs by Bacharach, Sager and Gerry Goffin, onetime husband and writing partner of Carole King. They would also write "Hang Your Teardrops Out to Dry" for the Stylistics and another number, "Feel the Love," that had no takers.

"Love Hurts" (Burt Bacharach)
From the Vestron motion picture *Love Hurts*
Recorded by Burt Bacharch, 1989, unreleased

Love Hurts was a much better film than Bud Yorkin's previous film, *Arthur 2,* but it made even less money and went straight to video after making its perfunctory rounds. Bacharach's involvement is virtually nil anyway—a pretty guitar, piano and string interlude that's heard for a mere two minutes in the middle of the film. A returned unused portion from *Arthur 2,* perhaps? Most of the music featured in the film consisted of previously released material by Rickie Lee Jones, Supertramp, Reba McIntire, Bruce Hornsby and Voices of the Beehive.

SECTION NINE
PAINTED FROM MEMORY (1991-2001)

...or the new songs of Bacharach & Costello

The Nineties get off to a rocky start with the split of Bacharach and Carole Bayer Sager and the shrinking pool of artists willing to cover new Bacharach material, a problem that persists to this day. But the use of old Bacharach-David material in a half-dozen movies jump-starts interest in the back catalog, as does a high profile collaboration with Elvis Costello, who encourages Bacharach to return to his old style for a collection of lost-love songs. The resulting album contains his best work since the split with Hal David, who returns to rekindle some of the old magic as well.

Setion Nine: Painted from Memory (1991–2001)

1. *"Obsession"* . . . . *Desmond Child*
2. *"Someone Else's Eyes"* . . . . *Aretha Franklin*
3. *"Hang Yor Teardrops Up to Dry"* . . . . *The Stylistics*
4. *"I Just Don't Know What to Do"* . . . . *The Stylistics*
5. *"The Power of Your Love (You and I)"* . . . . *Taja Sevelle*
6. *"A Higher Place"* . . . . *James Ingram*
7. *"Sing for the Children"* . . . . *James Ingram*
8. *"This Is the Night"* . . . . *James Ingram*
9. *"Sunny Weather Lover"* . . . . *Dionne Warwick*
10. *"Two Hearts"* . . . . *Earth, Wind & Fire*
11. *"Don't Say Goodbye Girl"* . . . . *Tevin Campbell*
12. *"This Doesn't Feel Like Love Anymore"* . . . . *Klymaxx*
13. *"Once Before You Go"* . . . . *Klymaxx*
14. *"If I Want To"* . . . . *Sandi Patti*
15. *"Captives of the Heart"* . . . . *Dionne Warwick*
16. *"Mulino Bianco"* . . . . *Burt Bacharach*
17. *"With a Smile"* . . . . *Burt Bacharach and Jene Miller*
18. *"Follow Your Heart" aka "Og Du Flyver Din Vej"* . . . . *Søs Fenger*
19. *"Stroke of Luck" aka "I Et Kort Sekund"* . . . . *Søs Fenger*
20. *"After All"* . . . . *Paul Anka*
21. *"Is There Anybody Out There"* . . . . *Mari Iijima*
22. *"Let Me Be the One"* . . . . *Marilyn Scott*
23. *"Like No One in the World"* . . . . *Johnny Mathis*
24. *"God Give Me Strength"* . . . . *Kristen Vigard*
25. *"You've Got It All Wrong"* . . . . *Burt Bacharach*
26. *"If Love Was That Way"* . . . . *Nana Mouskouri*
27. *"In the Darkest Place"* . . . . *Elvis Costello and Burt Bacharach*
28. *"Toledo"* . . . . *Elvis Costello and Burt Bacharach*
29. *"I Still Have That Other Girl"* . . . . *Elvis Costello and Burt Bacharach*
30. *"This House is Empty Now"* . . . . *Elvis Costello and Burt Bacharach*
31. *"Tears at the Birthday Party"* . . . . *Elvis Costello and Burt Bacharach*
32. *"Such Unlikely Lovers"* . . . . *Elvis Costello and Burt Bacharach*
33. *"My Thief"* . . . . *Elvis Costello and Burt Bacharach*
34. *"The Long Division"* . . . . *Elvis Costello and Burt Bacharach*
35. *"The Sweetest Punch"* . . . . *Elvis Costello and Burt Bacharach*
36. *"Painted from Memory"* . . . . *Elvis Costello and Burt Bacharach*
37. *"What's Her Name Today"* . . . . *Elvis Costello and Burt Bacharach*
38. *"Don't Give Up"* . . . . *Dave Koz*
39. *"If I Should Ever Lose You"* . . . . *Chicago*
40. *"Walking Tall"* . . . . *Lyle Lovett*
41. *"On My Way"* . . . . *Dionne Warwick*
42. *"Open Your Heart"* . . . . *Vanessa Williams*
43. *Isn't She Great (Original Soundtrack)* . . . . *Burt Bacharach*
44. *"Overture 2000"* . . . . *Burt Bacharach*
45. *"Nothing in This World"* . . . . *Engelbert*
46. *"Tell It to Your Heart"* . . . . *Randy Crawford*
47. *"Never Take That Chance Again"* . . . . *Diane Schuur*
48. *"Count on Me"* . . . . *Tonio K.*
49. *"In My Dreams"* . . . . *Tonio K.*
50. *"Someday"* . . . . *Carola*

"Obsession" (Burt Bacharach - Desmond Child)
Recorded by Desmond Child
From the album *Discipline,* Elektra 61048-2
Released June 1991

"It was a long period with Hal David and a long period with my ex-wife, Carole Bayer Sager," Bacharach told *GQ* magazine in 1996, "and now I like writing with a lot of people. I equate it to being married. Now I'm dating a lot."

As the last Bacharach-Sager material made its way to market, Bacharach teamed up with a diverse assortment of partners and even retained the kind of writing threesomes the couple helped popularize. One of the more interesting musical dates he kept was with Miami-born songwriter Desmond Child, who was releasing an album under his own name after over a decade of writing and producing for other artists.

Whenever a record executive informs a rock group "I don't hear the single," Child is one of an elite team of fixer-uppers enlisted to make that hit happen. But unlike David Foster, Diane Warren or Peter Wolf, Child was an active performing and recording artist before throwing himself fulltime into songwriting and producing for others. He'd released two Desmond Child & Rouge albums in 1979, but their slick boy-girl look and mix of singer-songwriter rock, urban dance, Latin and punk was perhaps too volatile during the intolerant "Disco Sucks" era. Before Rouge's collapse, Child coauthored Kiss's "I Was Made for Loving You," the costumed foursome's Top 10 quasi-dance hit. This led to a string of hugely successful hits cowritten by Child like "You Give Love a Bad Name" and "Livin' on a Prayer" with Bon Jovi, "Poison" with Alice Cooper, "I Hate Myself for Loving You" with Joan Jett, "Dude (Looks Like a Lady)" and "What It Takes" with Aerosmith and notable album tracks for Cher, Chicago, Roxette and Billy Squier.

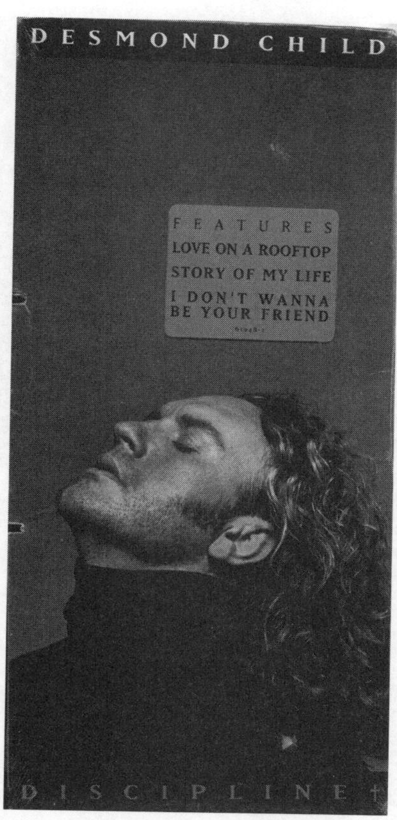

Desmond Child Sans Rouge. His former group Desmond Child and Rouge debuted in 1979, the same year the disastrous *Pink Lady and Jeff* premiered on television only to be yanked off the air a month later. After that, no one wanted to see a guy and a bunch of cute girls again. Ever.

Although Bacharach wasn't hanging around in heavy-metal circles in the Eighties, he did share some common ground with Child where quiet-storm and power ballads were concerned: Child authored Michael Bolton's ballistic "How Can We Be Lovers," a more than credible AC credential. Released as the third single from *Discipline*, the power ballad "Obsession" failed to follow its two predecessors into the Top 100, a dirty shame since it reunited him with Rouge girl Maria Vidal in a sensual duet that may owe more to Child and producer Sir Arthur Payson's input than to anything from Bacharach. After the album ran its course with this single, Child went back behind the scenes, fattening his bank account by penning and producing Ricky Martin's first international smash album, *Livin' La Vida Loca*, and opening the door for the Baha Men to ask "Who Let the Dogs Out."

Aretha Franklin. If they gave out Grammys for worst album title, *What You See Is What You Sweat* would have to qualify for a lifetime achievement award.

"Someone Else's Eyes" (Burt Bacharach - Carole Bayer Sager - Bruce Roberts)
Recorded by Aretha Franklin
From the album *What You See Is What You Sweat,* Arista 8628
Released July 1991

1991

Love Talk. It's Dress Casual Day in Philadelphia. Almost no one got the Stylistics' subtle homage to Emerson Lake & Palmer's *Love Beach* album. Until now.

Finally the practice of imposing a duet partner on every female Arista recording artist just to give Jeffery Osborne something to do seems to be losing ground. Aretha stands alone on this sister-must-do-it-for-herself anthem, giving notice that she can no longer let herself be defined by her mate. *"I can't love you, I can't love me / In someone else's eyes"* is a powerful I-gotta-be-me statement that Sager turns into one woman's declaration of independence. Although the lyrics strive not to place blame on her selfless self-image *("I've got to show myself I can still exist without a man....I was lost inside your name")*, Aretha inserts a few ad-libs that contradict the previous text, like *"I wanna be by your side / Aww, but you hurt this lady's pride."*

Those still clamoring for the return of Hal David (it's coming, it's coming) fail to account that with Sager's womanly insight and humor, Bacharach turned in a measurably different take on male-female relations than David could've gotten away with. Through Dionne Warwick, David was able to project strong philosophical beliefs and crushing vulnerabilities that weren't necessarily gender specific. But it's hard to imagine him writing a lyric like *"You were the sun and I was the one who just lay around you day and night"* for "Someone Else's Eyes" and not eliciting anger from women still incensed by Paul Anka's "(You're) Having My Baby." Once Bacharach terminated his writing and marital relationships with Sager, his subsequent songs with several methodically professional wordsmiths would miss the pushy humor of her best work. That is, until Bacharach arrived at the punning and cunning Elvis Costello.

"Hang Your Teardrops Up to Dry" (Burt Bacharach - Carole Bayer Sager - Gerry Goffin)
"I Just Don't Know What to Do"
(Burt Bacharach - Carole Bayer Sager)
Recorded by the Stylistics
From the album *Love Talk,* Amherst 4404
Released September 1991

Considering that the Stylistics' last flurry of hits was around the Bicentennial, it may have been an act of pure optimism for the Stylistics to give it the ol' Philly push. Thom Bell, their producer and guiding light, was long gone, working sporadically with the likes of Earth, Wind & Fire and James Ingram while Bell's longtime lyricist Linda Creed had passed away from breast cancer in 1986. The Stylistics went from a five- to a four-piece at the start of the Eighties, and after stints with producers Gamble and Huff and Maurice Starr, they were down to a trio by the Nineties. Compared to past hits, their trademark lush background vocals sound slightly anemic here at minus-two strength, but maybe the Stylistics just wanted an accurate record of their live sound that they could hawk at shows. Russell Thompkins Jr. retains his "betcha by golly wow" factor—reason enough for Bacharach and Sager to give the group their last compositions together. This brings everything full circle, since the Stylistics' recording of "You'll Never Get to Heaven" was the last Bacharach entry in the Top 40 before the long commercial drought leading up to meeting Sager.

Unlike the Hamlischs, the Bacharachs would not work together after their divorce, and if copyright records are any indicator, they only worked on these two songs and "The Power of Your Love" after 1989. Apparently, Gerry Goffin added additional words to an earlier registered song called "Teardrops," copyrighted in 1989 and credited solely to the Bacharachs. It's possible Bacharach finished these songs from sheets of unpublished Sager verse and called in collaborators when needed.

Given the circumstances, there's an understandable desire on Bacharach's part to revisit his older approach: the odd hanging chords on "Hang Your Teardrops Out to Dry" seem atypical of his more adventurous days. With commercial concerns not the driving motive behind such a low-profile release, both Bacharach and Sager loosened up enough to placate the nostalgia crowd. By titling one song "I Just Don't Know What to Do" after the familiar Dionne/Dusty refrain, it's as if both of them are daring the people who unfavorably compared their work with Bacharach-David's to make the comparisons in the eleventh hour.

"I Just Don't Know What to Do" is calmer and more accepting of a breakup than the earlier "I Just Don't Know What to Do with Myself," allowing that *"people change and nothing lasts forever"* and *"life goes on."* Although it's missing the dramatic climax of the Tommy Hunt classic, this new song has a more understated buildup, introducing a second Russell Thompkins Jr. vocal in the bridge and then a third in the closing choruses. Discounting the once modern, now antiquated sounding MIDI production, these recordings have held up quite nicely, even if few people know of their existence.

Taja Sevelle. Prince spotted Taja as an extra on the set of *Purple Rain* and encouraged her to sing on his Paisley Park label. Yeah, I know what you're thinking: when is Prince ever gonna discover someone who's really hideous looking?

"The Power of Your Love (You and I)" (Burt Bacharach - Carole Bayer Sager - Taja Sevelle)
Recorded by Taja Sevelle
From the album *Fountains Free,* Reprise 26724
Released October 1991

We're in the Nineties now, where the mere mention of the word "power" in a ballad could conjure up Celine Dion, who sings about the power of the heart and love as if they were Sherman tanks that could level villages. But since it's the early Nineties, we can relax and enjoy Taja Sevelle without any tangible threat of belligerence.

Discovered and signed by Prince, the Minneapolis radio DJ turned Paisley Park recording artist scored a hit right out of the box with the Purple One ("Love Is Contagious"), but Sevelle moved over to the Reprise label after her self-titled debut album. There's a noticeable drop of dance thrust on *Fountains Free*, with Sevelle playing to the quiet, cool, AC-conditioned crowd. Often sounding like a breathy Sheena Easton, Sevelle coaxes a better than average tune out of Bacharach and one of his better latter-day programmed productions. They would write together again with Denise Rich deputizing for the departed Sager on "Let Me Be the One."

1991

The Psychic Friends Network Kit. This package contains a 30-minute *Psychic Within* video, audio tape, daily inspirational guide and a special *Psychic Within* calling card you can never use because your psychic friend has the same idea and her phone is always busy. None of these artifacts contains any video or audio of Dionne. Or any mention of impending bankruptcy.

"A Higher Place" (Burt Bacharach - John Bettis - James Ingram)
Recorded by James Ingram, 1991
Unreleased demo

James Ingram rose to prominence as featured performer on his mentor Quincy Jones' 1980 Grammy Award–winning album *The Dude*. After two Top 20 hits from that album ("Just Once" and "One Hundred Ways"), Ingram became everyone's doubles partner, scoring big hits with Patti Austin, Michael McDonald and Linda Ronstadt, and in a big three-way face-off with Kenny Rogers and Kim Carnes, "What About Me." That's a question Ingram may well have asked himself after Quincy Jones crowded him onto a No. 1 R&B record with Al B. Sure, El DeBarge and Barry White. Finally in late 1990 the public remembered what Ingram sounded like singing alone and rewarded him with a No. 1 for "I Don't Have the Heart."

So why was this quality solo track left to gather dust? Recorded in 1991, the year Warner Brothers released *The Power of Great Music: The Best of James Ingram*, it should've been the enticing "previously unreleased" selection, especially with this song's early lyrical tie-in *"The power always lies in giving up the power."* What starts out like a million other nauseating Eighties phony Fender Rhodes ballads suddenly becomes something greater, once you realize that no nearby orchestra, choir or visiting diva is going to swoop in and sap Ingram of all his strength at the mike. Ingram can relax and build up steam, pacing his climax and crumbling like it's talent night at the Apollo and he's tired of going home empty-handed. He does his duty, the champion begging *"I'm reaching out my haaaands tooo-hooo yoooooo,"* and it's all magnificent.

John Bettis, onetime songwriting lyrical partner of Richard Carpenter, gives Ingram a politically correct forum to sing this incognito gospel number. For the "G" word, his text substitutes "a higher place" inside ourselves, which is what God is supposed to be anyway.

The four songs by Bacharach, Bettis and Ingram were written with all three present, affording Bacharach the luxury of having a singer of Ingram's ability there to make a song sound like a finished product at this early demo stage. If "A Higher Place" were ever recorded for an album, someone in the chain of command—perhaps even Bacharach, deep in his MIDI fascination—might have found a way to overthink and ruin it.

"Sing for the Children" and "This Is the Night" (Burt Bacharach - John Bettis - James Ingram)
Recorded by James Ingram
From the album *Always You,* Qwest 45275
Released May 1993

In the Bacharach annals, 1992 appears to be another year lost to tennis, concerts, horse racing, enjoying life or not enjoying life. With the concerns of a newly single father ever present, Bacharach wrote thoughtful music for a children's anthem that never caught on in inner-city grade schools. One would have a hard time disagreeing with the wisdom of

"We'll never stop our ways of war unless we love a child," but good intentions sometimes make for the blandest salads. All the truly compelling music is packed into a retro introduction that restores spiraling strings and the dearly departed flugelhorn to a front–and-center position on a Bacharach record. That it's a return to form for Philly producer and arranger Thom Bell, a Bacharach lover from back in the days, is a hopeful harbinger that the man himself would put his sequencing days behind him and stand, arms outstretched, in front of a real orchestra again.

With the kids safely tucked into bed, the choristers tiptoe downstairs and loosen their gowns for "This Is the Night," with Ingram belting out his nocturnal longings over a nice set of Bacharach changes and heavier than usual AOR guitar. And even if the *"if I lost you"* section of the explosive bridge apes the melody of "You Don't Know Me" from *Sometimes Late at Night*, the slow dancers don't mind.

Friends Can Be Lovers. Dionne's first album not to be released on vinyl featured some of her best material in ages—a great cover of Sting's "Fragile" and a sensual "Where My Lips Have Been." On the minus side, there's a dull duet with cousin Whitney Houston.

"Sunny Weather Lover" (Burt Bacharach - Hal David)
Recorded by Dionne Warwick
From the album *Friends Can Be Lovers,* Arista 18682
Released October 1993

Receiving ASCAP's prestigious Founders Award in 1993 was impetus enough for Burt Bacharach and Hal David to settle longstanding differences and write their first song together since 1978. Their acrimonious publishing dispute, in which David sued and Bacharach countersued, was settled out of court in 1979. Bacharach instigated the settlement, even agreeing to shell out more money than David just to have it over and done with. But resentment lingered, even after Bacharach resumed writing for Dionne again in 1985.

"It's all over now," Bacharach told the *Los Angeles Times* in May 1993, just before the awards ceremony. "I had a falling out with Dionne, then Hal got involved. And if I had to do it over again, I never, never would do it the same way. For whatever reason, it happened. But we finally made our settlement, Dionne and I are touring again, and Hal and I found a touch of the old spark when we wrote "Sunny Weather Lover" for Dionne's new album."

The pair's workday reunion actually took place in 1989, when the Bacharach-Sager marriage was showing the first signs of turbulence. This historic but private summit yielded only two songs, "How Can I Love You" (which remains unrecorded) and "Sunny Weather Lover," served up to the public as a Bacharach-David reunion offering some four years later.

It would be wonderful to report that the first song the pair assembled together in 11 years was phenomenally good. But much the same way the first batch of songs Bacharach and David wrote ("Peggy's in the Pantry," "The Morning Mail," etc.) were just average for 1956, "Sunny Weather Lover" just sounds like normal AC ventilation circa 1993. Without a third partner interjecting, Bacharach sounds temporarily tapped out for fresh musical ideas. David makes up for the lack with his customary sense of the occasion; the first words to come out of Dionne's mouth to break the threesome's long musical silence are a relieved *"Don't take the song out*

Tevin Campbell. Here are four fun facts learned off the fan website Tevin-Vision: (1) Tevin has a cocker spaniel; (2) when Tevin was little, kids called him Campbell Soup and Mr. T because he had the same haircut; (3) Tevin was going to star in a black version of *Oliver Twist* directed by Oliver Stone that never got made; and (4) if Tevin could be any animal, he would definitely be a dolphin.

of my life." More of a press release than a song, "Sunny Weather Lover" serves notice that their nearly 20-year estrangement has been permanently laid to rest and that friends don't let friends' attorneys do the talking for them.

"Two Hearts" (Burt Bacharach - Philip James Bailey - Maurice White)
Recorded by Earth, Wind & Fire
From the album *Millennium,* Reprise 45274
Released September 1993

The record industry's worst fears were realized on November 30, 1991, when *Billboard* began compiling its Hot 100 chart using data provided by BDS and Soundscan. Almost overnight, top-selling rap artists and emerging grunge-rock bands took their rightful spot in the upper echelon of the charts, where major label promotion money (or payola, take you pick) had dictated before. Suddenly Top 40 radio had a new calamity on its hands: how does one reconcile Nirvana, Vanessa Williams and Tupac on the same format? That no one seemed willing or able to offer a playlist that reflected the whole country's listening habits meant a lot more restrictive radio formats, and God help you if you're an evergreen act with a new album.

It's hard to believe, but in the Seventies, acts like Earth, Wind & Fire used to get crossover play on Top 40, R&B, rock and disco stations. With *Millennium*, the group's first album for Warner Brothers since 1972, EW&F managed to place a single in the Top 60, which was the group's chart average since the early Eighties, when Maurice White started pimping the group's trademark sound out to the likes of Phil Collins and Neil Diamond.

"Two Hearts," an irresistible slow cooker in the tradition of "That's the Way of the World," featured actual Bacharach presence in the studio for a change: the man himself is playing piano and presumably arranging the Earth, Wind & Fire horns to crest and dive. Urban contemporary listeners could do a lot worse.

"Don't Say Goodbye Girl"
(Burt Bacharach - Narada Michael Walden - Sally Jo Dakota)
Recorded by Tevin Campbell
Qwest 18254, from the album *I'm Ready,* Qwest 45388 (*Billboard* pop #71)
Released October 1993

Whether it was flutist Bobbi Humphrey, Quincy Jones or Prince who discovered Texas teen Tevin Campbell is a moot point: Campbell had all but shed his protégé shoes by the time *I'm Ready* arrived. Still only 15 years old, his maturity made Michael Jackson seem like a fetus, and the album spawned five hits over the next year, of which "Don't Say Goodbye Girl" was the fourth. If this mid-tempo grinder sounds like most mechanical pop of the day, there's beauty in the dependability of well-oiled machinery. Campbell's incredible bound from tenor to falsetto transfigures what was potentially a passionless piece of product into a work of undeniable urgency. Even the expected key shift offers some surprising delight.

It's hard to detect Bacharach's presence in all this, except in the selection of tasty chord changes. You might recognize Sally Jo Dakota as one of Narada Michael Walden's frequent collaborators: none of the songs they've ever written together lists fewer than three names in the parenthesis. Carole Bayer Sager, what have ye wrought?

Klymaxx. Joyce "Fenderella" Irby is credited for several significant R&B discoveries, including songwriter Debra "Shi" Killings, rapper Speech (of the group Arrested Development) and artist/producer Dallas Austin.

"This Doesn't Feel Like Love Anymore" and "Once Before You Go" (Burt Bacharach - Carole Bayer Sager - Joyce Irby)
Recorded by Klymaxx
From the CD *One Day,* Diva One Entertainment
Released May 1994, rereleased on Valley Vue 40001, January 1997

This was the last gasp from Klymaxx, an R&B girl group from Los Angeles that scored several sizable dance hits for MCA Records in the Eighties, including "I Miss You," "Man Size Love" and "I'd Still Say Yes." Motown, then owned and distributed by MCA, offered a solo record deal to the group's bassist and main vocalist Joyce "Fenderella" Irby. This shouldn't have spelled a permanent exodus from Klymaxx, but the other members of the band were so incensed she'd even considered a solo album that they booted her out. Once ejected, Irby enjoyed several solo dance-club hits with old-school rappers Doug E. Fresh and Doc Box.

Significantly, the hits ceased for Klymaxx, who were now a trio with the voluntary departure of drummer Bernadette Cooper, also embarking on a solo career. Without their original rhythm section, Klymaxx lost its funk and became a more conventional girl group, with the emphasis on vocals. The resulting 1990 album, *The Maxx Is Back*, didn't engender the comeback they'd hoped for (despite the presence of producers Jimmy Jam and Terry Lewis), so they welcomed Irby back to the fold. *One Day,* which Klymaxx released on its own dime after MCA dropped the group and invited Cooper back as a special guest, contained two standard sappy ballads likely written for Irby's second solo album but carried over to the reunion project.

"If I Want To" (Burt Bacharach - Will Jennings)
Recorded by Sandi Patti
From the album *Find It on the Wings,* Sony 66558
Released October 1994

First the evangelical world was rocked by the PTL scandals of 1987. The following year it was Jimmy Swaggart doing the fornicating and apologizing. That was enough to keep holier-than-thou tongues wagging for years. But who could've predicted that Sandi "The Voice" Patti, one of the biggest stars in Christian contemporary music, would confess to

1994

Definitely Maybe. The tiny inclusion of a Burt Bacharach poster on the lower-left-hand side of the cover of Oasis' debut album is credited with creating renewed interest in the composer and his work. This might never have happened if Oasis weren't trying to pay homage to Pink Floyd's *Ummagumma* cover by placing Bacharach in the same position of prominence the Floyds reserved for the soundtrack of *Gigi*.

having *two* extramarital affairs. Without this hidden rationale, her 1992 divorce came as a total shock to fans. Their shock turned to feelings of betrayal when the real story broke, shortly after the release of this secular CD. Knowing how hot under the collar the clergy can get, CCM stations quickly pulled her records out of holy rotation.

Find It on the Wings would've been one of the first pieces of trash to hit the anti-Sandi bonfire, and good riddance to "If I Want To," Bacharch's only collaboration with Will Jennings, the lyricist of such sappetizers as Barry Manilow's "Looks Like We Made It," Eric Clapton's "Tears in Heaven," Joe Cocker and Jennifer Warnes' "Up Where We Belong" and Celine Dion's blustering "My Heart Will Go On." Patti must've made this song's message of *"I can dream of a better world if I want to"* her mantra all through the controversy. Like most famous fallen Christians, she found her way to damage control by coming clean and asking her fans' forgiveness. She did this in, of all places, the liner notes to her 1995 Christmas album, accompanying her apology with a bewildering endorsement for the weight-loss company she began using after being born again, with enclosed discount coupons to melt the all-too-weak flesh. It must have worked, since her records eventually made their way back into CCM hearts. But there's no forgiving Jennings' clichéd greeting-card lyrics and Bacharach's equally monotonous music. This is tedious songwriting not even fit for a straight-to-video *Beauty and the Beast* sequel.

"If I Want To" was the only Bacharach song on *Dionne Sings Dionne* that wasn't a remake of a tune she did better somewhere else. Warwick once again took this opportunity to rewrite history and claim "What the World Needs Now" as her own, along with "All Kinds of People" and this drivel. Sandi Patti's dream of a better world isn't appreciably better dreamed Dionne's way. Bacharach and Jennings would pen another song, "There Is No Love Unless We Make It," that stayed unrecorded.

Other Versions: *Dionne Warwick (1998)*

"Captives of the Heart" (Burt Bacharach - John Bettis)
Recorded by Dionne Warwick
From the album *Aquarela do Brasil,* Arista 18777
Released October 1994

With Dionne having exhausted every conceivable duet partner, *Aquarela do Brasil* represents her last truly original album idea—an entire set of traditional Brazilian pop partly sung in Portuguese, with flashes of the Brazilian hip-hop that was just starting to come into fashion. Bacharach's music explored and exhausted both the *baion* beat and the bossa nova ages before Paul Simon's 1990 plundering of Brazilian idioms for *Rhythm of the Saints*: Dionne was just completing the musical voyage Bacharach had started with the ridiculous "Brigitte Bardot." But an album with a Jobim medley met with bewilderment from Arista, which failed to promote it and blamed her notoriety as an infomercial psychic as the reason they couldn't get anyone to play it. Warwick never recorded another note for the label.

Like "Sunny Weather Lover" on her previous album, "Captives of the Heart" is the most conventional selection here. Pleasant but ordinary, as if you played "Déjà Vu" like a samba.

"Mulino Bianco" (Burt Bacharach)
Recorded by Burt Bacharach
"With a Smile" (Burt Bacharach - John Bettis)
Recorded by Burt Bacharach and Jene Miller
From the album *Tribute to Burt Bacharach,* Nippon Columbia COCA-12166 199
Released 1994 (Japan only)

Bacharach's post-Sager output hadn't attracted much public support in the U.S., but Japanese recording artists were still hot enough on the writer of "Me Japanese Boy I Love You" to send some loving back his way. Nippon Columbia assembled a Japanese various-artists tribute album that included such modern-day space-age-bachelor-pad musical dwellers as the Pizzicato Five and Kyoto Jazz Massive. And though it's a clear conflict of interest to have the guest of honor perform on his own tribute album, no one minded that Bacharach used the opportunity to release two songs under his own name, something he hadn't done since the *Night Shift* soundtrack some 12 years before.

American celebrities who balk at doing commercials in the U.S. will happily shill for extra pocket yen in the Land of the Rising Sun. With that same sense of security, Bacharach allows himself to trade on his old signature sound without fear that it will be interpreted as a throwback. He turns in the very Bacharachesque "With a Smile," which skips along the street at the same velocity as "Raindrops Keep Falling on My Head" and has call-and-response trumpet, wispy female vocals that sound like the Breakaways, and the most prominent display of his whistling muse since "Odds and Ends." There's even a melodic passage that turns up again later in one of the new songs Bacharach and Costello would write, "Tears at the Birthday Party." The less notable "Mulino Bianco" resembles an *Arthur* instrumental outtake, from its alto sax to its standalone Richard Page– and Steve George–like backgrounds.

"Follow Your Heart" aka "Og Du Flyver Din Vej" (Burt Bacharach - Denise Rich)
"Stroke of Luck" aka "I Et Kort Sekund" (Burt Bacharach - Denise Rich - Taja Sevelle)
Recorded by Søs Fenger
From the CD *Et Kys Herfra,* Genlyd/BMG, released 1994

More exotic lost Bacharach obscurities! This time a pair of Denise Rich collaborations turn up on Danish soil, but this too should come as no surprise, as the first-ever full-length Bacharach-David tribute album—the hopelessly dorky *Gals & Pals*—was a product of Sweden. It's easier to enjoy the considerably calmer and lovelier-toned Søs Fenger singing "Og Du Flyver Din Vej," a lush ballad that comes dangerously close to familiar territory. The flugelhorn is flugelin', and wispy Fenger sings the same

Dionne Brazilian Style. Warwick songwriting credits became a regular occurrence starting with the *Friends Can Be Lovers* album. She shares songwriting duties on three songs from *Aquarela do Brasil.*

1995

Marilyn Scott. She was the only white cast member in the touring company of the musical *Selma*, which was about Dr. Martin Luther King Jr. and the march in Alabama. Scott first charted on *Billboard's* Top 100 back in 1977 with a single version of Brian Wilson's "God Only Knows" on Big Tree, the label that gave us Lobo's "Me and You and a Dog Named Boo."

three "just like me" notes found in "Close to You," just to let foreigners know they're in Bacharach country. "Stroke of Luck" would've made a fine mid-tempo AC number for cowriter Taja Sevelle, who sounds like Fenger's identical cousin.

"After All" (Burt Bacharach - Paul Anka)
Recorded by Paul Anka
From the album *After All,* Polydor 527430-2
Released April 1995

Sixteen years after merging talents for the *Together* score, Bacharach and Anka regroup somewhere off the deep end of the pop culture radar. The scarcity of this murky item only several years after its release indicates what minuscule attention the world at large accorded it. Another Anka-Bacharach effort, "Rainbow," has yet to turn up in recorded form.

"Is There Anybody Out There" (Burt Bacharach - John Bettis - James Ingram - Puff Johnson)
Recorded by Mari Iijima
From the album *Sonic Boom,* Moon 4226
Moon 4224 single (album version, Japanese version and TV mix)
Released September 1995 (Japan only)

The early Nineties was a time of frustration for Bacharach, writing adult contemporary music that Clive Davis was turning down for not being commercial enough. With a shrinking number of AC outlets in this country, Bacharach's publishers plugged into foreign markets with several unrecorded John Bettis collaborations.

"Is Anybody Out There" found its way to a Japanese singer living in the United States, Mari Iijima. Known to Japanese animation (*anime*) fans as the voice of Lynn Minmay in the classic *Macross,* series and a star on the USA Network series *Pacific Blue*, Iijima relocated to Los Angeles in 1989 to help further her singing career after years of superstardom in Japan. Almost immediately, Van Dyke Parks featured her on his *Tokyo Rose* album. She continued to record in Japanese and made tentative steps into English-language singing with this release in 1995.

"Doing Burt's song was my music publisher's suggestion," says Iijima, who selected the song from an assortment of demos. "'Is Anybody Out There' was the best one among them and I felt OK singing that one. There was something in common between my style and that song." Iijima recorded "Is Anybody Out There" in both English and Japanese for the CD single, translating the English lyric herself "with a little touch of Mari essence." Considering that the three-syllable "I love you" translates into the 14-syllable "Watashi wa anata wo aishite imasu," the Japanese translations require vigilant oversimplification.

Both versions were mixed and recorded in L.A., with Iijima stating a preference for the mix on the CD single. Bacharach's involvement did not extend beyond asking to Humbert Gatica produce it. "I was supposed to do a photo session with Burt for promotion purposes," says Iijima, "but it got canceled. It's a mystery. I was bummed when I heard the news that I wasn't going to see Burt."

The Bacharach-Bettis-Ingram axis featured a new name in the parenthesis—Sony recording artist Puff Johnson, a discovery of onetime Motown talent developer and president Suzanne de Passe. Johnson released a 1997 album called *Miracle,* produced by Narada Michael Walden. Another four-way committee collaboration entitled "Pride" was registered with BMI but not recorded.

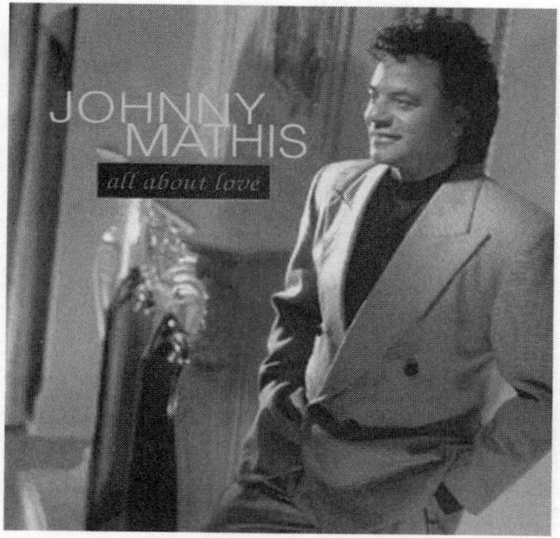

Johnny Mathis. Although this album didn't make much of a splash, Mathis soon remembered the theme albums that made him famous and enjoyed renewed sales with *Because You Loved Me: Songs of Diane Warren* (1998) and *Johnny Mathis on Broadway* (2000).

"Let Me Be the One" (Burt Bacharach - Denise Rich - Taja Sevelle)
First recorded by Marilyn Scott
From the Warner Bros. album *Take Me with You*
Released December 1995

Marilyn Scott, background vocalist turned foreground smooth-jazz stylist, released several recordings on Atco before signing with Warner Brothers. Her controlled, Gloria Estefan-style reading gives way to gutsy Gladys Knight ad-libs at the end of what would otherwise be another soporific installment in the Bacharach catalog. Cowriter Sevelle was readying her third album in 1995, and this standard AC fare would clash with the singer-songwriter persona she wanted to establish. But this song proved agreeable and anonymous enough for the latter-day Johnny Mathis to inject some warmth into.

Other Versions: *Johnny Mathis (1996)*

"Like No One in the World" (Burt Bacharach - John Bettis)
Recorded by Johnny Mathis
From the CD *All about Love,* Columbia 67509
Released summer 1996

"Like No One in the World" and "Let Me Be the One" bring Johnny Mathis into his fourth decade of Bacharach recording, after sitting out the Eighties and the entire Bacharach-Sager catalog. It's as if time has stood still on this placid acoustic number, a modern revision of something that would've been perfect for his classic smooching album *Open Fire, Two Guitars.*

Kristen Vigard. This former TV actress and Broadway understudy (for the musical *Annie*) gave up acting to focus on music. Her background vocals were heard by the millions who bought Red Hot Chili Peppers and Fishbone albums in the late Eighties and early Nineties. To date, this is her only solo album, released on Private Music in 1988.

"God Give Me Strength" (Burt Bacharach - Elvis Costello)
First recorded by Kristen Vigard
From the motion picture *Grace of My Heart*
From the original soundtrack album *Grace of My Heart,* MCA 11554
Released September 1996

Traditionally, rock biopics take so much dramatic license with their

Grace of My Heart. Although Bacharach and Carole Bayer Sager both worked on this soundtrack, they did not work together. Sager cowrote the song "I Do" with Dave Stewart of the Eurythmics.

real-life subjects that they might as well be fiction. The makers of *The Buddy Holly Story* thought it was more attention grabbing to have the likable Texan's life resemble an Elvis movie, where the King gets to whup everyone's ass. *La Bamba* left early-rock novices with the impression that Richie Valens was a guy obsessed with plane crash premonitions who just happened to play guitar. Alison Anders' film *Grace of My Heart* dealt only with hybrid luminaries. The film is very loosely structured around a Carole King–type songwriter who pairs up with a Gerry Goffin/Barry Mann–type lyricist; they write songs for a Phil Spector–type producer, and she gets romantically involved with a Brian Wilson–type wunderkind. Once Denise Waverly (sensitively portrayed by Illeana Douglas) sheds these bad boy/mad boy geniuses she's surrounded herself with, she finally finds the voice and the courage to sing her own songs her own way.

The film's climax required a pop pastiche that combined the hymnal quality of "You Make Me Feel Like a Natural Woman" with the despondency of "Anyone Who Had a Heart." Gerry Goffin, Carole King's former husband and lyricist, had already added three lyrical contributions to the score and had previously written with Bacharach and Sager (the inspired "Hang Your Teardrops Out to Dry" and the not-so-good "Take Good Care of You and Me"), so a Goffin-Bacharach tune would've been a logical choice to pencil in for the big song. Instead, Anders suggested that Bacharach team up with Elvis Costello, who'd already written one period piece for the film called "Unwanted Number," a revisionist Shirelles song that finds the girl of "Will You Still Love Me Tomorrow" unloved and pregnant three months later. While the song reads like one of Goffin and King's gritty bad girl/bad boy songs of 1962, the sound is pure "Baby It's You," right down to its cheddary organ.

"God Give Me Strength." Yet another live version of the *Grace of My Heart* highlight is featured in the April 8, 1988, Burt Bacharach tribute concert recorded at New York's Hammerstein Ballroom. Also scheduled to perform that amazing night was Noel Gallagher of Oasis, who was to reprise his 1996 Royal Albert Hall performance of "This Guy's in Love with You." Then came the March 16 announcement that he regretfully had to bow out owing to "rescheduled recording commitments"; curiously, the hit was not reassigned to someone else.

Bacharach had previously met Costello in a recording studio when the British singer-songwriter was recording his *Spike* album in 1989. Costello proceeded to play him a song he believed had a pseudo-Bacharach arrangement, and while Bacharach didn't much care for the tune ("Satellite"), Anders didn't have to ask him twice about working with Costello. "I loved the idea," Bacharach told the *Los Angeles Times*. "I think he is one of the great lyric writers. I love that he is an adventurer, that he takes chances as an artist."

Costello had performed a very early draft of the song "God Give Me Strength" in April of 1995, when he appeared as an unbilled opener for four Bob Dylan shows in Dublin and London. This early incarnation is probably what Costello first played into Bacharach's answering machine. With Costello in Dublin, Bacharach in Los Angeles and a four-day deadline to complete the song, there was no time for niceties like writing in the same room or country, so it was down to writing via phone and fax. According to Bacharach, "[Elvis] wrote a couple of verses and sent them to me, then I'd write a lead sheet and send them back, and it just snowballed. We never got together on that song until New York, when we made the record."

The resulting recording would not be Elvis's version: that wouldn't come for another three years. It was cut with Broadway understudy and TV actress turned singer Kristen Vigard providing the onscreen singing voice for Illeana Douglas. Her enthralling voice-and-piano reading lacks the Bacharachesque flugelhorn introduction at this stage, but it's more than made up for by the middle section, where Vigard's naked prayer for God to strengthen her has depreciated into a bitter request that the Almighty rub out her former lover as only He can. Forget the lipstick-on-his collar removal analogy just invoked: she requires Old Testament rage to match her own. *"I want him! I want him to hurt!"* she cries, in can't-live-with-him, can't-live-without-him agony that subsides into remorse and mumbled hopelessness. Seeking divine salvation in the annihilation of someone else helped catapult this movie beyond its jukebox soap-opera premise, but it may have prevented the song's consideration at Oscar time. Perhaps it's not so curious, when you consider that some shit song from *Pocahontas* walked away with the golden guy that year.

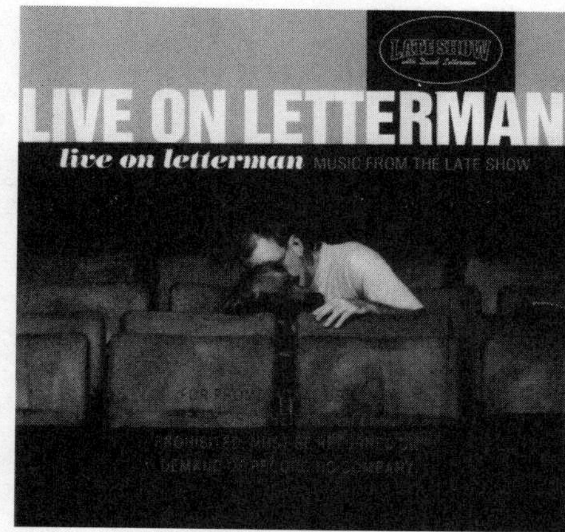

***Live on Letterman* (1997).** Those anxious to purchase Costello and Bacharach's version of "God Give Me Strength" got an advance opportunity when their February 25, 1997, *Late Night* appearance was included on this compilation that November, nearly a full year before the release of *Painted from Memory.*

Elvis's recording was worth the protracted wait, especially during that "I want him to hurt" exchange where he transmutes his anger from his departed lover to his replacement in the bedroom. After years of facile R&B and songs of polite heartbreak, it's as if Bacharach was reintroduced to the panic button that he jabbed liberally throughout all of his best songs to turn music into raw feeling. Before songwriting became a guessing game of "Who would sound good singing this with Aretha Franklin?" it used to be about writing something that could make the Queen of Soul weep. Costello was coming off his songwriting collaboration with Paul McCartney, where he managed to ease the former Beatle into writing Beatlesque songs and playing his Shea Stadium–era Hofner bass. Here he has brought Bacharach back to his old mode of studio instrumentation—a live orchestra to arrange and conduct, something one had to go to a concert hall to hear him do now.

It was almost a matter of duty for Bacharach and Costello to do a whole album of lost-love songs to satisfy the appetites they'd whetted. The trade ads for *Painted from Memory* explained their fateful mission best: "Together for the first time...because it's a lonely world."

Other Versions: *The Chubbies (2000) • Elvis Costello & Burt Bacharach (1996, live 1998) • Elvis Costello with the Swedish Radio Symphony Orchestra - live (2001) • Grant Geissman (1999) • Bill Frisell (1999) • Charles Lloyd (1999) • Bette Midler (2000)*

"You've Got It All Wrong" (Burt Bacharach - Hal David)
From the musical *Promises, Promises*
Recorded by Burt Bacharach (unreleased demo)
Show opened in March 1997

Promises, Promises. This is a 1968 souvenir book from the original show, which was briefly revived at New York City Center as a Sixties period piece. If the run had been extended, this little slice of nostalgic chauvinism would've probably been changed.

In a joint interview with the *Los Angeles Times* in May 1993, both Bacharach and David were receptive to writing more songs together after the cautious "Sunny Weather Lover." "Yeah, we'll probably write more songs," assured David. "Why not?" Bacharach stressed that "there has to be a real purpose—a reason to sit down for a specific project, like the title song for a film, or maybe even another Broadway show. That would really interest me."

With *Promises, Promises* about to be resurrected as part of New York City Center's "Encores!" series, the two men had an opportunity to write just such a situational song, with more bite than a latter-day Dionne album assignment would allow. "You've Got It All Wrong" comes in near

1997

Just Say Nana. That's what we Americans have been saying to her records for years, but guess what? She's the best-selling female artist of all time, regardless. Makes ya feel kinda unnecessary, don't it?

the end of Act One. In this singing dialogue, Miss Olson—one of Sheldrake's past office paramours and now his secretary—confronts Fran Kubelik about how she's just the latest link in Sheldrake's chain of fools, with Fran unwilling to listen. It finds the gentle David turning out bitter insinuations through the wisecracking Miss Olson *("He goes from floor to floor like an elevator man")*. Each time she bursts some more balloons *("You're now part of an ever growing cast")*, Fran shoots back with unconvincingly denials *("I don't know what you mean, I mean I think you've got it wrong")*. Unfortunately, the Martin Short–led revival was short-lived, and no new cast album or commercially available recording ever appeared. The best of the four Bacharach-David tunes from the last two decades remains a fantastic voice-and-piano demo, clandestinely circulated among collectors.

Two other proposed Bacharach musical projects in the Nineties didn't make their way to Broadway. One was a retelling of *Snow White,* with lyrics by B.A. Robertson (who cowrote "The Living Years" for Mike & the Mechanics), that was abandoned after a satisfactory book could not be provided. The other show, initially titled *Manhattan Girl*, evolved into *What the World Needs Now*, "a musical fable" built around preexisting Bacharach-David songs in much the way the 1974 Broadway production of *Sgt. Pepper's Lonely Hearts Club Band on the Road* connected some two dozen unrelated Beatles songs for no good reason. The male lead is of course named Alfie; he's caught cheating to the strains of "Are You There with Another Girl," and before the night is through, you've had 39 Bacharach-David songs crammed into two acts, sometimes not played out for more than 30 seconds.

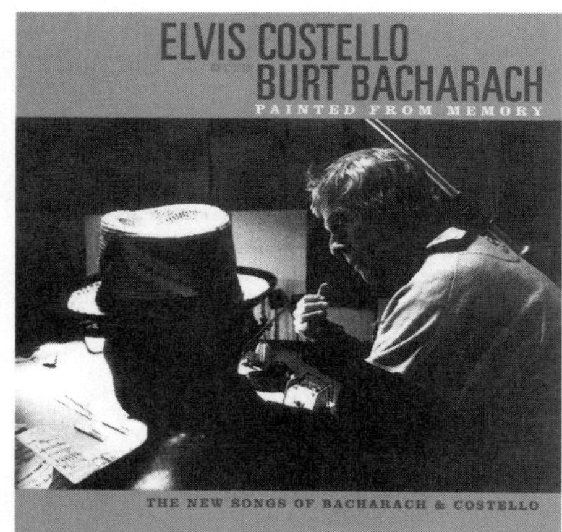

"In the Darkest Place." At one point this was considered as a possible album title, along with "Because It's Lonely World." But the more poetic and less pedantic *Painted from Memory* won out. Import copies of this album came bundled with a bonus disc containing live versions of "In the Darkest Place," "This House Is Empty Now," "I Still Have That Other Girl," "Painted from Memory" and "What's Her Name Today?"

Tryouts for *What the World Needs Now,* conceived by *Cats* and *Chorus Line* choreographer Gillian Lynne and book writer Kenn Solm, commenced on April 2, 1998, at the Roundabout Theatre in San Diego. After the show was savaged by the critics, plans to take it to New York's Roundabout Theater were cancelled. A second attempt was announced for the 1999–2000 Friends of Roundabout Playing Series but "The Burt Bacharach/Hal David Project" was quietly pulled with no explanation. However, when the Roundabout Theater Company announced it 2002-2003 season, the Burt Bacharach/Hal David musical was back on the boards, retitled *The Look of Love.*

"If Love Was That Way" (Burt Bacharach - Denise Rich - Taja Sevelle)
Recorded by Nana Mouskouri
From the CD *Return to Love,* Polygram 534573
Released April 1997

Nana Mouskouri is the best-selling female artist of all time, a huge star everywhere except the United States, where she's just some chick in Buddy Holly glasses. She's been recording since 1964, and her American licensees have tried at various times since the late Seventies to break her in this country. She serviced this intermittently pretty song, which always feels like the chorus is about to build up to something big but then stops and gives way to zilch, a design flaw that's glaringly apparent after the expected Barry Manilow key change.

"In the Darkest Place" (Burt Bacharach - Elvis Costello)
Recorded by Elvis Costello and Burt Bacharach
From the album *Painted from Memory*,
Mercury 314 538 0002-2
Released September 1998

The *Painted from Memory* songs were written over five or six sessions conducted in New York and Los Angeles. It was Costello who suggested that he and Bacharach create an entire cycle of lost-love songs, like Frank Sinatra's classic Gordon Jenkins albums (*No One Cares* and *Where Are You?*) and his Nelson Riddle–arranged *Only the Lonely,* long players designed to help you remember the lost love you're powerless to forget. Costello often mentioned *Only the Lonely* as one of his all-time favorites in promoting *Painted from Memory,* and while the latter seldom suggests Sinatra and Riddle, Costello establishes his sad Frank intentions right away with "In the Darkest Place," the song he always envisioned as the opening cut and at one point considered a possible title track. The guy in the song recalls the real-life Sinatra, a guy who could have any woman in the world but preferred to sit alone in the dark and shut out any light that's not a torch illuminating Ava Gardner's face. Of course, Costello is quick to puncture any ladies'-man pretense on his part; he even chooses to caption a giddy, grinning photo of him and Bacharach with *"Since you put me down / It seems I've been very gloomy / You might laugh but pretty girls look right through me"*—the only lyrics reprinted on the *Painted from Memory* CD booklet.

***A Singing Dictionary* (1980).** Anyone curious as to what sort of lyric Costello might've penned for Bacharach's "That's What Friends Are For" should dig out this sheet music collection containing Elvis's 1977 song of the same name. It's the only composition contained here that Costello himself never recorded. Georgie Fame *did* record it, in 1979.

While this album's unity of mood and plot development made it unlike any other in Elvis's discography, Bacharach had been down that road with Carole Bayer Sager's *Sometimes Late at Night*. The Sager suite of songs was stitched together to simulate one particularly turbulent night; *Painted from Memory* plays like a time-lapse movie where we get to see unrelieved sorrow played out for years afterward. If Dionne ever had a whole album of Bacharach-David torch songs—starting with "Are You There (With Another Girl)," swish panning to "Walk On By" and ending with "The Wine Is Young"—this would appear to be its sequel, with all the apologies delivered from the other side of the door, in letters never mailed from the dark end of the street.

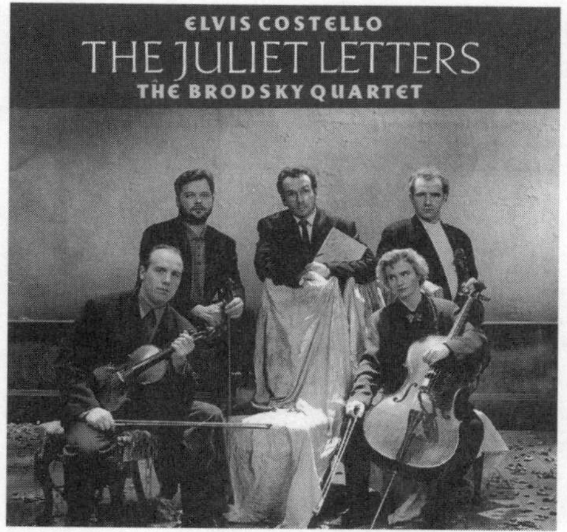

***The Juliet Letters* (1993).** Costello learned how to notate music while making this album with the Brodsky Quartet—his first collaboration with classically trained musicians.

One detects the flute traces of "Guy's Theme" from the *Isn't She Great* score in the intro and bridge of this number, which was reportedly written mainly by Costello before his first writing session with Bacharach. In a March 2002 *London Times* interview, Costello proudly insists, "I don't like people to be unaware of the fact that I wrote the music with him as well as the words. Each of the songs had a different proportion, but the material we brought to the piano may even have been a little in my favour. After the career he's had, he was willing to open himself up to a full-blooded collaboration, which was largely unprecedented. He had written one or two songs with other people, such as Neil Diamond, but nothing like to this extent."

Bacharachian instrumentation on this track includes tack piano, flugelhorn, girl gospel singers and the doorbell chimes of "One Less Bell to Answer" and "This House Is Empty Now" slowed down to a death knell. The uplifting ending offers some hope that the dark is a healing place and that he will eventually find his way back into the light.

Other Versions: *Bill Frisell (1999)*

1998

Holy "Toledo"! *Painted from Memory* sold half a million copies worldwide without any radio play. The most enthusiastic buyers were in Sweden, where it reached the Top 10, Australia (No. 22) and Britain (No. 32). The Americans lagged behind, only sending it as high as No. 78.

"Toledo" (Burt Bacharach - Elvis Costello)
Recorded by Elvis Costello and Burt Bacharach
From the album *Painted from Memory*,
Mercury 314 538 0002-2
Released September 1998

Much of the press brouhaha likening Bacharach and Costello to *The Odd Couple* was based on appearance, apparel and a false public image both men had cultivated and, in their own minds, discarded ages ago. The genial Costello was no more a vengeful punk than the driven workaholic Bacharach was some laid-back Martini & Rossi swinger who churned out easy-listening music. Musically speaking, they got on like Siamese twins: Costello fixates over the smallest lyrical detail the way Bacharach obsesses over a sixteenth note, and vice versa. "He's very precise," Costello told *Newsweek.* "Sometimes I tried to steal a couple of notes—you know, 'I've got this great line that would fit if you'd just give me another semiquaver!' But in the end I'd find a different way to say the same thing. It was good discipline."

Hal David could also be quite obsessive over a line; usually he put in his long hours struggling over how to say the strongest thing the simplest way. Costello matches David's zeal for providing detail (compare *"the music coming out of your radio"* and *"two silhouettes on the window shade"* from "Are You There with Another Girl" to *"the light beneath your the door and the laughter in your room"* from "In the Darkest Place"), but Costello gets even more specific, right down to the anxiously blinking red light on the answering machine. This is a song about an illicit affair that has come to light, and where David might simply have written about being untrue, Costello's betrayer confesses that *"it's no use saying that I love you and how that girl didn't mean a thing to me,"* continually ruminating over his guilt while watching other contented lovers able to go through life without having to make the phone call he cannot put off much longer.

Costello's metaphor of comparing Toledo, Spain, to Toledo, Ohio, in order to illustrate the distance his lies have followed him has the dual effect of separating him from his audience. Even if this is just a conversational tangent thrown in to keep the guy in the song from playing that dreaded recorded message, this added red herring smacks of elitism. Costello sounds a might too pleased with the conceit that people in Ohio are too ignorant to dream about Spanish citadels, even if it mirrors the wife's ignorance of his indiscretions in the song.

There's a coda on the song's fadeout, which you can hear in its entirety in live performances, where Elvis lists several other European vacation spots that are nothing like their American counterparts: *"But we still have Florence, Alabama / We don't have Paris and we don't have Rome / Or New York or even Amsterdam / None of these lonely towns will be my home."*

Costello sings that coda at full volume on *The Sweetest Punch,* the Bill Frisell reconstruction of the Bacharach and Costello material that was prepared concurrently with *Painted from Memory* and recorded without any knowledge of how Bacharach and Costello would ultimately arrange this material beyond their initial lead sheets. The composers, in turn, were not to hear Frisell's arrangements until after the Costello album was completed. Frisell's "Toledo" adds a darkly playful extended instrumental section that increases the drama considerably.

Other Versions: *Bill Frisell with Elvis Costello (1999)*

"I Still Have That Other Girl." The pair won a 1999 Grammy for this song, in the odd "pop collaboration with vocals" category.

"I Still Have That Other Girl" (Burt Bacharach - Elvis Costello)
Recorded by Elvis Costello and Burt Bacharach
From the album *Painted from Memory,* Mercury 314 538 0002-2
Released September 1998

On October 20, 1999, the Bravo cable network aired a documentary on the making of *Painted from Memory* entitled *Because It's a Lonely World,* with behind-the-scenes footage of the pair recording the album and discussing each track. Costello recalls that the construction of this song was a running dialogue of different musical ideas. "I nearly ruined it. We were trying to get to the chorus without going all the way through everything again.…I was sort of staring out the window in his writing room thinking about the lyric and Burt started playing the piano in this really beautiful way." Suddenly switched on again, Costello hears what his partner is playing and exclaims, "What's that? That's it. That's it." Bacharach, with eyes closed, was writing the now-familiar intro to "I Still Have That Other Girl," the team's Grammy winner for "pop collaboration with vocals."

The traveling adulterer of the previous song comes clean that his illicit affair was wrong and must now end, but the more one listens to the lyric, the more one wonders whether he isn't telling his wife that it's his legal marriage that must be terminated. Bacharach's exacting nature forced Costello to reign in the fancy wordplay that sometimes sounds like, in his own words, "a chainsaw running through a dictionary." This song demonstrates, as did past Tin Pan Alley appropriations like "Almost Blue" and "Baby Plays Around," that he is at his most effective with less fanciful verbiage.

The syllabic restrictions and Bacharach's conducting of the vocals allowed Elvis to stretch out his phrasing, achieving what *Rolling Stone* exclaimed was "the finest vocal performance of Costello's career." Certain elderly factions of Bacharach's fan base, his adult contemporaries, would audibly harrumph at the suggestion. You can see them at Bacharach concerts positively glowering at the intrusion of Elvis Costello's name and this song into the familiar, almost rote set list, although the less-jagged performance of this song by Bacharach's featured male vocalist John Pagano seems to quell their teeth gnashing. Given a chance to hear Bacharach's best work in decades, these fans chose to eject this out of the CD carousel in favor of *Dionne Sings Dionne*, an album of tepid Bacharach-David remakes that came out one week later.

1998

Ann Sofie von Otter Meets Elvis Costello: *For the Stars* (2001). This opera-meets-pop CD won the Edison Award for best classical album of 2001. It contains a stunning version of "This House Is Empty Now," which von Otter performed when Bacharach received the Polar Music Prize, also in 2001. It also features a Costello song called "Shamed into Love," whose opening melody apes the "as sure as I believe, there's a heaven above" line from "Alfie."

"I Still Have That Other Girl" is featured twice on *The Sweetest Punch*, once as an unsatisfying duet between Costello and Cassandra Wilson and again as a bizarre reprise that just explores the intro and winds up sounding like something David Lynch would commission from Angelo Badalamenti.

"This House is Empty Now" (Burt Bacharach - Elvis Costello)
Recorded by Elvis Costello and Burt Bacharach
From the album *Painted from Memory,*
Mercury 314 538 0002-2
Released September 1998

Although contractually a Costello album, *Painted from Memory* is also an artistic comeback album for Bacharach, whose name had been mostly hidden in album credits for over a decade. Unlike other return-to-active-duty albums (e.g., Roy Orbison's *Dream Girl*, John Fogerty's *Centerfield* or any Brian Wilson solo album), there are no deliberate rehashes of older songs to sucker you in. "This House Is Empty Now," the most mournful song on the album, comes closest. Thematically, it's almost another "House Is Not a Home," but the two are worlds apart. In the former song, Brook Benton had some sliver of hope that his love might return. A happy reunion is not likely for Costello's protagonist, who already surmised in "Toledo" that *"if anyone should look into your eyes, it's not forgiveness that they're gonna see."* So he is left in the empty house picking through the mementos she chose to abandon and wondering which of their friends will decide to retain him after the split.

On *Because It's a Lonely World*, Costello reveals Bacharach's lyrical input to this song: "He doesn't write lyrics but he has a very vocal sense. A lot of the instrumental lines have an underlying lyrical idea, maybe it's a dummy idea but it may be the key to the phrasing of the line.... When he played me the opening phrase, it had the word 'remember' in a very crucial place in the phrase and I couldn't get it out of my head. In fact, in the original manuscript of just the sketch of the opening ideas, we identified it with the word 'remember.'" The word "remember" was similarly used in the wistfully nostalgic "Making Love." One hears the Bacharach touch in two other instances that recall songs from his Carole Bayer Sager years. The phrase that follows "remember" in "This House" is reminiscent of the chorus of Neil Diamond's "I'll See You on the Radio (Laura)." Unfortunately, the rote-and-ready electric guitar solo also recalls his Eighties work, and it is an unwelcome intrusion.

Most of the cover versions of *Painted from Memory* songs seem personally sanctioned by Costello, except for that of legendary jazz bassist Ray Brown, who played on some of Costello's 1986 album *King of America*. Brown recorded a fine instrumental version of "I Still Have That Other Girl," playing Bacharach's splendid piano intro on the high strings of his upright bass, and combined it with the Cahn-Stordahl-Weston standard "I Should Care."

Other Versions: *Ray Brown (1999) • Elvis Costello & Anne Sofie von Otter (2001) • Bill Frisell (1999) • Ann Sofie von Otter with the Swedish Radio Symphony (2001)*

"Tears at the Birthday Party" (Burt Bacharach - Elvis Costello)
Recorded by Elvis Costello and Burt Bacharach
From the album *Painted from Memory,* Mercury 314 538 0002-2
Released September 1998

Bacharach's strident tack piano is prominent in the mix once more, but the musical question begging to be asked here is "What's Wrong, Pussycat?" On "Tears at the Birthday Party," Costello was writing from the viewpoint of someone recalling a childhood infatuation that he failed to cultivate into something lasting. In the album's development, it's possible to hear it as Elvis watching the ex-wife of "Toledo" at their own child's birthday party and seeing the new man in her life playing daddy to his kids. *"Now I see you share your cake with him / Unwrapping presents that I should've sent / Must I watch you?"* He jealously imagines that his successor will one day slip up in the same manner he did, as adults outgrow their childish penchant for hurting one another.

Other Versions: *Bill Frisell (1999)*

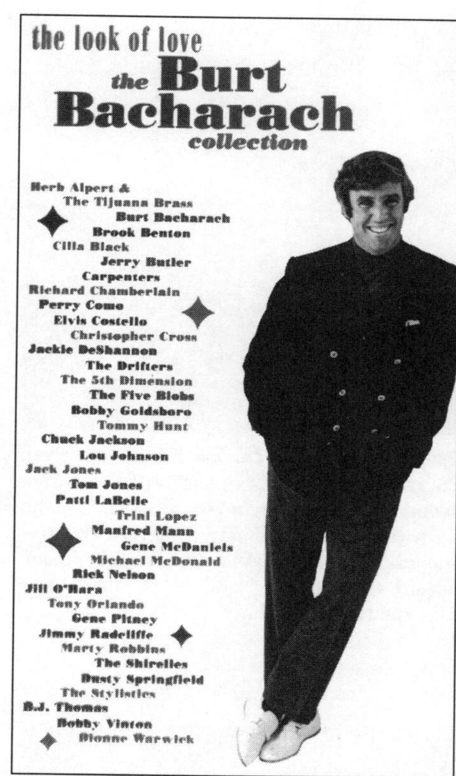

The Look of Love: The Burt Bacharach Collection. Brilliantly annotated by Alec Cumming, Patrick Milligan and Paul Grein, this smartly packaged 3-CD set is by far the best-ever gathering of Bacharach hits. A licensing nightmare, it was announced and delayed several times by Rhino before appearing hot on the heels of *Painted from Memory.* It concludes with Elvis's "God Give Me Strength."

"Such Unlikely Lovers" (Burt Bacharach - Elvis Costello)
Recorded by Elvis Costello and Burt Bacharach
From the album *Painted from Memory,* Mercury 314 538 0002-2
Released September 1998

Inserted into the album to provide some sunlight and relief as well as allude to the improbable pairing of two strange musical bedfellows, "Such Unlikely Lovers" offers us a romance, unfolding in the present tense, that Costello, four songs into his sad ennui, can't believe is happening. What a thrill it is to hear Bacharach putting the orchestra through its paces during the bridge, scoring the busy sounds of the city street. Costello slathers this track with several layers of irony. He's startled by violins appearing in doorways (which naturally appear on the track) and struggles with all the wonder and apprehension of someone about to lose control of his heart's internal functions. *"Though no one seems to notice as they hurry by / Ask me what I'm thinking and I won't deny it! I am bewildered,"* Costello exclaims at his most exasperated, punctuating it with a meek *"help me."* With the exception of "God Give Me Strength," it's his most exasperated singing on the album, but he clearly delighted in singing the song on the *Sessions at West 54th* TV show, even when certain notes failed to tumble out of his mouth as expected.

"My Thief" (Burt Bacharach - Elvis Costello)
Recorded by Elvis Costello and Burt Bacharach
From the album *Painted from Memory,* Mercury 314 538 0002-2
Released September 1998

The Sweetest Punch. Bill Frisell was given rough demos of every song on *Painted from Memory* as it was being written, and he came up with this album of vastly different arrangements. Costello guest-stars on the album, singing the lead on "I Still Have That Other Girl" and "Toledo."

Sadness returns once more like a bad reality check. Costello again invokes memories of "A House Is Not a Home, "that wonderful flash when "suddenly your face appears" only to disintegrate into "a crazy game." Here it's a crazy recurring nightmare, where the thief of Costello's affections visits him nightly. Even as she tells him she no longer loves him, he finds some consolation that she thinks enough of him to come all this way to return to the scene of the crime and rob him of peaceful sleep and any remaining hopeful dreams. In the sweetest voice imaginable, Lisa Taylor sings her evil lullaby of larceny in everybody, and Bacharach adds the uneasy epilogue, reminiscent of the equally bleak "Whoever You Are, I Love You."

Other Versions: *Bill Frisell (1999)*

"The Long Division" and "The Sweetest Punch" (Burt Bacharach - Elvis Costello)
Recorded by Elvis Costello and Burt Bacharach
From the album *Painted from Memory,* Mercury 314 538 0002-2
Released September 1998

Some critics of Costello's early work bemoaned his inability to resist a cheesy pun like "A wave of her hand could be so tidal" or "You lack lust, you're so lackluster." Often this is musicologist Costello's tip of the hat to the Smokey Robinson of "I Second That Emotion" and "What's So Good About Goodbye," the latter of which also wondered, 'How can farewell be fair?" In the tradition of his money punning in "Love for Tender," his camouflaging love songs in military fatigues for *Armed Force* and his exhausting every arithmetic analogy for "The Long Division," Costello turns in every boxing term he somehow missed on "T.K.O. (Boxing Day)" for "The Sweetest Punch."

Sessions at West 54th. The home video of the pair's appearance on this PBS series contained four Bacharach standards sung by Costello, including two ("Anyone Who Had a Heart" and "My Little Red Book") that he's never recorded.

"The Long Division," with its deliciously outdated moog-like solo, sounds more like one of Bacharach's better quiet-storm grooves of the Eighties than anything in Costello's catalog. If the two indeed fought over the white keys and the black keys on the *Sessions at West 54th* telecast, on this occasion Costello didn't put up much of a struggle. "The Sweetest Punch" also sounds like paydirt Bacharach, with Costello cramming in twice the number of words Carole Bayer Sager might've. Of all the Frisell refashionings, the guitarist's languid calculation of "The Long Division" seems the most indistinguishable from any Costello track.

Other Versions: *Bill Frisell (1999)*

"Painted from Memory" & "What's Her Name Today" (Burt Bacharach - Elvis Costello)
Recorded by Elvis Costello and Burt Bacharach
From the album *Painted from Memory,* Mercury 314 538 0002-2
Released September 1998

The only arrangement not of Bacharach's hand on *Painted from*

Memory was the title track. Johnny Mandell, the man who wrote "The Shadow of Your Smile," the song that beat Bacharach out of his first Oscar nomination, orchestrated what turns out to be the song's most Sinatraesque passage, especially the dramatic pause where Costello intones, *"She is gone and I must accept it."* The song centers on a man who carries around a photograph of his departed love and treats it as tenderly as if it were an art treasure. That sounds a lot like the Frank in Kitty Kelly's book *His Way,* whose nightly appointment of getting drunk in front of Ava Gardner's photo was interrupted by a blind rage that found him tearing up her photo and then desperately trying to reassemble it minutes later.

Costello ponders the woman who posed for this picture, whose eyes he cannot capture anymore and whose smiles are meant for someone else. Even though someone new has her, there's more gentility than jealousy here than on other tracks: it's years later and yet he still hasn't been able to mentally say goodbye to this woman. As on "In the Darkest Place" there's a possibility that keeping this memory will keep his heart from hardening until someone else comes along. This song provides the appropriate contrast to the cruel lover of "What's Her Name Today." As big a cad as Alfie was in his day, this guy can't even be trusted to remember a girl's name and is willing to take his rage out on every girl for not being the one who got away. The album concludes with the magnificent and previously discussed "God Give Me Strength," which the entire album was constructed to lead up to. This completion-backwards method of album making mirrors that of the Beatles, who usually arrived at the final track of a masterpiece early in the recording process. While Costello's 1981 album *Imperial Bedroom* was marketed as a masterpiece with a question mark, there's no questioning *Painted From Memory*'s masterpiece status five years later: it's a high-water mark that both men still wax euphoric over in interviews.

Repainted from Memory. This DVD collection of *Sessions at West 54th* contains 14 artists performing one song apiece. Lord knows why they thought we'd want an alternate version of "Painted from Memory" as a bonus cut instead of some other outtake, especially in light of all the other alternate versions of songs heard on the Bravo special *Because It's a Lonely World.*

"I'm very, very proud of the album, my work on it," says Bacharach on the Bravo special. "I feel it's some of the best work I've ever done, and hopefully Elvis feels the same."

The sight of two men with genuine affection for each other and for each other's talents was a healthy respite from the sight of Celine Dion in love with the sound of her own voice. Celine was a constant target for Costello's cutting jibes throughout the pair's tireless promotion for the album. "We're here to kick Celine Dion's ass," he'd joke, and while she won the song-of-the-year award for her *Titanic* love theme, it was a triumph of quality over commerce that "I Still Have That Other Girl," a song with no radio airplay, could win a Grammy.

In a better time, it would've been a Top 40 hit. "No. I don't think we even put out a single," Bacharach remarks. "That record company was going through a change. Mercury was falling apart; that was around the time everyone was getting fired. You can't do anything. It's out of your control." Coming off such an artistic triumph, the big question is, Will there ever be any more "new songs of Bacharach and Costello"? Bacharach was non-committal in 2000. "I don't know. It's always possible. That was a big one. It's a very expensive tour to put on the road but I saw him in Ireland about five weeks ago. I did three concerts there and Elvis lives in Dublin and he came onstage and did three songs with me and it was great."

1999

"Don't Give Up." President Bill Clinton, a Dave Koz fan, invited the saxophonist to play at his inaugural celebration in 1993—the same occasion where Fleetwood Mac reunited to play "'Don't Stop." Stevie Nicks became a Koz fan, too, and was a guest on his 1996 recording "Let Me Count the Ways."

Unlike Costello's collaborations with Paul McCartney, which have snuck out in dribs and drabs, nothing else by Bacharach and Costello has been issued on bootlegs, B-sides or bonus cuts. Costello's follow-up album, released in 2002, was a return to the raucous rock that he has sworn off several times already. The lesson here? Never say never.

Other Versions: *Bill Frisell (1999)*

"Don't Give Up" (Burt Bacharach - Dave Koz)
Recorded by Dave Koz
From the album *The Dance,* Capitol 99458
Released September 1999

A popular contemporary jazz artist and host of the syndicated program "The Dave Koz Radio Show," this saxophonist got the opportunity to produce, arrange and play with the man he calls "my idol" in his liner notes. On this sprightly R&B ballad, Bacharach plays a fine acoustic piano part, someone plays a triangle, and Koz switches from tenor to soprano saxophone. The main melody mostly hovers in the same range as Kenny G., that purveyor of smooth jazz whom rough-jazz purists enjoy deriding. Dave K. doesn't crowd each bar of music with millions of notes either, and if you removed his contribution, there would be nothing that would identify this as jazz at all. But it's a likeable enough for what it is—a smooth-jazz motivational record.

"If I Should Ever Lose You" (Burt Bacharach - Steve Krikorian)
Recorded by Chicago
From the album *Chicago 26: Live in Concert,* Chicago 3026
Released October 1999

If you hadn't let your subscription to the *International Trumpet Guild Journal* lapse, you'd know that the Chicago™ horn section has been together longer than any other section in the history of music. Longer than any big band outfit. Longer than Blood, Sweat & Tears. Longer than the careers of the Ides of March, Madness and the Baha Men combined.

But after the hits stopped coming as consecutively as the albums with Roman numerals did, the Nineties found Chicago™ in a curious holding pattern. For a while, Chicago™ the group became Chicago™ the record label, releasing countless greatest-hits collections, a big-band album, a Christmas album (the suitably named *Chicago XXV*, just like Jesus' birthday) and this live album, only their second in 35 years. *Chicago XXVI*, shockingly enough, proves that this band can still rock the rock in a live setting.

Two studio cuts were tacked on the end of the live set—a sorry-to-say-it's-sorry version of Jackie Wilson's "Higher and Higher," with lead vocals by Michael McDonald, and this ballad, which found Bacharach working with Steve Krikorian, better known as singer-songwriter Tonio K. Like Costello, Tonio K. emerged during the so-called new-wave movement, with sarcastically sharp pop sensibilities and an album called *Life in the Food Chain*. By the Nineties, he had shifted his focus to writing songs for others. Chicago™ has been receptive to outside material since the Eighties, when they became an outlet for David Foster ballads, with horns as an afterthought. "If I Should Lose You" puts the horns in front at the outset, as the group did with such great ballads of yesteryear as "Just You and Me" and "Wishing You Were Here," and it's the brass that provides the song's major hook.

Lee Loughnane on the Ballad Problem. "There wasn't a hell of a lot we could do about it, because how can you take success and say, 'You know what? I don't want that.' And when we did put out tunes that were up-tempo or medium tempo, we were told by radio and various other entities that it didn't sound like Chicago™. And that was always something of a dumbfounding comment."

According to Chicago™ trumpeter and flugelhornist Lee Loughnane, "Burt wrote the song, presented it to someone in the office, and we said, 'Yeah, this is a great tune.' And he was going to be putting it in a movie he was doing the music for. It turns out the director didn't think the song was good for the movie, so he pulled it."

The movie was the less-than-spectacular *Isn't She Great*. Both Bacharach's samey-sounding score and the listlessly dull movie could've used this song as a breather. "We wrote the brass parts, changed some of it chordally so as not to piss him off," laughs Loughnane. "As a writer should be, because if you change a song too much it's not their song anymore. He came in and played some keyboard parts, but I wasn't in that day so I didn't get to meet him, unfortunately."

"Walking Tall" (Burt Bacharach - Tim Rice)
Recorded by Lyle Lovett
From the original soundtrack *Stuart Little*, Polygram 542083
Released November 1999

How can your heart not go out to a computer-generated orphan mouse that only wants "a name to share, a heart to care"? Few resisted this charming and intelligent adaptation of E.B. White's classic children's story, which grossed a whopping $140 million and put a sequel into immediate production. Kicking the *Stuart Little* movie off was this Bacharach collaboration with Tim Rice, who initially teamed with Andrew Lloyd Webber for *Joseph and the Amazing Technicolor Dreamcoat, Jesus Christ Superstar* and *Evita* and in recent years became the Disney lyricist of choice. Rice won an Academy Award for best original song in 1992 ("A Whole New World," from *Aladdin*) and 1993 ("Can You Feel the Love Tonight?" written with Elton John for *The Lion King*).

Stuart Little. Another soundtrack featuring Bacharach and his ex-wife Carole Bayer Sager, but not together. It contains the Goss-Nelson-Sager composition "Lucky Day."

Unlike some of the previous Rice winners, this has an edginess Disney would never allow, like the questioning of the existence of a Supreme Being *("I wonder who arranges all our lives and sorts us out / Who chooses who")* and questioning the logic of a Creator who forgets to give someone a family *("I'm feeling relatively blue, oh how I'd love a next of kin or two")*. Musically, it sounds like a more realized version of "With a Smile," which only Japanese audiences would be familiar with. Its non-nomination at Oscar time is something of a mystery. Maybe the Academy worried that inviting Lyle Lovett to sing it meant that his ex-wife Julia Roberts might not show up.

2000

Isn't She Great. Both the DVD and VHS cassette of this film come in widescreen format to insure you can see any corner chairs and surplus shrubbery you might otherwise miss.

"On My Way" (Burt Bacharach - Hal David)
Recorded by Dionne Warwick
From the Universal motion picture *Isn't She Great*
Decca 289 466 981-2, released 2000

Bacharach and David remained true to their intent of getting together only to write for specific projects rather than just compose for some unnamed artist. Dionne Warwick's recent spate of theme albums (particularly her *Dionne Sings Dionne* rerecordings of old Bacharach-David favorites) precluded the necessity for any new Burt and Hal material. As is obvious with recordings like *Dionne Sings Dionne*, "On My Way" demonstrates how the passage of time and a chronic cigarette habit have grounded her once-soaring voice.

Bacharach and David may have spent nearly a lifetime hearing Dionne's voice in their heads while composing, but one wonders if it's the mature, hush-toned Dionne they heard when "On My Way" was on the drafting table. Dionne's reading is closer to Dusty Springfield's sotto voce "The Look of Love" than to her own version of that song. Had this pleasant ditty about wandering aimlessly but keeping a positive watch for a new life appeared in the days of *Valley of the Dolls*, it would've been given a perkier treatment by both singer and conductor. This track's mellow groove is soothing but hardly the stuff one would hope for to usher us into a biopic of shock 'n' sleaze novelist Jacqueline Susann. Unfortunately, the whole *Isn't She Great* project follows this misdirection, reducing the authoress' own larger-than-life story to a till-cancer-do-us-part flick with all the sin-sational sex, booze and drugs surgically removed.

"Open Your Heart" (Burt Bacharach - Hal David)
Recorded by Vanessa Williams
From the original soundtrack *Isn't She Great,*
Decca 289 466981-2
Released January 2000

Isn't She Great. One wonders if the versions of "Alfie" and "The April Fools" that Vanessa Williams cut in 1997 were training exercises for her performance on "Open Your Heart."

While Jacqueline Susann would've appreciated the singer of the *Valley of the Dolls* theme returning to sing her own story of naïve ambition, she would've salivated over the Vanessa Williams story, which reads like one of her books. A Miss America, disgraced by a pornographic past, is humiliated into giving up her crown, only to turn tragedy around and become a multi-platinum recording artist four years later. All that's missing is a vengeful Vanessa using her celebrity to settle old scores. Instead the real-life beauty simply persevered in establishing a credible singing career that made people forget the controversy.

Williams' easy-on-the-eye looks translate to the ear as well. When she coos, *"I looked at you, you looked at me and it just happened,"* it's hard to know what to do besides melt. You've got to wonder why it was so difficult to get Clive Davis to sign off on a Bacharach ballad for Whitney Houston, and you have your answer with this recording. Houston doesn't have the modesty to just lay back and let the song connect with the listener the way Williams does. She endows the movie's love theme with more sex appeal than it deserves. Bette Midler has more chemistry with her onscreen poodle than she does with Nathan Lane, who spends most of the film mooning "isn't she great," with nothing on the screen to back it up.

God Give Her Strength. Her *Bette* CD was timed to come out with her CBS television series of the same name. Despite the application of a lavender sticker reminding people to watch the show, few did. But she does a great version of "God Give Me Strength."

***Isn't She Great* (Original Soundtrack)**
Decca 289 466981-2, released January 2000

"On My Way" (Burt Bacharach - Hal David)
Performed by Dionne Warwick
"Open Your Heart" (Burt Bacharach - Hal David)
Performed by Vanessa Williams

"Love Theme (The Falling in Love)" • "Lunch at Lindy's" • "Guy's Theme" [Wordless] • "Mass Love" • "Sexual Me, Sexual You" • "Yes, They Said Yes!" • "The Big Pitch" • "Are You My Friend?" • "Hello Connecticut" • "For Mimsy" • "Heartache Revisited" • "The Book Tour (On My Way)" [Reprised] • "About Expectations" • "The Late Lunch" • Victory at a Price"
Written and performed by Burt Bacharach

What would've afforded Bacharach the perfect opportunity to write in his old style ends up a cluster of missed opportunities. Everything about the execution of this score postdates the era it's supposed to represent but is still too dated for the Nineties. Why are there Eighties urban-contemporary DX7 keyboard sounds and popping bass lines in the swinging Sixties? There's not even the slightest hint of rock or Motown, not one tambourine or a genuine Hammond organ in this digital sea.

The feeble attempts Bacharach makes at parodying himself don't go far enough, as if the composer is determined steer clear of any real excitement. "Sexual Me, Sexual You" is a passable stab at reprising "The Look of Love" but doesn't ever catch fire the way the original did. "The Big Pitch" and "The Book Tour" both start out with trumpet blasts that allude to "Promises, Promises" before caving into what sounds like a theme to some God-awful morning show like *Good Morning Rochester*. "The Big Pitch" could've been arranged to sound like Dave Brubeck's "Take Five"; instead it resembles an unused backing track to an Al Jarreau song. And there are way too many reprises of both the "Love Theme," played with a dissonant chord in the center to let you know that cancer is coming, and the mopey "Guy's Theme," to let you know Nathan Lane's sulking again. It's as if the movie and the music were geared toward elderly people who were young and vibrant in the turbulent Sixties but don't want to be reminded of it now.

"Overture 2000" (Burt Bacharach)
Performed at the 72nd annual Academy Awards by Bert Bacharach and Orchestra
Telecast on March 29, 2000

The news that Bacharach was composing an overture for the 2000 Oscar ceremony was overshadowed by the announcement that he and co-musical director Don Was were fashioning a medley of previously nomi-

2000

Engelbert. The smooth crooner vows to keep performing as long as people want to hear a romantic ballad. But you wonder how many of his millions of fans went to the movie *Beavis and Butt-Head Do America* to hear Engelbert perform the tender romantic ballad "Lesbian Seagull."

nated Oscar songs, sung by an all-star cast including Ray Charles, Garth Brooks. Queen Latifah, Isaac Hayes, Dionne Warwick (singing "Alfie," which she and Bacharach had performed together at the 1967 Oscar ceremony) and Whitney Houston.

Then the medley was overshadowed by reports in the *Los Angeles Times* and *New York Post* that Bacharach had fired Houston from the show because she flubbed her lines, missed cues and sang the wrong song after two nights of rehearsals. Unidentified sources quoted Bacharach as telling the singer, "Just leave. It's not going to work out," but the official Oscar account had Houston coming down with a sore throat and dropping out for the good of the show. Country singer Faith Hill substituted at the last minute to sing "The Way We Were" and "Somewhere Over the Rainbow."

Bacharach fans were probably the only people paying attention to the music playing underneath announcer Peter Coyote's reading of the academy's selection rules. They heard an invigorating Bacharach original with orchestration that resembled something off *Woman*—nothing like the cupboard-clearing sounds of *Isn't She Great*. It led to speculation that Bacharach might actually record a proper album of new songs under his own name for the first time since 1979. Not long after the Oscar telecast he conceded, "I've been approached by a couple of people. But for me to go in and make an album and put six or seven months into it and then they can't sell it, can't get it played on the right radio format at the right level. Or the company is suddenly acquired, taken over by somebody who doesn't give a shit about it....I'd rather just keep writing for other people."

"Nothing in This World" (Burt Bacharach - Nigel Lowis)
First recorded by Engelbert
From the CD *It's All in the Game,* Hip-O/Universal 440 013 307-2
Released 2001

I know what you're thinking: where's the Humperdinck? Since the late Eighties, Engelbert's been billing himself by one name only, like Cher, Madonna, Liberace, Elvis and Gallagher. But doesn't one do that at the peak of one's popularity, you ask? Yes, and don't let the lack of chart hits fool you: Engelbert is still huge at half the name size. He has the largest fan club in the world, with 250 chapters and around eight million members. And he plays sellout shows to screaming fans as if "Release Me" had just been released. How else can you explain his remaining on the Universal Records roster after the massive Seagram's shakedown and purge of 1999?

The smooth balladeer voice still carries quite a punch, though it has taken on a bit of a Kenny Rogers drawl in later years. There is nothing in "Nothing in This World" to discourage Engelbert lovers from loving him more. But if bland is not your brand, don't go looking for another "I'm a Better Man" here.

"Tell It to Your Heart" (Burt Bacharach - Steve Krikorian)
Recorded by Randy Crawford
From the album *Permanent,* Warner Bros. 89273
Released August 2001

Crawford first won notice as the female voice singing with the Crusaders on their 1979 hit "Street Life." Since then she's had considerable success overseas but hasn't manage to cross over into the pop market back in the States. Her eclectic albums are an opulent mix of funky numbers, power ballads and dance hits, but it's as if Warner Brothers isn't sure what she is and thinks that marketing her as a jazz singer is the cure-all. "Tell It to Your Heart" is a mainstream pop ballad all the way. Like Dionne Warwick, Crawford possesses a comforting voice that carries clout without tacking on any harshness. Bacharach crafts a chorus very similar to the coda on "My Thief," with all the malevolence of the former song removed. Rather than nurture romantic delusions, Tonio K. advises consulting your inner Magic 8-Ball for direction because *"love's gonna have its way no matter what you do."*

Diane Schuur. Talk about jazz elite! Schuur was the first recipient of the Montreal International Jazz Festival's annual Ella Fitzgerald Award for outstanding vocal performance in the tradition of Ella Fitzgerald. Mirroring Ella's infamous duet with Big Bird, Schuur visited *Sesame Street* twice to sing with Elmo. But the furry red castrato was less than tickled about being snubbed on the *Friends for Schuur* album.

"Never Take That Chance Again" (Burt Bacharach - Steven Krikorian)
Recorded by Diane Schuur
From the album *Friends for Schuur,* Concord Jazz 4898
Released September 2000

Often called "the new first lady of jazz," Diane Schuur is yet another singer whose jazz often veers off into pop airspace. As a result, her albums have been a curious mix of standards like "The Very Thought of You" and pop songs by the likes of Billy Joel and Jackson Browne. On *Friends for Schuur,* producer Phil Ramone repeats the popular *Duets* album format that was a great commercial success for Sinatra, but in a weird twist he pairs the blind singer-pianist with other sightless greats like Stevie Wonder and Ray Charles and adds an electronically engineered duet from the Great Beyond with her former mentor, the late Stan Getz. Bacharach was not one of the duet partners, but he sent his regards in the form of this ballad. The flavorless verses are offset by a majestic chorus, where the lyrics have Schuur calling out, *"Baby, can you save me from myself / help me to believe in someone else."* Schuur's perfect diction makes Tonio K.'s standard pop-vernacular lyrics (especially the word "baby") sound like a talking computer is translating from another language. Although the original first lady of jazz, Ella Fitzgerald, enunciated every syllable, too, it worked better with Cole Porter than it did with Cream's "Sunshine of Your Love."

2001

My Show. In Sweden and Norway, Carola's fans were almost a "no show" for this album, compared to their devotion in the past. Her millennium album didn't chart in Norway, where it sold roughly 10,000 copies. In Sweden, the tally was closer to 60,000.

"Count on Me," "Leave It to the Girls," and "In My Dreams" (Burt Bacharach - Steven Krikorian)
Recorded by Tonio K.
Unreleased Bacharach-Tonio K. demos, with Todd Herzog, vocals, 2001

Tonio K. likes to remark that he's probably the only artist to have collaborated with both Burt Bacharach and the Sex Pistols' Steve Jones. While we ponder that, we must note that none of the collaborations with Bacharach have yet appeared on a Tonio K. album, mostly because his last two albums have been Gadfly compilations of unreleased material left in the wake of folding record companies and lapsed contracts. Since Gadfly has taken an interest in rereleasing his entire recorded catalog, it's probable that K. will get around to releasing an album of new original material. All three ballads are appealingly Bacharachian: demo singer Todd Herzog adopts the upward inflections that are hallmarks of Bacharach's singing style for the soul ballad "Count on Me," while Bacharch brings back the *baion* beat of yesteryear for "In My Dreams" and "Leave It to the Girls." "In My Dreams" goes even further, with triggered timpani, a brooding horn part played on keyboards and the identical chorus melody line to "Long Ago Tommorrow," including the concluding line *"in my dreams"* that gives this song its title.

"Someday" (Burt Bacharach - Steven Krikorian)
Recorded by Carola
From the album *My Show,* Sonet/Universal 016 540-2 2001
Released in Sweden, November 2001

There's been a Eurovision Song Contest every year since 1958, and in that period Sweden has won four times, most notably in 1974, when a song called "Waterloo" brought ABBA international stardom. At the tender age of 17, Swedish singer Carola Häggkvist placed third with a song called "Främling" ("Love Isn't Love") but later won in 1991 with "Fångad av en Stormvind" ("Captured by a Lovestorm"). "Someday" sounds like the kind of song the betting parlors would offer as an odds-on favorite—a dreaming-of-a-better-world anthem that sounds like Miss World's platform for world peace *("Every one of us who's lost his way will find his way home someday...every baby's cry is gonna be answered").* Carola invests this someday place with considerable wonder and betrays some surprising doubt and fear when she admits, *"maybe I'm a million miles away from how it's gonna be."*

Carola traveled to London to record this track with producer Robert Smith (Spice Girls, Brandy, Michael Jackson). "Someday" received its world premiere at The Polar Music Prize Banquet in Stockholm on May 14, 2001. Following a Carola-led medley of his hits, Bacharach joined her onstage to perform this song and to collect his prize—1,000,000 Swedish kronor presented to each recipient by the king of Sweden.

"What's in Goodbye" (Burt Bacharach - Cathy Dennis)
Recorded by Will Young
From the album *From Now On,* BMG International 96959
Released October 22, 2002

2002

Will Young. In July of 2002, Will Young performed the song live at Burt Bacaharch concerts in Liverpool and London. The lyrics are by Cathy Dennis, who produces both Young and *American Idol* Kelly Clarkson.

Before *American Idol* consumed a nation's attention span for an entire summer, a similar reaction was engendered overseas by the UK prototype, *Pop Idol.* There on February 9, 2002, a 23-year-old singer named Will Young pulled in over four-and-a-half million viewer votes to win top honors. A week later, his rush-released first single, "Evergreen," went on to sell over a million copies to become the fastest-selling UK single of all time.

Bacharach, whose songs and participation were featured for the entire August 13 *American Idols* telecast, had already paired up with former dancepop diva turned Brit-teen writer/producer Cathy Dennis to come up with a song for Young shortly after his triumphant win. Young's voice is an engaging cross between Gilbert O'Sullivan and Glenn Tilbrook of Squeeze, and this soothing album track once again taps Bacharach's love for Antonio Carlos Jobim—it even includes a "How Insensitive" reference in the lyric. Tossing in the piano riff from "Don't Go Breaking My Heart" raises some questions. Is the composer comfortable enough in his celebrity to trade on his past, much the way Hitchcock casts himself as an extra in his own films, or it is a marketing department's desire to inform the audience it's a Burt Bacharach tune?

"Love's (Still) the Answer" (Burt Bacharach - Steven Krikorian)
Recorded by Ornella Vanoni
From the Sony/Epic album *Sogni proibiti—Ornella e le canzoni di Bacharach*
Released in Italy, December 2002

Torchy balladeer-ess Ornella Vanoni has been cooing Bacharach songs since 1964, when she turned "Don't Make Me Over" into "Non dirmi niente." Nearly forty years later came an album whose Italian title translates into *Forbidden Dreams - Ornella and the Songs of Burt Bacharach. You* could dismiss this as yet another surprise-free international collection of the usual Bacharach covers if not for the inclusion of this unheard Bacharach-and-Tonio-K. selection as the album's thoughtful finale. Written for Vanoni and arranged and played by the man himself, "Love's Still the Answer" is the only song on the album sung in English and its Tonio K. lyrics decide that twenty years of broken hearts and tears (forty years would've made Ornella sound too old) have not eroded the importance of love as the ultimate problem solver. Vanoni's odd pronunciations have an Old World charm that sounds rather sexy in this Mediterranean sea of digital keyboards. But because it's not a belter of a song, most American divas probably wouldn't even consider it.

SECTION TEN
QUESTION ME AN ANSWER

...or Odds and Ends

Our exclusive "Question Me an Answer" interview with Burt, followed by a complete listing of songs registered with the copyright office and a separate listing of all the missing songs not covered in this book and what little we know about them, plus a listing of recordings that include samples of Bacharach songs and a listing of all the Bacharach TV specials.

Bacharach Backchat

COLORADO, Thursday, March 27, 2002, 11 A.M.
"This ain't the most fun thing in the world for me. Some people really love to talk about the good old, tough old days."

While interviewing Burt Bacharach for this book, the old Davis Sisters' hit "I Forgot More Than You'll Ever Know" sprang to mind. After all, here's a man who has spent over 50 years creating and negating a body of work that I've been seriously collecting for roughly five. Much of our discussion, particularly concerning the Famous Music years, is literally asking someone to try and remember a day at the office 47 years ago. I'm not even 47, and I couldn't tell you why my grade point average in English may have dipped a little in the sixth grade. So I had no illusions about him remembering a lot of this musical minutia he's put behind him more than a lifetime ago and I've only bought on eBay last year.

Quite simply, it's not the artist's job to be sentimental about old records and concert programs: that duty falls to the fans who replace worn copies with clean ones and turn friends on to something if it strikes a chord. If Bacharach was ever that sentimental, he couldn't have produced this catalog of over 600 songs: it is simply too much to ask one mind to store that much music and still have enough brain capacity to create more—or even care about it. The earliest songs were naturally the first to go unremembered: a good half of these songs were written in 9-to-5 workaday fashion, only to be recorded and ruined by shortsighted A&R men and arrangers some evening thereafter. If any song Bacharach wrote did nothing upon release, what was the point of keeping it around mentally? Boom! It was vaporized and he was already pounding the piano and working up something else.

It must be just as taxing on the brain to carry around little anecdotes pertaining to the 150-odd songs that *did* do something—stories he has had to repeat over 30- or 40-odd years. How "Make It Easy on Yourself" was his first production *and* the first song he'd cut with Dionne. How he didn't write with Hal David after *Lost Horizon* until "Sunny Weather Lover." How he didn't want to show anyone "What the World Needs Now" because Dionne didn't like it. None of these stories turns out to be totally true when you lay all the records out, but they've become the standard answers, and it takes less time away from the now. Like you, Bacharach would rather live in the now. But with his resurgence in popularity, he's been asked to relive those early years more times than any sane man would care to. With a finite number of tomorrows and only so many hours in a day to enjoy his two young children from a fourth marriage to ski instructor Jane Hanson, it must be more than slightly irritating to keep being pulled into the past, especially when it's keeping you indoors instead of on the slopes.

"And for me, even with the Brill Building anthologies [which aired on A&E], and they want a tape from England for something on Karen Carpenter's life," he sighs, "it represents…not standing still, that represents going backwards. 'Let's talk about the Brill Building days,' you know? Shit. That was then. Right now, I'm more interested in right now. I'm really appreciative of the past and the interest in it. I'm proud of it. Do I love talking about it? No."

That said, on this occasion Bacharach graciously took the time to think about this stuff but could just as easily turn around and ask me, "Did I write that with Hal or Mack David?" simply because it wasn't something he'd ever been asked to remember. The questions worked their way chronologically up to the present day, where Bacharach has some genuinely exciting new projects to surprise us all with. And there'll be some parts I've left in that may read more like a session of Stump the Composer than a mutual exchange of information but sometimes led to something unexpected. I started by asking him about his first high-profile job working with Vic Damone.

SD: *Your first gig was conducting and playing piano for him. I've always read that you were army buddies with him.*

BB: We both got out of the army at the same time, but we didn't know each other. It was through a mutual friend, Ivan Mogul, who lived in the same building that my parents lived in, and I was living with my parents. And when Vic was discharged, Ivan intervened and thought working for Vic would be a great move.

SD: *But you got fired from that job. What happened?*

BB: You know, I think there was a certain inexperience on my part, though I didn't feel it at the time. I thought I was doing really well as far as handling the job. It wasn't the first time I'd been fired. I'd been fired from playing the Cape Playhouse up in Cape Cod when I was sort of in my high school years. Boy, that one really hurt, 'cause it was a really great place to play in; it was a friend of my Dad's who owned the place, and that's how I got the job. But maybe I didn't know enough show tunes. When you lose your job on summer vacation and it's your second or third year of high school, that hurts. You just don't want to come home. So I got another job, at a lesser-profile place on the Cape. At a place maybe called Captain Gray's in Barnstable.

Getting back to Vic. There was a certain inexperience; I never conducted an orchestra, though I learned some conducting at school in conservatory, watching and things like that. It's still...you get a baptism by fire doing it, getting up there and conducting guys that are much older than you that don't have that much respect for you, you know? "What's this kid telling us what to do?" I don't think that was the problem. I just think Vic went through a lot of people—32, 33 conductors. I think it was a personality thing, too. I had a tough time with it, 'cause that was horrible—getting fired—and I resented it because he didn't do it himself. He had his two managers come backstage at the Chicago Theater. Hey, that's a long time.

SD: *And he wound up recording one of your tunes five years later on a B-side—"Oooh My Love."*

BB: [surprised] I didn't know that. See, you know more about me than I do.

SD: *It came out in '58, "Ooh My Love"—one of the songs Mitch Miller would have brought him when he was recording for Columbia.*

BB: I was on tour with Dietrich by then. I thought the first time he recorded a song of mine is when I went in and recorded a version of "Wives and Lovers" with him. No, I don't remember that song. Totally undistinguishable, not recognizable and probably not very good, right?

SD: *Correct.*

BB: Right up there with "Peggy's in the Pantry"!

SD: *See, you keep bringing that song up in interviews. You're driving up the demand for it!*

BB: I never thought of that song, but the guy on the CBS *Morning Show* was so relentless. You didn't see the amount of footage [they shot], you only saw the final product on the *Morning Show,* and the way they handled it was kind of cute, but he must've come back to "Peggy's in the Pantry" 12 times during a two-hour interview.

SD: *Everything written about starting to write with Hal David has you writing with his brother Mack David first. But I've only been able to locate a couple of songs that you've written together.*

BB: There's "The Blob."

SD: *That was in '58, and you'd already been writing with Hal in '56. There's a song you wrote with Mack called "Third Window from the Right," which I haven't found a recording of.*

BB: I couldn't give you the first note. I remember a song called "Hot Spell" with him. I was writing with Hal, and Mack would come into New York, I think after "The Blob," though I don't know. "The Blob" happened after '58, 'cause I didn't have the first hit with Como in '58, right? And "The Story of My Life."

SD: *You'd written those with Hal in late '57—and the* Sad Sack *theme.*

BB: That's right. We were doing songs like movie promotional songs for hire. It'd be $500 a song. "Desperate Hours," I remember that.

SD: *You had some songs actually in movies. You had "I Cry More" with Al Dale, and "Warm and Tender" was in the movie* Lizzie, *with Johnny Mathis performing it on film.*

BB: It was in the movie? Wow, I didn't know that. See, I find out so much talking to you I never knew. [laughs] One story about "Warm and Tender" that you'll probably like and don't know is that when I first met Marlene Dietrich and decided to work for her, or she decided I was going to work with her, before going to Vegas, I was out of work. I'd come out to California to learn something about film scoring, 'cause I was still under contract with Famous Music at the time. I came out to learn and also to live with a girl, an actress I met in New York. We were gonna live together. And I got this call from Peter Matz at the airport in New York, that he couldn't work for Noel Coward and Marlene Dietrich. He was supposed to do both, and that's how I wound up with Dietrich. And I played this song for Dietrich after I got to know her a bit with rehearsals at the Beverly Hills Hotel, after a week. Oh, she like the song, she wanted to get it to Sinatra, who she was close to. She did get it to Sinatra just before Mathis had recorded it. And he turned it down, and she was so angry at him. "You'll be sorry one day!"

SD: *Do you remember what he said about the song?*

BB: No, he never spoke to me about it. It was their communication.

SD: *In trying to narrow down the first recorded appearance of a Bacharach-David song, I've narrowed it down to three records. There's one song called "You're the Dream" by the Marvellos, a black vocal group out of Chicago. There's some dispute as to whether you wrote it or not.*

BB: Doesn't ring a bell to me.

SD: *Then it must be "The Morning Mail" by the Gallahads.*

BB: Don't know that one either.

SD: Then there's a song called "Tell the Truth and Shame the Devil" that has you and Hal and Margery Wolpin credited as writers. Was that Eddie Wolpin's wife?

BB: [long pause] Margery Wolpin's credited as a writer? That doesn't make any sense at all.

SD: *That's what it says in the ASCAP files. Was she a writer? I don't know.*

BB: That's an interesting thing, because I don't know that she ever had a song at all.

SD: *Is she his wife?*

BB: Was his wife. I don't know what kind of marriage they had. I just know that Eddie was walking home from the Brill Building whatever day she jumped out the window, just about the time he'd be coming home at the Gotham Hotel, I think it was.

SD: *Maybe he just put her name on it.*

BB: Maybe. Was it for a picture?

SD: *It must be. It doesn't sound like it would've been a single by itself.*

BB: The fact that she's listed comes as a surprise to me. She was a bright woman, just pretty crazy. The only thing is, her ex-husband was [movie producer] Jack Cummings, so maybe there's a connection somewhere.

SD: *I have a recording of you playing piano with orchestration by Marion Evans. Two songs, "Searching Wind" and "Roseanne." Ring any bells?*

BB: [pause] These are sort of flimsy memories. But Marion Evans, he's a hell of an arranger.

SD: When you hit with [Marty Robbins' recording of] "The Story of My Life," did your publishers try to pitch you to other country artists?

BB: I don't think so. It was kind of a freakish thing. It's kind of amazing—your first hit after waiting all that time turns out to be a No. 1 country-and-western record.

SD: *Did you cut ever any recordings with your first wife, Paula Stewart? I haven't been able to find any recordings of her, but I've read that you used to be her accompanist.*

BB: No. I played auditions for her. I can't remember anything beyond playing auditions. She had a legit voice and she would do summer stock and things like that.

SD: *Starting in the Sixties, when you started working with Bob Hilliard, you start doing a lot of novelty records. Was this because it was a lukewarm period and you weren't having a lot of hits?*

BB: I'm not sure. I just know that Hilliard had a pretty out-there sense of humor and take on life. Stuff like

"Three Wheels on My Wagon." That was pretty brilliant. We didn't really write a lot together, Hilliard and me. He's a very gifted writer. Funny guy.

SD: *All the versions I've collected of "Please Stay," a lot of people seem to change the words. And they're great. It's something about the "canyon of doom" people don't like.*

BB: I don't know why they do. I forgot that I wrote that with him. "If I got down on my knees and I pleaded with you," that's pretty great."

SD: *Then there's your death disc, "Two Hour Honeymoon"—basically a spoken-word record with the car careening off the road.*

BB: Paul Hampton? Yeah, I remember. He was a cute kid from Oklahoma. Good-looking kid, blond. He was an actor named Paul Schwartz, but he changed his name to Paul Hampton. Nothing happened with any of those songs, right? I don't know that we wrote more than one or two songs, did we?

SD: *About seven or eight. One with Hal David called "Paradise Island."*

BB: I remember that one. He looked like he could be an artist after a minute and a half. I ran into him somewhere at a party, somewhere in the last five-year period. He introduced himself to me. I would've never recognized him.

SD: *When you and Hal start doing R&B, your tunes were cut by the Wanderers and the Turbans. They were really good doo-wop numbers. The Turbans did "Three Friends, Two Lovers."*

BB: Did I write that with Hal David? Good title! That doesn't jog my memory. It was just so much easier to get songs recorded then. [laughs]

SD: *For the first Bacharach-David production, I have two instrumental songs by the Rangoons—"Moon Guitar" and "My Heart Is a Ball of String." I was wondering what Hal David did on the production if there weren't any lyrics.*

BB: Why two instrumentals would have his name? I'm not sure, unless we were all just working as a team.

SD: *Usually when he's credited as producer, it's largely to maintain the integrity of the words, isn't it?*

BB: Well, you know, the relationship between Hal and

myself, the Dionne days, he was co-producer. But that was more like being there, being a filter and—

SD: *—sounding board?*

BB: Not so much the sound but a great buffer. He wouldn't work on the arrangements or anything like that, but he's very valuable in the sense of a support system in the studio. "What do you think, Hal?" "That's good." "That doesn't feel so good." "Should the strings be in there?"

SD: *The big turning point songs for you were "Make It Easy on Yourself" and "Any Day Now." There's a recording [by the Isley Brothers] of "Make It Easy" with different words called "Are You Lonely by Yourself." Was that an early version of the song?*

BB: I had nothing to do with it. Didn't know it even existed. The Isleys, they're good singers.

SD: *And there's a version of Tommy Hunt singing a different melody and words, called "Lover," that also surfaced in the Eighties. That wasn't an earlier draft either?*

BB: No. "Any Day Now" was "Any Day Now" from the get-go. So was "Make It Easy on Yourself."

SD: *Scepter liked to use interchangeable tracks.*

BB: Like at Motown. Maybe they learned it from them. They were trying to make a separate song and exclude us? That's possible. Unbelievable. Maybe Hal would know that. Gee, that's interesting.

SD: *These came out years after Scepter went under. It's hard to believe Scepter went under so soon after having all those hits.*

BB: You don't know what's going on in the books in a record company. What looks OK on the outside... I know we had to sue them. We weren't getting paid properly, or Dionne wasn't getting paid properly. Hal took care of most of that business end; we had to run an accounting. But they weren't doing anything too different than a lot of R&B companies were doing....I was just so happy to see the record in the Top 10.

SD: *I was wondering how come everything you cut with the Shirelles was just your demos with their vocals put on there.*

BB: [laughs] That's just the way it worked.

SD: *Before "Don't Make Me Over," you cut and released a Burt and the Backbeats record, "Move It on the Backbeat." Are you singing on that one?*

BB: I don't remember if I was singing on the Backbeats single. It was on another label and we used a couple of girls.

SD: *It was on Big Top.*

BB: Did I do that with "Brigitte Bardot"?

SD: *The serial numbers were consecutive.*

BB: There were nine singles on "Brigitte Bardot." Not mine. But nine different artists.

SD: *The credits list a Miguel De Souza. Is that a pseudonym?*

BB: It wasn't me. I didn't write the song.

SD: *But Hilliard's credited with writing the lyrics.*

BB: It had to have an English translation because it was a French song, and it was a hit in Europe. Everybody tried to cover it here. I remember using Joel Grey. Not a very good record.

SD: *When Dusty [Springfield] first came to the States in 1964, it was with the idea that you were going to show her some songs.*

BB: I thought I met Dusty initially taking her out to the Grammys in New York as my date. And I thought I tried to talk her into releasing "Wishing and Hoping," because she had some ambivalence about it.

SD: *Did you pitch any other songs to her, because everything before "The Look of Love" was things you'd already cut with other people?*

BB: She did eight things. I think a lot of our stuff was getting covered in England. I'm very grateful Dusty would cover my songs. That's terrific.

SD: *After that you go to England to do* Pussycat; *you start working with fully integrated bands like Manfred Mann. I've always read that that session was a little tense. Was that really difficult, going from session guys who would play exactly what you wanted to an independent rock group used to doing its own arrangements?*

BB: Manfred Mann was one of the roughest sessions I've ever had, because that's not the easiest tune—those kind of chord changes in "My Little Red Book." I think nine out of ten times I wound up playing keyboard...on whatever the date was. I sorta remember that date, and when I got the Polar Music Award last year, Manfred Mann was there, because he was going to do something [a tribute] in concert for Robert Moog, and he was brilliant. But backstage, you know, he came up to me and said, "Hey, you know, we hadn't met or talked in a long time," and he recounted this whole session and how polite I'd been in finally moving him off the piano bench. 'Cause I wasn't getting anywhere. It was an endless day.

SD: *Is it true you recorded the soundtrack in one night?*

BB: When I finally got into it and learned what I was

supposed to do, it was probably two and a half to three weeks. I was really under the gun, because I was walking around the park wondering what I was gonna do, because I didn't have a clue. Not a clue. I must've gone in with 40 different themes and recorded them—different sequences in the movie. None of them having anything to do [with it]. I didn't know. I didn't know how to score a picture. And then afterwards Charlie Feldman fell in love with the title song, and he took out all these pieces I'd written and stuck in instrumental versions of "What's New Pussycat?" Cop it from here, put it in there. I got really upset. I wanted to take my name off the picture. I was married to Angie at the time, and she said, "Don't be a fool. This picture's going to be a huge hit." So I was glad I listened to her.

SD: *Wasn't Angie was the one who ran into Charles Feldman in the first place and suggested he use you for the job?*

BB: Yeah. In the lobby of the Dorchester. Just luck that I got that picture.

SD: *Do you detect any influence of your sound on the Beatles? It's pretty pronounced on the Beach Boys.*

BB: I heard it more from the stuff coming out of Philadelphia. Not so much Gamble and Huff. The other guy, Thom Bell. Someone said, "It sounds like he's ripping you off." I said "Great."

SD: *Did psychedelic music have any influence on you?*

BB: I didn't pay much attention to it. I didn't like a lot of the music that was around then. I liked what was coming out of Philadelphia. I hated the 1-4-5 changes, like you take a Bill Haley groove or something like that—so unappealing to me. The Motown stuff was great, the Temptations' "Papa Was a Rolling Stone." Brilliant stuff. The Marvin Gaye stuff. Pretty great.

SD: *When you did* On the Flip Side, *were you and Hal actively looking for a book to score on Broadway? Was that like a dry run for you?*

BB: That was a one-time television thing. It wasn't a test run. Not in my mind, anyway.

SD: *Just something that came up?*

BB: Yeah. Nothing until [David] Merrick called me. He told me who he had in place. He had Neil Simon, and Neil would do it if we would do it. Before that, was I looking to do a show? No.

SD: *In terms of songs, I've got a listing of about five songs dropped. Were there even more that you remember writing?*

BB: No. We opened in Boston and it was pretty successful. A couple of things didn't work in rehearsal. It's a bit of a blur, because once we opened in Boston and I knew we had to write a couple of things, I wound up in the hospital with pneumonia and felt like shit the whole rest of the time on the road. No time to be sick, having to see that fucking show every night. And it's rough to be in the back of the house and even though the show's a hit, I don't like what's going on in the pit. What am I gonna do? Say, "OK, the only way to save this is to conduct every night"?

SD: *After you split up with Hal and Dionne, you got together with Hal again to write the Stephanie Mills album.*

BB: Oh yeah, yeah. Forgot about that. We were together for that? 'Cause that was after the split.

SD: *That was after Dionne filed suit. Were you actually in litigation with Hal while you were writing those songs?*

BB: I doubt it. I think it had been resolved, maybe.

SD: *From what I understand, it was settled out of court in '79. The Stephanie Mills album was in '75.*

BB: I didn't talk to Dionne for a long time. When we got back together, it was for the Aaron Spelling movie. I completely forgot about that Stephanie Mills album.

SD: *It's a really fine album. It's got two great songs you later rerecorded—"No One Remembers My Name" and "I Took My Strength from You."*

BB: That's a good one.

SD: *That wound up on* Futures, *another really good album.*

BB: I like that album, too. A&M was always supportive. You talk about the freedom…you mentioned two albums back-to-back, *Futures* and the Stephanie Mills album.…I was very conscious of people looking over my shoulder at Motown. I never had any experience working with them. I just know that one experience. A lot of looking over your shoulder. With *Futures*, those people were the best ever to work with—Herb and Jerry. You didn't have to play anything for anybody. You just played them the finished product. That kind of autonomy was basically [what we had] at Scepter. I don't think we had to play anything for anybody at Motown. We had to play it for Stephanie and her family and make sure she was OK with it. And I think we could've made a better album if we had really sat down and tried to understand her more, vocally, instead of remaking existing songs.

SD: *Were those all pre-existing songs?*

BB: Maybe not. Didn't we do "This Empty Place"?

SD: *And "Loneliness Remembers What Happiness Forgets," pretty much a note-for-note re-creation of the Dionne version.*

BB: Yeah, that's fudging a little bit in retrospect, looking back. Was I crazy about her as an artist? I thought she was pretty exciting in the show [*The Wiz*]. But it's very hard to follow Dionne.

SD: *Some writers have suggested the reason you did the album was because Dionne had just gotten her first No. 1 with the Spinners and this was a bit of one-upmanship on the part of you and Hal.*

BB: I don't think so. I think it was just a way for me and Hal to work together again. Or try to.

SD: *Before hooking up with Carole Bayer Sager, you did two interesting albums. Sometime after* Futures, *I have an interesting quote in a* GQ *interview where you say you thought the idea of writing with a woman was intimidating because you thought it would be like writing with your mother.*

BB: I'd written songs with women back in the Brill Building. Anita Jones—

SD: *"A Girl Like You," you wrote that with Anne Croswell.*

BB: Yeah, she was a nice lady. And I think that wasn't a bad song. Someone recorded it.

SD: *Larry Hall. And in England, Adam Faith and Cliff Richard recorded it.*

BB: [sings the melody of "Gotta Get a Girl"] Very common. Something like that. [sings] *"Gotta get a girl, someone to talk with."*

SD: *That's "Gotta Get a Girl," [which] you wrote with Hal for Frankie Avalon. Wow, I'm amazed you remember that one. 'Cause you wrote two songs for a couple of Frankie Avalon sound-alikes before finally doing one with the real deal.*

BB: Right. I think the demo on one of those two songs, one or the other, was done by Paul Simon. Under another name.

SD: *Jerry Landis?*

BB: Probably. [pauses and goes back to the earlier question] Intimidation? The power of a woman in the room if she was real strong? Yeah, I'm sure that is never as comfortable as writing with a guy. That's my own judgmental thing. I remember one time someone arranged a meeting with Carolyn Leigh for a possible collaboration. She wrote all those Broadway shows with Cy Coleman. Carolyn Leigh was the hottest Broadway writer at the time. She had a pop hit with "Young at Heart." But I went to her apartment and she was this heavy woman who died kind of young. I assumed she was going to write with me and she didn't like my stuff. She turned me down. It hurt. That didn't feel so good.

SD: *Before you meet Carole, you did the* Woman *album*

and wrote with three women.

BB: Yes, with Carly and Libby. There's some really nice things on that album and some things I can't believe I wrote. A little pretentious. But I had to do it. I had to get it out of my system.

SD: *Then you worked with Libby again on a song for the* Together *soundtrack, which is a really wonderful score. That's where you first worked with Michael McDonald.*

BB: Yeah. Wow. I thought a couple of songs were really good. The Jackie DeShannon one and the one with Michael. And the picture was hopeless, you know? It only played for one week and nobody paid any attention to it. I think it was the whole thing about maybe Jackie Bissett didn't work or do any promotion for it. Or it was a European thing and maybe they didn't have the money. I know I did the picture because I liked the picture and I wasn't doing anything and I practically did it for nothing. I mean, I wasn't doing so great at the time and I kind of welcomed the project 'cause I was gonna spend the summer in Jackson Hole and I thought, "Shit, why not do the picture up here?"

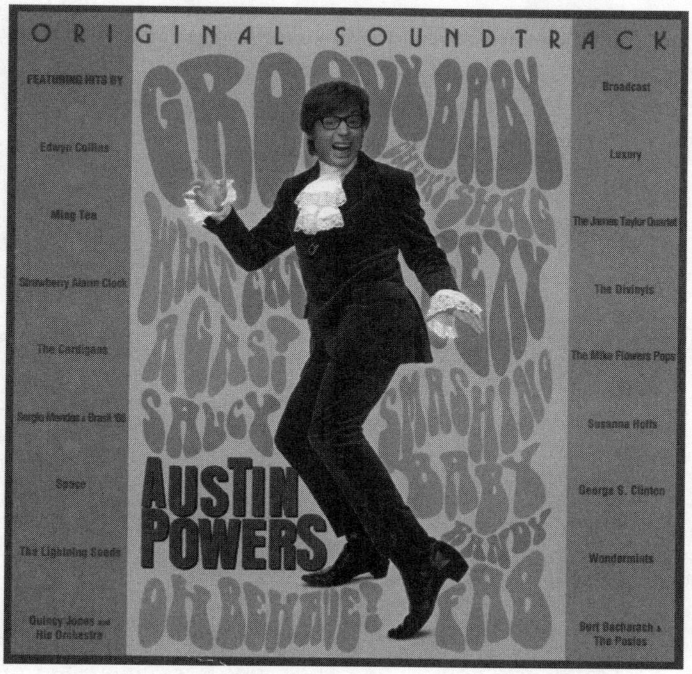

SD: *That had you writing with Paul Anka. What is it like for you writing with someone who writes words and music? Do you have to compromise more?*

BB: Not so much with Paul. Paul was really leaving the melody alone to me. Much more than Carole. Carole always wants to be a participant in the musical part, and that sometimes was good and sometimes was not good.

SD: *Is that why there are so many three-way compositions in the Eighties? Was the third guy there kind of like having a referee?*

BB: Listen, we had fun doing it. Wrote some cool songs with Carole and Peter Allen, and Peter was always a joy to be in the same room with because things would stay light, you know? And everybody was making a good contribution. Neil Diamond. Yes. What I didn't like was a couple of three- or four-way songs down the line...because...the artist...got credit because they recorded it and hardly contributed....They didn't even buy lunch.

SD: *Was that early on?*

BB: That could be anytime. Things started to get tougher, where you had a better chance of getting an artist by writing with him.

SD: *Ray Parker Jr. or someone like that?*

BB: Yes, if Ray was going into the studio, sure you write with Ray. He's a talent. He's good. Another situation, I mentioned Neil. James Ingram. We didn't do but a bunch of songs together, but James was great in the writing process, to sit in the room with John Bettis, and he's very creative just to hear him sing a line, so different from something I would sing, and just slam it so many different ways.

SD: *It's kind of like hearing the finished product while you're writing it.*

BB: It's a great concept because you can hear it right there and see what works and doesn't work. I could've made that album a little easier with Carole, *Sometimes Late at Night*—some of those songs.

SD: *Most of the best songs on that album were the ones with you and her writing together.*

BB: Yeah, but I think she went along with me and she's not a big singer and maybe I swamped her a little bit with orchestration and the demands vocally I was looking to make with her.

SD: *It's very well produced; you don't notice the vocals as being too swamped.*

BB: Hey, I always loved that record and the song "Stronger Than Before." It's really good.
SD: *It's kind of like* Painted from Memory *in that it kind*

of follows a plot line. You can imagine it's the same person throughout all the songs.

BB: Connected, yeah. I like that song "Stronger Than Before." Wrote that with Bruce Roberts, and we wrote "Making Love" with him. Very talented. We wrote maybe one song with Melissa [Manchester], which wasn't as much fun.

SD: *You also did one with Marvin Hamlisch—"Maybe."*

BB: That was a picture song they worked on [that] they brought me into just to add some input. I liked that song. [sings] *"Maybe there'll be no falling stars."*

SD: *So did she and Marvin continue to write together after they split up?*

BB: That's when I was living with Carole. He was scoring that movie (*A Romantic Comedy*). Sure, they continued to work on a project, like a picture. They'd write with David Foster or something. Carole's a really good writer.

SD: *She's on two soundtracks with you after the split—* The Grace of My Heart *soundtrack and* Stuart Little.

BB: Everybody's just doing their own thing. I had no connection with her at all on that.

SD: *You and Carole split in '91, but there are songs that continued to trickle out after that. Like the Stylistics. So were you two writing together during the divorce?*

BB: It was like '89 or '90 that we were coming apart. Hey, it's not easy writing, living and working together, you know? Compared to what other factors contribute to dismantling a relationship. It's a lot to ask. You get up in the morning. You go to the studio, you write a song, then we go to bed, get up and do the same thing. I like writing with different people. Hey, I'm writing songs with Tonio K. now. They brought this gal from England, Cathy Dennis, a month ago to write some songs with me. I've written now two songs with Jerry Leiber and his son Jeb, something Jerry and I always talked about.

SD: *Are you writing these Leiber songs for any project?*

BB: Independent. As songs. Which is tough today. Where do you take them? There are few artists. And they're good songs. Jerry Leiber is a great, great lyric writer. I think I've written some great songs with Jerry and Tonio K. And another song with Andreas Carlsson, the Swedish writer who's done stuff for the Backstreet Boys and *NSync. I think it's a pretty good song. I think the openings to place a song are very limited.

SD: *I remember reading you say in the Nineties that you'd bring a bunch of songs you'd written with John Bettis, and Clive Davis would turn them down as not being commercial enough.*

BB: Well, that was my speech for the lifetime achievement award for songwriters out in California. I was very appreciative but I said tomorrow morning I've still got to get up and try to sell songs to Clive Davis. Right now there are a lot of interesting things on the plate.

SD: *I heard you were writing for a young new British singer, Will Power.*

BB: That's what Cathy Dennis came over here for. And I'm in the new Austin Powers movie [*Austin Powers in Goldmember*].

SD: *Have you written a new song for it?*

BB: It's a remake, a song I've done before. I'm not allowed to say what old song we're doing. [In fact, it's "Alfie," with Susanna Hoffs singing "What's it all about, Austin?" in place of the original line.]

SD: *The new film is a blaxploitation spoof.*

BB: Well, Beyoncé Knowles got a big part. And I met with Dr. Dre to do something with him for the album [the soundtrack features Dr. Dre's remix of the Rolling Stones' "Miss You"]. So I've got 10 or 11 of his drum loops, which he gave me. And what I'm trying to do is not writing hit melodies but trying to write almost like I'm scoring a film and just do eight- or 10-bar sequences and put it in here or put it in there. Dre's a nice guy, very interested in branching out, and maybe some of my classical influences combined with my R&B or jazz leanings… It ain't like I'm trying to make a song I can get the Backstreet Boys on. No melodies like that.

SD: *You've been sampled so much the past 10 or 15 years, it's like creating your own samples.*

BB: We'll see how that works out.…But he's a nice guy; I think he's brilliant. And it's exciting and fun to work to his drum loops. They're very different. Dre has put some bass lines down, which tell me where the chord structures are, and some of these are good. And you write on top on that.

SD: *Any plans to write again with Elvis Costello?*

BB: Elvis and I talked. Wow, we worked so hard on that. He's an adventurer. We'd like to, but boy, that's like writing another show. It's not like Elton going in and making an album in 14 days. It's just not.

SD: He *said working with you was the first time he was ever conducted vocally. I'd be curious to see if he sounds any different on his latest album,* When I Was Cruel.

BB: I'll be curious to hear what he's done too. What label is it on?

SD: *Something on Universal. Island, since Mercury's been absorbed.*

BB: It's just a terrible time in the record business. Instead of trying to write, I should be out skiing with my kids every day. It's not just tough for me, it's tough for a lot of good writers out there—unless you get a movie. Diane [Warren] seems to do OK. I can't say I love every song she writes, but she's very talented.

SD: *What about the musical that was called* What the World Needs Now*? The Roundabout Theater has just announced it's going to be part of their 2002–2003 season, only now it's called* The Look of Love.

BB: I think they're taking it into the Roundabout. Just made a mental note, I haven't talked to Hal in a while. He'd be much more up-to-date on the project. Would I love to see it get on? Sure. It's something I haven't thought about in months, 'cause it's right up there with "Am I in the past or the present?" Ann Reinking had a workshop there, and if she still does, that would be a great plus, 'cause I heard what she did was really great. What they did out in California, the Gillian Lynne thing, was not so great. I haven't talked to Gillian in a long time. She was very hurt by the reception, the reviews that got out in California when it played in La Jolla. She wanted me to come to see it and I was out on the road, so I saw the second half of the show, and it's just for somebody who loved my music so much. I don't understand what they did to make it sound…like that.

SD: *Some of the reviews said they crammed too many songs in willy-nilly.*

BB: Nothing sat still for very long. And also I tried to say, Hey I'll help you. I'll come up with an idea for the pit band. I'm playing in Detroit. Why don't you send your musical director and the guy that's gonna be the programmer, who was involved with *Cats,* and we'll talk? And put a perfect eight-, nine-piece band structure in the pit. Two synthesizers, you cover a lot of the things. And use some pre-recorded stuff in addition. Or not. There were a lot of possibilities. But what I heard in San Diego—shit, man, it was like a band out of the Catskills. A saxophone, a trumpet and a rhythm section. And I said, Why did I do this, why did I spin my wheels? But I didn't say anything, I really didn't; I just know that the soul went out of the music.

SD: *There was another show you'd been working on.*

BB: There was one with BA Robertson, the *Snow White* thing. I put a lot of time into, spent a lot money going to England two or three times. Thought the songs were pretty good, never could get the book really straightened out. It's hard to take a standard fairy tale and put that into a different kind of setting. We didn't do it right. We did it musically OK. BA's a great writer. I haven't talked to him in a long time. That whole thing came down where we all didn't part the best of friends. Hey, anybody who can write a song like "The Living Years" is a great writer.

SD: *Have you written any songs with Hal since the* Isn't She Great *soundtrack?*

BB: We wrote one song for the *Promises, Promises* revival in New York, "I Think You've Got It Wrong." I thought that was terrific, and we never would've written it if Neil Simon hadn't said, "We need another song here. Put it in." And I like that. But witness that I never saw the New York production and I never saw the California production. And is it a little deliberate? Yeah, it's me. I guess if they get this revue at the Roundabout and I'm in New York, I'll go see it. I'd rather spend the time writing to the Dr. Dre loops.

Library of Congress List of Bacharach Songs

Here is a complete listing of Bacharach songs found in the copyright records of the Library of Congress. Although songs were copyrighted several times, this list includes the earliest registration date, only repeating a song if it was significantly modified at a later date (i.e., title changes, words added or another writer contributing). Some songs were registered long after they were written ("Something Bad," "Forgotten Music"), so it is not a 100 percent accurate gauge of when a song was written, but it's pretty close. It is also not a complete listing of songs, as there are movie instrumentals and cue music missing, and Bacharach seems to have been lax in registering songs from 1974 to 1978. But overall, this listing gives a fascinating overview of just how diligently Bacharach and David worked, particularly during the Famous Music years.

1951

"A Soldier's Prayer"
words William Stephen Quigley, music Burt Freeman Bacharach
Original registration date: 5 Oct. 51

1955

"Keep Me in Mind"
words Jack Wolf, music Burt Bacharach
Original registration date: 24 Feb. 55

"How About"
words Jack Wolf, music Burt Freeman Bacharach
Original registration date: 4 Apr 55

"The Secret of Love"
words Jack Wolf, music Burt Bacharach
Original registration date: 18 Apr 55

"Eye Witness"
words: Harry Ross, music Burt F. Bacharach
Original registration date: 16 May 55

"The Desperate Hours"
words Wilson Stone, music Burt F. Bacharach

"How About?"
words Jack Wolf, music Burt Freeman Bacharach
Original registration date: 18 Nov 55

1956

"Tell the Truth and Shame the Devil"
words & music Martita, Hal David & Burt Bacharach
Original registration date: 16 Mar 56
Martita, see Margery Cummings

"Peggy's in the Panty"
words Hal David, music Burt Bacharach
Original registration date: 9 May 56

"Beauty Isn't Everything"
words Edward Heyman, music Burt F. Bacharach
Original registration date: 8 Jun 56

"Presents from the Past"
words Hal David, music Burt Bacharach
Original registration date: 19 Aug 57

"The Morning Mail"
words Hal David, music Burt F. Bacharach
Original registration date: 5 Jul 56

"Warm and Tender"
words Hal David, music Burt Bacharach
Original registration date: 20 Jul 56

"Uninvited Dream"
words Sammy Gallop, music Burt Bacharach
Original registration date: 10 Aug 56

"I Cry More"
words Hal David, music Burt F. Bacharach
Original registration date: 27 Aug 56

"My Dreamboat Is Drifting (Down the River of Doubt)"
words Sammy Gallop, music Burt Bacharach
Original registration date: 28 Sep 56

1957

"Humble Pie"
words Hal David, music Burt F. Bacharach
Original registration date: 30 Jan 57

"Forever Faithful"
words Mack David, music Burt F. Bacharach
Original registration date: 28 Mar 57

"Love Bank"
words & music Hal David, Lou Melamed & Burt F. Bacharach
Original registration date: 28 Mar 57

"Your Lips Are Warmer Than Your Heart"
words Hal David, music Burt F. Bacharach
Original registration date: 28 Mar 57

"Wild Honey"
words Hal David, music Burt F. Bacharach
Original registration date: 8 Apr 57

"Underneath the Overpass"
words Hal David, music Burt F. Bacharach
Original registration date: 6 May 57

"Two Against the World"
words Hal David, Burt F. Bacharach
Original registration date: 29 May 57

"Magic Moments"
words Hal David, music Burt F. Bacharach
Original registration date: 29 May 57

"The Story of My Life"
words Hal David, music Burt F. Bacharach
Original registration date: 5 Jul 57

"Winter Warm"
words Hal David, music Burt F. Bacharach
Original registration date: 14 Aug 57

"Do You Remember As I Remember?"
words Buddy Bernier, music Burt F. Bacharach
Original registration date: 2 Oct 57

"Sad Sack"
words Hal David, music Burt F. Bacharach
Original registration date: 25 Oct 57

"Snowballs"
music Burt F. Bacharach
Original registration date: 18 Nov 57

1958

"Bottomless Cup"
words & music Hal David, Lou Melamed & Burt F. Bacharach
Original registration date: 3 Jan 58

"The Mission Bell by the Wishin' Well"
words Hal David, music Burt F. Bacharach
Original registration date: 3 Jan 58

"I'll Kiss You Goodnight in the Morning"
words Hal David, music Burt F. Bacharach
Original registration date: 3 Jan 58

"Ooooh, My Love"
words Hal David, music Burt F. Bacharach
Original registration date: 3 Jan 58

"Country Music Holiday"
words Hal David, music Burt F. Bacharach
Original registration date: 30 Jan 58

"Hot Spell"
words Mack David, music Burt F. Bacharach
Original registration date: 16 Apr 58

"It Seemed So Right Last Night"
words Hal David, music Burt F. Bacharach
Original registration date: 20 May 58

"Third from the Left"
words Hal David, music Burt F. Bacharach
Original registration date: 9 Jun 58

"Make Room for the Joy"
words Hal David, music Burt F. Bacharach
Original registration date: 9 Jun 58

"The Last time I Saw My Heart"
words Hal David, music Burt F. Bacharach
Original registration date: 9 Jun 58

"Sittin' in a Tree House"
words Hal David, music Burt F. Bacharach
Original registration date: 9 Jun 58

"The Night That Heaven Fell"
words Hal David, music Burt F. Bacharach
Original registration date: 9 Jul 58

"The Blob"
words Mack David, music Burt F. Bacharach
Original registration date: 1 Aug 58

"I Could Kick Myself"
words Hal David, music Burt F. Bacharach
Original registration date: 18 Aug 58

"Oh, Wendy, Wendy"
words Hal David, music Burt F. Bacharach
Original registration date: 18 Aug 58

"Saturday Night in Tia Juana"
music Burt F. Bacharach
Original registration date: 20 Aug 58

"Dream Big"
words & music Paul Hampton & Burt F. Bacharach
words Original registration date: 14 Nov 58

"Saturday night in Tia Juana"
words Hal David, music Burt F. Bacharach
Original registration date: 24 Dec 58

1959

"Paradise Island"
words & music Hal David, Burt F. Bacharach & Paul Hampton
Original registration date: 14 Jan 59

"The Windows of Heaven"
words Hal David, music Burt F. Bacharach
Original registration date: 23 Jan 59

"The Net"
words Hal David, music Burt F. Bacharach
Original registration date: 26 Jan 59

"That Kind of Woman"
words Hal David, music Burt F. Bacharach
Original registration date: 29 Jan 59

"Moon Man"
words Hal David, music Burt F. Bacharach
Original registration date: 5 Feb 59

"Loving is a Way of Living"
words Hal David, music Burt F. Bacharach
Original registration date: 10 Feb 59

"Write Me (Lonely Girl)"
words & music Paul Hampton & Burt Bacharach
Original registration date: 10 Feb 59

"What a Night"
words Hal David, music Burt F. Bacharach
Original registration date: 29 Feb 59

"Lorna Doone"
words Hal David, music Burt F. Bacharach
Original registration date: 25 Mar 59

"Young and Wild"
words Hal David, music Burt F. Bacharach
Original registration date: 3 Apr 59

"The Hangman"
words Hal David, music Burt F. Bacharach
Original registration date: 3 Apr 59

"Faker, Faker"
words Hal David, music Burt F. Bacharach
Original registration date: 20 Apr 59

"Don't Unless You Love Me"
words & music Burt Bacharach & Paul Hampton
Original registration date: 20 Apr 59

"You're the Dream"
words Hal David, music Burt Bacharach
Original registration date: 22 May 59

"With Open Arms"
words Hal David, music Burt F. Bacharach
Original registration date: 27 May 59

"Go 'Way, Mister Moon"
words Wilson Stone, music Burt F. Bacharach
Original registration date: 24 Jun 59

"The Woman Who Wasn't Mine"
words Wilson Stone, music Burt F. Bacharach
Original registration date: 24 Jun 59

"Happy and His One Man Band"
words Wilson Stone, music Burt F. Bacharach
Original registration date: 24 Jun 59

"Send Me Letters Filled with Kisses"
words Wilson Stone, music Burt F. Bacharach
Original registration date: 24 Jun 59

"Heavenly"
words Sydney Shaw, music Burt Bacharach
Original registration date: 13 Jul 59

"The Timeless Tide"
words Hal David, music Burt Bacharach
Original registration date: 30 Jul 59

"I Looked for You"
words Hal David, music Burt Bacharach
Original registration date: 22 Oct 59

"We're Only Young Once, Yeh Yeh Yeh"
words Robert Colby, music Burt Bacharach
Original registration date: 6 Nov 59

"A Girl Like You"
words Ann Croswell, music Burt Bacharach
Original registration date: 19 Nov 59

"Suddenly Last Summer"
words Hal David, music Burt Bacharach
Additional title: Long Ago Last Summer
Original registration date: 20 Nov 5

"In Times Like These"
words Hal David, music Burt F. Bacharach
Original registration date: 9 Dec 59

1960

"Faithfully"
words Sid Shaw (Sydney Shaw), music Burt Bacharach
Original registration date: 4 Jan 60

"Long Ago Last Summer"
words Hal David, music Burt Bacharach
Original registration date: 7 Jan 60
New matter: changed words

"I Cry Alone"
words Hal David, music Burt Bacharach
Original registration date: 21 Jan 60

"Crazy Times"
words & music Burt F. Bacharach & Paul Hampton
Original registration date: 5 Feb 60

"For All Time"
words Hal David, music Burt Bacharach
Original registration date: 11 Feb 60

"You Belong in Someone Else's Arms"
words Bob Hilliard, music Burt Bacharach
Original registration date: 16 Feb 60

"I'll Never, Never Forget 'What's Her Name'"
words Hal David, music Burt Bacharach
Original registration date: 17 Feb 60

"Indoor Sport"
words Fred Tobias, music Burt Bacharach
Original registration date: 4 Mar 60

"More and More"
words Nita Jonas, music Burt Bacharach
Original registration date: 18 Apr 60

"Two Figures on a Wedding Cake"
words Fred Tobias, music Burt Bacharach
Original registration date: 19 Apr 60

"Your Lips Are Warmer Than Your Heart"
words Hal David, music Burt Bacharach
Original registration date: 27 Apr 60

"Boys Were Made for Girls"
words Hal David, music Burt Bacharach
Original registration date: 16 May 60

"Two Hour Honeymoon"
words & music Burt F. Bacharach & Paul Hampton
Original registration date: 16 May 60

"Creams"
words & music Burt Bacharach & Paul Hampton
Additional Title: Cremes
Original registration date: 16 May 60

"Path of Pride"
words Fred Tobias, music Burt Bacharach
Original registration date: 9 Jun 60

"Close"
words Sydney Shaw, music Burt F. Bacharach
Original registration date: 9 Jun 60

"Out of My Continental Mind"
words Syd Shaw (Sydney Shaw), music Burt Bacharach
Original registration date: 15 Jun 60

"10,000 Years Ago"
words Bob Hilliard, music Burt Bacharach
Original registration date: 10 Aug 60

"One Really Big Chance"
words Bob Hilliard, music Burt Bacharach
Original registration date: 18 Aug 60

"I Could Make You Mine"
words Hal David, music Burt Bacharach
Original registration date: 21 Sep 60

"Cryin', Sobbin', Wailin'"
words Nita Jonas, music Burt Bacharach
Original registration date: 14 Oct 60

"Cross Town Bus"
words Hal David, music Burt Bacharach
Original registration date: 31 Oct 60

"Take Me to Your Ladder"
words & music Bob Hilliard & Burt Bacharach
Original registration date: 25 Nov 60

"Joanie's Forever"
words & music Bob Hilliard & Burt Bacharach
Original registration date: 25 Nov 60

1961

"One Part Dog, Nine Parts Cat"
words & music Burt Bacharach & Bob Hilliard
Original registration date: 6 Jan 61

"Three Wheels on My Wagon"
words & music Burt Bacharach & Bob Hilliard
Original registration date: 6 Jan 61

"And This Is Mine"
words & music Burt F. Bacharach & Hal David
Original registration date: 11 Jan 61

"Three Friends, Two Lovers"
words Hal David, music Burt Bacharach
Original registration date: 13 Jan 61

"Hideaway Heart"
words Hal David, music Burt Bacharach
Original registration date: 13 Feb 61

"Moon Guitar"
music Burt Bacharach
Original registration date: 9 Mar 61

"My Heart Is a Ball of String"
words Hal David, music Burt Bacharach
Original registration date: 14 Mar 61

"Along Came Joe"
words Hal David, music Burt Bacharach
Original registration date: 22 Mar 61

"Love in a Goldfish Bowl"
words Hal David, music Burt F. Bacharach
Original registration date: 6 Apr 61

"Forever, My Love"
words Hal David, music Burt F. Bacharach
Original registration date: 12 Apr 61

"Gotta Get a Girl"
words & music Burt Bacharach & Hal David
Original registration date: 24 Apr 61

"The Story Behind My Tears"
words Hal David, music Burt Bacharach
Original registration date: 4 May 61

"The Third Window from the Right"
words Mack David, music Burt F. Bacharach
Original registration date: 5 May 61

"Barracuda"
words & music Burt F. Bacharach, Paul Hampton
Original registration date: 8 May 61

"Too Late to Worry"
words Hal David, music Burt Bacharach
Original registration date: 9 May 61

"Don't Go, Please Stay"
words Bob Hilliard, music Burt Bacharach
Original registration date: 6 Jun 61

"I Wake Up Cryin'"
words Hal David, music Burt Bacharach
Original registration date: 19 Jun 61

"Love Lessons"
words Hal David, music Burt F. Bacharach
Original registration date: 26 Jun 61

"I'll Bring Along My Banjo"
words & music Burt Bacharach & Norman Gimbel
Original registration date: 27 Jun 61

"You're Following Me"
words & music Bob Hilliard & Burt Bacharach
Original registration date: 19 Jul 61

"You're Telling Our Secrets"
words Hal David, music Burt F. Bacharach
Original registration date: 2 Aug 61

"Tower of Strength"
words Bob Hilliard, music Burt Bacharach
Original registration date: 18 Aug 61

"Loneliness or Happiness"
words Hal David, music Burt Bacharach
Original registration date: 22 Aug 61

"Don't Do Anything Dangerous"
words Hal David, music Burt Bacharach
Original registration date: 22 Aug 61

"The Answer to Everything"
words Bob Hilliard, music Burt Bacharach
Original registration date: 24 Aug 61

"30 Miles of Railroad Track"
words Bob Hilliard, music Burt Bacharach
Original registration date: 25 Aug 61

"Deeply"
words Norman Gimbel, music Burt Bacharach
Original registration date: 8 Sep 61

"Move Me on the Backbeat"
words Mack David, music Burt F. Bacharach
Original registration date: 10 Oct 61

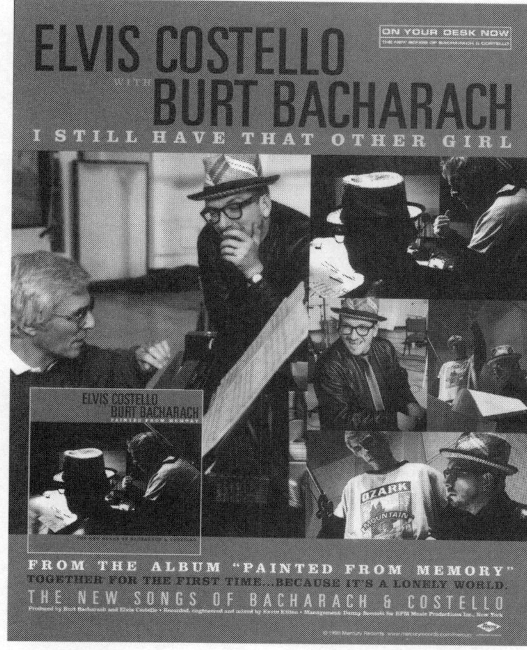

"The Breaking Point"
words Hal David, music Burt F. Bacharach
Original registration date: 16 Oct 61

"You Don't Have to Be a Tower of Strength"
words Bob Hilliard, music Burt F. Bacharach
Original registration date: 27 Oct 61

"Manpower"
words Bob Hilliard, music Burt Bacharach
Original registration date: 27 Oct 61

"Baby, It's You"
words & music Burt Bacharach, Mack David, Barney Williams
Original registration date: 15 Nov 61

"Miracle of St. Marie"
words & music Bob Hilliard & Burt Bacharach
Original registration date: 20 Nov 61

"Don't Envy Me"
words Hal David, music Burt F. Bacharach
Original registration date: 15 Dec 61

"Wastin' Away for You"
words Hal David, music Burt Bacharach
Original registration date: 21 Dec 61

1962

"Another Tear Falls"
words Hal David, music Burt F. Bacharach
Original registration date: 8 Jan 62

"Don't You Believe It"
words Bob Hilliard, music Burt F. Bacharach
Original registration date: 16 Jan 62

"Mexican Divorce"
words & music Bob Hilliard & Burt Bacharach
Original registration date: 18 Jan 62

"Waitin' for Charlie to Come Home"
words Bob Hilliard, music Burt Bacharach
Original registration date: 12 Jan 62

"Keep Away from Other Girls"
words & music Burt F. Bacharach & Bob Hilliard
Original registration date: 6 Feb 62
"Anonymous Phone Call"
words Hal David, music Burt F. Bacharach
Original registration date: 28 Feb 62

"I Just Don't Know What to Do with Myself"
words Hal David, music Burt F. Bacharach
Original registration date: 1 Mar 62

"The Man Who Shot Liberty Valance"
words Hal David, music Burt F. Bacharach
Original registration date: 1 Mar 62

"Any Day Now"
words & music Burt F. Bacharach & Bob Hilliard
Original registration date: 12 Mar 62

"Dreamin' All the Time"
words Bob Hilliard, music Burt F. Bacharach
Original registration date: 20 Apr 62

"Pick Up the Pieces"
words & music Bob Hilliard & Burt Bacharach
Original registration date: 30 Apr 62

"(There Goes) the Forgotten Man"
words & music Hal David & Burt F. Bacharach
Original registration date: 18 May 62

"Non Verra"
words Hal David, music Burt Bacharach
Additional title: "Make It Easy on Yourself"
Original registration date: 21 May 62

"If I Never Get to Love You"
words Hal David, music Burt F. Bacharach
Original registration date: 6 Jun 62

"Long After Tonight"
words & music Hal David, Burt Bacharach
Original registration date: 20 Jun 62

"Move Me on the Back Beat"
words & music Burt F. Bacharach & Mack David
Original registration date: 13 Jul 62

"I Forgot What It Was Like"
words Hal David, music Burt F. Bacharach
Original registration date: 15 Jul 63

"Only Love Can Break a Heart"
words Hal David, music Burt F. Bacharach
Original registration date: 23 Jul 62

"Forgive Me (For Giving You Such a Bad Time)"
words Hal David, music Burt F. Bacharach
Original registration date: 6 Aug 62

"Wonderful to Be Young"
words Hal David, music Burt F. Bacharach
Original registration date: 10 Aug 62

"The Love of a Boy"
words Hal David, music Burt F. Bacharach
Original registration date: 20 Aug 62

"It's Love That Really Counts (In the Long Run)"
words Hal David, music Burt F. Bacharach
Original registration date: 21 Aug 6

"Little Betty Falling Star"
words & music Bob Hilliard & Burt Bacharach
Original registration date: 10 Sep 62

"True Love Never Runs Smooth"
words Hal David, music Burt Bacharach
Original registration date: 13 Sep 62

"Don't Make Me Over"
words Hal David, music Burt F. Bacharach
Original registration date: 28 Sep 62

"I Smiled Yesterday"
words Hal David, music Burt F. Bacharach
Original registration date: 28 Sep 62

"Do I Have to Say More?"
words Hal David, music Burt F. Bacharach
Original registration date: 2 Oct 62

"An Errand of Mercy"
words Hal David, music Burt F. Bacharach
Original registration date: 18 Oct 62

"Call Off the Wedding (Without a Groom There Can't Be a Bride)"
words & music Hal David & Burt F. Bacharach
Original registration date: 8 Nov 62

"The Secret of Staying Young"
words Hal David, music Burt F. Bacharach
Original registration date: 16 Nov 62

"The Bell That Couldn't Jingle"
words & music Burt F. Bacharach & Larry Kusik
Original registration date: 27 Nov 62

"Rain from the Skies"
words Hal David, music Burt Bacharach
Original registration date: 31 Dec 62

1963

"That's Not the Answer"
words & music Hal David & Burt Bacharach
Original registration date: 10 Jan 63

"Wishin' and Hopin'"
words Hal David, music Burt Bacharach
Original registration date: 25 Jan 63

"A Message to Martha"
words Hal David, music Burt F. Bacharach
Additional titles: "A Message to Michael," "Kentucky Bluebird," "Send a Message to Martha"
Original registration date: 1 Feb 63

"This Empty Place"
words & music Hal David & Burt F. Bacharach
Original registration date: 1 Feb 63

"Make the Music Play"
words & music Hal David & Burt F. Bacharach
Original registration date: 8 Feb 63

"Lifetime of Loneliness"
words Hal David, music Burt Bacharach
Original registration date: 21 Mar 63

"Let the Music Play"
words & music Hal David & Burt F. Bacharach
Additional title: Make the music play
Original registration date: 26 Mar 63

"Feeling No Pain"
words Bob Hilliard, music Burt F. Bacharach
Original registration date: 27 Mar 63

"Blue on Blue"
music & arrangement Burt F. Bacharach, words Hal David
Original registration date: 27 Mar 63

"Reach Out for Me"
words Hal David, music Burt F. Bacharach
Original registration date: 15 Jul 63

"Magic Potion"
words Hal David, music Burt F. Bacharach
Original registration date: 15 Jul 63

"Who's Got the Action?"
words Bob Hilliard, music Burt F. Bacharach
Original registration date: 5 Aug 63

"The Right to Love You"
words Hal David, music Burt F. Bacharach
Original registration date: 9 Aug 63

"To Wait for Love (Is to Waste Your Life Way)"
words Hal David, music Burt F. Bacharach
Original registration date: 9 Aug 63

"Wives and Lovers"
words Hal David music, Burt F. Bacharach
Original registration date: 15 Aug 63

"Blue Guitar"
words Hal David, music Burt F. Bacharach
Original registration date: 29 Aug 63

"They Long to Be Close to You"
words Hal David, music Burt F. Bacharach
Original registration date: 29 Aug 63

"Twenty-Four Hours from Tulsa"
words & music Hal David & Burt Bacharach
Original registration date: 10 Sep 63

"Move Over and Make Room for Me"
words Hal David, music Burt F. Bacharach
Original registration date: 26 Sep 63

"Look in My Eyes, Maria"
words Hal David, music Burt Bacharach
Original registration date: 25 Oct 63

"Anyone Who Had a Heart"
words Hal David, music Burt Bacharach
Original registration date: 29 Oct 63

"In the Land of Make Believe"
words Hal David, music Burt Bacharach
Original registration date: 29 Oct 63

"Who's Been Sleeping in My Bed?"
words Hal David, music Burt F. Bacharach
Original registration date: 1 Nov 63

"Message to Michael"
words Hal David, music Burt Bacharach
Additional titles: "Message to Martha," "Kentucky Bluebird," "Send a Message to Martha"
Original registration date: 27 Nov 63
New matter: arrangement

"Be True to Yourself"
words Hal David, music Burt F. Bacharach
Original registration date: 30 Dec 63

"Building Walls"
words Hal David, music Burt F. Bacharach
Original registration date: 30 Dec 63

"Please Make Him Love Me"
words Hal David, music Burt F. Bacharach
Original registration date: 30 Dec 63

"Lost Little Girl"
words Hal David, music Burt F. Bacharach
Original registration date: 30 Dec 63

"Living without Love"
words Hal David, music Burt F. Bacharach
Original registration date: 30 Dec 63

"Everything Is Nothing Without You"
words Hal David, music Burt F. Bacharach
Original registration date: 30 Dec 63

"That's the Way I'll Come to You"
words Hal David, music Burt F. Bacharach
Original registration date: 30 Dec 63

"Saturday Sunshine"
words Hal David, music Burt Bacharach
Original registration date: 30 Dec 63

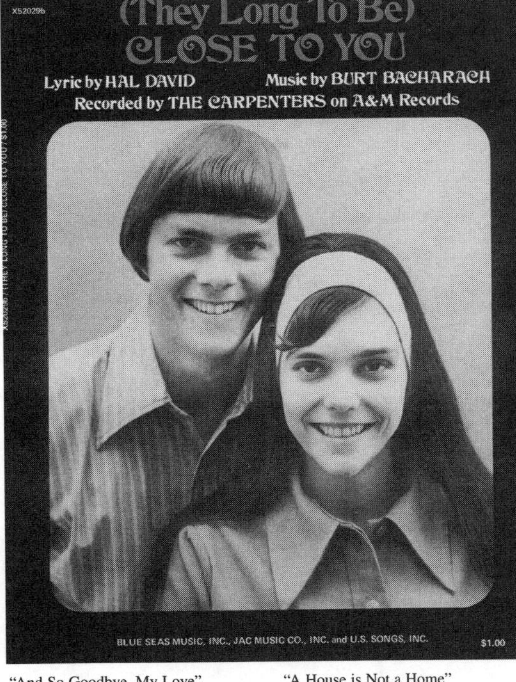

"And So Goodbye, My Love"
words & music Hal David & Burt Bacharach
Original registration date: 30 Dec 63

1964

"Trains and Boats and Planes"
words Hal David, music Burt F. Bacharach
Original registration date: 17 Jan 64

"Everyone Needs Someone to Love"
words Hal David, music Burt F. Bacharach
Original registration date: 17 Jan 64

"Accept It"
words Hal David, music Burt F. Bacharach
Original registration date: 17 Jan 64

"From Rocking Horse to Rocking Chair"
words Hal David, music Burt F. Bacharach
Original registration date: 17 Jan 64

"Any Old Time of Day"
words Hal David, music Burt F. Bacharach
Original registration date: 27 Jan 64

"I Fell in Love with Your Picture"
words Hal David, music Burt F. Bacharach
Original registration date: 6 Feb 64

"Lost Little Girl"
words Hal David, music Burt F. Bacharach
Original registration date: 17 Feb 64

"How Many Days of Sadness?"
words Hal David, music Burt F. Bacharach
Original registration date: 23 Mar 64

"Walk On By"
words Hal David, music Burt F. Bacharach
Original registration date: 23 Mar 64

"Rome Will Never Leave You"
words Hal David, music Burt F. Bacharach
Original registration date: 20 May 64

"Me Japanese Boy 'I Love You'"
words Hal David, music Burt F. Bacharach
Original registration date: 17 Jun 64

"A House is Not a Home"
words Hal David, music Burt F. Bacharach
Original registration date: 22 Jun 64

"You'll Never Get to Heaven (If You Break My Heart)"
words Hal David, music Burt F. Bacharach
Original registration date: 6 Jul 64

"(There's) Always Something There to Remind Me"
words Hal David, music Burt F. Bacharach
Original registration date: 22 Jul 64

"The Last One to Be Loved"
words Hal David, music Burt F. Bacharach
Original registration date: 27 Jul 64

"Send Me No Flowers"
words Hal David, music Burt Bacharach
Original registration date: 5 Aug 64

"Send Me No Flowers No. 2"
words Hal David, music Burt F. Bacharach
Original registration date: 5 Aug 64

"The Secret of Love"
words & music Jack Wolf & Burt Bacharach
Original registration date: 18 Aug 64

"Forgotten Music"
Jack Wolf & Burt Bacharach
Original registration date: 1 Sep 64

"The Eye of a Needle"
words Hal David, music Burt F. Bacharach
Original registration date: 2 Sep 64

"The Fool Killer"
words Hal David, music Burt F. Bacharach
Original registration date: 16 Sep 64

"Forever Yours I Remain"
words Hal David, music Burt F. Bacharach
Original registration date: 4 Dec 64

1965

"Don't Say I Didn't Tell You So"
words Hal David, music Burt F. Bacharach
Original registration date: 4 Jan 65

"Only the Strong, Only the Brave"
words Hal David, music Burt F. Bacharach
Original registration date: 4 Jan 65

"Is There Another Way to Love You?"
words Hal David, music Burt F. Bacharach
Original registration date: 4 Jan 65

"Long Day, Short Night"
words Hal David, music Burt F. Bacharach
Original registration date: 6 Jan 65

"Say Goodbye"
words Hal David, music Burt F. Bacharach
Original registration date: 8 Feb 65

"Don't Go Breakin' My Heart"
words Hal David, music Burt F. Bacharach
Original registration date: 15 Mar 65

"So Long, Johnny"
words Hal David, music Burt F. Bacharach
Original registration date: 15 Mar 65

"What the World Needs Now Is Love"
words Hal David, music Burt F. Bacharach
Original registration date: 15 Mar 65

"The Boss Is Not Here"
words Hal David & Burt F. Bacharach music Max Coplet & Lotar Olias
Additional title: "All at Once It's Sunday"
Original registration date: 21 May 65
New matter: English-language version

"Made in Paris"
words & music Hal David & Burt F. Bacharach
Original registration date: 21 May 65

"Here I Am"
words & music Hal David & Burt F. Bacharach,
Original registration date: 9 Jun 65

"My Little Red Book"
words & music Hal David & Burt F. Bacharach,
Additional title: "All I Do Is Talk about You"
Original registration date: 9 Jun 65

"Lookin' with My eyes, Seein' with My Heart"
words & music Hal David & Burt F. Bacharach
Original registration date: 25 Jun 65

"In Between the Heartaches"
words Hal David, music Burt F. Bacharach
Original registration date: 25 Jun 65

"Question of Love"
words Bob Hilliard, music Burt Bacharach
Original registration date: 6 Jul 65

"What's New, Pussycat?"
words & music Hal David & Burt F. Bacharach,
Original registration date: 7 Jul 65

"Dance Mama, Dance Papa, Dance"
words & music Hal David & Burt F. Bacharach,
Original registration date: 9 Aug 65

"Here Where There Is Love"
words Hal David, music Burt Bacharach
Original registration date: 15 Nov 65

"London Life"
words Hal David, music Burt F. Bacharach
Original registration date: 15 Nov 65

"If I Ever Make You Cry"
words Hal David, music Burt F. Bacharach
Original registration date: 15 Nov 65

"Are You There (With Another Girl)?"
words Hal David, music Burt F. Bacharach
Original registration date: 15 Nov 65

"How Can I Hurt You?"
words Hal David, music Burt Bacharach
Original registration date: 15 Nov 65

"Window Wishing"
words & music Hal David & Burt F. Bacharach
Original registration date: 16 Nov 65

"Promise Her Anything"
words & music Hal David & Burt F. Bacharach
Original registration date: 13 Dec 65

1966

"Alfie"
words & music Hal David & Burt F. Bacharach,
Original registration date: 20 Jan 66

"Trial by Jury"
words & music Hal David & Burt F. Bacharach,
Original registration date: 9 Feb 66

"More Time to Be with You"
music Burt Bacharach, words Bob Hilliard
Original registration date: 10 Feb 66

"Windows and Doors"
words Hal David, music Burt F. Bacharach
Original registration date: 1 Apr 66

"Come and Get Me"
words Hal David, music Burt Bacharach
Original registration date: 1 Apr 66

"Another Night"
words Hal David, music Burt Bacharach
Original registration date: 7 Jul 66

"Go with Love"
words Hal David, music Burt Bacharach
Original registration date: 1 Jul 66

"Walkin' Backwards Down the Road"
words Hal David, music Burt Bacharach
Original registration date: 1 Jul 66

"Juanita's Place"
words Hal David, music Burt Bacharach
Original registration date: 19 Sep 66

"They're Gonna Love It"
words Hal David, music Burt Bacharach
Original registration date: 19 Sep 66

"They Don't Give Medals (To Yesterday's Heroes)"
words Hal David, music Burt Bacharach
Original registration date: 19 Sep 66

"Fender Mender"
words Hal David, music Burt Bacharach
Original registration date: 19 Sep 66

"It Doesn't Matter Anymore"
words Hal David, music Burt Bacharach
Original registration date: 19 Sep 66

"Take a Broken Heart"
words Hal David, music Burt Bacharach
Original registration date: 19 Sep 66

"Try to See It My Way"
words Hal David, music Burt Bacharach
Original registration date: 19 Sep 66

"After the Fox"
words & music Hal David & Burt F. Bacharach
Original registration date: 22 Sep 66

"Weep"
words Hal David, music Burt Bacharach
Original registration date: 6 Oct 66

"The Beginning of Loneliness"
words Hal David, music Burt Bacharach
Original registration date: 14 Nov 66

"Walk, Little Dolly"
words Hal David, music Burt Bacharach
Original registration date: 14 Nov 66

"Nikki"
music Burt F. Bacharach
Original registration date: 14 Nov 66

"Love Was Here Before the Stars"
words Hal David, music Burt Bacharach
Original registration date: 14 Nov 66

"I Say a Little Prayer"
words Hal David, music Burt F. Bacharach
Original registration date: 28 Nov 66

1967

"Don't Count the Days"
words Hal David, music Burt F. Bacharach
Original registration date: 4 Jan 67

"Nikki"
words Hal David, music Burt F. Bacharach
Original registration date: 24 Apr 67
New matter: words

"One Less Bell to Answer"
words Hal David, music Burt F. Bacharach
Original registration date: 24 Apr 67

"Live Again"
words Hal David, music Burt F. Bacharach
Original registration date: 24 Apr 67

"Lisa"
words Hal David, music Burt F. Bacharach
Original registration date: 27 Apr 67

"The Windows of the World"
words Hal David, music Burt F. Bacharach
Original registration date: 27 Apr 67

"He Who Loves"
words Hal David, music Burt F. Bacharach
Original registration date: 15 Jun 67

"That Guy's in Love"
words Hal David, music Burt F. Bacharach
Original registration date: 15 Jun 67

"Where Would I Go?"
words Hal David, music Burt F. Bacharach
Original registration date: 6 Jul 67

"You Can't Build Happiness"
words Hal David, music Burt F. Bacharach,
Original registration date: 6 Jul 67

"Who Is Gonna Love Me?"
words Hal David, music Burt F. Bacharach
Original registration date: 6 Jul 67

"As Long As There's An Apple Tree"
words Hal David, music Burt F. Bacharach
Original registration date: 6 Jul 67

"Let Me Be Lonely"
words Hal David, music Burt F. Bacharach
Original registration date: 18 Jul 67

"Casino Royale"
words Hal David, music Burt F. Bacharach
Original registration date: 13 Jul 67

"Do You Know the Way to San Jose?"
words Hal David, music Burt F. Bacharach
Original registration date: 28 Jul 67

"Dream, Sweet Dreamer"
words Hal David, music Burt F. Bacharach
Original registration date: 28 Jul 67

"Bond Street"
music Burt F. Bacharach
Original registration date: 4 Sep 67

"A Sinner's Devotion"
words Bob Hilliard, music Burt F. Bacharach
Original registration date: 30 Nov 67

1968

"Promises, Promises"
words Hal David, music Burt F. Bacharach
Original registration date: 9 Feb 68

"What Am I Doing Here?"
words Hal David, music Burt F. Bacharach
Original registration date: 9 Feb 68

"You'll Think of Someone"
words Hal David, music Burt F. Bacharach
Original registration date: 9 Feb 68

"She Likes Basketball"
words Hal David, music Burt F. Bacharach
Original registration date: 9 Feb 68

"Let's Pretend We're Grownup"
words Hal David, music Burt F. Bacharach
Original registration date: 9 Feb 68

"Half As Big As Life"
words Hal David, music Burt F. Bacharach
Original registration date: 9 Feb 68

"Where Can You Take a Girl?"
words Hal David, music Burt F. Bacharach
Original registration date: 9 Feb 68

"A Young, Pretty Girl Like You"
words Hal David, music Burt Bacharach
Original registration date: 9 Feb 68

"Whoever You Are, I Love You"
words Hal David, music Burt Bacharach
Original registration date: 9 Feb 68

"Christmas Day"
words Hal David, music Burt Bacharach
Original registration date: 9 Feb 68

"Loyal, Resourceful and Cooperative"
words Hal David, music Burt Bacharach
Original registration date: 9 Feb 68

"Upstairs"
words Hal David, music Burt Bacharach
Original registration date: 15 Mar 68

"This Guy's in Love with You"
words Hal David, music Burt Bacharach
Original registration date: 15 Apr 68
New matter: arrangement

"Tick Tock Goes the Clock"
words Hal David, music Burt Bacharach
Original registration date: 16 Jul 68

"Turkey Lurkey Time"
words Hal David, music Burt Bacharach
Original registration date: 2 Oct 68

"Wanting Things"
words Hal David, music Burt Bacharach
Original registration date: 2 Oct 68

"A Fact Can Be a Beautiful Thing"
words Hal David, music Burt F. Bacharach
Original registration date: 2 Oct 68

"Hot Food"
words Hal David, music Burt F. Bacharach
Original registration date: 2 Oct 68

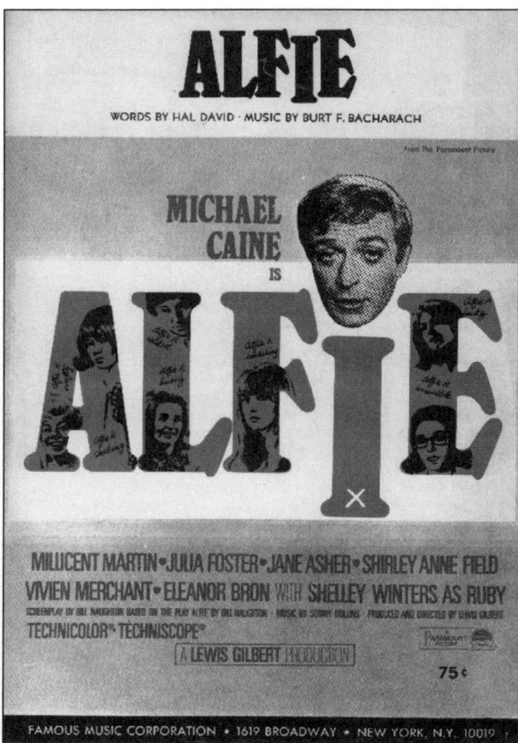

"Knowing When to Leave"
words Hal David, music Burt F. Bacharach
Original registration date: 2 Oct 68

"In the Right Kind of Light"
words Hal David, music Burt F. Bacharach
Original registration date: 30 Oct 68

"Phone Calls"
words Hal David, music Burt Bacharach
Original registration date: 12 Dec 68

"I'll Never Fall in Love Again"
words Hal David, music Burt Bacharach
Original registration date: 12 Dec 68

"It's Our Little Secret"
words Hal David, music Burt F. Bacharach
Original registration date: 12 Dec 68

1969

"Odds and Ends (Of a Beautiful Love Affair)"
words Hal David, music Burt F. Bacharach
Original registration date: 8 Apr 69

"Wouldn't That Be a Stroke of Luck?"
words Hal David, music Burt F. Bacharach
Original registration date: 22 Apr 69

"Pacific Coast Highway"
music Burt Bacharach
Original registration date: 19 May 69

"Loneliness Remembers (What Happiness Forgets)"
words Hal David, music Burt F. Bacharach
Original registration date: 29 May 69

"I'm a Better Man (For Having Loved You)"
words Hal David, music Burt F. Bacharach
Original registration date: 29 May 69

"The Wine Is Young (Our Dreams Are Old)"
words Hal David, music Burt F. Bacharach
Original registration date: 29 May 69

"She's Gone Away"
music Burt Bacharach
Original registration date: 13 Jun 69

"Grapes of Roth"
music Burt Bacharach
Original registration date: 29 Aug 69

"Raindrops Keep Fallin' on My Head"
words Hal David, music Burt F. Bacharach
Original registration date: 18 Sep 69

"How Does a Man Become a Puppet?"
words Hal David, music Burt F. Bacharach
Original registration date: 18 Sep 69

"April Fools"
words Hal David, music Burt F. Bacharach
Original registration date: 23 Sep 69

"Come Touch the Sun"
music Burt Bacharach
Original registration date: 2 Oct 69

"Butch Cassidy and the Sundance Kid"
music Burt Bacharach
Original registration date: 4 Dec 69

"Let Me Go to Him"
words Hal David, music Burt F. Bacharach
Original registration date: 15 Dec 69

"Paper Maché"
words Hal David, music Burt F. Bacharach
Original registration date: 15 Dec 69

"The Sundance Kid"
music Burt Bacharach
Original registration date: 23 Dec 69

1970

"Across the River, Round the Bend"
words Hal David, music Burt F. Bacharach
Original registration date: 12 Jan 70

"Three Important Things"
words Hal David, music Burt F. Bacharach
Original registration date: 12 Jan 70

"Hasbrook Heights"
words Hal David, music Burt F. Bacharach
Original registration date: 12 Jan 70

"Everybody's Out of Town"
words Hal David, music Burt F. Bacharach
Original registration date: 12 Jan 70

"Send My Picture to Scranton, PA"
words Hal David, music Burt F. Bacharach
Original registration date: 22 Jan 70

"Beads and Boots and a Green and Yellow Blanket"
words Hal David, music Burt F. Bacharach
Original registration date: 31 Jul 70

"The Very First person I Met (In California)"
words Hal David, music Burt F. Bacharach
Original registration date: 31 Jul 70

"Who Gets the Girl? Who Gets the guy?"
words Hal David, music Burt F. Bacharach
Original registration date: 31 Jul 70

"Walk the Way You Talk"
words Hal David, music Burt F. Bacharach
Original registration date: 31 Jul 70

"Ten Times Forever More"
words Hal David, music Burt F. Bacharach
Original registration date: 31 Jul 70

"Something Bad"
words Bob Hilliard, music Burt F. Bacharach
Original registration date: 5 Aug 70

"Check Out Time"
words Hal David, music Burt F. Bacharach
Original registration date: 28 Dec 70

"All Kinds of People"
words Hal David, music Burt F. Bacharach
Original registration date: 28 Dec 70

"My Rock and Foundation"
words Hal David, music Burt F. Bacharach
Original registration date: 28 Dec 70

"The Green Grass Starts to Grow"
words Hal David, music Burt F. Bacharach,
Original registration date: 10 Dec 70

1971

"Be Aware"
words Hal David, music Burt F. Bacharach
Original registration date: 18 Jan 71

"And the People Were with Her"
music Burt Bacharach
Original registration date: 14 Jun 71

"Free Fall"
music Burt Bacharach
Original registration date: 14 Jun 71

"Long Ago Tomorrow"
words Hal David, music Burt F. Bacharach
Original registration date: 15 Sep 71

"Something Big"
words Hal David, music Burt F. Bacharach
Original registration date: 15 Sep 71:

1972

"I Just Have to Breathe"
words Hal David, music Burt F. Bacharach,
Original registration date: 7 Mar 72

"If You Never Say Goodbye"
words Hal David, music Burt F. Bacharach,
Original registration date: 14 Mar 72

"The Balance of Nature"
words Hal David, music Burt Bacharach,
Original registration date: 14 Mar 72

"Lost Horizon"
words Hal David, music Burt Bacharach,
Original registration date: 16 Mar 72

"Reflections"
words Hal David, music Burt Bacharach,
Original registration date: 5 Jul 72

"The World is a Circle"
words Hal David, music Burt Bacharach,
Original registration date: 20 Oct 72

"Living Together, Growing Together"
words Hal David, music Burt Bacharach,
Original registration date: 26 Dec 72

1973

"Question Me an Answer"
words Hal David, music Burt Bacharach
Original registration date: 8 Feb 73

"I Come to You"
words Hal David, music Burt Bacharach
Original registration date: 22 Feb 73

"Where Knowledge Ends (Faith Begins)"
words Hal David, music Burt Bacharach
Original registration date: 22 Feb 73

"If I Could Go Back"
words Hal David, music Burt Bacharach
Original registration date: 22 Feb 73

"The Things I Will Not Miss"
words Hal David, music Burt Bacharach
Original registration date: 22 Feb 73

"I Might Frighten Her Away"
words Hal David, music Burt Bacharach
Original registration date: 22 Feb 73

"Share the Joy"
words Hal David, music Burt Bacharach
Original registration date: 22 Feb 73

"Monterey Peninsula"
music Burt Bacharach
Original registration date: 23 Oct 73

1978

"Looking Back over My Shoulder"
words Hal David, music Burt Bacharach
Created: 1978
Registered: 13 Feb 78

"You Learn to Love by Loving"
words Hal David, music Burt Bacharach
Created: 1978
Registered: 13 Feb 78

"Everybody Knows the Way to Bethlehem"
words Hal David, music Burt Bacharach
Created: 1978
Registered: 27 Apr 78

"Amnesia: The Inderal Song"
words Libby Titus, music Burt Bacharach
Created: 1978
Registered: 25 Sep 78

"Chicago Farewell"
words Libby Titus, music Burt Bacharach
Created: 1978
Registered: 25 Sep 78

"Single Girl"
words Libby Titus, music Burt Bacharach
Created: 1978
Registered: 25 Sep 78

"The Dancing Fool"
words & music Burt Bacharach & Anthony Newley
Created: 1978
Registered: 9 Jan 79

"Magdalena"
music Burt Bacharach
Created: 1979
Registered: 7 Feb 79

"There Is Time"
words Sally Stevens, music Burt Bacharach
Created: 1979
Registered: 7 Feb 79

"211: Two-Eleven"
music Burt Bacharach
Created: 1979
Registered: 7 Feb 79

"Your Life, My Life"
music Burt Bacharach
Created: 1979
Registered: 7 Feb 79

"Summer '77"
music Burt Bacharach
Created: 1979
Registered: 7 Feb 79

"Riverboat (Comes In)"
music Burt Bacharach, words Libby Titus
Published: 20 Apr 79
Registered: 23 Jul 79

"I Don't Need You Anymore"
words & music Burt Bacharach & Paul Anka
Created: 1979
Registered: 10 Dec 79

1980

"I think I'm Gonna Fall in Love"
words & music Paul Anka & Burt Bacharach
Created: 1980
Registered: 2 Mar 81

"Where Did the Time Go?"
words & music Burt Bacharach & Carole Bayer Sager
Created: 1980
Published: 22 Aug 80
Registered: 26 Jan 81

"The Love Too Good to Last"
words & music Burt Bacharach, Carole Bayer Sager & Peter Allen
Created: 1980
Published: 1 Aug 80
Registered: 12 Jan 81

"I Won't Break"
words & music Carole Bayer Sager, Peter Allen & Burt Bacharach
Created: 1980
Published: 6 Apr 81
Registered: 13 Apr 81

1981

"Just Friends"
music Burt Bacharach, words Carole Bayer Sager
Published: 23 Apr 81
Registered: 19 May 81

"Moving Pictures"
words & music Burt F. Bacharach & John Phillips
Created: 1981
Published: 24 Aug 81

"Tell Her"

words & music Burt Bacharach, Carole Bayer Sager & Peter Allen
Published: 23 Apr 81

"Somebody's Been Lying"
words C. Bayer Sager, music B. Bacharach
Published: 23 Apr 81
Registered: 19 May 81

"Wild Again"
words C. Bayer Sager, music B. Bacharach
Published: 23 Apr 81
Registered: 19 May 81

"Easy to Love Again"
words C. Bayer Sager, music B. Bacharach
Published: 23 Apr 81
Registered: 19 May 81

"Stronger Than Before"
words & music Burt Bacharach, Carole Bayer Sager & Bruce Roberts
Created: 1981
Published: 23 Apr 81
Registered: 19 May 81

"You Don't Know Me"
words & music B. Bacharach & C. Bayer Sager
Created: 1981
Published 23 Apr 81
Registered: 19 May 81

"Truth and Honesty"
words & music Burt Bacharach, Carole Bayer Sager & Peter Allen
Created: 1980
Published: 5 Aug 81
Registered: 30 Sep 81

"Arthur's Theme: Best That You Can Do"
words & music Burt Bacharach, Carole Bayer Sager & Christopher Cross & Peter Allen
Created: 1981
Published: 25 Aug 81
Registered: 30 Oct 81

"Come Make Me Over"
words Janice I. Spencer, music Burt Bacharach
Created: 1981
Registered: 24 Dec 81
New matter: changed words of "Don't Make Me Over" by Burt Bacharach and Hal David

"Making Love: Theme Song"
words & music Carole Bayer Sager, Burt Bacharach & Bruce Roberts
Created: 1981
Registered: 19 Jan 82

"Poor Rich Boy"
words David Pack & Joe Puerta, music Burt Bacharach
Music prev. reg. 1981
New matter: words

"It's Only Love"
words & music B. Bacharach, S. Bishop & C. B. Sager
Created 1981
Published: 12 Aug 81
Registered 7 Jan 82
New matter: words

"Money"
music Burt Bacharach
Created: 1981
Published: 31 Dec 81
Registered: 24 May 82

"Fool Me Again"
words & music B. Bacharach & C. B. Sager
Created 1981
Published 31 Dec 81
Registered: 24 May 82

1982

"That's What Friends Are For"
words C. Bayer Sager, music B. Bacharach
Created: 1982
Registered: 29 Jun 82
"Making Love"
words & music Carole Bayer Sager, Burt Bacharach & Bruce Roberts
Created: 1982
Published: 3 May 82
Registered: 13 Sep 82

"I'm Guilty"
words & music N. Diamond, B. Bacharach & C. B. Sager
Published: 26 Aug 82
Registered: 7 Sep 82

"Hurricane"
words & music N. Diamond, B. Bacharach & C. B. Sager
Published: 26 Aug 82
Registered: 7 Sep 82

"In Ensenada"
words & music N. Diamond, B. Bacharach & C. B. Sager
Published: 26 Aug 82
Registered: 7 Sep 82

"Heartlight"
words & music N. Diamond, B. Bacharach & C. B. Sager
Published: 26 Aug 82
Registered: 7 Sep 82

"Lost among the Stars"
words & music N. Diamond, B. Bacharach & C. B. Sager
Published: 23 Sep 82
Registered: 4 Oct 82

"Front Page Story"
words & music N. Diamond, B. Bacharach & C. B. Sager
Published: 23 Sep 82
Registered: 4 Oct 82

"It's All Up to You (Theme from Arthur)"
Prev. reg. 1982, PA 125-086
New matter: instrumental version

"Night Shift"
words & music Burt Bacharach, Carole Bayer Sager & Marv Ross
Created: 1982
Published: 20 Sep 82
Registered: 29 Jun 82

"That's What Friends Are For"
words & music Carole Bayer Sager & Burt Bacharach
Created: 1982
Published: 26 Nov 85
Registered: 29 Jun 82

1983

"Maybe"
words & music Marvin Hamlisch, Carole Bayer Sager & Burt Bacharach
Published: 22 Jul 83
Registered: 30 Sep 83

"Blame It on Me"
words C. Bayer Sager, music B. Bacharach
Published: 22 Jul 83
Registered: 5 Mar 84

"Time (All We Have Is Time)"
words & music Melissa Manchester, Carole Bayer Sager & Burt Bacharach
Created: 1983
Registered: 27 Jul 83

"Heart Strings"
music David Foster & Burt Bacharach
Published: 14 Oct 83
Registered: 2 Mar 84

1984

"Crazy"
words & music N. Diamond, B. Bacharach & C. B. Sager
Published: 23 Jul 84
Registered: 6 Aug 84

"Finders of Lost Love (Theme)"
words & music Burt Bacharach & Carole Bayer Sager
Created: 1984
Registered: 25 Sep 84
"Turn Around"
words & music Neil Diamond, Burt Bacharach & Carole Bayer Sager
Published: 8 Aug 84
Registered: 13 Jul 84

"A Chance for Heaven: Swimming Theme from the Official Music of the XXIIIrd Olympiad, Los Angeles, 1984"
words & music B. Bacharach, C. Bayer Sager & C. Cross
Published: 5 Jun 84
Registered: 14 Aug 86

1985

"Extravagant Gestures"
words & music Carole Bayer Sager & Burt Bacharach
Published: 21 Nov 85
Registered: 21 May 85

"On My Own"
words & music B. Bacharach & C. B. Sager
Created: 1985
Registered: 25 Nov 85

"Love Always"
words & music B. Bacharach, C. B. Sager & B. Roberts
Created: 1985
Registered: 25 Nov 85

"Love Will Show Us How"
words & music Michael Jay Margules (aka Michael Jay), Burt Bacharach & David Foster
Created: 1985
Registered: 17 Jun 85

"How Long?"
words C. Bayer Sager, music Burt Bacharach
Published: 21 Nov 85
Registered: 16 Dec 85

"Stay Devoted"
words Carole Bayer Sager, music Burt Bacharach
Published: 21 Nov 85
Registered: 16 Dec 85

1986

"Me Beside You"
words & music N. Diamond, B. Bacharach & C. B. Sager
Published: 5 May 86
Registered: 16 May 86

"I'll See You on the Radio (Laura)"
words & music N. Diamond, B. Bacharach & C. B. Sager
Published: 5 May 86
Registered: 16 May 86

"They Don't Make 'Em Like They Used To"
words Carole Bayer Sager, music Burt Bacharach
Published: 22 Sep 86
Registered: 5 Dec 86

1987

"Split Decision"
words C. Bayer Sager, music B. Bacharach
Published: 19 Jun 87
Registered: 6 May 87

"Perfect Lover"
words & music Carole Bayer Sager, Burt Bacharach & Nathan East
Created: 1987
Registered: 6 May 87
"In My Reality"
words C. Bayer Sager, music B. Bacharach
Published: 19 Jun 87
Registered: 11 Aug 87

"Over You"
words & music Ray Parker, Jr., Burt Bacharach & Carole Bayer Sager
Published: 8 Sep 87
Registered: 4 May 87

"In a World Such As This"
words & music Bruce Roberts, Burt Bacharach & Carole Bayer Sager
Published: 12 Jun 87
Registered: 4 May 87

"Overnight Success"
words & music Burt Bacharach & Carole Bayer Sager
Published: 16 Nov 87
Registered: 11 Jan 88

"Love Is Fire (Love Is Ice)"
words & music Burt Bacharach & Carole Bayer Sager
Published: 16 Nov 87
Registered: 4 May 87

"Love Power"
words & music Burt Bacharach & Carole Bayer Sager
Published: 13 Aug 87
Registered: 4 May 87

"Heartbreak of Love"
words & music Carole Bayer Sager, Burt Bacharach & Diane Warren
Published: 9 Jul 87
Registered: 4 May 87

1988

"Love is My Decision (Theme from Arthur 2: On the Rocks)"
words & music Burt Bacharach, Carole Bayer Sager & Chris de Burgh
Published: 5 Jul 88
Registered: 22 Jul 88

"Love Theme from Arthur"
music Burt Bacharach
Published: 5 Jul 88
Registered: 31 Oct 88

"The Best of Times"
music Burt Bacharach
Published: 5 Jul 88
Registered: 31 Oct 88

"You and Me for Always"
words C. Bayer Sager, music Burt Bacharach
Published: 20 Oct 88
Registered: 21 Dec 88

"Love Light"
words C. Bayer Sager, music Burt Bacharach
Published: 20 Oct 88
Registered: 21 Dec 88

"One More Time Around"
words & music Burt Bacharach, Carole Bayer Sager & Tom Keane
Published: 22 Sep 88
Registered: 27 Feb 89

"Why Can't We Be Together?"
words & music Carole Bayer Sager, Burt Bacharach & Bruce Roberts
Created: 1988
Published: 5 May 89
Registered: 23 Jun 89

1989

"Love Goes By"
words & music Burt Bacharach, Carole Bayer Sager & Bruce Roberts
Created: 1989
Registered: 14 Jul 89

"I'd Rather Sleep Alone"
words & music Burt Bacharach, Carole Bayer Sager & Gerry Goffin
Created: 1989
Registered: 5 Jul 89

"Here in Your Spotlight"
words & music Burt Bacharach, Carole Bayer Sager & Nathan East
Created: 1989
Registered: 5 Jul 89

"Take Good Care of You and Me"
words & music Burt Bacharach, Carole Bayer Sager & Gerry Goffin
Created: 1989
Registered: 5 Jul 89

"Someone Else's Eyes"
words & music Burt Bacharach, Carole Bayer Sager & Bruce Roberts
Created: 1989
Registered: 5 Jul 89

"Remember Me"
words & music Burt Bacharach, Carole Bayer Sager & Gerry Goffin
Created: 1989
Registered: 31 Jul 89

"Teardrops"
words & music Burt Bacharach & Carole Bayer Sager
Alternate title: "Hang Your Teardrops Up to Dry"
Created: 1989
Registered: 28 Aug 89

"Remember Me"

words & music Burt Bacharach & Carole Bayer Sager
Created: 1989
Registered: 28 Aug 89

"Everybody Knows"
words & music Burt Bacharach, Carole Bayer Sager & Adrienne Anderson
Created: 1989
Registered: 22 Sep 89

"Remember Me/All I Want from You"
words & music Burt Bacharach, Carole Bayer Sager & Sami McKinney
Created: 1989
Registered: 6 Nov 89

"Need a Little Faith"
words C. Bayer Sager, music Burt Bacharach
Published: 26 Jun 89
Registered: 10 Jul 89

"Hang Your Teardrops Up to Dry"
words & music Carole Bayer Sager, Burt Bacharach & Gerry Goffin
Created: 1989
Published: 6 Sep 91
Registered: 4 Nov 91

"How Can I Love You?"
words Hal David, music Burt Bacharach
Created: 1989
Registered: 24 Nov 89

"Sunny Weather Lover"
words Hal David, music Burt Bacharach
Created: 1989
Published: 8 Jan 93
Registered: 26 Mar 93

1990

"The Power of Your Love: You and I"
words & music Carole Bayer Sager, Burt Bacharach & Taja Sevelle
Created: 1990
Published: 15 Oct 91
Registered: 3 Sep 92

1991

"Obsession"
words & music Desmond Child & Burt Bacharach
Published: 14 Jun 91
Registered: 12 Aug 91

"I Just Don't Know What to Do"
words & music Carole Bayer Sager & Burt Bacharach
Published: 6 Sep 91
Registered: 4 Nov 91

"This Is the Night"
words & music Burt Bacharach, James Ingram & John Bettis
Created: 1991
Published: 25 May 93
Registered: 7 Sep 93

"Sing for the Children"
words & music Burt Bacharach, James Ingram & John Bettis
Created: 1991
Published: 25 May 93
Registered: 7 Sep 93

1993

"Two Hearts"
words & music Maurice White, Burt Bacharach & Philip Bailey
Published: 14 Sep 93
Registered: 30 Dec 93

"Don't Say Goodbye, Girl"
words & music Narada Michael Walden, Sally Jo Dakota & Burt Bacharach
Published: 26 Oct 93
Registered: 24 Apr 94

1994

"If I Want To"
words & music Will Jennings & Burt Bacharach
Published: 20 Oct 94
Registered: 4 Apr 95

1995

"Let Me Be the One"
words & music Burt Bacharach, Taja Seville & Denise Rich
Created: 1995
Published: 23 Apr 96
Registered: 16 Apr 97

"After All"
words & music Burt Bacharach & Paul Anka
Published: 3 Apr 95
Registered: 23 Feb 98

"God, Give Me Strength"
words & music Burt Bacharach & Elvis Costello
Created: 1995
Published: 10 Sep 96
Registered: 27 Apr 98

1997

"Such Unlikely Lovers"
words & music Burt Bacharach & Elvis Costello
Created: 1997
Published: 29 Sep 98
Registered: 23 Sep 99

"My Thief"
words & music Burt Bacharach & Elvis Costello
Created: 1997
Published: 29 Sep 98
Registered: 23 Sep 99

"What's Her Name Today?"
words & music Burt Bacharach & Elvis Costello
Created: 1997
Published: 29 Sep 98
Registered: 23 Sep 99

1998

"In the Darkest Place," "Toledo," "I Still Have That Other Girl," etc. 11 songs, performed by Elvis Costello with Burt Bacharach
Painted from Memory. Mercury 538 002-2. Compact disc
Created: 1998
Published: 29 Sep 98
Registered: 8 Mar 99

Bacharach Off the Record

Here is a chronological listing of all known Bacharach compositions that were never commercially made available, as well as songs that allegedly have been recorded but could not be located in time to list in the discography. Included is as much information as could be gathered from ASCAP, BMI, the Library of Congress, Warner/Chappell Music, the National Music Publishers' Association and the exhaustive Bacharach website *The Hitmaker Archive,* whose webmaster, Stefan Wesley, has spies working for him all over the world.

The Forties

The Night Plane to Heaven (Burt Bacharach)
According to the *Look of Love* liner notes, this was his first song, written while he was at McGill University in Montreal in the late Forties. It was published but never recorded.

The Fifties

A Soldier's Prayer (Burt Freeman Bacharach, William Stephen Quigley)
Bacharach's first copyrighted composition, written while he was in the army in 1951.

The Secret of Love (Burt F. Bacharach, Jack Wolf) ©1955

Forgotten Music (Jack Wolf, Burt Bacharach)
Most likely written in 1955 along with the above title and "Keep Me in Mind," it was registered with the Library of Congress for the first time in September 1964.

It's Great To Be Young (Jack Wolf, Burt Bacharach)
Ditto for this ditty, never copyrighted but registered with ASCAP. As for performers, it lists the mysterious R. Rogoo.

My Heart Will Still Be… (Jack Wolf, Burt Bacharach)
Another strange ASCAP composition, with the title variation "My Head [etc.]…."

Eyewitness (Burt F. Bacharach, Harry Ross) ©1955
This was possibly an exploitation song for the 1956 British thriller of the same name. In the film a woman witnesses a robbery, runs away, gets hit by a bus and then is terrorized in the hospital by the thieves, who return to kill her. It's doubtful the song can be as entertaining as that.

Forever Faithful. (Burt F. Bacharach, Mack David) ©1957

Love Bank (Burt F. Bacharach, Hal David & Lou Melamed) ©1957

Two Against the World (Hal David, Burt F. Bacharach) ©1957

My Dreamboat Is Drifting (Down the River of Doubt) (Sammy Gallop, Burt Bacharach) ©1956
From the same team that brought you "Uninvited Dream."

Do You Remember As I Remember? (Burt F. Bacharach, Buddy Bernier) ©1957

Snowballs (Burt F. Bacharach) ©1957

Bottomless Cup (Burt F. Bacharach, Hal David & Lou Melamed) ©1958

The Mission Bell by the Wishin' Well (Burt F. Bacharach, Hal David) ©1958

I'll Kiss You Goodnight In the Morning (Burt F. Bacharach, Hal David) ©1958

Third from the Left (Burt F. Bacharach, Hal David) ©1958

I Could Kick Myself (Burt F. Bacharach, Hal David) ©1958

What a Night. (Burt F. Bacharach, Hal David) ©1959

Lorna Doone (Burt F. Bacharach, Hal David) ©1959

You're the Dream (Burt F. Bacharach, Hal David) ©1959
There are some who allege that the Marvellos recorded it in 1956, but several doo-wop fans who own this rare record, the last to be released on the Theron label, say it's credited to someone else. Bacharach and David did write a song called "You're the Dream," copyrighted 1959, but if it indeed turns out to be the same song, its

writers will have to live with the knowledge that their song bankrupted the black-owned independent label shortly after its release.

Go 'Way, Mister Moon (Burt F. Bacharach, Wilson Stone) ©1959

The Woman Who Wasn't Mine (Burt F. Bacharach, Wilson Stone) ©1959

Happy and His One Man Band (Burt F. Bacharach, Wilson Stone) ©1959
Happy, you'll recall, was Bacharach's nickname.

I Need You (Burt F. Bacharach, Wilson Stone)
ASCAP also has this uncopyrighted song in its files with the title variant "I Need Your Love."

Send Me Letters Filled with Kisses (Burt F. Bacharach, Wilson Stone) ©1959

The Sixties

Across the River, Round the Bend (Burt Bacharach, Hal David)
Registered with the Library of Congress in 1970 but probably dated earlier. Supposedly John Ashley recorded this in 1960, but the single is harder to find than lips on chickens.

I'll Never Ever Forget "What's Her Name" (Hal David, Burt Bacharach) ©1960
There was a 1967 Oliver Reed film called *I'll Never Forget What's 'is Name,* which was a satire on the advertising world and was the first mainstream British film to utter the F-word. Whether there was any connection or a separate use of the same punch line is not known.

More and More (Nita Jonas, Burt Bacharach) ©1960

Cryin', Wailin', Sobbin' (Nita Jonas, Burt Bacharach) ©1960
An answer disc to Buddy Holly's posthumous 1959 recording of "Cryin', Waitin', Hopin'"?

Two Figures on a Wedding Cake (Fred Tobias, Burt Bacharach) ©1960
Path of Pride (Fred Tobias, Burt Bacharach) ©1960

One Really Big Change (Bob Hilliard, Burt Bacharach) ©1960

Manpower (Burt Bacharach, Bob Hilliard) ©1961

The Third Window from the Right (Mack David, Burt Bacharach) ©1961

Hideaway Heart (Hal David, Burt Bacharach) ©1961

Barracuda (Burt F. Bacharach, Paul Hampton) ©1961

Don't Do Anything Dangerous (Hal David, Burt Bacharach) ©1961

Thirty Miles of Railroad Track (Bob Hilliard, Burt Bacharach) ©1961

Something Bad (Bob Hilliard, Burt Bacharach)
Copyrighted in 1970, it was included on an album of early 1962 demos sung by Lonnie Sattin.

The Hurtin' Kind (Hal David, Burt Bacharach)
Also included on an album of early 1962 demos sung by Lonnie Sattin, but not copyrighted

Do I Have to Say More (Hal David, Burt Bacharach) ©1962

The Secret of Staying Young (Hal David, Burt Bacharach) ©1962

The Right to Love You (Hal David, Burt Bacharach) ©1963

Move Over and Make Room For Me. (Hal David, Burt Bacharach) ©1963

Building Walls (Hal David, Burt Bacharach) ©1963

Living Without Love (Burt Bacharach, Hal David) ©1963
This likely was recorded by someone, because it has turned up in several music books.

Everything Is Nothing Without You (Hal David, Burt Bacharach) ©1963

The Boss Is Not Here (All at Once It's Sunday) (Hal David & Burt F. Bacharach, music Max Coplet & Lotar Olias) ©1965
English translation.

Question of Love (Bob Hilliard, Burt Bacharach) ©1965
Written between 1960 and 1963.

Trial by Jury (Burt Bacharach, Hal David) ©1966

W.E.E.P. (Burt Bacharach, Hal David) ©1966
Brief radio jingle from *On the Flip Side* not included on the soundtrack. 1966

You Can't Build Happiness (Burt Bacharach, Hal David) ©1967

Alma Mater (Burt Bacharach, Murray Schisgal)

Love Cast its Shadow (Burt Bacharach, Murray Schisgal)

Luv (Cues) (Burt Bacharach, Murray Schisgal)
Murray Schisgal's play *Luv* was made into a movie starring Jack Lemmon in 1967. There are two a cappella songs written into the text of the play, and perhaps this was an attempt to improve upon them. Gerry Mulligan is credited with scoring the music, so it's possible Bacharach's input went either uncredited or unused. This Clive Donner film is also notable for containing the first brief onscreen appearance by a very young Harrison Ford.

Loyal, Resourceful and Cooperative (Burt Bacharach, Hal David) ©1968

Hot Food (Burt Bacharach, Hal David) ©1968
Above two tracks dropped from *Promises, Promises* after Boston tryouts.

In the Right Kind of Light (Burt Bacharach, Hal David) ©1968

Phone Calls (Burt Bacharach, Hal David) ©1968
As Bacharach and David wrote for nothing and no one else in 1968, these songs were probably intended for *Promises, Promises.*

Wouldn't That be a Stroke of Luck? (Burt Bacharach, Hal David) ©1969
A song called "A Stork of Luck" was listed in the Boston *Promises, Promises Playbill.*

The Seventies

Pussycat Pussycat I Love You (Cues) (Burt Bacharach, Hal David)
The failed 1970 sequel to *What's New Pussycat?* produced more variations on the hit but no soundtrack album.

Three Important Things (Burt Bacharach, Hal David) ©1970

Beads and Boots and a Green and Yellow Blanket (Burt Bacharach, Hal David) ©1970

The Very First Person I Met (In California) (Burt Bacharach, Hal David) ©1970

Peaches Don't Grow on a Cherry Tree (Burt Bacharach, Bobby Russell)
Said to be recorded by Bobby Russell in 1975, but the recording hasn't yet turned up.

Looking Back Over My Shoulder (Burt Bacharach, Hal David) ©1978

You Learn to Love by Loving (Burt Bacharach, Hal David) ©1978

Everybody Knows the Way to Bethlehem (Burt Bacharach, Hal David) ©1978
Possibly a Yuletide reworking of "Do You Know the Way to San Jose"

Chicago Farewell (Burt Bacharach, Libby Titus) ©1978

Single Girl (Burt Bacharach, Libby Titus) ©1978

Amnesia: The Inderal Song (Burt Bacharach, Libby Titus) ©1978
The above three Bacharach-Titus titles were copyrighted in advance of the *Woman* album but not returned to.

211: Two-Eleven (Burt Bacharach) ©1979

Your Life My Life (Burt Bacharach) ©1979
Two unused instrumentals from the *Woman* project.

The Eighties

Columbo (background cues) (Burt Bacharach, David Pack & Joseph Puerta)
Columbo, the Peter Falk TV and later TV-movie series that this would've been used for, often used preexisting music in its backgrounds. Most likely this is another instrumental arrangement of "Poor Rich Boy" from *Arthur,* as no other examples of Bacharach writing with Ambrosia exist.

Night Shift (cues) (Burt Bacharach)
Outside of "Street Talk" and an instrumental of "That's What Friends Are For," most of Bacharach's incidental music didn't make the soundtrack album.

Finder of Lost Loves (end credits, main title & background cues) (Burt Bacharach, Carole Bayer Sager)

I'd Rather Sleep Alone (Burt Bacharach, Carole Bayer Sager & Gerry Goffin) ©1989

Love Goes by (Burt Bacharach, Carole Bayer Sager & Bruce Roberts) ©1989

Here In Your Spotlight (Burt Bacharach, Carole Bayer Sager & Nathan East) ©1989

What I Like About You (Burt Bacharach, Carole Bayer Sager & Christopher Cross)

You Were There (Burt Bacharach, Carole Bayer Sager & Melissa Manchester)

I Tried (Burt Bacharach, Carole Bayer Sager & Julio Iglesias)
Julio gave Hal David his biggest non-Bacharach hit in the rock era. Maybe this was an attempt to even things up.

It's All Up To You (Burt Bacharach, Carole Bayer Sager & Stephen Bishop)

Love Hurts (cues) (Burt Bacharach)
Though Burt was credited for scoring the 1989 Bud Yorkin film, hardly any original music was used and no soundtrack was ever released.

The Nineties and Beyond

Music For Life (Burt Bacharach, BA Robertson)

Dead Serious (Burt Bacharach, BA Robertson)

Isn't it a Bliss (Burt Bacharach, BA Robertson)

Best We Ever Had (Burt Bacharach, BA Robertson)

Once Upon A Time (Burt Bacharach, BA Robertson)
The above five songs, from the shelved *Snow White* musical that Bacharach wrote with the Mike and the Mechanics lyricist in 1996, were registered with BMI.

Isn't She Great (score)
In the ASCAP files, nearly every song in this score has a different title except for "Mass Love" and "The Book Tour." There are 27 themes and cues as opposed to the 15 on the soundtrack: wherever it's obvious what the song turned out to be, the finalized title is listed in parentheses. And I gotta think "Sexual Me, Sexual You" is almost better served with the title "Dingle Blowingtits."

#1 Bestseller
#2 Bestseller
Blessed Event
Guy's Different (Guy's Theme)
The Book Tour
Dingle Blowingtits (ASCAP)
Drive to Connecticut (Hello Connecticut)
Gurney They Say Yes (Yes, They Said Yes)
Guy Revisited (Heartbreak Revisited)
Guy with Blocks
Henry's Fanfare
Irv Leaves Party
Irv Reads
Irv Wurn, Onassis Tag
Isn't She Great
J. In duck pond
Makeup
Mass Love
Montage Book #2
Pitching Book (The Big Pitch)
Pressteamsters
Proposal
Radio City
They Eat
The Tree
Valley Premiere
Visit Guy
You Wouldn't Use

Change My Mind (Burt Bacharach, Steven Krikorian)
Krikorian is Tonio K., and the song, which is listed with ASCAP, is probably late Nineties.

Find it in Your Heart (Burt Bacharach, Mark Cawley & Eliot John Kennedy)

Follow Your Heart (Burt Bacharach, Denise Rich)

I'll Never Be the Same (Burt Bacharach, John Bettis & Wendy Waldman)

Pride (Burt Bacharach, John Bettis, James Ingram & Puff Johnson)
Registered with BMI.

Overture 2000 or Bacharach Overture (Burt Bacharach)
Performed at the 72nd Annual Academy Awards.

Paint it Blue (Burt Bacharach, Tonio K.)

There Is No Love Unless We Make it (Burt Bacharach, Will Jennings)

True Love Was Meant For You and Me (Burt Bacharach, Allan Rich)

Dates Unknown

All I Ever Need Is You (Burt F. Bacharach)

Anthem (Burt Bacharach)
The title is listed with ASCAP, but no other information is given, not even the writer. According to the website *The Hitmaker Archive*, a recording of this song by Mel Tormé exists.

Before You Leave Me (Burt F. Bacharach, Hal David)

Big Band Dixieland (Burt F. Bacharach)

Night (Burt Bacharach, Norman Gimbel)

No Love Anywhere (Burt Bacharach, Norman Gimbel)
Being that Gimbel is the only person to write with Bacharach before 1963 and after 1975, it's hard to say when these songs were written.

Rainbow (Burt Bacharach, Paul Anka)

You Can't Buy Happiness (Burt Bacharach, Hal David)

These Just In...

When You Love Somebody (Burt Bacharach, Andreas Carlsson)
Carlsson wrote many tracks for the likes of the Backstreet Boys, *NSync and Britney Spears, and this formulaic exercise wouldn't be out of place on any of their albums. Which isn't saying much.

You Save Me (Burt Bacharach, Jerry Leiber & Jeb Leiber)

Fallin' Out Of Love (Burt Bacharach, Jerry Leiber & Jeb Leiber)
The recent A&E documentaries on the Brill Building, plus the *Biography* installments on Bacharach and Dionne Warwick, must've brought Bacharach and Jerry Leiber back to the idea of writing songs together, something they'd discussed but never actually done. Leiber's son Jeb is thrown in for good measure, and the results are two cozy if unspectacular ballads that stay in a mellow bag and never threaten to become power ballads. "You Save Me" is the better of the two, with a prettier melody and lyrics.

New Jack Bacharach: Always Sampling There to Remind Me

If you thought four people to write the "Theme from Arthur" was extravagant, how about 13 people to write "Mobbin' in My Old School"? Can it be—Hal David and Sean "P. Diddy" Combs bustin' rhymes? Hal and Carole Bayer Sager staging an intervention to help Little Bruce come up with alternate ways of saying motherfucker that mean the same thing? Burt getting "blue on blue" with some downbeat electronica outfit from Norway? Welcome to the wonderful world of sampling. Here's a partial listing of instances where Bacharach made it into the mix, even if good half of them are Isaac Hayes' version of "Walk On By."

Back at You (1996)
Writers: Burt Bacharach, Hal David, Albert Johnson & Kejuan Muchita
Performer: Mobb Deep
Album: *Sunset Park* soundtrack

Beautiful Ones (1999)
Writers: Burt Bacharach, Hal David, Rich Harrison & Cecil Ward
Performer: Mary J. Blige
Sample: "April Fools"
Album: *Mary*

Can I Live (1996)
Writers: Burt Bacharach, Hal David, Sean Carter & Irv Lorenzo
Performer: Jay-Z
Album: *Reasonable Doubt*

Can I Live (2000)
Writers: Burt Bacharach, Hal David, Sean Carter & Irv Lorenzo
Performer: L.O.X
Album: *We Are the Streets*

Candy (2001)
Writers: Burt Bacharach, Hal David & Ash
Sample: "Make It Easy on Yourself
Performer: Ash
Album: *Free All Angels*

Don't Rush the Night (1998)
Writers: Burt Bacharach, Hal David & Aaron Hall
Performer: Aaron Hall
Album: *Inside of You*

Do What I Gotta Do (2000)
Writers : Burt Bacharach, Hal David, Edward Ferrell, Clifton Lighty, Darren Lighty, Balewa Muhammad & J. Wilson
Performer: Donell Jones
Sample: "The Look of Love"
Album: *Shaft* soundtrack

Everybody Wanna Know (1999)
Writers: Burt Bacharach, Hal David, Carlos Broady, Sean Combs, Tiffany Lane, Chris Martin, Nashiem Myrick & Christopher Wallace
Performer: Charli Baltimore
Albums: *Cold As Ice, Trippin'* soundtrack

Everything Is Gonna Be Alright (1994)
Writers: Burt Bacharach, Hal David, Jimmy Jam & Terry Lewis
Sample: "Walk On By"
Performer: Sounds of Blackness
Album: *Africa to America: The Journey of the Drum*

Feel It
Writers: Burt Bacharach, Hal David & Joseph Kirkland

Find the Answer Within (1995)
Writers: Burt Bacharach, Hal David & James Martin Carr
Performer: Boo Radleys
Album: *Wake Up*

Gangsta's Boogie (1996)
Writers: Burt Bacharach, Hal David & Lawrence Sanders
Performer: L.V.
Sample: "The Look of Love"
Album: *Take a Ride*

The Gladiator (1992)
Writers: Burt Bacharach, Hal David, Michael Berrin, Alvin Lawson & Peter Nash
Performer: 3rd Bass
Album: *The Gladiator*

Hollis Goes to Hollywood (1995)
Writers: Burt Bacharach, Hal David, James Smith & Samuel Barnes
Sample: "The Look of Love"
Performer: LL Cool J
Album: *Mr. Smith*

Hype-Nitis (1998)
Writers: Burt Bacharach, Hal David, Jerry Duplessis & Germaine Williams
Performers: Canibus
Sample: "The Look of Love"
Album *Can-I-Bus*

I Can't Go to Sleep (2000)
Writers: Burt Bacharach, Hal David, Dennis Coles, Robert F. Diggs & Isaac Hayes
Performer: Wu-Tang Clan
Sample: "Walk On By"
Album: *The W*

If I Had You (1997)
Writers: Burt Bacharach, Hal David, Carl Thompson & Cecile Ward
Performer: Frankie
Album: *My Heart Belongs to You*

La Raza Part II (1995)
Writers: Burt Bacharach, Hal David, Julio Gonzalez, Arturo Molina & Alvin Trivette
Performer: Kid Frost
Album: *Smile Now Die Later*

Let Me Sing it 2 U (1996)
Writers: Burt Bacharach, Hal David, Duval Clear & Schea Boatwright
Performer: Leschea
Sample: "The Look of Love"
Album: *Rhythm & Beats*

Me Against the World (1994)
Performer: 2Pac
Writers: Burt Bacharach, Hal David, Minnie Riperton, Richard J. Rudolph, Tupac Shakur & LeonWare
Sample: "Walk On By"
Album: *Me Against the World*

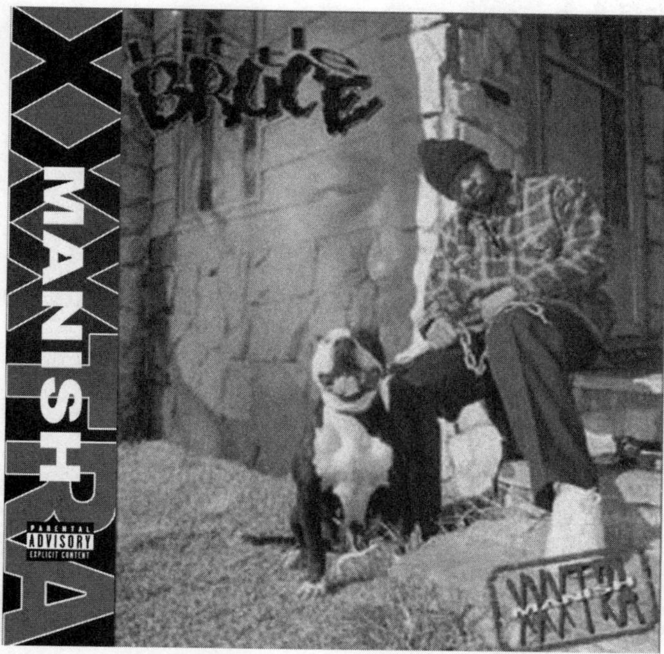

Little Bruce (1994). It took someone *XXXtra Mannish* like Little Bruce to get Burt and Hal and Carole Bayer Sager all together in one writing credit, along with nine other names!

Mobbin In My Old School (1994)
Performer: Little Bruce
Writers: Burt Bacharach, Hal David, Leroy Bonner, Eugene Marshall Jones, Ralph Middlebrooks, Walter Morrison, Bruce Napier, Andrew Noland, Marvin Pierce, Carole Bayer Sager, Bruce Thurman & Gregory Webster
Album: *XXXtra Mannish*

No Other Love (1995)
Performer: Faith Evans
Writers: Burt Bacharach, Hal David, Sean Combs & Faith Evans
Sample: "Walk On By"
Album: *Faith*

No Doubt (1996)
Performer: Heather B.
Writers: Burt Bacharach, Hal David, Heather Gardner, Kenny Parker, Christopher Wallace & Osten Harvey
Sample: Notorious B.I.G's "Warning," which sampled Isaac Hayes' "Walk On By"
Album: *Takin Mine*

Only God Knows (1995)
Performer: Bushwick Bill
Writers: Burt Bacharach, Hal David, Bryan Ross & Clement Burnett
Sample: "Walk On By"
From the album *Phantom of the Rapera*

Something B.I.G. The Notorious B.I.G., aka Chris Wallace, really dug Isaac Hayes' version of "Walk On By," as he sampled it on two separate occasions. Both "Warning" and "What's Beef" were issued posthumously. And Heather B. dug "Warning" so much, she sampled that, making this a thrice-removed Bacaharch interpolation!

Silicone (1997)
Performers: Mono
Writers: Burt Bacharach, Hal David, Roy Budd, Siobhan de Maré & Martin Virgo
Sample: "Walk On By"
Album: *La Femme Nikita* television soundtrack

So Easy (2001)
Writers: Burt Bacharach, Hal David & Röyksopp
Performer: Röyksopp
Sample: "Blue on Blue"
Album: *Melody A.M.*

Twiggy Twiggy (1993)
Writers: Burt Bacharach, Hal David, Nanako Sato, Lalo Schifrin & Morton Stevens
Performer: Pizzicato Five
Sample: "Another Night"
Album: *Expo 2001*

2 Wicky (1997)
Writers: Burt Bacharach, Hal David, Alex Callier & Raymond Geerts
Performer: Hooverphonic
Sample: "Walk On By"
Album: *A New Stereophonic Sound Spectacular*

Trippin (1996)
Performer: Horace Brown
Writers: Burt Bacharach, Hal David, Lee Drakeford & Tom Jefferson
Album: *Horace Brown*

Warning (1994)
Writers: Burt Bacharach, Hal David, Christopher Wallace & Osten Harvey
Sample: "Walk On By"
Performer: The Notorious B.I.G.
Album: *Ready to Die*

What's Beef? (1997)
Writers: Burt Bacharach, Hal David, Christopher Wallace, C. Broady, Sean Combs & Nashiem Myrick
Sample: "Walk On By"
Performer: The Notorious B.I.G.
Album: *Life After Death*

You're Gonna Love Me (1997)
Writers: Burt Bacharach, Hal David, George Pearson, Mary J. Blige, La Tonya Blige, Samuel J. Barnes & Jean Claude Olivier
Sample: "The Look of Love"
Performer: Allure
Album: *Allure*

Bacharach Network TV Specials

Try explaining the dazzle of the network variety show to a kid coming up now and he'll just shoot a look of puzzled bewilderment back at you. Sure there was the uncomfortable camaraderie between guests, the scripted banter, the canned laughter and applause, but those specials are what brought the name Burt Bacharach into millions of homes—sometimes twice and three times a year—and made him our first superstar songwriter. Did anyone even know what Richard Rodgers looks like? And if there were ever an Irving Berlin special, could he have been expected to play tennis with Chris Evert while a bunch of dancers in white fencing outfits pirouetted on a tennis court to one of his songs? I don't think so. Even with prewritten dialogue, these specials offer rare insight into Bacharach's charmed life as a songwriter. You get to meet some of his heroes, and you see and hear some incredible musical moments preserved only on videotape. Unfortunately, all the specials are tough to find, and some descriptions could only be transcribed from third-generation audio dubs. A word to Rhino DVD: a Bacharach Network Specials Boxed Set—think about it, OK?

Kraft Music Hall Presents The Sound Of Burt Bacharach

Air date: Wednesday, November 19, 1969, on NBC
Guests: Lena Horne, Tony Bennett, Edward Villela
This segment of the Kraft Music Hall won an Emmy for "outstanding directorial achievement in comedy, variety or music" (Dwight A. Hemion), "outstanding music direction" (Peter Matz) and "outstanding video tape editing."
Musical highlights: There must've been plenty, but not even a ninth-generation copy of this special could be located.

Kraft Music Hall Presents An Evening With Burt Bacharach

Air date: Wednesday, June 17, 1970, on NBC
Guests: Joel Grey, Dionne Warwick, Sacha Distel
Musical highlights: Burt and Sacha chat and sing "Raindrops" in two languages, and Burt and Dionne sing portions of her hits and recite scripted banter with Burt at the piano. Later, away from the canned laughter and applause, Dionne and Burt are videotaped at A&R Recording Studios rehearsing and recording "Loneliness Remembers What Happiness Forgets." Burt gives props to the songwriting of Paul Simon, then plays piano while Joel Grey sings "Bridge over Troubled Water." Joel sings "Anyone Who Had a Heart." Joel and Burt reminisce about working together in the Catskills, where Joel's act included singing "You Made Me Love You" to a life-size cutout of Betty Grable. Then the two perform "What's New Pussycat?" The show concludes with a concert segment where Burt and the Jack Parnell Orchestra perform "The Look of Love," "Bond Street" and "Reach Out."

Kraft Music Hall: Bacharach Is Back

Air date: Wednesday, July 29, 1970, on NBC
Guests: Dusty Springfield, Juliet Prowse, Mireille Mathieu
Musical highlights: Burt and the orchestra and chorus sing "There's Always Something There to Remind Me," "Alfie" and a medley of his hits. Dusty sings two Bacharach songs she's never recorded—"Knowing When to Leave" and a sensational duet with Burt on "A House Is Not a Home." Mireille sings the Tom Jones hit "I'm Coming Home." Juliet sings "Do You Know the Way to San Jose," and the whole gang engages in a Beatles medley.

Singer Presents Burt Bacharach: A Bacharach Potpourri

Air date: Sunday, March 14, 1971, on CBS
Guests: Rudolph Nureyev, Tom Jones, Barbra Streisand
Musical highlights: Tom sings "Any Day Now" in a slightly more modern arrangement than on the version he recorded in 1966. Then he and Burt are whisked by television magic to the Land of Song for a Welsh pub version of "Raindrops." In the Burt 'n' Barbara segment, Burt chides Babs for not recording "Alfie" before 64 other singers did. He also talks about how he sent her "One Less Bell to Answer" several years earlier, but she didn't do it because she liked the beginning and middle but not the end. This preamble neatly segues to her medley with "A House Is Not a Home." Barbra and Burt perform "Close to You," which was belatedly released on her *Streisand: Just for the Record* boxed set. The most exciting segment is her performance of the sensational "Be Aware," written especially for her, which Babs never wound up releasing on any of her albums. Rudolph Nureyev does strange cuckoo-clock choreography to "Never Goin' Home Anymore" and "N.Y. Sequence" from the *Butch Cassidy* score. The

show concludes with an in-studio concert segment of "Wives and Lovers," "This Guy's in Love with You" and "All Kinds of People."

Non-musical highlights: A filmed segment shows Bacharach at the racetrack with trainer Charlie Whittingham and jockey Bill Shoemaker, and we get to see the latest of Burt's seven horses, Loyal Ruler, race and lose. The horse, in fact, goes lame in the ankle and is relegated to the broodmare category.

Burt Bacharach: Close To You

Air date: Sunday, April 23, 1972, 8–9 P.M., on ABC
Guests: Rex Harrison, Isaac Hayes, Cilla Black
Musical highlights: "I long to be—close to you," sings Burt at the beginning of this, the most intimate of his TV specials. He thankfully dispenses with canned studio laughter and applause and just talks shop with his guests. Hayes performs "Shaft" and snippets of "Walk On By," "The Look of Love" and "The Windows of the World." Cilla Black stands near Burt's piano, and both sing "This Girl's in Love with You," with Burt courteously asking if she likes the key. They sing a brief snippet of "Anyone Who Had a Heart," with Cilla noting, "When I first heard this song I thought it was dead posh," as well as a fine new version of "Alfie," which prompts Cilla to remember, "You flew all the way from America to do 18 takes before you settled for the third." Rex and Burt sing "I'll Never Fall in Love Again" and "Everybody's Out of Town" and visit a rest home for racehorses. Burt rides a horse named "Raindrops" to the instrumental version of "Raindrops" from the *Butch Cassidy* soundtrack. He plugs the upcoming *Lost Horizon* and claims he never tried teaching a song to children before, "except to my daughter Nikki, but that's just for fun. Teaching a song to children for a movie is different. It has to be perfect."

Chevrolet Presents Burt Bacharach And Associates

Air date: Wednesday, November 15, 1972, on ABC
Guests: Vikki Carr, Anthony Newley, Sammy Davis Jr.
You get a great visual of Bacharach performing his extended "Wives and Lovers," as well as footage of him in the recording studio leading musicians through the remake of "Nikki." Otherwise, Bacharach seems more like a TV presenter in this show, with Newley and Davis vying to be his mid-season replacement. Newley and Davis perform songs from Newley's new musical *The Good Old Bad Old Days*, Davis tap dances to "Raindrops," and, yes children, there is a "Candy Man."

Burt Bacharach In Shangri-La

Air date: Friday, January 26, 1973, on ABC
Guests: Bobby Van, The 5th Dimension, Chris Evert, Richard Harris
This special was filmed before the *Lost Horizon* movie bombed but aired afterward. Burt explains the concept of Shangri-La over and over on the actual set of the film.
Musical highlights: Bobby Van dances to "This Guy's in Love with You" and reprises his "Question Me an Answer" routine. The 5th Dimension sneak through Shangri-La security and become the first recorded black people there: they dance and boogaloo to "Living Together." Later, there's a recording-studio segment where Bacharach leads the group through a vocal arrangement of the spiritual "Nobody Knows the Trouble I've Seen"; apparently it's too racy for Shangri-La. Richard Harris performs an excellent "If I Could Go Back" and "Didn't We." And Evert beats Bacharach, but unfortunately the dancers are not on the court during their volleys.

Burt Bacharach & Friends. Singer sold this specially produced A&M compilation for $1.29 the week the special aired. This album gives further proof to the argument that every artist who signed to A&M Records before 1968 was gently strong-armed into recording a Bacharach composition.

On the Move. Chevrolet sponsored Dionne's 1969 CBS special with guests Burt and Glen Campbell. This album contains only previously released selections from all three artists—songs not even performed on the show.

Burt Bacharach: Opus 3

Air date: 1973 on NBC
Guests: Peter Ustinov (as Beethoven), Bette Midler, Stevie Wonder, Gilbert O'Sullivan
Musical highlights: On his first special to not plug any new material, Bacharach performs several Bacharach and Beethoven pastiches and medleys, the most interesting of which is when he plays "Moonlight Sonata" like "The Look of Love." Burt talks about suicide and songwriting with Gilbert O'Sullivan. They perform "Alone Again Naturally" together and "Do You Know the Way to San Jose," which is interesting since Gilbert usually only sings his own songs. Bette Midler performs "Boogie Woogie Bugle Boy" and "Superstar," to which Bacharach adds an orchestral coda that includes Beethoven's "Ode to Joy"!

Chevrolet Presents Burt Bacharach '74

Air date: January 10, 1974, on NBC

Guests: Sandy Duncan, Roger Moore, the Harlem Globetrotters, Jack Jones
Musical highlights: There are none in this annoying special, which takes place in a park—make that a TV studio made up to look like a park. It opens with Burt and a kid chorus singing "The Green Grass Starts to Grow." Roger Moore plays a henpecked husband and father, to persistent canned laughter. Sandy Duncan and some dancers sing a distressing comical *Grease*-style oldies medley of "Magic Moments" and "I'll Never Fall in Love Again." Bacharach tries to strike up a conversation with Sandy Duncan, who plays a crazy, talkative book reader. The Harlem Globetrotters relive the moment when basketball was invented, and we get to relive the moment when Bacharach was their arranger with this video rendition of "Sweet Georgia Brown"

Burt Bacharach In Concert

Air date: 1977
Filmed in Edmonton Canada
Musical Highlights: All music and no talk. After a brief burst of "Alfie" and an announcer, the Maestro settles in for a medley of "Knowing When to Leave" and "I Say a Little Prayer," then another medley of "One Less Bell to Answer," "What's New Pussycat?" "Wives and Lovers" and "Do You Know the Way to San Jose." Burt sings "Raindrops Keep Falling on My Head," and Josie Armstead performs "I Took My Strength from You," followed by "Futures," "Another Spring Will Rise," "A House Is Not a Home," "No One Remembers My Name," "Charlie" (sung by Sally Stevens), "Alfie," "What the World Needs Now" and "Promises, Promises."